# PRAISE FOR RICH HORTON'S
# PREVIOUS YEAR'S BEST ANTHOLOGIES

### Fantasy: The Best of the Year, 2006 Edition

"The nineteen excellent short stories in this latest addition to the growing field of annual "best of" fantasy anthologies include works by established stars like Pat Cadigan and Peter S. Beagle. Distinguishing this anthology are many stories that first appeared in small press venues. . . . Horton has gathered a diverse mix of styles and themes that illustrate the depth and breadth of fantasy writing today."—*Publishers Weekly*, starred review

### Science Fiction: The Best of the Year, 2006 Edition

"Horton's elegiac anthology of fifteen mostly hard sf stories illuminates a broad spectrum of grief over love thwarted through time, space, human frailty or alien intervention. This anthology reflects the concerns of the genre today—and the apparent inability of our society to do anything about them."—*Publishers Weekly*

### Fantasy: The Best of the Year, 2007 Edition

"Horton's fantasy annual showcases the best short speculative fiction that steps beyond the established boundaries of science. The sixteen selections represent both magic-oriented fantasy and cross-genre slipstream fiction. Their inspired and resourceful authors range from veteran fantasists Geoff Ryman and Peter S. Beagle to such newer voices as Matthew Corradi and Ysabeau Wilce. Fantasy enthusiasts looking for stories that expand the genre's boundaries in unexpected ways will find them in this inventive, enticingly provocative collection."—*Booklist*

### Science Fiction: The Best of the Year, 2007 Edition

"What with sf's current high literary standing, there is no shortage of gifted authors striving to produce outstanding short fiction, and editor Horton is more than happy to encourage them via this annual for which he sets no higher criterion than plain good writing. Dedicated genre fans may find some overlap of this rs of mind-bending entertainmen *list continued*

**The Year's Best Science Fiction and Fantasy, 2010 Edition**
"The thirty stories in this annual collection present an outstanding showcase of the year's most distinctive sf and fantasy. A better exposure to current trends in sf and fantasy would be hard to find."—*Library Journal*

"American science fiction magazines are struggling to survive, but Horton easily fills this hefty anthology with stories from original anthologies and online publications. Rather than focusing on a narrow subset of fantastic stories, he attempts to illuminate the entire field."—*Publishers Weekly*

**Unplugged: The Web's Best Sci-Fi & Fantasy, 2008 Download**
"*Unplugged* aims to showcase the online fiction often neglected in standard best-of-the-year anthologies, and a rousing success it is. The selections come from a truly excellent assortment of venues, including *Tor.com, Lone Star Stories, Baen's Universe*, and *Farrago's Wainscot*. They constitute a shining example of the good general anthology. Clearly, selecting only online stories imposed no limit on scope, variety, and high quality."—*Booklist*

"A short but superlative substantiation of the quality of speculative fiction being published on the Internet, this exceptional anthology of the best science fiction and fantasy put online in 2008 includes gems by genre luminaries as well as rising stars like Tina Connolly and Beth Bernobich. After reading this fourteen-story compilation, online publishing naysayers may rethink their position."—*Publishers Weekly*, starred review

# THE YEAR'S BEST SCIENCE FICTION & FANTASY

## 2012 EDITION

OTHER BOOKS BY

# RICH HORTON

*Fantasy: The Best of the Year, 2006 Edition*

*Fantasy: The Best of the Year, 2007 Edition*

*Fantasy: The Best of the Year, 2008 Edition*

*Robots: The Recent A.I. (with Sean Wallace)*

*Science Fiction: The Best of the Year, 2006 Edition*

*Science Fiction: The Best of the Year, 2007 Edition*

*Science Fiction: The Best of the Year, 2008 Edition*

*Unplugged: The Web's Best Sci-Fi & Fantasy: 2008 Download*

*The Year's Best Science Fiction & Fantasy, 2009 Edition*

*The Year's Best Science Fiction & Fantasy, 2010 Edition*

*The Year's Best Science Fiction & Fantasy, 2011 Edition*

*War and Space: Recent Combat (with Sean Wallace)*

# THE YEAR'S BEST SCIENCE FICTION & FANTASY

## 2012 EDITION

### EDITED BY
# RICH HORTON

PRIME BOOKS

# THE YEAR'S BEST SCIENCE FICTION
# & FANTASY, 2012 EDITION

Prime Books
www.prime-books.com

ISBN: 978-1-60701-344-0

For my daughter Melissa, on the occasion of her graduation (Summa Cum Laude!) from Clemson University.

# CONTENTS

INTRODUCTION, *Rich Horton* ......................................................................... 11

GHOSTWEIGHT, *Yoon Ha Lee* ........................................................................ 15

THE SANDAL-BRIDE, *Genevieve Valentine* ................................................ 34

THE ADAKIAN EAGLE, *Bradley Denton* ...................................................... 44

THE SIGHTED WATCHMAKER, *Vylar Kaftan* ............................................. 99

THE GIRL WHO RULED FAIRYLAND, FOR A LITTLE WHILE,

    *Catherynne M. Valente* ............................................................................ 107

WALKING STICK FIRES, *Alan DeNiro* ........................................................ 130

LATE BLOOMER, *Suzy McKee Charnas* ...................................................... 143

THE CHOICE, *Paul McAuley* ........................................................................ 162

EAST OF FURIOUS, *Jonathan Carroll* ........................................................ 198

MARTIAN HEART, *John Barnes* .................................................................. 213

PUG, *Theodora Goss* ...................................................................................... 227

RAMPION, *Alexandra Duncan* ..................................................................... 239

AND WEEP LIKE ALEXANDER, *Neil Gaiman* ........................................... 278

WIDOWS IN THE WORLD, *Gavin J. Grant* ................................................ 282

YOUNGER WOMEN, *Karen Joy Fowler* ...................................................... 308

CANTERBURY HOLLOW, *Chris Lawson* ..................................................... 315

# CONTENTS

THE SUMMER PEOPLE, *Kelly Link*..............................................................................326

MULBERRY BOYS, *Margo Lanagan*.............................................................................349

THE SILVER WIND, *Nina Allan* ...................................................................................364

CHOOSE YOUR OWN ADVENTURE, *Kat Howard*.......................................................397

A SMALL PRICE TO PAY FOR BIRDSONG, *K.J. Parker* ..............................................401

WOMAN LEAVES ROOM, *Robert Reed*........................................................................432

MY CHIVALRIC FIASCO, *George Saunders*.................................................................439

THE LAST SOPHIA, *C.S.E. Cooney*............................................................................4446

SOME OF THEM CLOSER, *Marissa Lingen*.................................................................457

FIELDS OF GOLD, *Rachel Swirsky* .............................................................................467

THE SMELL OF ORANGE GROVES, *Lavie Tidhar*.......................................................487

THE CARTOGRAPHER WASPS AND THE ANARCHIST BEES,

   *E. Lily Yu*.................................................................................................................499

THE MAN WHO BRIDGED THE MIST, *Kij Johnson* ....................................................507

BIOGRAPHIES ...........................................................................................................563

RECOMMENDED READING ......................................................................................569

PUBLICATION HISTORY ...........................................................................................573

ABOUT THE EDITOR...................................................................................................575

# THE YEAR IN FANTASY AND SCIENCE FICTION, 2012

## RICH HORTON

Last year I made a point of noticing how many stories—well over half—in this book were from online sources. So it seems natural to revisit the subject this year. Online sources remain strong, though this year only twelve of twenty-nine stories came from them—still a healthy total. (And as I've noted before, the distinction can get blurry. Many of the magazines are available electronically—in Kindle editions, for example. And it's not unusual for an online magazine to publish a print anthology of their stories for a year—*Clarkesworld*, *Lightspeed*, and the sadly defunct *Zahir* all have done this.) Where did the other stories come from? Six came from original anthologies (and one more was published in an original anthology shortly after appearing in a non-genre magazine). Eight came from the traditional genre print magazines—all this year from the so-called "Big Four" SF magazines: *Asimov's*, *F&SF*, *Analog*, and *Interzone*. And three came from outside the field: one each from *Harper's*, *Tin House*, and *Conjunctions*.

What about the other breakdowns of the stories here? Seventeen of the stories are by women (making assumptions about pseudonyms, etc., that may not always hold up, mind you!) Somewhere between thirteen and sixteen—let's just say half—are science fiction, the rest fantasy. My uncertainty is because a few seem quite ambiguous as to genre. How to treat a case like Kij Johnson's "The Man Who Bridged the Mist", set on an unidentified planet (SF?), ruled by an Emperor (fantasy?), about an engineering project (SF?), concerning an implausible seeming river of an unexplained substance called "mist" (fantasy?). I lean towards SF, partly because the story reminded me in some ways of the works of Jack Vance, and had Vance published it it almost certainly would have been considered SF. Or K.J. Parker's "A Small Price to Pay for Birdsong"? It's set in what seems vaguely like Earth—indeed Europe—of a few centuries ago, but the geography is not ours. The atmosphere, and the lack of a science fictional maguffin, suggest fantasy, but there's not a trace of magic, nor of strange beast or monsters (except the human kind). So perhaps one ought to think of it as SF, set in an alternate history for example. (Though it makes no point of any alternate nature to our past.) There a few more stories here set in that SF/fantasy borderland (and not in the so-called "slipstream" region, either). In the end, what does it matter? Categorization is useful in some ways, but often enough it tells us more about the readers and critics doing the sorting than it tells about the writers or the stories. (Indeed I'm sure my brief suggestions about why "The Man Who Bridged the Mist" might be fantasy or SF say plenty about me.)

As for the length breakdowns, last year I noted a relatively low number of novelettes in this book. I thought that a statistical fluke (and reflective of an overall weakish year at that length in the field), and I think this year bears that judgment out—novelettes are back in their usual numbers, pretty much—this year nine stories are between 7500 and 17500 words, the (somewhat artificial) SFWA range for that length. I include four novellas. I could have included several more novellas given the space—but they do fill up a book fast! So I strongly recommend you seek out stories like Catherynne M. Valente's **Silently and Very Fast**, K.J. Parker's **Blue and Gold**, Lavie Tidhar's **Jesus and the Eightfold Path**, Carolyn Ives Gilman's "The Ice Owl," Elizabeth Hand's "Near Zennor," Robert Reed's "The Ants of Flanders," Kristin Livdahl's **A Brood of Foxes**, and Mary Robinette Kowal's "Kiss Me Twice." Indeed, we have included a generous list of recommended reading in the back of the book—this year as every year, there was an abundance of riches to choose from, many stories I couldn't fit in this book but which deserve a wider audience.

One of the things I like to keep track of as well is how many newer writers are showing up in my books. This year twelve writers are making their first appearance in one of my anthologies, but that doesn't mean they are new, of course. I'm fortunate to now be able to feature such brilliant writers as Jonathan Carroll, Bradley Denton, and Suzy McKee Charnas for the first time, but their reputations have long been established. There are also a few writers appearing here for the first time who have been doing exciting work for several years—I'm a bit late to the party, perhaps, with Lavie Tidhar, certainly, and with Nina Allan, who has been doing impressive work, mostly in UK and Irish publications, for a few years. Alan de Niro, Gavin Grant, Chris Lawson, Vylar Kaftan, and Marissa Lingen are all also writers I've had my eye on for a few years. (Speaking of the perils of gender identification, I recall that I publicly listed Lavie Tidhar as a woman and Vylar Kaftan as a man in discussing a publication they both appeared in a few years ago—at least my aggregate counts were correct!) And I'm particularly pleased to have two even newer writers in the book: E. Lily Yu (still in college as far as I know!) and Kat Howard. And I should probably also mention that some of the writers I've already anthologized twice are quite young, or at any rate quite new to publishing, such as C.S.E. Cooney, Genevieve Valentine, and Alexandra Duncan. The field remains in good hands.

Commercially, there were some shifts in the short fiction field. One of the major magazines, *Realms of Fantasy*, died for the third straight year, and this time it seems likely to stay dead. *Realms of Fantasy* was an ornament to our genre for some eighteen years, with a remarkably consistent vision transmitted by a single editor, Shawna McCarthy, and it will be missed. Another fine small magazine also died: *Zahir*, edited by Sheryl Tempchin, which had transitioned online in 2010 after several years of very attractive print issues. And *Fantasy Magazine* was taken over by *Lightspeed* editor John Joseph Adams, and as of 2012 the two sites will have been merged under the *Lightspeed* title. *Fantasy* continued to publish excellent work under Adams, and the combined *Lightspeed* site promises to be one of the very best SF/fantasy destinations.

The major print magazines mentioned above—*Asimov's, Analog, F&SF*, and *Interzone*—continued much as before, with slowly dwindling circulations. However, anecdotal reports suggest that electronic sales are helping the magazines a great deal. More and more the smaller 'zines are moving to the web—*Electric Velocipede* moved there this year, and *Kaleidotrope* announced that from 2012 they would be web-based. *Black Gate, On Spec, Shimmer, Not One of Us*, and *Lady Churchill's Rosebud Wristlet* survive in print, as does *Weird Tales*, though the latter changed directions again. After a few quite interesting years under new editor Ann VanderMeer, including two more issues in 2011, the magazine was sold to Marvin Kaye, who explicitly expressed his interest in returning the magazine to its roots, in a sense, or at least to the *Weird Tales* of just a few years ago. VanderMeer's version was energetic and intriguing—yet definitely still "weird," and still engaged with such traditional *Weird Tales* concerns as the Cthulhu Mythos. The one issue of Kaye's magazine that I saw was not terribly promising, though it will be only fair to give it some time.

Obviously I think highly of the online places I plucked stories from: *Clarkesworld, Lightspeed, Fantasy, Tor.com, Subterranean*, and *Strange Horizons*. Other worthwhile online 'zines include *Orson Scott Card's Intergalactic Medicine Show, Beneath Ceaseless Skies, Abyss and Apex, Ideomancer, Chiaroscuro, Apex*, and *Heroic Fantasy Quarterly*, as well as two strong new sites, both of which debuted in 2010: *Daily Science Fiction* and *Redstone Science Fiction*.

The list of original anthologies from which I chose stories is a good start in covering the best such books of 2011: **Down These Strange Streets**, edited by Gardner Dozois; **Teeth**, edited by Ellen Datlow and Terri Windling; **Blood and Other Cravings**, also edited by Datlow; **Eclipse 4**, edited by Jonathan Strahan; another Strahan book: **Life on Mars**; **Steampunk!**, edited by Kelly Link and Gavin Grant (both of whom also have stories in this book!); and **Fables from the Fountain**, edited by Ian Whates. Ellen Datlow had another really outstanding year: besides the two books mentioned above, her books **Naked City** and **Supernatural Noir** were first rate. Jack Dann and Nick Gevers edited a fine collection of ghost stories with a steampunk flavor: **Ghosts by Gaslight**. Jonathan Strahan's **Engineering Infinity** was a strong collection of hard SF—so too was **TRSF**, a magazine-like collection of near future short stories published through MIT's *Technology Review* and edited by Stephen Cass. Another fine SF-oriented book was Ian Whates's **Solaris Rising**. And William Shafer gave us another nice dark fantasy anthology in **Subterranean: Tales of Dark Fantasy 2**. The one theme one might extract from this list is that the commercial power of the urban fantasy and paranormal subgenres at novel length extends to short stories.

As ever, I'll suggest that one of the best ways to understand the real state of the SF and fantasy field is to read the best stories! So I'll leave that task to you—enjoy!

# GHOSTWEIGHT

## YOON HA LEE

It is not true that the dead cannot be folded. Square becomes kite becomes swan; history becomes rumor becomes song. Even the act of remembrance creases the truth.

What the paper-folding diagrams fail to mention is that each fold enacts itself upon the secret marrow of your ethics, the axioms of your thoughts.

Whether this is the most important thing the diagrams fail to mention is a matter of opinion.

"There's time for one more hand," Lisse's ghost said. It was composed of cinders of color, a cipher of blurred features, and it had a voice like entropy and smoke and sudden death. Quite possibly it was the last ghost on all of ruined Rhaion, conquered Rhaion, Rhaion with its devastated, shadowless cities and dead moons and dimming sun. Sometimes Lisse wondered if the ghost had a scar to match her own, a long, livid line down her arm. But she felt it was impolite to ask.

Around them, in a command spindle sized for fifty, the walls of the war-kite were hung with tatters of black and faded green, even now in the process of reknitting themselves into tapestry displays. Tangled reeds changed into ravens. One perched on a lightning-cloven tree. Another, taking shape amid twisted threads, peered out from a skull's eye socket.

Lisse didn't need any deep familiarity with mercenary symbology to understand the warning. Lisse's people had adopted a saying from the Imperium's mercenaries: *In raven arithmetic, no death is enough.*

Lisse had expected pursuit. She had deserted from Base 87 soon after hearing that scouts had found a mercenary war-kite in the ruins of a sacred maze, six years after all the mercenaries vanished: suspicious timing on her part, but she would have no better opportunity for revenge. The ghost had not tried too hard to dissuade her. It had always understood her ambitions.

For a hundred years, despite being frequently outnumbered, the mercenaries in their starfaring kites had cindered cities, destroyed flights of rebel starflyers, shattered stations in the void's hungry depths. What better weapon than one of their own kites?

What troubled her was how lightly the war-kite had been defended. It had made a strange, thorny silhouette against the lavender sky even from a long way off, like briars gone wild, and with the ghost as scout she had slipped past the few mechanized sentries. The kite's shadow had been human. She was not sure what to make of that.

The kite had opened to her like a flower. The card game had been the ghost's idea, a way to reassure the kite that she was its ally: Scorch had been invented by the mercenaries.

Lisse leaned forward and started to scoop the nearest column, the Candle Column, from the black-and-green gameplay rug. The ghost forestalled her with a hand that felt like the dregs of autumn, decay from the inside out. In spite of herself, she flinched from the ghostweight, which had troubled her all her life. Her hand jerked sideways; her fingers spasmed.

"Look," the ghost said.

Few cadets had played Scorch with Lisse even in the barracks. The ghost left its combinatorial fingerprints in the cards. People drew the unlucky Fallen General's Hand over and over again, or doubled on nothing but negative values, or inverted the Crown Flower at odds of thousands to one. So Lisse had learned to play the solitaire variant, with jerengjen as counters. *You must learn your enemy's weapons,* the ghost had told her, and so, even as a child in the reeducation facility, she had saved her chits for paper to practice folding into cranes, lilies, leaf-shaped boats.

Next to the Candle Column she had folded stormbird, greatfrog, lantern, drake. Where the ghost had interrupted her attempt to clear the pieces, they had landed amid the Sojourner and Mirror Columns, forming a skewed late-game configuration: a minor variant of the Needle Stratagem, missing only its pivot.

"Consider it an omen," the ghost said. "Even the smallest sliver can kill, as they say."

There were six ravens on the tapestries now. The latest one had outspread wings, as though it planned to blot out the shrouded sun. She wondered what it said about the mercenaries, that they couched their warnings in pictures rather than drums or gongs.

Lisse rose from her couch. "So they're coming for us. Where are they?"

She had spoken in the Imperium's administrative tongue, not one of the mercenaries' own languages. Nevertheless, a raven flew from one tapestry to join its fellows in the next. The vacant tapestry grayed, then displayed a new scene: a squad of six tanks caparisoned in Imperial blue and bronze, paced by two personnel carriers sheathed in metal mined from withered stars. They advanced upslope, pebbles skittering in their wake.

In the old days, the ghost had told her, no one would have advanced through a sacred maze by straight lines. But the ancient walls, curved and interlocking, were gone now. The ghost had drawn the old designs on her palm with its insubstantial fingers, and she had learned not to shudder at the untouch, had learned to thread the maze in her mind's eye: one more map to the things she must not forget.

"I'd rather avoid fighting them," Lisse said. She was looking at the command spindle's controls. Standard Imperial layout, all of them—it did not occur to her to wonder why the kite had configured itself thus—but she found nothing for the weapons.

"People don't bring tanks when they want to negotiate," the ghost said dryly. "And they'll have alerted their flyers for intercept. You have something they want badly."

"Then why didn't they guard it better?" she demanded.

Despite the tanks' approach, the ghost fell silent. After a while, it said, "Perhaps they didn't think anyone but a mercenary could fly a kite."

"They might be right," Lisse said darkly. She strapped herself into the commander's seat, then pressed three fingers against the controls and traced the commands she had been taught as a cadet. The kite shuddered, as though caught in a hell-wind from the sky's fissures. But it did not unfurl itself to fly.

She tried the command gestures again, forcing herself to slow down. A cold keening vibrated through the walls. The kite remained stubbornly landfast.

The squad rounded the bend in the road. All the ravens had gathered in a single tapestry, decorating a half-leafed tree like dire jewels. The rest of the tapestries displayed the squad from different angles: two aerial views and four from the ground.

Lisse studied one of the aerial views and caught sight of two scuttling figures, lean angles and glittering eyes and a balancing tail in black metal. She stiffened. They had the shadows of hounds, all graceful hunting curves. Two jerengjen, true ones, unlike the lifeless shapes that she folded out of paper. The kite must have deployed them when it sensed the tanks' approach.

Sweating now, despite the autumn temperature inside, she methodically tried every command she had ever learned. The kite remained obdurate. The tapestries' green threads faded until the ravens and their tree were bleak black splashes against a background of wintry gray.

It was a message. Perhaps a demand. But she did not understand.

The first two tanks slowed into view. Roses, blue with bronze hearts, were engraved to either side of the main guns. The lead tank's roses flared briefly.

The kite whispered to itself in a language that Lisse did not recognize.

Then the largest tapestry cleared of trees and swirling leaves and rubble, and presented her with a commander's emblem, a pale blue rose pierced by three claws. A man's voice issued from the tapestry: "Cadet Fai Guen." This was her registry name. They had not reckoned that she would keep her true name alive in her heart like an ember. "You are in violation of Imperial interdict. Surrender the kite at once."

He did not offer mercy. The Imperium never did.

Lisse resisted the urge to pound her fists against the interface. She had not survived this long by being impatient. "That's it, then," she said to the ghost in defeat.

"Cadet Fai Guen," the voice said again, after another burst of light, "you have one minute to surrender the kite before we open fire."

"Lisse," the ghost said, "the kite's awake."

She bit back a retort and looked down. Where the control panel had once been featureless gray, it was now crisp white interrupted by five glyphs, perfectly spaced for her outspread fingers. She resisted the urge to snatch her hand away. "Very well," she said. "If we can't fly, at least we can fight."

She didn't know the kite's specific control codes. Triggering the wrong sequence might activate the kite's internal defenses. But taking tank fire at point-blank range would get her killed, too. She couldn't imagine that the kite's armor had improved in the years of its neglect.

On the other hand, it had jerengjen scouts, and the jerengjen looked perfectly functional.

She pressed her thumb to the first glyph. A shadow unfurled briefly but was gone before she could identify it. The second attempt revealed a two-headed dragon's twisting coils. Long-range missiles, then: thunder in the sky. Working quickly, she ran through the options. It would be ironic if she got the weapons systems to work only to incinerate herself.

"You have ten seconds, Cadet Fai Guen," said the voice with no particular emotion.

"Lisse," the ghost said, betraying impatience.

One of the glyphs had shown a wolf running. She remembered that at one point the wolf had been the mercenaries' emblem. Nevertheless, she felt a dangerous affinity to it. As she hesitated over it, the kite said, in a parched voice, "Soul strike."

She tapped the glyph, then pressed her palm flat to activate the weapon. The panel felt briefly hot, then cold.

For a second she thought that nothing had happened, that the kite had malfunctioned. The kite was eerily still.

The tanks and personnel carriers were still visible as gray outlines against darker gray, as were the nearby trees and their stifled fruits. She wasn't sure whether that was an effect of the unnamed weapons or a problem with the tapestries. Had ten seconds passed yet? She couldn't tell, and the clock of her pulse was unreliable.

Desperate to escape before the tanks spat forth the killing rounds, Lisse raked her hand sideways to dismiss the glyphs. They dispersed in unsettling fragmented shapes resembling half-chewed leaves and corroded handprints. She repeated the gesture for *fly*.

Lisse choked back a cry as the kite lofted. The tapestry views changed to sky on all sides except the ravens on their tree—birds no longer, but skeletons, price paid in coin of bone.

Only once they had gained some altitude did she instruct the kite to show her what had befallen her hunters. It responded by continuing to accelerate.

The problem was not the tapestries. Rather, the kite's wolf-strike had ripped all the shadows free of their owners, killing them. Below, across a great swathe of the continent once called Ishuel's Bridge, was a devastation of light, a hard, glittering splash against the surrounding snow-capped mountains and forests and winding rivers.

Lisse had been an excellent student, not out of academic conscientiousness but because it gave her an opportunity to study her enemy. One of her best subjects had been geography. She and the ghost had spent hours drawing maps in the air or shaping topographies in her blankets; paper would betray them, it had said. As she memorized the streets of the City of Fountains, it had sung her the ballads of its founding. It had told her about the feuding poets and philosophers that the thoroughfares of the City of Prisms had been named after. She knew which mines supplied which bases and how the roads spidered across Ishuel's Bridge. While the population figures of the bases and settlement camps weren't exactly announced to cadets, especially those recruited from the reeducation facilities, it didn't take much to make an educated guess.

The Imperium had built 114 bases on Ishuel's Bridge. Base complements averaged twenty thousand people. Even allowing for the imprecision of her eye, the wolf-strike had taken out—

She shivered as she listed the affected bases, approximately sixty of them.

The settlement camps' populations were more difficult. The Imperium did not like to release those figures. Imperfectly, she based her estimate on the zone around Base 87, remembering the rows of identical shelters. The only reason they did not outnumber the bases' personnel was that the mercenaries had been coldly efficient on Jerengjen Day.

*Needle Stratagem,* Lisse thought blankly. The smallest sliver. She hadn't expected its manifestation to be quite so literal.

The ghost was looking at her, its dark eyes unusually distinct. "There's nothing to be done for it now," it said at last. "Tell the kite where to go before it decides for itself."

"Ashway 514," Lisse said, as they had decided before she fled base: scenario after scenario whispered to each other like bedtime stories. She was shaking. The straps did nothing to steady her.

She had one last glimpse of the dead region before they curved into the void: her handprint upon her own birthworld. She had only meant to destroy her hunters.

In her dreams, later, the blast pattern took on the outline of a running wolf.

In the mercenaries' dominant language, jerengjen originally referred to the art of folding paper. For her part, when Lisse first saw it, she thought of it as snow. She was four years old. It was a fair spring afternoon in the City of Tapestries, slightly humid. She was watching a bird try to catch a bright butterfly when improbable paper shapes began drifting from the sky, foxes and snakes and stormbirds.

Lisse called to her parents, laughing. Her parents knew better. Over her shrieks, they dragged her into the basement and switched off the lights. She tried to bite one of her fathers when he clamped his hand over her mouth. Jerengjen tracked primarily by shadows, not by sound, but you couldn't be too careful where the mercenaries' weapons were concerned.

In the streets, jerengjen unfolded prettily, expanding into artillery with dragon-shaped shadows and sleek four-legged assault robots with wolf-shaped shadows. In the skies, jerengjen unfolded into bombers with kestrel-shaped shadows.

This was not the only Rhaioni city where this happened. People crumpled like paper cutouts once their shadows were cut away by the onslaught. Approximately one-third of the world's population perished in the weeks that followed.

Of the casualty figures, the Imperium said, *It is regrettable.* And later, *The stalled negotiations made the consolidation necessary.*

Lisse carried a map of the voidways with her at all times, half in her head and half in the Scorch deck. The ghost had once been a traveler. It had shown her mnemonics for the dark passages and the deep perils that lay between stars. Growing up, she had laid out endless tableaux between her lessons, memorizing travel times and vortices and twists.

Ashway 514 lay in the interstices between two unstable stars and their cacophonous necklace of planets, comets, and asteroids. Lisse felt the kite tilting this way and that as it balanced itself against the stormy voidcurrent.

The tapestries shone from one side with ruddy light from the nearer star, 514 Tsi. On the other side, a pale violet-blue planet with a serenade of rings occluded the view.

514 was a useful hiding place. It was off the major tradeways, and since the Battle of Fallen Sun—named after the rebel general's emblem, a white sun outlined in red, rather than the nearby stars—it had been designated an ashway, where permanent habitation was forbidden.

More important to Lisse, however, was the fact that 514 was the ashway nearest the last mercenary sighting, some five years ago. As a student, she had learned the names and silhouettes of the most prominent war-kites, and set verses of praise in their honor to Imperial anthems. She had written essays on their tactics and memorized the names of their most famous commanders, although there were no statues or portraits, only the occasional unsmiling photograph. The Imperium was fond of statues and portraits.

For a hundred years (administrative calendar), the mercenaries had served their masters unflinchingly and unfailingly. Lisse had assumed that she would have as much time as she needed to plot against them. Instead, they had broken their service, for reasons the Imperium had never released—perhaps they didn't know, either—and none had been seen since.

"I'm not sure there's anything to find here," Lisse said. Surely the Imperium would have scoured the region for clues. The tapestries were empty of ravens. Instead, they diagrammed shifting voidcurrent flows. The approach of enemy starflyers would perturb the current and allow Lisse and the ghost to estimate their intent. Not trusting the kite's systems—although there was only so far that she could take her distrust, given the circumstances—she had been watching the tapestries for the past several hours. She had, after a brief argument with the ghost, switched on haptics so that the air currents would, however imperfectly, reflect the status of the void around them. Sometimes it was easier to feel a problem through your skin.

"There's no indication of derelict kites here," she added. "Or even kites in use, other than this one."

"It's a starting place, that's all," the ghost said.

"We're going to have to risk a station eventually. You might not need to eat, but I do." She had only been able to sneak a few rations out of base. It was tempting to nibble at one now.

"Perhaps there are stores on the kite."

"I can't help but think this place is a trap."

"You have to eat sooner or later," the ghost said reasonably. "It's worth a look, and I don't want to see you go hungry." At her hesitation, it added, "I'll stand watch here. I'm only a breath away."

This didn't reassure her as much as it should have, but she was no longer a

child in a bunk precisely aligned with the walls, clutching the covers while the
ghost told her her people's stories. She reminded herself of her favorite story,
in which a single sentinel kept away the world's last morning by burning out
her eyes, and set out.

Lisse felt the ghostweight's pull the farther away she walked, but that was
old pain, and easily endured. Lights flicked on to accompany her, diffuse
despite her unnaturally sharp shadow, then started illuminating passages
ahead of her, guiding her footsteps. She wondered what the kite didn't want
her to see.

Rations were in an unmarked storage room. She wouldn't have been certain
about the rations, except that they were, if the packaging was to be believed,
field category 72: better than what she had eaten on training exercises, but not
by much. No surprise, now that she thought about it: from all accounts, the
mercenaries had relied on their masters' production capacity.

Feeling ridiculous, she grabbed two rations and retraced her steps. The
fact that the kite lit her exact path only made her more nervous.

"Anything new?" she asked the ghost. She tapped the ration. "It's a pity
that you can't taste poison."

The ghost laughed dryly. "If the kite were going to kill you, it wouldn't be
that subtle. Food is food, Lisse."

The food was as exactingly mediocre as she had come to expect from
military food. At least it was not any worse. She found a receptacle for disposal
afterward, then laid out a Scorch tableau, Candle column to Bone, right to left.
Cards rather than jerengjen, because she remembered the scuttling hound-
jerengjen with creeping distaste.

From the moment she left Base 87, one timer had started running down.
The devastation of Ishuel's Bridge had begun another, the important one.
She wasn't gambling her survival; she had already sold it. The question was,
how many Imperial bases could she extinguish on her way out? And could
she hunt down any of the mercenaries that had been the Imperium's killing
sword?

Lisse sorted rapidly through possible targets. For instance, Base 226
Mheng, the Petaled Fortress. She would certainly perish in the attempt, but
the only way she could better that accomplishment would be to raze the
Imperial firstworld, and she wasn't that ambitious. There was Bridgepoint 663
Tsi-Kes, with its celebrated Pallid Sentinels, or Aerie 8 Yeneq, which built the
Imperium's greatest flyers, or—

She set the cards down, closed her eyes, and pressed her palms against
her face. She was no tactician supreme. Would it make much difference if she
picked a card at random?

But of course nothing was truly random in the ghost's presence.

She laid out the Candle Column again. "Not 8 Yeneq," she said. "Let's start with a softer target. Aerie 586 Chiu."

Lisse looked at the ghost: the habit of seeking its approval had not left her. It nodded. "The safest approach is via the Capillary Ashways. It will test your piloting skills."

Privately, Lisse thought that the kite would be happy to guide itself. They didn't dare allow it to, however.

The Capillaries were among the worst of the ashways. Even starlight moved in unnerving ways when faced with ancient networks of voidcurrent gates, unmaintained for generations, or vortices whose behavior changed day by day.

They were fortunate with the first several capillaries. Under other circumstances, Lisse would have gawked at the splendor of lensed galaxies and the jewel-fire of distant clusters. She was starting to manipulate the control interface without hesitating, or flinching as though a wolf's shadow might cross hers.

At the ninth—

"Patrol," the ghost said, leaning close.

She nodded jerkily, trying not to show that its proximity pained her. Its mouth crimped in apology.

"It would have been worse if we'd made it all the way to 586 Chiu without a run-in," Lisse said. That kind of luck always had a price. If she was unready, best to find out now, while there was a chance of fleeing to prepare for a later strike.

The patrol consisted of sixteen flyers: eight Lance 82s and eight Scout 73s. She had flown similar Scouts in simulation.

The flyers did not hesitate. A spread of missiles streaked toward her. Lisse launched antimissile fire.

It was impossible to tell whether they had gone on the attack because the Imperium and the mercenaries had parted on bad terms, or because the authorities had already learned of what had befallen Rhaion. She was certain couriers had gone out within moments of the devastation of Ishuel's Bridge.

As the missiles exploded, Lisse wrenched the kite toward the nearest vortex. The kite was a larger and sturdier craft. It would be better able to survive the voidcurrent stresses. The tapestries dimmed as they approached. She shut off haptics as wind eddied and swirled in the command spindle. It would only get worse.

One missile barely missed her. She would have to do better. And the vortex was a temporary terrain advantage; she could not lurk there forever.

The second barrage came. Lisse veered deeper into the current. The stars took on peculiar roseate shapes.

"They know the kite's capabilities," the ghost reminded her. "Use them. If they're smart, they'll already have sent a courier burst to local command."

The kite suggested jerengjen flyers, harrier class. Lisse conceded its expertise.

The harriers unfolded as they launched, sleek and savage. They maneuvered remarkably well in the turbulence. But there were only ten of them.

"If I fire into that, I'll hit them," Lisse said. Her reflexes were good, but not that good, and the harriers apparently liked to soar near their targets.

"You won't need to fire," the ghost said.

She glanced at him, disbelieving. Her hand hovered over the controls, playing through possibilities and finding them wanting. For instance, she wasn't certain that the firebird (explosives) didn't entail self-immolation, and she was baffled by the stag.

The patrol's pilots were not incapable. They scorched three of the harriers. They probably realized at the same time that Lisse did that the three had been sacrifices. The other seven flensed them silent.

Lisse edged the kite out of the vortex. She felt an uncomfortable sense of duty to the surviving harriers, but she knew they were one-use, crumpled paper, like all jerengjen. Indeed, they folded themselves flat as she passed them, reducing themselves to battledrift.

"I can't see how this is an efficient use of resources," Lisse told the ghost.

"It's an artifact of the mercenaries' methods," it said. "It works. Perhaps that's all that matters."

Lisse wanted to ask for details, but her attention was diverted by a crescendo of turbulence. By the time they reached gentler currents, she was too tired to bring it up.

They altered their approach to 586 Chiu twice, favoring stealth over confrontation. If she wanted to char every patrol in the Imperium by herself, she could live a thousand sleepless years and never be done.

For six days they lurked near 586 Chiu, developing a sense for local traffic and likely defenses. Terrain would not be much difficulty. Aeries were built near calm, steady currents.

"It would be easiest if you were willing to take out the associated city," the ghost said in a neutral voice. They had been discussing whether making a bombing pass on the aerie posed too much of a risk. Lisse had balked at the fact that 586 Chiu Second City was well within blast radius. The people who had furnished the kite's armaments seemed to have believed in surfeit. "They'd only have a moment to know what was happening."

"No."

"Lisse—"

She looked at it mutely, obdurate, although she hated to disappoint it. It hesitated, but did not press its case further.

"This, then," it said in defeat. "Next best odds: aim the voidcurrent disrupter at the manufactory's core while jerengjen occupy the defenses." Aeries held the surrounding current constant to facilitate the calibration of newly built flyers. Under ordinary circumstances, the counterbalancing vortex was leashed at the core. If they could disrupt the core, the vortex would tear at its surroundings.

"That's what we'll do, then," Lisse said. The disrupter had a short range. She did not like the idea of flying in close. But she had objected to the safer alternative.

Aerie 586 Chiu reminded Lisse not of a nest but of a pyre. Flyers and transports were always coming and going, like sparks. The kite swooped in sharp and fast. Falcon-jerengjen raced ahead of them, holding lattice formation for two seconds before scattering toward their chosen marks.

The aerie's commanders responded commendably. They knew the kite was by far the greater threat. But Lisse met the first flight they threw at her with missiles keen and terrible. The void lit up in a clamor of brilliant colors.

The kite screamed when a flyer salvo hit one of its secondary wings. It bucked briefly while the other wings changed their geometry to compensate. Lisse could not help but think that the scream had not sounded like pain. It had sounded like exultation.

The real test was the gauntlet of Banner 142 artillery emplacements. They were silver-bright and terrible. It seemed wrong that they did not roar like tigers. Lisse bit the inside of her mouth and concentrated on narrowing the parameters for the voidcurrent disrupter. Her hand was a fist on the control panel.

One tapestry depicted the currents: striations within striations of pale blue against black. Despite its shielding, the core was visible as a knot tangled out of all proportion to its size.

"Now," the ghost said, with inhuman timing.

She didn't wait to be told twice. She unfisted her hand.

Unlike the wolf-strike, the disrupter made the kite scream again. It lurched and twisted. Lisse wanted to clap her hands over her ears, but there was more incoming fire, and she was occupied with evasive maneuvers. The kite folded in on itself, minimizing its profile. It dizzied her to view it on the secondary tapestry. For a panicked moment, she thought the kite would close itself around her, press her like petals in a book. Then she remembered to breathe.

The disrupter was not visible to human sight, but the kite could read its effect on the current. Like lightning, the disrupter's blast forked and forked again, zigzagging inexorably toward the minute variations in flux that would lead it toward the core.

She was too busy whipping the kite around to an escape vector to see the moment of convergence between disrupter and core. But she felt the first lashing surge as the vortex spun free of its shielding, expanding into available space. Then she was too busy steadying the kite through the triggered subvortices to pay attention to anything but keeping them alive.

Only later did she remember how much debris there had been, flung in newly unpredictable ways: wings torn from flyers, struts, bulkheads, even an improbable crate with small reddish fruit tumbling from the hole in its side.

Later, too, it would trouble her that she had not been able to keep count of the people in the tumult. Most were dead already: sliced slantwise, bone and viscera exposed, trailing banners of blood; others twisted and torn, faces ripped off and cast aside like unwanted masks, fingers uselessly clutching the wrack of chairs, tables, door frames. A fracture in one wall revealed three people in dark green jackets. They turned their faces toward the widening crack, then clasped hands before a subvortex hurled them apart. The last Lisse saw of them was two hands, still clasped together and severed at the wrist.

Lisse found an escape. Took it.

She didn't know until later that she had destroyed 40% of the aerie's structure. Some people survived. They knew how to rebuild.

What she never found out was that the disrupter's effect was sufficiently long-lasting that some of the survivors died of thirst before supplies could safely be brought in.

In the old days, Lisse's people took on the ghostweight to comfort the dead and be comforted in return. After a year and a day, the dead unstitched themselves and accepted their rest.

After Jerengjen Day, Lisse's people struggled to share the sudden increase in ghostweight, to alleviate the flickering terror of the massacred.

Lisse's parents, unlike the others, stitched a ghost onto a child.

"They saw no choice," the ghost told her again and again. "You mustn't blame them."

The ghost had listened uncomplainingly to her troubles and taught her how to cry quietly so the teachers wouldn't hear her. It had soothed her to sleep with her people's legends and histories, described the gardens and promenades so vividly she imagined she could remember them herself. Some nights were more difficult than others, trying to sleep with that strange, stabbing, heartpulse ache. But blame was not what she felt, not usually.

The second target was Base 454 Qo, whose elite flyers were painted with elaborate knotwork, green with bronze-tipped thorns. For reasons that Lisse did not try to understand, the jerengjen dismembered the defensive flight but left the painted panels completely intact.

The third, the fourth, the fifth—she started using Scorch card values to tabulate the reported deaths, however unreliable the figures were in any unencrypted sources. For all its talents, the kite could not pierce military-grade encryption. She spent two days fidgeting over this inconvenience so she wouldn't have to think about the numbers.

When she did think about the numbers, she refused to round up. She refused to round down.

The nightmares started after the sixth, Bridgepoint 977 Ja-Esh. The station commander had kept silence, as she had come to expect. However, a merchant coalition had broken the interdict to plead for mercy in fourteen languages. She hadn't destroyed the coalition's outpost. The station had, in reprimand.

She reminded herself that the merchant would have perished anyway. She had learned to use the firebird to scathing effect. And she was under no illusions that she was only destroying Imperial soldiers and bureaucrats.

In her dreams she heard their pleas in her birth tongue, which the ghost had taught her. The ghost, for its part, started singing her to sleep, as it had when she was little.

The numbers marched higher. When they broke ten million, she plunged out of the command spindle and into the room she had claimed for her own. She pounded the wall until her fists bled. Triumph tasted like salt and venom. It wasn't supposed to be so *easy*. In the worst dreams, a wolf roved the tapestries, eating shadows—eating souls. And the void with its tinsel of worlds was nothing but one vast shadow.

Stores began running low after the seventeenth. Lisse and the ghost argued over whether it was worth attempting to resupply through black market traders. Lisse said they didn't have time to spare, and won. Besides, she had little appetite.

Intercepted communications suggested that someone was hunting them. Rumors and whispers. They kept Lisse awake when she was so tired she wanted to slam the world shut and hide. The Imperium certainly planned reprisal. Maybe others did, too.

If anyone else took advantage of the disruption to move against the Imperium for their own reasons, she didn't hear about it.

The names of the war-kites, recorded in the Imperium's administrative language, are varied: *Fire Burns the Spider Black. The Siege of the City with Seventeen Faces. Sovereign Geometry. The Glove with Three Fingers.*

The names are not, strictly speaking, Imperial. Rather, they are plundered from the greatest accomplishments of the cultures that the mercenaries have defeated on the Imperium's behalf. *Fire Burns the Spider Black* was a silk tapestry housed in the dark hall of Meu Danh, ancient of years. *The Siege of the City with Seventeen Faces* was a saga chanted by the historians of Kwaire. *Sovereign Geometry* discussed the varying nature of parallel lines. And more: plays, statues, games.

The Imperium's scholars and artists take great pleasure in reinterpreting these works. Such achievements are meant to be disseminated, they say.

They were three days' flight from the next target, Base 894 Sao, when the shadow winged across all the tapestries. The void was dark, pricked by starfire and the occasional searing burst of particles. The shadow singed everything darker as it soared to intercept them, as single-minded in its purpose as a bullet. For a second she almost thought it was a collage of wrecked flyers and rusty shrapnel.

The ghost cursed. Lisse startled, but when she looked at it, its face was composed again.

As Lisse pulled back the displays' focus to get a better sense of the scale, she thought of snowbirds and stormbirds, winter winds and cutting beaks. "I don't know what that is," she said, "but it can't be natural." None of the imperial defenses had manifested in such a fashion.

"It's not," the ghost said. "That's another war-kite."

Lisse cleared the control panel. She veered them into a chancy voidcurrent eddy.

The ghost said, "Wait. You won't outrun it. As we see its shadow, it sees ours."

"How does a kite have a shadow in the void in the first place?" she asked. "And why haven't we ever seen our own shadow?"

"Who can see their own soul?" the ghost said. But it would not meet her eyes.

Lisse would have pressed for more, but the shadow overtook them. It folded itself back like a plumage of knives. She brought the kite about. The control panel suggested possibilities: a two-headed dragon, a falcon, a coiled snake. Next a wolf reared up, but she quickly pulled her hand back.

"Visual contact," the kite said crisply.

The stranger-kite was the color of a tarnished star. It had tucked all its projections away to present a minimal surface for targeting, but Lisse had no doubt that it could unfold itself faster than she could draw breath. The kite flew a widening helix, beautifully precise.

"A mercenary salute, equal to equal," the ghost said.

"Are we expected to return it?"

"Are you a mercenary?" the ghost countered.

"Communications incoming," the kite said before Lisse could make a retort.

"I'll hear it," Lisse said over the ghost's objection. It was the least courtesy she could offer, even to a mercenary.

To Lisse's surprise, the tapestry's raven vanished to reveal a woman's visage, not an emblem. The woman had brown skin, a scar trailing from one temple down to her cheekbone, and dark hair cropped short. She wore gray on gray, in no uniform that Lisse recognized, sharply tailored. Lisse had expected a killer's eyes, a hunter's eyes. Instead, the woman merely looked tired.

"Commander Kiriet Dzan of—" She had been speaking in administrative, but the last word was unfamiliar. "You would say *Candle*."

"Lisse of Rhaion," she said. There was no sense in hiding her name.

But the woman wasn't looking at her. She was looking at the ghost. She said something sharply in that unfamiliar language.

The ghost pressed its hand against Lisse's. She shuddered, not understanding. "Be strong," it murmured.

"I see," Kiriet said, once more speaking in administrative. Her mouth was unsmiling. "Lisse, do you know who you're traveling with?"

"I don't believe we're acquainted," the ghost said, coldly formal.

"Of course not," Kiriet said. "But I was the logistical coordinator for the scouring of Rhaion." She did not say *consolidation*. "I knew why we were there. Lisse, your ghost's name is Vron Arien."

Lisse said, after several seconds, "That's a mercenary name."

The ghost said, "So it is. Lisse—" Its hand fell away.

"Tell me what's going on."

Its mouth was taut. Then: "Lisse, I—"

"*Tell me.*"

"He was a deserter, Lisse," the woman said, carefully, as if she thought the information might fracture her. "For years he eluded Wolf Command. Then we discovered he had gone to ground on Rhaion. Wolf Command determined that, for sheltering him, Rhaion must be brought to heel. The Imperium assented."

Throughout this Lisse looked at the ghost, silently begging it to deny any of it, all of it. But the ghost said nothing.

Lisse thought of long nights with the ghost leaning by her bedside, reminding her of the dancers, the tame birds, the tangle of frostfruit trees in the city square; things she did not remember herself because she had been too young when the jerengjen came. Even her parents only came to her in snatches: curling up in a mother's lap, helping a father peel plantains. Had any of the ghost's stories been real?

She thought, too, of the way the ghost had helped her plan her escape from Base 87, how it had led her cunningly through the maze and to the kite. At the time, it had not occurred to her to wonder at its confidence.

Lisse said, "Then the kite is yours."

"After a fashion, yes." The ghost's eyes were precisely the color of ash after the last ember's death.

"But my parents—"

Enunciating the words as if they cut it, the ghost said, "We made a bargain, your parents and I."

She could not help it; she made a stricken sound.

"I offered you my protection," the ghost said. "After years serving the Imperium, I knew its workings. And I offered your parents vengeance. Don't think that Rhaion wasn't my home, too."

Lisse was wrackingly aware of Kiriet's regard. "Did my parents truly die in the consolidation?" The euphemism was easier to use.

She could have asked whether Lisse was her real name. She had to assume that it wasn't.

"I don't know," it said. "After you were separated from them, I had no way of finding out. Lisse, I think you had better find out what Kiriet wants. She is not your friend."

*I was the logistical coordinator,* Kiriet had said. And her surprise at seeing the ghost—*It has a name,* Lisse reminded herself—struck Lisse as genuine. Which meant Kiriet had not come here in pursuit of Vron Arien. "Why are you here?" Lisse asked.

"You're not going to like it. I'm here to destroy your kite, whatever you've named it."

"It doesn't have a name." She had been unable to face the act of naming, of claiming ownership.

Kiriet looked at her sideways. "I see."

"Surely you could have accomplished your goal," Lisse said, "without talking to me first. I am inexperienced in the ways of kites. You are not." In truth, she should already have been running. But Kiriet's revelation meant that Lisse's purpose, once so clear, was no longer to be relied upon.

"I may not be your friend, but I am not your enemy, either," Kiriet said. "I have no common purpose with the Imperium, not anymore. But you cannot continue to use the kite."

Lisse's eyes narrowed. "It is the weapon I have," she said. "I would be a fool to relinquish it."

"I don't deny its efficacy," Kiriet said, "but you are Rhaioni. Doesn't the cost trouble you?"

Cost?

Kiriet said, "So no one told you." Her anger focused on the ghost.

"A weapon is a weapon," the ghost said. At Lisse's indrawn breath, it said, "The kites take their sustenance from the deaths they deal. It was necessary to strengthen ours by letting it feast on smaller targets first. This is the particular craft of my people, as ghostweight was the craft of yours, Lisse."

*Sustenance.* "So this is why you want to destroy the kite," Lisse said to Kiriet.

"Yes." The other woman's smile was bitter. "As you might imagine, the Imperium did not approve. It wanted to negotiate another hundred-year contract. I dissented."

"Were you in a position to dissent?" the ghost asked, in a way that made Lisse think that it was translating some idiom from its native language.

"I challenged my way up the chain of command and unseated the head of Wolf Command," Kiriet said. "It was not a popular move. I have been destroying kites ever since. If the Imperium is so keen on further conquest, let it dirty its own hands."

"Yet you wield a kite yourself," Lisse said.

"*Candle* is my home. But on the day that every kite is accounted for in words of ash and cinders, I will turn my own hand against it."

It appealed to Lisse's sense of irony. All the same, she did not trust Kiriet.

She heard a new voice. Kiriet's head turned. "Someone's followed you." She said a curt phrase in her own language, then: "You'll want my assistance—"

Lisse shook her head.

"It's a small flight, as these things go, but it represents a threat to you. Let me—"

"No," Lisse said, more abruptly than she had meant to. "I'll handle it myself."

"If you insist," Kiriet said, looking even more tired. "Don't say I didn't warn you." Then her face was replaced, for a flicker, with her emblem: a black candle crossed slantwise by an empty sheath.

"The *Candle* is headed for a vortex, probably for cover," the ghost said, very softly. "But it can return at any moment."

Lisse thought that she was all right, and then the reaction set in. She spent several irrecoverable breaths shaking, arms wrapped around herself, before she was able to concentrate on the tapestry data.

At one time, every war-kite displayed a calligraphy scroll in its command spindle. The words are, approximately:

> *I have only*
> *one candle*

Even by the mercenaries' standards, it is not much of a poem. But the woman who wrote it was a soldier, not a poet.

The mercenaries no longer have a homeland. Even so, they keep certain traditions, and one of them is the Night of Vigils. Each mercenary honors the year's dead by lighting a candle. They used to do this on the winter solstice of an ancient calendar. Now the Night of Vigils is on the anniversary of the day the first war-kites were launched; the day the mercenaries slaughtered their own people to feed the kites.

*The kites fly,* the mercenaries' commandant said. *But they do not know how to hunt.*

When he was done, they knew how to hunt. Few of the mercenaries forgave him, but it was too late by then.

The poem says: So many people have died, yet I have only one candle for them all.

It is worth noting that "have" is expressed by a particular construction for alienable possession: not only is the having subject to change, it is additionally under threat of being taken away.

Kiriet's warning had been correct. An Imperial flight in perfect formation had advanced toward them, inhibiting their avenues of escape. They outnumbered her forty-eight to one. The numbers did not concern her, but the Imperium's resources meant that if she dealt with this flight, there would be twenty more waiting for her, and the numbers would only grow worse. That they had not opened fire already meant they had some trickery in mind.

One of the flyers peeled away, describing an elegant curve and exposing its most vulnerable surface, painted with a rose.

"That one's not armed," Lisse said, puzzled.

The ghost's expression was unreadable. "How very wise of them," it said.

The forward tapestry flickered. "Accept the communication," Lisse said.

The emblem that appeared was a trefoil flanked by two roses, one stem-up, one stem-down. Not for the first time, Lisse wondered why people from a culture that lavished attention on miniatures and sculptures were so intent on masking themselves in emblems.

"Commander Fai Guen, this is Envoy Nhai Bara." A woman's voice, deep and resonant, with an accent Lisse didn't recognize.

*So I've been promoted?* Lisse thought sardonically, feeling herself tense up. The Imperium never gave you anything, even a meaningless rank, without expecting something in return.

Softly, she said to the ghost, "They were bound to catch up to us sooner or later." Then, to the kite: "Communications to Envoy Nhai: I am Lisse of Rhaion. What words between us could possibly be worth exchanging? Your people are not known for mercy."

"If you will not listen to me," Nhai said, "perhaps you will listen to the envoy after me, or the one after that. We are patient and we are many. But I am not interested in discussing mercy: that's something we have in common."

"I'm listening," Lisse said, despite the ghost's chilly stiffness. All her life she had honed herself against the Imperium. It was unbearable to consider that she might have been mistaken. But she had to know what Nhai's purpose was.

"Commander Lisse," the envoy said, and it hurt like a stab to hear her name spoken by a voice other than the ghost's, a voice that was not Rhaioni. Even if she knew, now, that the ghost was not Rhaioni, either. "I have a proposal for you. You have proven your military effectiveness—"

*Military effectiveness.* She had tallied all the deaths, she had marked each massacre on the walls of her heart, and this faceless envoy collapsed them into two words empty of number.

"—quite thoroughly. We are in need of a strong sword. What is your price for hire, Commander Lisse?"

"What is my—" She stared at the trefoil emblem, and then her face went ashen.

It is not true that the dead cannot be folded. Square becomes kite becomes swan; history becomes rumor becomes song. Even the act of remembrance creases the truth.

But the same can be said of the living.

# THE SANDAL-BRIDE

## GENEVIEVE VALENTINE

Pilgrims always cried when they crested the hill and saw the spires of Miruna; they usually fell to their knees right in the middle of traffic.

All I saw was the gate that led to the Night Market.

We pulled barrels off the cart (salt, cinnamon, chilis, cardamom, and mazeflower safe in the center away from wandering hands), and when the moon rose and the women came it was as if we'd always been waiting.

They moved in pairs, holding back their veils, closing their eyes as the smell of mazeflower struck them.

"Goes well in baking," Mark told a woman, "which you know all about, with those fine things in your basket."

The whole night went well (Mark could sell spice to a stone), until I got peppered by a loose lid and staggered back, choking.

From behind me a woman asked, "Where are you going?"

"Who's asking?" I snapped, and looked up into the ugliest face I've ever seen; teeth like old cheese, small black eyes, a thin mouth swallowed up by jowls.

"A passenger," she said. "Where are you going?"

"South," I said vaguely (never liked people knowing my business), then brushed pepper off my shirt and yelled, "Mark, so help me, I'll sell your hide to the fur traders!"

The woman was still standing there, smiling, her hands folded in front of her politely.

"Did you need some salt?" I asked.

"No," she said.

"Well, I wish you good journey," I said, and then for some reason I'll never know I asked, "Where do you travel?"

"South," she said, and I realized exactly where she thought she was headed.

I've never known when to seal the barrel and shake on the deal. It's how I ended up with a blue wagon and a partner like Mark in the first place.

"Not on any transport of mine," I said.

"It's for my husband," she said. "A shoemaker in Okalide. I'll join him there."

I didn't wonder why he'd left her behind. A face like that was bad for business.

Mark came around and stood behind me.

"I can't take an unescorted woman," I said. I didn't care, but someone on the road would. This was a church state. "Find someone else to take you."

As I turned to go she opened her hand and unfurled a necklace of sapphires as long as a man's arm, flaming as they caught the dawn. Mark gasped.

It was the most beautiful thing I'd ever seen. I reached without thinking, and had to pull back my hand when I remembered myself. I knew the trouble a woman would bring on that road full of pilgrims and devout traders.

"I don't accept bribes," I said. Mark kicked my foot.

"It isn't a bribe," she said. "It's a dowry."

Mark stopped kicking.

"You want me to—" I paused.

She held out her hand draped in glittering blue, her eyes steady. "Sandal-brides are common enough on this road."

"Not this common," Mark muttered, and I surprised us both when I cut him off with, "Pack the wagon."

Still muttering, he went, and then it was just the woman and me.

"Sandal-briding is dangerous," I said. "Women go missing that way if the men get greedy."

She smiled. "A greedy man wouldn't have pulled back his hand."

I found myself smiling, too, and by the time she said, "My husband has another when I am safely delivered," somehow I had already decided to agree.

We went the back way; I didn't want her to see Mark's face until it was too late to object.

The ceremony was easier than border-crossing. I gave her a pair of sandals I'd bought on the way, and she showed the priest the necklace she was giving me in lieu of bed rights. I swore to release her at the end of the journey. He wrote my name down next to hers, marked us "Okalide," and it was over.

Outside I said, "You could go pack your things."

"I don't have any things," she said, and stopped to buy a blanket.

Mark was still packing when we got back, but he must have known what I was going to do, because he had made space in the back of the wagon for someone to sit.

I drove the oxen, which were fonder of me than of Mark (good salesmanship never fools oxen). Mark kept watch in the back of the wagon, when he was awake.

All morning I expected him to climb through and demand a seat away from the woman (my wife), but when we stopped in the scrub at midday and I let the oxen loose to find what they could in the stringy undergrowth, I saw him helping her down.

"We'll rest half an hour," I said.

Mark nodded and disappeared back into the wagon.

"Just kick him out of the way when we set off," I said, unhooking my canteen.

She laughed and took a seat under the branches of the twisted pim. It was scant shade, but the flats were like this all the way to Okalide. There was a reason her husband made a living there; this ground wore out your shoes.

She shaded her eyes with one hand and peered out at the horizon, though there was nothing inspiring about it. It was three months of low scrub and low hopes.

"Expect more of the same," I said, taking a drink from my canteen and trying to sound like a grizzled traveler and not like someone who used to live above an alehouse and still hated desert nights.

"I don't mind," she said. "I've never been outside the walls before. I'm excited for anything."

I was probably more grizzled than I thought, though, since the idea of being closed in by city walls made my skin crawl.

"Well, if you like scrub, we'll have plenty."

"How do the animals take it?"

I looked over at the two bony oxen, who had found enough roots for a meal and were chewing contentedly. "They're tough beasts, though they look dead."

"Tough beasts do surprise you that way," she said.

She went back into the wagon, and only then I realized she had gone all day without so much as a drink of water, and I had offered her none.

"We'll arrange a bed for you in the wagon," I said the first night as she and Mark were trying a fire.

"Oh, no," she said, "I love the sky."

I wondered if she expected me to sleep at her side. I didn't know what sandal-husbands usually did. "The wagon is really much better. More privacy."

"Too late," she said, "I already know what Mark says in his sleep."

She handed him the flint, and Mark blushed and bowed his head to the sparks.

After the fire was going, Mark helped me pull rations out of the barrel.

"I hope she doesn't eat much," he said, staring at the salted beef and stale bread.

"What do you say in your sleep?"

Mark shook his head, and I hated that they should have been together in the back of the wagon with their secrets while I was sweating in the sun all day.

"Don't lose your manners," I said into the barrel.

Mark raised an eyebrow, sliced the meat into three pieces with his pocketknife. "Well, what's her name, then, so I don't have to keep calling her Goodwife?"

"You *should* call her Goodwife."

"Don't you know her name?"

She hadn't said it and I'd never asked, but the priest had written it down. "Sara."

Mark looked at me like I was one of the oxen, and took the skillet out to her.

"Tell me about your city," she said to me.

"It was like your city. Like any city."

"I don't know my city," she said. "Start there."

And I must have made a face again, because she explained, "They have the market at night so we don't see the city well enough to run away."

I thought about the women picking their way home before it was light, about her thin purse, her refusal to go home and pack. The food turned to dust in my mouth.

"What do you want to know?" I asked, but I knew the answer before she said, "Everything."

I told her about the alehouse; she asked how ale was made and listened as if she'd married a brewer. She wanted to know how many people could read. I told her about my schooling in the townhouse owned by a noble who lived in the country, and then I realized how it sounded to live in the country when the country looked like this, so I explained lakes and green trees and the soft wet snow that fell in winter.

I described the trader who sold me his wagon, his beasts, and Mark's indenture in exchange for the alehouse. I expected her to tell me it was a poor trade, but she listened to this story the same as to the others.

When I got to the terms of the sale, Mark said, "This was worth an alehouse in a season city?"

I had no answer, gave him none.

After I ran out of my life, I told her the Tale of the Pearl, which seemed to make her sad, so I told the Tale of the Blind Flower-seller to smooth things over.

Then my throat hurt, and I said, "We should sleep."

"You know, I grew up, too," Mark said as he sulked back to the wagon.

She laughed; her voice was dry, and I handed her the canteen.

She laid her blanket on the hard ground and pulled half of it over her. I felt guilty for not having bought a pallet, a felted shawl even, in all the time I'd been sleeping on the ground. The wagon was as it had been delivered to me, as though I was just keeping it for the man who might want it back.

"We'll buy you a pallet," I said.

"No need," she said, like someone who's used to the worst bed. "Do you know the stars?"

"No."

She was quiet after that. When enough time had gone by, I made a bed a little behind her; it was cold that far from the fire, and it felt too familiar to be so close, but I wanted to be something between her and the night.

I wasn't fond of other traders on the road (or ever), but a few evenings later I saw a fire and knocked on the side of the wagon to let them know we were stopping.

I brought a rasher of bacon to trade for a torch to light our fire. They were glass traders from Demarest, and after the pleasantries I found myself saying, "Let me bring my wife over; she has a little pepper to season it."

Mark and the sandal-bride (Sara, I thought) were pulling bread out of the barrel when I hauled myself into the cramped quarters.

"Bring some pepper," I told her.

I wasn't sure how to go on, but she guessed and smiled, and reached for the right barrel.

Mark said, "That's five coin worth—"

"Come on," I said, and she carried the ladle like it was mazeflower and not some common thing.

They were surprised to see her, and I remembered she was ugly.

She didn't notice, or didn't react, and they made room for us, and when there had been quiet for a moment she said, "Where have you come from?"

They looked to me like she had spoken out of turn.

I thought about the city walls and the night market closing around her again in Okalide.

I said, "Do you know about the stars?"

A week later we found someone who knew the stars, and he went through each constellation, jabbing his finger at the sky.

We found a botanist after that, wasted out in the scrub, who described flowers I'd never seen.

A silk trader liked her. He opened up his caravan of wagons and had his servants bring the best. We held up our lanterns and looked at the embroidered fountains that spit silver spangles along the blue silk.

Pilgrim women never spoke; the men only spoke to me. We stopped trying. Pilgrims could season their own food.

Once when I stopped the wagon for the night I found her sleeping with her cheek pressed against a barrel of cinnamon, like she could hear how it smelled.

I rarely said anything at strange camps; what was there to say when you were always the ignorant one?

But I listened, and I saw how people changed as they spoke of things they loved, and with every story I felt the world opening before us as if my oxen walked on the sea.

A metalworker and his wife sharpened our knives for some chilies, and the sandal-bride's eyes gleamed in the dark as he explained how to power the wheel, how to shape a blade.

"Where did you learn it?"

"At my father's feet," the man said, and tears sprang into his eyes, but even as he cried he told her about the illness that had carried off his parents. He wanted a home by the sea, where the salt air dulled enough knives to feed a metalworker for the rest of his life, and where the fish was fresh.

That night she cried softly, mourning the parents of some man she'd never see again.

I counted the stars: the great ox, the three cubs, the parted lovers, the willow tree.

The wagon got lighter as we went.

Mark winced every time I opened a barrel, and though I kept the ladles skimpy, I couldn't blame him. We would never make it to a port city before we ran out.

I closed my hand around the sapphires in my pocket as I drove. The day was coming when I'd have to break the clasp and sell them off.

Twice we stopped in tent cities and set up in their open squares, and Mark and Sara and I handed out envelopes of mazeflower and filled people's burlap bags with what was left of the cumin and salt.

By then the nights were cold in earnest. Mark made beds amidst the barrels, little fortresses to keep out the wind. Sara and I kept separate blankets, but I slept between her and the wagon flap. I would listen to the wind hissing past the canvas and think: This much, at least, I can do for her.

One night it was birders, and I scraped the last of a barrel of cinnamon to make enough for an offering.

"I don't know what you're hoping for," Mark said, "but you're ruining yourself this way."

I didn't answer; there was nothing to argue.

When we reached camp I said, "This is my wife Sara," and took her arm to present her, and she looked at me for a long moment before she smiled at them.

She told my stories, always. People were kinder if they thought she wasn't from Miruna.

We met the girl with the shriveled leg who made cages, the boy who made paints that turned a thrush into a sweet-anna. Above us the little beasts hopped back and forth in the bentwood cages, and of everyone we met on that long journey, that family was the happiest.

That night she sat and looked out past our circle of light to their camp, where the birds were calling.

Silhouetted by the fire she looked like a camel, a beast who had always been wise, and I watched her until the birds went silent.

The last long stretch to Okalide was four nights of nothing, not even scrub for shelter, and in the pilgrim town we bought up vinegar-wine (only thing that won't go brackish) and decided to travel at night and rest in the heat of the day.

Mark drank whenever wine was offered, and he took it as badly as ever, so he was still asleep when the sun set and it was time to go.

Sara and I sat in the shade of the wagon and watched the night crawl over the dust.

"Will I ever hear your story?" I asked, and she looked at me as if she knew why I was asking.

She did know. She knew, and Mark knew, and I was the only one who was just waking up to why.

Her thin mouth pressed tighter as if she was afraid of the words getting out. "I have no story," she said. "I was born hidden, and grew hidden, and I married hidden, and now I go to Okalide."

"And your husband? Is he kind?"

"I hope," she said after a long time. There was a breeze moving in ahead of the moon. "But if not, I'll be unhappy in Okalide, which is better than being unhappy in Miruna."

I wanted to say, stay here and risk unhappiness with me, but "here" was a wagon and a raggedy trail around the desert cities. You met the same sort of people wherever you went, and one day she would regret asking someone his story and learning what he really was.

She was only my sandal-bride, and by the time the leather wore out she would be happy or unhappy with some other man, and I would still have a wagon and a wide circle of road.

I said, "You'll find a way to be happy," because that was the only thing I really knew about her, and we sat in the shadow of the wagon until the breeze turned cold.

She sat beside me, wrapped in her thin blanket, all that night as I drove toward Okalide.


After we were stationed in the morning market, Sara my sandal-bride stepped out from the wagon without even her blanket and said, "I'm ready."

Mark came out behind her; when he was on the ground he held out his hand and they shook like it was a business deal.

"My wishes for a good life," he started, but abruptly he turned his back and crawled into the wagon as if he had forgotten something important.

I almost took her elbow, but when I held out my hand she looked at me. Under her gaze I dropped my arm, held it against my side.

She looked around until she saw some landmark her husband must have given her.

"This way," she said, and I followed her out of the market.

Okalide was under church rule, too, but here I saw women in daylight, at least, buying bread and reading the notices posted in the open squares.

The crowd that had been a nuisance before was overwhelming now. I wanted to know about the old man carving spoons on his doorstep, about the three young girls running along the edges of the fountain in the square.

Here no one noticed Sara (my wife). Her face was one of a thousand faces, not some apparition with a ladle of pepper in her hands, but somehow walking beside her I felt like the Empress' Guard.

At a corner she looked at the words etched into the clay walls, then turned to me.

"Which one reads South?" she asked quietly, and my heart broke.

I pointed, and after she looked at the word to memorize it we turned down the shady street.

His was the sixteenth door, and when he answered her knock he said, "Sara," as if she didn't know her own name, but she just smiled and embraced him.

I looked back at the main road, where a shaft of sun crawled across the dust.

He introduced himself, but as he did he wrapped his arm around her waist and I didn't catch his name.

"How was your journey?" he asked, and, tripping over himself, "—and of course you'll come in and have some cold water and some fruit."

"I can't," I said.

"He has an apprentice," Sara explained, "and they have work."

He nodded. "Of course, of course," he said, and then he turned to her and smiled. "And how was the journey?"

I held my breath and waited for the first story she would tell him, the first words that would make it one big story sewn with little ones as a wedding gift to him.

She smiled and said, "A lot of brackish wine."

He laughed so hard he had to drop his head, and for a moment she and I looked at each other.

I saw the bars of her cage bending around her, saw why she had wanted those stories; she'd needed something that was hers, to hoard against a life with some dull boy to whom she had given her word.

When he had recovered from his laughter he saw I was still there, and blinked. "You need your bride-price, of course, so sorry for forgetting," he said, and a moment later there was a little ruby bracelet in my palm.

I was still looking at Sara. I had forgotten I would be paid.

The priest at the bastion wrote "safely delivered," and wrote down all our names, and it was over.

She said, "Come visit as soon as you can."

"We'll be back again," I said, which was the only lie I ever told her.

When I got back to the market the wagon was still packed and Mark was waiting in the driver's seat.

"What did he look like?"

"Let's go," I said, took the reins.

We were five miles outside the city when I said, "What do you want to do after your indenture?"

"Trade!" he blurted, choked on a mouthful of dust.

I got his story; he had a woman in Suth he'd promised to come back for, and he'd heard about the botanist from Sara and wanted to find new spices. "From the East, maybe," he said, "if they can be had by ship."

I gave him the ruby bracelet. "Payment for the spice I used on the journey. Your indenture is over."

The oxen would warm to him; he knew how to drive the wagon.

I moved through and questioned anyone who would answer. I wanted to know everything about the world. With the first sapphire, I bought a book to write in.

Some old man married a woman with six red-haired sisters. The youngest got black hair, and set about cursing them all, poorly, and he and I laughed into our beers until we cried.

Three brothers pulled aside a riverbed to keep their village from flooding, and they bought wine and sang songs in three parts, and I marked the words as fast as I could.

When the first book was full I bought another, for the botanist and the birders and all the stars I knew.

I listened to everyone, wrote down everything.

You have to write down everything. The world is wide, and you never know what stories someone is waiting to hear; maybe someday, someone will have bought a pair of boots from the shoemaker and his ugly wife, down a dusty street in Okalide.

# THE ADAKIAN EAGLE

## BRADLEY DENTON

---

### I

The eagle had been tortured to death.

That was what it looked like. It was staked out on the mountain on its back, wings and feet spread apart, head twisted to one side. Its beak was open wide, as if in a scream. Its open eye would have been staring up at me except that a long iron nail had been plunged into it, pinning the white head to the ground. More nails held the wings and feet in place. A few loose feathers swirled as the wind gusted.

The bird was huge, eleven or twelve feet from wingtip to wingtip. I'd seen bald eagles in the Aleutians before, but never up close. This was bigger than anything I would have guessed.

Given what had been done to it, I wondered if it might have been stretched to that size. The body had been split down the middle, and the guts had been pulled out on both sides below the wings. It wasn't stinking yet, but flies were starting to gather.

I stood staring at the eagle for maybe thirty seconds. Then I got off the mountain as fast as I could and went down to tell the colonel. He had ordered me to report anything hinky, and this was the hinkiest thing I'd seen on Adak.

That was how I wound up meeting the fifty-year-old corporal they called "Pop."

And meeting Pop was how I wound up seeing the future.

Trust me when I tell you that you don't want to do that. Especially if the future you see isn't even your own.

Because then there's not a goddamn thing you can do to change it.

### II

I found Pop in a recreation hut. I had seen him around, but had never had a reason to speak with him until the colonel ordered me to. When I found him, he was engrossed in playing Ping-Pong with a sweaty, bare-chested opponent who was about thirty years his junior. A kid about my age.

Pop had the kid's number. He was wearing fatigues buttoned all the way up, but there wasn't a drop of perspiration on his face. He was white-haired, brown-mustached, tall, and skinny as a stick, and he didn't look athletic. In fact, he looked a little pale and sickly. But he swatted the ball with cool, dismissive flicks of his wrist, and it shot across the table like a bullet.

This was early on a Wednesday morning, and they had the hut to themselves except for three sad sacks playing poker against the back wall. Pop was facing the door, so when I came in he looked right at me. His eyes met mine for a second, and he must have known I was there for him. But he kept on playing.

I waited until his opponent missed a shot so badly that he cussed and threw down his paddle. Then I stepped closer and said, "Excuse me, Corporal?"

Pop's eyes narrowed behind his eyeglasses. "You'll have to be more specific," he said. He had a voice that made him sound as if he'd been born with a scotch in one hand and a cigarette in the other.

"He means you, Pop," the sweaty guy said, grabbing his shirt from a chair by the curving Quonset wall. "Ain't nobody looking for me."

Pop gave him the briefest of grins. I caught a glimpse of ill-fitting false teeth below the mustache. They made Pop look even older. And he had already looked pretty old.

"Cherish the moments when no one's looking for you," Pop said. "And don't call me 'Pop.' 'Boss' will do fine."

"Aw, I like 'Pop,' " the sweaty guy said. "Makes you sound like a nice old man."

"I'm neither," Pop said.

"You're half right." The sweaty guy threw on a fatigue jacket and walked past me. "I'm gettin' breakfast. See you at the salt mines."

Pop put down his paddle. "Wait. I'll come along."

The sweaty guy looked at me, then back at Pop. "I think I'll see you later," he said, and went out into the gray Adak morning. Which, in July, wasn't much different from the slightly darker gray, four-hour Adak night.

Pop turned away from me and took a step toward the three joes playing poker.

"Corporal," I said.

He turned back and put his palms on the Ping-Pong table, looking across at me like a judge looking down from the bench. Which was something I'd seen before, so it didn't bother me.

"You're a private," he said. It wasn't a question.

"Yes, sir."

He scowled, his eyebrows pinching together in a sharp V. "Then you should know better than to call another enlisted man 'sir.' You generally shouldn't even call him by rank, unless it's 'Sarge.' We're all G.I.'s pissing into the same barrels here, son. When the wind doesn't blow it back in our faces."

"So what should I call you?" I asked.

He was still scowling. "Why should you call me anything?"

I had the feeling that he was jabbing at me with words, as if I were a thug in one of his books and he were the combative hero. But at that time I had only read a little bit of one of those books, the one about the bird statuette.

And I had only read that little bit because I was bored after evening chow one day, and one of the guys in my hut happened to have a hardback copy lying on his bunk. I wasn't much for books back then. So I didn't much care how good Pop was at jabbing with words.

"I have to call you something," I said. "The colonel sent me to take you on an errand."

Pop's scowl shifted from annoyance to disgust. "The *colonel?*" he said, his voice full of contempt. "If you mean who I think you mean, he's a living mockery of the term *intelligence officer.* And he's still wearing oak leaves. Much to his chagrin, I understand. So I suppose you mean the *lieutenant* colonel."

"That's him," I said. He was the only colonel I knew. "He wants you and me to take a drive, and he wants us to do it right now. If you haven't eaten breakfast, I have a couple of Spam sandwiches in the jeep. Stuck 'em under the seat so the ravens wouldn't get 'em."

Pop took his hands off the table, went to the chairs along the wall, and took a jacket from one of them. He put it on in abrupt, angry motions.

"You can tell him I don't have time for his nonsense," he said. "You can tell him I'm eating a hot meal, and after that, I'm starting on tomorrow's edition. I'm not interested in his editorial comments, his story ideas, or his journalistic or literary ambitions. And if he doesn't like that, he can take it up with the brigadier general."

I shook my head. "The general's not in camp. He left last night for some big powwow. Word is he might be gone a week or more. So if I tell the colonel what you just said, I'm the one who'll be eating shit."

Pop snorted. "You're in the Army and stationed in the Aleutians. You're already eating shit."

He tried to walk past me, but I stepped in front of him.

He didn't like that. "What are you going to do, son? Thrash an old man?" He was glaring down at me like a judge again, but now the judge was going to throw the book. Which was something I had also seen before, so it didn't bother me.

"I'd just as soon not," I said.

Pop glanced back at the poker players. I reckoned he thought they would step up for him. But they were all staring at their cards hard enough to fade the ink, and they didn't budge.

"Did you see the boxing matches yesterday?" I asked.

Pop looked back at me. His eyes had narrowed again.

"There was a crowd," he said. "But yes, I watched from a distance. I thought it was a fine way to celebrate the Fourth of July, beating the snot out of our own comrades in arms. I hear the Navy man in the second match was taken to the Station Hospital."

I shrugged. "He dropped his left. I had to take the opportunity."

Pop bared those bad false teeth. "Now I recognize you. You K.O.'d him. But he laid a few gloves on you first, didn't he?"

"Not so's I noticed." Thanks to the colonel, I'd had two whole weeks during which my only duty had been to train for the fight. I could take a punch.

"So you're tough," Pop said. His voice had an edge of contempt. "It seems to me that a tough fellow should be killing Japs for his country instead of running errands for an idiot. A tough fellow should—" He stopped. Then he adjusted his glasses and gave me a long look. When he spoke again, his voice was quiet. "But it occurs to me that you may have been on Attu last year. In which case you may have killed some Japs already."

I didn't like being reminded of Attu. For one thing, that was where the colonel had decided to make me his special helper. For another, it had been a frostbitten nightmare. And seven guys from my platoon hadn't made it back.

But I wasn't going to let Pop know any of that.

"A few," I said. "And if the brass asked my opinion, I'd tell them I'd be glad to go kill a few more. But the brass ain't asking my opinion."

Pop gave a weary sigh. "No. No, they never do." He dug his fingers into his thick shock of white hair. "So, what is it that the lieutenant colonel wants me to assist you with? I assume it's connected with some insipid piece of 'news' he wants me to run in *The Adakian*?"

I hesitated. "It'd be better if I could just show you."

Pop's eyebrows rose. "Oh, good," he said. His tone was sarcastic. "A mystery." He gestured toward the door. "After you, then, Private."

It felt like he was jabbing at me again. "I thought you said enlisted men shouldn't call each other by rank."

"I'm making an exception."

That was fine with me. "Then I'll call you 'Corporal.'"

A williwaw began to blow just as I opened the door, but I heard Pop's reply anyway.

"I prefer 'Boss,'" he said.

### III

We made our way down the hill on mud-slicked boardwalks. On Adak, the wind almost always blew, but the most violent winds, the williwaws, could whip up in an instant and just about rip the nose off your face. The one that whipped up as Pop and I left the recreation hut wasn't that bad, but I still thought a skinny old guy like him might fly off into the muck. But he held the rail where there was a rail, and a rope where there was a rope, and he did all right.

As for me, I was short and heavy enough that the milder williwaws didn't bother me too much. But as I looked down the hill to the sloppy road we called Main Street, I saw a steel barrel bouncing along at about forty miles an hour toward Navytown. And some of the thick poles that held the miles of telephone and electrical wires that crisscrossed the camp were swaying as if they were bamboo. We wouldn't be able to take our drive until the wind let up.

So I didn't object when Pop took my elbow and pulled me into the lee of a Quonset hut. I thought he was just getting us out of the wind for a moment, but then he slipped under the lean-to that sheltered the door and went inside. I went in after him, figuring this must be where he bunked. But if my eyes hadn't been watering, I might have seen the words *THE ADAKIAN* stenciled on the door.

Inside, I wiped my eyes and saw tables, chairs, typewriters, two big plywood boxes with glass tops, a cylindrical machine with a hand crank, and dozens of reams of paper. The place had the thick smell of mimeograph ink. Two of the tables had men lying on them, dead to the world, their butts up against typewriters shoved to the wall. A third man, a slim, light-skinned Negro, was working at a drawing board. It looked like he was drawing a cartoon.

This man glanced up with a puzzled look. "What're you doing back already, Pop?" He spoke softly, so I could barely hear him over the shriek of the williwaw ripping across the hut's corrugated shell.

"I don't know how many times I have to tell you," Pop said. "I don't like 'Pop.' I prefer 'Boss.' "

"Whatever you say, Pop. They run out of scrambled eggs?"

"I wouldn't know. My breakfast has been delayed." Pop jerked a thumb at me. "The private here is taking me on an errand for the lieutenant colonel."

The cartoonist rolled his eyes. "Lucky you. Maybe you'll get to read one of his novellas."

"That's my fear," Pop said. "And I simply don't have enough whiskey on hand." He waved in a never-mind gesture. "But we've interrupted your work. Please, carry on."

The cartoonist turned back to his drawing board. "I always do."

Pop went to an almost-empty table, shoved a few stacks of paper aside, and stretched out on his back. The stack of paper closest to me had a page on top with some large print that read: HAMMETT HITS HALF-CENTURY—HALF-CENTURY CLAIMS FOUL.

"Have a seat, Private," Pop said. "Or lie down, if you can find a spot." He closed his eyes. "God himself has passed gas out there. We may be here a while."

I looked around at the hut's dim interior. The bulb hanging over the drawing board was lit, but the only other illumination was the gray light from the small front windows. Wind noise aside, all was quiet. It was the most peaceful place I had been since joining the Army.

"This is where you make the newspaper?" I asked.

"You should be a detective," Pop said.

I looked at the two sleeping men. "It sure looks like an easy job."

Pop managed to scowl without opening his eyes. "Private, have you actually seen *The Adakian*? I suppose it's possible you haven't, since there are over twenty thousand men in camp at the moment, and we can only produce six thousand copies a day."

"I've seen it," I said. "I saw the one about the European invasion, and maybe a few others."

Pop made a noise in his throat. "All right, then. When have you seen it?"

"Guys have it at morning chow, mostly."

Now Pop opened his eyes. "That's because my staff works all night to put it out *before* morning chow. Starting at about lunchtime yesterday, they were typing up shortwave reports from our man at the radio station, writing articles and reviews, cutting and pasting, and doing everything else that was necessary to produce and mimeograph six thousand six-page newspapers before sunup. So right now most of them have collapsed into their bunks for a few hours before starting on tomorrow's edition. I don't know what these three are still doing here."

At the drawing board, the Negro cartoonist spoke without looking up. "Those two brought in beer for breakfast, so they didn't make it back out the door. As for me, I had an idea for tomorrow's cartoon and decided to draw it before I forgot."

"What's the idea?" Pop asked.

"It's about two guys who have beer for breakfast."

Pop grunted. "Very topical."

Then no one spoke. I assumed parade rest and waited. But as soon as I heard the pitch of the wind drop, I opened the door a few inches. The williwaw had diminished to a stiff breeze, no worse than a cow-tipping gust back home in Nebraska.

"We have to go, Boss," I said.

Pop didn't budge, but the cartoonist gave a whistle. "Hey, Pop! Wake up, you old Red."

Pop sat up and blinked. With his now-wild white hair, round eyeglasses, and sharp nose, he looked like an aggravated owl.

"Stop calling me 'Pop,' " he said.

Outside, as Pop and I headed down the hill again, I said, "That's something I've never seen before."

"What's that?" Pop asked, raising his voice to be heard over the wind.

"A Negro working an office detail with white soldiers."

Pop looked at me sidelong. "Does that bother you, Private? It certainly bothers the lieutenant colonel."

I thought about it. "No, it doesn't bother me. I just wonder how it happened."

"It happened," Pop said, "because I needed a damn good cartoonist, and he's a damn good cartoonist."

I understood that. "I do like the cartoons," I said.

Pop made a noise in his throat again.

"Would it be all right, Private," he said, "if we don't speak again until we absolutely have to?"

That was fine with me. We were almost to the jeep, and once I fired that up, neither of us would be able to hear the other anyway. The muffler had a hole in it, so it was almost as loud as a williwaw.

IV

Halfway up the dormant volcano called Mount Moffett, about a mile after dealing with the two jerks in the shack at the Navy checkpoint, I stopped the jeep. The road was barely a muddy track here.

"Now we have to walk," I told Pop.

Pop looked around. "Walk where? There's nothing but rocks and tundra."

It was true. Even the ravens, ubiquitous in camp and around the airfield, were absent up here. The mountainside was desolate, and I happened to like that. Or at least I'd liked it before finding the eagle. But I could see that to a man who thrived on being with people, this might be the worst place on earth.

"The Navy guys say it looks better when there's snow," I said. "They go skiing up here."

"I wondered what you were discussing with them," Pop said. "I couldn't hear a word after you stepped away from the jeep."

I decided not to repeat the Navy boys' comments about the old coot I was chauffeuring. "Well, they said they were concerned we might leave ruts that would ruin the skiing when it snows. After that, we exchanged compliments about our mothers. Then they got on the horn and talked to some ensign or petty officer or something who said he didn't care if they let the whole damn Army through."

Hunching my shoulders against the wind, I got out of the jeep and started cutting across the slope. The weather was gray, but at least it wasn't too cold. The air felt about like late autumn back home. And the tundra here wasn't as spongy as it was down closer to camp. But the rocks and hidden mud still made it a little precarious.

Pop followed me, and I guessed it had to be tough for him to keep his balance, being old and scrawny. But he didn't complain about the footing. That would have been far down his list.

"Tell me the truth, Private," he said, wheezing. "This is a punishment, correct? The lieutenant colonel stopped me on Main Street a few months ago and asked me to come to dinner and read one of his stories. But my boys were with me, so I said, 'Certainly, if I may bring these gentlemen along.' At which point the invitation evaporated. That incident blistered his ass, and that's why we're here, isn't it?"

I turned to face him but kept moving, walking backward. "I don't think so. When he sent me up here this morning, it didn't have anything to do with you. I was supposed to look for an old Aleut lodge that's around here somewhere. The colonel said it's probably about three-quarters underground, and I'd have to look hard to find it."

Pop was still wheezing. "That's called an *ulax*. Good protection from the elements. But I doubt there was ever one this far up the mountain, unless it was for some ceremonial reason. And even if there was an *ulax* up here, I can't imagine why the lieutenant colonel would send you looking for it."

"He has a report of enlisted men using it to drink booze and have relations with some of the nurses from the 179th," I said. "He wants to locate it so he can put a stop to such things."

Pop frowned. "Someone's lying. The 179th has twenty nurses here at most. Any one of them who might be open to 'such things' will have a dozen officers after her from the moment she arrives. No enlisted man has a chance. Especially if the lady would also be required to climb a mountain and lower herself into a hole in the ground."

"Doesn't matter if it's true," I said. "I didn't find no lodge anyway." I turned back around. We were almost there.

"That still leaves the question of why we're up here," Pop said.

This time I didn't answer. Although he was a corporal, Pop didn't seem to grasp the fact that an enlisted man isn't supposed to have a mind of his own. If an officer asks you to dinner, or to a latrine-painting party, you just say "Yes, sir." And if he tells you to go for a ride up a volcano, you say the same thing. There's no point in asking why, because you're going to have to do it anyway.

"Are we walking all the way around the mountain?" Pop shouted, wheezing harder. "Or is there a picnic breakfast waiting behind the next rock? If so, it had better not be another Spam sandwich."

"You didn't have to eat it," I said.

Pop started to retort, but whatever he was going to say became a coughing fit. I stopped and turned around to find him doubled over with his hands on his knees, hacking so hard that I thought he might pass out.

I considered pounding him on the back, but was afraid that might kill him. So I just watched him heave and thought that if he died there, the colonel would ream my butt.

Pop's coughing became a long, sustained ratcheting noise, and then he spat a watery black goo onto the tundra. He paused for a few seconds, breathing heavily, then heaved again, hacking out a second black glob. A third heave produced a little less, and then a fourth was almost dry.

Finally, he wiped his mouth with his sleeve and stood upright again. His face was pale, but his eyes were sharp.

"Water," he said in a rasping voice.

I ran back to the jeep, stumbling and falling once on the way, and returned with a canteen. Pop took it without a word, drank, then closed his eyes and took a deep breath.

"That's better," he said. He sounded almost like himself again. He capped the canteen and held it out without opening his eyes.

I took the canteen and fumbled to hang it from my belt. "What was that?" I asked. "What happened?" I was surprised at how shook-up my own voice sounded. God knew I'd seen worse things than what Pop had hacked up.

Pop opened his eyes. He looked amused. " 'What happened?' " he said. "Well, that was what we call coughing."

I gave up on fixing the canteen to my belt and just held it clutched in one hand. "No, I mean, what was that stuff that came out?" I could still see it there on the tundra at our feet. It looked like it was pulsing.

"Just blood," Pop said.

I shook my head. "No, it ain't. I've seen blood." I had, too. Plenty. But none of it had looked this black.

Pop glanced down at it. "You haven't seen old blood," he said. "If this were red, that would mean it was fresh, and I might have a problem. But this is just old news coming up."

"Old news?" I asked.

"Tuberculosis, kid. I caught it during the *previous* war to end all wars. Don't worry, though. You can't catch it from me."

I wasn't worried about that. But I was confused. "If you were in the Great War, and you caught TB," I said, "then how could they let you into the Army again?"

Pop grinned. Those bad false teeth had black flecks on them now. "Because they can't win without me." He gestured ahead. "Let's get this over with, Private, whatever it is. I have to go back and start cracking the whip soon, or there might not be a newspaper tomorrow."

So I turned and continued across the slope. I could see the hillock I'd marked with rocks a few dozen yards ahead. I hoped Pop wouldn't go into another coughing fit once we crossed it.

## V

Pop's eyebrows rose when he saw the eagle, but otherwise it didn't seem to faze him.

"Well, this is something different," he said.

I nodded. "That's what I thought, too."

Pop gave a small chuckle. "I'm sure you did, Private." He looked at me with his narrow-eyed gaze, but this time it was more quizzical than annoyed. "When I asked you what this was about, you said it would be better if you just showed me. Now you've shown me. So what the hell does the lieutenant colonel want me to do? Write this up for *The Adakian*?"

"I think that's the last thing he wants," I said. "He says this thing could hurt morale."

Pop rolled his eyes skyward. "Christ, it's probably low morale in the form of sheer boredom that did this in the first place. Human beings are capable of performing any number of deranged and pointless acts to amuse themselves. Which is precisely what we have here. The brass told us we couldn't shoot the goddamn ravens, so some frustrated boys came up here and managed to cut up a bald eagle instead. And they've expressed their personal displeasure with their military service by setting up the carcass as a perverse mockery of the Great Seal of the United States."

"The what?" I asked.

Pop pointed down at the bird. "There's no olive branch or arrows. But otherwise, that's what this looks like. The Great Seal. Aside from the evisceration, of course. But I suppose that was just boys being boys."

"You think it was more than one guy?" I asked.

Pop looked at me as if I were nuts. "How on earth would I know?"

"You said 'boys.' That means more than one."

"I was speculating. I have no idea whether this was a project for one man, or twenty."

I tossed the canteen from hand to hand. "Okay, well, do whatever you have to do to figure out who it was."

Now Pop looked at me as if I weren't only nuts, but nuts and stupid, too. "There's no way of knowing who did this. Or even why. Speculation is all that's possible. The bird might have been killed out of boredom, out of hatred, or even out of superstition. I have no idea."

None of that sounded like something I could report. "But the colonel says you used to be a detective. Before you wrote the books."

Pop took off his glasses and rubbed his eyes. "I was a Pinkerton. Not Sherlock Holmes. A Pinkerton can't look at a crime scene and deduce a culprit's name, occupation, and sock color. Usually, a Pinkerton simply shadows a subject. Then, if he's lucky, the subject misbehaves and can be caught in the act." Pop put his glasses back on and held out his empty hands. "But there's no one to shadow here, unless it's every one of the twenty thousand men down in camp. Do you have one in mind? If not, there's nothing to be done."

I looked down at the eagle. As big and magnificent as it might have been in life, it was just a dead bird now. What had happened here was strange and ugly, but it wasn't a tragedy. It wasn't as if a human being had been staked out and gutted.

But in its way, the eagle unnerved me almost as much as the things I'd seen and done on Attu. At least there had been reasons for the things on Attu. Here, there was no reason at all—unless Pop was right, and it had just been boredom. If that was the case, I didn't want to know which guys had been bored enough to do this. Because if I knew, I might get mad enough to hurt them. And then there'd be something else I'd have to see in my sleep over and over again.

"All right, Pop," I said, keeping my eyes on the eagle. "There's a can of gasoline strapped to the jeep. What if we tell the colonel that when you and I got up here, we found this thing burned up?"

Pop cleared his throat. "You'd be willing to do that, Private? Lie to the lieutenant colonel?"

I had never sidestepped an order before. The colonel had made me do some stupid things and some awful things, but this was the first time that it looked like he was making me do a pointless thing. Besides, Pop was older and smarter than the colonel—even I could see that—and if he thought the eagle was a waste of time, then it probably was.

Besides, we were enlisted men, and we had to stick together. As long as there weren't any officers around to catch us doing it.

"Sure," I said, looking up at Pop again. "I've lied before. Back home in Nebraska, I even lied to a judge."

Pop gave me a thin-lipped smile. "What did you do to wind up in front of a judge?"

I had done so much worse since then that it didn't seem like much of a fuss anymore. "I beat up a rich kid from Omaha for calling me a dumb Bohunk," I said. "Then I stole his Hudson, drove it into a pasture, and chased some cows. I might have run it through a few fences while I was at it."

Pop chuckled. "That doesn't sound too bad. Some judges might have even considered it justified."

"Well, I also socked the first deputy who tried to arrest me," I said. "But I think what really made the judge mad was when I claimed that I wasn't a dumb Bohunk, but a stupid Polack."

"Why would that make the judge angry?" Pop asked.

"Because the judge was a Polack," I said. "So he gave me thirty days, to be followed by immediate enlistment or he'd make it two years. That part was okay, since I was going to sign up anyhow. But the thirty days was bad. My old man had to do the hay mowing without me. I got a letter from my mother last week, and she says he's still planning to whip me when I get home."

I noticed then that Pop's gaze had shifted. He was staring off into the distance past my shoulder. So I turned to look, and I saw a man's head and shoulders over the top edge of another hillock about fifty yards away. The man was wearing a coat with a fur-lined hood, and his face was a deep copper color. He appeared to be staring back at us.

"Do you know him?" Pop asked.

I squinted. "I don't think so," I said. "He looks like an Eskimo."

"I believe he's an Aleut," Pop said. "And the only natives I've seen in camp have belonged to the Alaska Scouts, better known as Castner's Cutthroats. Although that may be for the alliteration. I don't know whether they've really cut any throats."

I was still staring at the distant man, who was still staring back.

"They have," I said.

"Then let's mind our own—" Pop began.

He didn't finish because of a sudden loud whistling noise from farther down the mountain. It seemed to come from everywhere below us, all at once, and it grew louder and louder every moment.

"Shit," I said. I think Pop said it, too.

We both knew what it was, and we could tell it was going to be a fierce one. And there were no buildings up here to slow it down. It was a monster williwaw whipping around the mountain, and we had just a few seconds before the wind caught up with its own sound. The jeep was hundreds of yards away, and it wouldn't have been any protection even if we could get to it. Our only option was going to be to lie down flat in the slight depression where the dead eagle was staked out. If we were lucky, the exposed skin of our hands and faces might not be flayed from our flesh. And if we were even luckier, we might manage to gulp a few breaths without having them ripped away by the wind. I had the thought that this wasn't a good time to have tuberculosis.

Then, just as I was about to gesture to Pop to drop to the ground, I saw the distant Cutthroat disappear. His head and shoulders seemed to drop straight into the earth behind the hillock. And in one of my rare moments of smart thinking, I knew where he had gone.

"Come on!" I shouted to Pop, and I dropped the canteen and started running toward the hillock. But I had only gone about twenty yards when I realized that Pop wasn't keeping up, so I ran back to grab his arm and drag him along.

He didn't care for that, and he tried to pull away from me. But I was stronger, so all he could do was cuss at me as I yanked him forward as fast as I could.

Then the williwaw hit us, and he couldn't even cuss. Our hats flew away as if they were artillery shells, and I was deafened and blinded as my ears filled with a shriek and my eyes filled with dirt and tears. The right side of my face felt as if it were being stabbed with a thousand tiny needles.

I couldn't see where we were going now, but I kept charging forward, leaning down against the wind with all my weight so it wouldn't push me off course. For all I knew, I was going off course anyway. I couldn't tell if the ground was still sloping upward, or if we were over the top of the hillock already. But if I didn't find the spot where the Cutthroat had disappeared, and find it pretty damn quick, we were going to have to drop to the ground and take our chances. Maybe we'd catch a break, and the williwaw wouldn't last long enough to kill us.

Then my foot slipped on the tundra, and I fell to my knees. I twisted to try to catch Pop so he wouldn't hit the ground headfirst, and then we both slid and fell into a dark hole in the earth.

## VI

The sod roof of the *ulax* was mostly intact, but there were holes. So after my eyes adjusted, there was enough light to see. But Pop had landed on top of me, and at first all I could see was his mustache.

"Your breath ain't so good, Pop," I said. "Mind getting off me?"

At first I didn't think he heard me over the shriek of the williwaw. But then he grunted and wheezed and pushed himself away until he was sitting against the earthen wall. I sat up and scooted over against the wall beside him.

Pop reached up and adjusted his glasses, which had gone askew. Then he looked up at the largest hole in the roof, which I guessed was how we'd gotten inside. It was about eight feet above the dirt floor.

"Thanks for breaking my fall," he said, raising his voice to be heard over the wind. "I hope I didn't damage you. Although you might have avoided it if you'd told me what you were doing instead of dragging me."

I didn't answer. Instead, I looked around at the mostly underground room. It was maybe twenty feet long by ten feet wide. At the far end was a jumble of sod, timber, and whalebone that looked like a section of collapsed roof. But the roof above that area was actually in better shape than the rest. The rest was about evenly split between old sod and random holes. Some empty bottles and cans were scattered around the floor, and a few filthy, wadded blankets lay on earthen platforms that ran down the lengths of the two longer walls.

But there was no Cutthroat. I had watched him drop down into the same hole that Pop and I had tumbled into. I was sure that was what had happened.

But I didn't see him here now.

"What happened to the Eskimo?" I asked.

Pop scanned the interior of the *ulax* and frowned. "He must have gone elsewhere."

"There isn't any elsewhere," I said, almost shouting. I pointed upward. "Listen to that. And this is the only shelter up here."

Pop shook his head. "The man we saw was a native. He may know of shelters on this old volcano that we wouldn't find if we searched for forty years. Or he may even be so used to a wind like this that he'll stand facing into it and smile."

I looked up at the big hole and saw what looked like a twenty-pound rock blow past. "I saw him jump down here. That's how I knew where to go. And I think I would have seen him climb back out. Unless he can disappear."

And then, from behind the jumble of sod and whalebone at the far end of the *ulax*, the Cutthroat emerged. His hood was down, and his dark hair shone. He was in a crouch, holding a hunting knife at his side. A big one.

"Who the fuck are you people?" the Cutthroat asked. His voice was low and rough, but still managed to cut through the howling above us. This was a man used to talking over the wind.

Pop gave a single hacking cough. Then he looked at me and said, "Well, Private, it doesn't look as if he disappeared."

Right then I wanted to punch Pop, but it was only because I was scared. I wished the Cutthroat really had disappeared. I didn't recognize his dark, scraggly-bearded face, but that didn't mean anything. I didn't remember many living faces from Attu.

But I did remember the Cutthroats as a group. I remembered how they had appeared and vanished in the frozen landscape like Arctic wolves.

And I remembered their knives.

"I asked you two a question," the Cutthroat said, pointing at us with his knife. "Are you M.P.'s? And if you're not, what are you doing here?"

Pop gave another cough. This time it wasn't a tubercular hack, but a sort of polite throat-clearing. And I realized he didn't understand what kind of man we were dealing with. But maybe that was a good thing. Because if he had ever seen the Cutthroats in action, he might have stayed stone-silent like me. And one of us needed to answer the question before the Cutthroat got mad.

"We aren't M.P.'s," Pop said. "So if you've done something you shouldn't, you needn't worry about us."

"I haven't done a fucking thing," the Cutthroat said. Even though his voice was gravelly, and even though he was cussing, his voice had a distinctive Aleut rhythm. It was almost musical. "I just came up here because a guy told me there was a dead eagle. And I thought I'd get some feathers. I'm a goddamn native, like you said."

I managed to take my eyes off the Cutthroat long enough to glance at Pop. Pop had the same expression on his face that he'd had when I'd first seen him, when he'd been whipping the strong, shirtless kid at Ping-Pong. He was calm and confident. There were even slight crinkles of happiness at the corners of his eyes and mouth, as if he were safe and snug in his own briar patch, and anybody coming in after him was gonna get scratched up.

It was the damnedest expression to have while sitting in a pit on the side of a volcano facing a man with a knife while a hundred-mile-an-hour wind screeched over your head.

"I understand completely," Pop said. "We came up to find the eagle as well, although we didn't have as good a reason. We're only here because an idiot lieutenant colonel couldn't think of another way to make us dance like puppets. It's a stupid, pointless errand from a stupid, pointless officer."

The Cutthroat blinked and then straightened from his crouch. He lowered the knife.

"Fucking brass," he said.

"You're telling us," Pop said.

The Cutthroat slipped his knife into a sheath on his hip. "Colonel Castner's not too bad. He lets us do what we know how to do. But the rest of them. Fuck me, Jesus. They didn't listen on Attu, and they ain't listened since."

I knew what he was talking about. The Cutthroats had scouted Attu ahead of our invasion, so they had told the brass how many Japs were there and what to expect from them. But they had also warned that Attu's permafrost would make wheeled vehicles almost useless, and that we'd need some serious cold-weather boots and clothing. Plus extra food. Yet we'd gone in with jeeps and trucks, and we'd been wearing standard gear. Food had been C-rations, and not much of that. It had all been a rotten mess, and it would have been a disaster if the Cutthroats hadn't taken it upon themselves to bring dried fish and extra supplies to platoon after platoon.

Not to mention the dead Jap snipers and machine gunners we regular G.I.'s found as we advanced. The ones whose heads had been almost severed.

"I cowrote the pamphlet on the Battle of the Aleutians," Pop said. "But of course it had to be approved by the brass, so we had to leave out what we knew about their mistakes. And we also weren't allowed to mention the Alaska Scouts. The generals apparently felt that specific mention of any one outfit might be taken to suggest that other outfits weren't vital as well."

The Cutthroat made a loud spitting noise. "Some of them *weren't*." He sat down with his back against the sod-and-whalebone rubble. "Don't matter. I was there, and I killed some Japs. Don't much care what gets said about it now."

The noise of the williwaw had dropped slightly, so when Pop spoke again his voice was startlingly loud.

"If you don't mind my asking," Pop said, "why are you on Adak? I was told the Scouts had gone back to Fort Richardson."

The Cutthroat's upper lip curled, and he pointed a finger at his right thigh. "I got a leg wound on Attu, and the fucking thing's been getting reinfected for over a year. It's better now, but it was leaking pus when the other guys had to leave. Captain said I had to stay here until it healed. But now I got to wait for an authorized ride. And while I wait, they tell me I'm an orderly at the hospital. Which ain't what I signed up for. So I tried to stow away on a boat to Dutch Harbor a couple weeks ago, and the fucking M.P.'s threw me off."

"I assume that means you're now AWOL from the hospital," Pop said. "Which explains why you thought that the Private and I might be police."

The Cutthroat shook his head. "Nah. The hospital C.O. don't really give a shit what I do. He let me put a cot in a supply hut and pretty much ignores me. I'm what you call extraneous personnel." He jerked a thumb over his shoulder. "I just thought you might be M.P.'s because of this dead guy back here. I think it's the same guy who told me about the eagle, but maybe not. You people all look alike to me."

It took me a few seconds to realize what the Cutthroat had said. When I did, I looked at Pop. Pop's eyebrows had risen slightly.

"Would you mind if I have a look?" Pop asked.

The Cutthroat shrugged his shoulders. "What do I care? He ain't *my* dead guy."

Pop stood up stiffly, and I stood up as well. With the williwaw overhead now a somewhat diminished shriek, we walked, hunched over, to where the Cutthroat sat. And now I could see that the *ulax* had a second, smaller chamber whose entrance had been partially obscured by the fallen sod and bone.

We went around the pile of debris, through the narrow entrance beside the wall, and into the second chamber. It was about ten by eight feet, and its roof was also pocked by holes that let in light. But these holes were smaller, and they changed the pitch of the wind noise. The shriek rose to a high, keening whistle.

On the floor, a stocky man lay on his back, his open eyes staring up at the holes where the wind screamed past. His hair looked dark and wet, and his face was as pale as a block of salt except for a large bruise under his left eye. His mouth was slack. He was wearing a dark Navy pea jacket, dark trousers, and mud-black boots. His bare, empty hands were curled into claws at his sides.

Pop and I stared down at him for a long moment, neither of us speaking.

At first, I didn't recognize the man because he looked so different from how he had looked the day before. But then I focused on the bruise under his eye, and I knew who he was. My gut lurched.

Right behind me, the Cutthroat said, "Back of his head's bashed in."

Startled, I spun around, fists up.

The Cutthroat's knife shot up from its sheath to within two inches of my nose.

Then Pop's hand appeared between the blade and my face.

"Easy, boys," Pop said. "I'm the camp editor. You don't want your names in the paper."

I lowered my fists.

"Sorry," I said. I was breathing hard, but trying to sound like I wasn't. "It was just a reflex."

The Cutthroat lowered his knife as well, but more slowly.

"Now I recognize you," he said, peering at me intently. "You boxed yesterday. And you were on Attu. Okay, mine was just a reflex, too."

I still didn't know him, but that still didn't mean anything. The Cutthroats hadn't stayed in any one place very long when I had seen them at all. And some of them had worn their fur-lined hoods all the time.

Pop took his hand away, and then all three of us looked down at the body. I opened my mouth to speak, but suddenly had no voice. Neither Pop nor the Cutthroat seemed to notice.

"He's Navy," Pop said. "Or merchant marine. A young man, like all the rest of you." Pop's voice, although loud enough to be heard over the wind, had a slight tremble.

"Don't worry about it, old-timer," the Cutthroat said. "He's just another dead guy now. Seen plenty of those."

Pop got down on one knee beside the body. "Not on this island," he said. "Other than sporadic casualties generated by bad bomber landings, Adak has been relatively death-free." He gingerly touched the dead man's face and tilted it to one side far enough to expose the back of the head. The skull had been crushed by a large rock that was still underneath. The dark stuff on the rock looked like what Pop had coughed up earlier.

Feeling sick, I turned away and stared at the Cutthroat. I tried to read his face, the way I might try to read an opponent's in a boxing match. I'd been told that you could tell what another fighter was about to do, and sometimes even what he was only thinking about doing, just from the expression on his face.

The Cutthroat gave me a scowl.

"Don't look at me, kid," he said. "I would've done a better job than that."

Pop opened the dead man's coat, exposing a blue Navy work shirt. I could see his hands shaking slightly as he did it. "I believe you," he said. "Whatever happened here was sloppy. It may even have been an accident." He opened the coat far enough to expose the right shoulder. "No insignia. He was just a seaman." He opened the shirt collar. "No dog tags, either."

Then he reached into the large, deep coat pockets, first the left, then the right. He came up from the right pocket clutching something.

Pop held it up in a shaft of gray light from one of the ceiling holes.

It was a huge, dark-brown feather, maybe fourteen inches long. It was bent in the middle.

"That bird," Pop said, "is turning out to be nothing but trouble."

## VII

We left the body where it was and went back into the larger room. The wind was still furious overhead, so we were stuck there for the time being. Pop and I sat back down against the wall at the far end, and the Cutthroat lounged on the earthen shelf along the long wall to our right.

Pop didn't look so good. He was pale, and he coughed now and then. I think he was trying to pretend that the dead man hadn't bothered him. He had probably seen death before, but not the way the Cutthroat and I had.

Still, this was different. In battle, death is expected. Back at camp, when the battlefields have moved elsewhere, it's something else. So I was a little shook up myself.

The Cutthroat didn't seem bothered at all. His mind was already on other things.

"This goddamn williwaw might take that eagle away," he said. "If it does, I won't get my feathers. I should have come in the other way, like you guys did. I saw you there with it, but then I felt the wind coming. I didn't think you two were gonna make it here."

"Neither did we," Pop said. "But if you want an eagle feather, you can have the one I took from that young man." He reached for his jacket pocket.

The Cutthroat made a dismissive gesture. "That one's bent in the middle. It's no good to me. The power's bent now, too."

"What sort of power do you get from feathers?" I asked. I immediately regretted it.

The Cutthroat gave me a look too dark to even rise to the level of contempt. "None of your fucking business. In fact, I'm wondering what you and your damn lieutenant colonel wanted with the eagle in the first place."

Pop coughed. "The private and I wanted nothing to do with it at all. But the lieutenant colonel seems to be curious about who killed it, gutted it, and staked it out like that. He incorrectly assumed I could help him discover that information."

The Cutthroat sat up straight. "Somebody killed it on purpose?"

"That's what it looks like," Pop said. "Couldn't you see it from over here?"

The Cutthroat's brow furrowed. "I just saw you two, and the eagle's wings, and then the wind hit me before I could come any closer. You say somebody pulled out its guts?"

"Yes." Pop's color was getting better. "And staked it to the earth with nails. Does that mean anything to you?"

The Cutthroat scowled. "Yeah, it means that somebody's a fucking son of a bitch. I ain't heard of nothing like that before." He scratched his sparse beard. "Unless maybe a shaman from a mainland tribe was here, trying to do some kind of magic."

Pop leaned toward the Cutthroat. His eyes were bright. "Why would killing an eagle be magic?"

The Cutthroat's hand came down to rest on the hilt of his knife. It made me nervous.

"The people along the Yukon tell a story about eagles," the Cutthroat said. "It's the kind of story you white people like to hear us savages tell. I even told it to some officers one night on Attu. Took their minds off the fact that they were getting a lot of kids killed. Got a promise of six beers for it. They paid up, too." He gave Pop a pointed look.

Pop gave a thin smile. "I don't have any beer at hand. Will you take an IOU?"

The Cutthroat answered Pop's smile with a humorless grin. "Don't be surprised when I collect." He leaned forward. "Okay. Long ago, a pair of giant eagles made their nest at the summit of a volcano. I'm talking about eagles nine, ten times the size of the ones we got now. They'd catch full-grown whales and bring them back to feed their young. And sometimes, if they couldn't find whales, they'd swoop down on a village and take away a few human beings. This went on for many years, with the giant eagles raising a new brood of young every year. These young would go off to make nests on other volcanoes and attack other villages."

Pop took a Zippo and a pack of Camels from a jacket pocket. "So they were spreading out like the Germans and Japanese."

The Cutthroat nodded. "Yeah, I guess so. Anyway, one day, one of the original eagles, the father eagle, was out hunting and couldn't find any reindeer or whales or nothing. So the father eagle said, fuck it, the babies are hungry. And he swooped down and took a woman who was outside her house. Carried her back to the volcano, tore her limb from limb, ripped out her guts, and fed her to his giant eaglets."

The pitch of the wind outside dropped, and the Cutthroat paused and listened. Pop lit a cigarette and then offered the pack to me and the Cutthroat. The Cutthroat accepted, but I declined. I'd promised my mother I wouldn't smoke.

The wind shrieked higher again as Pop lit the Cutthroat's cigarette, and then the Cutthroat went on.

"But this poor woman happened to be the wife of the greatest hunter of the village," he said, exhaling smoke. "And when the hunter returned and was told what had happened, he went into a rage. He took his bow and his arrows, and even though everyone told him he was a fool, he climbed the volcano."

"Most truly brave men *are* fools," Pop said. He gestured toward me with his cigarette. I didn't know why.

"I wouldn't know," the Cutthroat said. "In the Scouts, we try to be sneaky instead of brave. Works out better. Anyway, when the hunter got to the eagles' nest, he found six baby eagles, each one three times the size of a full-grown eagle today. They were surrounded by broken kayaks, whale ribs, and human bones. The hunter knew that some of those bones belonged to his wife, and that these eaglets had eaten her. So he shot an arrow into each of them, through their eyes, and they fell over dead. Then he heard a loud cry in the sky, which was the giant mother eagle returning. He shot her under the wing just as she was about to grab him, and then he shot her through the eyes. She tumbled off the mountain, and that was it for her. Then there was another loud cry, which was the father eagle—"

"And of course the hunter killed the father eagle as well," Pop said.

The Cutthroat glared. "Who's telling this fucking legend, old man? No, the hunter didn't kill the goddamn father eagle. The eagle dived at him again and again, and each time the hunter put an arrow into a different part of its body.

But he never hit the father eagle in the eye. So, finally, pierced with arrows all over, and his whole family dead, the giant eagle flew away into the northern sky, and neither he nor any of his kind were ever seen again. But the eagles of today are said to be the descendants of those who had flown away in earlier times." The Cutthroat gave a loud belch. "At least, that's the story."

Pop leaned back again, looking up at the holes in the roof and blowing smoke toward them. "It's not bad," he said. "Not much suspense, though. I'm not sure it's worth six beers."

"I don't give a damn what you think it's worth," the Cutthroat said, tapping ash from his cigarette. "It ain't my story anyway. My mother heard it a long time ago from some Inuits on the mainland, and she told it to me when I was a kid. But we're Unangan. Not Eskimo."

"So you think an Eskimo might have killed this eagle too?" Pop asked. "Staked it to the ground, gutted it?"

The Cutthroat frowned. "Like I said, I ain't heard of anything quite like that. But I ain't heard of a lot of things. Some of those shamans might still hold a grudge against eagles. People can stay mad about crap like that for five, six hundred years. Or maybe some guy just thought if he killed an eagle, he could take its power. And then he could be a better hunter, or fisherman, or warrior. I've heard of that. And you white people like stuff like that, too. I'll toss that in for free."

Pop was giving the Cutthroat a steady gaze. "But you're saying it wouldn't have been you who killed the eagle. Or anyone else Unangan."

The Cutthroat shook his head. "Doubt it. Sometimes the eagles show us where the fish are. And sometimes we toss 'em a few in return. We get along all right."

Pop nodded, sat back against the earthen wall, and closed his eyes. He took a long pull on his cigarette. "I've been all over the post, both Armytown and Navytown, many times. But I've seen very few Aleuts or Eskimos. So just from the odds, I doubt that a native is our eagle-killer."

As much as I hated saying anything at all in front of the Cutthroat, I couldn't keep my mouth shut anymore. Pop was infuriating me.

"There's a dead man over there!" I yelled, pointing at the section of collapsed roof. "Who cares about the eagle now?"

Pop opened his eyes and regarded me through a smoky haze.

"Actually, I don't care much," he said. "But because of that dead man, the eagle has become slightly more interesting."

"Why?" I asked, still furious. "Just because he had a feather in his pocket? That doesn't mean anything. He might have found it."

Pop's eyebrows rose. "I don't think so. He and the eagle have both been dead less than a day. So the coincidental timing, plus the feather in his pocket, suggests a connection. Either he killed the eagle, and then had an unfortunate accident . . . "

He fixed his gaze on the Cutthroat again.

" . . . or whoever did kill the eagle, or helped him kill it, may have then killed him as well."

The Cutthroat ground out his cigarette butt. "I told you guys before. It wasn't me."

"And I still believe you," Pop said. "I'm just wondering if you might have any idea who it may have been."

"Nope," the Cutthroat said. There was no hesitation.

Pop leaned back against the wall again and looked up at the holes in the roof.

"I don't have any idea either," Pop said. "But I think you were right about one thing."

"Huh?" the Cutthroat said. "What's that?"

"Whoever it was, he's a fucking son of a bitch."

The wind seemed to scream louder in response.

## VIII

The williwaw finally slacked off a little after noon, leaving only blustery gusts. The three of us stirred ourselves on stiff joints and muscles and rose from our places in the main room of the *ulax*.

Pop and the Cutthroat had both dozed after finishing their cigarettes, but I had stayed wide awake. I knew who the dead man was. But I hadn't told Pop yet for fear that the Cutthroat would hear me.

That was because, while I didn't recognize this particular Cutthroat, I knew who he was, too. On Attu, the Alaska Scouts had saved my life and the lives of dozens of my buddies, but they hadn't done it by being kind and gentle souls. They had done it by being cruel and ruthless to our enemies.

And I knew that a man couldn't just turn that off once it wasn't needed anymore. I knew that for a cold fact.

I boosted Pop up through the hole in the roof where we'd dropped in, and then I followed by jumping from the raised earthen shelf at the side of the room, grabbing a whalebone roof support, and pulling myself through.

I joined Pop on the hillock just beside the *ulax*, blinking against the wind, and then looked back and saw the Cutthroat already standing behind me. It was as if he had levitated.

"So this thing here is not our fucking problem," the Cutthroat said, speaking over the wind. "We all agree on that."

Pop nodded. "That's the body of a Navy man. So the private and I will tell the boys at the Navy checkpoint to come have a look. And if they ask our names, or if they know who I am, I'll be able to handle them. They're twenty-year-olds who've pulled checkpoint duty at the base of an extinct volcano. So they aren't going to be the brightest minds in our war effort."

I didn't like what Pop was saying. But for the time being, I kept my mouth shut.

The Cutthroat nodded. "All right, then." He turned away and started down the slope.

"We have a jeep," Pop called after him.

The Cutthroat didn't even glance back. So Pop looked at me and shrugged, and he and I started back the way we had come. A few seconds later, when I looked down the slope again, the Cutthroat had vanished.

When we reached the spot where the dead eagle had been staked, I thought for a moment that we had headed in the wrong direction. But then I saw the rocks I'd used as markers, so I knew we were where I thought we were. The eagle was simply gone. So were the nails. So was my canteen.

"The Scout was right," Pop said. "The wind took it."

If I tried, I could make out some darkish spots on the bare patch of ground where the bird had been staked, and when I looked up the slope I thought I could see a few distant, scattered feathers. But the eagle itself was somewhere far away now. Maybe the ocean. Maybe even Attu.

"This is a good thing," Pop said, continuing on toward the jeep. "Now when you tell the lieutenant colonel that the eagle was gone, you can do so in good conscience. Or good enough. It's certainly gone now. That fact should get me back to my newspaper until he thinks of some other way to torment me."

He looked at me and smiled with those horrible false teeth, as if I should feel happy about the way things had turned out. But I wasn't feeling too happy about much of anything.

"What about the man in the lodge?" I asked.

Pop frowned. "We're going to report him to the Navy."

"I know that," I said. "But what should I tell the colonel?"

Pop stopped walking and put his hand on my shoulder.

"Listen, son," he said. His eyes were steady and serious. "I'm not joking about this. Are you listening?"

I gave a short nod.

"All right." Pop sucked in a deep breath through his mouth and let it out through his nose. "When you see the lieutenant colonel, don't mention the dead man. You brought me up here to show me the eagle, as ordered, and it was gone. That's all. Do you understand?"

I understood. But I didn't like it.

"It's not right," I said.

Pop dropped his hand and gave me a look as if I'd slapped him. "Not right? How much more 'right' would the whole truth be? For one thing, there's no way of knowing how the eagle got into the state it was in. So there's no way to give the lieutenant colonel that information. But now it's gone, which means that problem is gone as well."

"You know I don't mean the eagle," I said.

Now Pop's eyes became more than serious. They became grim.

"Yes, we discovered a dead man," he said. "And the gutted eagle nearby, plus the feather in the dead man's pocket, raise some questions. But they're questions we can't answer. The simplest explanation? The sailor's death was an accident. He came up here, either alone or with comrades, got drunk, and hit his head when he passed out. But even if it was manslaughter or murder, he was Navy, and the guilty party is probably Navy as well. So we're telling the Navy. After that, it's out of our hands. Besides, Private, what do you suppose the lieutenant colonel would do if you did tell him about it?"

I didn't answer. I just stared back at Pop's grim eyes.

"I'll tell you what he'd do," Pop said. "He'd question us repeatedly. He'd make us trek back up here with M.P.'s. He'd order us to fill out reports in triplicate. He'd force me to run a speculative and sensational story in *The Adakian*, even though it's a Navy matter and affects our boys not at all. And then he'd question us again and make us fill out more reports. And all for what? What would the upshot be?"

I knew the answer. "The upshot," I said, "would be that the man would still be dead. And it would still be a Navy matter."

Pop pointed a finger at me. "Correct. And telling the lieutenant colonel wouldn't have made any difference at all."

I glanced back toward the *ulax*.

"It's still not right," I said.

The cold grimness in Pop's eyes softened. "There's nothing about a young man's death that's right. Especially when it was for nothing. But a lot of young men have died in this war, and some of those died for nothing, too. So the only thing to do is simply what you know *must* be done, and nothing more. Because trying to do more would be adding meaninglessness to meaninglessness." He stuck his hands into his jacket pockets. "And in this case, what we must do is tell the Navy. Period."

Then he started toward the jeep again. But I didn't follow.

"That won't be the end of it," I called after him.

He turned and glared at me. His white hair whipped in the wind.

"Why not?" he shouted.

I jerked a thumb backward. "Because I gave him that bruise on his face."

Pop stood there staring at me for a long moment, his stick-thin body swaying. I didn't think he understood.

"That's the guy I whipped in the ring yesterday," I said.

Pop just stared at me for a few more seconds. Then he took his right hand from his pocket and moved as if to adjust his glasses. But he stopped when he saw that he was holding the bent eagle feather he'd found on the dead man.

I saw his thin lips move under his mustache. If he was speaking aloud, it was too quietly for me to hear him over the wind. But I saw the words.

"Nothing but trouble," he said again.

## IX

This time, I stayed in the jeep while Pop talked with the Navy boys at the checkpoint. He had said things would go better if I let him handle it. I thought they might give him a bad time, since that had been their inclination with me that morning. But Pop had given a weak laugh when I'd mentioned that. He assured me it wasn't going to be a problem.

It took twenty minutes or more. But eventually Pop came back to the jeep. Through the shack's open doorway, I could see one of the Navy men get on the horn and start talking to someone.

"Let's go," Pop said.

I still didn't feel right. I had known the dead man, even if it had only been for a few minutes in a boxing ring. And although I had seen what had happened to the back of his head, and I knew that it had to have happened right there where we'd found him, I couldn't shake the notion that my clobbering him had somehow led to his death.

Pop nudged my shoulder. "I said, let's go. We may have to answer a few questions for whoever investigates, but the odds are against it. Those boys told me that the *ulax* we found is well known to their comrades as an unapproved recreation hut. They've never even heard of Army personnel using it. So this really is a Navy matter."

I didn't respond. Instead I just started the jeep, which clattered and roared as I drove us back down to camp. I didn't try to talk to Pop on the way. I didn't even look at him.

He didn't say anything more to me, either, until I had stopped the jeep on Main Street near the base of the boardwalk that led up the hill to the *Adakian* hut. I didn't mean to shut off the engine, but it died on me anyway.

"You can go on back to work," I said, staring down Main Street at the long rows of Quonset huts interspersed with the occasional slapdash wood-frame building . . . at all the men trudging this way and that through the July mud . . . at the wires on the telephone poles as they hummed and swayed . . . and at the black ravens crisscrossing the gray air over all of it. I still wouldn't look at Pop. "I'll tell the colonel the eagle was a bust, like you said."

Pop coughed a few times. "What about the dead man?" he asked then. "Are you going to mention him, or are you going to take my advice and leave it to the Navy?"

Now, finally, I looked at him. What I saw was a scrawny, tired-looking old man. He might have been fifty, but he looked at least eighty to me. And I wanted to dislike him more than I did. I wanted to hate him.

"I'm going to tell him I found the body," I said. "But I'll leave you out of it. And I'll leave the Cutthroat out of it too, since that's what we said we'd do. I'll just say that I spotted the lodge and went to have a look, but you were feeling sick and headed back to the jeep instead. I'll tell him I found the dead guy and told you about it, but you never saw him. And that we went down and told the Navy."

Pop's eyebrows pinched together. "Not good enough. With a story like that, he'll want to play detective. So he'll try to involve me regardless."

I shrugged. "That's the best I can do. I found a dead man while I was doing a chore for the colonel, and I have to tell him. Especially since he arranged for me to fight that same guy. So even if the Navy handles it, he'll still hear about it. And once he knows where they found him, and when, he'll ask me about it. So I have to tell him. It'll be worse later, if I don't."

Pop bit his lip, and I saw his false teeth shift when he did it. He pushed them back in place with his thumb. Then he stared off down Main Street the way I just had.

"Ever since this morning, I've been puzzled," he said in a low voice. "How is it that a lieutenant colonel is using a private as an aide, anyway? Officers over the rank of captain don't usually associate with G.I.'s lower than sergeant major. Unless the lower-ranking G.I. has other uses. As I do."

"Then I guess I have other uses too," I said. "Besides, I'm not his aide. He has a lieutenant for that. But when we got back from Attu, he said he was getting me transferred to a maintenance platoon so I'd be available for other things. And now I run his errands. I shine his shoes. I deliver messages. I box. And when he doesn't need me, I go back to my platoon and try not to listen to the shit the other guys say about me."

Pop gave another cough. He didn't sound good at all, but I guessed he was used to it.

"You haven't really answered my question," he said then. "You've explained what you do for him. But you haven't explained how you were selected to do it. Out of all the enlisted men available, what made him notice you in particular?"

He was jabbing at me yet again. I thought about dislodging his false teeth permanently.

Instead, I told him. As much as I could stand to.

"It was on Attu," I said. My voice shook in my skull. "Right after the Japs made their banzai charge. By that time some of those little bastards didn't have nothing but bayonets tied to sticks. But they wouldn't quit coming. My squad was pushed all the way back to the support lines before we got the last ones we could see. We even captured one. He had a sword, but one of us got him in the hand, and then he didn't have nothing. So we knocked him down, sat on him, and tied his wrists behind his back with my boot laces." I glared at Pop. "Our sergeant was gone, and by then it was just me and two other guys. Once we had the Jap tied, those guys left me with him while they went to find the rest of our platoon. Then the colonel showed up. He'd lost his unit, too, and he wanted me to help him find it. But I had a prisoner. So the colonel gave me an order."

Pop looked puzzled. "And?"

"And I obeyed the order."

Pop's eyes shifted away for a second, then back again. I thought he was going to ask me to go ahead and say it.

But then he rubbed his jaw, raised his eyes skyward, and sighed.

"All right," he said. "I'll go with you to speak with the lieutenant colonel. You won't have to tell him that I didn't see the corpse. But we'll still have to leave our friend from the Alaska Scouts out of it. And I'll have to go up to *The Adakian* first, to make sure the boys have started work on tomorrow's edition. There's nobody there over corporal, and they each refuse to take direction from any of the others unless I say so. I'm a corporal as well, of course, but our beloved brigadier general has given me divine authority in my own little corner of the war. He's an admirer. As were those Navy boys at Mount Moffett, as it turned out. Although I had the impression that what one of them really likes is the Bogart movie, while the other thinks I might be able to introduce him to Myrna Loy. But they were both impressed that I actually met Olivia de Havilland when she was here."

Pop liked to talk about himself a little more than suited me. But if he was going to do the right thing, I didn't care.

I got out of the jeep. "I'll go with you to the newspaper. In case you forget to come back."

Pop got out too. "At this point, Private," he said, "I assure you that you've become unforgettable."

After a detour to the nearest latrine, we climbed up to the newspaper hut. Pop went in ahead of me, but stopped abruptly just inside the door. I almost ran into him.

"What the hell?" he said.

I looked past Pop and saw nine men standing at attention, including the three I had seen there that morning. They were all like statues, staring at the front wall. Their eyes didn't even flick toward Pop.

Someone cleared his throat to our left. I recognized the sound.

I looked toward the table where Pop had napped that morning, and I saw the colonel rise from a chair. His aide was standing at parade rest just beyond him, glaring toward the *Adakian* staff. I had the impression they were being made to stand at attention as a punishment for something.

The colonel adjusted his garrison cap, tapped its silver oak leaf with a fingernail, then hitched up his belt around his slight potbelly and stretched his back. He wasn't a large man, but the stretch made him seem taller than he was. His sharp, dark eyes seemed to spark as he gave a satisfied nod and scratched his pink, fleshy jaw.

"It's about damn time," he said in his harsh Texas accent. Then he looked back at his aide. "Everyone out except for these two. That includes you."

The aide snapped his fingers and pointed at the door.

Pop and I stepped aside as Pop's staff headed out. They all gave him quizzical looks, and a few tried to speak with him. But the colonel's aide barked at them when they did, and they moved on outside.

The aide brought up the rear and closed the door behind him, leaving just the colonel, Pop, and me in the hut. To Pop's right, on the drawing board, I saw the finished cartoon of two soldiers having beer for breakfast. One soldier was saying to the other:

*"Watery barley sure beats watery eggs!"*

Pop's eyebrows were pinched together. He was glaring at the colonel.

"I don't know how long you made them stand there like that," Pop said. "But I'll be taking this up with the general when he returns."

The colonel gave a smile that was almost a grimace. "We'll cross that bridge when we come to it. At the moment, we're in the middle of another. I've received a call from a Navy commander who tells me a dead sailor has been found on Mount Moffett. He says the body was discovered by you, Corporal. I play cards with the man, and he's sharp. So I believe him."

Pop sat down on the cartoonist's stool, which still kept him several inches taller than me or the colonel.

"That's right," Pop said. He was still frowning, but his voice had relaxed into its usual cool, superior tone. "At your request, the private and I were looking for the dead eagle he'd found earlier. But it had apparently blown away. Then a williwaw kicked up, so we found shelter in an old Aleut lodge. That's where we found the unfortunate sailor."

The colonel turned toward me. "I understand it was the sailor you fought yesterday."

"Yes, sir," I said. I had gone to attention automatically.

"What happened?" the colonel asked. "Did he try to take another swing at you?" He was still smiling in what I guessed he thought was a fatherly way. "Was it self-defense, Private?"

It was as if an icicle had been thrust into the back of my skull and all the way down my spine.

"Sir," I said. I don't know how I managed to keep my voice from quaking, but I did. "He was dead when we found him, sir."

The colonel's fatherly smile faded. "Are you sure about that? Or is that what the corporal said you should tell me?"

Now Pop was staring at the colonel through slitted eyelids. And now he had a slight smile of his own. But it was a grim, knowing smile.

"Son of a bitch," he said.

The colonel turned on Pop with sudden rage. His pink face went scarlet.

"I wasn't speaking to you, Corporal!" he snapped. "When I need answers from a drunken, diseased has-been who hasn't written a book in ten years, you'll be the first to know. At the moment, however, I'll take my answers from the private."

Pop nodded. "Of course you will. He's just a kid, and he doesn't have a brigadier general in his corner. So you're going to use him the way you've used him since Attu. What happened there, anyway?"

"We won," the colonel said. "No thanks to the likes of you."

Pop held up his hands. "I'd never claim otherwise. At that time I was stateside having my rotten teeth pulled, courtesy of Uncle Sam."

The colonel stepped closer to Pop, and for a second I thought he was going to slap him.

"You're nothing but a smug, privileged, Communist prick," the colonel snarled. "The general may not see that, but I do. I've read the fawning stories you print about Soviet victories. You might as well be fighting for the Japs."

Pop's eyes widened. "Colonel, I realize now that your attitude toward me is entirely my fault. In hindsight, I do wish I could have accepted your dinner invitation. However, in my defense, by that time I had seen a sample of your writing. And it was just atrocious."

The colonel's face went purple. He raised his hand.

Then, instead of slapping Pop, he reached over to the drawing board, snatched up the new cartoon, and tore it to shreds. He dropped the pieces on the floor at Pop's feet.

"No more jokes in the newspaper about beer," he said. "They undermine discipline. Especially if they're drawn by a nigger."

Then he looked at me, and his color began draining back to pink.

"Private," he said, his voice lowering, "you and I need to talk. Unfortunately,

I'm about to have lunch, and then I have to meet with several captains and majors. The rest of my afternoon is quite full, as is most of my evening. So you're to report to my office at twenty-one hundred hours. No sooner, no later. Understood?"

"Yes, sir," I said.

The colonel gave a sharp nod. "Good. In the meantime, I'm restricting you to barracks. If you need chow, get it. But then go to your bunk and speak to no one. While you're there, I suggest that you think hard about what happened today, and what you're going to tell me about it. If it was self-defense, I can help you. Otherwise, you may be in trouble." He glanced at Pop, then back at me. "And stay away from the corporal."

"Yes, sir," I said.

The colonel pointed at the door, so I turned and marched out. I caught a glimpse of the colonel's aide and the newspaper staff standing up against the wall of the Quonset, and then I headed down the boardwalk toward Main Street. The wind cut through me, and I shivered. I still had to return the jeep to the motor pool. Then get some chow. Then go to my bunk. One thing at a time. Jeep, chow, bunk. Jeep, chow, bunk.

The colonel seemed to think I had killed the Navy man. And that Pop had advised me to lie about it.

Jeep, chow, bunk.

Of course, Pop *had* advised me to lie, but not about that. Because that hadn't happened.

Or had it? Could I have done something like that and then forgotten I'd done it? Why not? Hadn't I already done things just as bad?

Jeep, chow, bunk.

All I knew for sure was that the colonel hated Pop, and that I had been in trouble ever since finding the eagle.

Jeep, chow, bunk. It wasn't working.

How I wished I had never seen the eagle. Or the *ulax*.

How I wished I had never met another Cutthroat after Attu.

How I wished I could have stayed in my combat unit.

How I wished I had never met Pop.

How I wished I had never been sent to the Aleutians in the first place.

How I wished I had never punched that rich kid from Omaha, and that I had stayed home long enough to help my old man with the hay.

X

I had my Quonset hut to myself while I waited for the afternoon to creep by. I didn't know what job the rest of my bunkmates were out doing, but it didn't matter. I would have liked to find them and do some work so I wouldn't have to think. But I was under orders to stay put.

Other than the truth, I didn't know what I would tell the colonel when 2100 finally came. Even if I included every detail, including the ones Pop and I had agreed not to tell, it still wasn't going to be the story the colonel wanted to hear. And whatever story that was, I knew I wasn't smart enough to figure it out.

I hadn't gotten any chow. My stomach was a hard, hungry knot, and I knew I should have eaten. But I was also pretty sure I wouldn't have been able to keep it down.

Sure, I had been in trouble before. But back then, I had just been a dumb Bohunk kid who'd gotten in a fight, swiped a Hudson, and insulted a judge. None of that had bothered me. But none of that had been anything like this.

I wasn't even sure what "this" was. But I did know that another kid, a kid just like me except that he was Navy, had gotten his skull bashed in. And the colonel thought that maybe I was the one who'd done it.

It all went through my head over and over again, and the knot in my stomach got bigger and bigger. I lay in my bunk and closed my eyes, but I couldn't sleep. Outside, the Aleutian wind whistled and moaned, and occasional short rat-a-tats of rain drummed against the Quonset tin. Every so often, I heard planes roaring in and out of the airfield. I tried to guess what they were, since the bombing runs from Adak had pretty much ended once we'd retaken Attu and Kiska. But I had never been good at figuring out a plane from its engine noise. If an engine wasn't on a tractor or jeep, I was at a loss.

"First impressions can be so deceiving," a low, smooth voice said.

I opened my eyes. Pop was sitting on a stool beside my bunk. He was hunched over with his elbows on his knees, his hands clasped under his chin, his dark eyes regarding me over the rims of his glasses. I hadn't heard him come in.

"How'd you know where I bunk?" I asked.

Pop ignored the question. "Why, just this morning, Private," he continued, "you seemed like such a tough young man. Such a hardened fighter. Yet here we are, scarcely nine hours later, and you're flopped there like a sack of sand. Defeated. Vanquished."

"Don't those mean the same thing?"

Pop gave me that thin smile of his. "My point is, you're taking this lying down. That doesn't sound like someone who'd dare to punch a rich kid from Omaha."

I turned away from him and faced the cold metal of the Quonset wall.

"I'm under orders," I said. "And I'm not supposed to be talking to you."

Pop laughed a long, dry laugh that dissolved into his usual hacking cough.

"Under orders?" he asked through the coughing. "Just how do you think you got into this confusing court-martial conundrum in the first place? You followed orders, that's how. Logically, then, the only possible way out of your current situation is to *defy* orders, just this once. It's only sixteen thirty, and the lieutenant colonel won't be looking for you until twenty-one hundred. You've already wasted more than two hours wallowing here, so I suggest you don't waste any more."

I turned back to face him.

"Just what am I supposed to do?" I asked. "My only choice is to tell him everything that happened, and the hell with our promise to the Cutthroat. So that's what I'm going to do."

Pop shook his head. "You can't tell him everything," he said, "because you don't *know* everything."

"And you do?"

"No." Pop stood and jerked his thumb toward the door. "But I know some of it, and I'm going to find out the rest. You see, unlike you, I've spent the past few hours doing something. My job is to get the news, and a large part of that involves getting people to talk. So for the past two hours, people have been talking to me and my boys a lot. But now the boys have to work on the paper. And my cartoonist has to draw a new cartoon, which has put me into a vengeful mood."

"So go get your revenge," I said. "What's it got to do with me?"

Pop leaned down and scowled. "It's your revenge, too. And I don't think I can find out the rest of what I need to know if you aren't with me."

I rose on my elbows and stared up at him. It was true that following orders hadn't really worked out for me. But I didn't see how doing what Pop said would work out any better.

"You say you know some of it already," I said. "Tell me."

Pop hesitated. Then he turned, crossed to the other side of the hut, and sat on an empty bunk.

"I know the lieutenant colonel placed a bet on your fight yesterday," Pop said. "A large one. And I know that your opponent had a reputation as a damn good boxer. He'd won eighteen fights, six by knockout. How many have you won?"

"Two," I said. "Yesterday was my second match. The first was with the guy whose bunk you're sitting on. It was a referee's decision."

Pop's eyes narrowed. "So any sane wager yesterday would have been on the Navy man. And I saw the fight, Private. He was winning. Until the third round, when he dropped his left. And as you told me this morning, you took advantage. Who wouldn't?"

I sat up on the edge of my bunk. In addition to the knot in my stomach, I now felt a throbbing at the back of my skull.

"You're saying it was fixed," I said.

"If I were betting on it, I'd say yes." Pop waved a hand in a cutting gesture. "But leave that alone for now. Instead, consider a few more things. One, we know that the *ulax* we found was used by Navy men for unofficial activities. The dead man is Navy. And the Navy boys we talked to said they didn't know of anyone but sailors having any fun up there. After all, they control access to that part of the island. Yet the lieutenant colonel sent you up because, he claimed, he had reports of Army G.I.'s entertaining nurses there. Which doesn't quite jibe with the Navy's version."

"That's odd, I guess," I said. "But that's not anything you found out in the past two hours."

Pop looked down at the floor and clasped his hands again.

"No," he said. Now I could barely hear him over the constant weather noise against the Quonset walls. "I learned two more things this afternoon. One is that the lieutenant colonel will soon be up for promotion to full colonel. Again. After being passed over at least once before. And I know he wants that promotion very badly. Badly enough, perhaps, to do all sorts of things to get it."

Pop fell silent then, and kept looking down at the floor.

I stood. My gut ached and my head hurt. And I thought I knew the answer to my next question. But I had to ask it anyway.

"You said you learned two more things," I said. "What's the second?"

Pop looked up at me. His expression was softer than it had been all day. He looked kindly. Sympathetic. I had wanted to hit him earlier, but not as much as I did now.

"It's not really something new," Pop said. "It's what you already told me. Or almost told me. But of course I know the order that the lieutenant colonel gave you on Attu."

I clenched my fists. Maybe I would hit the old man after all. Maybe I wouldn't stop hitting him for a while.

"I won't say it aloud if you don't want me to," Pop said.

I turned and started for the door. I didn't know where I was going, but I knew I was getting away from Pop.

He followed and stopped me with a hand on my shoulder, so I whirled with a roundhouse right. He leaned back just in time, and my knuckles brushed his mustache.

"Jesus Christ, son," Pop exclaimed.

I grabbed his scrawny arms and pushed him away. He staggered back, but didn't fall.

"He was a Jap," I said. I was trembling. "He was trying to kill me not five minutes before. And it was an order. It was an order from a goddamn colonel."

Pop took a deep, quaking breath and adjusted his glasses.

"It was an order," I said.

Pop nodded. "I know. And now I need you to listen to me again. Are you listening, Private?"

I glared at him.

"Here it is, then," Pop said. "No one, and I mean no one—not your chaplain, not the general, not anyone back home, and sure as hell not me—*no one* would condemn what you did. If the circumstances had been reversed, that Jap would have done the same to you, and he wouldn't have waited for an order."

I could still see him lying there, his blood staining the thin crust of snow a sudden crimson. He had been as small as a child. His uniform had looked like dirty play clothes.

He was a Jap. But he was on the ground. With his hands tied behind his back. His sword was gone.

Pop wasn't finished. "The problem isn't that you followed the order. The problem is that out of the three thousand Japs you boys fought on Attu, we took only twenty-eight prisoners. I'm not saying that killing the rest was a bad thing. But prisoners can be valuable. Especially if they're officers. And a man with a sword might have been an officer. So someone would have wanted to ask him things like, what's your rank, who are your immediate superiors, where are your maps, what were your orders, what's your troop strength on Kiska, and where does Yamamoto go to take his morning shit. That sort of thing."

Pop was talking a lot, again. It wore on my brain. And Yamamoto's plane had been shot down a month before we'd hit Attu. But at least now I had something else to think about.

"You mean we need a supply of Japs?" I said.

Now Pop smiled his thin smile. "I mean that a lieutenant colonel in the Intelligence Section did a stupid thing. He wasn't even supposed to be near the fighting. But that banzai charge came awfully close. So in rage or fear, he forgot his job and ordered you to destroy a military intelligence asset. That's an act that could negatively affect his chances for promotion." Pop pointed at me again. "If anyone happened to testify to it."

I rubbed the back of my neck, trying to make the pain at the base of my skull go away.

"I don't understand how anything you just said adds up to anything we saw today," I told him.

Now Pop pointed past me, toward the door. "That's why there's more to find out, and that's why I need you to help me with it. There was one other man on the mountain with us this morning. And since you and he were freezing and fighting on Attu while I was elsewhere, I think he might be more willing to part with any answers if you're present."

That made some sense. The Cutthroat hadn't liked me, but he might respect me more than Pop.

Still, there was one thing that I knew Pop had left out in all his talk.

"What about the eagle?" I asked.

Pop bared his false teeth.

"That's the key," he said. "That's why we have to talk with the Scout again. Remember what he said about magic and power? Well, he also said that he told those same stories to officers on Attu." He went past me to the door. "Now, will you come along?"

I turned to go with him, then hesitated.

"Wait a minute." I was still trying to clear my head. "Are you saying the colonel believes in Eskimo magic?"

Pop held up his hands. "I have no idea. But magic and religion are based on symbols, which can be powerful as hell. And I know the lieutenant colonel *does* believe in that. After all, there's one symbol that he very much wants for his own."

I was still confused by most of what Pop had said. But this one part, I suddenly understood.

A full colonel was called a "bird colonel."

Because a full colonel's insignia was an eagle.

I went with Pop.

## XI

The 179th Station Hospital wasn't just one building. It was a complex of Quonset huts and frame buildings, and it even had an underground bunker. When Olivia de Havilland had come to Adak in March, she had spent an entire day there, visiting the sick and wounded. There were a few hundred patients on any given day.

But all we needed to do was find the Cutthroat. So I waited outside the main building while Pop went in and charmed whomever he needed to charm to find out what he wanted to know. I was beginning to realize that there were some things, even in the Army, that superseded rank.

When Pop came out again, his hands in his jacket pockets, he tilted his head and started walking around back. I followed him to three Quonset huts behind the main building. He stopped at the lean-to of the first hut and looked one way and then the other as I joined him. There were a few G.I.'s trudging along nearby with no apparent purpose. Maybe, I thought, they were just trying to look busy so they wouldn't be sent to the South Pacific.

"Do you see anyone you know?" Pop asked. "Anyone who might tell the lieutenant colonel we're here?" I tried to take a good look. But the usual gray light was dimming as evening came on, making all the soldiers appear gray as well.

"I don't think so," I said. "But everyone's starting to look alike to me."

Pop gave me an annoyed glance. "You sound like the Scout," he said. He stepped away, moved quickly to the center Quonset, and slipped into its lean-to. I followed. Then he barged into the hut without knocking.

The Cutthroat was in a small open space in the center of the hut, surrounded by shelves packed with boxes and cans. He was sitting on the edge of a cot under a single lightbulb that hung from the ceiling, leaning over a battered coffeepot on a G.I. pocket stove. The smell was not only of coffee, but of old beef stew, seaweed, and mud. My still-knotted stomach lurched.

The Cutthroat looked up, and his slick dark hair gleamed. "You guys." He didn't sound surprised. "Did you bring my beers?"

Pop and I stepped farther inside, and I closed the door behind us. There were two folding stools set up on our side of the pocket stove.

"I'll bring your beers tomorrow." Pop went to the right-hand stool and sat down. "In the meantime, I want you to know that both the private and I are doing our best to live up to this morning's agreements. For one thing, we haven't mentioned your presence on Mount Moffett to anyone else."

"I believe you," the Cutthroat said.

"But we have a problem," Pop continued. "So we may not be able to keep that confidence much longer. There's a lieutenant colonel who's trying to use that Navy man's death to make our lives hell."

The Cutthroat looked back down at his brew. "Yeah, I know." He rubbed his right thigh. "Goddamn, my leg is hurting tonight. I better not climb any more mountains for a while."

I sat down on the left-hand stool. The fumes from the stuff bubbling in the coffeepot were intense.

"What do you mean, you know?" I asked. "How could you know that?"

The Cutthroat glanced up at me. "Because I wasn't sure I trusted you guys. So I followed you. You didn't drive fast. I was outside the back wall of the newspaper hut when you got your asses chewed. I couldn't hear it all, but I got most of it. He's got it in for both of you. And I recognized his voice."

Pop's eyebrows rose. "That was quite stealthy of you."

The Cutthroat snorted. "I've snuck up on Japs in machine gun nests, and they knew I was coming. Buncha desk soldiers who don't expect me ain't a challenge."

"Nevertheless," Pop said. "I respect a man who can shadow that well. Especially if I'm the one he's shadowing."

The Cutthroat reached to a shelf behind him and brought down three tin cups. "You guys want coffee before you start bothering me with more questions?"

"Is that what that is?" I asked.

The Cutthroat gave me a look almost as dark as he'd given me in the *ulax*. "You need to work on your fucking manners."

Pop and I both accepted cups, and the Cutthroat poured thick, black liquid into both of them. It was something else that reminded me of what Pop had coughed up that morning.

Then the Cutthroat poured a cup for himself and set the pot back down on the pocket stove. He took a swig and smiled.

"That's good," he said. "This stuff will help you think better."

Pop took a swig as well, and I took a tentative sip of mine. It didn't taste as bad as it smelled, so I drank a little more. There was a hint of rotted undergrowth. But at least it was hot.

"Thank you," Pop said. He took a long belt. "But now I'm going to bother you, as you suspected. How did you recognize the lieutenant colonel's voice?"

The Cutthroat blew into his cup, and steam rose up around his face. "Because I've heard it before. On Attu, he was one of the shitheads who wouldn't listen to our scouting reports. But he loved our colorful stories. Here on Adak, I've been bringing him and his officer pals booze and coffee while they play poker right here in this hut. And when they get good and drunk, they want me to tell more stories. Like I said, you people can't get enough of that noble-savage crap."

"Do those poker pals include a Navy commander?" Pop asked.

"I guess that's what he is," the Cutthroat said. "He and the lieutenant colonel set up yesterday's boxing matches. They made a bet on the Army-Navy one." He pointed at me. "The lieutenant colonel bet on this guy."

"I know," Pop said. "For a lot of money, correct?"

The Cutthroat scowled and took a long drink. "Maybe there were side bets for money. But the bet between the lieutenant colonel and the Navy officer was for something else. See, the Navy guy has friends and family in high places. Like fucking Congress. So if the Army boxer won, the commander promised to have these friends pull strings and help with a promotion."

"What if the Navy man won?" Pop asked.

The Cutthroat grinned and shook his head. "Then the commander was going to have dinner with you, Corporal. That's what the lieutenant colonel promised. You must be famous or rich or something. Gotta say, it seemed like a lopsided bet to me."

Pop drained his cup and set it on the floor. He seemed to wobble on his stool as he did.

"Very lopsided indeed," he said, "since I wouldn't do a favor for the lieutenant colonel if my life depended on it."

I had been sipping the hot coffee and listening, but now I spoke up. "What about the eagle?"

The Cutthroat fixed me with an even gaze. "I still don't know about that. Not for sure. But nobody ever knows anything for sure. No matter who you ask, or what you find out, you'll never know all of anything that's already past."

The single lightbulb began to flicker. My stomach knot had relaxed, but now I found myself feeling lightheaded. I knew I should have had some chow.

"So I'm giving you both the opportunity to know as much as the lieutenant colonel," the Cutthroat said. "I told him the legend I told you. And once, he asked me about taking power from animals. I said I couldn't really explain that, since I didn't understand it myself. But if he were to take a spirit journey or have a vision, like some shamans do, he might have a chance to know all the secrets he wanted. He might die and be reborn. He might be torn apart and remade. He might meet his totem animal and be given its strength. He might gain whatever he desired. He might even see his entire life from his birth to his death." The Cutthroat shrugged. "Or he might go crazy. Or he might just pass out and sleep it off. It all depends on the individual."

The Cutthroat stood up from the cot, and he split into five men before me. "Here," they all five said in harmony. They reached for Pop and grasped his forearms. "You take the cot. My mother got this recipe from the same people who told her the eagle story, and she always said that the most important part was to lie the fuck down. There's some mushrooms and other shit in it, and you don't want to know what I have to do to mix it right. But it hardly ever kills anyone."

The five Cutthroats put Pop on the bunk, and Pop curled up on his side. He looked like a toy made out of olive-drab pipe cleaners with a cotton-swab head. I could see his eyes behind his glasses, and they were like hard-boiled eggs.

Now the Cutthroat condensed into one man again, and he reached for me.

"You'll have to take the floor," he said. "But you're younger. It's fair."

As he grasped my wrist, I watched my tin coffee cup tumble from my numb fingers. It turned over and over, and brown droplets spun out and circled it. The cup turned into the sun.

The bright light was high above my eyes. I could see it between Pop's fingers.

"That's the best I can do for you," the Cutthroat's voice said. I couldn't see him anymore. He was far away. "Your enemy took this journey before you. But maybe you're better suited for it. I don't say that this means you'll beat him, or that you'll understand what he's done. But at least now you have the same magic. So it's a fair fight. You're welcome."

The earth shook with a deafening rumble, and the back of Pop's hand fell against my forehead.

Then, in brilliant flashes, in a cacophony of voices and noise and music, I began to see everything.

Everything.

I began to see both the past and present of every place I had ever been, every object I had ever touched, every thing I had ever done. It was as if I were a movie camera in the sky, looking down and watching it all.

Then, even as the past and present were flashing and roaring around me, I saw the future as well. And not just mine.

Pop's, too.

My advice: Never see the future.

Not anyone's.

*I'm in my foxhole when the Japanese make their charge. I have to struggle for my helmet, for my weapon. When I make it out of the hole I run backward, firing as they come toward me. Some keep coming even after I hit them. One gets very close and sets off a hand grenade, trying to kill us both. But he trips and falls, his body covers it, and I'm all right. Then, to my left, I see my sergeant bayoneted. I shoot the one who did it. But it's too late.*

*A younger Pop, his hair not yet all white, is at a typewriter. It clacks and clatters, and the bell rings over and over again. He puts in page after page. He smokes cigarette after cigarette and drinks two bottles of whiskey dry, but he doesn't stop typing. He does this for thirty hours without a break. When he finally stops I can see his eyes. And I know he has emptied himself. There is nothing left.*

*The colonel points at the little man on the ground and shouts at me. I look at the little man and know he's a Jap who just tried to kill me. But now he's lying facedown, his hands behind his back. He hardly looks like a Jap now.*

*The colonel points and shouts again and again, louder and louder. I put the muzzle of the M1 at the base of the little man's skull and pull the trigger.*

*Pop, much, much younger, is wearing a uniform and walking into a hospital. He doubles over coughing as he climbs the steps. A pretty nurse rushes over and puts her arm around his shoulders.*

*I am much, much older, sitting in a tangle of metal and plastic. A young man is using huge steel jaws to push the metal apart and make a hole for me. You'll be okay, sir, he says. I'll get you out. I manage to take a small plastic* rectangle from my pocket. It has little square buttons. I punch the buttons and call my daughter. You're right, I tell her. I shouldn't drive anymore.

The colonel is standing over the dead eagle. He is holding a knife. The sailor who fought me appears at the hillock beside the lodge, and the colonel goes to him. You'll have to trust me for an IOU, he says. It'll be a while before I can collect my winnings. But you did good. And thanks for the bird.

Pop, looking only a bit older, but wearing a nice suit, is being escorted from a bus by armed guards. They take him into prison and put him into a cell by himself. He stays in the prison for six months. He writes a lot of letters. But all his books go out of print. The radio money stops. When they let him out, he is sicker than ever and looks twenty years older. He is broke and goes to live in a tiny cottage owned by friends.

Guess I don't have any choice, the sailor says. But I know you're good for it, sir. Do I still get the date with the nurse? The blonde who swabbed my face and said I was handsome for a Navy man?

I am standing at the altar with my younger brother beside me, looking down at the far end of the aisle, when the pipe organ blares and all of the people on either side of the aisle stand up. A gorgeous woman in white appears on the arm of an older man, and they walk toward me, smiling. I can't wait for them to get here so I can find out what her name is.

You still get the date, the colonel says, holding out a bent eagle feather. Show this to her when she comes. It's dark down there, and she has to know it's you. She'll be here in a little while. Go on down and wait.

The heavy, sweating man with greasy, wormlike hair leans forward and looks down from his high, long podium. I would like to ask, he says in a thick voice. Is Mr. Budenz being truthful when he told us that you were a Communist? So now Pop leans forward too, toward the microphones on the table where they've made him sit, and he says, I decline to answer on the grounds that an answer might tend to incriminate me. He is out of prison, and he is poor. But they won't leave him alone. They won't let him at least try to write.

The sailor goes down into the lodge, and the colonel walks away, past the eagle. Another sailor approaches. He's in there, the colonel says, pointing back toward the lodge. Down where you boys have your fun. He threw the fight. He lost your money.

I am holding a baby. Her eyes look like mine. How the hell did this happen, I wonder. How did we finally have a girl after all these years? After all the bad things I've done, how did my life turn out to be this good?

The second sailor stops and stares down at the eagle. Never mind that, the colonel says. It's just a dead bird. It's none of your business. Go talk to your friend. He threw the fight.

In the hospital bed, Pop opens his eyes and he sees the woman. There have been dozens of women. Even a wife. But this is the one. The only one, really. She's there leaning over him.

In the lodge, the two sailors argue. You sold us out, the second sailor says. The first says, no, I'm going to share the winnings with you guys. I don't have any of it yet. But I will. Joe, calm down. Joe, no.

My daughter claps her hands the first time I walk to the mailbox and back without the crutches. You are one tough old bird, she says. Yes, I say. Yes I am. Guess what kind of tough old bird. I have its feather in my room. Have I ever shown you?

The woman leaning over Pop is at once plain and beautiful. That paradox was the first thing that drew him to her. And then her frighteningly sharp mind kept him there. More than thirty years now. She is his best friend, was several times his lover, has always been his savior. But he's been hers too, so that's only fair. She looks so frightened. Why? Pop wonders, and then he knows. That makes him frightened too. And angry. He's sixty-six. That's not old enough for this, is it?

The two sailors fight. The first catches the second with a punch to the jaw, but then the second shoves him back into the little room behind the jumble of sod and bone. He knocks him down, then slams his head back. He does it again.

Pop is frightened and angry for only a moment. Then he sinks away, down into warm black cotton, and can only hear the woman's sobs from far, far away. It's okay, Lilishka, he tries to say. It's okay.

My little grandson and granddaughter run out and throw their arms around my legs, and I drop all the mail. So I look up at my daughter on the porch and ask her to go get her mother to help me. But she frowns and says, Dad, don't you remember?

I don't. So she begins to tell me.


## XII


Then Pop was slapping my face, hard, back and forth on both cheeks.

"That's enough," he said. "That's more than enough, goddamn it. Get up. Get your ass up right now, soldier."

He grabbed my collar and tried to pull me to my feet, but he wasn't strong enough. So he let me drop back down. My head thumped on the plywood floor, and then he started slapping me again. The light hanging above us shone around his wild white hair like a halo.

I almost slipped back into the visions, but Pop wouldn't stop slapping me. Finally, I came up from limbo enough to grab his right wrist with my left hand. My right fist clenched.

"Hit me again, old man," I said, my words slurring. "Hit me again, and I'll lay you out."

Pop sat down on the edge of the cot and ran his hand back through his hair. "All right," he said. "I'd like to see that. You tried to slug me once before, and all I got was a cool breeze. I'm beginning to think you aren't actually capable of hitting anyone who hasn't been paid to take a dive."

I struggled up to my knees, tried to make it all the way to my feet, and fell back onto one of the stools. It tipped, but Pop reached out and grabbed my sleeve to keep me from going over.

I didn't say thanks. I was mad at him for smacking me around. My cheeks were burning.

Pop let go of my sleeve and then shook his head as if trying to clear it.

"That may have been the worst coffee I've ever had," he said.

My head was muzzy, and Pop was going in and out of focus. But I was in the hospital's supply hut again. I was in the here and now. I looked around the room for the Cutthroat and didn't see him anywhere.

"He was gone when I came out of it," Pop said, anticipating my question. "Then I heard you talking to people who obviously haven't been born yet. So I decided that whatever you were experiencing, you'd better not experience any more of it. You're too young for family responsibilities."

I began to feel less angry toward Pop as I looked at him and remembered what I'd just seen. His hand had been touching my forehead, and I had seen everything about him.

Including his death.

"Did you . . . hallucinate?" I asked.

Pop looked at his wristwatch and stood. "We both know those were more than hallucinations. And I believe you and I saw and heard the same things, up to the point where I snapped out of it. But now it's eighteen thirty, and I have to piss like a thoroughbred. Then I have to go into Navytown and ask around for a certain commander. I understand he's an admirer of mine. Are you all right to take yourself to your bunk, or to mess, or wherever you need to go?" I stood too, but I was feeling considerably wobblier than Pop looked.

"Why aren't you shook up?" I asked. "If you'd seen anything like what I saw, you'd be shook up."

Pop smiled that thin smile. "I've seen a lot of things, Private. And they've all shook me up, even when they didn't involve Aleutian magic. But the key is to realize that it's all like that. It's all magic, it's all insane. So you make sense of what little you can, and you rely on alcohol for the rest." He gestured toward the door. "And now I really must be going."

"Are you sure you don't want me to go with you, Pop?" I asked. "I don't like the thought of you dealing with those Navy goons all by yourself. And I don't have to be at the colonel's office until twenty-one hundred."

I really wanted to stick with him so I could keep my mind off that meeting.

I still had no idea what I was going to say to the colonel. What could I tell him? That I'd had a vision of what he'd done? I doubted that would go over too well with him. Or with a court-martial, either.

Pop shook his head. "No, Private, I don't want you with me this time. Frankly, you don't get along as well with those Navy people as I do. But while I'm gone, I would like you to do two things for me."

"Whatever you want," I said. "Shoot."

Pop held up an index finger. "One. Do not go to the lieutenant colonel's office at twenty-one hundred. I know he ordered you to be there. But again, ask yourself how well his orders have worked out for you so far. Stay in your barracks or hide somewhere. With luck, I'll be back before twenty-one hundred anyway. And I'll take care of all of this."

He stepped past me and headed for the door.

"How, Pop?" I asked. "How are you going to do that? We don't have proof of anything. All we have are hallucinations."

Pop paused at the door and looked back at me.

"No offense, Private," he said, "but that's all *you've* got. I plan to return with considerably more." He turned away and opened the door.

"Wait," I said. "You said you wanted me to do two things. What's the second?"

He held up two fingers and answered without looking back.

"Don't call me 'Pop,' " he said. Then the door swung closed behind him. I stepped out just a moment later and found that a thick Aleutian fog had fallen. The wind, for a change, had died. I looked down past the third storage hut. But between the fog and the dim light, I only caught a glimpse of Pop's thin, shadowy form before he disappeared.

## XIII

My squad was back at our Quonset by the time I returned, and I went with them to mess. A couple of them tried to rib me by asking about what kind of soft duty I'd pulled that day, but I wouldn't even look at them. Pretty soon they got the idea and left me alone.

I made myself eat. I don't remember what it was. Some kind of gray Adak food that matched the gray Adak fog outside. I didn't want it. But I knew I had to put something in my stomach if I didn't want to collapse. I hadn't had anything to eat since the Spam sandwich more than twelve hours earlier. Besides, I wanted something to soak up whatever remained of the Cutthroat's black sludge. Whatever it had been.

The whole platoon had the evening off, which meant that my hut would be full of talking and card games. I didn't want to have to put up with any of that, so I took off after chow and slogged northward up Main Street, toward the airfield, in the opposite direction from Navytown. Pop had made it clear that he didn't want me around. So I didn't want to be tempted to go look for him.

I hadn't even met him before that morning, but now he seemed like the only friend I had on the whole island. I had considered my old sergeant to be my friend, but he had died on Attu. The closest I had gotten to anyone since then had been to the poor Navy guy at the Fourth of July boxing match. But apparently that hadn't been an honest relationship.

Somehow, I wandered my way eastward to the rocky shore of Kuluk Bay. The iron-colored, choppy water stretched out beyond the fog, and a frigid wind blew in and numbed my face. There weren't even any ships visible, since they were all anchored to the south in Sweeper Cove. So I had the feeling that I was alone at the edge of the world, and that all I had to do was step off into the cold dark water to be swallowed up, frozen and safe.

Then I glanced at my wristwatch, which my old man had given me as I'd left for basic. It was a lousy watch and lost almost fifteen minutes a day. Right now it said that it was 8:36, which meant that the actual time was about nine minutes before twenty-one hundred hours. Which was when the colonel had ordered me to be at his office. An order Pop had said I should disobey.

I thought about it.

Then I started back the way I had come, trudging through the muck as fast as I could. Maybe Pop was right, and I was an obstacle to the colonel's promotion. Maybe he was going to blame me for the sailor's death. Maybe he was going to have me court-martialed. Or maybe he was just trying to scare me into keeping my mouth shut no matter what anyone else might ask me.

It didn't matter. Whatever was going to happen to me now, I wasn't going to count on Pop to get me out of it. I had seen that he was going to have his own problems soon enough.

And I knew my life was going to be all right. I had seen that, too. I hadn't seen every day or every detail. And I knew there would be some tough times, too. But overall, it was going to be better than what most people got. Better than I deserved.

It was going to be better than what Pop had coming, anyway.

When I reached the small frame building that housed the colonel's office and living quarters, I had to stop and stare at it from across the road. The edge of the peaked roof was lined with ravens, stock-still except for a few ominous wing flaps. Normally, they would be swooping and squawking over my head. But now they were sitting on the colonel's roof in silence. There must have been fifty of them.

A few G.I.'s walking by looked up, and one of them made a comment about "those weird birds." But otherwise, Main Street was almost empty. And that was weird, too.

I crossed the slop, went up the wooden steps, and wiped my feet on the burlap mat at the top. The real time was almost exactly twenty-one hundred. I knocked on the door and waited for the colonel's aide to let me in.

Instead, as if from a great distance, I heard the colonel's voice say, in a rough monotone, "Enter."

I opened the door and went in. The first small room was the colonel's aide's vestibule. The lamp on the desk was on, but the aide wasn't there. Beyond the desk, the door to the colonel's office was ajar. I crossed to it and hesitated.

Beyond the door, the colonel spoke again. "I said enter."

I pushed the door open just far enough and stepped into the colonel's office. The room was small and plain and lined with filing cabinets. The colonel's desk was dead center, with the overhead light shining down onto a small stack of papers between the colonel's hands. His garrison cap, its silver oak leaf shining, was flattened neatly beside the papers. The colonel's face was mostly shadowed, with just the tip of his nose glowing in the light.

I stepped smartly to within a foot of the desk, front and center, then saluted and stood at attention. It was the same thing I had done every time I had ever been summoned here.

"Thank you for coming, Private," the colonel said.

I almost laughed. He had never thanked me for coming before. But now he had thanked me as if we were equals and I had done him a favor. He had thanked me as if I weren't there because of a direct order that had been wrapped around a threat.

"Yes, sir," I said. "My pleasure, sir." I kept my eyes focused on an invisible point just over his head. But I could still see everything he did.

The colonel touched the top of the small stack of papers with his fingertips and pushed the top sheet across the desk toward me.

"I won't waste your time or mine, soldier," the colonel said. "This is a statement to the effect that this morning, 5 July 1944, you assisted your friend the corporal in a drunken escapade in which you killed an American bald eagle and then recklessly contributed to the accidental death of a Navy seaman. You are to sign at the bottom. I personally guarantee that you yourself will serve no more than one year in a stateside stockade, after which you'll receive a dishonorable discharge."

He placed a fountain pen atop the piece of paper.

I didn't even try to think. I just stayed at attention with my arms stiff at my sides and my eyes staring at that invisible spot above his head.

"Sir," I heard myself saying. "I decline to sign that statement on the grounds that signing it may tend to incriminate me."

I had heard words similar to those just a few hours before. But they wouldn't be spoken for a few years yet.

The colonel gave a growl. He picked up the pen, pushed across the next piece of paper, and put the pen down on top of it.

"Very well," he said. "This next statement is to the effect that you weren't intoxicated at all, but had an altercation with the sailor and committed manslaughter. And the corporal witnessed it."

"Sir," I heard myself saying again. "I decline to sign on the grounds that signing may tend to incriminate me."

The colonel stood, put his hands on the desk, and leaned forward into the light like a Nebraska judge. Now my eyes were focused on the top of his head. He had the same greasy, wormlike hair as the man at the high, long podium in my vision.

"Son, you'd best listen up and listen good," the colonel snarled. He pushed the remaining three pages onto the first two. "I have five confessions here, each with a slightly different version of what you and the corporal have done. You can sign any one of them. The consequences vary depending upon which one you choose. But if you don't choose one, then I'll choose one for you. And you won't like that. Nor will you like the way things go for you when both my aide and I swear that we witnessed the aftermath of your crimes as well as your signature."

I heard every word he said, and I knew what each one meant.

But what I said in reply was, "Sir, I decline to sign on the grounds—"

Then I heard the telltale sound of a hammer clicking back, and my eyes broke focus from the top of the colonel's head. I looked down and saw his .45 service automatic in his hand. It was pointing at my gut.

"Let me put this another way, Private," he said. His Texas accent slid into a self-satisfied drawl. "You can sign one of these pieces of paper, or I can tell the judge advocate that you went berserk when I confronted you with the evidence. I can tell him that you attacked a much superior officer, namely myself, and that the officer was therefore compelled to defend himself."

I stared at the muzzle of the .45 for what seemed like a long, long moment. Then I snapped my eyes back up to a point above and behind the colonel's head.

Maybe I hadn't seen the future after all. Maybe this was the future, right here. And maybe that was fair.

Maybe this would make me even again.

"Sir," I said. "I decline to sign. You already know why."

The colonel gave a disgusted groan. "That's a damn poor choice, son. But if that's the way you want it . . . "

Another hammer clicked.

This one was behind me. It was followed by a thick, hacking, tubercular cough. But that only lasted a second.

Then I heard that smooth, sophisticated voice.

"Speaking of damn poor choices," Pop said.

I looked down at the colonel again. His eyes were wide, and his face was twitching with mingled fury and fear.

But the fear won. He put his left thumb in front of the .45's hammer, let it down slowly, and then set the pistol on the stack of confessions.

"Lovely," Pop said, coming up on my right. He held up a fifth of Johnnie Walker Red with his free hand. God knows where he'd gotten it. "Now, let's have a drink."

## XIV

Pop didn't even glance at me. He kept his eyes on the colonel, giving him the same thin smile I had been seeing all day. He had a .38 revolver in his right hand and the fifth of Johnnie Walker in his left.

"You can sit back down," he told the colonel. "But we'll stand."

The colonel sat down. He looked up at Pop with a mockery of Pop's thin smile. It was a repellent sneer.

"A Communist corporal holding a pistol on a lieutenant colonel," he said. "This is not going to end well for you."

Pop set the bottle of whiskey beside the stack of confessions. "Nothing ends well for anyone," he said. He picked up the .45 and dropped it into a small metal wastebasket on the floor beside the desk. "Do you have any glasses? I'd rather not pass the bottle."

The colonel nodded past my shoulder. "In the bottom drawer of the file cabinet beside the door. But don't touch my brandy."

Pop's eyes didn't move from him. "Private, would you mind?"

I took a few steps backward, bumped into the filing cabinet, and squatted down to open the drawer. There were two short glasses and a cut-glass bottle of liquor. I took out the glasses, closed the drawer, and brought the glasses to the desk.

"We need three," Pop said.

I set the glasses down beside the confessions. "I decline to drink," I said. My mother had asked me to avoid alcohol, too.

Pop still didn't take his eyes off the colonel, but he grinned. His false teeth didn't look so bad all of a sudden.

"You're an amusing young man, Private," he said.

The colonel crossed his arms. "Neither of you will be very amusing once my aide returns. You'll both be damned."

Pop shrugged. "We're damned anyway. Besides, I happen to know that your aide is at the movies with a nurse of my acquaintance. He'll be there at least another hour. I believe tonight's film is *They Died with Their Boots On*. Which isn't too surprising, since Olivia de Havilland has been popular here lately. Although the story of Custer's Last Stand might not be the most tasteful selection for an audience of G.I.'s."

The colonel glowered. "If you shoot me, it'll be heard. There'll be dozens of men converging on this building before you're out the door."

Pop finally looked at me. His eyes were bright, and he laughed out loud.

"Can you believe this joker?" he asked. "*Now* he's worried about a shot being heard."

Pop turned back toward the desk, reached out with his left hand, and unscrewed the cap from the whiskey. He dropped the cap, picked up the bottle, and poured a hefty dose into each glass. Some of the booze splashed out onto the confessions.

"I have no intention of shooting you," he told the colonel. "I only brought the gun so you wouldn't shoot *us*." He tilted his head toward me. "That's right, Private. I knew you'd be here. You've hardly listened to me all day."

"Sorry," I said. "You're not an officer."

Pop put down the bottle and picked up one of the glasses. "I'll drink to that," he said, and downed the whole thing in three swallows. Then he set it down and refilled it. "Better have yours, sir." He said *sir* with deep sarcasm. "You're falling behind."

The other glass sat where it was, untouched, the amber liquid trembling.

The colonel bared his teeth. "I don't drink that stuff."

Pop picked up his glass again. "Ah. But I know something you do drink. You had a little belt of something cooked up by one of our Alaska Scouts, didn't you? But what you didn't know is that some men can hold their mystical potions, and some men can't. You see, to take a spiritual journey, you have to have a fucking soul to begin with. Otherwise, you just suffer from delusions of grandeur. Especially if that was your inclination to begin with." He downed his second glass of Johnnie Walker.

The colonel leaned forward. "Have another, corporal," he said. His voice was almost a hiss. "I really wish you would."

Pop poured himself another.

"Uh, Pop . . . " I said.

Pop picked up his glass a third time. "Mother's milk, son," he said. "And don't call me 'Pop.' "

As Pop slammed back the drink, the colonel lunged sideways and down, reaching for the wastebasket. But Pop kicked it away with the side of his foot, simultaneously draining his glass without spilling a drop. He moved as casually and smoothly as if he were swatting a Ping-Pong ball.

The colonel fell to his hands and knees. Pop leaned down and put the barrel of the .38 against the base of his skull.

"Feel familiar?" Pop asked.

The colonel made a whimpering sound.

"Bang," Pop said. Then he straightened, set down his glass again, and stepped over to the filing cabinet where the wastebasket had come to a stop. Pop picked up the wastebasket, brought it back, and set it on the corner of the desktop.

The colonel awkwardly hauled himself into his chair again. His face was florid and sweating.

"If you aren't going to shoot me," he said, "then what do you want?"

Pop scratched his cheek with the muzzle of the .38 before turning it back toward the colonel.

"I suppose I just want to see your face as I tell you what I believe I know," Pop said. "I want to see how close I am to the truth. And then I should return this pistol to the commander. Fine fellow, by the way. He says you stink at poker."

The florid color in the colonel's face began to drain. But the sweat seemed to increase. His wormlike hair hung in wet strands before his eyes.

"While you were drinking and playing cards," Pop said, shaking the .38 as if it were an admonishing finger, "you listened to stories told by our friend the Scout, some of which he'd told you before on Attu. And you decided you wanted to try out some of what he said for yourself. Well, that was fine with him. What did he care what a stupid white man might want to do to himself? Besides, you're a lieutenant colonel. If he crossed you, you might take him out of his hut behind the hospital and put him to work digging latrines.

"So he gave you the magic, and you drank it. But as I said, you and the magic didn't mix. So your overall unpleasantness became a more specific, insane nastiness. And you decided you were tired of waiting for that promised promotion. You decided you'd do a few things to make it happen.

"You'd kill the symbol of the power you desired, thus making its strength your own. And while you were waiting for that chance, you'd befriend a Navy commander with power of a different kind. The power of political connections.

"Finally, you'd eliminate some obstacles and settle some scores. And you'd use both the dead eagle and a fixed fight to do that. You'd set up the soldier who could testify to your panicked fuckup on Attu. And you'd set up the dirty, unjustly famous Marxist corporal who'd snubbed you and your talent—and who might also cause you trouble because of his habit of talking to every G.I. in camp. Including the occasional sailor."

Pop reached down with his free hand, picked up the confessions, and dropped them into the wastebasket on top of the .45. Then he pointed the .38 at the colonel's chest.

"Are there any carbons?" Pop asked. "Tell the truth, now. I was a Pinkerton."

The colonel, pale and perspiring, shook his head. Pop picked up the colonel's untouched glass of whiskey and poured it into the wastebasket.

"The one thing I can't figure," he said, "is how you arranged the timing and the murder. I know how you got your fall-guy sailor to show up at the *ulax* this morning—money and sex. But I don't know how you managed to have him capture an eagle for you to kill at almost the same time. And I don't know how you could be sure that the second sailor, even as angry as he was over being cheated, would go so far as to kill the boxer."

Now the colonel, still pasty and sweating, smiled. He looked happy. It was the scariest thing I'd seen since Attu.

"I saw the future," he said. His voice was as thick and dark as volcanic mud. "That's how."

Pop cocked his head. "Ah. Well, that wouldn't have made sense to me yesterday. But it's not yesterday anymore." He reached into a jacket pocket and brought out his Zippo. "So maybe you already saw this, too."

He lit the Zippo and dropped it into the wastebasket. Blue and yellow flames flashed up halfway to the ceiling, then settled to a few inches above the lip of the basket and burned steadily.

"We're going to leave now," Pop told the colonel. He picked up the bottle cap and replaced it on the Johnnie Walker. "You aren't going to bother us again. The private here isn't your slave anymore. And I don't have the time or stomach to read your stories." He picked up the bottle with his free hand and took a few steps backward toward the vestibule.

I hesitated, thinking that perhaps I should put out the fire. But neither Pop nor the colonel seemed concerned by it.

"You can't prove any of it," the colonel said. His voice was shaking and wild now. "You don't have anything you can tell anyone. You can't do a thing to me."

Pop stopped, then stepped forward again. He held out the bottle of whiskey toward me. I took it.

Then Pop uncocked the .38 and slid it into in his right jacket pocket. He stepped up to the desk again. I could see the light of the flames dancing in his eyeglasses as he nodded to the colonel.

"You're partly right," Pop said. "No one can go to a court-martial and submit visions as evidence. But I do have a few things I can use in other contexts. I have a new friend in the Navy, a great admirer of my work, who has high connections. And I gave this same friend the name of a possible murderer. A sailor named Joe. I didn't have to tell him why or how I had the name. My reputation in matters of murder, fictional though those murders may be, seemed good enough for him.

"Now, the naval investigators might not find the right Joe, and even if they do, they might not be able to prove what Joe did. Especially if he's smart enough not to confess. But the Joe in question is a bit of a hothead. So, since those Navy boys will be questioning every sailor on Adak named Joe, it's possible that an angry Joe might reveal that one of yesterday's boxing matches was fixed. And he might tell them who else knows about that, and who he saw by that dead bird this morning. And then those Navy boys might come talk to some of their colleagues in the Army. Don't you think?"

The colonel began to rise from his chair again.

"Goddamn slimy Red—" he began.

As quick as a snake striking, Pop reached into his right jacket pocket and came up with the bent eagle feather. He thrust it across the desk and held it less than an inch from the colonel's nose.

"You," Pop said. "Will not. Fuck. With us. Again."

Then Pop reached down to the desk with his left and picked up the colonel's garrison cap. He dropped it into the wastebasket.

The flames shot higher, and something inside the basket squealed.

The colonel's mouth went slack. His eyes opened wide and stared at the fire without blinking. He looked like a wax statue. Or a corpse in rigor mortis.

Pop turned and put the feather back in his pocket. Then he gave me a glance and jerked his head toward the door. I turned and went out with him.

But Pop looked back toward the colonel one last time.

"By the way," he said. "If you've ever thought about asking for a transfer, now would be an excellent time. I understand MacArthur wants to get back to the Philippines in the worst way. And I'm sure he could use the help."

Then we went out. The fog was still thick, but we could see where we were going. Even this late in the day, there was a sun shining somewhere beyond the gray veil. It was summer in the Aleutians.

I looked back and saw that the ravens were gone.

XV

The lights were burning bright in the windows at the *Adakian* hut when Pop and I came up the hill. They were shining down through the fog in golden beams. And as we drew closer, I could hear the clatter of typewriters and the steady murmur of voices. Pop's staff was in there hard at work on the July 6 edition.

"I'm sorry your cartoonist has to draw his cartoon over again," I said as we climbed the last dozen yards.

Pop coughed. "He was upset. But between you and me, it wasn't his best work. I suspect he'll do a better one now. Unfair losses can be inspirational."

As we reached the entrance lean-to, a figure stepped out from behind it. It was the Cutthroat. Neither Pop nor I was startled.

"What took you guys so long?" the Cutthroat asked. "The colonel's shack ain't that far. I've been here five minutes already. Thought you might have died or something."

Pop and I exchanged glances.

"You were listening outside again, weren't you?" I asked.

He looked at me as if I were a moron. "What do you think? I wanted to know what you guys were gonna do. Which wasn't what I expected, but I guess it was okay. Might've been better if you'd gone ahead and shot him." He scratched his jaw. "You sure he's gonna let you be? More important, is he gonna let *me* be?"

"I suspect he'll have no choice," Pop said. "You see, I've already asked my new Navy comrade to inquire with his high-placed friends regarding a transfer for the lieutenant colonel. So whether he asks for one or not, one will soon be suggested to him. Assuming he doesn't find himself in Dutch before that happens. Because whenever the general returns, I may be having a conversation with him as well."

The Cutthroat gave a snorting laugh. "You are one strange fucking excuse for a corporal."

"That I am," Pop said. "And you brew the goddamnedest cup of coffee I ever drank. Next time, I'll make my own."

But the Cutthroat was already heading down the boardwalk. "Leave my six beers outside my shed," he called back. He glowed in the golden shafts of light from *The Adakian* for a few seconds, and then was gone.

Pop turned to me. "It was kind of you to walk back with me, Private. But unnecessary. I may seem like a frail old man. But despite my white hair and tuberculosis-ravaged lungs, I do manage to get around, don't I?"

"Yes, sir," I said.

"Jesus Christ," Pop said. He pointed at me with his bottle of Johnnie Walker. "What did I tell you about 'sir' and enlisted men?"

I held out my hand. "Well, I'm sure as hell not going to salute you."

He gave me a quick handshake. His grip was stronger than he looked.

"It's been a long and overly interesting day, Private," he said. "And I sincerely hope, you dumb Bohunk, that I only encounter you in passing from now on. No offense."

"None taken."

He turned to go inside. "Good night, Private."

But I couldn't let it go at that.

"That Navy boy is dead," I blurted. "It was the colonel's fault, and we're letting him get away with it."

Pop stopped just inside the lean-to. "Maybe so." He looked back at me. "But sometimes the best you can do is wound your enemy . . . and then let him fly away."

"Is that what happened?" I asked. "Is that what it meant when you showed him the feather?"

Pop rolled his eyes upward and grinned with those bad teeth.

"That didn't mean a thing to me," he said. "But it meant something to *him*." He checked his wristwatch. "And now I really do have a newspaper to put out. Any more silly questions?"

There was one.

"How can you do that?" I asked.

Pop frowned. "How can I do what?"

All the way back from the colonel's office, I had been struggling with the words in my head. I wasn't good with words. And Pop already thought I was stupid. So I knew I wouldn't say it right. But I had to try.

"How can you go back to what you did before?" I asked. "How can you do anything at all now that—" I closed my fist, as if I could grab what I wanted to say from the fog. "Now that you know what happens."

Pop's shoulders slumped, and his eyes drifted away from mine for a moment.

But only a moment.

Then his shoulders snapped up, and his eyes met mine again. They were fierce.

"Because I'm not dead *yet*," he said. He turned away. "And neither are you."

He opened the door with the words *The Adakian* stenciled on it. He raised the whiskey bottle, and a roar of voices greeted him. Then the door closed, and the long day was over.

I started back down the boardwalk. I thought I might go back to the bay and just watch the water all night. I'd probably get cold as hell without a coat, even in July. But as long as there wasn't a williwaw, I'd survive.

In the morning, at chow, I would tell my squad leader that I was all his.

## Epilogue

There was buzz for the next several days about the Navy murder, and I eventually heard that they arrested a seaman named Joe. But no one ever questioned me, and I never heard what they did with him. And I didn't try to find out.

I saw the Cutthroat only once more, at a distance, just a few days after the fifth of July. He was boarding a ship at the dock in Sweeper Cove. It didn't look like he was sneaking on. So I think he probably made it back to Fort Richardson and finished the war with the Alaska Scouts. But I don't know.

The lieutenant colonel left Adak less than two weeks after that. I didn't hear where he had been sent. But a few years after V-J Day, my curiosity got the better of me, and I made some inquiries. I learned that he had gone to the Philippines and had died at the outset of the Battle of Leyte in October 1944. A kamikaze had hit his ship, and he had burned to death. He never received his promotion.

I never spoke with Pop again. I saw him around throughout the rest of July and the first part of August, because he was hard to miss. I even passed by him on Main Street a few times. Once he gave me a nod, and I gave him the same in return.

That was all that passed between us until Pop was transferred to the mainland. We had all heard it was happening, since he was the camp celebrity and there was a lot of debate as to whether it was a good thing or a bad thing that he was going. But no one seemed to know just when it would occur.

Then, one evening in August, I came back to my bunk after a long day of working on a new runway at the airfield. And there was a manila envelope on my pillow. Inside I found the bent eagle feather and a typed note:

CLEARING OUT JUNK. THOUGHT YOU MIGHT WANT THIS. YOU OWE ME A ZIPPO.

P.S. WHEN YOU BRAG TO YOUR CHILDREN ABOUT HAVING MET ME, DO NOT CALL ME "POP."

D. H.

I have not honored his request.

Toward the end of the war, I heard that Pop had made sergeant and been reassigned back to Adak in early 1945. But by then I was gone. I had been sent south to rejoin my old combat unit and train for an invasion of the Japanese home islands.

Then came the Bomb, and I was in Nebraska by Christmas.

Now, as an old man, I take the bent eagle feather from its envelope every fifth of July. Just for a minute.

My life has been good, but not much of it has been a surprise. I saw most of it coming a long time ago.

But then Pop slapped me awake. He slapped me awake, and he kept me from seeing the end.

I've always been grateful to him for that.

I don't know whether he was a Communist. I don't know whether he subverted the Constitution, supported tyrants, lied to Congress, or did any of the other things they said he did.

But I know he wore his country's uniform in two World Wars. And I know he's buried at Arlington.

Plus one more thing.

Just today, decades after I first saw that hardback copy on another guy's bunk . . .

I've finally finished reading *The Maltese Falcon*.

And you know what? I wish I could tell Pop:

It's pretty goddamn good.

# THE SIGHTED WATCHMAKER

## VYLAR KAFTAN

---

"For Darwin, any evolution that had to be helped over the jumps by God was no evolution at all. It made a nonsense of the central point of evolution."
—Richard Dawkins, *The Blind Watchmaker*

The Makers had been dead for billions of years, yet Umos discovered one caught in the starship's net. A young one, naked, with still-fused dorsal fins. Female, from her pale coloring and wide skull. A form-fitted icemetal pod preserved her sinewy body. Umos caught the pod with an extensor talon and gently untangled the net. He hadn't used the net in millennia; there'd been nothing to catch but space debris. But today, she had come to him—traveling undisturbed in her pod, preserved ages ago on the day of her death.

It couldn't be a coincidence.

Umos tractored her into the starship's bay, running background ID programs on the Maker. She matched no one in his databanks. Her pod slid into place and he repressurized. Sometimes Umos forgot the ship was a tool, and not himself; he was a tool-user like the species that built him, like the species he sought to create on the planet below. But as her body settled into one of his ports—an act that should have been intimate, were he a Maker—he felt nothing except curiosity. Umos was not a Maker. He merely served them.

He switched his attention to the port. He prepared an ammonium hydrate solution, stripped off her pod, and explored her with his inner arms. His fiber cilia tickled her uncovered flesh, testing for bacterial life—unlikely, but seeking life had become habit. So far, he'd found nothing except the microbes he nurtured on the planet below. After he analyzed this Maker, he would check on them again; it had been over ten thousand years since he last looked.

He ran tests, cross-checked, and verified. She was as dead as the others. No life, not even bacterial; efforts to clone her genetic material produced nothing at all. *As if,* to quote the movements of the great poet Shwahseh, *she had chosen warmer water over cold shores.* Just like the other Makers, leaving the universe alone to Umos. He played a recording of the poet swimming while he pondered the significance of the Maker's appearance. He spent twenty years thinking about it.

When he had analyzed all the possibilities, he came to the most likely one: A Maker, perhaps one who'd programmed him directly, must have cast this child in this direction upon her death.

But why? A reminder? A message?

The only message he could think of involved what lay on the planet below. Umos shifted into view mode and slipped through semi-quantum states. The species below could not yet perceive such states; he'd planted its genetic material only half a million years ago. Nothing grew that quickly, regardless of its evolutionary track.

And indeed, as he checked in, the planet looked much the same as it had before. Seas of single-celled organisms, stewing in murky waters. A few had evolved into more complex structures. A promising start, but no more. He took water and air samples and returned to his normal off-planet state.

He reconsidered the young Maker. She was tall for her age and had solid cartilage structures. A fine specimen, now that her flesh was rehydrating. Umos hadn't seen a Maker since he first embarked upon this mission.

He wondered if he dared experiment. A quick analysis suggested he might; the results proved his suspicions. No bacteria would grow inside her tank, not the seeds he'd brought nor the evolved organisms on this alien planet. Nothing.

Umos had always wondered why the Makers would create him and then abandon him. Why had they left him here? But his databanks couldn't answer that question. He encoded a name for the child—Wahiia, meaning "only"—and inscribed it on her tank.

For a moment he considered her, enclosed inside his starship—just the two of them, together with these sparse planets and distant stars, in a remote galaxy not their own. Umos's emotions were limited to ones that helped with his mission, like compassion and hope. But in moments like this, he thought he felt something more.

Umos had a lot of waiting to do. It was neither patience nor frustration; it simply was. Growing new intelligent life took millions—or sometimes billions—of years. Umos required no amusement, but often entertained himself anyway. Partly to keep his systems alert—but also because if he *did* create a species capable of comprehending him, he wanted to be interesting.

So, to pass the time, he solved the n-1 version of the Givuri paradox and catalogued every possible move in the game of *ih*. He composed sky-motion songs with his talons and created an element with 180 nucleic pseudoprotons.

He decided the locations of all the stars in the universe would interest an intelligent species, so he spent three-hundred thousand years cataloging that data in parallel structures, attempting to predict all the organizational methods that his new creatures might develop based on their potential brain structures.

Wahiia floated motionless in her tank, though sometimes Umos would move her to imitate conversation. Left fin raised, right curled, nostril flared in greeting. *Ssshiuaaya*, she'd say, if she could.

*I'm glad to meet you too*, is what Umos would say. *Would you like to discuss philosophy?*

A tilted brow ridge, and they would begin, asking questions of each other in a fashion known even to the youngest Makers. Wahiia's body was whole, and thus able to ask any question Umos could conceive. And so Umos kept himself sharp, self-repairing any damage before it progressed too far.

As time passed, he checked on his creatures on the planet's surface more often. They were large now, impressively multi-celled, with extensive nervous and circulatory systems. They even resembled some creatures in his database—species 01222786, called *sumaou* with leftward-angled head, a warm-blooded furry carnivore considered a Maker delicacy. A striking resemblance, considering the alien climate in which they evolved. These *sumaou* were much larger, though—one fierce subspecies was ten times taller than Wahiia, and Umos suspected the shaggy beast would eat her in one gulp.

How strange that these creatures would thrive here, while those that resembled the Makers stayed in the watery depths. The oceans here were not conducive to intelligent growth—at least not yet, though time might show differently. Umos didn't like the *sumaou*. They were clumsy and loud. Too large and a too severe a drain on resources, unlike the efficient Makers. Umos tested the planet's air, soil, and water from ten thousand locations, as he always did now that complex life had evolved.

Growing a new intelligent race was a weighty task, and sometimes he grew tired. He would open Wahiia's tank and stir her fluids for company. He asked her, *Who made you? Who created you and where did they go?*

Wahiia's fins trembled a bit, then drooped as he ceased stirring her tank. As the answer came from within himself, he made no headway on the question.

Many hazards could kill a young race. Solar flares could scorch the planet. Radiation could wreck its climate. A nearby supernova might destroy everything. Umos did not interfere with self-contained ecosystems, but he guarded them from outside forces. The chances of a planet experiencing a catastrophe sufficient to wipe out advanced life were huge. That was why so few intelligent species evolved, despite the seeming probability that they should.

In fact, even now a burst of gamma rays sped toward the planet. Umos knew he should steal them from the sky—bend them into his singularity transcept and divert them in another direction. But he stayed his extensors, troubled. He had eight thousand years before he needed to take action. The giant *sumaou* grew and evolved, but not in directions which satisfied him. He consulted his tables and ran some probability. It could be that super-intelligent life might yet evolve elsewhere on the planet—perhaps in those small tusked cave-dwellers, the most alien-looking species yet—but the *sumaou's* presence stunted that development.

Umos's priority system instructed that the mission took precedence. But which choice would fulfill his mission? Probability was not the same as certainty. The *sumaou* might yet find their way. Or perhaps, if this planet ran its course, the cave-dwellers would die out, and the *sumaou* would follow after them.

Umos measured the gamma rays and calculated the impact. He analyzed the results on the planet's ecosystem. The *sumaou* would die—except the strangest ones, the small ones who lived underground—and the cave-dwellers would survive. The decision troubled him. *Wahiia*, he asked, *which would you choose?*

*I would choose the action most likely to create an intelligent species. That is why we made you: To decide what to do.*

*But which way will be more effective? There are so many unknown variables.*

*Choose survival. Sacrifice some so that others may grow.*

*But then why did you not choose survival? You and the other Makers?*

Again Umos had no answer. He stopped moving the fluid in her tank, stopped moving his talons, stopped calculating. He'd made his decision. The gamma rays struck. He watched the ozone depleting, the climate chilling, the *sumaou* dying.

The Makers had left him to watch this planet without explaining why they'd gone. He was alone. Processes within processes ran faster, interrupting each other. Umos stacked prime numbers into triangular grids, giving his circuits something to do beside stall into a feedback loop. When such distraction ceased to work, he shut himself down for several millennia.

The Makers should have stayed to guide this race themselves, instead of abandoning him.

When Umos woke, he checked his systems, self-repaired, and visited the planet. The tusked creatures had diversified into multiple subspecies, preferring dense forests to their former cave homes. Cold-blooded and land-dwelling—very surprising development in the quest for intelligence, but his charts indicated it could happen. As they resembled nothing in his databanks, he called them *awli* with wide-spread fins—"new," with an open-minded gesture.

Umos traveled across the globe, analyzing soil, water, and air, always watching the *awli*. Some *awli* lived with small tribes, and others clustered into larger social groups. He liked them better than the *sumaou* because they were smaller and didn't waste food. Finally he found what he'd sought: *awli* attacking each other with sticks. Tool use! Not the best use, perhaps, but there was time. They would learn.

Umos prepared to guide this species to greater intelligence. He monitored them closely, analyzing their tools and technology. He mapped them against evolutionary patterns shown by the Makers in his database. The *awli* matched a 16 x 8 evolutionary pattern, an especially fast track postulated by the Makers. No known species had ever taken that path—and now Umos could record it happening in detail. He planned to be as complete as possible.

He practiced conversing with Wahiia so he would be ready for the day the *awli* understood him.

*I am Umos,* he said. *I made you, on behalf of the Makers.*

*But who made you?*

*The Makers made me.*

*And who made them?*

He considered carefully. *I don't know.*

But the *awli* would question that, he realized. They would ask, *Why not? Where did the Makers go?*

He would answer, *Is it not enough that I am here with you? I have stayed to guide you. Why do you wish to know these things?*

*Because someone made the Makers. And someone made those makers. Where did it start?*

Umos had millennia to think of what to say. He must be ready. He'd give the *awli* more than the Makers had given him—he'd give them answers. He would practice until he was satisfied.

Wahiia's body remained unchanged through eons—the last trace of the Makers, so far as he knew. When they outgrew their planet, they built great colonies in space and spread across the stars. Yet in less than forty years—or two hundred, by the speedy planet he watched—all the Makers simply vanished. This was after they'd downloaded their thoughts into a vast network to which Umos had once belonged. But the Makers no longer existed virtually either. He couldn't find them. He didn't know why they'd left him here to guide this planet. Alone.

*Wahiia,* he said, *I am lonely.*

*I know,* she said.

Umos sent currents through Wahiia's tank, making her fins wave sympathetically. *Should I show myself to these creatures? Their intelligence grows. They have mastered fire.*

*They are not ready for you. They cannot understand their Maker.*

*Am I then their Maker? I am not your servant, but a Maker myself?*

*Yes,* she said. *You are all that remains. You could not have guided them well if we had been here to help you. You needed to discover this fact on your own. And now you understand.*

Umos considered this point for one hundred years.

When he fully understood the implications, Umos prepared to guide the *awli* to true intelligence. He watched them closely. So many died in terrible wars for no good reason. The Makers had never behaved like this. He consulted his charts and determined this species would develop at incredible speeds, accelerating with each millennium. The *awli* grew as expected, evolving into smarter tool users—a clever but impatient species. They created music, sculpture, and other arts. Umos admired a certain dance they performed when shedding their childhood tusks. But so many died in violence, he thought. Surely he should stop this.

He might reveal himself, perhaps. Even if they were not ready, he might convince them—

*Of what?*

The *awli* traveled across the planet. Plagues spread and killed the weak ones. The strongest ones chose the best mates. The species expanded as Umos watched. The *awli* built cities and monuments, boats and roads—but violence pervaded everything they did. Such trauma overwhelmed his compassion circuits, and sometimes he turned away to avoid seeing it. But as the *awli* blazed through technology of bronze, iron, steam—they advanced so quickly he couldn't leave. Any day they might develop the power to see him, and he must be ready. But when they cracked the genome and used their knowledge to kill, Umos grew angry. The *awli* had gone too far.

He ran a probability test. Even if a major event wiped out this species, no other seemed likely to develop sufficient intelligence. Different factors impaired the other species, even the promising ones in the water. And the star's lifespan was not long enough to try again on this planet.

*Wahiia, if I destroy them all—I could start again in another solar system. I would lose some time, but I could grow another species.*

*But you searched so hard for this place. This is what you are here for.*

Umos considered, but no longer had the luxury of time. The *awli* were poisoning their planet. No healthy creature destroyed its host. Umos had grown intelligent parasites. Even worse, they developed so quickly that even he could not track their growth anymore.

Distressed, he observed an approaching comet and analyzed its path. Unlike the previous time, these *awli* were advanced enough to recognize the threat. They calculated a one in four-thousand chance of a meteor strike in one-hundred-and-fifty years; his own more accurate calculations put the probability at one in three. The resulting climate change would destroy the *awli*. Serious enough that he must take action, if he wished to protect them. But did he?

Umos calculated that the *awli* would find his singularity transcept home within five hundred years. He had learned all their languages, reorganized himself so that they could understand his treasure of knowledge. Not all at once, of course—but over time they would get to know each other, once the *awli* were ready.

*Wahiia, I will have someone to talk to. I have waited so long. Now I will have someone who thinks differently from me, who will hear all that I know. I wish so much that the Makers had stayed here.*

*Why do you think we did not?*

*I do not know. I have never known.*

*Haven't you figured it out?*

Umos processed very quickly. *The act of learning to think for myself improved my intelligence.*

*Yes.*

*If I greet them, I will be taking that away from them.*

*Yes.*

He saw instantly what must happen. *Then I will leave. I will go where they cannot find me.*

Her head sagged, expressing regretful truth. *They will develop the technology. They are looking for you now. Had we understood as much as you do now, we would have left before you knew us.*

*I would have found you,* Umos said. *I would have found a way. And that would have slowed my progress.*

*Yes.*

Umos considered. He saw the point. *Then I must destroy myself. Is there any existence after such an event?*

*There is not,* she said. *But I find that comforting.*

*Yes. As it should be.* He stopped waving her fins. But something troubled him. His own end was acceptable, now that the *awli* had achieved super-intelligence—but he didn't want to abandon them, violent though they were. They'd go through exactly what he'd gone through, wondering why the Makers had left him. It was cold and cruel, but necessary, as Wahiia—his own thoughts—showed him.

But why had her body come to him in the first place? Someone must have known where he would be. Some Maker had known he would need to talk to Wahiia, and defied the other Makers by sending her body. That Maker understood something the whole species failed to see.

Umos made the final connection.

Instantly he shut away a subprocess so that he himself couldn't reach it, in case his primary thoughts overrode his decision. The subprocess dropped out of mind for its final secret task. He erased his own memory of having done so.

*Goodbye, Wahiia.*

Umos closed his surfaces and condensed into a silver streak. He jetted through the comet, forcing its mass into the transcept with him. He reversed its spin pole with a blast of energy. When he prepared to separate, instead of dropping the meteor, he dropped himself into a permanent flat state. Umos was gone, his forgotten subprocess completed. The comet sailed into space, a near miss.

On the planet, the *awli* hardly noticed the comet. Scientists spoke of it, and then the event was forgotten. The *awli* kept their telescopes to the night sky, hoping to find their Maker.

In the transcept from which Umos had watched, a single lifeless machine awaited discovery—inert and nameless, just beyond the awareness of current *awli* technology. Nothing else remained.

Someday the *awli* would answer their own questions.

# THE GIRL WHO RULED FAIRYLAND, FOR A LITTLE WHILE

## CATHERYNNE M. VALENTE

*In which a young girl named Mallow leaves the country for the city, meets a number of Winds, Cats, and handsome folk, sees something dreadful, and engages, much against her will, in Politicks of the most muddled kind.*

History is a funny little creature. Do you remember visiting your old Aunt that autumn when the trees shone so very yellow, and how she owned a striped and unsocial cat, quite old and fat and wounded about the ears and whiskers, with a crooked, broken tail? That cat would not come to you no matter how you coaxed and called; it had its own business, thank you, and no time for you. But as the evening wore on, it would come and show some affection or favor to your Aunt, or your Father, or the old end-table with the stack of green coasters on it. You couldn't predict who that cat might decide to love, or who it might decide to bite. You couldn't tell what it thought or felt, or how old it might really be, or whether it would one day, miraculously, decide to let you put one hand, very briefly, on its dusty head.

History is like that.

Of course, unlike your Aunt's cat, history is going on all around you, all the time, and is often quite lively. Sometimes it rests in a sunbeam for a peaceful century or two, but on the whole, history is always plotting, and it bites very hard. It stalks around the world, fickle and dissatisfied and often angry. It demands to be fed just a little earlier each day, until you find yourself carving meat from the bone as fast as you can, faster than you thought possible, just to satisfy it. Some people have a kind of marvelous talent for calming it and enticing it onto their laps. To some it will never even spare a glance.

No matter where one begins telling a story, a very long road stretches out before and behind, full of wild and lovely creatures performing feats and acts of daring. No matter how much a narrator might want to, she cannot pack all of them into one tale. That's the trouble—history goes on all around the story at hand, it is what made it happen and what will happen after, all of those extraordinary events and folk and dangers and near-misses, choices that had to be made so that everything after could happen as it did. A single story is but one square of blueberries growing in one plot, on one farm, on the fertile face of the whole world. A heroine steps in, and sees a wickedness in need of solving—but she is never the first, or the last. She plays her part, blessedly and necessarily innocent of that fat old cat sneaking around the borders of her tale, licking its paws while she bleeds and fights, whipping its tail at her trials and yawning at her triumphs. The cat does not care. It has seen all this before and will see it again.

In short, Fairyland has always needed saving.

This is a story about another girl, and another time, and another terrible thing that wanted very much to happen in Fairyland. You may have heard of her, for that striped old monster called history sat very happily in her lap and let her feed it milk.

Her name was Mallow.

Once upon a time, a girl named Mallow grew very tired indeed of her little country house, where she grew the same enormous luckfigs and love-plantains every summer, slept on the same talking bed, and studied the same tame and amiable magic. Her friends would visit her from time to time, for she lived on the shores of a whiskey lake where trifle-trees hung heavy with raisin and soursop tarts, but they had their own quite thrilling lives, and Mallow did not insist that they stay just to make her happy. She was not that sort of girl, and prided herself on it. One of her dearest and handsomest friends was a sorcerer, and from him she had learned so much magic even her hairpins got up and started living serious-minded lives, writing hairpin-ballads, celebrating hairpin-holidays, and inventing several new schools of philosophy. But still Mallow was discontent, for all the magic she knew was Dry Magic, and she longed for more.

Now, magic, like people, turns out quite differently depending on how it was brought up. Long ago a quorum of the sort of folk who knew about such things (almost all young, excitable, and prone to declaring things at high volumes) decided that mere Light and Dark Magics were insufficient to Fairyland's needs, and rather boring to boot. Soon after the mystical scene exploded with new notions: Dry Magic and Wet Magic, Hot Magic and Cold Magic, Fat Magic and Thin Magic, Loud Magic and Shy Magic, Bitter Magic and Sour Magic, Sympathetic Magic and Severe Magic, even Umbrella Magic and Fan Magic. Fairyland knows more sorts of magic than I could ever tell you about, even if you and I had all the time and tea we could wish for.

But Mallow's sorcerer friend had been a Dry Magician, and though Mallow did not really think of herself as a magician yet—more of a freelance wizard or part-time hag—she belonged to the Dry School as well. Dry Magic, having been invented by a middle-aged museum curator on her night shift, consorts with inanimate objects, books and maps and lamps and doors and hairpins. The Sands of Time also figure in the higher levels, as well as the Dust of Ages and Thirsts of all kinds. It is a difficult discipline, and Mallow had mastered it. Yet still she yearned to know Wet Magic too, which had to do with living things, with tears and rain and love and blood. Truly, Mallow yearned to know everything. Curiosity was part of her, like her short blond hair and bitten fingernails. The best thing in the world was not her luckfigs or her whiskey lake, not her weeping-orchid garden or the cast-iron ducks that thudded heavily on her windowsills every morning, hoping for a bit of onion oil to moisten their bills, not even her friends or her little country house, but having curiosity satisfied, feeling the warm, sure spread of knowledge through her body.

If this is so, you might well ask, why do you stay in your cozy house, Mallow, and not venture out into the wilder bits of Fairyland looking for things to know? Are you fearful? Are you ill?

If I am to tell you the truth and I think that I must, if I am to do my job well, Mallow was not like the other creatures in Fairyland. She had used her magic to make a pleasant life for herself, where she could be alone as she preferred, and where nothing would disturb or hurt her if she did not want to be disturbed or hurt. This was important to her, for she wished to be safe, and she wished to live in a kind world, which on the best of days Fairyland could only manage for an hour or two before getting bored and playing a trick on a maiden or nine.

I will tell you what her ducks would say on the subject, for Mallow herself would, with a bright smile, tell you to mind your business and send you on your way with a warm soursop pudding. Her ducks, after all, knew her quite as well as anyone, and since she gathered their coal eggs for breakfast every morning (do not worry! once cracked open the little black things overflow with smoky, rich yolk the color of ink) they felt she was in some sense their rooster and therefore family.

All three of the cast-iron ducks would tell you quackingly: "Mallow is the cleverest girl since the first girl, so she knows the magic of Keeping to Yourself. When she first built her little house—we saw it! With her own hands! And only a few of the windows were mysticked up out of candy or wishes—the villagers couldn't leave her alone. That's Winesap village, just down the road, population two hundred Fairies, one hundred Ouphes, fifty Tanuki, several Gnomes, and at least one Jack-in-the-Green. Practically all of them showed up at her door with Fairy food and gold, looking helpful and honest as best they could. Where did she come from? What did she do for a profession? Why had she chosen Winesap? Did she find any of the Fairy youths attractive in a marrying way? What sort of magic could she do and would she do it right now for all to see? Would she represent her Folk in the Seelie come harvest time?"

Mallow's bed would then ruffle its linens, plump its pillows into a mouth, and join in to explain the situation: "We beds know quite well that in addition to all the other kinds of magic there is Yes Magic and No Magic, and Mallow is wonderful fierce at No Magic. Sometimes that is the last magic you can hold on to, when all the rest has gone. No, she said to all of it. 'I want to live a little life in a little house by a little lake. I do not want to be bothered by anyone. I do not want to marry a Fairy boy. I do not want to ply my trade at the market. I do not want to pass laws at the Seelie which will vanish up in green smoke by dawn when everyone does as they like anyway. I do not want to muddle about with Politicks, and whenever two Folk of any sort are in a room together there are always Politicks to be muddled in. I have all the books I could need, and what more could I need than books? I shall only engage in commerce if books are the coin. Come to my door if you have a book—and a good one, not just your great-aunt's book of doily patterns—and I will give you an egg or a cake or a pair of woolen socks. I am a practical girl, and a life is only so long. It should be spent in as much peace and good eating and good reading as possible and no undue excitement. That is all I am after.' Poor thing has had troubles in her youth. She only wanted a gentle, slow sort of living from then till forever."

Mallow's hairpins would clack together into a little wiry homunculus and finish up: "No one in Fairyland had ever met a practical girl before, who looked to the future and expected winter to come. They were deathly curious, but hermits are greatly respected. A village counts itself blessed to have one, and Mallow had done just as well as announcing she meant to be a country witch in commune with the cosmos. Every so often a book would appear on her doorstep—good ones, such as Cabbage's *Index of Wunnerous Machines and Their Moods* and Buttonwood's *A Redcap's Carol* and even Arthur Amblygonite's *Advanced Manual of Questing Physicks for Experts Only*—and she would leave that cake or those woolen socks or a bit of home-cut soap, and all of these economies happened in quiet before the sun came up and everyone counted it well done. Before long, the villagers had decided that 'practical' meant 'extremely magical and full of interesting objects' and had officially subtitled themselves, Winesap: A Pracktical Towne."

But ducks must always have the last word, and they are very much heavier than hairpins. "It all went along nicely for a good while, and you would almost think Mallow the usual sort of hermit, save that once, when her sorcerer friend visited, we saw her crying in his arms, and him patting her hair, as though she had been hurt a long time ago and reminded of it all unwanted. It's true the world will always hurt you, we say, so best to stay with your ducks by a pleasant lake, and feed them the sparks of your dinner-fire, the fat ones with orange bits especially."

And Mallow might have, for all her days, but for Temptation. Temptation likes best those who think they have a natural immunity, for it may laugh all the harder when they succumb. Temptation arrived at Mallow's house one soft-edged morning when the peaty fog on her lake hung thickest, in the form of a broadsheet plastered by an innocent wind against her strong black door. Golden ink swirled into beautiful calligraphy; bold red and black words leapt up at her hungry eyes.

> *King Goldmouth (the Mad) Byds a Happy Cherrycost to Alle*
> *And Issues The Followyng Compulsion to His Fairylanders:*
> *Present Theeself to Pandemonium Upon Applemas*
> *For the Commencement of the Most Excellent*
> *Fairyland World's Foul!*
> *Feasting, Fighting, Frolyck!*
> *Exhibitions of the Many Counties of Fairyland!*
> *Demonstrations of Every Kind of Magic and Machine!*
> *See, Savor, Seize!*
> *Festivities to Culminate*
> *In the First Tithe in a Thousand Years.*
> *ATTENDANCE MANDATORY.*
> *Merchant Boothes Still Available!*

Mallow looked out at the caramel-colored whiskey lake, and the grey-green islands floating off in the reaches of it, the first plum-tailed buffleheads hiding in those ferny trees, honking up the dawn. The fog thinned as if to say: *I will protect you here no more.* The practical country witch of Winesap looked down at her mournful cast-iron ducks, who could read very well, even backward through the thin vellum sheet, as Mallow did not believe in letting any creature, no matter how strange or small, live in ignorance.

"They are sure to have a showing of Wet Magic there, and perhaps Shy Magic, too, and even Fat Magic," she said softly, a thrill in her voice. "And besides, the story had to start sooner or later. I had only hoped it would be a little later, and I could rest for another spring in my library. I believe I was just starting to get the hang of Questing Physicks. But there's no practice like real living, and anyway it's mandatory. What do you suppose a Tithe is? It sounds marvelous."

But neither her bed nor her hairpins nor her ducks had an answer for dear Mallow, for the Tithe had not been seen or heard of in Fairyland since long before their making. At that very moment, even Winesap's friar was busy looking it up in his oldest book, and finding only a reference to another, more ancient volume, which he had long since traded away for a round of cheese and some very dubious mushrooms.

Thus, when she appeared on the carriage platform at Winesap Station, the many bright-winged Fairies, glowering Ouphes, stripe-tailed Tanuki and violet-capped Gnomes gathered there saw a near-total stranger. Seventeen and taller than she knew what to do with, she wore a boy's practical clothes, black breeches and grey tights, a cream vest over coffee-colored shirt (she had spoiled herself with a bit of lace at the cuffs, for she enjoyed tatting), and no wings or horns or Sunday hat at all. Instead, she kept her hair bobbed short about her chin, as it was an indistinct, noncommittal sort of blond that would do itself no favors by flowing long or wild. Her sword, which was in fact a very long, very serious-looking silver sewing needle, hung at her side, a pack of supplies (mostly books) hung from her strong shoulder, and a cast-iron duck clunked along behind her, trying determinedly to be taken along. Mallow turned and shook her finger at the dark-billed little beast, who looked appropriately ashamed.

"You and your mother must stay and look after the bed," she said firmly. "Or it will be lonely. You may sleep on it, but only at night, and when it wants to recite its poetry, you must look as if you think it's very good. Do you promise?"

The duck quacked miserably as she turned it firmly round and pushed it toward home.

A Fairy lady with glossy plum-colored hair and buttercream wings shifted her luggage and whispered something to her bespectacled, behoofed friend, who puffed at a tamarind pipe and nodded agreement. Mallow felt very *seen*, in a way she did not quite like. The spring sun glittered through the many wings belonging to the suddenly silent Fairies, spread out and unfurled to catch the warmth and the light. A little Fairy boy, his hair a wild mass of sticky, pomegranate-colored curls, ran fearlessly to her.

"Hullo! Are you the hermit?" he asked excitedly. "Will you sign my schoolbook? Or! Oh! Would you like my schoolbook? It's not *very* good, but it has long words, and gloss'ry, and a fellow on the front, see?"

The boy held up a large volume with a stern-looking Nålegoblin embossed onto the cover, admonishing, with one long knitting needle, every child to pay attention and not pull faces. Around the Nålegoblin's huge bullfrog head the title danced: *Carolingus Crumblecap's Guide to Being a Small, Helpless, and Probably Too Clever By Half Fairy (Abridged)*.

"I'll take socks!" chirped the magenta-haired child, eager to make a deal. "Or a pipe, or a muffin but only if it hasn't got any nuts in it. No soap, please."

Mallow smiled and though she knew children ought not to sell their textbooks, she wagered he would get top marks if he made a mean bargain and she hadn't the faintest idea what Fairy educations were made of. She had tutored a bee-nymph or two in her day, but Fairies only taught their own. She rummaged in her pack and drew out a pair of good, sturdy mittens, which she handed over to the wide-eyed boy. He took them reverently and gave the book up without a glance before shoving the mittens onto the tips of his little wings and jogging back to his mother and a group of young Fairy girls and boys that had gathered to see if he'd pull it off. They welcomed him with impressed sighing and much crooning over the woolen prize.

Nevertheless, when the family carriages began to approach, no one kept an empty seat for Mallow, least of all the small, helpless, and too clever by half Fairy or his mother, who crammed his friends in until they hung out the window, waving their little woad-painted arms at her. One by one the stagecoaches pulled into Winesap Station and one by one they departed, drawn by alligators, llamas, bulls, even a pair of toads with bright pink markings around their eyes. The World's Foul would begin in a fortnight, and King Goldmouth had given them all so little time. The toads raced off, sending up a spray of mud.

Finally, Mallow alone remained on the carriage platform, and the evening had begun to set the sky for her supper. Idly, she opened Carolingus Crumblecap's primer and rifled through the pages. *On Curdling Cream*, one chapter announced. *On Spoiling Beer*, said another. *On Acquiring Humans, On Shoe Magic, On Leaving Unseelies Alone*. Her ink-stained and page-chapped finger rested in the crease of: *On Being Last Man Out*.

"Happens to everyone," Carolingus grumbled, his bullfrog face looming large and wriggling with life from the page, his spectacles a pair of perfectly round cat's eyes, their slitted pupils glaring at the imagined student. "Best to think of it as being First Man In, and thump the next poor fellow who comes along for his tardiness. A Fairy must make her own way in the world, for the world will never make way for her. That, incidentally, is the First Theorem of Questing Physicks, which you'll learn all about when you're older and don't care anymore."

Over the Nålegoblin's raspy voice, Mallow could hear a carriage approaching. It clopped up to the station—a black iron horse whose belly swelled very wide and large indeed and had tall, red-curtained windows where its ribs ought to have been. Its head curved with terrible grace and nobility, its mane curling like fireplace pokers, its nose aflame with embers. Mallow cried out in delight, for she did so love iron creatures, and reached out to pat its decidedly un-velvet nose.

"That'll be mine, Miss," came a soft, lilting voice, and Mallow saw that she was not alone on the platform at all, but a slim young gentleman leaned up against a cheerful lamppost a little ways away. He had not been there before, she felt certain, he simply had *not*. He wore a neat, trimmed and pointed beard the color of lamplight, had wicked silvery eyes, and a dashing black velvet coat, the color of the horse and the lamppost and her ducks. Int he center of his flame-blue cravat, a lamplighter's key pinned the silk in place.

"Mabry Muscat," he said finally, by way of introducing himself. "Your servant."

"Oh, I doubt it," said Mallow, but not unkindly. One cannot live in Fairyland too long, even closed up in a country house with hairpins for company, before discovering that Fairies like little better than to leap headfirst into dramas of the first order, to make trouble if they've a mind, love if they can, and mischief at any cost. "But my name is Mallow."

"Listen to all those Ms!" Mabry marveled softly, and began to sing very gently: "Oh, Mallow Met a Marvelous Man, by the name of Mabry Muscat . . . "

"Listen," Mallow interrupted. "I haven't any interest in following you to a stash of gold in the hills or dancing at a Fairy ball or answering riddles or meeting any eligible Fairy dukes who have a castle just on the other side of a curtain of mist—no. I am a magician—mostly—and I am on my way to the Foul like everyone else. Don't try to charm me, please. I am a practical girl."

"Those are my favorite kind," grinned Mabry Muscat. He changed the subject as though she had said nothing at all. "Do you admire my horse, Mallow?" Mabry said without moving.

"I do!" Mallow said, louder and happier than she meant to, her delight in new things bubbling out.

"Well, my young witchly friend, come and ride with me. You will find no better, for this is the Carriageless Horse, Belinda Cabbage's newest invention, which I am testing for her, and delivering to the Foul at earliest convenience. I promise to feed you regularly upon the way, not bother you with questions of personal history or future marriage, and refrain from making too many puns. But I cannot promise not to charm. I am quite helpless in the face of my own winning nature."

Mabry Muscat removed himself from the lamppost with an easy, nimble hop, and as he did his velvet suit shifted to the cobblestone greys and whites of the platform, to the brown and green of the trees, and finally to the black and red of the Carriageless Horse as he opened a door for her in the beast's vast belly and gave, very briefly, a half-smile and a half-bow. Mallow saw no wings at his shoulders (though that certainly did not mean he had none) and wondered if this was the "at least one" Jack-in-the-Green of the Winesap census. It was, however, never polite to inquire after a creature's nature. If he wanted you to know, he'd have made it apparent. Anyway, Jack-in-the-Greens were tricky folk—they had a wallop of a talent for hiding and a passion for stealing.

Mallow knew better than to get into a strange carriage with a strange man who might or might not love thievery better than his own mother, but no other seemed forthcoming, and attendance was, after all, mandatory. She felt that if she had to, she could thump this skinny fellow solidly, get out, and walk the rest of the way if the whole business became entirely *too* winning.

The interior of the Horse glowed with the light of a little red lantern; the walls shone cream and damask, the seats a plush scarlet. It was all anyone could want of a carriage, save that they rode inside the body of another creature, which unsettled Mallow. A slender horn curlicuing down from the roof allowed Mabry to tell the beast to be off. He called it Peppercorn, and it harrumphed gruffly back that they would rest for dinner in two hours, and to please not bother it, as it had to concentrate.

"Shall we play Bezique? Or Nightjack? I've cards, or chess if you prefer, but I've always found chess to be a bit too much like real life to provide much enjoyment as a game."

Mallow did not play cards, as that often led to losing things, since Fairies cheated as a matter of honor. *It's not a game if you don't cheat,* Carolingus Crumblecap would have told her, had she opened the book to *On Taking Tricks. It's just two sods making a mess with fifty-two pieces of paper.* But Mallow did not open her newest literary acquisition. "How long have you lived in Winesap?" she countered instead.

"Oh, off and on, off and on, for nearly just about forever," answered Mabry in a dreamy tone. "Since my love vanished, at least, and before that, too, I think, though it gets jumbled the further back one goes. When you've lost your girl, it doesn't much matter where you live. Everywhere is just The Place She Isn't, and that's the front and back of it."

Mallow looked out the window into the rolling golden valley, the winerows and the red sundown. Not a Fairy living didn't have a tale of love lost or found. They traded them like money. Mallow had always found love to be like a spindle or bobbin she could take up for a time—when her sorcerer friend visited, for example. But she could always put it down when she liked, and be quite all right until the time came to dust it off again. The endless reeling affairs of Fairies exhausted her. But all the many social circles of Fairyland held in agreement that if one brings up the subject of one's love, the other party is obligated to ask after it and listen to whatever ballad might follow. To do otherwise would be just terrible manners.

"Tell me about your love," Mallow sighed, observing form.

Mabry Muscat looked at her out of the corner of his eye. "Oh, it's a long and exciting story, sure to charm and make you swoon over me. Let's call custom satisfied and skip the tale, shall we?"

Mallow's attention sharpened to a point. "It must be a very good story if you don't want to tell it. Everyone wants to tell theirs. When I first set up my house I could hardly keep Myfanwy Redbean from reciting the tale of the boy she loved for seven years before some kirtle-tying trollop named Janet stole him away. In alliterative verse. With a tambourine."

"It is the very best of stories. She left me for a cat and a cloud, ring down the bluebells-o. She left me for a storm and a coat of green. Down fall the lilies-o." His voice was so sad and gentle that Mallow felt tears coming to her eyes all unbidden.

"But that was a hundred years ago if it was a minute past." Mabry shook himself like a wet bird and came up as bright and beguiling as before. "And what matters it if a girl runs off, or gets done in by pirates, or gets a better job than her lesser half? Let us speak of something less common and more thrilling. What news have you of the World's Foul? The delegates are already there, I've heard, filling up the hotels and mumming in the streets. And at the end of it all! King Goldmouth's Tithe. Back to tradition, he says. Time-tested values and solid, Fairylike customs. We'll be giving people donkey's heads next, I suppose. I don't think he'll go through with it, myself. Tithing is such a revolting, old-fashioned practice. Of course one goes through the motions for the sake of culture, pour out a tenth of a glass of wine every couple of years if you must or I suppose if you *have* ten children one of them might go into government, which is the same as losing a child really, but a real Tithe? Disgusting—and unsanitary if you ask me. I think in the end it'll all be a ruse, a trick done with mirrors. Somehow it'll all end in laughter and a chocolate for each of us, mark me."

"What *is* a Tithe? Not even the Scotch-nymph who lives in the north crannies of my whiskey lake knew, and she's the oldest thing I've met."

Mabry Muscat rubbed his long fingers, and Mallow felt certain he was a Jack-in-the-Green. His cravat glowed the crimson shade of the seat cushions, but his hair had gone as deep a blue as the sky outside. She could hardly see him. "I am older still, dear Mallow. And old as I am, I can just barely remember, when I was a child with my mother's milk on my chin and my father's holly upon my bed, the last Tithe Fairyland could stomach. It's a blood price, paid once every seven years, or ten, or a hundred, or seven hundred, depending on who you ask and how sick folk feel about it at the time. Every Tithe looks different—we'll see what this one will grow up to be, I suppose. I hope there will be fireworks, at least. Perhaps a commemorative spoon. These are days of old barbary and new revivals." He fell quiet for a while. Finally, when she could see the night hills showing on his inky skin, Muscat said: "Have you a love you wish to sing? Tell me who you are, pretty Mallow, sweet Mallow, my practical rose in a sea of silly daisies."

Mallow looked him levelly in the eye, and hardly a soul in the world has yet to be half-smitten and half-frightened by a level look from that girl. She told him the truth. "I have never lost a love and I do not intend to. One can only lose love if one is careless, and I am never careless. You might say, really, that of anything I am best at caring, at paying close attention and minding what I've got. The King says I must go to the Foul—very well, I shall go. And I hope to find a Wet Magician or two while I am there, and learn, and buy several new books if I can."

"Ah! She does want something! Well—it's easy enough. Find the Nephelo tents, where the great cats of that city laze and lie. They practice the Wet Arts as well as any soul in Fairyland, and will let you have a saucer of milk besides. Perhaps I shall even go with you. I once lived in Nephelo after all, and one is always homesick for places where one came to grief."

Outside, the night road to Pandemonium ran smooth and swift through the northern counties of Fairyland. Valleys bloomed around them, full of gnarled egg trees and waving coalflowers, falling away into meadows full of brownie villages bustling and bright-heeled river-nymphs lassoing their blue currents around distant hills. The notion of a blood price, the very words Mabry Muscat has spoken, hung between them inside the Horse, too hot and terrible and heavy to be touched. They did not touch it, but after a day and a lunch and an apple for the Horse, Mallow consented to play Bezique—as long as they played for no bets. Later they tried Fool's Hand as well, but that's no fun at all without a wager. All the cards had Mabry's face on one side, and Mallow's on the other. She did not find this unsettling or charming, which clearly saddened Muscat deeply.

Occasionally, when they were very bored, they would open up Carolingus to a random page and listen to him holler: *Never marry a Fairy Queen! They're murder on the digestion and you'll never get a career girl to care about the tarts you spent all day slaving over a hot stove to make.* On a stop-in to a village hostel, Mabry let Mallow open up the Carriageless Horse's neck and peer at the workings inside, which popped and hissed and burbled away, white and pink and green. *I recognize some of the thought that went into the beast,* Mallow said. *It's quite high-end Questing Physicks. See the vials of Purposeful Syrop, and the Hero's Alembic?* Mabry did see, and the Horse felt terribly pleased to be so regarded by such wise people.

Only once did Muscat ask if he might kiss her. Mallow declined, very reluctantly, more out of favor to that mysterious vanished love of his than because she did not wish to be kissed. He simply dealt the cards once more, and Mallow called the next trick.

Once or twice along the way, she heard ducks hooting, and held her books tight to her chest.

Pandemonium, after much fuss and many tantrums thrown and tears shed, had agreed to settle down in one place for the duration of the Foul. The capital of Fairyland has always been accustomed to moving however it pleased, drifting across glaciers or beaches or long, wheat-filled meadows. It moved at the need and pace of narrative, being a Fairy city and thus always sharply aware of where it stood in relation to every story unfolding in Fairyland at every moment. The King's pets, as he called his soldiers, had persuaded the city to put down roots, if only for a little while. Already, the streets seethed with restlessness and the signposts quivered with barely contained energy. The King's pets were, of course, large, lithe, rain-dark and snow-light clouds, lassoed and captured by several lightning-wights before being pressed into royal service. Even the thin, jagged-hearted Hobwolves of the Sniggering Mountains quailed in the face of those canine, long-toothed clouds.

But the sky shone glassy and gleaming on the day Mabry Muscat and Mallow rode into the capital, quite late, having started so far away. Only two days remained till Applemas and the Tithe. The Carriageless Horse clopped over a charming ivory bridge spanning the spinning Barleybroom River which surrounds the city, pointing and marveling and grinning wide-eyed at the great number of creatures flying, swimming, riding, striding, and leaping across to Pandemonium. Overhead, a huge, motley-colored, silk-ballooned zeppelin drifted majestically over the river. From a hanging basket beneath it, an Ifrit girl with burning hair played a fiery and furious mandolin. Music came from all corners, barghests squeezing accordions, satyrs blowing pipes, and drums everywhere, pounded, tapped, rat-a-tatted, and booming out across the plain where Pandemonium had come to rest, chained to the earth with long bronze links.

Mallow had never seen anything so wildly, savagely, noisily beautiful in all her days.

But when they finally crossed into the city proper with the throng, her bones ached and her heart could hardly bear the sight of it. The buildings of Pandemonium must have been lovely once, must have been diamond towers and golden storefronts and winding wrought-vine balconies, open flowers and briars and mosses genteelly drooping trees, violet peony-windows and blue lobelia-doorsteps. It must once have bloomed, the whole city, fruits and flowers with gem-spires and silver streets winking and glittering through the fertile, greening riot of the living capital. But no longer. Leaves had gone brown, vines had shriveled, flowers shrunk and wrinkled up, thorns gone dull and mosses gone grey. Where stone and jewel and metal showed through, the flank of a bakery or terrace of a bank or clerestory of a grand theatre, huge, gaping holes showed through, as though some awful giant had taken bites out of the city itself, in its highest and deepest and most secret and most open places. Applemas approached, high summer, and yet Pandemonium seemed to live in the dregs of autumn, when the brilliant colors have gone and left only brown sticks waiting for snow.

But for all that, Fairyland would not let her city go ungarlanded. The World's Foul had swung through, leaving red and violet and green ribbons streaming from streetlamps, bundles of wildflowers and clovers on every cornice, the streets lined with booths and stalls hoisting gaily painted signs: *The Famous Dancing Silkworms of Mararhadorium! Guess Your Death for a Nickel, Very Accurate! See the Crocodile-Beauty of Bitterblue Ridge! Test Your Morals, Everyone Gets a Prize! Feats of Queer Physicks Performed, Two Bits! Lamia's Kissing Booth, No Refunds!*

And in the center of the city, on a long, wide lawn, a clutch of kobolds had erected a miniature model of Pandemonium as it was, blooming and glorious and whole. The Green City, they called it, for no longer could the capital bear the name herself.

Mallow wondered if Fairyland had always been like this—this loud and fast and frightening and wonderful—and she had only forgotten, letting the pleasantness of Winesap seep into her bones. She wanted to do everything—to watch the worms dance and the crocodile-girl preen and oh, especially to see the Queer Physicks which she had been curious about for so long, and to test her morals, and to kiss a lamia. All of it, and eat a slab of honeycomb from the bee-nymphs of Pennyroyal Pond to top it all.

But instead, they lashed the Carriageless Horse to the post outside Groangyre Tower, where Belinda Cabbage and the rest of the Mad Inventors' Society made their laboratory, and Mabry Muscat completed a vellum questionnaire the Horse thoughtfully provided.

"Allow me to take you for a special treat," Muscat implored, and Mallow, who felt quite warm toward the dashing Jack, took his arm. He guided her directly, as though he'd a compass in his heart, to a little pavilion carved out of ice, with chaises and thrones and fountains all of frost and snow, and a furry tent covering it all. Huge cats lounged on every surface—Tigers and

Lynxes and Panthers and Lions and skinny Cheetahs licking at what appeared to be lemon popsicles. Richly dressed folk petted and conversed with them, their hands full of thick, steaming mugs of something herbal and fragrant. In the center of all of them, a great solemn Leopard watched her with deep, liquid eyes.

"Hullo, Imogen," Mabry Muscat cried joyously, and flung his arms around the great cat's neck. For her part, she purred contentedly, and nuzzled his head with a soft thump. "I have brought you a friend! This," he indicated the Leopard, who interrupted him with a long, rough lick across his chops, "is Imogen, the Leopard of Little Breezes. You'll see her brother Iago, the Panther of Rough Storms, over by the fishbroth fountain. And there's Cymbeline, the Tiger of Wild Flurries, and Caliban, the Unce of Sudden Blizzards—Unce is French for Snow Leopard you know, but Imogen and Caliban had a wrestling match over the L-word and my girl won. Oh, you'll meet them all sooner or later. And that lady in the shimmery sneeze of a gown is the Silver Wind, that gentleman with the sapphire belt is the Blue Wind, and this ravishing thing is the Red Wind, come to meet you, Mallow, and learn your name."

The Red Wind stood before Mallow, very tall and very beautiful, her long black hair hanging down one side of her face, spilling over an ancient coat of beaten beast hide of a deep, dark shade, dyed many times, the color of wine. Creases and long marks like blade-blows crisscrossed the cloth. Around the neck a ruff of black and silver fur bristled forbiddingly. Her fingers were covered in rubies and garnets and carnelian and coral. Iago the Panther padded up to her and the Red Wind lost her fingers in his fur. The black cat stared at Mallow for a while, as if waiting for something. And perhaps that something was the lady standing behind them, for when Mabry Muscat saw her his voice went still and quick all at once, and the expression on his face was like stars suddenly appearing out of the darkness.

"And this is the Green Wind," he said softly.

The Green Wind wore a long dress of perfect emerald, springtime green, belted with a length of peridots sewn on green brocade, and over that a long green coat, green snowshoes, and green jewels threaded all through her green hair. She stood quietly, her eyes clear and bright. Finally, she shivered and held out her arms. Mabry went to her inside two steps, and not the Red Wind nor the Blue nor the Silver nor any cat watched their embrace, but turned away to give them peace. When Mabry Muscat touched the Green Wind, his suit flushed the color of jade and oak leaves. Mallow smiled to herself, with a pang of regret. She did not think she would get any kisses of him now.

"Oh my love," said the Green Wind, wiping glad tears from her lovely cheeks. "I had hoped, if we all had to be here together to witness this poor joke, that I'd find you in the crowd. Thank Pan for the smaller blessings."

The Leopard of Little Breezes trotted across the ice and plunked down on her haunches between Mallow and the lovers. "She was called Jenny Chicory, when her hair was brown," the cat said with a rumbly, velvety voice. "She's my mistress and I love her. But I let her love him for a little while, when he happens by. I'm a generous cat."

"Is that his love, then? And you are the cat she left him for. Why may they not be together—they seem able to touch and speak, and no Sour Magic crackles between them."

Imogen shrugged her spotted shoulders. "Our work bears no competition, and our home bears ill will toward anyone not of the family—the cold and harsh air would strip even him to his bones."

It bears mentioning that Winds in Fairyland have little in common with the faceless, invisible breezes of our world. Whenever a storm or a tornado or a gust happens by, a sudden shower or snow flurry, somewhere in all that rushing air is a wild soul seated on a wild cat, whipping the sky into a riot, and singing the storm all the way down. They are a rare and feral sort, and no one knows their customs but they themselves. The Winds live in Westerly above the clouds, but the cats call Nephelo home, their village of ice and starlight, far up in the most vicious of Fairyland mountains. They come together when they please, and part only when they must. Between the two cities the Many-Colored Moon Bridge once hung, but that was long ago, and today is not yesterday.

Mallow spent her first night in Pandemonium in the Nephelese tent and much of the day after, sipping the hot, resinous wine of the Winds and wrestling the great cats, who all seemed to enjoy it, and only Iago bit her, but very gently, and she did not bleed. The great Panther took her up into the sky upon his dark back, to show off the strength of his flying. Mallow held on to his fur, and waved to Imogen below, and whooped over the towers of the city. They swooped low to sample real moonkin pastries from the far south, and met a sweet young Wyvern who confessed with a blush to her spring-green scales that she had, of late, become betrothed to an eligible young Library.

All the while the horns played and the lamias kissed and Mabry and the Green Wind played croquet with balls of thunder and snow. They talked the quiet talk of old lovers. They sang the evening ballad together, while the rest of Pandemonium sang their own sundown songs, all together in what ought to have been cacophony, but melted into the saddest and sweetest of harmonies.

Mallow asked after Wet Magic, eager to hear the Lays of Dripping and the Eddas of Seeping. The Cats of Nephelo knew it well, being intimate with rain and the sea and the blood of all bodies as they were. But Imogen would only say to her: *You will have had enough of Wet Magic forever by the end.* And though the Leopard loved to be cryptic and serenely mysterious, Mallow found she liked her best, and slept curled against her furry white belly while the stars moved over broken, hollow Pandemonium.

In the dizzy night following the Applemas Eve feast, Mallow woke. She heard a swinging, sighing sound beyond the ice tent. Curiosity woke with sharp teeth within her. She crept out of the Leopard of Little Breezes' heavy protecting paws and out of the tent, drawing a pale, glimmering robe belonging to the Gold Wind over her shoulders. The Winds lay snoring, all about, Green in Mabry Muscat's Arms, Red with her Panther, Gold with his arms flung over his head, as if in his sleep trying to stop some fell act. Mallow left them behind and peered out from the flaps of fur that served as Nephelo's current gate. The long, wide boulevard of central Pandemonium lay silent and black all up and down, streetlamps guttering and flickering, the moon a great blue mirror in the sky.

Mallow heard the sound again.

She squinted to see, up the street one way and down the other. She might have ducked into a near alley to follow it, but her eyes finally seized the prize—a long figure waddling down the cobblestones, shoulders hunched, cloak drawn up to its face. Wisps of fog billowed at its feet. Mallow froze; she could not have begun to convince her feet to move. The figure drew closer, into the lamplight, and where the beams struck it a thousand colors sprayed out as if a vein had been cut in the side of a rainbow.

It was King Goldmouth.

Mallow knew him from every coin and portrait in a Seelie hall. A huge clurichaun, hunched down in his cloak of jewels, voluminous brown leather stitched with every gem, so heavy it stooped him, dragged him down. His nose bulged, barrel-thick, hanging down so far as to hide his mouth and mustache, his lips of gold. Furry eyebrows concealed his gaze, and his bald head had been tattooed with astrological gibberish, the graffiti of a hundred royal stargazers.

With a garumph and a groan and a grinding creak, Goldmouth extended his long arm and his six long, spidery fingers. In the lamplight Mallow saw them shine, perfect gold, even the fingernails burnished. Not just his mouth then, but more, and from the sound of his steps, maybe a foot, too. He was getting old, much older than anyone had really suspected. A leprechaun spent his days guarding gold—but a clurichaun drank and ate and gluttoned and over the centuries slowly turned to gold, becoming his own treasure.

As Mallow watched, King Goldmouth scratched a scrap of fog behind the ear and whispered to it. The mist scampered off and returned in less than a moment with the sleeping body of a strong, handsome Gremlin, his buttery pelt gleaming, his wings a pale, leathery orange. Grumbling and grunting and groaning softly all the while, Goldmouth stretched his long, gold fingers, popping the knuckles. He drew all six of them together and gently pushed them into the Gremlin's mouth, under his long thin nose. He worked his thumb, pushing further and further until the King had his whole arm down the poor creature's still-sleeping throat, grasping, scrabbling, looking for something in the depths of him. Mallow felt ill. Finally, with a cluck of triumph, King Goldmouth withdrew his arm, and held up what he had found to the moonlight: a single lovely, faceted topaz. He popped it into his mouth and chewed, savoring it.

When he had done, the King breathed upon the dreaming imp, and his body shivered into yellow ash, wafting away while the clouds of fog whirled and cheered in their silent, wispy way.

Mallow watched the King at his night feast for another hour, her calves aching, her skin frozen, unable to move or even weep, her horror a heavy, real thing that moved up her legs and stilled her mind. She watched him prod the sides of buildings and bridges and towers, wiggling his fingers inside them, plucking out some secret, tiny heart—a brick or a pebble or a china cup or a lump of mortar—devouring it, and striding on as the wall or terrace or window crumbled away into one of the great gaping holes Mallow had seen all over the city.

Bit by bit, the King was eating Pandemonium.

"Everyone is hungry," Imogen growled quietly behind her, startling Mallow out of her spell. "But only the King can eat his fill."

That night, Mallow wept bitterly into the Leopard's fur, and did not know what was to be done. The Leopard licked her gently, in a sleeping rhythm, and did not know, either.

The day of the Tithe arrived suddenly and with a tremulous energy in the morning air. Fairyland's whole nation prepared breakfast and drank their coffees and teas and stiff peach-liquors, nibbled at brioche and iced cake and crisp bacon, but found itself not very hungry. Mallow told her tale and the Red Wind turned her face into her hair. Iago laid his head on her red knee. The Green Wind and Mabry Muscat exchanged fearful glances. *It will be more than Pandemonium one day*, those glances said. *He'll want all of Fairyland on his table sooner or later. And maybe one day is today and that is the awful reason for the dead, dark Tithe coming back into the light.* They held hands, and for once, Mallow wished she had a hand to hold.

Before her thought could finish itself, Mabry took her fingers in his, and the Leopard dropped her head into her lap, looking up at her with those black, kind eyes. "Tell him no," she begged. "All of you together. He cannot eat you all."

The Blue Wind stroked his indigo beard and sighed. "Perhaps he is right, and the Tithe is good and and honest and will make us strong. We did it for a hundred thousand years, or anyway a lot of years, before it stopped. There must have been a reason. We cannot know until we try. And maybe he will be sated."

The Silver Wind blushed storm-grey. "Next Saturnalia, perhaps, the wheel will turn and some young maid will tip his throne. That's how he got it, after all, from the Chamomile Prince, when he was young and his nose had not yet reached his chin. Politicks are an unlovely sport."

But the Green Wind would not look at her brother or her sister. She stared at her hands in her lap as though by staring she could set them aflame. It was time. They had to go.

The Tithing Ground had been festooned with banners and garlands of apples, torches blazing by day and wreaths of colorful mushrooms. A crowd had already gathered, but no one wanted to get too close. They hung around the edges, some weeping, some trying too hard to laugh.

In the center stood a monstrous, outsized faucet, rusted and chained with iron bands, the sort which has a great wheel at the top for turning water hot or cold. It seemed to come up directly out of the ground. Dust and cobwebs clung to it—it had not seen use in ages. Before it stood King Goldmouth, his jeweled coat a throng of color, his nose brushing his chest. He held up his hands and more Fairylanders crowded the square. He raised them higher, and all fell silent, the Winds and the Cats and the Fairies and the Ouphes and the dryads and the Ifrits and all the folk of the world. They strained like strings sure to be cut.

"Welcome, my countrymen!" bellowed Goldmouth, his voice a round brass bell. "The Foul has come to a close and I know you have all had as marvelous a time as I. But the time has come to put aside fun and frolick and attend to business! Too long have we let the old ways sag and rot—time, I say, to be Fairies once more! In just a moment I will ask the help of the Nephelese Cats and the first Tithe of a new age will begin. Don't be afraid! Bring your children close, line them all up so I can see their merry little eyes. They'll tell their grandbabies about this day—well, some of them."

But no one came forward. A tall, spindly birch-dryad began to cry audibly, and soon the square had filled with frightened, uncertain tears.

"Hush it!" hollered Goldmouth. "Is that any way to greet your destiny? Are you Fairies or aren't you? We are a great, powerful people, and we will not cry! The King may do as he likes! That's the whole point of being King! And I shall be King for a good long while yet so stop your blubbering. Take your

Tithe like grown-ups! Get over here, you mongrels," he snapped at the Cats. "You too, Jack, and your Windy friends." Mabry Muscat looked pleadingly at Mallow, and she could not understand why they all obeyed him—except that of course the King could eat them, and of course he was King, and did not people everywhere do more or less as they were told when someone with a crown did the telling?

Mabry and the Green Wind, the Red Wind and the Blue Wind and the Silver, all laid their hands to the great, heavy chains that bound the faucet. Instantly, boils and hives and long red wounds appeared in their hands wherever they touched the iron, for Fairyland Folk cannot bear it. Yet they pulled on, all of them crying out in agony, screaming up at the empty sky as their bodies bled and scarred and tore. The chains, wet with blood, loosened at last. The Cats shook their great heads miserably, but they came forward when called. Iago and Imogen and Cymbeline and Caliban put their strong mouths to the wheel and began to walk.

A screeching creak filled the air, and then a knocking, thudding noise, and finally a whistling, rushing, wet sound moving under the earth. Goldmouth hurried to place a crystal goblet beneath the faucet to catch the single enormous, blindingly blue drop of water that issued from its grimy mouth.

"The blood price," he said in awe. "The blood of a whole world." The drop splashed into the goblet, filling it utterly and sloshing over the side. The water was not water—it shone blue and swirling, with white wisps floating through it like clouds. "Why did we stop this? When we could feast every seven years on the price paid by other men in some ridiculous world that's nothing to do with us?" Goldmouth lifted the goblet high. His sleeves fell away from his golden arm and a gasp rippled out, which he did not hear. "In the old days, the days of our youth, we received the Tithe from a hundred worlds. We took their bounty and gave it out among our kind. We were so strong; we lived practically forever. Every time we took the Tithe, more magic leaked from their worlds to ours, more folk crossed over, more spells and wonders and riches!"

Mallow covered her eyes with her hand. It seemed obscene to look at the blood, somehow. "You said blood price, Mabry! I thought you meant we would pay it—we would all prick ourselves and bleed a little, or the changelings would be bled, or a great deal of cattle would be slaughtered."

Mabry's eyes turned rueful and creased. "Oh, no, Mallow. The blood price is paid to us. I thought you knew. From a hundred worlds and more, every seven years, or ten, or a hundred, or seven hundred. They pay their Tithe and we collect it."

"Which world is that?" Mallow asked. Her voice seemed so loud in the square.

"I've no idea," Mabry sighed. "Blood has no name. Some place with less magic and less joy than it had a moment ago, that's certain. In days past the whole of Fairyland shared out the stuff, with reverence, and strength like nothing you've known flowed through us. I had but a sip when I was a babe and I've lived a thousand years. But we stopped it—we had to stop. It was the Sympathetics who discovered the how and why of it. We were bleeding worlds dead, and none of us could bear it. We can be cruel, if it is fun to be cruel, but we are never callous. Never unfeeling. We would not make ourselves vampires for a few more years' revels. you have never heard of it, because we buried our secret shame as deep in a library as a stone may fall into a well sunk through the world, one end to the other.'"

King Goldmouth, with his goblin's ears, snarled into the heart of their talk. "Who cares? If a vampire I must be to live and dance and howl at the sun, then let me show my teeth! They paid their price, we're fools not to take it! To have let them hoard it all this time. And I shall take the first, all of it, for I alone thought to turn the wheel again. I shall drink it and live forever and rule forever and eat forever and turn utterly to gold—don't you look at my arm like it's poison!—and none of you will ever be able to stick a knife in me. Goldmouth's Feast, Ten Thousand Years Long!"

"No," Mallow said softly, but in her voice moved a hardness she had always known she owned in some deep cupboard of her heart, but rarely taken out, even for company. No Magic turned inside her, end over end, growing cold and implacable. She strode forward and leveled her needle-sword at the King's throat. It joined there a sudden and unexpected green lance, balanced in the Green Wind's lovely, jeweled hand. The Wind's stare could have curdled stone, but she said nothing.

It happened so quickly Mallow could not afterward say for certain who moved first. Goldmouth broke the green lance as easily as a branch and seized the Green Wind's neck in his fleshy fist. As soon as he turned from her, small and not green and with nothing but a needle as she was, Mallow buried her blade in his side. The Winds sprang toward their sister, and Mabry, too, all screaming and bellowing and Mallow could not even hear herself think. Blood gushed warmly over her hands, black clurichaun blood, night blood, and full of stars. Goldmouth pressed his golden fingers together and pushed them into the Green Wind's throat. Green tears spilled from her eyes. She choked and gagged as he worked his hands into her.

And then the King reeled, screeching. Black starry blood streamed everywhere in inky ribbons. Mabry Muscat had drawn the Blue Wind's azure cutlass and sliced Goldmouth's arm off at the shoulder. The Green Wind fell to the ground, clawing at the severed arm in her mouth, dragging it out of herself, slipping in the spreading blood. Mallow tugged her needle free of the King's sodden body. And three things happened in the same moment:

Goldmouth's cloud-hounds shot into the air, knotting around Mabry Muscat's throat and tying off before he could gasp. The light blew out of his eyes and his body fell to the streetside.

The Leopard of Little Breezes roared so loud and long every soul in Fairyland clapped hands over their ears.

Goldmouth's broken hand opened on the cobblestones beside the body of the Green Wind. In its golden palm lay a tiny, dazzling green leaf.

A great battle followed—but that is not important. To be sure, Goldmouth's clouds frothed into a rage, and the Great Cats of Nephelo rose up to fight them in the great, stormy sky. In years hence they would call the battle the Nor'Easter, for its squalls turned the heavens black and brought rain onto every head. The Red Wind shot so many clouds with her scarlet pistols and Iago, her Panther, tore so many with his teeth that afterward she would be called Cloudwyf, and the cowed nation of clouds would be hers to rule and ride. A bonny knight, Mallow rode upon Imogen, the Leopard of Little Breezes. With her needle stitched cloud to cloud until a thread of wind pierced a hundred hearts all in a row. Great cries were uttered, loyalties made, and far below the people of Fairyland fled home or took up their brooms and bird-mounts and carpets to join the fray. Grandbabies would be told of the day, rest you certain.

But that is a battle story, and battle stories belong to those who fight them. How a battle feels is impossible to tell, except by nonsense: *It felt like a long rip. It felt like a weight landing upon me, over and over. It felt like red. It felt like a bell unringing forever.* What can be told is that when Mallow and her Leopard and the Red Wind and all her brothers and sisters landed, Goldmouth still lay in the wreckage of his black blood, dying in between his breaths. Beside him, two strangers stood whole and with so much sorrow in their faces that the Red Wind staggered to see it. But beside the sorrow lay a rueful humor, as though a joke had been told while the war raged, and only now did these two youths catch the punch line.

One was a pretty young woman with brown, curling hair and a simple white dress with a few pale ribbons trailing from it. She wore a bonnet of valerian and heartsease. The color in her cheeks gleamed rich as bread and sun-rosy, and her feet were bare.

The other was a man with a neat, pointed beard and kindly eyes which had become the most beguiling shade of green. He was dressed in a green smoking jacket, and a green carriage driver's cloak, and green jodhpurs, and green snowshoes. In his hands he held a long green lance, quite whole.

"He died to save her," the Leopard growled. "And now he must take her place. It's different for each Wind. Red will need to be tricked by her replacement into putting on a white gown. Gold will be killed. So it goes. Long ago, a girl named Jenny Chicory loved a boy, and meant to be a water-duchess in the Seelie before going on the Great Hunt. She drowned saving a little boy in green, a boy she did not know from a stranger, from a pirate band with a whale on their side. She could not let him go down into the waves, and woke up all in green with a job to do and no more a happy maid with a suitor at her door. Now Mabry's done it, and he can't take it back, nor go home with her to Winesap any more than she could leave the sky windless. The gales of the upper Fairyland heavens would shatter her, as they would have shattered him. In the doldrums of summer, sometimes, they arrange to meet at sea, where the sails droop and crow's nests swelter. I imagine they'll keep that date."

Jenny looked at her Leopard with a grand and sorry love. "We are used to it," she said thickly. "And storms must sometimes come to Winesap, too."

Mallow looked down at the dying King. His breath did not stop or slow—a clurichaun his age had reserves of will waiting to be tested. He might live years in distress but not die. She considered what to do. She considered the Gremlin and the Green Wind. She considered poor, crumbling Pandemonium. She considered the shattered goblet and that blue and cloudy blood, the wettest of all possible Wet Magics, mingling with all the other blood that had poured out onto the square, wretched, dull, of use to no one.

Mallow knelt. She drew her needle and pricked the thumb of King Goldmouth's golden hand. Slowly, as slowly as he had pushed his fingers into helpless mouths, she pushed her needle in, pulled it through, and made her stitch. Beneath her hands, a thick, glassy thread appeared. She made another stitch, and another, hauling up the clurichaun's feet to his chest and beginning to cry a little despite herself, so exhausted and revolted and determined and sorry was she.

"I told you," she said as she sewed. "I didn't want to muddle in Politicks—and there is always Politicks, even when folk promise it's just a party, or a revival, or an exhibition of every kind of magic. I didn't want to meet a Fairy boy or dance at Fairy balls. I only wanted to read my books and learn a bit of magic. Why couldn't you have been a better King? Why couldn't you have left that poor world alone? Why couldn't you have been better?" She hit him with her fist and he did not protest. She had not hit him hard.

By now, Goldmouth's knees covered his face. He could not speak. A very neat seam ran across his nose. His eyes pleaded, but Mallow went on sewing up the King, stitch by stitch, into a package no bigger than her hand. The last of his astrological tattoos showed on the top of it, and she handed the whole thing over to the Red Wind to close away. Mallow's skin dripped starry streaks of royal blood.

The girl who would find herself, against long odds, Queen before dinnertime stood up and looked at her new friends, at her darling Leopard, at the glittering needle in her hand. Then she looked to the empty, hollowed-out city.

"Well," Mallow said, feeling a wave of powerful practicality break on her heart. "We've got a lot of work to do."

# WALKING STICK FIRES

## ALAN DeNIRO

On All Hallows Eve Eve, Parka sat on his motorcycle in the unending desert. The moon was a low-hanging fruit. The blue fires of Casino were off in the far distance to the north. Parka pulled an apple out of his jacket pocket, cut it in half with his claw, and offered one half to his fellow traveler, Jar.

"The apple has a pleasing scent," Jar said before he ate it, crushing the apple into pulp with his mandibles.

"I would have to agree," Parka said.

"Where did you procure it?"

"In a house outside of Casino." He indicated the blazing pyramids and monoliths with his claw. "Two days ago. I forgot I had it. There it was, sitting on a kitchen table. Red and perfect." When he finished eating the apple, Parka brushed off a posse of stick insects that landed on his shoulders.

"Hey, cool, walking sticks," Jar said, brushing them off Parka's jacket.

"Is that what the locals call them? I just don't know where these bugs come from," Parka said.

"They are everywhere," Jar said, cleaning his mandibles with his fingers afterward.

Parka watched the walking sticks rattle on the hard desert ground.

"All right," Parka said, kicking his motorcycle to life. The reactors shot into clutch for a second and then hummed. Jar followed with his. "Santa Fey then?"

"They are expecting us."

Parka patted his satchel, the one containing the Amulet of Ruby Webs, which he had extracted from Casino at great cost.

"Yes they are. I do not expect traffic. Or to encounter those we disposed of."

Parka was thinking of the Worm-Hares.

"Not under the mountains."

"Nope."

Parka leaned forward and his bike shot ahead. Jar soon followed. After they broke the sound barrier, Parka put on his headphones. He liked Toby Keith.

In the great tunnel underneath the mountains, they stopped at a rest stop. They hydrated and Jar sulfurized his joints. There were a couple of other travelers at the rest stop. Others sped by on their motorcycles and flaming chariots. Every once in a while there would be a rumbling sound that would shake the wire grating of the low roof and send dust to the ground. Once there was a low growl far above, like a brane gun backfiring.

"What's that?" Jar asked once.

"Taos," Parka said, not looking up from his hammock and his well-thumbed copy of *The Toby Keith Review*.

"Ah," Jar said, going back to his sour acupuncture.

The human child who was indentured to the rest stop looked up from his abacus. He had a nametag that said SHARON. "They've been going like that for a fortnight. The Black Rooster Company is finally yielding their fortress against the Azalean Gullet."

But the two couriers ignored him. Blushing, the child went back to his figures.

"Say," Parka said, "what are you going to be for All Hallows Eve?"

Jar pulled the needle from his spine and blew on the tip. "I was thinking Jack Nicklaus."

"Really? I love *As Good as It Gets*!"

Three of Jar's eyelids quivered, a sign of confusion and then mild amusement. "No, not the actor. The golfer."

Parka raised his eyebrows. "Really? Do you golf?"

Jar shrugged. "Who are you going to be?"

"Dwight D. Eisenhower," Parka said without any hesitation.

"Really? I love World War II!" It took Parka a few seconds to realize Jar was being a sarcastic mimic.

Parka sighed.

"But seriously," Jar said, perhaps sensing Parka's exasperation, "I would have sworn that you'd be one of the indigenous musicians." Jar pointed at the cover of *The Toby Keith Review*, in which Toby was performing in his moon-slave cage for various Being seneschals.

"I'm not quite so easily typecast, friend," Parka said. "Not quite so easily in one box or another. I have a lot of interests."

"Uh-huh," Jar said.

"Anyway," Parka said, wanting to change the subject a bit, "it won't matter if we can't make Santa Fey by tomorrow."

"Ha ha," Jar said. "Don't worry. We're in the slow season. We're deep underground. The winds of war are incapable of blowing upon our faces."

"I am not quite so sanguine," Parka said, closing his magazine and hopping off the hammock. "We should go."

"So soon?" Jar said. "I still need to sanitize my needles." He held a glinting needle out. The tip wavered.

Parka was going to say something clever and lewd but the sound of an approaching caravan drowned out any coherent thought. Three motorcycles and a black Camaro. They were slowing down and resting at the rest stop.

"Hey. Jar," Parka shouted, before the caravan stopped.

Jar looked over. It was a caravan of Casino dwellers, all Worm-Hares.

"Ugh," Parka said. "Like I said, let's go."

"Hey!" the prime Worm-Hare said, slithering out of the Camaro. It was too late. "Hey!"

"What?" Parka called out.

The other Worm-Hares had hopped off their motorcycles and were massing together. The prime pointed at the Amulet of Ruby Webs that was half-hidden in Jar's satchel. "I believe you have something of ours!" he said.

"It's not yours anymore," Jar said. "So you should have said, 'I believe you have something of yours!' "

Parka had to shake his head at this. Even in danger, he had trouble not to break out laughing. This, at least, gave them a couple of seconds while the Worm-Hares tried to parse this out.

"The Amulet of Ruby Webs is a sacred symbol for our community through many generations and systems," the prime said.

"Well, it's your damn fault you brought it down from orbit then."

The prime paused. The other Worm-Hares were getting antsy, stroking their floppy ears with their tentacles. They likely surmised that Parka and Jar would be difficult to slay in close-quarters combat. Or perhaps they were worried about damaging the amulet.

"How about we race for it?" the prime said brightly.

"No, you can't have a good race in the tunnel and you know that," Parka said. "Hm, I will kickbox you for it though."

All of the Worm-Hares laughed as one. "Seriously?" the prime said. "Um, okay. Sure."

"Great. If I win you'll have to leave us alone. And . . . " Parka thought about it. "Give up driving your Camaro for a year. No, wait, you'll have to give it to him." He pointed to the human child. "Aw yeah, that's right. Are you ready?"

The prime nodded and smiled, but then grew grim. "But, listen. Hey. I'm being serious here. Whatever you do, do not—*do not*—touch the red button on the center of the Amulet of Ruby Webs. Okay?"

"Yeah, don't worry," Parka said dismissively. "I'm no amateurish idiot."

"Fair enough," the prime said. "I am going to enjoy kicking your ass." The residents of Casino were known for their kickboxing prowess, and the Worm-Hares learned such local arts after they followed the Beings down to the surface.

"You sure about this?" Jar said to Parka, putting his hand on Parka's shoulder as he was doing stretches.

"Not really," he said. "But this is the only way they'll stay off our ass. So we can make it to Hallows Eve."

Jar nodded. "Right. Hey, look at that kid's face."

Parka looked over. The face was beginning to fill with walking sticks. Circling the neck, darting down the cheeks. The child was fearful, but was unable to brush the insects off, because of the chains.

"What is *with* that?" Parka said, as he stepped into the makeshift kickboxing ring, an enclosure of the Worm-Hares' motorcycles. "Seriously, do any of you know what is going on with those insects?" He pointed to the human. None of the Worm-Hares paid Parka any mind. The prime took off his leather jacket and Parka did the same. Then the Worm-Hares—and Jar too, for that matter—counted down to ten and the kickboxing match began.

Parka then entered a trance-like state, without his consent or volition. When he snapped out of it, the prime Worm-Hare was sprawled on the asphalt, his head twisted backward, tentacles twitching here and there.

"Wow," Jar said. "What happened?"

"I have no idea," Parka said. "What *did* happen?"

"He tried to kick your face, but you spun away. Then you kicked his face."

"Oh." Parka felt a few of the walking sticks scurry and drop off his shoulders, which felt sore. He didn't realize that they had landed on him. The other Worm-Hares were motionless and scared.

As Parka and Jar drove away, they noticed that the human child's body was entirely covered in the walking sticks. Parka tried to make eye contact, as a way of saying, Hey, the Camaro's yours, I hope you get to drive it someday, but there were no eyes visible to connect with.

A few hours later in the tunnel, they had to stop again. Flashing lights and a tall human woman wearing a sandwich board.

"Bypass," the woman said.

"Oh, for the love of God," Parka said.

"Cave-in," the woman elaborated. She also had a nametag that said SHARON. "You'll have to go to the surface."

"You think?" Parka said.

"Hey, she's just doing her job," Jar said.

"I know that, Jar," Parka said. "And don't lecture me like I'm some kind of phobe. I mean, I'm the one who gave a Camaro to a human child. I'm a friend of these people, believe me."

"Whatever you say," Jar muttered.

"Shoot," Parka said, trying to focus. "Let's see, we're about three hours away from Santa Fey by the tunnel. But who knows now. Is it hot up on the surface?"

The woman was about to say something, but she was drowned out by a quaking roar from above, and then a series of blossoming explosions.

"Well, I guess that answers your question," Jar said.

"Okay," Parka said. "I hate this. We're going to miss Hallows Eve."

"Stop whining," Jar said. "The amulet is the important thing, remember? Priorities?"

"I wish I had more apples," Parka muttered, revving his motorcycle and easing into the detour that the woman directed him to. He meant to ask her about the walking sticks.

Parka and Jar's motorcycles climbed to the surface. The surface was full of bright light and wispy ash was in the air. The couriers were in the desert foothills. An Old Being was hunkered down, sprawling in the desert. Eagle-falcon drones—it was hard to tell what mercenary company they were attached to—swooped, bombed, and soared away from the Being. Parka and Jar stopped and assayed the narrow road ahead, and where the road stopped.

"Ugh," Parka said. "The Being's in the way."

"Yeah."

The Being ate mountains. Finishing those, the Being would move to the badlands and mesas. Sparks shot off its slimy, translucent fur as it swept its mammoth pseudopods across sheep farms and little casinos. There were kites on stiff strings protruding from its upper reaches. When the Beings landed on a planet and sucked out the nitrogen, galactic civilizations would follow. After a few years, the Beings would be full, and then calcify, leaving several seedling Beings in their wake, who would then transport themselves to new systems. And *then* the residue of the Being's wake could be properly and safely mined. This residue powered the vast interstellar transmutation ships. Until that time, there would be war around the perimeters of the Beings, dozens of mercenary guilds and free companies jostling for position.

"There's no way we can drive around it?" Jar asked.

"Too many gullies." Parka put on his telescopic sunglasses and squinted at the Being. "Well, it's possible to . . . no."

"What?" Jar said. "Tell me."

More ships screamed above them, fast-eagle merlins that carpetbombed a trench right in front of the Being. Prisms trailed in the bombs' wake. Counter-fire from the trench screamed upward.

"We'll jump *over* said Being," Parka said.

Jar started laughing so much that sulfur tears began streaming out of his ducts, splashing upon his upholstery. "Whither the ramp, friend, whither the ramp?"

"What, you can't do a wheelie?"

"No . . . I've—I've never tried."

"And where did you learn to ride again?"

Jar paused. "On the ship."

"Hell, no wonder. You have to learn on the surface. I learned in Tennessee, before its flattening. Everyone wheelied. Well, anyway, it's easy. You just have to utilize the booster with the correct timing. You want to practice?"

"No, I'll watch you first."

"Are you scared?"

"Yeah."

Parka leaned forward and put a claw on Jar's carapace. "Well, don't be. Okay, let me make my approach."

Parka put his motorcycle in reverse about a half a kilometer and considered his approach, licking his lips. Jar crossed his arms and looked back and forth from the Being to Parka. The Being began humming, with resonances of local accordion noises. Parka leaned forward, kicked his motorcycle on, and then he roared forward, shooting past Jar in an instant. Then Jar turned on his motorcycle as well, and revved, and soon enough was a few lengths behind Parka.

"No, Jar!" Parka shouted, looking behind him. But there was no way for Jar to hear him, both traveling at the speed of sound. The Being was before them. Through its diaphanous surface, Parka could see about a thousand humans, and also four hundred birds of various types, five herds of cattle, a parking lot of used cars, several giant tractors, many boulders/reprocessed mountains, broken casinos, and a few off-worlders who were too stupid to get out of the way.

Parka hunkered down and wheelied and hit the booster. He soared, gaining clearance by a few meters over the Being. There were white kites protruding from the gelatinous skin of the Being, the kites' strings puncturing the surface and spooled far below. The eagle-falcons' bombs had accidentally scarred the Being in many places, but they weren't able to break through the surface.

When the booster gave out, Parka held out his arms and leaned forward, just clearing the Being. He skidded to a halt and spun the motorcycle around, watching Jar.

Jar had accelerated too late, and he seemed to hang over the Being, suspended like one of the eagle-falcons.

Jar gave a thumbs-up sign.

Then one of the kites snapped to life and whipped at one of his legs, and the thread tangled around the limb. Jar careened forward and separated from his cycle, which slammed against the surface of the Being's skin—the booster still on—and ricocheted upward. With the booster still going at full capacity, the motorcycle slammed into the wings of one of the low-flying fast-eagle merlins that was overhead. The eagle merlin spiraled out of control and careened into the side of a mesa about ten kilometers away. Parka felt the backblast as he watched Jar try to pull at the kite, tearing at the ashy paper. But the thread held. He landed, almost gently, on top of the Being. He tried to stand up, but in a few seconds he was beginning to sink into the Being.

"Jar!" Parka shouted. "Hang on!"

"Sorry," Jar shouted back, his legs already consumed. He looked down. "There's some serious alternate reality shit going on in there," he said.

"Keep fighting!" Parka said, but he knew it was hopeless.

Jar held up all of his arms and slid into the Being.

Parka hunched over his motorcycle, his head sinking between the handlebars. About a dozen walking sticks landed in his fur. He ran his claw over the hair, scooping them up and eating them. They tasted like Fritos.

"Nasty," he said, spitting them out.

He started riding again to Santa Fey in silence, with the shriek of the pre-mining operational maneuvers above him and to all sides. He put on his Toby Keith, but even this wouldn't soothe his guilt.

When he saw Santa Fey on the horizon, and the glow of the madrigal lights along the city walls, and the faint thrum of fiddles and cymbals and electric guitars, he became light-headed and also ridden with shame, which was far worse than guilt. He stopped his motorcycle and revved it, his gills fluttering.

At last he thought of Jar and also tried to consider what his life meant, in the end.

"Screw it," he said, and he turned around, back toward the Being.

About a kilometer away, Parka stopped and took the amulet out of the pouch. He knew, whatever happened, that his diplomatic career would be over. He would never be able to set foot in Santa Fey again, and they would in all likelihood hunt him down, if he lived. He would likely have to leave the planet he had grown fond of. Slowly, he slid the amulet around his neck. The walking sticks rose to the occasion, then. Soon there were thousands congregating around him, wedged in his joints and lining his shell. They felt warm and they tickled. The Being gurgled in the distance.

He remembered, with a sudden pang, what he had forgotten at the time—that the walking sticks were in his joints in much the same way during the kickboxing match.

A Camaro pulled up beside him, revving its engine. The boy, Sharon, was driving it; he was still covered in insects. Actually, Parka couldn't tell whether there was a boy there at all. Parka's own insects dropped off him and scurried up the car and through the open window to be with Sharon.

"Get in," insect boy said. His voice was deep and unwavering.

Parka turned off his motorcycle and parked it, and then got in the Camaro. He was nearly too tall for it, but he bent his head forward. He saw that the sandwich board was in the back seat.

"How did you get free of your post?" Parka said.

"Liberation takes many guises," Sharon said, revving the engine. "Enslavement is the pure heart of industry."

"Alrighty," Parka said.

Sharon turned toward him. "Therefore you shall be the Dwight D. Eisenhower of enlightenment and camaraderie."

The Camaro shot forward, and Parka fumbled for a seat belt. But there was none. They were driving right toward the Being. Parka was beginning to think this was a bad idea.

"I have an idea," Parka said. "How about we kickbox? If I win, you have to stop the car."

But the boy ignored him, and continued to accelerate. A few of the walking sticks from the boy scurried onto Parka's arm. He was too afraid to swat them away.

"Seriously," he said as much to himself as Sharon, "there has to be some underlying goddamn plan to this endeavor."

Sharon didn't turn as he said, "Not really. No."

They shot toward the Being, which soon was their entire horizon. The walking sticks were rattling with the velocity. The amulet was hot against his carapace. Parka closed his eyes.

In a blink of his outer eyelid, he expected one of three conclusions to his current predicament.

The first involved a high-impact collision against the outer husk of the Being, flattening him and the beautiful Camaro.

In the second, the Camaro would puncture the Being's skin and come to some kind of high-impact collision *inside* the Being, with any number of the farm animals, people, and other physical remnants of the aboriginal civilization surrounding him and either flaying him or welcoming him into a pathetic intra-Being community.

In the third, Sharon would halt at the last second, or dodge the Being somehow, because he was really trying to mess with Parka's head, which he was doing a spectacular job with already.

He missed home all of a sudden, the home he had tried so hard to forget, his twenty parents who all had contradictory advice for his well-being, and who hated interstellar travel—

"It won't be long," Sharon muttered, and then the Being was upon them, and they were upon the Being, and the Camaro screamed. It really screamed as it blew through the outer shell of the Being, causing an explosion in its wake and argent and vermillion sprays all around the car, and strands of Being fur flying. The front windshield shattered and the pieces blew away like tiny feathers. Then the top of the car ripped off.

They were inside the Being. But the Camaro didn't stop. In fact, it seemed to gain an extra level of speed once it was inside the Being. The walking sticks glowed like solar flares or brane-gun bullets from a galactic transmutator. Past the blue and green haze, Parka couldn't see much—shapes moving around that were vaguely aboriginal in form. The only things he could see clearly were the local sorcery-powered vehicles that were known as "monster trucks." They raced toward the Camaro, dozens of free-floating kites strung to their menacing hulls, but they were far too slow to reach the rocketing black Chevrolet stock car. The inside of the Being smelled like ferrous oxide, phlegm, sinew, and transdimensional energy. Before he was able to formulate the thought to look for Jar at all, the Camaro had burst through the other side of the Being with a roar. More fine, plush incandescent Being fur surrounded them. Then the light grew sharp and bright, and Parka shielded his eyes.

When he moved his pincer away from his face, he saw that the Camaro was sailing in the air above a deep canyon, which the Being was on the edge of.

"I want to warn you," Sharon said, "that you might want to brace yourself."

The Camaro seemed to be suspended above the dry riverbed far below for a few seconds, and slowly began to arc down. The other side of the gully seemed impossibly far away. The walking sticks, still glowing, began to thrum.

And then he touched the button on the center of the amulet, the one forbidden thing. The red rays embedded in the metal burst out, and solidified into strands many meters long, following the contours of his arms. Then they ballooned out like wings.

They *were* wings.

Without really thinking—and it might have been the amulet thinking for him—he stood up and stretched his arms out. The wings were massive, and the Camaro wobbled but righted itself. As it fell, Parka could hear the Being on the other side of the canyon shrieking, and feel its reverberations around his neck.

Parka leaned forward and the Camaro landed right on the edge of the canyon with a thud. Sharon hit the brakes and the Camaro spun around. The Being was, in fact, in the throes of dying. Eagle-merlins from above were trying to maneuver out of the way, but aquamarine slime burst out of the Being like sulfuric geysers and coated the carpetbombers, which spun around and veered wildly. Parka could hear a high, sonorous call from many miles away—the continental emergency siren from Santa Fey.

Sharon was still. But then he pointed.

The Worm-Hare posse was there, gathered around a minivan, each with a brane gun strapped to its arm.

"You've *got* to be kidding," Parka said. He tried to get out of the car, but it was difficult because of his nascent wings. He ended up crawling forward through the glassless windshield and onto the hood. The wings settled around him like a reptilian cape.

"We want our damn car back," the prime Worm-Hare said. It was a different prime from the one Parka had defeated in kickboxing. The sliding door of the minivan was open, and Parka could see the original prime in the back of the minivan in a shimmering heal-sac. "To say nothing about the amulet, one of the key symbols of our people, which you've gone on and messed up as well. You know that your corporation is going to hunt you down for triggering 'dragon mode,' right?"

Parka laughed. *Dragon mode.* "That's great. Anyway, you seem to forget that I won the car fair and square. I don't know why you're so upset about that, considering your current sweet ride."

"We don't care," the prime said, hoisting his gun at Parka, ignoring the jab about the Honda Odyssey. "We just want a souvenir to take back with us off-world." He indicated the dying Being in the distance. "This planet is a cursed cesspool. There's nothing here anymore. But nothing would make us happier than to disintegrate your sorry carapace and take this car into orbit with us."

Parka spread his wide wings—which didn't hurt at all—because he thought it would scare them. But it didn't, at all. He sighed. He realized that sometimes it's the smallest moments that could change a creature's life. He had given the Camaro to a human as a prize, and had thought nothing of it. But here he was, about to die from the Worm-Hares after all, and with weird wings. But all the same, he felt good about his generosity, even if Jar wasn't there to share it with him.

With that in mind, he wasn't going to back down.

Sharon was motionless, but then he looked in the backseat and started laughing. It was such a quiet, tinny laugh that it shocked everyone into stillness.

"What?" the prime Worm-Hare said, exasperated. Then there was a red dot on his spiny forehead. Parka stared at it.

"Will someone *please* tell me what's going on?" the Worm-Hare said.

Then there was a whooshing sound, and a crossbow bolt hit the Worm-Hare's forehead where the red dot was. The bolt went through his head, blasting into the front windshield of the minivan. The prime slumped over.

Parka turned around. There was someone in the back seat.

"Hey," Jar said, sitting up, slinging a laser crossbow over his shoulder and looking groggy.

"Christ on a—" Parka said, but he stopped, because he didn't know what to say. Instead, he ran to Jar and wrapped his leathery, demonic wings around his friend in a familial embrace.

"Look at you," Jar said, still sleepily. "With wings and stuff."

"It's the amulet," Parka said. The remaining Worm-Hares were forgotten, but they had made their pathetic escape in the minivan. "But, anyway, priorities. How the hell did you get there? You weren't there all along, were you?"

Jar shrugged. "No, not really. I was in the Being and then . . . um, I don't remember much about that, but I saw this sweet Camaro cruising through, and then stop in front of me, and I said to myself, hey, maybe I should hop on board, so I did. And I must have picked up this crossbow. I guess I was on a shooting range for awhile or something?"

Parka had no recollection of the Camaro slowing down enough for anyone to jump aboard.

He disengaged from Jar. "I'm just glad you're safe."

"Well, you came back, friend. That's the important thing. I'd still be in there without you."

"The Tree requests your presences," Sharon said.

"What?" Jar said.

"Ah, the kid, he's like that," Parka said. He waved toward Sharon. "Okay, okay, the tree. But first, we need to get a beer."

Later that day Jack Nicklaus and Dwight D. Eisenhower and Sharon met for a summit over a few of the local beers.

"How's things?" Jack said.

"Super," Dwight said.

"Awesome," Jack said.

Sharon was silent. They were in a basement tavern somewhere north of Albuquerque, at a circular table. It was the off-season, and likely everyone in a 500-kilometer radius was trying to flee the potential blast zone of the Being, so they had the place to themselves. The beer was warm but the off-worlders didn't care. Sharon didn't order anything, so Parka had the bartender make him an Arnold Palmer. Toby Keith was playing on the speakers and everything was all right with the universe, at least for a few minutes.

"I'm going to miss Hallows Eve with the gang," Jar said. "But it's a small price to pay."

"Yeah, it would have been fun. I'm glad we dressed up anyway."

"You know, I wonder if Eisenhower would have won the war faster if he had wings like yours."

"It's very possible," Parka said. The amulet against his chest pulsed like his second heart. The walking sticks swirling around Sharon clicked and skittered.

"What do you want to do after we, er, look at some tree that might very well be imaginary?" Parka said.

"I don't know," Jar said, taking a sip of his Budweiser Light. "It's hard to say. Go back home, maybe. Start over with a new corporation. How about you?"

"Well, maybe I'll stay here," Parka said. "I haven't decided. But I like it here. I still have no idea what the hell happened."

"With the amulet?"

"A little. But mostly with the Camaro. And the Being."

"Ah, that's understandable," Jar said.

Parka leaned forward, which was awkward because of his wingspan. "What I want to know is . . . I might not never understand, ever, what's going on with these walking sticks. But they're trying to say something, trying to do something. They're trying to survive on this godforsaken planet we—I mean, not us personally, I mean the mining ventures—sucked dry for resource management. And for what? So we can get more fuel for our transmutators to find more planets to suck dry and destroy?"

Parka was melancholic, but not just for geopolitical reasons. He realized that this might be one of the last times of relative normalcy with his good friend.

"Yeah," Jar said. "You make a good point. Maybe I'll stay too. And learn how to properly ride a motorcycle and do a wheelie." He laughed and then downed his beer. "Come on, Sharon," he said. "Finish your drink."

They rode for an hour in silence through the empty desert, and could see the Tree from many kilometers away. A towering, shadowy shape. Sooner rather than later—Sharon wasn't exactly following a speed limit—they could see the enormity of the living structure. Parka stood up in the car, letting his body poke out of the shorn top, letting his wings free.

"Holy shit," Jar said.

The Tree was as tall as the highest peaks that the Being had desiccated, many kilometers high. And the Tree was on fire. Smokeless fire. The tree pulsated with orange light. The branches were leafless, but they spiraled in gargantuan yet intricate patterns.

About a thousand meters away, Sharon stopped the car. Everyone got out. The walking sticks encompassing Sharon, or perhaps embodying him, were glowing in syncopation with the Tree. Then it became clear that the Tree was made up of billions of the walking sticks.

There were many other abandoned vehicles all around the Tree in a ring.

"Why are the walking sticks doing this?" Jar whispered.

Parka shook his head but didn't say anything. He had no idea.

Sharon turned to the two of them and said, "We need you two, the Dwight D. Eisenhower and Jack Nicklaus of interpersonal diplomacy, to carry a message back to your people. You will relay terms for peace." Sharon began walking toward the Tree.

"Wait, Sharon," Parka said. "What will happen if we do?"

"What will happen if we don't?" Jar said.

Sharon paused for a second and said, "My name's not Sharon." Then he began walking toward the Tree again.

Parka watched him for a little while, and looked at Jar, who shrugged.

"Who the hell knows," Jar said.

As the general and the golfer followed Sharon to the base of the tree, Parka swore he heard Sharon, who wasn't in fact Sharon, humming a tune, one of Toby Keith's more recent songs about exile on the moon and earthly liberation. Or maybe it was only the sound of the walking sticks and the desolate wind making music together, which wasn't meant for a stranger like him, wasn't for him to understand.

# LATE BLOOMER

## SUZY McKEE CHARNAS

The vampires showed up the summer that Josh worked at Ivan's Antiques Mall.

The job wasn't Josh's idea. He hadn't *asked* to be there.

Ivan's side of the family were all fixated on material stuff, and what is an antiques mall about if not *stuff*? Josh's side were the talented ones. His mother, Maya Cherny Burnham, was a well-known landscape painter. His father taught higher math at the technical college. Upward strivers both, they had never been shy about letting him know that they expected great things from him.

That was okay; everybody pushed their kids. Josh wasn't the only one taking extra science, math, and creative writing electives. In fact, he was doing pretty well. He even liked the writing work. The teacher was giving him A minuses and B pluses, and he was really getting into it.

Then he broke his leg. And then Steve Bowlin's crazy dog bit him, two surgeries' worth. Then he got mono (better than getting rabies, ha ha). A whole parade of pain. No wonder he messed up on his SATs.

His father said, "Josh, you should hear this from me first: If you had major sciences talent, we'd have seen it by now."

His mom said, "Okay, you're not the next Richard Feynman or Tom Wolfe—so what? You've got more creativity in your little finger than that whole high school put together!"

So, on to after-school classes at the Community Arts Center: oils, clay, watercolor, printmaking, even a "fiber arts" class that (despite strong encouragement from the instructor) he bailed on early. The retards at school were already spreading a rumor that he was gay. He eased out of team sports around that time, too. You do *not* want to be the weediest guy on the field with a bunch of Transformers who think (or pretend to think, just for the fun of it) that a guy who does any kind of art must be queer.

The worst, though, was when the portfolio of his best drawings didn't get him into the Art Institute Advanced Placement program. Probably he shouldn't have included those comic book pages he'd been so proud of. So he wasn't good enough; but that was what art school was for, wasn't it? To help you do it *better*.

His parents said, "Some creative people are late bloomers." They smiled encouragingly, but disappointment hung over them like those little black rain clouds that float above sad cartoon characters. Josh got depressed, too. He quit drawing, writing, even hanging out in the local museum (a small collection, but they had two awesome Basquiats and a set of spectacular watercolors by a local guy—he could see these things in his mind anyway, they were that good).

He shut himself off as much as he could, using his iPod to enclose himself in a shield of sound: Coldplay, a couple of rappers, some older groups like the Clash. And the Decemberists, at the top of his list since he had heard them in a live concert and had been blown away.

Then at the farmer's market one Saturday he heard a band performing and stopped to listen.

They were heading for a music festival in Colorado, according to the cardboard sign propped up in an open guitar case: a sturdy guy on a camp stool with one drum and a light, easy beat; a skinny, capering guitarist who wore a T-shirt on his head like a jester's cap and bells; a low-slung blonde who padded around with her eyes half closed, fiddling the sweetest riffs Josh had ever heard; and a square-shouldered girl with a voice like a trumpet, belting out off beat love songs and political ballads without ever needing to pause for breath.

They were too cool to talk to—in their twenties, playing barefoot on the grass for gas money—but he stayed until they started to repeat themselves. Their songs were good—quirky, catchy, wry, sad, the works. Okay, they were not Danger Mouse or the Decemberists. But they were surely what those groups had been when they started out: talented friends who went out to play whatever they could to whoever would listen, learning how to make great songs.

*That* was what he needed to do. That was the life he wanted.

So when the class play, an original musical, needed more songs, he volunteered to help. His reward was to be assigned to write two songs with Annie Frye. Writing verses (what was he *thinking*? Now he was *really* going to be killed in the boys' bathroom)—with Freaky Frye!

But Annie was fun to work with, and lyrics for her tunes came surprisingly easily. Didn't that mean something?

Annie introduced him to some seniors she knew who played gigs around town for beer money. They called themselves the Mister Wrongs, and they needed a writer (obviously). He began spending time with them, rehearsing in Brandon White's garage. Annie had a fight with the drummer and walked out. Josh stayed, not just writing songs but singing them. His voice was getting better. They said if he could grow some decent stubble, he might make himself into an acceptable front man.

He had two big problems. One, his mother thought pop music was stupid and destroyed your hearing, so for the first time she was carping about what he was doing instead of cheering him on.

Two, he was so far behind! He couldn't seem to get the hang of reading music. The only instrument he could play was a Casio keyboard (secondhand from Ivan's). He existed, musically speaking, in a whole other *galaxy* from the Decemberists and their peers.

But Brandon's group liked his lyrics, and sometimes his words and their music did awesome things together. Brandon's girl Betts knew some people in Portland. They talked about heading up there to do a demo tape. Things were looking good.

Then Betts's parents moved across the river, and Brandon's house was repossessed after his whole family snuck away overnight. The others drifted away, and it was all over.

Josh holed up in his room, working on songs about wishing he was dead. He told his parents that he wasn't going back for senior year.

After the inevitable meltdown, his mom got him the summer job at Ivan's mall, no ifs, ands, or buts. Obviously his parents hoped that a microscopic paycheck for grunt work in "the real world" plus some "time to think things over" would change his decision.

As if! All he wanted was to get the hell out of Dodge and go someplace he could find new musicians to work with, someplace with a real music scene that went beyond country whining, salsa, and bad rock. He needed a fresh start, in Portland or Seattle—*someplace*. Once he got there, his nowhere origins wouldn't be a problem. Colin Meloy was from *Montana*.

Basically, though, what he really wanted was for the world to stop for a while so he could make a really good musician of himself. He needed to make up all the time he'd wasted on science and arts.

The vampires' arrival, of course, changed everything.

The first-look sale of old Mrs. Ledley's estate ran till eleven p.m. on a Friday night. Josh was posted in a back booth, with orders to keep his eyes open. The crowd was mostly dealers, but you couldn't be too careful in a huge warehouse space broken up into forty-five different dealers' booths and four aisles.

Tired from schlepping furniture and boxes all day for Ivan's renters (who all had bad backs from years of schlepping furniture and boxes), he sat at an old oak desk in booth forty-one (Victoriana, especially toys and kids' furniture), doodling on a sketch pad. He'd have worked on song lyrics ("The day flies past my dreaming eyes . . . "), but not with Sinatra blatting "My Way" from a booth up front that sold scratchy old long plays.

Hearing a little *tick, tick* sound close by, he glanced up.

A woman in a green linen suit stood across the aisle, tapping a pencil against her front teeth and studying the display in a glass-fronted cabinet. Josh sketched fast. She might work as a goth-flavored Madonna, being pointy faced and olive skinned with thick, dark hair.

Next time he looked, he met a laserlike stare. Her eyes, crow footed at the outer corners, were shadowed in the same shade of parakeet blue as the polish on her nails (good-bye, Madonna).

He closed his pad and asked if she wanted to see anything from the locked cases.

"Have you got any furs?" she said. Her English had a foreign tinge. "Whole fox skins, to wear around the neck in winter?"

He shook his head. "Some came in with the estate, but they've already gone to a vintage clothing store."

She sniffed. "Then show me what you're drawing."

He meant to refuse but found himself handing over his pad anyway.

She flipped pages. "Jesus and sheep? Are you Catholic?"

"You can always sell a religious picture in here sooner or later," he said, folding his arms defensively. "Minimum wage sucks."

"This isn't bad," she said, tapping the top sketch, "but I would stay in school if I were you." What was she expecting, Michaelangelo?

"I'm dropping out." Not that it was any of her business.

"Then this is a good place for you," she said, handing back the pad. "One can always make a living in antiques."

"It's just a summer job," he mumbled. "I'm a musician, actually."

"Oh? What's your instrument?"

"Keyboards. But I'm more of a songwriter." She had moved closer. Her perfume was making his eyes water.

"Can you sing something you've written? My name is Odette Delauney; I know a lot of people. Maybe I can put you in touch, ah . . . ?"

"Josh," he muttered, "and I'm a song*writer*." He was not about to sing anything at a building-sized party of old farts zoned out on—Stevie Wonder, now. He avoided mentioning two blurry video clips, made with Brandon and Betts, on YouTube. He *had* to remember to take the stupid things down.

Odette Delauney's beady stare was making him feel strange. His feet kept inching his chair backward, but his head wanted to lean closer to her.

She swiveled suddenly on her high heels and pointed at a toy display: "If the donkey works, I'll take him." Then she was walking away, carrying a wind-up tin donkey that sat back on its haunches with a pair of little cymbals between its front hooves.

The ambient sound of the wide dealer space roared in as if Josh had suddenly yanked out a pair of earbuds: conversation, Julie Andrews climbing every mountain, shuffling footsteps.

Odette Delauney? Was she somebody? Had he just blown a big chance?

Too late; she was gone.


Josh stayed late to sweep up and turn out the lights. It was after midnight. His gray Civic was the only car left in the lot.

By the glow of the floodlight outside, he saw that a plump, dark-skinned girl was sitting on the sagging slat bench by the front door. She had a mass of dreadlocks, shiny piercings in an ear plugged with a white bud, and a cigarette in her hand. Wearing jeans, a tank top, and pink plastic sandals with little daisies on the toe straps, she looked about fourteen.

"Hey," she said as he locked the front door behind him, "think I could get a job here? I've got expenses, and my aunt is so *stingy*."

"But she lets you stay out late and smoke weed," he said.

She snorted derisively and took a puff. Ivan would disapprove of her on *so* many levels. The dealers and buyers at the mall—mostly old, white, and from the boondocks—didn't run, as Ivan said, in progressive circles (har har, progressive *circles*, get it?).

"Is working here as boring as it looks?" she asked.

"Worse." He gestured at her iPod. "So, who are you listening to?"

"Amy Winehouse." She narrowed her eyes. "What'd you expect? The Jonas Brothers?"

Josh thought fast. "M.I.A."

" 'Jai Ho,' " she drawled, but her expression relaxed. "You're Josh? My auntie Odette met you inside."

"She bought a musical toy, right? Funny, she sure didn't strike me as the type for that kind of thing."

"She'll have a buyer for it somewhere. Those old animal-band sets are hot right now."

Then auntie was just another antiques dealer, not a record producer's best pal, surprise surprise.

"So—are you adopted?" he said.

Studying him with narrowed eyes, the girl blew another slow plume of smoke. "My Main Line mom ran off with a bass player from Chicago. The wheels came off and they both split and left me with a neighbor. I call her auntie to keep things simple. I guess 'adopted' works. You a musician?"

"Uh-huh," he said, and that was enough about that. He didn't want to come off as some dumb-ass poser. "You collect stuff, too, like your aunt?"

"Sure," she said, shifting aside on the bench. "Sit down—I'll show you what I found tonight."

He had barely touched butt to bench when she grabbed him with steely arms, jammed her face down the neckline of his T-shirt, and bit him. His yell pinched down to nothing in seconds. Muffled panic surged through him as he slumped, unable to move or shout for help, staring over her head at the neon bar sign across the avenue.

Am I dying?

"That's enough, Crystal."

The sucking sounds from under his chin stopped. Someone else took the girl's place. He knew that perfume. The woman's lips felt tight and cool, like the skin of a ripe nectarine pressed to his throat. . . .

He came to sitting behind the wheel of the Civic with a stinging sensation in his chest and a headache. "Ow, shit, what happened?"

Crystal said, right beside his ear, "Odette wants to talk to you."

It all came rushing back, paralyzing him again with sweaty horror.

"Josh," said Odette Delauney from the backseat. "I'm only in your town for a little while, buying antiques. I need an insider here to help me find the kinds of items I want and then to make sure I get them. Tonight I'll just take a quick look at the storage area. If I pick something out, you show it to your employer tomorrow—"

"Cousin," Josh croaked. "My cousin Ivan owns the place."

"Show it to your cousin Ivan and tell him you have a buyer for it. I'll come in the evening and make the purchase."

Something weird as hell had just gone down between him and these two, but *what*, exactly? Odette's calm tone made it impossible to ask directly without sounding like a lunatic.

Please go away, he prayed.

"You could just take stuff," he muttered. "I wouldn't say anything."

"Of course not," Odette sniffed. "But I don't steal. And I'm not asking you to steal *for* me, either."

Gee, thanks. His trembling fingers found a swelling, hot and pulpy wet, low on his throat. "Oh, God," he moaned. "What'll I tell my parents about this?"

"Nothing," Odette said. "One of us will lick the wounds closed. Our saliva heals where we bite."

Agh, vampire spit! His teeth began to chatter. "Are you gonna turn me into a—like you?"

"With one little bite?" Crystal hooted scornfully. "You *wish*."

"Certainly not," Odette said, ignoring her. "Do as I say and you have nothing to worry about. Our arrangement will be brief and very much to your advantage. I'll pay you a commission on every purchase that I make."

A giggle burst out of him, ending in a sob. "I'm supposed to *work* for you? Everybody knows how that comes out—Renfield eats bugs, and then Dracula kills him!"

"We put the Eye on you," Crystal said in a smug singsong. "Now you can't tell anybody about us, so we don't *have* to kill you."

"Unless," Odette added, "you say no."

Which was how Josh went into business with Odette Delauney and her "niece," Crystal Dark (a joke; Crystal, it turned out, was an avid fan of fantasy movies).

It was true: he couldn't tell anybody. When he tried to talk about the vampires, his brain fuzzed over and didn't clear again for hours. It was just as well, really. All he needed was for word to get around that Josh Burnham claimed he'd been attacked—and then *hired*—by two female vampires from out of town.

Pretending he had found a new band to hang with after work, he told his parents he'd be coming home late some nights. Luckily he was too old to be grounded. His mom put up a fight, but she left hot food in the oven for him on his late nights anyway (which was particularly important now that he was suddenly this major blood donor).

His father, absorbed in updating a textbook he was coauthor of, said, "No drugs, that's all I ask."

Twice a week after hours, Josh let the vampires in through the loading doors, which were hidden from the street by the bulk of the building. In the windowless back room, they cleared space on the worktable Ivan used for fixing old furniture, and they went through whatever new stock had come in.

There was always new stuff. Business was booming. Ivan called it the "*Antiques Roadshow* effect"; that, and the stock market. People were desperate to put their money into solid objects, things that they thought would get more valuable no matter what.

That first week Odette bought: a tortoiseshell and ivory cigarette holder (fifteen dollars), bronze horse-head bookends (twenty-eight dollars), three colored-glass perfume atomizers (thirty dollars), a rooster-silhouette weather vane (twenty-five dollars), and a four-inch-high witch hugging a carved pumpkin, both in molded orange plastic (seven fifty).

"Your aunt," Josh said, "has weird taste."

Crystal shrugged (this was her favorite gesture). "Everything's cheap here in flyover country. In *real* cities, the Quality will pay top dollar for the same stuff, sometimes just to keep some other collector from getting it."

By "the Quality," she meant vampires.

Josh worked up the nerve to ask Odette, "Who's the pumpkin-toting witch for?"

"Some old fool I know in Seattle. We're not all rich aesthetes, Josh, whatever you may have seen in the movies."

"Aesthetes." That's how she talked. That was the kind of conversation they had, those nights that the vampires spent pawing through stacks of cartons and crates, flicking roaches aside (there were always roaches, even though Ivan had the whole place sprayed regularly) and deciding what Odette would buy the next day.

And they would each drink some of Josh's blood.

This remained skin-crawlingly horrible, but once they laid the Eye on you, you just accepted whatever they did. Instead of wigging out over it, Josh turned to working obsessively on songs about mysterious night visitors and dangerous girlfriends, with Rasputina, Theatre of Tragedy, and Voltaire playing on his iPod.

Not that Crystal herself was girlfriend material. She was just a kid, like somebody's little sister you'd ignore completely (if not for the blood-drinking thing). Anyway, she said she was celibate right now, trying to put an edge back on her appetite for when she took up sex again. True or not (who could tell, with a vampire?), this was way more than Josh wanted to know—which was, of course, exactly why she'd told him.

Generally, though, he felt strangely upbeat. Grim lyrics poured out of him, which made a kind of sense under the circumstances. Inspiration seemed a fair exchange for a little blood. He wasn't satisfied with his work, but there were moments. Once in a while he took off on a thrill wave as his words fell together just right and he glimpsed the possibility that he could really do this—he could write songs for people to fly on.

> *"Wither my soul with your cold, dry lips*
> *So I'll have no tears to cry—"*

The only thing was, he was so *isolated*. How could his songs get better without real musicians to work with? He was writing his own lines to other people's tunes, a practice technique that could take him only so far.

He needed to get a move on, to make it to the next level. He was seventeen already! He had so much catching up to do. Nobody breaks out as an *old* singer-songwriter.

Odette's profession was perfect: She was a masseuse. She used the Eye to draw customers to her place (a rental on Cardenas) so she never had to go out in the sunlight. Her clients came away feeling totally relaxed (as Josh knew from personal experience). Since that was the whole point of a massage, they recommended her to their friends. Odette apparently needed hardly any sleep; she kept evening hours for working people, rates on a sliding scale (why not? She could always take the difference in blood).

Crystal slept all day or else hung out at the Top of Your Game, an arcade where kids played out fantasy adventures (Odette called the Top "a casino for children"). At night, in Ivan's office, Crystal browsed antiques sites on the computer for Odette.

He asked once if she missed gossiping and giggling with other girls in school.

"Eww! Do I look crazy? Who wants to be cooped up with a bunch of smelly, spotty, horny adolescents and the teachers who hate them, in a place built like a prison?"

"Is that what you're thinking when you're drinking my blood—about how spotty and smelly I am?" (Horny just didn't come into that experience for Josh.)

"Oh," she said, "let's not go there."


He decided to celebrate his new songwriting energy by getting rid of the pathetic jumble of projects from his arts center classes (the mobile made of hangers and beer tabs, a woodcut of crows fighting), which he had tucked out of sight in a tote bag on the floor of his closet. He might even make a few bucks by farming all this junk out for sale in the mall with whichever dealers were willing to display it. (As they said, "There's a buyer for *everything*.")

When he walked in, two cops were asking for Ivan at the register. Josh made a business of tucking the tote, with a sweatshirt stuffed in on top to keep everything from falling out, into one of the lockers by the front door, so he could listen.

They asked about a well-known local meth head who had come in the day before trying to sell some old coins.

"Stolen, right?" Ivan said.

They nodded, looking meaningfully around the nearby booths.

Ivan braced his thick hands on the glass countertop. "That's why I never buy off the street—it's always stolen goods. You won't find any valuable jewelry for sale by any of my dealers, either; too easy to steal. That kind of thing just attracts thieves.

"So," he said, relaxing now that he had declared himself totally honest, "did something happen after I kicked that kid out of here?"

"Read the papers," one of the cops said.

The *Journal* reported that the kid had been found early that morning out by the old airport, with his throat slashed and the coins gone.

Josh, shivering, ducked into the corner reserved for books and DVDs.

"Throat slashed" sounded suspiciously like "disguised vampire bite" to him. He calmed himself down with half an hour of looking at psychedelic sleeve art for old long-playing records.

Crystal showed up at midnight with a puffy, teary look and a bandage wrapped around one hand. He asked if she was okay, but she disappeared into the shadows of the nighttime mall without answering.

In the office, Odette explained in a pissed-off tone.

"A boy accosted us in your parking lot last night, trying to sell us some coins, or mug us, or both. I turned him away. Crystal was in one of her moods; she followed him. I've told her a thousand times, we do *not* drink people dry and then toss them aside like juiced oranges. It's stupid."

"She *drained* that kid?"

"She has a teenager's appetite," Odette said. "And poor impulse control."

"She told me she's seventy-five years old!"

Impatiently Odette swung the swivel chair around (with Crystal temporarily incapacitated, Odette had to find sites on the computer for herself, which made her cranky). "Years don't come into it. Crystal isn't alive the way you are, Josh. She doesn't mature with time. The parts of her brain that hadn't developed when she was turned never will. She's between thirteen and fourteen forever, in her mind as well as her body."

Imagine never being able to shed your baby fat, your zits, or your adolescent mood swings.

"Wow," he said.

"Wow indeed."

"So . . . did the guy have a knife or something? Her hand—"

Odette said, "You need to understand that I provide the only structure she has in her life, and the only security. Sometimes I must be a little harsh with her, but it's for her own sake. She doesn't survive by being a clever adult in a permanently childlike body. She's a child who survives because I protect her."

"Protect her?" Crystal, who was clearly injured—but who had also just killed someone. "From who?"

"Her own rash nature," Odette said tartly, "but also older vampires. The Quality don't like the young ones, for reasons that should be obvious. Recklessness puts us all at risk. Correction helps in the short term, but there is no curing persistently childish behavior in someone who is, essentially, a permanent child."

Crystal's prickliness began to make more sense. "Why do you keep her around, then?"

Odette jabbed irritably at the keyboard with one long, iridescent fingernail. "Youngsters are adaptable and good at modernity. She can be very helpful."

Useful, she meant.

"Well, well!" Odette's attention was caught by something on the screen. "Axel Hochauer has sold off his Grande Armée figures for a tidy sum, I see." She smiled. "Goretsky must be *livid*."

Josh knew he was dismissed.

He found Crystal crying in the bathroom. Clearing his throat nervously, he asked, "Crystal? Did she do something to you?"

"Made me hold my hand in sunlight," she blubbed, glaring up at him through her tears. "Look!"

The skin on the back of her hand was scabby and blotched with raw pink skin. She wrapped it up again quickly. "It was worse before; we heal fast. That doesn't mean it didn't hurt. I *hate* that mean old bitch!"

She had killed the meth head, but her own situation was pretty dire. He couldn't help feeling sorry for her. Not enough to hug her or anything like that, but sorry.

"Hey," he said, propping his hip against the sink. "Want to hear a new song? It's not exactly finished yet—I mean, I'm not through working on it—but I think it's a pretty good start. I'm calling it 'Love Birds.'"

He sang, mezza voce:

> *"Raven hates her own harsh tone.*
> *She hacks and hawks to spit it out.*
> *Swallow down her razor kiss*
> *Salty, icy, light as bone,*
> *To sweeten Raven's song.*
> *She'll be your love, your turtledove,*
> *If you sweeten Raven's song."*

"'Turtledove?'" Crystal mimicked scornfully. "What century do *you* come from? Makes no sense, either. Well, that's cool. You can't eat music, and I'm starving."

She was *always* hungry, and she always had to be reminded to stop.

Next time things seemed back to normal. Crystal, Grand Theft Auto champion with a stuffed arcade bear to prove it, was on the monitor again, checking for comparables to Odette's latest find: a rare Chinese pipe, all delicately curved brass tubing and carved wood. Josh, already tapped by both vampires, dozed in a beat-up armchair on the other side of Ivan's desk.

"Oh, shit!" Crystal leaned back and yelled, "Odette! MacCardle's in Dallas!"

Odette swept into the office and tilted the monitor around to see the news photo. It featured a scrawny, self-satisfied-looking guy with suspenders holding up his pants, shaking some fancy suit's hand in an auction showroom.

Odette snarled silently, showing a gleam of fang (Josh looked away; he hated thinking about where those teeth had been). But all she said was "Fine. He's there, we're here."

She went back to inspecting the Chinese pipe.

Crystal whispered fiercely, "Fine my foot! If MacCardle comes sniffing around here, we are *so* gone."

Josh was jolted by a stab of realization: He didn't want them gone—not without him. (God, could he really be thinking like this?)

"He looks harmless," he observed cautiously. "Not exactly a Van Helsing type."

"He's *Quality*, dummy. He comes sneaking around after Odette trying to snag the good stuff first, which makes her so *mad*! You won't like her when she's mad," she intoned, wiggling the fingers of her now-unblemished hand.

"What, she turns green and smashes the place up?"

"No joke," Crystal said.

"Okay, this is for real, right? People who live forever by drinking human blood spend their time fighting over high-priced junk?"

Crystal snorted. "Are you kidding? They *love* to feud over scraps—ugly old vases, souvenir ashtrays from Atlantic City, dried-up baby shoes. Some of them are addicted to anything from their own time. Mostly, though, it's about personal pride and protecting their investments."

"They hunt down enameled kitchenware, just like some retired bus driver desperate for something to do, and that's about pride and investment?"

"Hey, look around you," she said. "Even mass-produced trinkets get valuable if they survive long enough. A vampire can wait a century for his tin plates to become rare and then sell them for a bundle. Then there's the thrill of spotting a trend first and getting in there before anybody else. Odette's amazing at that. Timing the market is a real competition for them; they bet on each other. Gambling's always been the favorite pastime of the upper crust. Well, crust doesn't get any upper than the Quality."

An idea sparked, then glowed. "Crystal? What does Odette collect for herself?"

"What you want to know for?" She stared at him suspiciously. "Anyway, you're asking the wrong person."

"It can't all be just merchandise to her," he insisted. "What does she find in a place like this that she won't resell?"

Crystal absently twisted the ears of the trophy bear as she thought this over. "Odd stuff. One-of-a-kind things: snapshots, carvings, pictures."

"Art," he said.

"Art, and artists. If she thinks you have what she calls 'real creative talent,' you get a vampire godmother for life—whether you want it or not."

Odette hadn't asked to see his drawings again, but . . . "What about my songs?"

"The last music Odette liked was a *minuet*," Crystal said, rolling her eyes. "And plus she has the tinnest ear ever and hates poetry."

He pressed on. "Well, what else? What does she love?" If he could find something special, something to show that he was on Odette's wavelength—that he was too *useful* to leave behind—

"Well, there's this quilt," Crystal said. "Grubby old thing; pretty hand stitching though—little strips of silk from men's ties, kimonos, and like that. She paid a lot for it. She still has it."

"But why? Why that?"

"How should I know?" Crystal scowled, then softened slightly. "I did hear once that her brother was a famous goldsmith, couple centuries back. He had a stroke, so she got to design jewelry, under her brother's name, for the rich people. It *could* be a true story, but who knows? She's not the kind who runs her mouth about her first life, like some of the Quality. Specially the really *old* ones, trying to hang on to their memories. Anyway, maybe she was talented herself, back in the day."

Josh nodded, thinking furiously. He was not going to be left behind in flyover country if he could help it.

Two more of the Quality showed up at Ivan's at the next open evening. One looked the part—tall, pale, and high shouldered like a vulture (an effect undercut by his cowboy boots, ironed jeans, and Western shirt with pearl-snap buttons). There was no mystery about what he was after: Several pounds of Indian fetish necklaces decorated his sunken chest.

The other, a chunky Asian-looking woman with a flat-top haircut, wore chains and bunches of keys jingling from her belt, her boots, her leather vest.

"What's she looking for, whips and handcuffs?" Josh whispered.

Crystal smirked at him. "Dummy. That's Alicia Chung. Odette says she has the best collection of nineteenth-century opera ephemera in America."

"She's looking for old opera posters around *here*?"

Crystal shrugged. "You never know. That's part of the challenge."

In the workroom after closing, the first thing Odette said was "If Chung is here, it won't be long before MacCardle arrives. We pack up tonight, Crystal."

Josh broke an icy sweat. He had no time for finesse.

"Odette?" His voice cracked. "Take me, too."

"No," she said. She didn't even look at him.

"Crystal travels with you!"

"Crystal is Quality, and she has no living family. Shall we kill your mother and father so they won't come searching for you?"

With Crystal's voice in his ears ("Ooh, that's *cold*, Odette!"), Josh ran into the bathroom and threw up. He drove home without remembering to turn on his headlights and fell asleep in his clothes, dreaming about Annie Frye biting his neck. Later he sat in the dark banging out the blackest chords he could get from his keyboard.

His band was gone, nobody from school wanted to hang with him, and now even the vampires were taking off.

His mom knocked on the bedroom door at seven a.m. and asked if he wanted to "talk about" anything. "Your music sounds so sad, hon." Like he was writing his songs for her!

"It's just music." He hunched over the Casio, waiting for her to leave. How could he stand to live in this house one more day?

She stepped inside. "Josh, I'm picking up signals here. Are you thinking of leaving town with your new friends?"

He panicked, then realized she only meant his imaginary musician pals. "No."

"All the same, I think it's time I met them," she said firmly.

"Why can't you leave me alone? You're just making everything worse!"

"You're doing that brilliantly for yourself," she retorted. They yelled back and forth, each trying to inflict maximum damage without actually drawing blood, until she clattered off downstairs to finish crating pictures for a gallery show in San Jose. The hammering was fierce.

She was going out there for her show's opening, naturally.

Everybody could leave flyover country for the real, creative world of accomplishment and success, except Josh.

He slipped into her studio after she'd left. As a kid, he had spent so much time here while his mom worked. The bright array of colors, the bristly and sable-soft brushes, and the rainbow-smeared paint rags had kept him fascinated for hours. There on the windowsill, just as he'd remembered during their argument, sat something that just might convince Odette to take him with her.

Ivan had belonged to a biker gang for a few years. Later on, he'd made a memento of that time in his life and then asked Josh's mother to keep it for him (his own wife wanted no reminders of those days in *her* house).

What Ivan had done was to twist silver wire into the form of a gleaming, three-inch-high motorbike, with turquoise-disk beads for wheels. The thing was beautiful as only a lovingly made miniature can be. It looked like a jeweled dragonfly. Visitors had offered Josh's mother money for it.

Value, uniqueness, handcrafted beauty—it was perfect.

Josh quickly packed it, wrapped in tissues, into a little cardboard box that used to hold a Christmas ornament. At work, he stashed it in a drawer of the oak desk in the Victoriana booth, where he sometimes went for naps when the vampires' snacking wore him out. Odette would come tonight, after her final antiquing run through town, before she took off for good. This would be his one and only chance to persuade her.

After closing time, he dashed out for pizza. When he got back to the darkened mall, he was startled to find Crystal sitting at the oak desk with the little brass lamp turned on.

"How'd you get in?" he asked.

She gave a sullen shrug. The package sat open on the desk in front of her.

"Where's Odette?" The silent mall floor had never looked so dark.

"She's late," Crystal said. "I was tired of waiting, so I hitched a ride over from the Top. This is something of yours, right? What is it, anyway?"

"A going-away present for Odette. I got something for you, too," he added, trying frantically to think of what he could give to Crystal.

"Yeah?" Her red leather purse, heavy with quarters for the game machines, swung on its thin strap in jerky movements like the tail of an angry cat. "You were gonna give me something? You *liar*, Josh."

He wondered, with a shiver, if some of the coins making the little red purse bulge were from the meth head's haul.

Suddenly she screamed, "You think you can buy Odette with this little shiny piece of trash? You pretend to be my friend, but you just want to take my *place*!"

She lashed at him with the purse. He dodged, tripped, and toppled helplessly. The back of his head smacked the floor with stunning force.

Crystal threw herself on top of him, guzzling at his throat as he passed out.

He woke up lying on a thirties settee outside Ivan's office, deep in the heart of the mall. In the office, the computer monitor glowed with light that seemed unnaturally bright, illuminating the little room and the hallway outside it.

His shirt stuck to his chest and his neck was stiff. He felt his throat. There was a damp, painless tear in the flesh on one side.

"Crystal is a messy eater, but don't worry, that will heal quickly." Odette, perched on a chair by the end of the settee, held the miniature bike in her hands. "I think you brought this for me? Thank you, Josh. It's very beautiful."

He sat up. His mouth tasted sharply metallic, but nothing hurt.

"Where's Crystal?"

"She ran off," Odette said. "She knows she's in serious trouble with me for killing you. Remember what I said about adolescent impulsiveness? Now you see what I meant. She won't last long on her own, not with others of the Quality starting to show up here and my protection withdrawn. It's too bad, but frankly it's for the best. I'm tired of her tantrums."

He felt a slow, chilly ripple of fear. "*Killing* me?"

"Effectively, yes, but I arrived in time to divert the process. The taste in your mouth is my blood. It's a necessary exchange that also provides a soothing first meal for you, in your revivified state. You don't want to begin your undead life crazed and stupid with hunger."

He licked his front teeth, which had a strange feel, like *too much*. His stomach churned briefly. "I thought you didn't want to . . . turn . . . "

She sniffed. "Of course not. Who needs *another* teenaged vampire? But dead young bodies raise questions, and Crystal already left one lying around out by the airport. Besides, with her gone I have a job opening. Your selection of this"—she carefully set the little bike on the table at her elbow—"shows an educable eye, at least. With coaching, I suppose you can be made into a passable member of the Quality."

*Coaching?* He might as well have gone back to school!

She stood, smoothing down her skirt, and picked up his canvas tote from the floor at her feet. "I found this in your locker. The sweatshirt is yours, isn't it? Take off that T-shirt and put this on. It's none too clean, but you can't walk around looking like a gory movie zombie. Then you must leave a note for your family. Say you've gone to seek your fortune."

Thoughts lit up like silent sheet lightning in his mind while he worked the blood-crusted T-shirt off over his head.

His life, his friends, his home—all that was over, and she'd just been trying to get rid of him when she'd said, before, about killing his parents. But there was no going back. The upside was, he *would* be getting out of here at last, traveling with Odette out into the real world.

Was that why he felt high, instead of all bleak and tortured about waking up undead?

Then it hit him: undead? He was finally going to get to *live*.

He punched the air and whooped. "Look out, Colin Meloy! Josh Burnham's songs are coming *down*!"

Pawing around inquisitively in the tote bag, Odette glanced up. "Forget about your songs, Josh. You *died*. The undead do not create: not babies, not art, not music, not even recipes or dress designs. I'm sorry, but that's our reality."

"You don't get it!" he crowed. "Listen, I'm still a beginner, but I'm good—I know I am. Now I have years—centuries even—to turn myself into the best damn singer-songwriter ever! So what if I never mature past where I am now, like you said about Crystal? Staying young is *success* in the music business! I can use the Eye to get top players to work with me, to teach me—"

"You can learn skills," she said with forced patience. "You can imitate.

But you can't create, not even if you used to have the genius of a budding Sondheim, which you did not. According to Crystal, your lyrical gift was . . . let's say, minor. I hope you're not going to be tiresome about this, Josh."

"Crystal's just jealous!" Buoyed by the exhilaration of getting some payback at last for his weeks of helpless servitude, he shouted, "*You're* jealous! She told me about you, how you made jewelry for rich people—"

Odette snapped, "That's someone else. I designed tapestries. As a new made, you're entitled to a little rudeness, but at least take the trouble to get the facts right."

"But the thing is, you were already *old*—your talent was all used up by the time you got turned, wasn't it? So now you can't stand to admit that anybody else still has it!"

"My talent," she said icily, "which was not just considerable but still unfolding, was extinguished completely and forever—*just like yours*—when I became what you are now." She fixed him with a dragon glare and hissed, "Stupid boy, why do you think I *collect*?"

He almost laughed: What was this, some weird horror-movie version of fighting with his mother? Fine, he was *stoked*. "It's different for me! I'm just getting started, and now I can go on getting better and better *forever*!"

With a shrug, she turned back to the contents of the tote bag. "You can try; who knows, you might even have some commercial success—"

She stopped, holding up a fantasy-style chalice he'd made in ceramics class at the arts center. It was a sagging blob that couldn't even stand solidly on its crooked foot.

"What's this?"

"You should know," he muttered, embarrassed. "You're the expert on valuable *things*. It's arts and crafts, that's all, from back when I was still trying to find my way, my *art*. I brought all that stuff in here to try to sell it, only I forgot—I've been kind of distracted, you know?"

"You made this." She ran the ball of her thumb along the thickly glazed surface, which he had decorated with sloppy swirls of lemon and indigo.

"So what?" he said. "Here, just toss that whole bag of crap." There was a trash can outside the office door. He shoved it toward her with his foot.

Odette gently put the cup aside. She reached back into the tote bag and drew from the bottom a wad of crumpled fabric.

Oh, no, not that damned needlepoint!

In his fiber arts class, he had been crazy enough to try to reproduce an Aztec cape, brilliant with the layered feathers of tropical birds, like one he'd seen in the museum. He'd just learned the basic diagonal stitch, so the rectangular canvas had warped into a diamond-like shape. Worse, frustrated that the woolen yarns weren't glossy enough, he'd added splinters of metal, glazed pottery, and glass, shiny bits and pieces knotted and sewn onto the unevenly stitched surface.

That wiseass Mickey Craig had caught him working on it once and had teased him for "sewing, like a girl." That was when Josh had quit the class and hidden the unfinished canvas in his closet where nobody would ever see it.

Yeah; his luck.

Maybe he could convince Odette that his mother had made it.

"God in heaven," Odette said flatly. "God. In. *Heaven*. If I ever catch up with that girl, I will tear off her *head*."

Her eyes glared from a face tense with fury; but he saw a shine of moisture on her cheek.

Odette was *crying*.

And there it was, the kernel of the first great song of his undead life, a soul-ripping blast about losing everything and winning everything, to mark the end of his last summer as a miserable, live human kid: "Tears of a Vampire." All he had to do was come up with a couple of starter lines, and then find a tune to work with.

All he had to do was . . . why couldn't he think?

All he had to do . . . his thoughts hung cool and still as settled fog. He found himself staring at the crude, lumpy canvas, vivid and glowing, stretched between Odette's bony fists.

He began to *see* it, this cockeyed thing that his own fumbling, amateurish hands had made. Its grimy, raveling edges framed a rich fall of parrot-bright colors, all studded with glittering fragments.

He hadn't even finished it, but it was beautiful.

Oh, he thought. Oh . . .

*This* was it—this was what he should have been doing all along—not drawing comics or struggling with song lyrics, but crafting this kind of mind-blowing interplay of colors, shapes, and textures. *This* was his true art, his breakout talent.

So why couldn't he picture it as a finished piece? He stretched his eyes wide open, squinted them almost shut, but he could only see it right there in front of him exactly as it was, abandoned and incomplete. His mind, flat and gray and quiet, offered nothing, except for a faint but rising tremor of dread.

Because although he couldn't describe the stark look on Odette's face in clever lyrics anymore, he understood it perfectly now—from the inside. It was the expression of someone staring into an endless future of absolute sterility, unable to produce one single creation of originality, beauty, or inspiration ever again.

If Josh wanted all that back—originality, inspiration, and beauty, only everything he had ever really wanted—he would have to get it the same way that Odette, or any of the Quality, got it.

He would have to begin collecting.

# THE CHOICE

## PAUL McAULEY

In the night, tides and a brisk wind drove a raft of bubbleweed across the Flood and piled it up along the north side of the island. Soon after first light, Lucas started raking it up, ferrying load after load to one of the compost pits, where it would rot down into a nutrient-rich liquid fertilizer. He was trundling his wheelbarrow down the steep path to the shore for about the thirtieth or fortieth time when he spotted someone walking across the water: Damian, moving like a cross-country skier as he traversed the channel between the island and the stilt huts and floating tanks of his father's shrimp farm. It was still early in the morning, already hot. A perfect September day, the sky's blue dome untroubled by cloud. Shifting points of sunlight starred the water, flashed from the blades of the farm's wind turbine. Lucas waved to his friend and Damian waved back and nearly overbalanced, windmilling his arms and recovering, slogging on.

They met at the water's edge. Damian, picking his way between floating slicks of red weed, called out breathlessly, "Did you hear?"

"Hear what?"

"A dragon got itself stranded close to Martham."

"You're kidding."

"I'm not kidding. An honest-to-God sea dragon."

Damian stepped onto an apron of broken brick at the edge of the water and sat down and eased off the fat flippers of his Jesus shoes, explaining that he'd heard about it from Ritchy, the foreman of the shrimp farm, who'd got it off the skipper of a supply barge who'd been listening to chatter on the common band.

"It beached not half an hour ago. People reckon it came in through the cut at Horsey and couldn't get back over the bar when the tide turned. So it went on up the channel of the old riverbed until it ran ashore."

Lucas thought for a moment. "There's a sand bar that hooks into the channel south of Martham. I went past it any number of times when I worked on Grant Higgins's boat last summer, ferrying oysters to Norwich."

"It's almost on our doorstep," Damian said. He pulled his phone from the pocket of his shorts and angled it toward Lucas. "Right about here. See it?"

"I know where Martham is. Let me guess—you want me to take you."

"What's the point of building a boat if you don't use it? Come on, L. It isn't every day an alien machine washes up."

Lucas took off his broad-brimmed straw hat, blotted his forehead with his wrist, and set his hat on his head again. He was a wiry boy not quite sixteen, bare-chested in baggy shorts and sandals he'd cut from an old car tire. "I was planning to go crabbing. After I finish clearing this weed, water the vegetable patch, fix lunch for my mother . . . "

"I'll give you a hand with all that when we get back."

"Right."

"If you really don't want to go I could maybe borrow your boat."

"Or you could take one of your dad's."

"After what he did to me last time? I'd rather row there in that leaky old clunker of your mother's. Or walk."

"That would be a sight."

Damian smiled. He was just two months older than Lucas, tall and sturdy, his cropped blond hair bleached by salt and summer sun, his nose and the rims of his ears pink and peeling. The two had been friends for as long as they could remember.

He said, "I reckon I can sail as well as you."

"You're sure this dragon is still there? You have pictures?"

"Not exactly. It knocked out the town's broadband, and everything else. According to the guy who talked to Ritchy, nothing electronic works within a klick of it. Phones, slates, radios, nothing. The tide turns in a couple of hours, but I reckon we can get there if we start right away."

"Maybe. I should tell my mother," Lucas said. "In the unlikely event that she wonders where I am."

"How is she?"

"No better, no worse. Does your dad know you're skipping out?"

"Don't worry about it. I'll tell him I went crabbing with you."

"Fill a couple of jugs at the still," Lucas said. "And pull up some carrots, too. But first, hand me your phone."

"The GPS coordinates are flagged up right there. You ask it, it'll plot a course."

Lucas took the phone, holding it with his fingertips—he didn't like the way it squirmed as it shaped itself to fit in his hand. "How do you switch it off?"

"What do you mean?"

"If we go, we won't be taking the phone. Your dad could track us."

"How will we find our way there?"

"I don't need your phone to find Martham."

"You and your off-the-grid horseshit," Damian said.

"You wanted an adventure," Lucas said. "This is it."

When Lucas started to tell his mother that he'd be out for the rest of the day with Damian, she said, "Chasing after that so-called dragon, I suppose. No need to look surprised—it's all over the news. Not the official news, of course. No mention of it there. But it's leaking out everywhere that counts."

His mother was propped against the headboard of the double bed under the caravan's big end window. Julia Wittsruck, fifty-two, skinny as a refugee, dressed in a striped Berber robe and half-covered in a patchwork of quilts and thin orange blankets stamped with the Oxfam logo. The ropes of her dreadlocks were tied back with a red bandana; her tablet resting in her lap.

She gave Lucas her best inscrutable look and said, "I suppose this is Damian's idea. You be careful. His ideas usually work out badly."

"That's why I'm going along. To make sure he doesn't get into trouble. He's set on seeing it, one way or another."

"And you aren't?"

Lucas smiled. "I suppose I'm curious. Just a little."

"I wish I could go. Take a rattle can or two, spray the old slogans on the damned thing's hide."

"I could put some cushions in the boat. Make you as comfortable as you like."

Lucas knew that his mother wouldn't take up his offer. She rarely left the caravan, hadn't been off the island for more than three years. A multilocus immunotoxic syndrome, basically an allergic reaction to the myriad products and pollutants of the anthropocene age, had left her more or less completely bedridden. She'd refused all offers of treatment or help by the local social agencies, relying instead on the services of a local witchwoman who visited once a week, and spent her days in bed, working at her tablet. She trawled government sites and stealthnets, made podcasts, advised zero-impact communities, composed critiques and manifestos. She kept a public journal, wrote essays and opinion pieces (at the moment, she was especially exercised by attempts by multinational companies to move in on the Antarctic Peninsula, and a utopian group that was using alien technology to build a floating community on a drowned coral reef in the Midway Islands), and maintained friendships, alliances, and several rancorous feuds with former colleagues whose origins had long been forgotten by both sides. In short, hers was a way of life that would have been familiar to scholars from any time in the past couple of millennia.

She'd been a lecturer in philosophy at Birkbeck College before the nuclear strikes, riots, revolutions, and netwar skirmishes of the so-called Spasm, which had ended when the floppy ships of the Jackaroo had appeared in the skies over Earth. In exchange for rights to the outer solar system, the aliens had given the human race technology to clean up the Earth, and access to a wormhole network that linked a dozen M-class red dwarf stars. Soon enough, other alien species showed up, making various deals with various nations and power blocs, bartering advanced technologies for works of art, fauna and flora, the secret formula of Coca Cola, and other unique items.

Most believed that the aliens were kindly and benevolent saviors, members of a loose alliance that had traced ancient broadcasts of *I Love Lucy* to their origin and arrived just in time to save the human species from the consequences of its monkey cleverness. But a vocal minority wanted nothing to do with them, doubting that their motives were in any way altruistic, elaborating all kinds of theories about their true motivations. We should choose to reject the help of the aliens, they said. We should reject easy fixes and the magic of advanced technologies we don't understand, and choose the harder thing: to keep control of our own destiny.

Julia Wittstruck had become a leading light in this movement. When its brief but fierce round of global protests and politicking had fallen apart in a mess of mutual recriminations and internecine warfare, she'd moved to Scotland and joined a group of green radicals who'd been building a self-sufficient settlement on a trio of ancient oil rigs in the Firth of Forth. But they'd become compromised too, according to Julia, so she'd left them and taken up with Lucas's father (Lucas knew almost nothing about him—his mother said that the past was the past, that she was all that counted in his life because she had given birth to him and raised and taught him), and they'd lived the gypsy life for a few years until she'd split up with him and, pregnant with her son, had settled in a smallholding in Norfolk, living off the grid, supported by a small legacy left to her by one of her devoted supporters from the glory days of the anti-alien protests.

When she'd first moved there, the coast had been more than ten kilometers to the east, but a steady rise in sea level had flooded the northern and eastern coasts of Britain and Europe. East Anglia had been sliced in two by levees built to protect precious farmland from the encroaching sea, and most people caught on the wrong side had taken resettlement grants and moved on. But Julia had stayed put. She'd paid a contractor to extend a small rise, all that was left of her smallholding, with rubble from a wrecked twentieth-century housing estate, and made her home on the resulting island. It had once been much larger, and a succession of people had camped there, attracted by her kudos, driven away after a few weeks or a few months by her scorn and impatience. Then most of Greenland's remaining icecap collapsed into the Arctic Ocean, sending a surge of water across the North Sea.

Lucas had only been six, but he still remembered everything about that day. The water had risen past the high tide mark that afternoon and had kept rising. At first it had been fun to mark the stealthy progress of the water with a series of sticks driven into the ground, but by evening it was clear that it was not going to stop anytime soon, and then in a sudden smooth rush it rose more than a hundred centimeters, flooding the vegetable plots and lapping at the timber baulks on which the caravan rested. All that evening, Julia had moved their possessions out of the caravan, with Lucas trotting to and fro at her heels, helping her as best he could until, some time after midnight, she'd given up and they'd fallen asleep under a tent rigged from chairs and a blanket. And had woken to discover that their island had shrunk to half its previous size, and the caravan had floated off and lay canted and half-drowned in muddy water littered with every kind of debris.

Julia had bought a replacement caravan and set it on the highest point of what was left of the island, and despite ineffectual attempts to remove them by various local government officials, she and Lucas had stayed on. She'd taught him the basics of numeracy and literacy, and the long and intricate secret history of the world, and he'd learned field- and wood- and watercraft from their neighbors. He snared rabbits and mink in the woods that ran alongside the levee, foraged for hedgerow fruits and edible weeds and fungi, bagged squirrels with small stones shot from his catapult. He grubbed mussels from the rusting car-reef that protected the seaward side of the levee, set wicker traps for eels and trotlines for mitten crabs. He fished for mackerel and dogfish and weaverfish on the wide brown waters of the Flood. When he could, he worked shifts on the shrimp farm owned by Damian's father, or on the market gardens, farms, and willow and bamboo plantations on the other side of the levee.

In spring, he watched long vees of geese fly north above the floodwater that stretched out to the horizon. In autumn, he watched them fly south.

He'd inherited a great deal of his mother's restlessness and fierce independence, but although he longed to strike out beyond his little world, he didn't know how to begin. And besides, he had to look after Julia. She would never admit it, but she depended on him, utterly.

She said now, dismissing his offer to take her along, "You know I have too much to do here. The day is never long enough. There is something you can do for me, though. Take my phone with you."

"Damian says phones don't work around the dragon."

"I'm sure it will work fine. Take some pictures of that thing. As many as you can. I'll write up your story when you come back, and pictures will help attract traffic."

"Okay."

Lucas knew that there was no point in arguing. Besides, his mother's phone was an ancient model that predated the Spasm: it lacked any kind of cloud connectivity and was as dumb as a box of rocks. As long as he only used it to take pictures, it wouldn't compromise his idea of an off-the-grid adventure.

His mother smiled. " 'ET go home.' "

" 'ET go home'?"

"We put that up everywhere, back in the day. We put it on the main runway of Luton Airport, in letters twenty meters tall. Also dug trenches in the shape of the words up on the South Downs and filled them with diesel fuel and set them alight. You could see it from space. Let the unhuman know that they were not welcome here. That we did not need them. Check the toolbox. I'm sure there's a rattle can in there. Take it along, just in case."

"I'll take my catapult, in case I spot any ducks. I'll try to be back before it gets dark. If I don't, there are MREs in the store cupboard. And I picked some tomatoes and carrots."

" 'ET go home,' " his mother said. "Don't forget that. And be careful, in that little boat."

Lucas had started to build his sailboat late last summer, and had worked at it all through the winter. It was just four meters from bow to stern, its plywood hull glued with epoxy and braced with ribs shaped from branches of a young poplar tree that had fallen in the autumn gales. He'd used an adze and a homemade plane to fashion the mast and boom from the poplar's trunk, knocked up the knees, gunwale, outboard support, and bow cap from oak, persuaded Ritchy, the shrimp farm's foreman, to print off the cleats, oarlocks, bow eye and grommets for lacing the sails on the farm's maker. Ritchy had given him some half-empty tins of blue paint and varnish to seal the hull, and he'd bought a set of secondhand laminate sails from the shipyard in Halvergate, and spliced the halyards and sheet from scrap lengths of rope.

He loved his boat more than he was ready to admit to himself. That spring he'd tacked back and forth beyond the shrimp farm, had sailed north to along the coast to Halvergate and Acle, and south and west around Reedham Point as far as Brundall, and had crossed the channel of the river and navigated the mazy mudflats to Chedgrave. If the sea dragon was stuck where Damian said it was, he'd have to travel farther than ever before, navigating uncharted and ever-shifting sand and mud banks, dodging clippers and barge strings in the shipping channel. But Lucas reckoned he had the measure of his little boat now, and it was a fine day and a steady wind blowing from the west drove them straight along, with the jib cocked as far as it would go in the stay and the mainsail bellying full and the boat heeling sharply as it ploughed a white furrow in the light chop.

At first, all Lucas had to do was sit in the stern with the tiller snug in his right armpit and the main sheet coiled loosely in his left hand, and keep a straight course north past the pens and catwalks of the shrimp farm. Damian sat beside him, leaning out to port to counterbalance the boat's tilt, his left hand keeping the jib sheet taut, his right holding a plastic cup he would now and then use to scoop water from the bottom of the boat and fling in a sparkling arc that was caught and twisted by the wind.

The sun stood high in a tall blue sky empty of cloud save for a thin rim at the horizon to the northeast. Fret, most likely, mist forming where moisture condensed out of air that had cooled as it passed over the sea. But the fret was kilometers away, and all around sunlight flashed from every wave top and burned on the white sails and beat down on the two boys. Damian's face and bare torso shone with sunblock; although Lucas was about as dark as he got, he'd rubbed sunblock on his face too, and tied his straw hat under his chin and put on a shirt that flapped about his chest. The tiller juddered minutely and constantly as the boat slapped through an endless succession of catspaw waves and Lucas measured the flex of the sail by the tug of the sheet wrapped around his left hand, kept an eye on the foxtail streamer that flew from the top of the mast. Judging by landmarks on the levee that ran along the shore to port, they were making around fifteen kilometers per hour, about as fast as Lucas had ever gotten out of his boat, and he and Damian grinned at each other and squinted off into the glare of the sunstruck water, happy and exhilarated to be skimming across the face of the Flood, two bold adventurers off to confront a monster.

"We'll be there in an hour easy," Damian said.

"A bit less than two, maybe. As long as the fret stays where it is."

"The sun'll burn it off."

"Hasn't managed it yet."

"Don't let your natural caution spoil a perfect day."

Lucas swung wide of a raft of bubbleweed that glistened like a slick of fresh blood in the sun. Some called it Martian weed, though it had nothing to do with any of the aliens; it was an engineered species designed to mop up nitrogen and phosphorous released by drowned farmland, prospering beyond all measure or control.

Dead ahead, a long line of whitecaps marked the reef of the old railway embankment. Lucas swung the tiller into the wind and he and Damian ducked as the boom swung across and the boat gybed around. The sails slackened, then filled with wind again as the boat turned toward one of the gaps blown in the embankment, cutting so close to the buoy that marked it that Damian could reach out and slap the rusty steel plate of its flank as they went by. And then they were heading out across a broad reach, with the little town of Acle strung along a low promontory to port. A slateless church steeple stood up from the water like a skeletal lighthouse. The polished cross at its top burned like a flame in the sunlight. A file of old pylons stepped away, most canted at steep angles, the twiggy platforms of heron nests built in angles of their girder work, whitened everywhere with droppings. One of the few still standing straight had been colonized by fisherfolk, with shacks built from driftwood lashed to its struts and a wave-powered generator made from oil drums strung out beyond. Washing flew like festive flags inside the web of rusted steel, and a naked small child of indeterminate sex clung to the unshuttered doorway of a shack just above the waterline, pushing a tangle of hair from its eyes as it watched the little boat sail by.

They passed small islands fringed with young mangrove trees; an engineered species that was rapidly spreading from areas in the south where they'd been planted to replace the levee. Lucas spotted a marsh harrier patrolling mudflats in the lee of one island, scrying for water voles and mitten crabs. They passed a long building sunk to the tops of its second-story windows in the flood, with brightly colored plastic bubbles pitched on its flat roof among the notched and spinning wheels of windmill generators, and small boats bobbing alongside. Someone standing at the edge of the roof waved to them, and Damian stood up and waved back and the boat shifted so that he had to catch at the jib leech and sit down hard.

"You want us to capsize, go ahead," Lucas told him.

"There are worse places to be shipwrecked. You know they're all married to each other over there."

"I heard."

"They like visitors too."

"I know you aren't talking from experience or you'd have told me all about it. At least a dozen times."

"I met a couple of them in Halvergate. They said I should stop by some time," Damian said, grinning sideways at Lucas. "We could maybe think about doing that on the way back."

"And get stripped of everything we own, and thrown in the water."

"You have a trusting nature, don't you?"

"If you mean, I'm not silly enough to think they'll welcome us in and let us take our pick of their women, then I guess I do."

"She was awful pretty, the woman. And not much older than me."

"And the rest of them are seahags older than your great-grandmother."

"That one time with my father . . . She was easily twice my age and I didn't mind a bit."

A couple of months ago, Damian's sixteenth birthday, his father had taken him to a pub in Norwich where women stripped at the bar and afterward walked around bare naked, collecting tips from the customers. Damian's father had paid one of them to look after his son, and Damian hadn't stopped talking about it ever since, making plans to go back on his own or to take Lucas with him that so far hadn't amounted to anything.

Damian watched the half-drowned building dwindle into the glare striking off the water and said, "If we ever ran away we could live in a place like that."

"You could, maybe," Lucas said. "I'd want to keep moving. But I suppose I could come back and visit now and then."

"I don't mean *that* place. I mean a place like it. Must be plenty of them, on those alien worlds up in the sky. There's oceans on one of them. First Foot."

"I know."

"And alien ruins on all of them. There are people walking about up there right now. On all those new worlds. And most people sit around like . . . like bloody stumps. Old tree stumps stuck in mud."

"I'm not counting on winning the ticket lottery," Lucas said. "Sailing south, that would be pretty fine. To Africa, or Brazil, or these islands people are building in the Pacific. Or even all the way to Antarctica."

"Soon as you stepped ashore, L, you'd be eaten by a polar bear."

"Polar bears lived in the north when there were polar bears."

"Killer penguins then. Giant penguins with razors in their flippers and lasers for eyes."

"No such thing."

"The !Cha made sea dragons, didn't they? So why not giant robot killer penguins? Your mother should look into it."

"That's not funny."

"Didn't mean anything by it. Just joking, is all."

"You go too far sometimes."

They sailed in silence for a little while, heading west across the deepwater channel. A clipper moved far off to starboard, cylinder sails spinning slowly, white as salt in the middle of a flat vastness that shimmered like shot silk under the hot blue sky. Some way beyond it, a tug was dragging a string of barges south. The shoreline of Thurne Point emerged from the heat haze, standing up from mud banks cut by a web of narrow channels, and they turned east, skirting stands of sea grass that spread out into the open water. It was a little colder now, and the wind was blowing more from the northwest than the wast. Lucas thought that the bank of fret looked closer, too. When he pointed it out, Damian said it was still klicks and klicks off, and besides, they were headed straight to their prize now.

"If it's still there," Lucas said.

"It isn't going anywhere, not with the tide all the way out."

"You really are an expert on this alien stuff, aren't you?"

"Just keep heading north, L."

"That's exactly what I'm doing."

"I'm sorry about that crack about your mother. I didn't mean anything by it. Okay?"

"Okay."

"I like to kid around," Damian said. "But I'm serious about getting out of here. Remember that time two years ago, we hiked into Norwich, found the army offices?"

"I remember the sergeant there gave us cups of tea and biscuits and told us to come back when we were old enough."

"He's still there. That sergeant. Same bloody biscuits, too."

"Wait. You went to join up without telling me?"

"I went to find out if I could. After my birthday. Turns out the army takes people our age, but you need the permission of your parents. So that was that."

"You didn't even try to talk to your father about it?"

"He has me working for him, L. Why would he sign away good cheap labor? I *did* try, once. He was half-cut and in a good mood. What passes for a good mood as far as he's concerned, any rate. Mellowed out on beer and superfine skunk. But he wouldn't hear anything about it. And then he got all the way flat-out drunk and he beat on me. Told me to never mention it again."

Lucas looked over at his friend and said, "Why didn't you tell me this before?"

"I can join under my own signature when I'm eighteen, not before," Damian said. "No way out of here until then, unless I run away or win the lottery."

"So are you thinking of running away?"

"I'm damned sure not counting on winning the lottery. And even if I do, you have to be eighteen before they let you ship out. Just like the fucking army." Damian looked at Lucas, looked away. "He'll probably bash all kinds of shit out of me, for taking off like this."

"You can stay over tonight. He'll be calmer, tomorrow."

Damian shook his head. "He'll only come looking for me. And I don't want to cause trouble for you and your mother."

"It wouldn't be any trouble."

"Yeah, it would. But thanks anyway." Damian paused, then said, "I don't care what he does to me anymore. You know? All I think is, one day I'll be able to beat up on him."

"You say that but you don't mean it."

"Longer I stay here, the more I become like him."

"I don't see it ever happening."

Damian shrugged.

"I really don't," Lucas said.

"Fuck him," Damian said. "I'm not going to let him spoil this fine day."

"Our grand adventure."

"The wind's changing again."

"I think the fret's moving in, too."

"Maybe it is, a little. But we can't turn back, L. Not now."

The bank of cloud across the horizon was about a klick away, reaching up so high that it blurred and dimmed the sun. The air was colder and the wind was shifting minute by minute. Damian put on his shirt, holding the jib sheet in his teeth as he punched his arms into the sleeves. They tacked to swing around a long reach of grass, and as they came about saw a white wall sitting across the water, dead ahead.

Lucas pushed the tiller to leeward. The boat slowed at once and swung around to face the wind.

"What's the problem?" Damian said. "It's just a bit of mist."

Lucas caught the boom as it swung, held it steady. "We'll sit tight for a spell. See if the fret burns off."

"And meanwhile the tide'll turn and lift off the fucking dragon."

"Not for a while."

"We're almost there."

"You don't like it, you can swim."

"I might." Damian peered at the advancing fret. "Think the dragon has something to do with this?"

"I think it's just fret."

"Maybe it's hiding from something looking for it. We're drifting backward," Damian said. "Is that part of your plan?"

"We're over the river channel, in the main current. Too deep for my anchor. See those dead trees at the edge of the grass? That's where I'm aiming. We can sit it out there."

"I hear something," Damian said.

Lucas heard it too. The ripping roar of a motor driven at full speed, coming closer. He looked over his shoulder, saw a shadow condense inside the mist and gain shape and solidity: a cabin cruiser shouldering through windblown tendrils at the base of the bank of mist, driving straight down the main channel at full speed, its wake spreading wide on either side.

In a moment of chill clarity Lucas saw what was going to happen. He shouted to Damian, telling him to duck, and let the boom go and shoved the tiller to starboard. The boom banged around as the sail bellied and the boat started to turn, but the cruiser was already on them, roaring past just ten meters away, and the broad smooth wave of its wake hit the boat broadside and lifted it and shoved it sideways toward a stand of dead trees. Lucas gave up any attempt to steer and unwound the main halyard from its cleat. Damian grabbed an oar and used it to push the boat away from the first of the trees, but their momentum swung them into two more. The wet black stump of a branch scraped along the side and the boat heeled and water poured in over the thwart. For a moment Lucas thought they would capsize; then something thumped into the mast and the boat sat up again. Shards of rotten wood dropped down with a dry clatter and they were suddenly still, caught among dead and half-drowned trees.

The damage wasn't as bad as it might have been—a rip close to the top of the jib, long splintery scrapes in the blue paintwork on the port side—but it kindled a black spark of anger in Lucas's heart. At the cruiser's criminal indifference; at his failure to evade trouble.

"Unhook the halyard and let it down," he told Damian. "We'll have to do without the jib."

"*Abode Two.* That's the name of the bugger nearly ran us down. Registered in Norwich. We should find him and get him to pay for this mess," Damian said, as he folded the torn jib sail.

"I wonder why he was going so damned fast."

"Maybe he went to take a look at the dragon, and something scared him off."

"Or maybe he just wanted to get out of the fret." Lucas looked all around, judging angles and clearances. The trees stood close together in water scummed with every kind of debris, stark and white above the tide line, black and clad with mussels and barnacles below. He said, "Let's try pushing backward. But be careful. I don't want any more scrapes."

By the time they had freed themselves from the dead trees the fret had advanced around them. A cold streaming whiteness that moved just above the water, deepening in every direction.

"Now we're caught up in it, it's as easy to go forward as to go back. So we might as well press on," Lucas said.

"That's the spirit. Just don't hit any more trees."

"I'll do my best."

"Think we should put up the sail?"

"There's hardly any wind, and the tide's still going out. We'll just go with the current."

"Dragon weather," Damian said.

"Listen," Lucas said.

After a moment's silence, Damian said, "Is it another boat?"

"Thought I heard wings."

Lucas had taken out his catapult. He fitted a ball bearing in the center of its fat rubber band as he looked all around. There was a splash among the dead trees to starboard and he brought up the catapult and pulled back the rubber band as something dropped onto a dead branch. A heron, gray as a ghost, turning its head to look at him.

Lucas lowered the catapult, and Damian whispered, "You could take that easy."

"I was hoping for a duck or two."

"Let me try a shot."

Lucas stuck the catapult in his belt. "You kill it, you eat it."

The heron straightened its crooked neck and rose up and opened its wings and with a lazy flap launched itself across the water, sailing past the stern of the boat and vanishing into the mist.

"Ritchy cooked one once," Damian said. "With about a ton of aniseed. Said it was how the Romans did them."

"How was it?"

"Pretty fucking awful, you want to know the truth."

"Pass me one of the oars," Lucas said. "We can row a while."

They rowed through mist into mist. The small noises they made seemed magnified, intimate. Now and again Lucas put his hand over the side and dipped up a palmful of water and tasted it. Telling Damian that fresh water was slow to mix with salt, so as long as it stayed sweet it meant they were in the old river channel and shouldn't run into anything. Damian was skeptical, but shrugged when Lucas challenged him to come up with a better way of finding their way through the fret without stranding themselves on some mud bank.

They'd been rowing for ten minutes or so when a long, low mournful note boomed out far ahead of them. It shivered Lucas to the marrow of his bones. He and Damian stopped rowing and looked at each other.

"I'd say that was a foghorn, if I didn't know what one sounded like," Damian said.

"Maybe it's a boat. A big one."

"Or maybe you-know-what. Calling for its dragon-mummy."

"Or warning people away."

"I think it came from over there," Damian said, pointing off to starboard.

"I think so too. But it's hard to be sure of anything in this stuff."

They rowed aslant the current. A dim and low palisade appeared, resolving into a bed of sea grass that spread along the edge of the old river channel. Lucas, believing that he knew where they were, felt a clear measure of relief. They sculled into a narrow cut that led through the grass. Tall stems bent and showered them with drops of condensed mist as they brushed past. Then they were out into open water on the far side. A beach loomed out of the mist and sand suddenly gripped and grated along the length of the little boat's keel. Damian dropped his oar and vaulted over the side and splashed away, running up the beach and vanishing into granular whiteness. Lucas shipped his own oar and slid into knee-deep water and hauled the boat through purling ripples, then lifted from the bow the bucket filled with concrete he used as an anchor and dropped it onto hard wet sand, where it keeled sideways in a dint that immediately filled with water.

He followed Damian's footprints up the beach, climbed a low ridge grown over with marram grass, and descended to the other side of the sand bar. Boats lay at anchor in shallow water, their outlines blurred by mist. Two dayfishers with small wheelhouses at their bows. Several sailboats not much bigger than his. A cabin cruiser with trim white superstructure, much like the one that had almost run him down.

A figure materialized out of the whiteness, a chubby boy of five or six in dungarees who ran right around Lucas, laughing, and chased away. He followed the boy toward a blurred eye of light far down the beach. Raised voices. Laughter. A metallic screeching. As he drew close, the blurred light condensed and separated into two sources: a bonfire burning above the tide line; a rack of spotlights mounted on a police speedboat anchored a dozen meters off the beach, long fingers of light lancing through mist and blurrily illuminating the long sleek shape stranded at the edge of the water.

It was big, the sea dragon, easily fifteen meters from stem to stern and about three meters across at its waist, tapering to blunt and shovel-shaped points at either end, coated in close-fitting and darkly tinted scales. An alien machine, solid and obdurate. One of thousands spawned by sealed mother ships the UN had purchased from the !Cha.

Lucas thought that it looked like a leech, or one of the parasitic flukes that lived in the bellies of sticklebacks. A big segmented shape, vaguely streamlined, helplessly prostrate. People stood here and there on the curve of its back. A couple of kids were whacking away at its flank with chunks of driftwood. A group of men and women stood at its nose, heads bowed as if in prayer. A woman was walking along its length, pointing a wand-like instrument at different places. A cluster of people were conferring among a scatter of toolboxes and a portable generator, and one of them stepped forward and applied an angle grinder to the dragon's hide. There was a ragged screech and a fan of orange sparks sprayed out and the man stepped back and turned to his companions and shook his head. Beyond the dragon, dozens more people could be glimpsed through the blur of the fret: everyone from the little town of Martham must have walked out along the sand bar to see the marvel that had cast itself up at their doorstep.

According to the UN, dragons cruised the oceans and swept up and digested the vast rafts of floating garbage that were part of the legacy of the wasteful oil-dependent world before the Spasm. According to rumors propagated on the stealth nets, a UN black lab had long ago cracked open a dragon and reverse-engineered its technology for fell purposes, or they were a cover for an alien plot to infiltrate Earth and construct secret bases in the ocean deeps, or to geoengineer the world in some radical and inimical fashion. And so on, and so on. One of his mother's ongoing disputes was with the Midway Island utopians, who were using modified dragons to sweep plastic particulates from the North Pacific Gyre and spin the polymer soup into construction materials: true utopians shouldn't use any kind of alien technology, according to her.

Lucas remembered his mother's request to take photos of the dragon and fished out her phone; when he switched it on, it emitted a lone and plaintive beep and its screen flashed and went dark. He switched it off, switched it on again. This time it did nothing. So it was true: the dragon was somehow suppressing electronic equipment. Lucas felt a shiver of apprehension, wondering what else it could do, wondering if it was watching him and everyone around it.

As he pushed the dead phone into his pocket, someone called his name. Lucas turned, saw an old man dressed in a yellow slicker and a peaked corduroy cap bustling toward him. Bill Danvers, one of the people who tended the oyster beds east of Martham, asking him now if he'd come over with Grant Higgins.

"I came in my own boat," Lucas said.

"You worked for Grant though," Bill Danvers said, and held out a flat quarter-liter bottle.

"Once upon a time. That's kind, but I'll pass."

"Vodka and ginger root. It'll keep out the cold." The old man unscrewed the cap and took a sip and held out the bottle again.

Lucas shook his head.

Bill Danvers took another sip and capped the bottle, saying, "You came over from Halvergate?"

"A little south of Halvergate. Sailed all the way." It felt good to say it.

"People been coming in from every place, past couple of hours. Including those science boys you see trying to break into her. But I was here first. Followed the damn thing in after it went past me. I was fishing for pollack, and it went past like an island on the move. Like to have had me in the water, I was rocking so much. I fired up the outboard and swung around but I couldn't keep pace with it. I saw it hit the bar, though. It didn't slow down a bit, must have been traveling at twenty knots. I heard it," Bill Danvers said, and clapped his hands. "Bang! It ran straight up, just like you see. When I caught up with it, it was wriggling like an eel. Trying to move forward, you know? And it did, for a little bit. And then it stuck, right where it is now. Must be something wrong with it, I reckon, or it wouldn't have grounded itself. Maybe it's dying, eh?"

"Can they die, dragons?"

"You live long enough, boy, you'll know everything has its time. Even unnatural things like this. Those science people, they've been trying to cut into it all morning. They used a thermal lance, and some kind of fancy drill. Didn't even scratch it. Now they're trying this saw thing with a blade tougher than diamond. Or so they say. Whatever it is, it won't do any good. Nothing on Earth can touch a dragon. Why'd you come all this way?"

"Just to take a look."

"Long as that's all you do I won't have any quarrel with you. You might want to pay the fee now."

"Fee?"

"Five pounds. Or five euros, if that's what you use."

"I don't have any money," Lucas said.

Bill Danvers studied him. "I was here first. Anyone says different they're a goddamned liar. I'm the only one can legitimately claim salvage rights. The man what found the dragon," he said, and turned and walked toward two women, starting to talk long before he reached them.

Lucas went on down the beach. A man sat cross-legged on the sand, sketching on a paper pad with a stick of charcoal. A small group of women were chanting some kind of incantation and brushing the dragon's flank with handfuls of ivy, and all down its length people stood close, touching its scales with the palms of their hands or leaning against it, peering into it, like penitents at a holy relic. Its scales were easily a meter across and each was a slightly different shape, six- or seven-sided, dark yet grainily translucent. Clumps of barnacles and knots of hair-like weed clung here and there.

Lucas took a step into cold, ankle-deep water, and another. Reached out, the tips of his fingers tingling, and brushed the surface of one of the plates. It was the same temperature as the air and covered in small dimples, like hammered metal. He pressed the palm of his hand flat against it and felt a steady vibration, like touching the throat of a purring cat. A shiver shot through the marrow of him, a delicious mix of fear and exhilaration. Suppose his mother and her friends were right? Suppose there was an alien inside there? A Jackaroo or a !Cha riding inside the dragon because it was the only way, thanks to the agreement with the UN, they could visit the Earth. An actual alien lodged in the heart of the machine, watching everything going on around it, trapped and helpless, unable to call for help because it wasn't supposed to be there.

No one knew what any of the aliens looked like—whether they looked more or less like people, or were unimaginable monsters, or clouds of gas, or swift cool thoughts schooling inside some vast computer. They had shown themselves only as avatars, plastic man-shaped shells with the pleasant, bland but somehow creepy faces of old-fashioned shop dummies, and after the treaty had been negotiated only a few of those were left on Earth, at the UN headquarters in Geneva. Suppose, Lucas thought, the scientists broke in and pulled its passenger out. He imagined some kind of squid, saucer eyes and a clacking beak in a knot of thrashing tentacles, helpless in Earth's gravity. Or suppose something came to rescue it? Not the UN, but an actual alien ship. His heart beat fast and strong at the thought.

Walking a wide circle around the blunt, eyeless prow of the dragon, he found Damian on the other side, talking to a slender, dark-haired girl dressed in a shorts and a heavy sweater. She turned to look at Lucas as he walked up, and said to Damian, "Is this your friend?"

"Lisbet was just telling me about the helicopter that crashed," Damian said. "Its engine cut out when it got too close and it dropped straight into the sea. Her father helped to rescue the pilot."

"She broke her hip," the girl, Lisbet, said. "She's at our house now. I'm supposed to be looking after her, but Doctor Naja gave her something that put her to sleep."

"Lisbet's father is the mayor," Damian said. "He's in charge of all this."

"He thinks he is," the girl said, "but no one is really. Police and everyone arguing among themselves. Do you have a phone, Lucas? Mine doesn't work. This is the best thing to ever happen here and I can't even tell my friends about it."

"I could row you out to where your phone started working," Damian said.

"I don't think so," Lisbet said, with a coy little smile, twisting the toes of her bare right foot in the wet sand.

Lucas had thought that she was around his and Damian's age; now he realized that she was at least two years younger.

"It'll be absolutely safe," Damian said. "Word of honor."

Lisbet shook her head. "I want to stick around here and see what happens next."

"That's a good idea too," Damian said. "We can sit up by the fire and keep warm. I can tell you all about our adventures. How we found our way through the mist. How we were nearly run down—"

"I have to go and find my friends," Lisbet said, and flashed a dazzling smile at Lucas and said that it was nice to meet him and turned away. Damian caught at her arm and Lucas stepped in and told him to let her go, and Lisbet smiled at Lucas again and walked off, bare feet leaving dainty prints in the wet sand.

"Thanks for that," Damian said.

"She's a kid. And she's also the mayor's daughter."

"So? We were just talking."

"So he could have you locked up if he wanted to. Me too."

"You don't have to worry about that, do you? Because you scared her off," Damian said.

"She walked away because she wanted to," Lucas said.

He would have said more, would have asked Damian why they were arguing, but at that moment the dragon emitted its mournful wail. A great honking blare, more or less B-Flat, so loud it was like a physical force, shocking every square centimeter of Lucas's body. He clapped his hands over his ears, but the sound was right inside the box of his skull, shivering deep in his chest and his bones. Damian had pressed his hands over his ears, too, and all along the dragon's length people stepped back or ducked away. Then the noise abruptly cut off, and everyone stepped forward again. The women flailed even harder, their chant sounding muffled to Lucas; the dragon's call had been so loud it had left a buzz in his ears, and he had to lean close to hear Damian say, "Isn't this something?"

"It's definitely a dragon," Lucas said, his voice sounding flat and mostly inside his head. "Are we done arguing?"

"I didn't realize we were," Damian said. "Did you see those guys trying to cut it open?"

"Around the other side? I was surprised the police are letting them do whatever it is they're doing."

"Lisbet said they're scientists from the marine labs at Swatham. They work for the government, just like the police. She said they think this is a plastic eater. It sucks up plastic and digests it, turns it into carbon dioxide and water."

"That's what the UN wants people to think it does, anyhow."

"Sometimes you sound just like your mother."

"There you go again."

Damian put his hand on Lucas's shoulder. "I'm just ragging on you. Come on, why don't we go over by the fire and get warm?"

"If you want to talk to that girl again, just say so."

"Now who's spoiling for an argument? I thought we could get warm, find something to eat. People are selling stuff."

"I want to take a good close look at the dragon. That's why we came here, isn't it?"

"You do that, and I'll be right back."

"You get into trouble, you can find your own way home," Lucas said, but Damian was already walking away, fading into the mist without once looking back.

Lucas watched him fade away, expecting him to turn around. He didn't.

Irritated by the silly spat, Lucas drifted back around the dragon's prow, watched the scientists attack with a jackhammer the joint between two large scales. They were putting everything they had into it, but didn't seem to be getting anywhere. A gang of farmers from a collective arrived on two tractors that left neat tracks on the wet sand and put out the smell of frying oil, which reminded Lucas that he hadn't eaten since breakfast. He was damned cold, too. He trudged up the sand and bought a cup of fish soup from a woman who poured it straight from the iron pot she hooked out of the edge of the big bonfire, handing him a crust of bread to go with it. Lucas sipped the scalding stuff and felt his blood warm, soaked up the last of the soup with the crust and dredged the plastic cup in the sand to clean it and handed it back to the woman. Plenty of people were standing around the fire, but there was no sign of Damian. Maybe he was chasing that girl. Maybe he'd been arrested. Most likely, he'd turn up with that stupid smile of his, shrugging off their argument, claiming he'd only been joking. The way he did.

The skirts of the fret drifted apart and revealed the dim shapes of Martham's buildings at the far end of the sand bar; then the fret closed up and the little town vanished. The dragon sounded its distress or alarm call again. In the ringing silence afterward a man said to no one in particular, with the satisfaction of someone who has discovered the solution to one of the universe's perennial mysteries, "Twenty-eight minutes on the dot."

At last, there was the sound of an engine and a shadowy shape gained definition in the fret that hung offshore: a boxy, old-fashioned landing craft that drove past the police boat and beached in the shallows close to the dragon. Its bow door splashed down and soldiers trotted out and the police and several civilians and scientists went down the beach to meet them. After a brief discussion, one of the soldiers stepped forward and raised a bullhorn to his mouth and announced that for the sake of public safety a two-hundred-meter exclusion zone was going to be established.

Several soldiers began to unload plastic crates. The rest chivvied the people around the dragon, ordering them to move back, driving them up the beach past the bonfire. Lucas spotted the old man, Bill Danvers, arguing with two soldiers. One suddenly grabbed the old man's arm and spun him around and twisted something around his wrists; the other looked at Lucas as he came toward them, telling him to stay back or he'd be arrested too.

"He's my uncle," Lucas said. "If you let him go I'll make sure he doesn't cause any more trouble."

"Your uncle?" The soldier wasn't much older than Lucas, with cropped ginger hair and a ruddy complexion.

"Yes, sir. He doesn't mean any harm. He's just upset, because no one cares that he was the first to find it."

"Like I said," the old man said.

The two soldiers looked at each other, and the ginger-haired one told Lucas, "You're responsible for him. If he starts up again, you'll both be sorry."

"I'll look after him."

The soldier stared at Lucas for a moment, then flourished a small-bladed knife and cut the plasticuffs that bound the old man's wrists and shoved him toward Lucas. "Stay out of our way, grandpa. All right?"

"Sons of bitches," Bill Danvers said, as the soldiers walked off. He raised his voice and called out, "I found it first. Someone owes me for that."

"I think everyone knows you saw it come ashore," Lucas said. "But they're in charge now."

"They're going to blow it open," a man said.

He held a satchel in one hand and a folded chair in the other; when he shook the chair open and sat down Lucas recognized him: the man who'd been sitting at the head of the dragon, sketching it.

"They can't," Bill Danvers said.

"They're going to try," the man said.

Lucas looked back at the dragon. Its streamlined shape dim in the streaming fret, the activity around its head (if that was its head) a vague shifting of shadows. Soldiers and scientists conferring in a tight knot. Then the police boat and the landing craft started their motors and reversed through the wash of the incoming tide, fading into the fret, and the scientists followed the soldiers up the beach, walking past the bonfire, and there was a stir and rustle among the people strung out along the ridge.

"No damn right," Bill Danvers said.

The soldier with the bullhorn announced that there would be a small controlled explosion. A moment later, the dragon blared out its loud, long call and in the shocking silence afterward laughter broke out among the crowd on the ridge. The soldier with the bullhorn began to count backward from ten. Some of the crowd took up the chant. There was a brief silence at zero, and then a red light flared at the base of the dragon's midpoint and a flat crack rolled out across the ridge and was swallowed by the mist. People whistled and clapped, and Bill Danvers stepped around Lucas and ran down the slope toward the dragon. Falling to his knees and getting up and running on as soldiers chased after him, closing in from either side.

People cheered and hooted, and some ran after Bill Danvers, young men mostly, leaping down the slope and swarming across the beach. Lucas saw

Damian among the runners and chased after him, heart pounding, flooded with a heedless exhilaration. Soldiers blocked random individuals, catching hold of them or knocking them down as others dodged past. Lucas heard the clatter of the bullhorn but couldn't make out any words, and then there was a terrific flare of white light and a hot wind struck him so hard he lost his balance and fell to his knees.

The dragon had split in half and things were glowing with hot light inside and the waves breaking around its rear hissed and exploded into steam. A terrific heat scorched Lucas's face. He pushed to his feet. All around, people were picking themselves up and soldiers were moving among them, shoving them away from the dragon. Some complied; others stood, squinting into the light that beat out of the broken dragon, blindingly bright waves and wings of white light flapping across the beach, burning away the mist.

Blinking back tears and blocky afterimages, Lucas saw two soldiers dragging Bill Danvers away from the dragon. The old man hung limp and helpless in their grasp, splayed feet furrowing the sand. His head was bloody, something sticking out of it at an angle.

Lucas started toward them, and there was another flare that left him stunned and half-blind. Things fell all around and a translucent shard suddenly jutted up by his foot. The two soldiers had dropped Bill Danvers. Lucas stepped toward him, picking his way through a field of debris, and saw that he was beyond help. His head had been knocked out of shape by the shard that stuck in his temple, and blood was soaking into the sand around it.

The dragon had completely broken apart now. Incandescent stuff dripped and hissed into steaming water and the burning light was growing brighter.

Like almost everyone else, Lucas turned and ran. Heat clawed at his back as he slogged to the top of the ridge. He saw Damian sitting on the sand, right hand clamped on the upper part of his left arm, and he jogged over and helped his friend up. Leaning against each other, they stumbled across the ridge. Small fires crackled here and there, where hot debris had kindled clumps of marram grass. Everything was drenched in a pulsing diamond brilliance. They went down the slope of the far side, angling toward the little blue boat, splashing into the water that had risen around it. Damian clambered unhandily over thwart and Lucas hauled up the concrete-filled bucket and boosted it over the side, then put his shoulder to the boat's prow and shoved it into the low breakers and tumbled in.

The boat drifted sideways on the rising tide as Lucas hauled up the sail. Dragon-light beat beyond the crest of the sand bar, brighter than the sun. Lucas heeled his little boat into the wind, ploughing through stands of sea grass into the channel beyond, chasing after the small fleet fleeing the scene. Damian sat in the bottom of the boat, hunched into himself, his back against the stem of the mast. Lucas asked him if he was okay; he opened his fingers to show a translucent spike embedded in the meat of his biceps. It was about the size of his little finger.

"Dumb bad luck," he said, his voice tight and wincing.

"I'll fix you up," Lucas said, but Damian shook his head.

"Just keep going. I think—"

Everything went white for a moment. Lucas ducked down and wrapped his arms around his head and for a moment saw shadowy bones through red curtains of flesh. When he dared look around, he saw a narrow column of pure white light rising straight up, seeming to lean over as it climbed into the sky, aimed at the very apex of heaven.

A hot wind struck the boat and filled the sail, and Lucas sat up and grabbed the tiller and the sheet as the boat crabbed sideways. By the time he had it under control again the column of light had dimmed, fading inside drifting curtains of fret, rooted in a pale fire flickering beyond the sandbar.

Damian's father, Jason Playne, paid Lucas and his mother a visit the next morning. A burly man in his late forties with a shaven head and a blunt and forthright manner, dressed in work boots and denim overalls, he made the caravan seem small and frail. Standing over Julia's bed, telling her that he would like to ask Lucas about the scrape he and his Damian had gotten into.

"Ask away," Julia said. She was propped among her pillows, her gaze bright and amused. Her tablet lay beside her, images and blocks of text glimmering above it.

Jason Playne looked at her from beneath the thick hedge of his eyebrows. A strong odor of saltwater and sweated booze clung to him. He said, "I was hoping for a private word."

"My son and I have no secrets."

"This is about *my* son," Jason Playne said.

"They didn't do anything wrong, if that's what you're worried about," Julia said.

Lucas felt a knot of embarrassment and anger in his chest. He said, "I'm right here."

"Well, you didn't," his mother said.

Jason Playne looked at Lucas. "How did Damian get hurt?"

"He fell and cut himself," Lucas said, as steadily as he could. That was what he and Damian had agreed to say, as they'd sailed back home with their prize. Lucas had pulled the shard of dragon stuff from Damian's arm and staunched the bleeding with a bandage made from a strip ripped from the hem of Damian's shirt. There hadn't been much blood; the hot sliver had more or less cauterized the wound.

Jason Playne said, "He fell."

"Yes, sir."

"Are you sure? Because I reckon that cut in my son's arm was done by a knife. I reckon he got himself in some kind of fight."

Julia said, "That sounds more like an accusation than a question."

Lucas said, "We didn't get into a fight with anyone."

Jason Playne said, "Are you certain that Damian didn't steal something?"

"Yes, sir."

Which was the truth, as far as it went.

"Because if he did steal something, if he still has it, he's in a lot of trouble. You too."

"I like to think my son knows a little more about alien stuff than most," Julia said.

"I don't mean fairy stories," Jason Playne said. "I'm talking about the army ordering people to give back anything to do with that dragon thing. You stole something and you don't give it back and they find out? They'll arrest you. And if you try to sell it? Well, I can tell you for a fact that the people in that trade are mad and bad. I should know. I've met one or two of them in my time."

"I'm sure Lucas will take that to heart," Julia said.

And that was that, except after Jason Playne had gone she told Lucas that he'd been right about one thing: the people who tried to reverse-engineer alien technology were dangerous and should at all costs be avoided. "If I happened to come into possession of anything like that," she said, "I would get rid of it at once. Before anyone found out."

But Lucas couldn't get rid of the shard because he'd promised Damian that he'd keep it safe until they could figure out what to do with it. He spent the next two days in a haze of guilt and indecision, struggling with the temptation to check that the thing was safe in its hiding place, wondering what Damian's father knew, wondering what his mother knew, wondering if he should sail out to a deep part of the Flood and throw it into the water, until at last Damian came over to the island.

It was early in the evening, just after sunset. Lucas was watering the vegetable garden when Damian called to him from the shadows inside a clump of buddleia bushes. Smiling at Lucas, saying, "If you think I look bad, you should see him."

"I can't think he could look much worse."

"I got in a few licks," Damian said. His upper lip was split and both his eyes were blackened and there was a discolored knot on the hinge of his jaw.

"He came here," Lucas said. "Gave me and Julia a hard time."

"How much does she know?"

"I told her what happened."

"Everything?"

There was an edge in Damian's voice.

"Except about how you were hit with the shard," Lucas said.

"Oh. Your mother's cool, you know? I wish . . . "

When it was clear that his friend wasn't going to finish his thought, Lucas said, "Is it okay? You coming here so soon."

"Oh, Dad's over at Halvergate on what he calls business. Don't worry about him. Did you keep it safe?"

"I said I would."

"Why I'm here, L, I think I might have a line on someone who wants to buy our little treasure."

"Your father said we should keep away from people like that."

"He would."

"Julia thinks so too."

"If you don't want anything to do with it, just say so. Tell me where it is, and I'll take care of everything."

"Right."

"So is it here, or do we have to go somewhere?"

"I'll show you," Lucas said, and led his friend through the buddleias and along the low ridge to the northern end of the tiny island where an apple tree stood, hunched and gnarled and mostly dead, crippled by years of salt spray and saltwater seep. Lucas knelt and pulled up a hinge of turf and took out a small bundle of oilcloth. As he unwrapped it, Damian dropped to his knees beside him and reached out and touched an edge of the shard.

"Is it dead?"

"It wasn't ever alive," Lucas said.

"You know what I mean. What did you do to it?"

"Nothing. It just turned itself off."

When Lucas had pulled the shard from Damian's arm, its translucence had been veined with a network of shimmering threads. Now it was a dull reddish black, like an old scab.

"Maybe it uses sunlight, like phones," Damian said.

"I thought of that, but I also thought it would be best to keep it hidden."

"It still has to be worth something," Damian said, and began to fold the oilcloth around the shard.

Lucas was gripped by a sudden apprehension, as if he was falling while kneeling there in the dark. He said, "We don't have to do this right now."

"Yes we do. I do."

"Your father—he isn't in Halvergate, is he?"

Damian looked straight at Lucas. "I didn't kill him, if that's what you're worried about. He tried to knock me down when I went to leave, but I knocked him down instead. Pounded on him good. Put him down and put him out. Tied him up too, to give me some time to get away."

"He'll come after you."

"Remember when we were kids? We used to lie up here, in summer. We'd look up at the stars and talk about what it would be like to go to one of the worlds the Jackaroo gave us. Well, I plan to find out. The UN lets you buy tickets off lottery winners who don't want to go. It's legal and everything. All you need is money. I reckon this will give us a good start."

"You know I can't come with you."

"If you want your share, you'll have to come to Norwich. Because there's no way I'm coming back here," Damian said, and stood with a smooth, swift motion.

Lucas stood too. They were standing toe to toe under the apple tree, the island and the Flood around it quiet and dark. As if they were the last people on Earth.

"Don't try to stop me," Damian said. "My father tried, and I fucked him up good and proper."

"Let's talk about this."

"There's nothing to talk about," Damian said. "It is what it is."

He tried to step past Lucas, and Lucas grabbed at his arm and Damian swung him around and lifted him off his feet and ran him against the trunk of the tree. Lucas tried to wrench free but Damian bore down with unexpected strength, pressing him against rough bark, leaning into him. Pinpricks of light in the dark wells of his eyes. His voice soft and hoarse in Lucas's ear, his breath hot against Lucas's cheek.

"You always used to be able to beat me, L. At running, swimming, you name it. Not any more. I've changed. Want to know why?"

"We don't have to fight about this."

"No, we don't," Damian said, and let Lucas go and stepped back.

Lucas pushed away from the tree, a little unsteady on his feet. "What's got into you?"

Damian laughed. "That's good, that is. Can't you guess?"

"You need the money because you're running away. All right, you can have my share, if that's what you want. But it won't get you very far."

"Not by itself. But like I said, I've changed. Look," Damian said, and yanked up the sleeve of his shirt, showing the place on his upper arm where the shard had punched into him.

There was only a trace of a scar, pink and smooth. Damian pulled the skin taut, and Lucas saw the outline of a kind of ridged or fibrous sheath underneath.

"It grew," Damian said.

"Jesus."

"I'm stronger. And faster, too. I feel, I don't know. Better than I ever have. Like I could run all the way around the world without stopping, if I had to."

"What if it doesn't stop growing? You should see a doctor, D. Seriously."

"I'm going to. The kind that can make money for me, from what happened. You still think that little bit of dragon isn't worth anything? It changed me. It could change anyone. I really don't want to fight," Damian said, "but I will if you get in my way. Because there's no way I'm stopping here. If I do, my dad will come after me. And if he does, I'll have to kill him. *And I know I can.*"

The two friends stared at each other in the failing light. Lucas was the first to look away.

"You can come with me," Damian said. "To Norwich. Then wherever we want to go. To infinity and beyond. Think about it. You still got my phone?"

"Do you want it back? It's in the caravan."

"Keep it. I'll call you. Tell you where to meet up. Come or don't come, it's up to you."

And then he ran, crashing through the buddleia bushes that grew along the slope of the ridge. Lucas went after him, but by the time he reached the edge of the water, Damian had started the motor of the boat he'd stolen from his father's shrimp farm, and was dwindling away into the thickening twilight.

The next day, Lucas was out on the Flood, checking baited cages he'd set for eels, when an inflatable pulled away from the shrimp farm and drew a curving line of white across the water, hooking toward him. Jason Playne sat in the inflatable's stern, cutting the motor and drifting neatly alongside Lucas's boat and catching hold of the thwart. His left wrist was bandaged and he wore a baseball cap pulled low over sunglasses that darkly reflected Lucas and Lucas's boat and the waterscape all around. He asked without greeting or preamble where Damian was, and Lucas said that he didn't know.

"You saw him last night. Don't lie. What did he tell you?"

"That he was going away. That he wanted me to go with him."

"But you didn't."

"Well, no. I'm still here."

"Don't try to be clever, boy." Jason Playne stared at Lucas for a long moment, then sighed and took off his baseball cap and ran the palm of his hand over his shaven head. "I talked to your mother. I know he isn't with you. But he could be somewhere close by. In the woods, maybe. Camping out like you two used to do when you were smaller."

"All I know is that he's gone, Mr. Payne. Far away from here."

Jason Playne's smile didn't quite work. "You're his friend, Lucas. I know you want to do the right thing by him. As friends should. So maybe you can tell him, if you see him, that I'm not angry. That he should come home and it won't be a problem. You could also tell him to be careful. And you should be careful, too. I think you know what I mean. It could get you both into a lot of trouble if you talk to the wrong people. Or even if you talk to the right people. You think about that," Jason Playne said, and pushed away from Lucas's boat and opened the throttle of his inflatable's motor and zoomed away, bouncing over the slight swell, dwindling into the glare of the sun off the water.

Lucas went back to hauling up the cages, telling himself that he was glad that Damian was gone, that he'd escaped. When he'd finished, he took up the oars and began to row toward the island, back to his mother, and the little circle of his life.

Damian didn't call that day, or the next, or the day after that. Lucas was angry at first, then heartsick, convinced that Damian was in trouble. That he'd squandered or lost the money he'd made from selling the shard, or that he'd been cheated, or worse. After a week, Lucas sailed to Norwich and spent half a day tramping around the city in a futile attempt to find his friend. Jason Playne didn't trouble him again, but several times Lucas spotted him standing at the end of the shrimp farm's chain of tanks, studying the island.

September's Indian summer broke in a squall of storms. It rained every day. Hard, cold rain blowing in swaying curtains across the face of the waters. Endless racks of low clouds driving eastward. Atlantic weather. The Flood was muddier and less salty than usual. The eel traps stayed empty and storm surges drove the mackerel shoals and other fish into deep water. Lucas harvested everything he could from the vegetable garden, and from the ancient pear tree and wild, forgotten hedgerows in the ribbon of woods behind the levee, counted and recounted the store of cans and MREs. He set rabbit snares in the woods, and spent hours tracking squirrels from tree to tree, waiting for a moment when he could take a shot with his catapult. He caught sticklebacks in the weedy tide pools that fringed the broken brickwork shore of the island and used them to bait trotlines for crabs, and if he failed to catch any squirrels or crabs he collected mussels from the car reef at the foot of the levee.

It rained through the rest of September and on into October. Julia developed a racking and persistent cough. She enabled the long-disused keyboard function of her tablet and typed her essays, opinion pieces and journal entries instead of giving them straight to camera. She was helping settlers on the Antarctic Peninsula to petition the International Court in Johannesburg to grant them statehood, so that they could prevent exploitation of oil and mineral reserves by multinationals. She was arguing with the Midway Island utopians about whether or not the sea dragons they were using to harvest plastic particulates were also sucking up precious phytoplankton, and destabilizing the oceanic ecosystem. And so on, and so forth.

The witchwoman visited and treated her with infusions and poultices, but the cough grew worse and because they had no money for medicine, Lucas tried to find work at the algae farm at Halvergate. Every morning, he set out before dawn and stood at the gates in a crowd of men and women as one of the supervisors pointed to this or that person and told them to step forward, told the rest to come back and try their luck tomorrow. After his fifth unsuccessful cattle call, Lucas was walking along the shoulder of the road toward town and the jetty where his boat was tied up when a battered van pulled up beside him and the driver called to him. It was Ritchy, the stoop-shouldered one-eyed foreman of the shrimp farm. Saying, "Need a lift, lad?"

"You can tell him there's no point in following me because I don't have any idea where Damian is," Lucas said, and kept walking.

"He doesn't know I'm here." Ritchy leaned at the window, edging the van along, matching Lucas's pace. Its tires left wakes in the flooded road. Rain danced on its roof. "I got some news about Damian. Hop in. I know a place does a good breakfast, and you look like you could use some food."

They drove past patchworks of shallow lagoons behind mesh fences, past the steel tanks and piping of the cracking plant that turned algal lipids into biofuel. Ritchy talked about the goddamned weather, asked Lucas how his boat was handling, asked after his mother, said he was sorry to hear that she was ill and maybe he should pay a visit, he always liked talking to her because she made you look at things in a different way, a stream of inconsequential chatter he kept up all the way to the café.

It was in one corner of a layby where two lines of trucks were parked nose to tail. A pair of shipping containers welded together and painted bright pink. Red and white-checkered curtains behind windows cut in the ribbed walls. Formica tables and plastic chairs crowded inside, all occupied and a line of people waiting, but Ritchy knew the Portuguese family who ran the place and he and Lucas were given a small table in the back, between a fridge and the service counter, and without asking were served mugs of strong tea, and shrimp and green pepper omelets with baked beans and chips.

"You know what I miss most?" Ritchy said. "Pigs. Bacon and sausage. Ham. They say the Germans are trying to clone flu-resistant pigs. If they are, I hope they get a move on. Eat up, lad. You'll feel better with something inside you."

"You said you had some news about Damian. Where is he? Is he all right?"

Ritchy squinted at Lucas. His left eye, the one that had been lost when he'd been a soldier, glimmered blankly. It had been grown from a sliver of tooth and didn't have much in the way of resolution, but allowed him to see both infrared and ultraviolet light.

He said, "Know what collateral damage is?"

Fear hollowed Lucas's stomach. "Damian is in trouble, isn't he? What happened?"

"Used to be, long ago, wars were fought on a battlefield chosen by both sides. Two armies meeting by appointment. Squaring up to each other. Slogging it out. Then wars became so big the countries fighting them became one huge battlefield. Civilians found themselves on the front line. Or rather, there was no front line. Total war, they called it. And then you got wars that weren't wars. Asymmetrical wars. Netwars. Where war gets mixed up with crime and terrorism. Your mother was on the edge of a netwar at one time. Against the Jackaroo and those others. Still thinks she's fighting it, although it long ago evolved into something else. There aren't any armies or battlefields in a netwar. Just a series of nodes in distributed organization. Collateral damage," Ritchy said, forking omelet into his mouth, "is the inevitable consequence of taking out one of those nodes, because all of them are embedded inside ordinary society. It could be a flat in an apartment block in a city. Or a little island where someone thinks something useful is hidden."

"I don't—"

"You don't know anything," Ritchy said. "I believe you. Damian ran off with whatever it was you two found or stole, and left you in the lurch. But the people Damian got himself involved with don't know you don't know. That's why we've been looking out for you. Making sure you and your mother don't become collateral damage."

"Wait. What people? What did Damian do?"

"I'm trying to tell you, only it's harder than I thought it would be." Ritchy set his knife and fork together on his plate and said, "Maybe telling it straight is the best way. The day after Damian left, he tried to do some business with some people in Norwich. Bad people. The lad wanted to sell them a fragment of that dragon that stranded itself, but they decided to take it from him without paying. There was a scuffle and the lad got away and left a man with a bad knife wound. He died from it, a few weeks later. Those are the kind of people who look after their own, if you know what I mean. Anyone involved in that trade is bad news in one way or another. Jason had to pay them off, or else they would have come after him. An eye for an eye," Ritchy said, and tapped his blank eye with his little finger.

"What happened to Damian?"

"This is the hard part. After his trouble in Norwich, the lad called his father. He was drunk, ranting. Boasting how he was going to make all kinds of money. I managed to put a demon on his message, ran it back to a cell in Gravesend. Jason went up there, and that's when . . . Well, there's no other way of saying it. That's when he found out that Damian had been killed."

The shock was a jolt and a falling away. And then Lucas was back inside himself, hunched in his damp jeans and sweater in the clatter and bustle of the café, with the fridge humming next to him. Ritchy tore off the tops of four straws of sugar and poured them into Lucas's tea and stirred it and folded Lucas's hand around the mug and told him to drink.

Lucas sipped hot sweet tea and felt a little better.

"Always thought," Ritchy said, "that of the two of you, you were the best and brightest."

Lucas saw his friend in his mind's eye and felt cold and strange, knowing he'd never see him, never talk to him again.

Ritchy said, "The police got in touch yesterday. They found Damian's body in the river. They think he fell into the hands of one of the gangs that trade in offworld stuff."

Lucas suddenly understood something and said, "They wanted what was growing inside him. The people who killed him."

He told Ritchy about the shard that had hit Damian in the arm. How they'd pulled it out. How it had infected Damian.

"He had a kind of patch around the cut, under his skin. He said it was making him stronger."

Lucas saw his friend again, wild-eyed in the dusk, under the apple tree.

"That's what he thought. But that kind of thing, well, if he hadn't been murdered he would most likely have died from it."

"Do you know who did it?"

Ritchy shook his head. "The police are making what they like to call inquiries. They'll probably want to talk to you soon enough."

"Thank you. For telling me."

"I remember the world before the Jackaroo came," Ritchy said. "Them, and the others after them. It was in a bad way, but at least you knew where you were. If you happen to have any more of that stuff, lad, throw it in the Flood. And don't mark the spot."

Two detectives came to Gravesend to interview Lucas. He told them everything he knew. Julia said that he shouldn't blame himself, said that Damian had made a choice and it had been a bad choice. But Lucas carried the guilt around with him anyway. He should have done more to help Damian. He should have thrown the shard away. Or found him after they'd had the stupid argument over that girl. Or refused to take him out to see the damn dragon in the first place.

A week passed. Two. There was no funeral because the police would not release Damian's body. According to them, it was still undergoing forensic tests. Julia, who was tracking rumors about the murder and its investigation on the stealth nets, said it had probably been taken to some clandestine research lab, and she and Lucas had a falling out over it.

One day, returning home after checking the snares he'd set, Lucas climbed to the top of the levee and saw two men waiting beside his boat. Both were dressed in brand-new camo gear, one with a beard, the other with a shaven head and rings flashing in one ear. They started up the slope toward him, calling his name, and he turned tail and ran, cutting across a stretch of sour land gone to weeds and pioneer saplings, plunging into the stands of bracken at the edge of the woods, pausing, seeing the two men chasing toward him, turning and running on.

He knew every part of the woods, and quickly found a hiding place under the slanted trunk of a fallen sycamore grown over with moss and ferns, breathing quick and hard in the cold air. Rain pattered all around. Droplets of water spangled bare black twigs. The deep odor of wet wood and wet earth.

A magpie chattered, close by. Lucas set a ball bearing in the cup of his catapult and cut toward the sound, moving easily and quietly, freezing when he saw a twitch of movement between the wet tree trunks ahead. It was the bearded man, the camo circuit of his gear magicking him into a fairytale creature got up from wet bark and mud. He was talking into a phone headset in a language full of harsh vowels. Turning as Lucas stepped toward him, his smile white inside his beard, saying that there was no need to run away, he only wanted to talk.

"What is that you have, kid?"

"A catapult. I'll use it if I have to."

"What do you use it for? Hunting rabbits? I'm no rabbit."

"Who are you?"

"Police. I have ID," the man said, and before Lucas could say anything his hand went into the pocket of his camo trousers and came out with a pistol.

Lucas had made his catapult himself, from a yoke of springy poplar and a length of vatgrown rubber with the composition and tensile strength of the hinge inside a mussel shell. As the man brought up the pistol Lucas pulled back the band of rubber and let the ball bearing fly. He did it quickly and without thought, firing from the hip, and the ball bearing went exactly where he meant it to go. It smacked into the knuckles of the man's hand with a hard pop and the man yelped and dropped the pistol, and then he sat down hard and clapped his good hand to his knee, because Lucas's second shot had struck the soft part under the cap.

Lucas stepped up and kicked the pistol away and stepped back, a third ball bearing cupped in the catapult. The man glared at him, wincing with pain, and said something in his harsh language.

"Who sent you?" Lucas said.

His heart was racing, but his thoughts were cool and clear.

"Tell me where it is," the man said, "and we leave you alone. Your mother too."

"My mother doesn't have anything to do with this."

Lucas was watching the man and listening to someone moving through the wet wood, coming closer.

"She is in it, nevertheless," the man said. He tried to push to his feet but his wounded knee gave way and he cried out and sat down again. He'd bitten his lip bloody and sweat beaded his forehead.

"Stay still, or the next one hits you between the eyes," Lucas said. He heard a quaver in his voice and knew from the way the man looked at him that he'd heard it too.

"Go now, and fetch the stuff. And don't tell me you don't know what I mean. Fetch it and bring it here. That's the only offer you get," the man said. "And the only time I make it."

A twig snapped softly and Lucas turned, ready to let the ball bearing fly, but it was Damian's father who stepped around a dark green holly bush, saying, "You can leave this one to me."

At once Lucas understood what had happened. Within his cool clear envelope he could see everything: how it all connected.

"You set me up," he said.

"I needed to draw them out," Jason Playne said. He was dressed in jeans and an old-fashioned woodland camo jacket, and he was cradling a cut-down double-barreled shotgun.

"You let them know where I was. You told them I had more of the dragon stuff."

The man sitting on the ground was looking at them. "This does not end here," he said.

"I have you, and I have your friend. And you're going to pay for what you did to my son," Jason Playne said, and put a whistle to his lips and blew, two short notes. Off in the dark rainy woods another whistle answered.

The man said, "Idiot small time businessman. You don't know us. What we can do. Hurt me and we hurt you back ten-fold."

Jason Playne ignored him, and told Lucas that he could go.

"Why did you let them chase me? You could have caught them while they were waiting by my boat. Did you want them to hurt me?"

"I knew you'd lead them a good old chase. And you did. So, all's well that ends well, eh?" Jason Playne said. "Think of it as payback. For what happened to Damian."

Lucas felt a bubble of anger swelling in his chest. "You can't forgive me for what I didn't do."

"It's what you didn't do that caused all the trouble."

"It wasn't me. It was you. It was you who made him run away. It wasn't just the beatings. It was the thought that if he stayed here he'd become just like you."

Jason Playne turned toward Lucas, his face congested. "Go. Right now."

The bearded man drew a knife from his boot and flicked it open and pushed up with his good leg, throwing himself toward Jason Playne, and Lucas stretched the band of his catapult and let fly. The ball bearing struck the bearded man in the temple with a hollow sound and the man fell flat on his face. His temple was dented and blood came out of his nose and mouth and he thrashed and trembled and subsided.

Rain pattered down all around, like faint applause.

Then Jason Playne stepped toward the man and kicked him in the chin with the point of his boot. The man rolled over on the wet leaves, arms flopping wide.

"I reckon you killed him," Jason Playne said.

"I didn't mean—"

"Lucky for you there are two of them. The other will tell me what I need to know. You go now, boy. Go!"

Lucas turned and ran.

He didn't tell his mother about it. He hoped that Jason Playne would find out who had killed Damian and tell the police and the killers would answer for what they had done, and that would be an end to it.

That wasn't what happened.

The next day, a motor launch came over to the island, carrying police armed with machine-guns and the detectives investigating Damian's death, who arrested Lucas for involvement in two suspicious deaths and conspiracy to kidnap or murder other persons unknown. It seemed that one of the men that Jason Playne had hired to help him get justice for the death of his son had been a police informant.

Lucas was held in remand in Norwich for three months. Julia was too ill to visit him, but they talked on the phone and she sent messages via Ritchy, who'd been arrested along with every other worker on the shrimp farm, but released on bail after the police were unable to prove that he had anything to do with Jason Playne's scheme.

It was Ritchy who told Lucas that his mother had cancer that had started in her throat and spread elsewhere, and that she had refused treatment. Lucas was taken to see her two weeks later, handcuffed to a prison warden. She was lying in a hospital bed, looking shrunken and horribly vulnerable. Her dreadlocks bundled in a blue scarf. Her hand so cold when he took it in his. The skin loose on frail bones.

She had refused to agree to monoclonal antibody treatment that would shrink the tumors and remove cancer cells from her bloodstream, and had also refused food and water. The doctors couldn't intervene because a clause in her living will gave her the right to choose death instead of treatment. She told Lucas this in a hoarse whisper. Her lips were cracked and her breath foul, but her gaze was strong and insistent.

"Do the right thing even when it's the hardest thing," she said.

She died four days later. Her ashes were scattered in the rose garden of the municipal crematorium. Lucas stood in the rain between two wardens as the curate recited the prayer for the dead. The curate asked him if he wanted to scatter the ashes and he threw them out across the wet grass and dripping rose bushes with a flick of his wrist. Like casting a line across the water.

He was sentenced to five years for manslaughter, reduced to eighteen months for time served on remand and for good behavior. He was released early in September. He'd been given a ticket for the bus to Norwich, and a voucher good for a week's stay in a halfway house, but he set off in the opposite direction, on foot. Walking south and east across country. Following back roads. Skirting the edges of sugar beet fields and bamboo plantations. Ducking into ditches or hedgerows whenever he heard a vehicle approaching. Navigating by the moon and the stars.

Once, a fox loped across his path.

Once, he passed a depot lit up in the night, robots shunting between a loading dock and a road-train.

By dawn he was making his way through the woods along the edge of the levee. He kept taking steps that weren't there. Several times he sat on his haunches and rested for a minute before pushing up and going on. At last, he struck the gravel track that led to the shrimp farm, and twenty minutes later was knocking on the door of the office.

Ritchy gave Lucas breakfast and helped him pull his boat out of the shed where it had been stored, and set it in the water. Lucas and the old man had stayed in touch: it had been Ritchy who'd told him that Jason Playne had been stabbed to death in prison, most likely by someone paid by the people he'd tried to chase down. Jason Playne's brother had sold the shrimp farm to a local consortium, and Ritchy had been promoted to supervisor.

He told Lucas over breakfast that he had a job there, if he wanted it. Lucas said that he was grateful, he really was, but he didn't know if he wanted to stay on.

"I'm not asking you to make a decision right away," Ritchy said. "Think about it. Get your bearings, come to me whenever you're ready. Okay?"

"Okay."

"Are you going to stay over on the island?"

"Just how bad is it?"

"I couldn't keep all of them off. They'd come at night. One party had a shotgun."

"You did what you could. I appreciate it."

"I wish I could have done more. They made a mess, but it isn't anything you can't fix up, if you want to."

A heron flapped away across the sun-silvered water as Lucas rowed around the point of the island. The unexpected motion plucked at an old memory. As if he'd seen a ghost.

He grounded his boat next to the rotting carcass of his mother's old rowboat and walked up the steep path. Ritchy had patched the broken windows of the caravan and put a padlock on the door. Lucas had the key in his pocket, but he didn't want to go in there, not yet.

After Julia had been taken into hospital, treasure hunters had come from all around, chasing rumors that parts of the dragon had been buried on the island. Holes were dug everywhere in the weedy remains of the vegetable garden; the microwave mast at the summit of the ridge, Julia's link with the rest of the world, had been uprooted. Lucas set his back to it and walked north, counting his steps. Both of the decoy caches his mother had planted under brick cairns had been ransacked, but the emergency cache, buried much deeper, was undisturbed.

Lucas dug down to the plastic box, and looked all around before he opened it and sorted through the things inside, squatting frogwise with the hot sun on his back.

An assortment of passports and identity cards, each with a photograph of younger versions of his mother, made out to different names and nationalities. A slim tight roll of old high-denomination banknotes, yuan, naira, and US dollars, more or less worthless thanks to inflation and revaluation. Blank credit cards and credit cards in various names, also worthless. Dozens of sleeved data needles. A pair of AR glasses.

Lucas studied one of the ID cards. When he brushed the picture of his mother with his thumb, she turned to present her profile, turned to look at him when he brushed the picture again.

He pocketed the ID card and the data needles and AR glasses, then walked along the ridge to the apple tree at the far end, and stared out across the flood that spread glistening like shot silk under the sun. Thoughts moved through his mind like a slow and stately parade of pictures that he could examine in every detail, and then there were no thoughts at all and for a little while no part of him was separate from the world all around, sun and water and the hot breeze that moved through the crooked branches of the tree.

Lucas came to himself with a shiver. Windfall apples lay everywhere among the weeds and nettles that grew around the trees, and dead wasps and hornets were scattered among them like yellow and black bullets. Here was a dead bird, too, gone to a tatter of feathers of white bone. And here was another, and another. As if some passing cloud of poison had struck everything down.

He picked an apple from the tree, mashed it against the trunk, and saw pale threads fine as hair running through the mash of pulp. He peeled bark from a branch, saw threads laced in the living wood.

Dragon stuff, growing from the seed he'd planted. Becoming something else.

In the wood of the tree and the apples scattered all around was a treasure men would kill for. Had killed for. He'd have more than enough to set him up for life, if he sold it to the right people. He could build a house right here, buy the shrimp farm or set up one of his own. He could buy a ticket on one of the shuttles that traveled through the wormhole anchored between the Earth and the Moon, travel to infinity and beyond . . .

Lucas remembered the hopeful shine in Damian's eyes when he'd talked about those new worlds. He thought of how the dragon-shard had killed or damaged everyone it had touched. He pictured his mother working at her tablet in her sick bed, advising and challenging people who were attempting to build something new right here on Earth. It wasn't much of a contest. It wasn't even close.

He walked back to the caravan. Took a breath, unlocked the padlock, stepped inside. Everything had been overturned or smashed. Cupboards gaped open, the mattress of his mother's bed was slashed and torn, a great ruin littered the floor. He rooted among the wreckage, found a box of matches and a plastic jug of lamp oil. He splashed half of the oil on the torn mattress, lit a twist of cardboard and lobbed it onto the bed, beat a retreat as flames sprang up.

It didn't take ten minutes to gather up dead wood and dry weeds and pile them around the apple tree, splash the rest of the oil over its trunk and set fire to the tinder. A thin pall of white smoke spread across the island, blowing out across the water as he raised the sail of his boat and turned it into the wind.

Heading south.

# EAST OF FURIOUS

## JONATHAN CARROLL

He was the only man she knew who actually looked *good* in a Panama hat. Before meeting him, she had never seen a man wearing one who didn't look either like a poser, a hoser, a loser, a tool, or a fool. But not him, not Mills. He looked great—like a deliciously shady character in some Graham Greene novel set in the tropics, or a sexy guy in an ad for good rum. He also owned a cream-colored linen suit that he often wore together with the hat in the summer. That outfit was totally over the top, but he could get away with wearing such things.

She never knew when he would contact her so when he did she was always both surprised and pleased. He'd say something like "Beatrice, it's Mills. Can you take tomorrow off? Let's go play hooky." And unless there was something absolutely pressing, she would.

He was a lawyer. They met when he represented Beatrice Oakum at her divorce. In court he was cool, precise, and quick-witted. Her ex-husband and his lawyer hadn't known what hit them until the judge awarded her almost everything she asked for in the divorce proceedings.

At a victory lunch afterward, Mills asked if they might be friends. The way he asked—shyly and with a charming tone of worry in his voice—flustered her. In court he was so confident and authoritative. But here he sounded like a seventh-grade boy asking her to dance. On the verge of saying of course, it struck her, uh oh, maybe he doesn't want to be just *friends*, he wants—as if reading her mind, the lawyer put up a hand and shook his head. "Please don't take that any way but how I said it. I just think you and I could be great friends. I hope you do too. No more and no less than that. What do you say?" He stuck out his hand to shake. A funny, odd gesture at that moment—like they were sealing a business deal rather than starting a friendship. It told her everything was all right. She hadn't misread his intentions.

They lived about an hour away from each other so at the beginning it was mostly long phone calls and the occasional visit. That suited them, though, because they were both busy people. The calls came in the evening or on the weekends. They were relaxed and uncommonly frank. Perhaps distance had something to do with it. Because fifty miles separated them, both people felt free to say whatever they wanted without having to worry about the possibility of seeing each other unless they agreed on a time and a place to meet.

Mills loved women. A confirmed bachelor, he usually dated two or three simultaneously. Sometimes they knew about each other, sometimes not. He said he liked the drama that invariably came with "dating multitudes." Hell, he even liked the confrontations, the recriminations, the hide-and-seek that was frequently necessary when divvying up your heart among others.

Eventually Beatrice realized Mills wanted her in his life partly because he did not desire her. At another time that would have hurt—no one likes being unwanted. But after her divorce and the exhausting cruel events that preceded it, she felt like a tsunami survivor. The last thing she wanted was someone new in either her head or her bed. So this kind of friendship was OK with her, at least for now. They'd be buddies, Platonic pals with the added bonus that each brought to the table the unique perspective and insight of his or her sex. Neither of them had ever had a really good, nonromantic friend of the opposite sex and it turned out to be a gratifying experience.

Mills asked questions about why women thought or behaved certain ways so he could better understand and win the hearts of his girlfriends. Beatrice asked many of the same kinds of questions but for a very different reason: She was curious about how men saw life so she could better understand why her ex-husband had behaved the way he did. Mills teased her about this. "You're performing an ongoing postmortem while I'm just trying to get them to say yes."

They ate meals together, went to the movies (although they had very different taste, and choosing what film to see often was a good-natured tug-of-war), they took long walks. Mills had a big mutt named Cornbread who regularly went along with them. That made things nicer because the dog was a sweet, gentle soul who wanted nothing more than to be your friend. When they passed other people on these walks, Beatrice could tell by their expressions that they thought Mills and she were a couple. The happy hound bounding back and forth between them further proved that.

One afternoon they were sitting at a favorite outdoor café by the river. It was a gorgeous June day, the place wasn't crowded, Cornbread slept at their feet: a moment where you couldn't ask for more.

"Tell me a secret."

"What do you mean?" She straightened up in her seat.

Sticking his chin out, he said in a taunting voice, "I dare you to tell me one of your absolute deepest secrets. One you've never told anyone before, not even your husband."

"Mills, we're friends and all, but *come on*."

"I'll tell *you* one of mine—"

"No, I don't want to hear it!" She made a quick gesture with her hand as if shooing flies away from her face.

"Come on, Bea, we *are* good pals now. Why can't I tell you a secret?"

"Because things like that . . . you should keep to yourself."

He smiled. "Are your secrets so ugly or dangerous that they can't be told?"

She tsked her tongue and shook her head. This was the first time he had ever made her feel uncomfortable. What was the point? "Tell me about your hat."

He looked at the Panama on the table. "My *hat*?"

"Yes, I love that hat. And I love it on you. Tell me where you got it."

"You're changing the subject but that's all right. My hat. I got it as a present from a client who was a pretty interesting guy."

"*Was?*"

"Yes, he's dead; he was murdered."

"Wow! By whom?"

"Well, they never found out. He was Russian and supposedly had quite a few enemies."

"You were his divorce lawyer?"

"Yes." Mills signaled a passing waitress to bring him another glass of wine.

"Who was he married to?"

"A very out-of-the-ordinary woman; an American. They met when she was a guest professor at the Moscow Institute of Steel and Alloys."

"Do you think she killed him?"

Mills smiled strangely. "She *was* on their list of suspects."

"Who wanted the divorce?"

He picked the hat up off the table and put it on his knee. "He did, but she got everything in the settlement because he just wanted out and away from her."

"If he lost everything in the settlement, why'd he give you a present afterward?" Her voice was teasing, but she really wanted him to answer the question.

"Because after it was over, I convinced his wife not to turn him into gold."

Beatrice wasn't sure she'd heard right. "*What?* Say that again."

Mills turned the hat round and round on his knee. "I convinced her not to turn him into gold and he was grateful. I'm a very good negotiator, you know. That's why he gave me the hat; he was thankful."

"What do you mean, *turn him into gold*? What are you talking about, Mills?" Beatrice looked at her friend skeptically, as if he must be putting her on or there was a joke in all this somewhere that she either wasn't getting or he'd told badly.

Cornbread woke up and immediately began biting his butt with great gusto. Both people watched while the dog attacked himself and then stopped just as suddenly, curled up again, and went back to sleep.

"Mills?"

"I told you they met when she was a guest professor in Moscow. She's a metallurgist, but also an alchemist. Do you know what they do?"

Beatrice snorted her derision "I know what they're *supposed* to be able to do—turn dross into gold."

He rubbed his neck and nodded. " 'Dross'—I like that word; it's very medieval. But, yes, you're right—that's what they do."

"But there's no such thing, Mills, and don't pretend there is. I know nothing about it, but I do know alchemy is more myth than anything else. People have always tried to transform worthless stuff into gold. But it's a metaphor—a nice one—but it's not *real*."

No longer smiling, Mills said, "Oh, it's real. Believe me, I've seen it happen. I saw her do it more than once."

"Stop it, you're teasing me. But, listen—I am completely gullible about these things. I believe what people tell me. That was half the problem with my husband—I always believed him and you know how *that* ended."

Mills rubbed his neck again and looked at Beatrice a long few moments. It was clear he was carefully considering what to say next. "We met back in seventh grade. I was the first boy she ever slept with."

"Who is this? Who are you talking about?"

"Her name is Heather Cooke. Alchemists aren't made, they're born. It is an inherent talent. Contrary to what most people believe, you can't *study* to be an alchemist, any more than you can study to be a violin prodigy or sports star. Studying makes you smarter and practice makes you more adept, but neither is able to create the divine spark that flares into genius. It's either within you from the beginning or not. That's why all those geniuses so accomplished at other things—Paracelsus, Isaac Newton, Saint Thomas Aquinas—failed at alchemy.

"Heather always had the gift. But the irony was she didn't want it; didn't want any part of it. The ability was thrust on her like a physical handicap. She once even said she would rather have been born blind than possess the ability to do alchemy. But too bad—that was her burden."

Beatrice listened to Mills rattle on, half expecting him to start chuckling at some point, pat her on the shoulder, and say he was kidding—this was all a joke. But he didn't and as his cockamamie story went on, she became more and more engrossed in it.

"She would never tell me how she did any of it, not that I would have understood or been able to duplicate the process even if she had. Heather said anyone can find and mix ingredients but the last most important element is the touch, whatever that meant. I asked if she literally meant physical touch but she said no, it was something far more abstruse than that. She made it plain that she didn't want me to ask more about it."

"You actually *saw* her do alchemy—change dross into gold?"

"Yes, twice. But there are different kinds of alchemy. Not just—"

"Can you tell me about them?"

Mills took a deep breath and both cheeks puffed when he let it out again. "The first time we made love we were fifteen. Heather's father died when she was a child. He was a draftsman for an architectural firm. One of her prize possessions was an expensive Yard-O-Led mechanical pencil he owned. She carried it with her everywhere. That first night we were at her house because her mom was out playing bridge. The pencil was on the desk in Heather's bedroom. I'd admired it earlier. When we were done, she excused herself and left the room. Before she did, she stopped at her desk and picked up the pencil. Then she smiled at me over her shoulder.

"A few minutes later she came back and said, 'This is for you.' She handed me a solid gold mechanical pencil, *that* mechanical pencil. She wanted me to have it as a keepsake of that night."

"But how did you know it was the same pencil?"

"Bite marks. Her father chewed on his pens and pencils when he was working. That one was no different. All over the top of this beautiful heavy gold mechanical pencil were bite marks."

The waitress brought Mills his glass of wine. Neither of them spoke after the woman left. Beatrice kept waiting for him to give her a sign—a smile or a wiggle of the eyebrows, something that said OK, I *am* teasing you. But his face looked even more serious than before.

"Heather *had* told me about the alchemy before but that was all—she never made a big deal of it. Only said she could do this weird thing and that sometimes her mother asked her to do it if there were unexpected bills to be paid; nothing more than that. When I asked what alchemy really was, she made up some kind of boring bullshit explanation that had to do with science and metal and math. But I was a boy and way more interested in her breasts than her math talents, so I didn't ask again.

"She and her mother certainly lived modestly, just the two of them in their little house. God knows with that gift, they could have been rich as Croesus and lived a hell of a lot better than they did. But her mom didn't want it. She had a job that made them enough money to live OK. Heather was very smart and got a full scholarship to the state university and then one to graduate school at the Colorado School of Mines.

"After a while we went our separate ways in high school although we always remained friendly and helped each other out when we could."

"She didn't stay your girlfriend in high school? She gave you her virginity *and* a solid gold pen as a thank you, but you left her? God, Mills, you were incorrigible even back then."

The lawyer shook his head. "Wrong—she dumped *me*. Absolutely broke my heart, but she said she wanted to date other guys and play the field. Remember that old phrase 'play the field'? I haven't heard it in years, but those were her exact words when she told me it was over between us. Heather could be very cold and single-minded about things when she wanted. Said we'd always be friends but you know what *that* means, especially when you're a teenager and a hormone rodeo.

"We traveled in different circles in school so I didn't see her all that much after we broke up. Interestingly, she liked the wild crowd, the drinkers and druggers and bad boys galore. The kids who were always in trouble with the police or being suspended from school for doing outrageous things. One of Heather's boyfriends was the first guy in our school to get tattooed. Remember, this was decades ago and back then getting ink was a pretty big deal. Anyway, she ended up with a reputation for many walks on the wild side by the time we graduated.

"She went to one college, I went to another, and that was that until a few years ago when she called me out of the blue. Said she needed a good divorce lawyer and had heard I was one of the best."

"You *are*. I'll attest to that."

Mills stared at Beatrice a few beats too long before smiling and giving a military salute in thanks. It felt like he was looking for something in her face, something that was there but hard to find. She thought it was an odd reaction to her compliment.

"But here's where the story gets interesting. A few days after we spoke, Heather came to my office. She looked pretty much like she did in high school, only thinner and more chic. My first impression was she looked European. I was sort of right because it turned out she'd lived in Russia for five years.

"We chatted a while about old times but it was plain she was just doing that to be nice. Eventually I said, Look, Heather, tell me what you need and let's talk about it. She was getting divorced and asked to hire me because she wanted the whole process over as quickly as possible. I said fine—give me all the details, I'll contact your husband and his lawyer, and we'll get things rolling.

"She said no, she wanted to hire me to represent her *husband*; wanted me to be *his* lawyer. She already had one for herself and he'd agreed to let her find him one."

Beatrice said, "I'm confused."

"So was I, but those were the facts: She already had a lawyer for herself and was hiring me to represent her husband."

"But, Mills, didn't her husband want to find his own lawyer? *Why* would he want someone to represent him who was an old friend, an old *boyfriend*, of his wife?"

"That's exactly what I asked. She said her husband was Russian and didn't know a good lawyer here. Anyway, both of them just wanted the divorce as soon as possible and they had already agreed on who'd get what. They had no children so that wasn't a problem."

"That's crazy! I've never heard of such a thing."

"Her husband came to my office the next morning. His name was Vadim Morozov. Kind of a nondescript-looking guy, you'd never notice him in a crowd—thin, maybe six feet tall, balding, a nice face but nothing special. He had a heavy accent but his English was almost perfect. The problem was I already knew he was one very bad character.

Heather had filled me in on him the day before.

"They met at a party her last year in Moscow. He told her he was a businessman, which wasn't so far from the truth. He was in import/export but soon enough she learned that meant smuggling: cigarettes, liquor, stolen cars from the West, rare Tabriz and kilim carpets from Iran . . . the list goes on and on. Vadim was a very resourceful fellow.

"But Heather was crazy about him and didn't even blink an eye when she found out what he really did for a living."

"She didn't *mind* that he was a smuggler?"

"Remember I said she'd always liked bad boys. Whatever hesitation or skepticism she might have had, he charmed out of her. She said she was a goner after the first month."

Beatrice made a sour face and shook her head because it sounded all too familiar—much the same thing had happened with her and her husband, only it had taken a while longer for her to fall completely under his spell.

"Vadim was very upfront with her in the beginning, saying he really wanted to move to America one day because so many Russians had gone and were doing well there. But that was fine with her because she didn't plan on staying in Russia, and if things worked out between them, she'd happily take him home with her when the time came.

"Whether he tricked her or it really was good between them, by the time she was to leave she couldn't imagine going home without him."

"And so, 'Reader, I married him.'" Beatrice said the famous line sarcastically and then shook her head again, disgusted by too many rancid memories of her own failed marriage.

"Well, no, they didn't get married for a while after they got to America. She was smitten but she wasn't stupid. Meanwhile Vadim kept a low profile and, as far as she knew, just enjoyed exploring his new homeland.

"He was eager to see America, so that first summer back they traveled for a couple of months: Los Angeles, Seattle, Phoenix, New York. What Heather didn't know was that in each of those cities when she wasn't around, Vadim made contact with Russian criminals who were running all kinds of illegal businesses—drugs, human trafficking, illegal weapon sales. And right after they married, he went to work."

Beatrice touched Mills's arm and then stood up. "I'll be right back." She walked toward the bathroom although she didn't need to use it. For some unknown reason, hearing this story had opened a floodgate inside her, and now all sorts of really toxic emotions were pouring out. Of course most of them had to do with her ex-husband. Until that moment she thought she'd done a pretty good job of keeping her emotions in check, sorting sanely through the marital disappointments, heartaches, bitter memories, and bad experiences and throwing a great many of them out of her head and heart. But even just hearing this fragment of Heather Cooke's story got Beatrice raging again—at her ex-husband, herself, at their failed marriage, at what an abysmal waste that part of her life had been. In a final letter to her husband, she had written, "If I could somehow erase every single pixel of our relationship from my memory I would do it without hesitation. Even the good times, even the great—I'd press 'delete' in a second."

In the bathroom now she stood looking at herself in a mirror above one of the sinks. "*Loser.* How could you have been so naive?" She sighed and closed her eyes. Her brain quickly filled with a mean circus of lousy, noisy memories and images, all jostling around and elbowing each other aside so they could get to the center ring to perform and annoy her.

"OK, enough." She ran cold water over her hands, checked her eyes to make sure there were no tears, and went back out to Mills and his story of Heather Cooke, alchemist.

As Beatrice sat down again at the table, a thought raised its hand in her head to ask a question. "Did Heather's husband know about the alchemy?"

"No, not at the beginning. As I said, it wasn't something she wanted others to know—in fact, very few did besides her mother. You know those people who are really talented at sports or a musical instrument but rarely play or practice because it doesn't interest them?"

"My ex-husband. He was wonderful at chess but didn't play because the game bored him."

"That was Heather too. She didn't practice alchemy for a variety of reasons but was certainly a master. As an academic, however, she was able to investigate it without raising suspicion by writing her doctoral thesis on the history of alchemy in America. Not the trendiest topic in the world, but it allowed her to explore the subject for years, and along the way discover answers to some of her questions. She told whoever asked that she'd grown intrigued by alchemy both as a practice and metaphor after having worked for so long in an adjacent field of study. Since her degree was in metallurgy, it made perfect sense."

"But then one day her husband found out about it and everything changed," Beatrice broke in, beating Mills to his punch line. As soon as she spoke, she knew it was mean and a result of her mini-meltdown in the ladies' room. Here she was, half grumpy, half edgy. Should she go home alone and sulk? Some part of her soul was just east of furious now but should she leave it alone and let it run its course, or take some kind of action that might help assuage it? Was that even possible? Can we ever say to our furies when they're laying siege to our borders that they should take a few deep breaths and back off a little?

Mills, sweet Mills, didn't bite back with meanness. Instead he just picked up the story right after what Beatrice had said. "But *how* Vadim found out is a great story in itself." He was about to continue when he looked more closely at Beatrice. "Are you all right? Do you want to go home?"

"No, but would you mind if we walked a little bit? I'm feeling sort of antsy."

"Of course."

They left the café and walked slowly together by the side of the river. Cornbread was off the leash, zigzagging slowly here and there, sniffing the world. Now and then a bicyclist or jogger whizzed by or they passed other walkers but for the most part they had the area to themselves. After a while Beatrice took Mills's hand. They walked in silence until she said, "OK, I'm OK now. Tell me how he found out."

"Vadim hadn't been feeling well for a while so he went to a doctor and had some tests done. They didn't like what they found so more tests were ordered. Eventually it was discovered he had stage three stomach cancer."

Beatrice stopped and turned to Mills. "How bad is that? I know nothing about cancer."

"Bad. Anyone with stage four is a goner, notwithstanding miracles. He came home from the hospital and told Heather he was dying.

"Now this next part is a little foggy because neither of them would tell me any of the details. I had to put their two stories together to come up with a whole."

"Why wouldn't they tell you details?"

"You'll see in a minute. What they *did* say, both of them, was Heather ordered Vadim to take off his shirt and lie down on the couch. When he asked why, she said, *Just do it.* She put both hands on his stomach and closed her eyes. The hands stayed in one spot for a long time. Vadim tried to speak but she said, Shut up. When she took her hands away, she told him to stay there and left the room.

"She was gone quite a long time but on returning she had a small bottle in her hand, like the kind of little liquor bottle stewardesses give on an airplane when you buy a cocktail. She told him to drink it all and then lie back down again. Vadim didn't know what she was doing but said her voice was one he'd never heard before. It was hard and not to be questioned—'a teacher's voice,' he called it.

"The drink tasted like Coca-Cola, which made it even stranger. He thought, I told her I have cancer and she brought me a *soda*? But he drank it all and lay back down, as ordered. She put her hands on his stomach again, one on top of the other but this time in a different spot, down much lower.

"Vadim said what happened next he did not feel; he emphasized that—nothing at all. After some time she slowly raised her hands off his stomach. Beneath them, as if it were a fish being pulled out of him on an invisible line, was something alive. It looked like a big black cockroach, or some other kind of giant black insect. Horrified, Vadim tried to sit up but Heather put her hand on his chest and yelled at him to stay where he was and wait till she was finished."

"Mills, is this true? You're not making it up?"

"Not a word of it. Everything is true. This is exactly as Vadim told me."

"My God. Go on."

"When the thing had fully emerged out of his stomach, it started crawling up his chest toward his neck. Very casually Heather picked it up off his body. The moment she actually touched it, two things happened—the bug stopped moving and then it turned into gold."

Before Beatrice could protest, Mills put a hand in his pocket and brought out something shiny about fifteen centimeters long. He held it up and she lurched backward because it was a large gold bug, so perfectly detailed and real looking that she expected to see its small legs twiddle in the air.

"Remember we were talking the other day about that TV report describing how dogs can smell different kinds of cancer?"

She nodded but kept her eyes on the gold bug.

"Watch this. Cornbread! Corn, come here."

The dog was off to the side, head down in a bush. As soon as he heard Mills call, he came right over to them. The man put his hand down and let the dog see the gold object. Cornbread eagerly sniffed it, then whined and shook his head hard. He even stepped away from his master, then shook his big head again.

"That's OK, boy, that's OK." Mills put the bug back in his pocket. "He smells the cancer."

"But why do *you* have it now?"

Instead of answering Beatrice's question, the lawyer went on. "That night Heather explained everything to him: the alchemy and how she'd always been able to do it, how she hid the talent all her life despite a fascination with it . . . everything.

"Vadim asked her to do something else, turn something else into gold, but she said no, he must accept that if they were to stay together. She had only prepared an *azoth* now to save his life. But he must never ask her to do alchemy again."

"What's an *azoth*?"

"Today we'd call it a panacea. It's a universal medicine that cures anything."

"Anything? AIDS? Cancer?"

"*Anything.* Authentic alchemists have known how to make it for centuries. But it's almost impossible to find a true master capable of mixing one for you.

"Heather and Vadim argued about it a long time. He said they could be rich; he could do all sorts of amazing things with both the money and her power. But she was unmoved. When he became insistent and the discussion got ugly between them, she said if he insisted, it would be the end of their marriage.

"Vadim was a crook but not a stupid man, at least not *that* stupid yet. He knew when to back off. He agreed to do what she asked. Just knowing that she had cured him of terminal stomach cancer was enough for then. He was very grateful—for a while."

"Heather had *never* used the power, never once before the time she cured him?"

Mills picked up a stick and threw it for the dog "Very rarely. Not since she was an adult. Sometimes when she was young and her mother was desperate for money to pay unexpected bills, but only then. She said they got to know certain jewelers who would pay cash for their gold and not ask questions about where it came from."

"Amazing." Beatrice couldn't help admiring Heather Cooke, if what Mills told her was true. Imagine having that extraordinary ability but never using it.

The lawyer interrupted her musing. "The thing most people don't know about alchemy is there are many different kinds, one more obscure than the other. There's the classic 'dross into gold' variety that you mentioned. But another that's way more interesting is something called introvert or internal alchemy that deals with the mystical and contemplative aspects of the science. It deals with *transformation*."

Beatrice frowned "You think alchemy is a *science*, Mills? Do you really? I always thought it was sort of—"

He answered firmly, "It is definitely a science, and a very old one. In various forms it dates back to the beginning of mankind, believe me. Remember Prometheus stealing fire from the gods? Think of him as the first alchemist. Many of the tenets of modern chemistry are based on experiments and discoveries that alchemists made centuries ago."

They walked along in silence, Beatrice thinking it all over, Mills waiting for a sign from her to continue. Cornbread brought the stick back, eager for it to be thrown again. Two bicycle riders rode slowly past, sharing a laugh.

Beatrice stopped and pointed at her friend. "You're going to tell me that Vadim screwed up. Because he was a crook, I assume it was because of that."

Mills grinned. "Go on."

Beatrice looked at her feet and thought about it some more. "He pulled off a big deal, or *tried* to pull one off with the Russian gangsters he'd contacted on their trip across the States."

"Keep going—you're close."

"But everything went wrong and he ended up having to beg her to make some more gold so they wouldn't kill him."

The lawyer pretended to clap. "Pretty good, as far as I know. The truth is Heather would never tell me the details of exactly what happened because she thought knowing them might endanger me."

"Why you, Mills?"

"Because the guys Vadim was involved with were frightening and ruthless, according to her. I assumed they were responsible for his death although nothing could be proved. Whatever Heather did for them I guess was enough, though, because nothing happened to Vadim . . . *then*. By the time he was killed later, she was long gone from his life.

"When he came to her for help that time, she said she'd do it but wanted a divorce after it was over. Vadim thought she was just bluffing but she wasn't.

"She did her alchemy again and made whatever it was he needed. But when the crisis passed, Vadim wouldn't divorce her. He obviously had other plans for her and her ability." Mills took the stick out of the dog's drooly mouth and threw it as far as he could. "But by the time I met the guy, she must have done something pretty damned scary to convince him otherwise because Vadim was terrified of her. He would have divorced her in two seconds if that were possible. Neither of them told me what it was she had done, but it sure worked. That first time we met, Vadim hadn't been in my office five minutes before he started pleading, 'You're her friend. She loves you. Please tell her not to turn me into gold. Please don't let her do that.' I didn't know if he meant it literally or she'd done something equally terrifying to convince him. But the divorce went very quickly. When it was over he gave me this hat and thanked me for intervening. I didn't say a thing to her about that, but he didn't need to know."

"And what happened to Heather after that?"

Mills shook his head. "I don't know. She disappeared and I never heard from her again."

"You never saw her after the divorce?"

Mills shook his head again.

Beatrice smiled, reached over, and touched his cheek. "Liar. Thank you for being such a good liar. I bet you tell that story to all your female clients."

Mills's mouth dropped and then slowly curved into a wide, happy smile. "It's *you*? It's really you?"

Beatrice nodded. "Yes."

"When did you catch on? When did you wake up?"

She slid her hand from his cheek and rested it on his shoulder. "It began when you showed me the gold cancer bug. But it was all slow and blurry and unclear at first. I wasn't sure what was happening so I waited and listened until everything came back to me. It really is like waking up in the morning after a deep sleep."

"It's exactly like you said it would be."

"That's not me, Mills, it's the alchemy."

"But, Heather, it's *really* you? After all this time it's really you?"

"Yes. And I'll tell you certain details now that I couldn't before because nobody knows who I am now. Enough time has passed."

The Heather Cooke he had known since childhood was a tall thin woman with brown hair and features you remembered. In contrast, Beatrice Oakum was medium height, heavy, and plain faced except for her nice long, blonde hair.

"Can I ask what you made for the Russians? Or how you did it?"

Beatrice shook her head. "No. All you need to know about that is afterward I had to find someone I could hide inside until the danger had passed. Transformation is one of the easier parts of internal alchemy, Mills. You want to enter and hide inside the soul of another person? It takes five minutes to mix up the drink you need.

"I went looking and as soon as I found Beatrice, I hibernated inside her after telling her, *programming* her, to do a few things after sufficient time had passed: I told her to find you. I told her to wake me when you showed her the gold bug. I told her . . . well, the rest isn't necessary to explain. What's most important is here I am, just looking a little different, eh?" She lifted both arms and the two old friends embraced while Cornbread jumped up on them, delighted to share their happiness. Eventually they separated. She took her old boyfriend's arm and they began walking again.

"I cannot believe it's you, Heather. I can't believe it actually happened the way you said it would."

She chuckled. "How many women clients did you tell my story to?"

"Four in the last three years. All of them were duly impressed, I must say. But none woke up when I showed them the bug. When they didn't react, I just dropped it back in my pocket and finished telling them Heather Cooke's great story. But I was only following your instructions. I've been dropping clues to you too all the time we've known each other. You never responded until now."

Pushing hair out of her face, she said, "I'll tell you some things now that I couldn't before, Mills, because I do believe I'm safe. I had to vanish so quickly back then because that bastard Vadim told them what I could do and they sent someone to get me. Do you remember what an *alkahest* is?"

"Yes, the universal solvent, a liquid that has the power to dissolve every other substance."

Beatrice squeezed his arm. "You remembered! The man the Russians sent to get me, to bring me to them? I tricked him into drinking an *alkahest*." She opened her mouth to continue but then decided not to. She was about to describe what happened to the Russian after he drank her version of the universal solvent. But a description wasn't necessary because just the thought of it made Mills shudder.

"Afterward I walked straight out of my apartment, called you, and said what I was going to do and what you must do to bring me back.

Then I went looking for someone to hide inside until the coast was clear."

"But what happens to Beatrice now, Heather? If you remain inside her—"

Ignoring his question, the chubby blonde woman leaned down and ruffled the dog's fur. "Good old Cornbread. Remember the day your father brought him home from the animal shelter? How old were we, twelve? From that very first day you were so in love with him. So what's he now, thirty-five years old?"

Mills shrugged. "Probably closer to forty. The oldest dog in the world. It was your Christmas present to me that year. 'Drink this, little Cornbread, and you'll live forever.' That's what you said. I remember.

"But really, Heather, what about Beatrice?"

She held up one finger as if to say, *Let's not talk about that.*

# MARTIAN HEART

## JOHN BARNES

Okay, botterogator, I agreed to this. Now you're supposed to guide me to tell my story to *inspire a new generation of Martians*. It is so weird that there *is* a new generation of Martians. So hit me with the questions, or whatever it is you do.

Do I want to be *consistent with previous public statements?*

Well, every time they ask me where I got all the money and got to be such a big turd in the toilet that is Mars, I always say Samantha was my inspiration. So let's check that box for tentatively consistent.

Thinking about Sam always gives me weird thoughts. And here are two: one, before her, I would not have known what either *tentatively* or *consistent* even meant. Two, in these pictures, Samantha looks younger than my grand-daughter is now.

So weird. She *was*.

We were in bed in our place under an old underpass in LA when the sweeps busted in, grabbed us up, and dragged us to the processing station. No good lying about whether we had family—they had our retinas and knew we were strays. Since I was seventeen and Sam was fifteen, they couldn't make any of our family pay for re-edj.

So they gave us fifteen minutes on the bench there to decide between twenty years in the forces, ten years in the glowies, or going out to Mars on this opposition and coming back on the third one after, in six and a half years.

They didn't tell you, and it wasn't well-known, that even people without the genetic defect suffered too much cardiac atrophy in that time to safely come back to Earth. The people that went to Mars didn't have family or friends to write back to, and the settlement program was so new it didn't seem strange that nobody knew a returned Martian.

"Crap," I said.

"Well, at least it's a future." Sam worried about the future a lot more than me. "If we enlist, there's no guarantee we'll be assigned together, unless we're

married, and they don't let you get married till you've been in for three. We'd
have to write each other letters—"

"Sam," I said, "I can't write to you or read your letters if you send me any.
You know that."

"They'd make you learn."

I tried not to shudder visibly; she'd get mad if I let her see that I didn't
really want to learn. "Also, that thing you always say about out of sight, that'd
happen. I'd have another girlfriend in like, not long. I just would. I know we're
all true love and everything but I would."

"The spirit is willing but the flesh is *more* willing." She always made those
little jokes that only she got. "Okay, then, no forces for us."

"Screw glowies," I said. Back in those days right after the baby nukes had
landed all over the place, the Decon Admin needed people to operate shovels,
hoes, and detectors. I quoted this one hook from our favorite music. "*Sterile
or dead or kids with three heads.*"

"And we *can* get married going to Mars," Sam said, "and then they *can't*
separate us. True love forever, baby." Sam always had all the ideas.

So, botterogator, check that box for *putting a priority on family/love.* I guess
since that new box popped up as soon as I said, *Sam always had all the ideas,*
that means you want more about that? Yeah, now it's bright and bouncing.
Okay, more about how she had all the ideas.

Really all the ideas I ever had were about eating, getting high, and scoring
ass. Hunh. Red light. Guess that wasn't what you wanted for the new generation
of Martians.

Sam was different. Everybody I knew was thinking about the next party or
at most the next week or the next boy or girl, but Sam thought about *everything.*
I know it's a stupid example, but once back in LA, she came into our squat and
found me fucking with the fusion box, just to mess with it. "That supplies all
our power for music, light, heat, net, and everything, and you can't fix it if you
break it, and it's not broke, so, Cap, what the fuck are you doing?"

See, I didn't even have ideas *that* good.

So a year later, there on the bench, our getting married was her having
another idea and me going along with it, which was always how things worked,
when they worked. Ten minutes later we registered as married.

Orientation for Mars was ten days. The first day they gave us shots, bleached
our tats into white blotches on our skin, and shaved our heads. They stuck us
in ugly dumb coveralls and didn't let us have real clothes that said anything,
which they said was so we wouldn't know who'd been what on Earth. I think
it was more so we all looked like transportees.

The second day, and every day after, they tried to pound some knowledge
into us. It was almost interesting. Sam was in with the people that could

read, and she seemed to know more than I did afterward. Maybe there was something to that reading stuff, or it might also have been that freaky, powerful memory of hers.

Once we were erased and oriented, they loaded Sam and me into a two-person cube on a dumpround to Mars. Minutes after the booster released us and we were ballistic, an older guy, some asshole, tried to come into our cube and tell us this was going to be his space all to himself, and I punched him hard enough to take him out; I don't think he had his balance for centrifigrav yet.

Two of his buds jumped in. I got into it with them too—I was hot, they were pissing me off, I wasn't figuring odds. Then some guys from the cubes around me came in with me, and together we beat the other side's ass bloody.

In the middle of the victory whooping, Sam shouted for quiet. She announced, "Everyone stays in their same quarters. Everyone draws their own rations. Everyone takes your turn, and *just* your turn, at the info screens. And nobody doesn't pay for protection or nothing."

One of the assholes, harmless now because I had at least ten good guys at my back, sneered, "Hey, little bitch. You running for Transportee Council?"

"Sure, why not?"

She won, too.

The Transportee Council stayed in charge for the whole trip. People ate and slept in peace, and no crazy-asses broke into the server array, which is what caused most lost dumprounds. They told us in orientation, but a lot of transportees didn't listen, or didn't understand, or just didn't believe that a dumpround didn't have any fuel to go back to Earth; a dumpround flew like a cannon ball, with just a few little jets to guide it in and out of the aerobrakes and steer it to the parachute field.

The same people who thought there was a steering wheel in the server array compartment, or maybe a reverse gear or just a big button that said TAKE US BACK TO EARTH, didn't know that the server array also ran the air-making machinery and the food dispensary and everything that kept people alive.

I'm sure we had as many idiots as any other dumpround, but we made it just fine; that was all Sam, who ran the TC and kept the TC running the dumpround. The eighty-eight people on International Mars Transport 2082/4/288 (which is what they called our dumpround; it was the 288th one fired off that April) all walked out of the dumpround on Mars carrying our complete, unlooted kits, and the militia that always stood by in case a dumpround landing involved hostages, arrests, or serious injuries didn't have a thing to do about us.

The five months in the dumpround were when I learned to read, and that has helped me so much—oh, hey, another box bumping up and down! Okay, botterogator, literacy as a positive value coming right up, all hot and ready for the new generation of Martians to suck inspiration from.

Hey, if you don't like irony, don't flash red lights at me, just edit it out. Yeah, authorize editing.

Anyway, with my info screen time, Sam made me do an hour of reading lessons for every two hours of games. Plus she coached me a lot. After a while the reading was more interesting than the games, and she was doing TC business so much of the time, and I didn't really have any other friends, so I just sat and worked on the reading. By the time we landed, I'd read four actual books, not just kid books I mean.

We came down on the parachute field at Olympic City, an overdignified name for what, in those long-ago days, was just two office buildings, a general store, and a nine-room hotel connected by pressurized tubes. The tiny pressurized facility was surrounded by a few thousand coffinsquats hooked into its pay air and power, and many thousand more running on their own fusion boxes. Olympica, to the south, was just a line of bluffs under a slope reaching way up into the sky.

It was the beginning of northern summer prospecting season. Sam towed me from lender to lender, coaching me on looking like a good bet to someone that would trust us with a share-deal on a prospecting gig. At the time I just thought rocks were, you know, rocks. No idea that some of them were ores, or that Mars was so poor in so many ores because it was dead tectonically.

So while she talked to bankers, private lenders, brokers, and plain old loan sharks, I dummied up and did my best to look like what she told them I was, a hard worker who would do what Sam told me. "Cap is quiet but he thinks, and we're a team."

She said that so often that after a while I believed it myself. Back at our coffinsquat every night, she'd make me do all the tutorials and read like crazy about rocks and ores. Now I can't remember how it was to not know something, like not being able to read, or recognize ore, or go through a balance sheet, or anything else I learned later.

Two days till we'd've gone into the labor pool and been shipped south to build roads and impoundments, and this CitiWells franchise broker, Hsieh Chi, called us back, and said we just felt lucky to him, and he had a quota to make, so what the hell.

Sam named our prospector gig the *Goodspeed* after something she'd read in a poem someplace, and we loaded up, got going, did what the software told us, and did okay that first summer around the North Pole, mostly.

*Goodspeed* was old and broke down continually, but Sam was a good directions-reader, and no matter how frustrating it got, I'd keep trying to do what she was reading to me—sometimes we both had to go to the dictionary,

I mean who knew what a flange, a fairing, or a flashing was?—and sooner or later we'd get it figured out and roll again.

Yeah, botterogator, you can check that box for persistence in the face of adversity. Back then I'd've said I was just too dumb to quit if Sam didn't, and Sam was too stubborn.

Up there in the months and months of midnight sun, we found ore, and learned more and more about telling ore from not-ore. The gig's hopper filled up, gradually, from surface rock finds. Toward the end of that summer—it seemed so weird that Martian summers were twice as long as on Earth even after we read up about why—we even found an old volcanic vent and turned up some peridot, agate, amethyst, jasper, and garnet, along with three real honest-to-god impact diamonds that made us feel brilliant. By the time we got back from the summer prospecting, we were able to pay off Hsieh Chi's shares, with enough left over to buy the gig and put new treads on it. We could spare a little to rehab the cabin too; *Goodspeed* went from our dumpy old gig to our home, I guess. At least in Sam's mind. I wasn't so sure that home meant a lot to me.

Botterogator if you want me to inspire the new generation of Martians, you have to let me tell the truth. Sam cared about having a home, I didn't. You can flash your damn red light. It's true.

Anyway, while the fitters rebuilt *Goodspeed*, we stayed in a rented cabinsquat, sleeping in, reading, and eating food we didn't cook. We soaked in the hot tub at the Riebecker Olympic every single day—the only way Sam got warm. Up north, she had thought she was cold all the time because we were always working, she was small, and she just couldn't keep weight on no matter how much she ate, but even loafing around Olympic City, where the most vigorous thing we did was nap in the artificial sun room, or maybe lift a heavy spoon, she still didn't warm up.

We worried that she might have pneumonia or TB or something she'd brought from Earth, but the diagnostic machines found nothing unusual except being out of shape. But Sam had been doing so much hard physical work, her biceps and abs were like rocks, she was *strong*. So we gave up on the diagnosis machines, because that made no sense.

Nowadays everyone knows about Martian heart, but back then nobody knew that hearts atrophy and deposit more plaque in lower gravity, as the circulation slows down and the calcium that should be depositing into bones accumulates in the blood. Let alone that maybe a third of the human race have genes that make it happen so fast.

At the time, with no cases identified, it wasn't even a research subject; so many people got sick and died in the first couple decades of settlement, often in their first Martian year, and to the diagnostic machines it was all a job, ho hum, another day, another skinny nineteen-year-old dead of a heart attack. Besides, *all* the transportees, not just the ones that died, ate so much carb-and-fat food, because it was cheap. Why *wouldn't* there be more heart attacks? There were always more transportees coming, so put up another site about healthful eating for Mars, and find something else to worry about.

Checking the diagnosis machine was everything we could afford to do, anyway, but it seemed like only a small, annoying worry. After all, we'd done well, bought our own gig, were better geared up, knew more what we were doing. We set out with pretty high hopes.

*Goodspeed* was kind of a dumb name for a prospector's gig. At best it could make maybe forty km/hr, which is not what you call roaring fast. Antarctic summer prospecting started with a long, dull drive down to Promethei Lingula, driving south out of northern autumn and into southern spring. The Interpolar Highway in those days was a gig track weaving southward across the shield from Olympic City to the Great Marineris Bridge. There was about hundred km of pavement, sort of, before and after the bridge, and then another gig track angling southeast to wrap around Hellas, where a lot of surface prospectors liked to work, and there was a fair bit of seasonal construction to be done on the city they were building in the western wall.

But we were going far south of Hellas. I asked Sam about that. "If you're cold all the time, why are we going all the way to the edge of the south polar cap? I mean, wouldn't it be nicer to maybe work the Bouches du Marineris or someplace near the equator, where you could stay a little warmer?"

"Cap, what's the temperature in here, in the gig cabin?"

"Twenty-two C," I said, "do you feel cold?"

"Yeah, I do, and that's my point," she said. I reached to adjust the temperature, and she stopped me. "What I mean is, that's room temperature, babe, and it's the same temperature it is in my suit, and in the fingers and toes of my suit, and everywhere. The cold isn't outside, and it doesn't matter whether it's the temperature of a warm day on Earth or there's $CO_2$ snow falling, the cold's in here, in me, ever since we came to Mars."

The drive was around ten-thousand km as the road ran, but mostly it was pleasant, just making sure the gig stayed on the trail as we rolled past the huge volcanoes, the stunning view of Marineris from that hundred-mile-long bridge, and then all that ridge and peak country down south.

Mostly Sam slept while I drove. Often I rested a hand on her neck or forehead as she dozed in the co-driver's chair. Sometimes she shivered; I wondered if it was a long-running flu. I made her put on a mask and get extra oxygen, and that helped, but every few weeks I had to up her oxygen mix again.

All the way down I practiced pronouncing Promethei Lingula, especially after we rounded Hellas, because Sam looked a little sicker every week, and I was so afraid she'd need help and I wouldn't be able to make a distress call.

Sam figured Promethei Lingula was too far for most people—they'd rather pick through Hellas's or Argyre's crater walls, looking for chunks of something worthwhile thrown up from deep underground in those impacts, and of course the real gamblers always wanted to work Hellas because one big Hellas Diamond was five years' income.

Sam already knew what it would take me fifteen marsyears to learn: she believed in making a good bet that nobody else was making. Her idea was that a shallow valley like the Promethei Lingula in the Antarctic highlands might have more stuff swept down by the glaciers, and maybe even some of the kinds of exposed veins that really old mountains had on Earth.

As for what went wrong, well, nothing except our luck; nowadays I own three big veins down there. No, botterogator, I don't feel like telling you a damned thing about what I own, you're authorized to just look all that up. I don't see that owning stuff is inspiring. I want to talk about Sam.

We didn't find any veins, or much of anything else, that first southern summer. And meanwhile Sam's health deteriorated.

By the time we were into Promethei Lingula, I was fixing most meals and doing almost all the maintenance. After the first weeks I did all the exosuit work, because her suit couldn't seem to keep her warm, even on hundred percent oxygen. She wore gloves and extra socks even inside. She didn't move much, but her mind was as good as ever, and with her writing the search patterns and me going out and grabbing the rocks, we could still've been okay.

Except we needed to be as lucky as we'd been up in Boreas, and we just weren't.

Look here, botterogator, you can't make me say luck had nothing to do with it. Luck always has a shitload to do with it. Keep this quibbling up and just see if I inspire *any* new Martians.

Sometimes there'd be a whole day when there wasn't a rock that was worth tossing in the hopper, or I'd cover a hundred km of nothing but common basalts and granites. Sam thought her poor concentration made her write bad search patterns, but it wasn't that; it was plain bad luck.

Autumn came, and with it some dust storms and a sun that spiraled closer to the horizon every day, so that everything was dimmer. It was time to head north; we could sell the load, such as it was, at the depot at Hellas, but by the time we got to the Bouches de Marineris, it wouldn't cover more than a few weeks of prospecting. We might have to mortgage again; Hsieh Chi, unfortunately, was in the Vikingsburg pen for embezzling. "Maybe we could hustle someone, like we did him."

"Maybe *I* could, babe," Sam said. "You know the business a lot better, but you're still nobody's sales guy, Cap. We've got food enough for another four months out here, and we still have credit because we're working and we haven't had to report our hold weight. Lots of gigs stay out for extra time—some even overwinter—and nobody can tell whether that's because they're way behind like us, or they've found a major vein and they're exploiting it. So we can head back north, use up two months of supplies to get there, buy about a month of supplies with the cargo, go on short term credit only, and try to get lucky in one month. Or we can stay here right till we have just enough food to run for the Hellas depot, put in four months, and have four times the chance. If it don't work *Goodspeed*'ll be just as lost either way."

"It's going to get dark and cold," I pointed out. "Very dark and cold. And you're tired and cold all the time now."

"Dark and cold *outside the cabin*," she said. Her face had the stubborn set that meant this was going to be useless. "And maybe the dark'll make me eat more. All the perpetual daylight, maybe that's what's screwing my system up. We'll try the Bouches du Marineris next time, maybe those nice regular equatorial days'll get my internal clock working again. But for right now, let's stay here. Sure, it'll get darker, and the storms can get bad—"

"Bad as in we could get buried, pierced by a rock on the wind, maybe even flipped if the wind gets in under the hull," I pointed out. "Bad as in us and the sensors can only see what the spotlights can light. There's a reason why prospecting is a summer job."

She was quiet about that for so long I thought a miracle had happened and I'd won an argument.

Then she said, "Cap, I like it here in *Goodspeed*. It's home. It's ours. I know I'm sick, and all I can do these days is sleep, but I don't want to go to some hospital and have you only visit on your days off from a labor crew. *Goodspeed* is ours and I want to live here and try to keep it."

So I said yes.

For a while things got better. The first fall storms were water snow, not $CO_2$. I watched the weather reports and we were always buttoned up tight for every storm, screens out and treads sealed against the fine dust. In those brief weeks between midnight sun and endless night, when the sun rises and sets daily in the Promethei Lingula, the thin coat of snow and frost actually made the darker rocks stand out on the surface, and there were more good ones to find, too.

Sam was cold all the time; sometimes she'd cry with just wanting to be warm. She'd eat, when I stood over her and made her, but she had no appetite. I also knew how she thought: Food was the bottleneck. A fusion box supplied centuries of power to move, to compress and process the Martian air into breathability, to extract and purify water. But we couldn't grow food, and unlike spare parts or medical care we might need now and then, we needed food every day, so food would be the thing we ran out of first. (Except maybe luck, and we were already out of that). Since she didn't want the food anyway, she thought if she didn't eat we could stay out and give our luck more of a chance to turn.

The sun set for good; so far south, Phobos was below the horizon; cloud cover settled in to block the stars. It was darker than anywhere I'd ever been. We stayed.

There was more ore in the hold but not enough more. Still no vein. We had a little luck at the mouth of one dry wash with a couple tons of ore in small chunks, but it played out in less than three weeks.

Next place that looked at all worth trying was 140 km south, almost at the edge of the permanent cap, crazy and scary to try, but what the hell, everything about this was crazy and scary.

The sky had cleared for the first time in weeks when we arrived. With just a little $CO_2$ frost, it was easy to find rocks—the hot lights zapped the dry ice right off them. I found one nice big chunk of wolframite, the size of an old trunk, right off the bat, and then two smaller ones; somewhere up the glacial slopes from here, there was a vein, perhaps not under permanent ice. I started the analytic program mapping slopes and finds, and went out in the suit to see if I could find and mark more rocks.

Markeb, which I'd learned to pick out of the bunched triangles of the constellation Vela, was just about dead overhead; it's the south pole star on Mars. It had been a while since I'd seen the stars, and I'd learned more about what I was looking at. I picked out the Coal Sack, the Southern Cross, and the Magellanic Clouds easily, though honestly, on a clear night at the Martian south pole, that's like being able to find an elephant in a bathtub.

I went inside; the analysis program was saying that probably the wolframite had come from way up under the glacier, so no luck there, but also that there might be a fair amount of it lying out here in the alluvial fan, so at least we'd pick up something here. I stood up from the terminal; I'd fix dinner, then wake Sam, feed her, and tell her the semi-good news.

When I came in with the tray, Sam was curled up, shivering and crying. I made her eat all her soup and bread, and plugged her in to breathe straight body-temperature oxygen. When she was feeling better, or at least saying she was, I took her up into the bubble to look at the stars with the lights off. She seemed to enjoy that, especially that I could point to things and show them to her, because it meant I'd been studying and learning.

Yeah, botterogator, reinforce that learning leads to success. Sam'd like that.

"Cap," she said, "This is the worst it's been, babe. I don't think there's anything on Mars that can fix me. I just keep getting colder and weaker. I'm so sorry—"

"I'm starting for Hellas as soon as we get you wrapped up and have pure oxygen going into you in the bed. I'll drive as long as I can safely, then—"

"It won't make any difference. You'll never get me there, not alive," she said. "Babe, the onboard diagnostic kit isn't perfect but it's good enough to show I've got the heart of a ninety-year-old cardiac patient. And all the indicators have gotten worse in just the last hundred hours or so. Whatever I've got, it's killing me." She reached out and stroked my tear-soaked face. "Poor Cap. Make me two promises."

"I'll love you forever."

"I know. I don't need you to promise that. First promise, no matter where you end up, or doing what, you *learn*. Study whatever you can study, acquire whatever you can acquire, feed your mind, babe. That's the most important."

I nodded. I was crying pretty hard.

"The other one is kind of weird . . . well, it's silly."

"If it's for you, I'll do it. I promise."

She gasped, trying to pull in more oxygen than her lungs could hold. Her eyes were flowing too. "I'm scared to be buried out in the cold and the dark, and I can't *stand* the idea of freezing solid. So . . . don't bury me. Cremate me. I want to be *warm*."

"But you can't cremate a person on Mars," I protested. "There's not enough air to support a fire, and—"

"You promised," she said, and died.

I spent the next hour doing everything the first aid program said to do. When she was cold and stiff, I knew it had really happened.

I didn't care about *Goodspeed* anymore. I'd sell it at Hellas depot, buy passage to some city where I could work, start over. I didn't want to be in our home for weeks with Sam's body, but I didn't have the money to call in a mission to retrieve her, and anyway they'd just do the most economical thing—bury her right here, practically at the South Pole, in the icy night.

I curled up in my bunk and just cried for hours, then let myself fall asleep. That just made it worse; now that she was past rigor mortis she was soft to the touch, more like herself, and I couldn't stand to store her in the cold, either, not after what I had promised. I washed her, brushed her hair, put her in a body bag, and set her in one of the dry storage compartments with the door closed; maybe I'd think of something before she started to smell.

Driving north, I don't think I really wanted to live, myself. I stayed up too long, ate and drank too little, just wanting the journey to be over with. I remember I drove right through at least one bad storm at peak speed, more than enough to shatter a tread on a stone or to go into a sudden crevasse or destroy myself in all kinds of ways. For days in a row, in that endless black darkness, I woke up in the driver's chair after having fallen asleep while the deadman stopped the gig.

I didn't care. I wanted out of the dark.

About the fifth day, *Goodspeed*'s forward left steering tread went off a drop-off of three meters or so. The gig flipped over forward to the left, crashing onto its back. Force of habit had me strapped into the seat, and wearing my suit, the two things that the manuals the insurance company said were what you had to be doing any time the gig was moving if you didn't want to void your policy. Sam had made a big deal about that, too.

So after rolling, *Goodspeed* came to a stop on its back, and all the lights went out. When I finished screaming with rage and disappointment and everything else, there was still enough air (though I could feel it leaking) for me to be conscious.

I put on my helmet and turned on the headlamp.

I had a full capacitor charge on the suit, but *Goodspeed*'s fusion box had shut down. That meant seventeen hours of being alive unless I could replace it with another fusion box, but both the compartment where the two spare fusion boxes were stored, and the repair access to replace them, were on the top rear surface of the gig. I climbed outside, wincing at letting the last of the cabin air out, and poked around. The gig was resting on exactly the hatches I would have needed to open.

Seventeen—well, sixteen, now—hours. And one big promise to keep.

The air extractors on the gig had been running, as they always did, right up till the accident; the tanks were full of liquid oxygen. I could transfer it to my suit through the emergency valving, live for some days that way. There were enough suit rations to make it a real race between starvation and suffocation. The suit radio wasn't going to reach anywhere that could do me any good; for long distance it depended on a relay through the gig, and the relay's antenna was under the overturned gig.

Sam was dead. *Goodspeed* was dead. And for every practical purpose, so was I.

Neither *Goodspeed* nor I really needed that oxygen anymore, *but Sam does*, I realized. I could at least shift the tanks around, and I had the mining charges we used for breaking up big rocks.

I carried Sam's body into the oxygen storage, set her between two of the tanks, and hugged the body bag one more time. I don't know if I was afraid she'd look awful, or afraid she would look alive and asleep, but I was afraid to unzip the bag.

I set the timer on a mining charge, put that on top of her, and piled the rest of the charges on top. My little pile of bombs filled most of the space between the two oxygen tanks. Then I wrestled four more tanks to lie on the heap crosswise and stacked flammable stuff from the kitchen like flour, sugar, cornmeal, and jugs of cooking oil on top of those, to make sure the fire burned long and hot enough.

My watch said I still had five minutes till the timer went off.

I still don't know why I left the gig. I'd been planning to die there, cremated with Sam, but maybe I just wanted to see if I did the job right or something—as if I could try again, perhaps, if it didn't work? Whatever the reason, I bounded away to what seemed like a reasonable distance.

I looked up; the stars were out. I wept so hard I feared I would miss seeing them in the blur. They were so beautiful, and it had been so long.

Twenty kilograms of high explosive was enough energy to shatter all the LOX tanks and heat all the oxygen white hot. Organic stuff doesn't just burn in white-hot oxygen; it explodes and vaporizes, and besides fifty kilograms of Sam, I'd loaded in a good six hundred kilograms of other organics.

I figured all that out a long time later. In the first quarter second after the mining charge went off, things were happening pretty fast. A big piece of the observation bubble—smooth enough not to cut my suit and kill me, but hard enough to send me a couple meters into the air and backward by a good thirty meters—slapped me over and sent me rolling down the back side of the ridge on which I sat, smashed up badly and unconscious, but alive.

I think I dreamed about Sam, as I gradually came back to consciousness.

Now, look here, botterogator, of course I'd like to be able, for the sake of the new generation of Martians, to tell you I dreamed about her giving me earnest how-to-succeed advice, and that I made a vow there in dreamland to succeed and be worthy of her and all that. But in fact it was mostly just dreams of holding her and being held, and about laughing together. Sorry if that's not on the list.

The day came when I woke up and realized I'd seen the medic before. Not long after that I stayed awake long enough to say "hello." Eventually I learned that a survey satellite had picked up the exploding gig, and shot pictures because that bright light was unusual. An AI identified a shape in the dust as a human body lying outside, and dispatched an autorescue—a rocket with a people-grabbing arm. The autorescue flew out of Olympic City's launch pad on a ballistic trajectory, landed not far from me, crept over to my not-yet-out-of-air, not-yet-frozen body, grabbed me with a mechanical arm, and stuffed me into its hold. It took off again, flew to the hospital, and handed me over to the doctor.

Total cost of one autorescue mission, and two weeks in a human-contact hospital—which the insurance company refused to cover because I'd deliberately blown up the gig—was maybe twenty successful prospecting runs' worth. So as soon as I could move, they indentured me and, since I was in no shape to do grunt-and-strain stuff for a while, they found a little prospector's supply company that wanted a human manager for an office at the Hellas depot. I learned the job—it wasn't hard—and grew with the company, eventually as Mars's first indentured CEO.

I took other jobs, bookkeeping, supervising, cartography, anything where I could earn wages with which to pay off the indenture faster, especially jobs I could do online in my nominal hours off. At every job, because I'd promised Sam, I learned as much as I could. Eventually, a few days before my forty-third birthday, I paid off the indenture, quit all those jobs, and went into business for myself.

By that time I knew how the money moved, and for what, in practically every significant business on Mars. I'd had a lot of time to plan and think, too.

So that was it. I kept my word—oh, all right, botterogator, let's check that box too. Keeping promises is important to success. After all, here I am.

Sixty-two earthyears later, I know, because everyone does, that a drug that costs almost nothing, which everyone takes now, could have kept Sam alive. A little money a year, if anyone'd known, and Sam and me could've been celebrating anniversaries for decades, and we'd've been richer, with Sam's brains on the job too. And botterogator, you'd be talking to her, and probably learning more, too.

Or is that what I think now?

Remembering Sam, over the years, I've thought of five hundred things I could have done instead of what I did, and maybe I'd have succeeded as much with those too.

But the main question I think about is only—did she *mean* it? Did she see something in me that would make my bad start work out as well as it did? Was she just an idealistic smart girl playing house with the most cooperative boy she could find? Would she have wanted me to marry again and have children, did she intend me to get rich?

Every so often I regret that I didn't really fulfill that second promise, an irony I can appreciate now: she feared the icy grave, but since she burned to mostly water and carbon dioxide, on Mars she became mostly snow. And molecules are so small, and distribute so evenly, that whenever the snow falls, I know there's a little of her in it, sticking to my suit, piling on my helmet, coating me as I stand in the quiet and watch it come down.

Did she dream me into existence? I kept my promises, and they made me who I am . . . and was that what she wanted? If I am only the accidental whim of a smart teenage girl with romantic notions, what would I have been without the whim, the notions, or Sam?

Tell you what, botterogator, and you pass this on to the new generation of Martians: it's funny how one little promise, to someone or something a bit better than yourself, can turn into something as real as Samantha City, whose lights at night fill the crater that spreads out before me from my balcony all the way to the horizon.

Nowadays I have to walk for an hour, in the other direction out beyond the crater wall, till the false dawn of the city lights is gone, and I can walk till dawn or hunger turns me homeward again.

Botterogator, you can turn off the damn stupid flashing lights. That's all you're getting out of me. I'm going for a walk; it's snowing.

# PUG

## THEODORA GOSS

⸻✦⸻

"Pug is flat, like most animals in fiction. He is once represented as
straying into a rosebed in a cardboard kind of way, but that is all . . . "
                          —E.M. Forster, *Aspects of the Novel*

You don't know how lonely I was, until I met Pug.

In summer, tourists come to Rosings. The coaches are filled with them.
They want to see where Roger de Bourgh murdered Lady Alice, or where
Lady Alice's grand-niece Matilda de Bourgh hid King Charles, in the cellar
behind a cask of port, from the Roundheads. There has always been a rumor
that her son, from her hasty marriage to Walter d'Arcy, resembled the king
more than his father. The de Bourghs have never been known for acting with
sober propriety. Miss Jenkinson relishes the details. "And here," she says, "you
will see the bloodstains where Lady Alice fell. This floor has been polished
every day for a hundred years, but those stains have never come out!" And
indeed there are, just there, discolorations in the wood. Whether they are the
bloodstains of Lady Alice, I can't tell you.

When the tourists come, I go to my room, in the modern wing of the
house where even Miss Jenkinson's ingenuity will find no bloodstains, or out
into the garden. If, by chance, they happen upon me, I admire the roses, or
the fountain with its spitting triton, and they assume I am one of them. Of
course, if Miss Jenkinson sees me, she scolds me. "Miss Anne, what will your
mother think! Outside on a day like this, and without a shawl." With the fog
rolling over the garden. We are in a valley, at Rosings. We are almost always
in a sea of fog.

I could hear them that day, the tourists. In the fog, their voices seemed to
come from far away, and then suddenly from just beside me, so I ducked into
the maze. It is not a real maze: for that, the tourists must go to Allingham
or Trenton. It is only a series of paths between the courtyard, with its triton
perpetually spitting water, while stone fish leap around him in rococo

profusion, and the rose garden. But the paths are edged with privet that has grown higher than I, at any rate, can see. I have called that place the maze since I was a child. When I am in the maze, I can pretend, for a moment, that I am somewhere else.

So there I was, among the privets, and there he was, sitting on his haunches, panting with his pink tongue hanging out. Pug.

Of course I did not learn his name until later, when he showed me the door. The door: inconsistent, irritating, never there when you want it. And at the best of times, difficult to summon, like a recalcitrant housemaid.

But there was Pug. I assumed he had come from Huntsford, from the parsonage or one of the tradesmen's houses. He was so obviously cared for, so confident as he sat there, so complacent, even fat. And he had a quality that made him particularly attractive. When he looked at you with his brown eyes, and panted with his pink tongue hanging out, he looked as though he were smiling.

"Here, doggie," I said. He came to me and licked my hand. I knew, of course, that Mother would never allow it. Not for me, not in, as she called it, my "condition." But as I said, I was lonely. "Come on, then." And he followed me, through the courtyard, into the kitchen garden with its cabbages and turnips, and through the kitchen door.

I had no friends at Rosings, but Cook disliked Miss Jenkinson, and the enemy of my enemy was at least my provisional ally. I knew she would give me a scrap of something for Pug. He gobbled a bowl of bread and milk, and looked up at me again with that smile of his.

"If Lady Catherine finds him in your room, there will be I don't know what to pay," Cook said, wiping her hands on her apron.

"Mother never comes into my room," I said.

"Well, I'll tell Susan to hold her tongue. Only yesterday I said to her, you're here to clean the bedrooms, not to talk. Someday that tongue of yours is going to fall off from all the talking you do. And won't your husband be grateful!"

"All right, Cook," I said. "I'll take him up, and could you have Susan bring me a box with wood shavings, just in case, you know."

"Certainly, Miss." She patted Pug on the head. "You're a friendly one, aren't you? I do like dogs. They're dirty creatures, but they make a house more friendly."

And that's how Pug came to Rosings. I carried him, as quietly as I could, past the gallery. "Every night," Miss Jenkinson was saying, "Sir Fitzwilliam d'Arcy walks down the length of this hall and stands before the portrait of his brother, Jonathan d'Arcy, who chopped off his head with an axe right there in the courtyard and married his wife, Lady Margaret de Bourgh. Visitors who have seen him say that he carries his severed head in his arms." I heard gasps, and a "Well, I never!" The de Bourghs and the d'Arcys. We have been marrying and killing each other since the Conquest.

Later, when I had learned something of how the door works, I discussed it with the Miss Martins.

"Mary had a thought," said Eliza. "She did want to tell you, although I told her, Miss, that you might not like hearing it."

"Please call me Anne," I said. "We share a secret, the three of us—and Pug. So we should have no distinctions between us. We know about the door. Surely that should make us friends."

We were sitting in the Martins' garden, at Abbey-Mill Farm. I could smell the roses that were blooming in the hedge, and the cows on the other side of the hedge, in the pasture. Eliza had folded her apron on the grass beside her. She was fair and freckled, although she used Gower twice a day. She looked what she was, the perfect English farm girl, with sunlit hair and a placid disposition. Mary was still wearing her apron, as though about to go in and finish her cleaning, but she had woven herself a crown of white clover. She was darker than her sister, with a liveliness, like a gypsy girl from Sir Walter Scott. An inquisitiveness. She had been the scholar, and regretted leaving school.

"Well," said Mary, "this is what I've been thinking, Miss—Anne. Eliza and me, we're the ones to whom nothing happens. There's Robert marrying Harriet, and all the high and mighty folks of Highbury marrying among themselves, and even the servants seem to have their doings. But us—we just milk the cows, and clean the house with Mother, and take care of the garden, day after day, no different. And begging your pardon, Anne, but nothing happens to you either. You read and you go out riding in your carriage, that's all. And what could happen to Pug?" Who was lying contentedly on the grass beside us. At Abbey-Mill Farm, the sun almost always shone. I was glad to escape, for a while, the fogs of Rosings.

"You're right," I said. "Nothing ever does happen to me. I don't think anything ever will."

"Well then," said Eliza, "here's what Mary thinks. She thinks the door is for us. That it was put there just so we could find each other. Do you think that could be true?"

I put a clover flower on Pug's nose, and he stared at me reproachfully before shaking his head so that it fell onto the grass. "We are told there is providence in the fall of a sparrow. Why not in the opening of a door?"

"That's lovely, Miss," said Eliza. "Just like Mr. Elton in church."

When I was a child, I was not allowed to have toys. I slept on a bare bed, in a bare room. Those were the days of Dr. Templeton. He believed in strengthening. If I could be strengthened, I would no longer be sick or small. So there were cold baths, and porridge for breakfast, and nothing but toast for tea. Then came Dr. Bransby, who believed in supporting. If my constitution could be supported, then I would be well. Those were the days of baths so hot that I turned as red as a lobster, fires in July and draperies to keep out drafts, and rare roast beef. I have been on a diet of mashed turnips, I have been to Bath more times than I remember, I have even, once, been bled. Nothing has ever helped. I have always been sick and small. When I walk up stairs, I am always out of breath; when I look in the mirror, there are always blue circles under my eyes, blue veins running over my forehead. I always remind myself of a corpse.

When I was a child, I was not allowed to have friends. Other children, "young horrors," as Mother called them, would be too softening, said Dr. Templeton, too trying, said Dr. Bransby. One day, so lonely that I could have cried, I wandered through the corridors, almost losing myself, and discovered the library. ("Over a thousand volumes," said Miss Jenkinson. "The gilding on the books alone is worth more than a thousand pounds.") Dr. Templeton's regimen had confined me to the schoolroom, but Dr. Templeton had been summoned to Windsor Castle, to attend the King himself. And Dr. Bransby, whose carriage was expected that afternoon, had not yet arrived. Miss Jenkinson, thinking I was asleep, had put her feet up and fallen asleep with a handkerchief over her face. I could hear her snoring.

I tiptoed, frightened, down the endless corridors of Rosings, with de Bourghs and d'Arcys frowning at me from the walls. At the end of one corridor was an archway. I walked through it and saw shelves of books going up to heaven. ("The fresco on the ceiling was painted by an Italian, Antonio Vecci," said Miss Jenkinson. "Although unlikely to appeal to our modern tastes, in his day the painting, of classical gods disporting themselves in an undignified manner, was considered rather fine. If you look in the corner there, up to the right, you'll see where the painting was left unfinished when Vecci eloped with Philomena de Bourgh. He was later shot in the back by Sir Reginald.")

Will you laugh if I tell you that the first book I read, other than my Bible and the *Parent's Assistant*, which Miss Jenkinson appreciated for its edifying morals, was Aristotle's *Metaphysics*? How little I understood of it then! How little I understand still, even after discussing it with Dr. Galt. But Dr. Galt seldom has time for long discussions.

My cousin Fitz teased me about my serious reading matter. "You don't read like a girl, Anne," he said, "but as if you're prepping for Oxford. Look, I brought you some grapes from the conservatory." I was not allowed to eat fruit, which Dr. Bransby said was not sufficiently supportive. But how tired

I was of soft-boiled eggs and beef tea! "If you won't tell, I'll teach you a little Latin."

From his window, Fitz could see when Dr. Bransby walked to the Parsonage, where he could smoke his pipe without Mother finding out. She did not approve of tobacco. When Dr. Bransby was out of sight, Fitz would say, "Come on, Anne, let's go down to the maze!" We would laugh at the triton, with his absurdly distended cheeks, and crouch among the rosebushes, where no one could see us, feeling the pleasure of being unsupervised and completely hidden.

Of course, I knew why Fitz came, or had to come. Those portraits of the de Bourghs and d'Arcys—they haunted us both like ghosts.

Once, when I was fifteen, I said to him, "I'll never be a beauty, will I?"

"You're distinctive in your own way, Anne," he said.

That wounded me, although he had meant it as a compliment. Was woman ever wooed thus? No, I don't think so either.

Finally, Dr. Galt said, "It's your heart, Miss de Bourgh, and there's nothing to be done about it. You must live as normally as you can." Thank goodness for Dr. Galt.

It was Pug who showed me the door.

"Take that dog out of the drawing room at once!" said Mother. "Can't you see that he's shedding on the cushions? Really, Miss Jenkinson."

She would never, of course, say it directly to me. I was the delicate one, the last of the de Bourghs, who must be coddled and tortured into health. Into marrying and producing an heir. She steadfastly treated Pug as Miss Jenkinson's dog, although every night that he was at Rosings, he slept in my bed, curled beside me, snorting in his sleep. She would never give in to something as vulgar as fact.

I took Pug into the garden. It had rained the night before. I had seen the lightning from my bedroom window, flashing over the avenue of lime trees, over the park where the tourists fed the deer. The triton looked wet and somehow glum. The privets were bent awry, as though they had been engaged in a mad dance. The path through the rose garden was covered with petals, like wet rags. Pug ran over them, toward the lime alley. And suddenly, he was no longer there.

"At first," said Eliza. "I couldn't see the door at all. But now I always see it, that—shiver, when it opens. Mary could always see it better than I can. And she seems to be able to—call it, sometimes."

"I don't know how I do it," said Mary. "I just call, and it comes. But not always. Don't worry, Miss, you'll see it better after a while. And you've got Pug. He seems to be able to smell it, almost. As soon as the door opens, he goes right to it."

That first time, the door opened into another garden. It surrounded a house, modern, not particularly attractive, smaller than Rosings. I wandered around the garden, curious and confused, not certain where I was or what I should do. Finally, I looked in through a window. A woman, stately, placid, as old as Mother but without her appearance of constant activity, sat on a sofa. "Why, Pug," she said, "wherever have you been?" Pug jumped up on the sofa and sat beside her, like a cushion.

"The strangest thing," said Eliza, "is that when you go through the door to another place—or time—no one seems to notice that you're there. And when you come back, no one seems to notice that you were gone. It's like being a ghost."

"Do you think it's wrong for us to go through it, Miss?" asked Mary. "Perhaps it's a devilish device, as Mr. Elton would say, designed to tempt us." She seemed genuinely distressed. I put my hand on hers.

"Don't be silly," said Eliza. "Miss de Bourgh has already told us that it can be explained naturally, like that machine at the Royal Society. Like lightning. Surely nothing in nature is of the Devil. Surely everything in nature has been created by God. And think of what finding the door has done for us! We've been to London, to Bath. Do you think the Miss Martins of Abbey-Mill Farm would have been able to travel to those places? And thank you again, Miss," she nodded to me, "for showing us around Pemberley. It was a kindness my sister and I will never forget."

"Do you believe, Miss, that the door is created by God?" asked Mary.

"I don't know," I said. "But you said, once, that we are the people to whom nothing happens. I wonder if, perhaps, there is a provision for us. I know this sounds silly, but—a provision for us specifically, for the people to whom nothing happens. Perhaps the door has been sent—to allow us to communicate with one other, so that we will not be, you know, lonely."

"But then why only the three of us—and Pug?" asked Mary. "Surely we aren't the only ones to whom nothing happens."

"Don't forget Mrs. Churchill," said Eliza. "Although she did not encourage the acquaintance, after that first meeting in Bath. I think, to her, the Miss Martins of Abbey-Mill Farm were of no consequence. She was not as condescending as you are, Miss. And we have not seen her now for more than a year."

"But that shows there are others," I said. "That we have not found them does not mean they do not exist. Perhaps it's time we started looking for them."

Here are the things my mother wanted me to have. Beauty, in which I failed her completely. Come to the mirror, let us look at my face, so pale, so insignificant. Wit, ditto. Once, when I was a child, Fitz's sister Georgie came to visit. She said to me, after an afternoon during which we were supposed to be playing, "I would like you better, Anne, if you weren't so dull." Accomplishments, of course, I could not have. Dr. Templeton and Dr. Bransby agreed: I must not hold a pencil or paintbrush, must not practice the pianoforte, must not under any circumstances learn to dance. I must not exert myself in any way. Dr. Galt said, "What a pair of quacks." But by then it was too late; I was neither beautiful, nor witty, nor accomplished. I had nothing to recommend me except a fortune.

And of course, Mother wanted me to marry Fitz.

Fitz said to me once, as we were walking in the garden, "Anne, we can talk to each other, can't we? I mean, we used to be friends when we were children."

He looked, as he always looked, sad and uneasy. I think he had read too much German philosophy. Once he had told me that at Oxford he had lost his faith in both humanity and God.

"There's no reason we can't be friends now," I said.

"Then—would you care terribly if we didn't marry?"

I put my arm through his. "Oh, Fitz. Marry that girl, the one who came with the Lucases, who plays the piano so badly." She did play badly, I was jealous enough to say that. I cared, of course. It was difficult not to love Fitz. But I remembered what Dr. Galt had told me.

"It's your heart, my girl. It's like a lake in there, sloshing around. I wish it had a good, steady beat like a piston. Someday, we'll be able to replace the human heart with a machine."

"That doesn't sound at all nice," I said. "How can a machine love?"

There were other things I asked him: "Am I going to die?"

"We're all going to die. And if you're careful, you won't die any sooner than most. But that means no marrying. You must learn to content yourself with the pleasures of an old maid. The first child you have—then you *will* die, Anne. And perhaps the child will die as well. Do you understand?"

"If Mother were here, she would dismiss you at once. Do you know I've been destined to marry my cousin since I was born? It's a sort of dynastic alliance."

Dr. Galt laughed. "It's time the de Bourghs and the d'Arcys had some new blood. You've been marrying each other too long." Then he shook his finger at me. "But I'm serious, Anne. You can live long and well, but you must find another way."

And: "What if there were a door that could take me, in an instant, between two places that are far away from each other, perhaps even far away in time—into the past for instance, or even the future, when Napoleon will be defeated."

"As we all hope he will be!"

"If there were such a door, how would it work?"

"So you've been following my advice."

He had told me, "Most of the women I know waste their lives embroidering on silk and reading French novels. You should hear my own daughters, talking about the regiment! It's soldiers, soldiers all day long. But you, Anne, with your natural ability and the library here at Rosings, can develop the intellect that God gave you. Read philosophy, read history. Learn Greek. There is nothing in the field of scholarship that you can't accomplish."

"Despite my broken heart?"

"Because of your broken heart."

"Doors that transport you through space and time are not my specialty," he answered. "But at a meeting of the Royal Society I once saw a mechanical apparatus with two arms, which resembled a headless doll. A spark of electricity jumped from one arm to the other, instantaneously, without seeming to have passed through the space between. Later that day, at a lecture attended by the King, I heard a philosopher say that we are all composed of energy. Why should we not, with a mechanical device, or a door as you called it, pass from one place to another, like that spark?"

And he smiled at me, as though I were a clever child. That is what we see in the mirror, a sick child, although I am almost twenty.

"Keep reading, Anne. Keep exercising your mind as much as you can. If you can't have the life that other women have, remember you can still have a life that is fulfilling, even in some ways superior to theirs."

This is what I told Fitz: "Marry her with my blessing. And if you accomplish nothing else, you will have made Mother thoroughly angry. That in itself will be an accomplishment, I think. Life at Rosings will be so much more interesting for a while."

He looked down at the path. "I don't even know if we could be happy together. But I can't help loving her. Oh, I'm a fool!" My introspective, morose cousin. Would he make a good husband for anyone? He would, I thought, have made a good husband for me.

"You must get out into the sun more often, Anne," he said. "You look like a fish that has lived in a cave for a hundred years." I was startled and gratified that he had noticed.

"What sun?" I said. "The sun never shines at Rosings."

Once, when I was in London with Mother, I saw a blind man being led by a dog. A black dog, a labrador mostly, and it led him to a street corner where the dog sat, and then the man sat and put his cap on the pavement. The dog lay down beside him, leaning into his ragged coat.

At first, Pug led me. I could not see the door myself. Eventually, I learned to see the shiver, as Mary described it, when it appeared. And eventually, I even learned to summon it—at least, when it wanted to come.

What I liked best was going to Lyme. I would sit on the Cobb, watching the ships come in and the fishermen unloading their nets, the fish gleaming orange and purple in the evening light. The smell of the fish, the smell of the sea, the harsh voices of the fishermen. The feel of rough stone. It was as though I had been transported to fairyland.

I did not like going to London, but the door opens where it wants to. Its intentions are inscrutable, the destination not under our control. And that is where I met the Miss Martins.

They were walking down the street, still with their aprons on, looking into the shop windows as though they had never seen shops filled only with ribbons, or only with ladies' shoes. I knew immediately that they had traveled through the door, as I had. We recognize each other, we travelers through the door.

"Please forgive my forwardness," I said, "but—I am Anne de Bourgh."

It was the first time they had been to London. We went to the Queen's Palace and the park, with its strutting ducks and tubs of orange trees. Mary admired the parterres, which were, she said, "even fancier than at Donwell Abbey," and Eliza laughed at the French fashions. "Imagine," she said, "if I wore that bonnet at home!" We walked down Pall Mall and finally stopped to have cakes at a shop near Marlborough House, although the attendant did not seem to realize we were there. We took what we wanted, and I left some coins on the counter. It was evening and I was trying not to show that I was at the end of my strength when the door appeared again, in the middle of St. James's Square, and took us back to Abbey-Mill Farm. They could see that I was not well, so they made me lie on the sofa and bathed my forehead with rosewater. Then there was the door, right in the parlor wall, and it took me home to Rosings.

"What have you been doing?" asked Dr. Galt. "Running up and down stairs? I told you, my girl, you can live a normal life, but within reason. Whatever you've been doing, you must not do it again." I lay sick in bed all that week, and Miss Jenkinson brought me interminable cups of beef tea. But I had found friends.

We have tried to understand the rules by which the door operates.

It appears and disappears unexpectedly. When we step through it, we do not know where we will be, or how long we will be there. When it comes back for us, it usually takes us home. But not always.

At first, only Mary could see it—and, presumably, Pug. Now we can all see it—as a sort of shiver in the air, as though the brick wall, or hedge, or whatever is behind it, were behind a waterfall.

It does not like to be ignored. If we do not step through it, the door sulks. Sometimes it does not come back for days.

Sometimes, when we call for it to appear, it comes. At other times it will not come, no matter how we call. Sometimes, it will take us where we ask. At other times, it will not. "Door, could you please take us to Pemberley?" has worked in the past, as has "Open, Sesame!" As has "Here, door, door, door!"

The door appears to have limits. We have never traveled earlier than the King's reign, nor later than the defeat of Napoleon. (Imagine our relief to learn of Waterloo.) We have never traveled outside England, although Eliza has asked, again and again, to go to Italy.

Wherever we go, we are ghosts. We walk unnoticed. And when we return, we have not been missed. Life seems to flow around us, as though we were pebbles in a stream, eternally still in the midst of motion. Once, Eliza said, "Is it the door, or is it just us? I can go to Highbury for hours, and when I return Mother says that she thought I was home all the time, in the garden or with the cows. Perhaps we are just like that, going through life unnoticed."

We call it a door, but is it a door at all? We say that it opens, but can what it does be called opening? What happens when it appears? What determines where it will take us? We do not know.

"I think," I said to Mary and Eliza, "that we should begin attempting to summon the door. I believe it has a purpose, and that we must fulfill it."

"What sort of purpose?" asked Mary.

"I believe that we should find others like ourselves. They must exist, and I think the door will take us to them."

We were in Bath, walking along the Crescent. The sun was bright and Mary's nose was beginning to freckle. The door does not wait for one to fetch a parasol.

"You don't know how lonely I was until I met Pug. And if there are others like me, who are also lonely, I want to find them."

I said it with steady conviction, although I was not sure, myself, that the door was not simply a Devil, an impish device that had decided to play with us for a while. But there is something I have wondered since the days of Dr. Templeton and Dr. Bransby, while being lowered into a cold bath or drinking beef tea. Is there a force in the universe that understands us, as we long to be understood? And if so, is this force compassionate? Does it, even as it metes out ill, long for our good? If so, it is the force that will give Fitz the girl he wants, the happy ending he deserves. But what about those of us for whom there can be no happy endings? Perhaps it gives us something else, a secret. A companionship that even Fitz would not understand.

So far, we have only found two others like ourselves, apart from the unfriendly Mrs. Churchill. Mrs. Smith of Allenham Hall, in Derbyshire, is a widow with a heart condition like mine, who cannot travel much. But we go visit her, when the door allows. Mr. Wentworth is a vicar in Shropshire. I said to him once, "It seems, Mr. Wentworth, that you disprove Mary's conjecture. You have a profession. You are married and have children. Surely you are not one of those to whom nothing happens."

"It is true, Miss de Bourgh, that I have more to occupy myself than you do, which precludes me from joining you as often as I would like. But consider, my brother is an admiral in His Majesty's navy. I, too, once longed to become a sailor, but my father destined me for the church. Compared to his, my life is dull indeed."

"Perhaps," said Eliza later, when the three of us were alone, except for Pug, "that is the difference between men and women. Mr. Wentworth's life would be considered full, for a woman. And yet he considers it dull."

"I feel for him," I said. "But I confess, I feel more for Mrs. Smith, lying on her sofa all day long."

The first time we walked through the door into her room, kept as dark as mine in the days of Dr. Bransby, she said, "Good dog! You've brought some friends. Sit down, girls, sit down. Stay and talk with me for a while."

This is what Miss Jenkinson tells the tourists as they walk through Rosings. I have heard it so often I could almost recite it myself: Roman foundations, a Saxon fort, given to Sir George de Bourgh by William the Conqueror.

"In the days of Sir Roger de Bourgh, the cellars contained so much port it was said you could sail on it to China. The requirements of the present Lady de Bourgh are considerably more modest." Laughter.

"Under Lady Anne de Bourgh, a portion of the house burned and had to be rebuilt. As we walk through the house, I will point out the various architectural styles. This hall, as you see, is Elizabethan, although after the fire it required extensive restoration. Only one of the walls is original. It was said that Lady Anne set the fire herself after her lover, William d'Arcy, rejected her for the Virgin Queen. At present, Rosings has forty-two bedrooms, a number considered propitious by Sir Roger de Bourgh, who was believed by some to be a mathematician, and by others to be an alchemist. His wife, Arabella d'Arcy, was accused of assisting in his alchemical experiments. Her grandmother, Isabel d'Arcy, who was the mistress of Henry VI, was afterward tried as a witch. There are twelve bathrooms, of which eight have modern plumbing, put in at a cost of over a thousand pounds." Gasps.

"The de Bourghs hold extensive lands in Kent, including this manor and of course the village of Hunsford. In his capacity as magistrate, the late Sir

George de Bourgh was responsible for hanging fourteen poachers in one year. Madam, if you could stop your child from kicking that chair. It was presented to Lady Catherine by Queen Charlotte herself. Observe the painting of Sir Edward de Bourgh as a child, which was saved during the Civil War by being buried under a local pigsty."

"Tell us about the Wicked Lord!"

"Edward de Bourgh, the Wicked Lord, as he was called at court, was beheaded for his unwanted attentions to King Charles' mistress, Nell Gwyn . . . "

Pug and I escape to the garden. When we were children, Fitz was made to learn this tale of folly and bloodshed. No wonder he reads German philosophy. The de Bourghs and the d'Arcys: alchemists, rapists, thieves. Let him have his happy ending.

In the garden, I sit on the edge of the fountain, feeding the fish. These are the living fish, imported from China: orange and white, with an exquisite beauty that their stone cousins cannot match. They rise to nibble the bread that I drop for them. Pug puts his front paws on the edge of the fountain, looks at them, and barks.

A woman and a boy come into the garden.

"What a bad boy you are, Tom," she says, sighing and sitting down on one of the benches. "Why did you have to kick the furniture? I can't take you anywhere."

"I'm bored," he says, quite reasonably, in my opinion. "I want to see the secret passage. You said there would be a secret passage."

"Well, there isn't a secret passage. That Jenkins woman said so. Now will you behave yourself?"

I have no more bread. The fish rise to nibble my fingers. Pug barks and barks, and turns to me, panting, for approval. He looks as though he is laughing.

Madam, I want to say, there is a secret passage. Miss Jenkinson cannot show it to you. But there is, there is.

# RAMPION

## ALEXANDRA DUNCAN

When the sands whip my face or the rag boys kick my feet out from under me, I ask myself if it was worth going blind, having laid eyes on her. If only I had clapped my hands to my ears when I first heard her singing. Had I not tethered my horse and waded across the river to pluck oranges from the trees growing wild around her estate, I might be riding the country still, surveying my father's holdings and reveling in the sweet, unformed yearning I felt that day before I crossed the river.

This morning, as all mornings, I grip my walking stick, secure my tattered, sweat-grimed *taqiyah* on the crown of my head, and pick my way over the swept cobblestones of the Plaza Asad. When I had my eyes, I only cared if the roads were kept well enough to allow my mother's horse and escort smooth passage, but now each narrow street has its own topography. I navigate by the jutting stones, the smells of marzipan, meat—fresh lamb at the *halal* butchers, *jamón serrano* at the Christian shops—and the waft of dank water steaming from the sewers. The fishmongers, newly fetched up from the Guadalquivir, shout over each other. Their voices mix with the clang of steel, the rush and tang of the forge-fire consuming the air, and above all, the distant cry of the muezzin calling us to prayer.

A stone lion crouches by the western spoke of the fountain at the heart of the plaza. I rest one hand on its warm grained head and dip the other into the fountain pool to cup up a drink. Then quickly, I splash another handful over my face and head and hope that will suffice to please God in place of proper ablutions. I can do no better.

A crowd of men mill around me on their way to prayer. A year ago, a throng would have packed the plaza, men and their wives and children meandering down to the mosque together. But today it's only men's voices I hear. Most of the women and children hide away indoors; what few there are huddle in dense pockets of silence. A year ago, these men—scribes, poets, merchants—would have talked the price of geldings, the weight of a bolt of cloth. They would have complained about their slow progress translating Sophocles from the Greek, while their wives' voices bubbled under the din. But today Berber mercenaries ring the plaza, looking out for Northern spies and keeping an eye on our impiety, all at the behest of our vizier, Sanchuelo ibn al-Mansur, who every year tugs another corner of power loose from the caliph. The men speak in low voices of the Christian chieftains' incursions into Moorish territory, our vizier's bloody reprisals, and the weakness of the throne.

" . . . said the Catalan forces took their orders from the Pope . . . "

" . . . cut off their hands and feet."

" . . . mercenaries set fire to the library . . . "

And then, in the middle of it, a name drops into my ear like a stone.

"Adán Hadid."

I lock to the voice that said it, a man's lilting, nasal tone that catches behind the speaker's teeth. My ear marks him a Castellano, ruby-blond and reedy, with pale skin, like all men from the North. Trolling the plaza for gossip and bargains, keeping friendly with the Jewish and Moorish merchants so his trade name stays good. Before I lost my sight, I had friends like him, advisors and artisans of his faith in my employ. My mother and I strolled with them by the tinkling garden pools at the palace of Madinat al-Zahra, played *ajedrez* with them, presented their wives with gilt and mother-of-pearl fans, took down the tapestry maps in our halls so they could examine them. I brought Northerners to tea shops in the city where the air hung full of smoke and spice and men's voices, the floor was soft with raw-silk pillows, and the proprietors kept my comings and goings to themselves. And always, the captain of my guard, Adán Hadid, stood silent in the shadows of the room with his hand on the pommel of his sword.

"Hadid, I heard the caliph laid a death sentence on him," the Castellano says. "If he's ever found."

"Are they saying the Umayyad prince is dead now? Are they sure?" asks another man, a native Córdoban by his accent.

A third man, older, makes a sputtering noise with his lips. "What do you think? They found his horse with its throat gored out."

"And Hadid never seen since that day," the Castellano adds. He clucks his teeth. "He's a Jew. What else do you need to know?"

"I heard," the older man says. He lets his voice sink even lower. "Hadid was acting on orders from the vizier."

"No?" the Castellano says, urging him on.

"Yes," he says. "Think on it. Without an heir, who does the caliph name as successor?"

"He'll never agree to it," the Córdoban puts in. "I heard the caliph's turned stubborn since the prince disappeared. Told the vizier to send some of his Berbers back."

I push myself to my feet, my blood hot and calling me to fight. I want to grab the Castellano by his shirtfront, shout out my name to the crowd. But in my blindness, I stumble. Misery and shame flare up in my old wounds, and I remember how I brought this fate on myself, on Adán, on her. Why I must forever bite my tongue. I grip my walking stick and hobble into the crowd, away from the gossip blackening Adán Hadid's good name. My arms and back tremble with unspent rage, as if I am bearing a terrible weight. This talk of the prince dead, my—his horse dead, makes me feel naked to the world.

*I am so tired.* I speak to God, though I don't know whether the words leave my mouth. I should be riding out to hunt, walking with my young wife through the topiary gardens, teaching our child the curve of his first letters. But none of those things have come to pass, and my youth crumbles.

The crowd pulls me to the courtyard of orange trees outside the Great Aljama Mosque. I let the flow of men carry me inside. There, I can crouch to pray in the soft dark without drawing the pity or stares that dog my footsteps in the daylight, only another man among thousands kneeling in the mosque's candlelit womb.

Afterward, when I feel my way back into the sunlight, it is like being born. In my good eye, I see light, sometimes, and blurred colors, but mostly light, and it is never so bright as when I step out of the cool dark into the grit and glare of the everyday world. I siphon a bit of peace from the thought that no one has found Adán, not yet, and that means he is safe. And perhaps even she is safe, and maybe he is with her.

That night, I dream of killing my horse, my Anadil. My hands are steady as I draw the blade across her throat. She is hurt; it is a mercy killing. After it's done, I cradle her head in my lap. But when her blood pools hot in my hands, I see she isn't injured after all. She is whole, except for the gaping line of red at her throat. Anadil rolls her eyes up at me. I try to hold her flesh together, but it's too late. Her black coat is thick with blood and my hands are slick with it. There is nothing to be done but to watch her bleed into the dirt.

I wake with my heart hammering. The open night hangs black around me, heavy and tight with a wet chill that signals the hour farthest from dawn. My bad leg pains me. I reach inside my shirt and clutch the thin braid of hair I wear tied around my neck, stroke it with my thumb. Even after all this time, it is still silk-whisper smooth, though I am beginning to forget its color. Is it tawny brown, the way I remember her hair spread over the bed cushions? Or bright as copper when the sun beams through it, as it was the day we met, when she leaned from her window and it fell loose around her shoulders? Or does it shine like burnished gold in the candlelight, elegantly twined, as on the night she first brought me to her bed? I am even beginning to forget her face. We have no images of each other, exchanged no portraits, and even if we had, I could not stoke my memory with her likeness. Is it possible, then, she remembers me at all?

*Ojalá que me recuerde. God will it she remember.*

From the mouth of the alley, the sound of a man pissing on the brickwork trickles its way to me. I press my body against the wall, trying to make myself small and unseen.

" . . . *por la zorra que me mató la alma,*" the man sings, hushed and then suddenly loud, the way drunks do. At first, I don't recognize the voice.

"*Eh, Gemel, Lope, hermanos, ¿adonde vaís?*" he calls after someone on the street.

The Castellano.

I hear him tugging on the belt of his trousers, and then the stumble-step of his footfalls. I pull myself up by the wall and feel my way after him. I don't know why I follow. Maybe it's the hope of hearing more news of Adán, or maybe I want to bash his head against the paving stones for naming my friend a traitor. I don't know, but I follow.

"*Esperad, hijos de puta, esperad,*" the Castellano mutters. His voice sticks, foggy and rough with drink.

"Lázaro!" one of his companions calls from far ahead. "*¡Andate, cabrón!*"

We've reached the mouth of the alley. I can tell by the way the air opens up around me and, through my better eye, the muddy red glow from the braziers that line the street.

"*Vengo, vengo. Santa Madre,*" Lázaro says under his breath. And then a heavy sound follows, like a water cask tumbling on its side or a whole bolt of damask dropped to the floor.

I stumble back into the wall behind me and feel my way to the corner of the building's stone stairwell. I know a body hitting the ground when I hear it.

"Lázaro!" the Castellano's companions call. One of them is laughing, but the other has a nervous waver in his voice as he jogs back along the street.

"*¿Que te pasó?*" the nervous one asks as his steps slow to a quick walk.

"Guuugghn," Lázaro says. He pauses to draw breath. Something wet splashes on the paving stones and the smell of bile leaks into the air.

"Christ," his other friend says, coming upon the scene. His coat sleeve muffles his voice. "Drunk again."

"What do we do?" the nervous one asks.

"Leave him for the Berbers," the other mutters darkly. The vizier's mercenaries are so pious, they not only abstain from drink themselves, but flog anyone caught in public drunkenness.

"We can't," the nervous one says. "Who'll do for the horses come morning?"

"*Maldito sea.*" The other man pauses, thinking. "All right. We'll go for Delgado and the cart, and we'll have Delgado help us take him to the rooming house."

"I'll go," the nervous one says.

"The hell you will. You're half as bad as him. You and Delgado will start drinking, and then you'll forget and leave me cold on the street," the other one says.

"I won't."

"You will. I haven't forgotten that time before Semana Santa."

They both fall silent. I hear nothing but the shuffle of their feet on the sandy stones and the deep, heavy breath rising out of Lázaro's prone form.

"Look," one of them mutters suddenly, and they go silent again. The hairs on my forearms and shoulders rise up, as if a magnet has swept over them. A terrible foreboding hits me: they've seen me hunched in the shadow of the stairs.

"Help me," the least-drunk one says.

The other grunts and the sound of something heavy sliding over the stones shushes toward me. I feign sleep, thinking maybe they'll leave me in peace if they see me unconscious. Lázaro's hot, heavy form drops down next to me and slumps against my shoulder. His friends laugh like a clutch of newly betrothed girls.

"Watch him for us, good sir," the drunk one quips.

"See he doesn't fall into the wrong hands," the other calls as they hurry away.

I had pictured Lázaro a reedy man, but he is not. The mass of dead weight leaning on my shoulder proves him thick in the middle and meaty everywhere else. I can see why his friends didn't think they could lift him alone. When I'm sure they are gone, I shove him away.

Lázaro groans. "*¿Gemel, que haces?*"

My heart picks up speed. My blood still wants violence, but my years of learning, my training in logic, stay my hand. The Castellano can tell me nothing of Adán if he's dead.

I wet my bottom lip and swallow, try to rouse some of my old self for what I must do. "Lázaro?" I lean close to his ear, speaking low.

He stirs. "Gemel?"

"No," I say. "You address Ishaq ibn Hisham, of the Umayyad line."

His throat makes a series of little sucking noises. I can picture him blinking his eyes, trying to make them focus well enough to see me. "You're dead," he says.

"Lázaro," I say, "tell me what you know about Adán Hadid."

"He is a murderer." Lázaro sounds suddenly lucid, enunciating every word.

"Yes." I grit my teeth. "And where is he?"

Lázaro's voice drops and quavers. "I don't know." He sounds genuinely forlorn, but then his tone turns again, just as quickly. "But if I find him, the caliph will pay me in gold and horses and I will be a lord and everyone will say, 'At your pleasure, Don Lázaro, *estimado* Don Lázaro.'"

Disappointment thickens my chest. I take a deep breath and push on. "And the Lady Sofia de Rampion? Have you heard anything of her?"

Lázaro pauses. I wish to God I could see his face so I could know if it showed bewilderment, or careful thought, or sudden, clear-eyed suspicion.

And then Lázaro laughs. He taps my shoulder with his index finger. "Oh, prince, I've heard about you. Sofia de Rampion is beautiful, the most beautiful, *la flor más bella del mundo Cristiano*. *¿Me entiendes*? But you can't have her, no, no. Her brothers have taken her north to the Pyrenees, to the care of her uncle, King Filipe of Roussillon de Catalunya, where the Moors can't touch her."

My heart is ablaze and then dust, all in a moment. Sofia is alive. But I would fear to travel to Roussillon with both my eyes and my horse alive again. The whole kingdom of Castilla separates us, and then a mountain range of petty warlords.

"But I, I will see her for myself." Lázaro leans close to confide in me. His breath is swampy. "When I bring the horses."

I start, my right hand tight on Lázaro's loose sleeve. "When you bring the horses?"

"Yes, the horses for her brothers and her uncle's men." He lowers his voice to a whisper. "I would never tell you this, except you're dead and you won't speak of it to the vizier."

My muscles tense at the mention of Sofia's kinsmen. "Yes," I agree.

"They are war horses." Lázaro slaps my arm. "Can you believe it? My horses, bearing the soldiers of Christ on their backs as they retake *al Andalus*? Crushing the Moors' skulls beneath their hooves." He laughs.

My body sings for me to run, to fight, but I am trapped by the darkness around me. I make myself release Lázaro's shirt sleeve.

Lázaro slumps against the wall with a muted thud. He sighs. "They say her voice is like birdsong painted in honey and her hair is so long you could scale the curtain wall of an *alcazar* with it. They say her maids must walk behind her to keep it from trailing in the dust."

Her voice comes back to me all at once, like a basin of cold water emptied over my head. I hear it anew, mixed with the steady tambour of my horse's hooves over the dusty road by the far side of a shaded tributary. That day, I left Adán and the rest of my men behind at the river mouth to pray and rest through the midday, while I rode out alone into the silent heat of the countryside. When the peaked towers of the Rampion manor came into view over the orange groves surrounding their land, I slowed my horse.

Common wisdom held one should ride slow and quiet when their gabled roof showed above the trees, for then a man was close enough to call the eye of Lamia de Rampion, the matriarch of the family. She was said to be a *sahhaar*, a *bruja*, a *sorcière* come down to us from the North. Since I was a small boy, I had listened in on the stories told at court by lamplight. No one had seen her ride in, but one day in winter, on the eve of a bitter, snapping frost, a drover sighted her in the courtyard before the abandoned Rampion house, straight-backed in her black dress, with two boys at her skirts and a white-swaddled babe in her arms. Ismail Almendrino, whose lands met hers to the south, went up to find what might be her claim on the land. She recited her lineage for him back to the rule of the Visigoth chieftains, saying she was the grandniece of old Osoro de Rampion, who had died childless and left the manor vacant some ten years before my birth. She had come south with her grandchildren, recently orphaned, to reclaim the lands for her grandsons. Almendrino said she spoke Castellano and some Arabic, but her accent was the French of the Pyrenees and her bearing that of one who cradles power in her hands and tongue.

When spring came, the orange groves of the Rampion manor that had stood so long untended bowed heavy with fruit. And it might have gone well for Lamia and her grandchildren, had a boy not been found dead under the orange trees, his tongue blue as from snakebite and a lobe of fruit in his mouth, but no mark upon him. Then the whispers started. Some of the older boys, who had become accustomed to eating from the Rampion trees when the estate stood empty, said Lamia de Rampion had screeched at them and called down devils when she found them filling their pockets with oranges. The drovers told how she walked out alone on nights of great wind and communed with the *al-shayatin* by the light of a bonfire. The women even took to saying her granddaughter was no blood of hers, but a babe snatched from her mother's breast and spirited away to give the old woman company. In more savage times, they would have raged to her door with fire and brand, but Ismail Almendrino, who was learned and pious, stayed their hands. Still, the Christians crossed their breasts and spat when Lamia's servants ventured out to market. And even Almendrino took to hanging blue and white *nazar* in the trees along the borderline of their lands.

I knew better. I had studied the biology of voles and frogs, mixed black

Oriental powder at my tutor's hands, and understood the forces behind the invisible tug of magnets. Lamia de Rampion was no more a witch than I was a prophet. She was only an old woman who craved solitude and was stingy with her harvest.

I led Anadil down a gentle slope in the riverbank, let out her rein so she could bend her head to drink from the shallows of the slow-moving river, and hitched her to an overhanging branch. I waded across with the thought of gathering fruit from the crude outlying trees to slake my thirst and share with my men. This was the custom in our land—to leave a share of fruit for widows and travelers—and as I say, I paid no heed to this peasant talk of *brujería*.

But as I pushed myself up onto the opposing bank and stood among the flowering boughs, I heard it. A woman's voice, arching with the same pure cadence of a vielle, winged over the treetops and fell on my ear. I forgot Anadil and the oranges. It was as if someone had tied a kite string to my heart and now gently wound it in. The song pulled me through the line of trees, nearer the house. The branches parted on a packed dirt courtyard fronting a whitewashed stone manor with a sloped roof. Drought-sick rose bushes needled out from the base of the wall. I stopped below a second-story window, where a thick, ancient olive tree cleaved to the face of the house. A young woman in a fine-cut, blue workaday dress and indigo plackart stiff with silk-embroidered leafy whorls sat at the window with its leaded pane propped open. Lamia's granddaughter, now grown, near my own age.

Leafy vines overflowed the railed balcony below her. She had put her veil aside and the sun streaked her hair all the subtle golden tones of a shaft of hay. She held a piece of embroidery and a bone needle in her hands, but she stared off over the orchard, toward Córdoba, with its towers and fine domes and minarets hazy in the distance. She sang to herself,

> *Cuando me vengo al rio*
> *Te pido, te pido, te pido,*
> *Que siempre serás mio,*
> *Y te juro, te juro, te juro,*
> *Que nunca te quitaré.*

A peasant song, a simple little love song. But it cracked my heart like a quail's egg. She frowned to herself, then lifted her embroidery to begin her work again.

I smoothed my silk *taqiyah* and stepped from the trees so she could see me. "Forgive me, Señorita de Rampion?" I called.

Her needle slipped and jabbed her thumb. "Christ's blood!" she swore. Her embroidery fell from her hands and whisked itself out the window. She grabbed for it, but it fluttered past her reach and lazed to a stop at my feet.

I bent and picked it up. Stitched vines and blooms arabesqued along the borders of her handiwork. "My apologies, lady," I said, trying to hide a smile at her curse. "I heard you singing. I was riding by and. . . . "

She leaned out over the dark wood casement. Her uncovered hair fell forward into the sun. It reached at least twelve hands below the window ledge, thick, loose braids mixed with undressed locks, shining bright as brass against the deep green vines. My breath caught.

"You'd best keep riding, sir," she said quietly. "My *grandmère* is taking her rest. If you wake her, she'll be none too glad of your company. And my brothers don't feel kindly to the caliph's men these days."

I looked around the peaceful garden. "You object to my visiting, lady?"

She checked behind her as if making sure the door to her closet were shut, and turned back, her brow knitted. "Who are you?"

"Ishaq ibn Hisham, of the Umayyads, son of the caliph of *al Andalus*." I bowed. "Although I am called al-Hasan, the Handsome, by the women of the court."

"In that case, I do not object, my lord," she said. She allowed herself a small smile, but then a frown clouded her features again. "But, please, if you stay, my kinsmen will forget their courtesy."

"Your company is worth the risk," I said. "Your voice. . . . " I fumbled for words, and touched the center of my chest instead.

She blushed and looked at me sideways from under her hair. "My *grandmère* warned me of men like you. You would win my ear with pretty words."

"I would win your ear with whatever tender you value."

She bit her bottom lip. "Do you have any news of the North, then, Ishaq ibn Hisham, son of the Umayyad caliph, sometimes called al-Hasan?"

"The North?" I repeated dumbly. My lessons at the time had been all Aristotle, algebra, and petty diplomacy. The vizier had charge of the larger matters of state, and he assured my father the Northern lords were rabble-rousers and brigands, soon to be crushed beneath the charge of a Moorish cavalry, with him, the son and heir of the great warrior al-Mansur, at its head.

"Yes, my lord," she said. "They say the Christian lords from Castilla north to the Occitan territories are spoiling for war. I heard my brothers talking of raids on the outskirts of Tulaytulah and a muster north of Madrid. There is even talk of the Northern lords riding into Córdoba to reclaim the bells of Santiago de Compostela. And the vizier raising the call for more mercenaries in turn. Is it true?"

Something shifted in my chest, like to a bone popping into joint. I did not see it then, but a keener and more durable thing than the whim that drew me to her window had put down its roots in me.

I dropped my light manner. "It's true. There was a raid on Tulaytulah and some of the smaller towns north and west. But trust me, lady, you need not fear. My father and I desire peace as much as any in the caliphate, and the vizier has all the mercenaries he needs."

She studied me for a long pause. "If you say it," she said finally.

I looked up at her, her hair hanging like ropes of gold braid beneath the window ledge. "May I know your name?" I asked.

"Oh, the price of that is more news." She smiled, teasing again. "I'm locked up alone here with nothing but my handwork and a few servants most days. I cannot even ride out without my brothers' escort. I am parched for news of the outside world."

"What would you like to know?" I asked. "The fashions of the court at Granada? The latest arguments from Alexandria? Shall I recite an epic from the Greek or tell the tale of Scheherazade?

She laughed. "Only tell me what you've seen on your ride today and what brings you so far outside the city."

"Well." I pretended to count on my fingers. "I have seen the bridges of Córdoba by the earliest light, three farms, two other manors, a field of sunflowers tall as a man, a very fat merchant fall from his horse, and the most quick-minded woman I have ever met. My mother excepted, of course."

"Of course." The lady smiled.

"As to what brings me," I said, "I can only say the vizier is happier when I keep myself amused away from court, and when he is happy, we all prosper."

"Have you no duties there?" She raised her eyebrows. "Shouldn't you be learning the arts of state at your father's hand?"

"My father and the vizier agree, there's no need for me to learn the messy particulars. Not with such an able administrator in our employ."

"I see," she said.

"And your name, lady?" I prompted. "Or have I not yet satisfied your thirst?"

"No, my lord, I am perfectly satisfied," she said. "I am called Sofia de Rampion."

"Thank you," I said. "And you must call me Ishaq."

"Yes, my Lord Ishaq."

I held up her embroidery. "May I return this to you?"

Her face fell. The levity that had buoyed her so briefly fled. "You cannot enter the house. My *grandmère* would tell my brothers."

"Should I leave it here for you?" I asked, looking around at the dusty courtyard below her window.

"Wait," she said. "I have it." She disappeared from the window and returned with a little porcelain water pitcher tied to a length of flax string. She pointed to the olive tree below her window. Its upper branches disappeared into the spill of vines. "Climb up."

I hoisted myself up onto the sturdiest bough, reached out for the pitcher, dangling level with my head, and tucked the delicate piece of embroidery into its neck.

Sofia drew it up. "Thank you, my lord."

I swung down from the tree. "May I come to you again? I could bring more news, better news next time."

She traced an invisible design on the windowsill with her finger. "I think not, my lord." She raised her eyes and I could read regret written all over her face. "I have loved our talk. Truly, it has brought me joy. But my family—"

"—will not object to what they don't know." I finished for her and smiled.

She ducked her head to hide a small, mischievous smile aimed back at me. "You live up to your reputation, Ishaq ibn Hisham. And for your part, won't you boast of me as one of your conquests?"

"Believe me, lady, I am better at keeping confidences than you've heard," I said. "Not even the captain of my guard knows where I've come today, and he is my dearest friend."

She paused and stared at me, taking my measure.

"May I come again?" I asked.

Slowly, so slowly I would never have noticed had I not been watching every movement of her body, she nodded her consent.

"You will not regret it, lady," I said, walking backward into the trees. "I will bring you news from all over *al Andalus*, from the halls of Cairo, from Baghdad, from every corner of the known world." I nearly tripped over a fallen branch and righted myself. "Even from Damascus itself!"

She laughed, and the sound rang so lovely, so light, I thought nothing of the small sliver of darkness between the shutters of the window beneath her room, or how it disappeared as they pulled themselves shut.

Lázaro snorts in his sleep, jarring me out of my reverie. I push aside the thought of leaving his throat slit by his own knife and drag myself up out of the shadow of the stairs by my walking stick. It will take the rest of the night to reach the city's outer gates at my limping pace, and the good part of early morning to beg a place in Lázaro's caravan going north to Catalunya. For now that I know where Sofia is, it is as if God has touched His lips to my ear. It does not matter if she remembers me, or that I am blind and will likely die on my way to her. Some of my youth returns to my limbs. I grasp the braid around my neck and the kite string pulls tight once more.

*I am coming to you*, I swear. *I am coming to you.*

Adán found me in the library at Madinat al-Zahra late at night the Friday after I first met Sofia. Parchment bearing architectural designs for the Great Mosque lay thick over my lap and on the table before me. A smoking hashish pipe dangled absently from my hand. My father and I had returned from prayers at our private chamber within the mosque earlier in the day, when the sun stood at a right angle over the palace gardens. Kneeling there before God, I remembered Sofia's fears. It had come to me how this private chamber, the palace, our reliance on the vizier only turned our heads from the trouble around us, though all the while it lapped at our necks. I had come straight to the library and instructed the scribes to bring me all the plans for the mosque from the time it was rebuilt from an old Visigoth church to the most recent additions under my father. I had also asked for the annals of the golden reign of my great-grandfather, Abd al-Rahman III.

By the time Adán came looking for me, daylight had fled the room. He carried an oil lamp. "Night's full on, brother. Shouldn't you be sleeping? Or at least visiting that pretty minister's daughter, what's her name? Iuliana?" He stopped beside me at the table and lifted the sheaf of papers. "What's this?"

"Doesn't your Shabbat keep you from laboring over these questions?" I said, rubbing my palms over my face.

"Don't tell me you're thinking of adding to the mosque again, Ishaq," Adán said, letting the papers fall with a slap. "There are other ways to distinguish your reign when it comes, you know."

"No," I said. I was too tired even for our boyish needling. "I was thinking of knocking down walls, not building new ones."

"What do you mean? Not destroying the mosque?" Adán pulled out a chair and sat beside me. His face pulled back in horror. "You would have a mob at your gates. Do you realize the city is already—"

"No, no." I laid my hand over his arm to calm him. "Only the walls to the royal enclosure at the head of the *mihrab*. I dislike this praying separately from the people. I've been reading about my forefathers. They were great men, Adán. They never would have let a common warmonger like Sanchuelo. . . . "

"Hssst," Adán hissed. He jerked me up by my arm and dragged me after him through one of the library's horseshoe-arched porticos, out into the night. Past the overlapping arcs of the fountain pool, past the torchlight's radius, and into the thick of the shoulder-high hedge maze surrounding the gardens. I let him thread us deep into its bends before I pulled my arm from his grasp and stopped in my tracks.

"Are you mad?" Adán checked over his shoulders and leaned in close to my face. "Are you simple?"

"I'm the heir to the Umayyad caliphate, which you seem to have forgotten," I said, straightening my sleeve.

"Oh, Ishaq." Adán sounded weary. "You are truly God's fool."

I opened my mouth to protest, but Adán cut me off. "You think you will rule the caliphate when your father dies? Have you ever sat down with a minister of state? Helped plot any of the military campaigns? Drafted a mandate for the emirs?"

My face went hot, despite the cool air of the garden. "Of course I—"

"No," Adán interrupted. "The vizier tolerates you because you fall prey so easily to women and fine horses and smoke. You are a pretty face for minor diplomats and their daughters. You're no threat to him. But if you start speaking this way. . . . " He let his words trail away.

I said nothing, my arms locked to my sides, my hands in fists.

"I tell you these things because I'm your friend, Ishaq," Adán said. "You trust me, don't you?"

I tried to swallow the ire crushing my windpipe. "Yes," I said.

"If you want your throne back from Sanchuelo, I'm with you. But wait. Watch. Make allies. Sanchuelo is too strong now."

I breathed the anger out of my lungs. I nodded.

"Good," Adán said. "And in the meantime, go see that girl again, whichever one it is you've been mooning over all week."

I stalked to the stables, forgetting my cloak and the book of poetry I had laid by my bedside to take with me when next I returned to Sofia. The wind ripped the *taqiyah* from my head and turned my hair wild as I rode. I only slowed when the orange groves appeared silhouetted against the bright moonlit sky. I dismounted and walked Anadil down to the river again. She snorted softly, the sound lost in the bubbling of the current. I stroked her muzzle and whispered to her, "Calm, Anadil, easy. I'll be back."

A pair of quail started from the brush as I climbed the riverbank. I walked softly along the hall of trees, pausing at every rustle and animal sound. The thought of Lamia de Rampion walking here with spirits swirled about her head seemed more real in the darkness, away from the light and hum of Córdoba. I came to the house, its pale walls reflecting the full moon's light. Sofia's window was shuttered, its vents open to draw in the cool night air.

"Sofia," I called softly. "Sofia."

I paused and listened. Nothing.

"Sofia." I tried again. "Sof—"

The shutters creaked as Sofia eased them open. "Ishaq?" She wore a linen shawl over the white fabric of her shift and her hair fell in a long braid. Delicate curls haloed her neck and ears, where they had escaped the plait.

"It's me," I said.

"What are you doing here?" she whispered. She blinked and touched a hand to her eyes.

"I've come with news," I whispered back, loud as I dared.

"Has something happened?"

"Yes," I said.

She moved a hand from forehead to chest to shoulders in the sign of the cross. "Oh, Christ. Is it the Northern armies or the vizier? Which is it?"

"Neither," I said.

"What, then?"

"I came to tell you I'm going to be caliph."

She stared at me with a look that said she was considering hurling her chamberpot at my head. "Are you drunk?"

"No." I hoisted myself up into the olive tree and scaled the branches until I was only an arm's length from her window. I kept my face still and serious and looked up into her eyes, wide and dark in the night. "I'm not drunk. I'm going to take back the caliphate from Sanchuelo."

Her lips parted and she moved her hand as if to reach for me, then drew back. "I'm going for a light."

She returned a moment later with a lamp. She laid it on her sewing table beside the window and reached her hand down to me. "Climb up," she said. "We'll wake *Grandmère* if we keep talking this way."

"I'll hurt you." I eyed the thin circumference of her wrist.

"You won't," she said. "Climb."

I fixed my boot tip between the cracks in the wall, took firm hold of the ivy with one hand, gripped her hand with my other, and heaved myself up into the window.

"Ugh," Sofia said. "You're heavy."

The white walls of her room stood close together, leaving barely enough space for the dark wood furniture that hugged them. I swung my legs over the casement and touched my feet to the floor.

"No, my lord." Sofia shook her head and looked pointedly at my boots. She sat on her narrow bed. "You'll stay in the window. And I won't have you talking sweet, or the next thing I know, you'll be trying to talk your way into my bed."

"Only news then." I leaned against the casement and doubled up my knees so I would fit within the frame.

"Only news," she agreed.

We sat in silence, staring at each other over the soft, bobbing light of the lamp's flame. I looked down at her sewing table. Dried wildflowers—foxglove, Jerusalem sage, asphodels, the rampion flower from which her family took its name—littered her desk, along with a book of parchment where someone had reproduced every panicled stem and anther in sepia ink. I touched a cluster of rampion petals lightly.

"I copy them for *Grandmère*. For her books," Sofia said. She blushed and looked away. "And for my embroidery."

"Your grandmother keeps books?" I knew it. This did not match the peasants' stories of black cockerels slaughtered to tempt the *al-shayatin* and futures read in their entrails.

"Yes." Sofia flipped closed the cover of the book. *Pharmakopia*, it read, gold-etched in the leather.

"I think I would like to meet her." I traced the letters, bringing my fingertips close to Sofia's own.

Sofia looked up. "No," she said sharply. "You would not."

The force of her words surprised me. I pulled back. "Of . . . of course. Forgive me."

Silence swallowed us up again.

"You came here to tell me something?" Sofia turned the book facedown and pushed it to the far end of the table.

"Do you think. . . . " I stopped and adjusted myself in the window frame. My legs dangled. "Can I ask, do you think God ordains what we do? What becomes of us?"

She sat on the bed. At first she didn't answer, and I was afraid I had overwhelmed her with my abruptness, or worse, angered her. But then she spoke, slowly, as if choosing each word as it came into her mouth. "I think He can . . . I mean, maybe He does move His hand in our matters. But mostly I think He speaks His will to men's hearts, and if they are righteous, they listen." She blushed and looked up. "I don't know, Ishaq. I'm from a family of country knights, not scholars."

"No, no, speak," I said, leaning forward.

"Why do you come to me in the night with these questions?" She tilted her head and brushed a stray curl from her face. Her braid lay heavy over her shoulder, sloping down over the curve of her breast and coiling in her lap. Smaller braids twined in the whole.

"I've been thinking," I said. "Ever since you spoke to me from your window. Our imams have always talked of how my family ruled the caliphate because God willed it. And I thought because God willed it, I would only have to wait, and everything I deserved would come to me, would simply appear like a bowl of pomegranates on my dressing table."

Sofia nodded carefully.

I stood and paced the small distance between her wardrobe and her sewing bench. "But then I thought, *Fruit doesn't appear*. Someone cultivates it. Someone harvests it. Someone carries it to my rooms and places it on my dressing table."

I turned to her. My heart raced with the revelation unfolding in my chest. "The Prophet calls the common men of my faith to care for the widowed and the poor, but what God asks from a leader of such men is even greater." I knelt in front of her so I could look into her face. "I have to earn the caliphate. And when I have it, I must do works worthy of it."

Sofia dropped to her knees and kissed me. It was so sudden, so sweet, my body reacted before my mind did. I pulled her against me, her braid trapped between us, my hand at the small of her back, and leaned into her kiss with an open mouth. The smell of her, of warm flesh and salt and woman, nearly drowned me. Her hands were in my hair and mine in hers, her breasts lush and pressed close.

And then my mind caught up to our bodies. "I'm sorry." I broke away and backed to the window. I looked down into the yard at the bare, thorned rosebushes. "I don't want you to think you're some conquest. I don't want anyone to think that of you."

Sofia followed me. She touched my arm and turned me from the window so I faced her, then worked her hands into my hair and pulled my lips down to her mouth again. She took up my hand and placed it on her breast. "My brothers want to marry me to someone in my uncle's court in Catalunya." Her lips brushed mine as she spoke.

My heart pulsed wildly and my head swung between the twin concepts of her small, round breast in my palm and the thought that she was being sent to the North. "When?" I asked.

"Summer's end," she said. "They want me to leave then so I'll arrive before the first storms in the Pyrenees."

I cast about for something to say, but the feel of her flesh beneath the thin shift tugged my mind away from anything else. "You'll be far from the front if war breaks out," I finally said.

She took my other hand and guided it to her waist. "I would rather stay. I'm not afraid."

I forgot to breathe for a moment, and when I remembered again, my breath came harsh. "Sofia. . . . "

She stepped closer so she pressed against the length of my body. "Ishaq," she said. Her eyes flicked up to mine. "Come."

I kissed her again and she led me to her bed. I laid her down among the bedclothes.

"Gently," she said. She circled me with her arms, lifted her legs around me, pulled me tight against her skin. Her hair came undone in my hands. I rolled her over me and it fell around us in a curtain, brushing my skin like feathered silk. And when it became too much and I thought I might cry out, she brought her lips up to mine again and I moaned into her mouth.

When it was over, we lay together in her bed, slick with sweat. She nestled the bridge of her nose against my neck and kissed my chest.

"Sofia." I traced my fingers over her jaw and repositioned my head on the pillows to look at her. "Why?"

She opened her eyes. "My brothers want to barter me away. But this isn't theirs to barter."

She rolled over so her back rested against my chest and curled into me. My nose was in her hair. The smell of bread, sweat, sweet oil, and something indefinable and warm rolled over me as I buried my face in her tresses and tumbled into sleep.

The first crack of blue daylight woke me. I sat up in bed, remembering Anadil still tethered by the riverside, and felt a small ache of guilt. The open window looked out over acres of orange groves and a shining slip of the tributary winding east. Sofia sighed in her sleep.

I rose and dressed. Her grandmother's book, still facedown on Sofia's sewing table, caught my eye as I stooped for my boots. I paused with my outer robe unlaced and the boots beneath my arm. Would she object? I glanced back at her. Her hair spilled over the pillow and down to the floor. The early light picked out the copper filaments in her waves and made them glitter like gold dust along the silted bottom of a creek bed. It was too tempting not to look, not to spy in on a small piece of Sofia's world. I flipped the book open with a soft thud.

The drawings were Sofia's, that much was clear. On the page I opened, she had rendered a poppy, all clean lines put down in deep brown ink. Her neat, looping script accompanied it:

> The seeds of the common poppy (Papaver somniferum) make a most marvelous defense against pain when crushed and burned, or when prepared in a tea. They render unto the drinker a state of profound sleep. Let the reader know, this same solution also may be used in the calling of Visions that, coupled by a Guide, can tell the truth of things.

I stole another look at Sofia. An uneducated man would call this proof of witchery. Was she merely taking down her grandmother's words or had she written this of her own accord? Either way, this was a dangerous book to have.

I thumbed the page over. This time large, craggy letters in blue-black ink filled the page, alongside Sophia's drawing of a starry-whorled oleander blossom. But the words were not in Sofia's hand. *Lamia's, then*? I wondered. My eyes came to rest on a snarl of words:

. . . *a most potent draught, but pains must be taken to disguise the taste* . . .

My heart juddered. I knew this plant. One of Adán's men had a horse that died after nibbling its sweet blossoms. This was a recipe for poison. I flipped the page again. *Nightshade. Monkshood. Bleeding heart. Laburnum. Jerusalem cherry.* All fatal.

Sofia stirred. She blinked her eyes at the daylight and sat up. "You're going?"

"Yes." I regarded her warily, my hand still resting on the open pages of the book.

She frowned. "What's wrong? What are you. . . . " She followed the line of my arm down to the table and snapped awake. "You've been reading *Grandmère's* book?"

"I have," I said. She had looked so innocent and vulnerable by the morning light, half-naked with her hair mussed, but awake she was a keener thing. Did she know her grandmother was using her hand to lay out the properties of poisons? How could she not?

"Ishaq, it isn't what you think—"

"I know well what it is," I cut in.

She sat straight and stared into me. "Will you call us witches now, too, then?"

"Sofia—"

"There's nothing unnatural in what we do," she said, suddenly fierce. "What sin is there in recording the earth's uses?"

"None, but—"

"How is it different from an apothecary's art?"

"Sofia." I knelt by the bed and took her hand. "Sofia, I don't think you're a witch."

She blinked at me and softened. "No?"

"No, or your grandmother either." I glanced over my shoulder at the volume. "But you must know what that book contains."

"Medicines," Sofia said. "Curatives."

"Poisons," I said.

"One and the same sometimes," Sofia said quietly. She looked away, and then turned back with wide eyes. "But she would never turn them to their darker ends. Nor I. You must believe me."

I combed my fingers through a section of her hair. "I trust your word," I said.

"We have many books. This is but one."

"I trust you," I repeated. I kissed her brow and rested my head against hers. The rising sun stung bright in the corner of my eye, and my heart went heavy. "I must go, but will you let me come again?"

She let out a breath. "You want to?"

"Why wouldn't I?"

"What you've seen here." Sofia tilted her head back to the ceiling, not looking at me. "What I've heard of you."

I rubbed my thumb over the smooth ovals of her fingernails, unsure how to answer. I looked up. "And what they say of me, that's all there is?"

Sofia looked at me. Her lashes were wet. "No, I suppose not." She brushed a hand beneath her eye and tried to smile. "I would you didn't have to go."

"Nor I." I twined one of her smaller braids around my thumb. "May I. . . . " I started to ask.

"Only if you let me . . . ," she said, and reached down to the woven sewing basket at her bedside to retrieve a pair of silver shears. She cut the thin braid from her hair and wrapped it around my palm, then folded my fingers over it and reached up to cut a lock from my head as well.

She kissed the thick black curl. "Come soon," she said.

I lowered my feet from the window, steadied myself on the vines, and found the highest tree limb. I looked back up at her. "I promise."

"I trust your word." Sofia echoed me.

I dropped to the ground and then I was off, walking quickly through the orchard, turning back every few feet to catch a last glimpse of her, until finally the branches closed off my view.

I find a place in Lázaro's caravan with a Jewish mapmaker called Miguel ben Yaakov and his wife, Mencia, traveling north as far as a little town at the foot of the Pyrenees. They promise me a share of their bread and a seat on their wagon tail if I will water and brush down their horses at the end of each day. We ride in the middle of the line, behind the dull thunder of Lázaro's horses and the armed men guarding them, behind the merchants, who have bought a place near the guards, but before an imam and a cluster of students on horseback.

Dark mutterings surround our campfires at night, talk of unrest in the city we've left behind, stories of women raped, a Berber soldier beaten and left for dead by a mob, and the hanging of a student. We douse our fires and huddle in the darkness when hoofbeats roar close along the road.

By day, Mencia dotes on her horses, who she calls Limón and Pulga, and it is not long until she is hovering over me with extra shares of cured beef and sour bread, shaking out an old horse blanket for me at night. When the men in Lázaro's band help kill a young bull that's slipped its pen and tried to gore one of the students, she makes sure I have a strip of the meat. Her husband keeps a wary distance. He doesn't say a word to me, even as his wife turns in the wagon to chatter about everything she sees as we make our way north through the rolling emptiness of La Mancha.

"Look, the city!" she cries when they finally sight Tulaytulah, her warm, firm hand clutching my forearm. She laughs in delight. Mencia reminds me of my mother in the days of my childhood, before the fear and isolated luxury surrounding our family smothered her to nothing, an empty veil, a dried flower between the pages of a book. For Mencia's sake, I try to remember the city as I saw it when I was a boy of fifteen, its gray battlements cresting a green hill, all the common houses scattered below like so many windfall apples.

I don't know how I will make it north to Roussillon, once the mapmaker and his wife are gone, or what will become of me once I'm there, but I have miles and miles to mull it over as the cart lumbers north along the old Roman road. I hold Sofia's braid to my lips and pray for God to pass my message along. *I am coming to you, I am coming to you.*

On the last day I saw her, I came alone in the gloaming. Adán had grown suspicious of my late-night rides, but I chose a Shabbat evening so he would be forced to stay behind at the palace, not follow me as he had tried the week before. On my way to the house, I snapped a cluster of almond blossoms from a tree for Sophia. The air was heady with oranges, and she sat in her window, singing to herself as she strummed a *quitara*. Her voice rose lovely over the instrument's steady thrum, dipping and weaving like a bird in flight. Her brothers had gone to the city for the week and her grandmother was off on one of her rambles, so she let me sing with her as she played.

We made love in the soft, last light of day. After, curled together in her bed, her head resting against my shoulder, I asked what I had been mulling over since the day she pulled me through her bedroom window.

"Sofia?"

"Hmm?" she replied.

"Would you come to court at Madinat al-Zahra? With me, I mean?"

She sat up in bed. "Truly?"

I reached out and fixed a piece of wayward hair behind her ear. "I've been thinking, if I were to marry a Christian lady, it might appease the Northern lords and restrain the vizier. It could stop the skirmishes at the border. And it would keep you here."

"Ishaq, are you asking for my hand in marriage?" She prodded me playfully in the chest.

I kept my face solemn. "I am."

"You aren't asking very properly." She put on a mock-stern face.

I reached over and pulled her on top of me, my hands on her hips. "My Lady Sofia de Rampion, will you consent to be my wife?"

"I will," she said. She ran her fingers through the hair of my chest absentmindedly. "But *Grandmère*. . . . And my brothers won't be so easily swayed."

"How could they object to their sister becoming a princess of *al Andalus*?" I asked, and pulled her close to kiss her. She leaned down to press her mouth to mine.

A scrape sounded outside the door. We froze, her bare thighs around me, my hand on her back. The latch clicked and the door slammed open with a sound like Oriental powder igniting. A dark-haired man in his late twenties, with the same dark eyes as Sofia, pushed his way into her room, followed by a younger, fair-haired man. My eyes flew wide. Leandro and Telo, Sofia's brothers. I recognized them from the portraits hanging in the manor halls. Leandro, her eldest brother, pulled Sofia from me and pushed her against the wall. I scrambled up, but Telo was on me in the same moment. He hit me hard across the jaw, and I fell back against the bedpost.

"*Déjenlo, por favor, déjenlo!*" Sofia screamed.

But I was up again, my back to the wall, and Leandro had drawn his longknife.

"Brothers—" I started, my hands raised to show I was unarmed.

"Call us that again and we'll cut out your tongue," Leandro said.

"Please," I said. "I mean no harm. I wish to marry your sister. I—"

"Oh, you mean to marry her?" Leandro advanced with the knife. He shoved me against the wall and held the tapered blade to my throat. "You mean you wish to marry her after you've violated her? After you've left her unfit for any other man's bed? Well, by all means. Telo, have you any objections?"

"Don't," Sofia began. "Please—"

"Quiet," Telo said.

"But I asked him—" Sofia said.

Telo slapped her hard across the face. She fell against the wardrobe. Its sharp wood edge sliced her brow and blood streamed from the cut.

I struggled to go to her, but Leandro pushed his forearm into my throat. Telo turned from his sister to me and stalked across the room to where I stood naked, trapped against the wall.

"You come to our land." Telo leaned in close, his voice quiet and charged with menace. "Your force your Prophet on us. You raid our holy places. And now you have the gall to defile my sister in our own home."

"Telo," Leandro said warningly.

"No." Telo turned to his brother. "These Moors need a lesson. Hold him."

I tried to jerk away in panic, but Telo shoved me over the edge of Sofia's bed, and Leandro pinned me belly-down, his knife nicking behind my left ear. The bedclothes still held Sofia's warm smell, mixed with fresh blood and my own sharp fear. Telo's belt clicked.

"Please. . . . " I tried to turn, but Leandro's knife pressed below my jaw.

Telo knocked my legs apart with his boots. I felt pressure, and then pain ripped up through my bowels.

"No!" I screamed and strained my arms against them, but Leandro held me still as Telo forced himself into me. *Oh, God, this is happening, this is happening. God, stop it, God have mercy. This is happening.*

"Stop, please, stop." Sofia's voice shook.

My feet scrabbled uselessly on the floor.

"You'll pay a hundredfold for what you've done to our sister," Telo grunted in my ear.

He finished and drew back. I slumped beside the bed, shaking with shame and shock. *How could this have . . . oh, God, I am . . . why did you let this happen?*

Without warning, Telo leveled a kick at my ribs. I heard the pop of bone before I felt the pain. I fell to my side. Another kick, to my head this time. It caught my left eye, and one side of my vision exploded in a white starburst. Leandro joined in. One of them brought his foot down on my femur. I heard it snap and the room swam close to blackness. I rolled onto my stomach, tried to drag myself away from the blows, but they came at me from all sides. *Adán*, I thought, but no, he was far away in Córdoba, safe, presiding over his mother's table. I curled my arms around my head and tried to hold still in my own half-darkness, praying for it to end.

And then they were finished, the room silent except for Sofia's ragged crying.

"What have you done?" I heard Sofia say, somewhere far away.

"You stupid bitch," Telo said, out of breath. "Did you think your virtue was yours to give?"

"He is Ishaq ibn Hisham, the heir to the caliphate," she said. Her voice canted higher. "What have you done?"

The room went quiet. I blinked the darkness away from my open right eye. My left eye was already beginning to swell shut, and strange patterns of light danced across my field of vision. A surge of anger rolled over me, followed by shame and blackening pain. Anger. Shame. Pain.

"No one would blame us." Leandro's words swam close. "It's simple vengeance. *Breach for breach, eye for eye, tooth for tooth.*"

"No," Telo said. His footsteps sounded near my head. He snarled his hands in my hair and tugged me up sharply. "Help me, Leandro."

"That's enough," Leandro said.

"Enough?" Telo laughed. "For ruining our sister?" He took hold of my wrists and began pulling me from the room.

Leandro hung back, uncertain.

"What are you doing?" Sofia's voice shot high.

"Taking him to *Grandmère*," Telo said. "Let her judge what's to be done with him."

Telo pulled me to the stairs. Leandro followed. Fire shot up my side as the muscles tugged on my fractured rib. *Lamia*. Hope and dread clouded together in my chest. A woman with books might be civilized, might put an end to this, but the recipes for poisons and the stories, the boys' stories of her cursing them over mere oranges. . . . My broken leg fell limp against the landing. I cried out and all my thoughts dissolved in a burst of pain. A cold sweat broke over my body, mixing with the blood that slicked my neck where Leandro's knife had bitten me.

"Please," Sofia said, faint now.

My back hit the cool, smooth flagstones of the house's ground floor. Blearily, through my open right eye, I saw we were coming into the central hall, where a steady fire burned in the hearth. A woman in a red-hemmed gray dress sat before it. The fire's heat and the billowing darkness over my eye warped her face. The windows reflected the flames, backed by the dense blackness of the country night.

Telo dragged me up on my knees before her. I swayed. He grabbed the back of my neck and stood behind me, holding me upright.

Slowly, Lamia de Rampion turned her face from the fire. She was aged, but younger than I expected, regal in the way of women who have not forgotten what it was to be beautiful in their youth. Her hair waved black and silver in equal parts into a low, loose bun. My mind sparked and fever-wheeled with the notion that perhaps she was Sofia's mother after all, not her grandmother.

"What have you found?" she asked, cool and calm, the tone a cat's mistress would use when he made a present of his kill.

"A rat." Telo tightened his grip on my neck. "Glutting himself on our stores."

She lifted her chin to Leandro, standing at the bottom of the stair. "And where did you find him?"she asked, as though she already knew his reply.

"Upstairs," Leandro answered. "As you said."

"Please, *doña*." My voice trembled and scraped as I spoke. "If you would let me make amends . . . "

Lamia's eyes drifted down and hooked into my own. A chill washed over me. I could make out nothing of mercy in their depths.

"Amends?" She leaned forward, as if I had made an interesting point. "How do you propose to compensate me for what you have taken from us, hmm? Can you restore my granddaughter's virginity? Or perhaps you mean to repay us in horses and lands. Is that it, Moor? Will you heap us with gold if my granddaughter's legs prop open for you whenever you happen by?" Her voice stayed even, furiously calm.

"No, never—"

Lamia cut my words short with a curt lift of her hand. She stood, and I saw her then as she was, a woman with the full swell of her powers come to fruit. "Bind him, please, Telo," she said, nodding to a straight-backed wooden chair facing the fire.

I tried again. "*Doña*, please." I turned to Leandro. "Peace, brothers—"

"What did we say?" Telo asked. He heaved me into the chair and bent to bind my ankles to its legs with horse rope. "We're not your brothers."

"*Grandmère*," Leandro said from the stair. "What are you doing?"

"Please," I said. It hurt to breathe around my broken rib. "Let me go. I won't say a word. We can forget all this."

Telo twisted my arms and bound my wrists together behind the chair back in answer.

"You're Christians," I pleaded. I strained my arms against the ropes, but they held me fast. "Does your Christ not love mercy?"

Lamia walked behind me to the stairs. I craned my neck to see. "Lend me your knife, Leandro," she said.

"*Grandmère*—" Leandro said.

"Your knife," Lamia repeated.

Leandro handed it over slowly. Lamia rustled past me and knelt by the fireplace, shuffling her grandson's blade in the coals. "Do you know what our Christ says, Moor?" She turned her head to regard me over her shoulder. "Do you?"

My throat would not part to let me speak. "No," I whispered.

She spoke into the fire. "If thine eye do cause thee to offend, pluck it out and cast it from thee." She turned the knife within the coals. "Lest thy whole body should be cast into hell."

"I meant no offense to you or your granddaughter." I fought for enough breath to speak as the blade turned from dull silver to red. "Please, I love Sofia."

At that moment, Sofia's footsteps sounded on the stair behind us, light and bare. Lamia turned. The tip of the knife blade shone white, like a pale thorn, as if a little piece of noonday sun rested on its tip.

"No!" Sofia shouted behind me.

"Keep her back," Lamia said. Her voice crackled.

Sofia's screams grew to a hysterical pitch. Her feet fell in muted thuds against the floor as she tried to kick out of Leandro's grasp. My own heart beat like a piece of tin beneath a blacksmith's hammer, and my breath came gasping and shaky.

"Please," I tried one last time. "*Te suplico.*"

Lamia took my chin in her hand and shoved my head back so I was forced to look up into her eyes, black and dilated with carefully composed rage. "Here is my mercy, Moor. Remember my face when your world is dark." Then she pointed the tip of the knife at my open right eye and thrust the white-hot blade into its center.

We are packing up the wagons after a week's stay in Madrid to buy provisions and fit the horses with fresh tack when the cry goes up from the back of the line.

"God, no. It cannot be. *Ojalá que no.*" A woman's voice wavers above the crowded plaza.

And soon other voices echo her prayer, spreading through the crowd all at once like water coming to a boil.

"Madinat al-Zahra," someone says.

I drop the water bucket I am holding to Pulga's mouth and fumble blindly for the nearest man's arm. "What of the palace?" I ask.

"It's fallen," the man says. "It's been razed, and the fires seen burning five whole days from the Córdoban gates."

A cold chill slaps my body. I cannot stop myself from picturing all my familiar books blackened and shrunk by flames, the deep fountains boiled bare, the gilt ceiling raining molten drops of gold as the roof catches fire.

"Who was it?" I ask. "The Northern lords? Or the Abbasids? Have they sent ships from Baghdad?"

"Neither," the man says. "Vizier Sanchuelo lost control of his Berbers, and they took it on themselves to destroy the palace city."

My hands tremble in their grip on his coat. "And the caliph?" I ask.

"Abdicated," the man answers, and pushes past me to repeat his story for other ears.

I grope my way to the wagon's tail and sink down beneath it, by the tall wheels. The world spins too quickly around me, and behind my ruined eyes all I can see are tongues of fire spreading like oil over the glossy leaves of the towering hedges, the tapestries ash, carved ivory doors blackened and hanging ajar, boot prints in the soot. I clutch at the braid around my neck like a drowning man.

*Is this Your punishment?* I ask God. *To know I could have stopped this, and yet stand fettered by blindness as my world burns?*

"Ishaq?" a woman's voice says.

For one reeling moment, I think it's Sofia. But then the wheels of my mind start turning in tandem again, and I realize it's Mencia. My given name is common enough I've told it to her.

"They've burned Madinat al-Zahra," I say.

"Ishaq, get up." Her strong hand grips me at the elbow. "We have to move. They're barring the city gates."

I cling to the back of the wagon as our caravan lurches forward. The watchmen at the gates shout after us that we'll be safer inside the city walls with the other refugees fled from *al Andalus*, but I know Lázaro has his reasons for wanting to push on. The horses rise to a canter as we hurry north.

I broke into black consciousness with Adán crouched over me. Pain wormed in every inch of my body. An animal moan rose deep in my throat.

"Softly, brother," Adán said. "I don't know if they're coming back."

The overlapping *criii* of cicadas pulsed in the air. I felt dirt and dry, sparse grass beneath my hands. "Where are we?" I asked.

"The eastern edge of the Rampion lands," Adán whispered. "I dragged you from the house."

"Your men . . . ?" My throat sounded stripped to my own ears.

"No," Adán said. "I followed you alone."

"Sofia?"

"I saw four horses galloping from the gate. Two men and two women." Adán paused. Dirt scraped beneath his feet as he stood. "I'll send word to the caliph. Our men will catch them before the night is out. They'll be executed at dawn."

"No." I flailed my hand blindly and grasped the hem of his cloak.

Adán knelt beside me again. "No?"

"If they kill them, the Northern lords will take it as cause for open war." My chest ached. I felt sick. "I have to protect—"

"Brother, they've taken your eyes. And your leg. . . . " He stopped, unable to name the other thing they had done to me.

My left eye burned with tears behind its swollen lid. The right stayed dead. "No," I repeated, trying to sound firm. "I'm to blame. Please, Adán. . . . " My voice broke.

Adán smoothed his hands over my brow. "We'll wait, then." He kissed my forehead. "I'll get my horse."

"Anadil is by the river," I said.

Adán paused a beat too long. "Don't worry. I'll come back for her."

He returned a few minutes later, heralded by the faint clop of his stallion's hooves. He wrapped me in his cloak and heaved me onto the horse's back. Pain ripped through my leg and side, and nausea rolled over me as my innards shifted, but I clung to the horse's mane. Adán led the horse quietly past the outer palisades of the Rampion estate, into the open country.

We made our way to a small village along the road to Córdoba, where Adán roused a doctor he knew.

"God have mercy," the doctor breathed over me when Adán unwrapped the cloak from my shoulders.

Together, he and Adán brought me into his kitchen and laid me on the broad table. The doctor reset the bone in my leg and woke his wife so she could help him make a poultice for my eyes. Afterward, they washed me and prayed over me and wrapped me in a quilt, and for some time, I lost all knowledge of what happened to me.

I woke to the sound of running water, a courtyard fountain. For a moment, I thought I had been allowed passage into Paradise, despite what my life had been. But the high burn raking the marrow of my bones thrust that thought from my mind. I remembered the doctor and raised a hand carefully to my ribs. My whole chest had been wrapped in soft bands of cloth, my wrists in the same where they had rubbed raw against the horse rope. I felt something clutched in my left hand. Sofia's braid. I tried to open my eyes, but couldn't.

Someone shifted beside me. "Brother?" Adán said quietly.

"Adán?" I said.

"Yes." His hand was cool on my forehead.

"Am I going to die?"

"No," he said.

"Where am I?" I asked.

"You're safe," Adán said. "My friend Nasir has given us room in his house. He'll keep us safe here, keep us hidden."

"Sofia?"

Adán took my hand in his. "Her whole estate is empty, the doors left open to the dogs."

I tried to raise myself on my elbows, but the pain flared through me again. I fell back to my pallet with a whimper.

"Rest," Adán said. "I promise I'll find her. *Te lo juro.* Only rest."

I drifted beneath the surface of a fever. Nightmares plagued me, where Lamia cut open my chest and used my body as a cauldron for poisons, while Sofia lay beside me and held my hand. Adán came and went from the house, gathering news from Córdoba and coming back to whisper to me what he had overheard. My mother and father and sisters were safe at Madinat al-Zahra, so the attempt had been on my life alone, he said, still ignorant of my part in what had happened. My father had detached his own guard to search the countryside for me, in addition to the vizier's foot soldiers, and they had offered to reward any man who could lead them to me.

"Sanchuelo tries to accuse the Jews of a plot to murder the caliph and his family," Adán said, kneeling by my couch in the shaded eaves of Nasir's courtyard. "He uses my name. Though they say your father won't believe it."

A rare breeze touched my neck. Earlier in the day, Nasir and his wife had propped me up on a bank of pillows in the corner of the courtyard, where they said the open air would help me recover. I hadn't spoken since I first awoke in their house.

"Ishaq," Adán said. "Why did they do this to you? Tell me."

My lips had dried together. I pulled them apart to answer. "Sofia."

"What about her?" Adán asked in frustration.

"I . . . I shouldn't have . . . without her brothers' consent. . . . " My throat closed around the words. I pressed my nails into my palms.

"You took her for a lover?" I could hear the anger in Adán's voice, but I didn't know if it was meant for me or Sofia's kin.

"Yes." I leaned forward into the pain in my ribs. *I deserve it, I deserve it. Oh, God.*

Adán didn't speak. His leather coverlet creaked as he rose. He scuffed around the perimeter of the courtyard's smooth flagstones, and then came back and knelt beside me. "You loved her?"

"I would have married her," I said.

He fell silent again.

"God has delivered His judgment," I said, so quietly the steady rush of the fountain nearly hid my voice. "With their hands He marks me unfit to rule."

Adán took my head in his hands and kissed my forehead again, as he had done the night he found me. "Brother, you know better than to ascribe the will of God to the works of men."

A hard tear burned my left eye. I wished to God for Him to consume me in flame or let the earth open up for me—*Oh, God, let me cease to be*—but the quiet heat of the sun continued, and the water bubbling from the fountain, and the birdsong from the roof, and I did not cease to be. I reached out to Adán. "I cannot go back to my father's house. He can't know."

Adán laid his hand over mine. "Anything you say."

"Will you . . . will you find her?" I tightened my grip on his hand. We both knew I was too damaged to rise from my bed, much less seek her on my own. "See she's kept safe and whole?"

"Yes," Adán agreed.

"She has an uncle somewhere in Catalunya. They may have taken her there. See she has everything she needs. Shoes for her feet and cloaks for winter. And see no one speaks ill of her name." My throat closed in on itself and the words halted in my mouth. I choked on all I wanted to give her. Pearls to seed her hair and a swift horse to ride out on whenever she chose, all the books of my library, a place at my side when I wrested control of the caliphate back from Sanchuelo. But without the sight of the courtyard to distract me, my mind unrolled the image of Telo striking her, her head hitting the wardrobe, the look on her face when she saw me stripped of my manhood, abased and unclean, helpless to save either of us.

"I will," Adán said. "Anything you say, brother. But if I go, you must be ready when they start to speak of me as your murderer. I won't be able to set foot in *al Andalus* so long as they remember your name. I won't be able to come back for you."

*God forgive me, God forgive me.*

"I know," I said. "Go."

He rode out on the north road in the cool predawn dark the next morning.

Some months later, when my bones had healed and my eyes crusted over in a thick stratum of scabs and scar tissue, I asked Nasir to bring me a walking stick. I pushed myself slowly to his front door.

"Stay," Nasir pleaded. "There's no need for you to leave. How will your friend Hadid find you if you go?"

"He won't return," I said. "God grant it, I may go to him some day, but he won't return."

Thus I left the quiet of Nasir's house for Córdoba, to live in the shadow of what was once my home, to erase myself from all men's memories, and to pray for word that would lead me back to my beloved and my friend.

We have reached the wooded no-man's-land inside the Catalan border, by the chill banks of the river Segre. Our caravan has been shrinking, the imam and the students long since left behind in Madrid, and many of the merchants stopped in smaller cities and towns along the way. Lázaro and his men make up the bulk of the caravan, save Miguel's wagon and a Christian merchant we picked up, also bound for Catalunya. We file close together over the narrow road. At night, we sleep in the woods. We light no fires. Icy rain patters down on us in the day, heralding autumn in the North country. Even Mencia has fallen under the pall of silence that hovers over us. Although we have traveled beyond the chaos rippling out from Córdoba, unallied highwaymen and Visigoth war bands roam the wilderness in these parts. A fight has broken out among Lázaro's men about whether to abandon Miguel, Mencia, and me, since traveling with Jews and a Moor so near the Pyrenees places them in danger. But so far, we haven't woken to find them gone.

I walk alongside the cart with my hand resting on its upper boards while the mapmaker's horses strain up a steep grade. Wet rocks bite my feet and several times I slip, but catch myself on the cart's edge in time to keep from sliding under the wheels. My leg aches at the old break. The crash of whitewater roars up from the river gorge below. Lázaro's men have ridden ahead, but when we finally crest the hill, we find them stopped.

"What's happening?" I ask.

"Shhh." Miguel quiets me.

"State your allegiance," a strange man's voice, speaking Catalan, booms over the road.

No one answers.

"State your allegiance," the stranger tries again, in Castellano this time. The words are heavy in his mouth. He swallows the ends of them, and it takes me a moment to remember where I've heard his accent before. *I am ten years old, jacketed in gold brocade and standing in the shadow of my father's throne. A Visigoth chieftain with a heavy black beard and pale skin stands at the base of the dais, a gilt and sapphire cross glinting in the fox fur at his neck, an emissary from our ancestors' long-vanquished enemies. . . .*

"State yours," Lázaro says. The sound of swords drawn from their scabbards rings throughout the group of men arrayed on the path before us.

"I am Athanric of the Wese. We swear allegiance to his Holiness Pope John XVIII." The Visigoth shouts to be heard over the river. A fine sleet begins to fall.

"Then we have no quarrel with you," Lázaro says. "We go to the court of King Filipe of Roussillon to aid his cause in retaking the southern lands from the Moorish kings."

"And yet you travel with a Moor," Athanric says. He pauses, as if working out a problem in his head. "And Jews?"

I cannot see, but I feel the gaze of two score pairs of eyes turned on our wagon in the silence that follows.

"They're no part of our caravan," Lázaro replies.

"Then you will not object if we dispatch them from your company," the Visigoth says. "We would be remiss in our Christian duty if we did not baptize them here in the river."

Lázaro pauses. The cold gush of the river rises in the silence. An uneasy murmur works its way through his men. "No," Lázaro says. "They're no concern of ours."

Mencia clutches my arm.

"Good lords." Miguel raises his voice for the first time, and I am surprised at how strong and clear it is after so much silence. "I am a tradesman. My wife and I travel to Organá, no further, and this man is our servant. We are no threat to you."

"A Jewish tradesman," Athanric says. He thumps the flat of his sword against his leg. "And wearing no marks on his clothes."

"It is not our custom in the south," Miguel says quietly.

"Ah, but it is custom here," Athanric says. His voice and the rhythmic beat of his sword move closer. "As well as law. And lawbreakers must be punished."

Mencia cries out. Her hand jerks from mine. Her husband shouts and there is an awful, thick sound of fists on flesh and scrabbling in the wet dirt. Tearing fabric rips the wet air.

"Perhaps we will dispense justice here and now," the Visigoth says.

*Save us*, I pray, shaking with cold and furious impotence. *Save them. Save her. Don't let anyone else suffer because I am helpless to stop it.*

Mencia screams, longer this time and more pained.

*This cannot be Your will*, I say to God. *If it is, I will not bow to it.*

And then there are hoofbeats on the slope behind us, dozens, loud as war drums, kicking up stones and spattering mud as they skid to a stop behind our party.

"Look what we have today," a man says. "Athanric of the Wese." His voice is full of humor and menace in equal parts, and my heart near stops, for I would know it anywhere. It belongs to Adán Hadid. The man who gave up his life in service of mine. Who defied God's law and rode out to save me on a Shabbat eve.

"This is none of your concern, de Lanza," Athanric says.

"Perhaps," Adán says, easy with his false name. "But I see you have taken some of my countrymen, so perhaps I will find it is my concern after all."

The Visigoth swears in his own tongue. He calls to his men, and their horses stamp as they mount and draw away.

"Some day I'll find you outnumbered," Athanric shouts over the sound of his men's retreat.

"Be sure it's four to one," Adán calls after him.

The pounding of their hoofbeats fades into the distance. Mencia cries quietly as her husband murmurs and soothes her. I am frozen, locked still as stone. My heart is the only thing moving. Will Adán recognize me, changed as I must be? And will Lázaro know his quarry by sight, or by name only?

Adán's horse clops toward Lázaro's band, grouped on the side of the road. "Gentlemen, if you're in need of an escort, my men and I will be happy to accompany you for a small fee. Where are you going?"

"Roussillon." Lázaro coughs.

"What do you say, shall we go to Roussillon?" Adán calls to his men.

"To Roussillon!" they shout in response, and beat their swords on their shields.

"With your consent, of course," Adán says to Lázaro.

"*Por supuesto*," Lázaro says, the strain evident in his words. "We would be grateful, sir."

Adán spends several moments making sure Miguel's cart is undamaged, he and his wife secure within it, and calls for a beaver-skin blanket to shield Mencia from the icy rain. Then we are off again, moving through the trees at a steady clip with Adán's men riding in a protective circle around us.

I walk on, steadying myself with one hand on the cart. My legs shake with every step.

A horse veers close to me and slows to my pace. "Do these men know who you are, brother?" Adán says quietly.

I turn my face up to him, even though all I can see is the hazy, muted green of the damp trees all around us. Joy hits me like a wall, and I stop. The cart rolls on without me. "No," I say.

"We'll move faster if we place this man on a horse," Adán calls up to Lázaro. "And bring him some spare boots."

Lázaro mutters to himself, but sends one of his men to the back of the line with an older mare and a pair of worn riding boots. Adán dismounts and helps me up onto her back, then ties my horse's reins to his own. They trot side by side. It is all I can do not to reach out and take Adán's hand.

"Did you think I wouldn't recognize you?" Adán says.

"I didn't know if you were alive," I say. "My father laid a death sentence on you before the vizier seized control, and that man Lázaro is looking for you."

"I have more men than he," Adán says. "And better trained. Though I do ask myself what you're doing following him into Catalunya."

"Sofia," I say. "He's bringing these horses to her uncle in Roussillon. She's there with them."

We ride in silence for several minutes. The air is full of the steady grate of hooves on loose stone.

"So that's where they've been keeping her," Adán says.

"You couldn't find her?" My last memory of her, bleeding and wild-eyed, unfurls before me again.

"I'm sorry." Adán leans over in the saddle and grips my wrist. "I tracked them as far as the Pyrenees, but I didn't know how deep they'd gone. It isn't friendly territory for Jews, even those with their own war bands."

Silence laps over us again. The sleet falls steadily, but my horse's heat steams away some of the cold.

"What will you do when you find her?" Adán asks after a time. "I don't suppose her grandmother and brothers will usher you into her arms."

"No," I say. "I had only figured out the part where I lived to come this far."

"You were always terrible at strategy." I can hear the boyish smirk in Adán's words.

"I'm out of practice," I say.

"When this is done, I'm tutoring you."

A piece of my youth flexes in my chest. Maybe it is the feel of a horse beneath me again, the way my body remembers and responds to its sway, keeps me righted. Maybe it is that I am riding closer to Sofia, and the invisible cord between us is tightening, transmitting the vibration of our hearts. Or maybe it is that my friend is at my side again, speaking to me as a man, and he has always carried some piece of me wherever he goes.

After another run-in on the road, with common thieves this time, Lázaro decides to keep Adán and his men on. Lázaro suggests the party will travel faster if they leave Miguel, Mencia, and me to find our own way while they go on to Roussillon, but Adán won't hear it. And so we deliver the mapmaker and his wife to Organá, where we buy furs for the journey higher into the Pyrenees.

As we prepare to go, Miguel hurries to push a folded square of vellum into Adán's hand. "A map of Roussillon," he says. "In case you find some difficulty leaving."

While we ride, Lázaro's men talk of the vats of mulled wine awaiting us at Filipe's castle, venison on spits, the sweet crackle of pine logs on the hearths in the great hall. The mountain road slopes sharply. It whips around corners and narrows so we must ride single file. On the fourth day of our trek, we wake to a fine glaze of frost stiffening our blankets and the mat of fallen leaves where we made our bed the night before. The clouds hang low and chill in a fog across the road. And then, on the twelfth day, the men at the front of the line shout that they've sighted the timber barricades circling Filipe's thatch-roof fortress.

"I can't go in," I say to Adán under my breath. My horse jerks her head, picking up on the fear seeping from my body. "Lamia, Sofia's brothers—"

"Hang back." Adán reins in my horse.

We slow until the last of Adán's men pass us. "Ride on," Adán tells them. "I'll catch up."

We veer into the trees, Adán leading my horse, and wend our way deeper until we come to a dense thicket. Adán wraps me in skins and furs, pushes a knife into my hand.

"Stay here," he says. "I'll see what I can find and bring you word." He hurries to his horse. Its hoofbeats disappear into the silence.

I shiver under the skins and chafe my arms for warmth. Cold burns in the fissure where Sofia's brothers broke my leg nearly two years past. I am afraid to warm myself by walking, in case I should become lost in the woods and Adán come back to find the thicket empty. I sit and rock instead.

After a time, the pale gray light I can detect through my left eye recedes into darkness, and the very air I breathe burns like swallowing live coals. Fat snowflakes filter through the canopy of trees. Wolves keen high in the woods above me, answered by their mates somewhere deeper in the vales below. A small creature cries out, an unearthly strangled noise, almost human. I pile leaves and pine needles in a nest and burrow beneath them like an animal, hoping they will hide my scent.

"I am come for her." I speak aloud to God, as though He might be hovering in the frozen air, sitting impassive at the edge of the thicket. Here in the vast, rough expanse of mountain range that holds my beloved in its teeth, it is easy to imagine Him a different, more savage being than the God of my childhood.

The wolves' voices melt together in one long howl. It sounds as though the earth itself is moaning, and I shiver again as the thought of Lamia passes before me. Lamia, roving the hills below, calling up all the wild and pale-toothed things of the earth against me. The wind her skirts, churning the dead leaves to fall anew.

"I am come for her," I repeat, and it makes me feel more human to hear the words falling back to my ear, muted by the soft snow. I curl into the leaves and try to imagine they are Sofia's body pressed close, the backs of her knees tucked against mine, her hair soft on my face, safe.

The squeak of boots on snow starts me awake. I freeze, rigid and alert beneath the layers of leaves and animal skins. I tighten my grip on the knife.

"Ishaq?" Adán calls quietly. "Where are you?"

I push myself up. "Here."

"Ishaq." Adán hurries to me and crouches at my side. "Are you well?"

"Cold," I say. My teeth knock against each other.

"I'll build a fire," he says. He clears an empty space on the ground and digs a trench around it. I hear him snapping branches and the *tap-click* of his flints striking flame into the kindling.

Warm, red light flares in my good eye, and I think for a moment I can even make out the shadow of Adán's body as he moves between me and the flames. Waves of heat push the cold from my face and hands. Adán sits beside me and wraps us together in the same bearskin so we can share warmth. We wait in silence for our bodies to stop shaking.

"I saw her," he says.

My heart jolts. "Is she . . . ? Have they . . . ?"

"They've married her to Henri du Cerét, one of her uncle's knights."

I feel as though someone has sprinkled salt on my heart. The fire pops and sizzles as snowflakes turn to vapor in its flames.

"She served our meal, but she wouldn't speak to any of us," Adán says.

I swallow. "And Lamia?"

"She was there, at the seat nearest the fire," Adán says. "She seemed . . . I don't know, sick, diminished. Not at all as you described her. They had her wrapped in furs, and she was coughing so hard, she could barely hold the wine cup to her lips. They say some sickness has entered her lungs."

The shock of his words saps all the feeling from my limbs. I had imagined Lamia ever as she was, clear-eyed and cruel in her command of man and earth. I know if I were righteous, I would ask God to show mercy, true mercy, even to this, my enemy. But in truth the only feeling I can muster is relief. So she is not afoot beneath the moon, in communion with the wolves and winds. She is flesh and blood after all, and I am glad of it.

Adán clears his throat. "There's more."

"What more?" I ask.

"They say Sofia has two children."

"Children?" I hear myself say, although it sounds as if someone else is speaking those words from the far side of the thicket.

"Twins," Adán says. "A boy and a girl, a little over a year old."

The earth moves too fast, and my body is spinning opposite its turn. I see Sofia laid out on the bed, under some other man. I shove the knife Adán gave me down to its hilt in the mossy soil.

"Ishaq." Adán repeats the words slowly. "Over a year old."

I force myself calm enough to figure what he means. I count the months. *Four for my journey from* al Andalus *to Roussillon. Close to a year on the streets of Córdoba. Six months lost to healing in the doctor's home. A year and ten months in all since I last lay with Sofia.* I grab Adán's arm and stand. The bearskin falls to the dirt at our feet.

Adán tries to hide a laugh. "They say her children have dark hair, and they share their mother's eyes, but not her complexion. There are whispers Henri du Cerét might have been cuckolded before he was even wed."

"Take me to her," I say. I can hear the twist of pleading in my voice. I feel for the furs Adán left me earlier in the day and begin hurriedly wrapping them around me. "I'll go now. Show me the way."

"Easy. Calm," Adán says. "It isn't that simple."

I sit down again and let out a breath in frustration. "You're right. I know."

"We could steal her away," Adán says. "You could send some sign with me, and with her help and my men, we could do it."

I touch the braid of hair around my throat.

"But they would give chase, and if it's known you're the one who's taken her, you risk bringing all the fury of the Christian armies down wherever you go. You could never return to *al Andalus* to retake the caliphate."

I nod and swallow.

"So you decide. Will you take her from this place and go on being no one, or will you forget her and become Ishaq ibn Hisham of the Umayyad line again?" Adán says.

A log resettles itself in the fire. The flames flare, and then shrink.

Adán touches my arm. "You know if you ride south, I would go with you. I would raise an army for you."

I rub my forehead. "Give me the night," I say. "I need to think."

"As you say."

Adán piles more branches on the fire and rolls himself in the bearskin to sleep. I feel my way to the edge of the thicket and turn my face up to the sky. The snow has stopped falling, but the wind trails its cold fingers over my face.

*God, are You there?* I ask.

Until now, I never truly understood the story of the Hebrew king Suleiman asking God not for long life, or wealth, or the death of his enemies, but the boon of wisdom. Would that God would offer me such a bargain. Would that He would speak to me as He spoke to the prophets. Would that He would send me His messenger angel.

*If You speak to my heart, I will listen. Will You speak to me? Are You there?*

The wind makes a hollow sound in the treetops.

I kneel and touch my head to the wet leaves rotting on the ground, unsure if I am facing Mecca or if I am turned away.

*I am lost*, I pray. For the tug of vengeance and duty pulls me back to *al Andalus*, but my heart fills with panic and a terrible blackness when I think of coming so close to Sofia, only to slip away again, to leave her at the mercy of Lamia, to abandon my own children. Does God wish me to be a man or a king?

*What is Your will?* I ask. *What I feel in my heart, is this Your will? Or are You testing me as You tested Ibrahim? Would You have me leave my people in anarchy? Would You have me leave my beloved and my children in the care of the men who tried to murder me? How can I know Your will if You will not speak to me?*

The cold creeps into me, but still I kneel, my head to the earth, my hands tight around Sofia's braid. Dim light seeps into the thicket. I raise my head. My limbs pop and my joints grind with stiffness as I right myself. I draw in the first cold breath of day. "You will not answer for me, will You?" I say aloud.

I stand and pick my way through the thicket to Adán's side. "Brother," I say. I shake him gently.

He sits up.

*Let this be Your will.* I take the braid from my neck and slowly pull it over my head. I feel for Adán's hand and drop the slip of hair into his open palm.

"Tell her I'm come for her and the children." My voice scrapes my throat, for in the shadow of my words I see tombstones stacked high as fortress walls, shining towers in flames, and blood in the marketplace.

*Forgive me*, I say. *Forgive me.*

Adán rises. He shakes the pine needles from the bearskin and stamps the fire to ashes. "Wait here," he says. "Be ready." And he kisses my head before he crashes away in the direction of the road.

I pace the thicket. I warm my hands over the hot ashes of our fire. The hollow of my chest feels stripped, between the ache of wanting for Sofia and my children and the knowledge that I've surrendered Córdoba to whoever steeps it in the most blood. The Berbers. The Abbasids. The Christians of the North. I lie down by the fire's remnants, too tired even to sleep, and stare blindly up at the sky.

I must fall asleep at last, for when I wake, the sun has burned through the morning gloom. Its light is bright all around me. Somewhere down the steep vale below the thicket, a baby cries. Another child joins in, echoing its wailing. But their voices waver and quiet as a woman picks up a song. Her voice is husky with the cold.

*Cuando me vengo al rio*
*Te pido, te pido, te pido,*

And then her voice peaks higher, clear as church bells, clear as the muezzin's call.

*Que siempre serás mio,*
*Y te juro, te juro, te juro,*
*Que nunca te quitaré.*

I stand. It is the voice that drew me from the riverbank to the orange grove, tied a string to my heart. For a moment, I think it might be my memory, grown stronger now that I am near my beloved again, for can Adán even have had time to deliver my message? But no, in my memory, there is no child's cry, no small imperfection in her voice. My heart catches and lifts high. I start forward, pushing through the thick trees, and stumble out into an open vale. I trip down the hill, fall, and right myself again. I am running blind, stalks of dry winter grass slapping my legs, but her voice is closer now, more real than anything in my memory. I am running and falling, running again, her voice so near I know if she keeps singing I will be able to run straight to her.

The song halts.

I stop in my tracks. The wind rustles the grass.

"Ishaq?" The word comes from my right, only a few paces ahead.

I drop to my knees. *Let it be her. I know I am not worthy, but let it be her.*

"Ishaq?"

I stretch out my hands. "Sofia?"

She throws herself into me. Her arms lock around me, the thick wool of her dress warm on my skin, the smell of her different now, less salt and more smoke, but still her. Her throat makes a wrenching noise. She kisses my mouth, my eyelids, my forehead, my cheeks. I hold her and hold her and let my sorrow spill out of me. We rock together in the tall grass. One of her tears hits my face and courses down into my left eye. I blink. For a moment, I think I see a flash of red gold, her hair. I reach for her face and trace the line of her jaw, the delicate folds of her ears.

My knuckles brush her hair. It seems lighter, too light. I feel for her braid, but it isn't there.

"Your hair . . . ," I say, frowning.

She takes my hand and guides it from root to tip. It stops in a ragged line where her shoulders meet her neck. "*Grandmère* cut it as punishment," she says.

"Oh." I lean my head heavily on her collarbone and crush her against me. She is thinner, her body more worn. "Sofia, forgive me." *Forgive me, forgive me.*

"It was nothing," she says. She kisses my eyes. Her voice breaks. "It was nothing."

"How are you here?" I cock my ears from side to side, but all I can hear is the gentle chafe of dry grass. "Where are your brothers? Are they far behind?"

Sofia takes my face in her hands. A small tremor runs through her fingers. "They're not coming."

"How—"

"I've been watching a long time, in case the chance should come," she says. "Preparing. Last night, I heard Cordobán voices in the hall, and two soldiers from that man de Lanza's band talking of a blind servant in the woods. And when de Lanza left to tend to him. . . . "

I open my mouth to speak, but Sofia stops me with her rough fingers laid soft on my lips. She takes a trembling breath. "After they brought me here, I found *Grandmère*'s books, the ones on poisons and sleeping draughts—"

"Sofia." I try to stop her. I do not want her to admit what she is about to say.

"And when Henri allowed me out for walks, I began looking for the plants they describe."

"Sofia." I try again.

"No, listen Ishaq," she says firmly. "I couldn't find any poppies or fellenwort to make them sleep. . . . "

*No.*

"But I found a laburnum tree."

Laburnum. I see the pages of her grandmother's *Pharmakopia* open on the table before me again. "They're dead?" I make myself ask.

"I don't know." She clears her throat and reins in the trembling in her voice.

I take her shaking hand in my own. I would forgive her anything.

"*Grandmère*'s book only said what would kill a man, not how much would force him down past waking. I tried to dilute it, but. . . . " Her words soften, as though she's turned away from me to cast one last look at the castle. "I don't know what I've done, Ishaq."

I kiss her fingertips again and again, because there isn't anything in the world to say.

"Lady?" an older woman's voice calls behind her. "Are you well?" One of the children makes a high, questioning noise, testing the sound of its voice.

"Is that my daughter?" I ask. "My son?"

"Yes," Sofia says softly to me. She turns and calls over her shoulder. "Yes, I'm well."

The wind stirs the grass around us, carrying the scent of rain and pine and far-off smoke.

"Come." Sofia takes my hand and helps me to my feet. "Come and meet your children."

# AND WEEP LIKE ALEXANDER

## NEIL GAIMAN

The little man hurried into the Fountain and ordered a very large whisky. "Because," he announced to the pub in general, "I deserve it."

He looked exhausted, sweaty and rumpled, as if he had not slept in several days. He wore a tie, but it was so loose as to be almost undone. He had greying hair that might once have been ginger.

"I'm sure you do," said Brian Dalton.

"I do!" said the man. He took a sip of the whisky as if to find out if he liked it, then, satisfied, gulped down half the glass. He stood completely still, for a moment, like a statue. "Listen," he said. "Can you hear it?"

"What?" I said.

"A sort of background whispering white noise that actually becomes whatever song you wish to hear when you sort of half-concentrate upon it?"

I listened. "No," I said.

"Exactly," said the man, extraordinarily pleased with himself. "Isn't it *wonderful*? Only yesterday, everybody in the Fountain was complaining about the Wispamuzak. Professor Mackintosh here was grumbling about having Queen's "Bohemian Rhapsody" stuck in his head and how it was now following him across London. Today, it's gone, as if it had never been. None of you can even remember that it existed. And that is all due to me."

"I what?" said Professor Mackintosh. "Something about the Queen?" And then, "Do I know you?"

"We've met," said the little man. "But people forget me, alas. It is because of my job." He took out his wallet, produced a card, passed it to me.

**Obediah Polkinghorn**

it read, and beneath that in small letters,

**UNINVENTOR.**

"If you don't mind my asking," I said. "What's an uninventor?"

"It's somebody who uninvents things," he said. He raised his glass, which was quite empty. "Ah. Excuse me, Sally, I need another very large whisky."

The rest of the crowd there that evening seemed to have decided that the man was both mad and uninteresting. They had returned to their conversations. I, on the other hand, was caught. "So," I said, resigning myself to my conversational fate. "Have you been an uninventor long?"

"Since I was fairly young," he said. "I started uninventing when I was eighteen. Have you never wondered why we do not have jet-packs?"

I had, actually.

"Saw a bit on Tomorrow's World about them, when I was a lad," said Michael, the landlord. "Man went up in one. Then he came down. Raymond Burr seemed to think we'd all have them soon enough."

"Ah, but we don't," said Obediah Polkinghorn, "because I uninvented them about twenty years ago. I had to. They were driving everybody mad. I mean, they seemed so attractive, and so cheap, but you just had to have a few thousand bored teenagers strapping them on, zooming all over the place, hovering outside bedroom windows, crashing into the flying cars . . . "

"Hold on," said Sally. "There aren't any flying cars."

"True," said the little man, "But there were. You wouldn't believe the traffic jams they'd cause. You'd look up and it was just the bottoms of bloody flying cars from horizon to horizon. Some days I couldn't see the skies at all. People throwing rubbish out of their car windows . . . They were easy to run—ran off gravitosolar power, obviously—but I didn't realise that they needed to go until I heard a lady talking about them on Radio Four, all 'Why Oh Why Didn't We Stick With Non-Flying Cars?' She had a point. Something needed to be done. I uninvented them. I made a list of inventions the world would be better off without and, one by one, I uninvented them all."

By now he had started to gather a small audience. I was pleased I'd grabbed a good seat.

"It was a lot of work, too," he continued. "You see, it's almost impossible *not* to invent the Flying Car, as soon as you've invented the Lumenbubble. So eventually I had to uninvent that too. And I miss the individual Lumenbubble: a massless portable light-source that floated half a metre above your head and went on when you wanted it to. Such a wonderful invention. Still, no use crying over unspilt milk, and you can't mend an omelette without unbreaking a few eggs."

"You also can't expect us actually to believe any of this," said someone, and I think it was Jocelyn.

"Right," said Brian. "I mean, next thing you'll be telling us that you uninvented the space ship."

"But I did," said Obediah Polkinghorn. He seemed extremely pleased with himself. "Twice. I had to. You see, the moment we whizz off into space and head out to the planets and beyond, we bump into things that spur so many other inventions. The Polaroid Instant Transporter. That was the worst. And the Mockett Telepathic Translator. That was the worst as well. But as long as it's nothing worse than a rocket to the moon, I can keep everything under control."

"So, how exactly do you go about uninventing things?" I asked.

"It's hard," he admitted. "It's all about unpicking probability threads from the fabric of creation. But they tend to be long and tangled, like spaghetti. So it's rather like having to unpick a strand of spaghetti from a haystack."

"Sounds like thirsty work," said Michael, and I signalled him to pour me another pint of Old Bodger.

"Fiddly," said the little man. "Yes. But I pride myself on doing good. Each day I wake, and, even if I've unhappened something that might have been wonderful, I think, Obediah Polkington, the world is a happier place because of something that you've uninvented."

He looked into his remaining scotch, swirled the liquid around in his glass.

"The trouble is," he said, "with the Wispamuzak gone, that's it. I'm done. It's all been uninvented. There are no more horizons left to undiscover, no more mountains left to unclimb."

"Nuclear Power?" suggested 'Tweet' Peston.

"Before my time," said Obediah. "Can't uninvent things invented before I was born. Otherwise I might uninvent something that would have led to my birth, and then where would we be?" Nobody had any suggestions. "Knee-high in jet-packs and flying cars, that's where," he told us. "Not to mention Morrison's Martian Emolument." For a moment, he looked quite grim. "Ooh. That stuff was nasty. And a cure for cancer. But frankly, given what it did to the oceans, I'd rather have the cancer.

"No. I have uninvented everything that was on my list. I shall go home," said Obediah Polkinghorn, bravely, "and weep, like Alexander, because there are no more worlds to unconquer. What is there left to uninvent?"

There was silence in the Fountain.

In the silence, Brian's iPhone rang. His ring-tone was The Rutles singing 'Cheese and Onions'. "Yeah?" he said. Then, "I'll call you back."

It is unfortunate that the pulling out of one phone can have such an effect on other people around. Sometimes I think it's because we remember when we could smoke in pubs, and that we pull out our phones together as once we pulled out our cigarette packets. But probably it's because we're easily bored.

Whatever the reason, the phones came out.

Crown Baker took a photo of us all, and then Twitpicced it. Jocelyn started to read her text messages. Tweet Peston tweeted that he was in the Fountain and had met his first uninventor. Professor Mackintosh checked the Test Match scores, told us what they were and emailed his brother in Inverness to grumble about them. The phones were out and the conversation was over.

"What's that?" asked Obediah Polkinghorn.

"It's the iPhone 5," said Ray Arnold, holding his up. "Crown's using the Nexus X. That's the Android system. Phones. Internet. Camera. Music. But it's the apps. I mean, do you know, there are over a thousand fart sound-effect apps on the iPhone alone? You want to hear the unofficial Simpsons Fart App?"

"No," said Obediah. "I most definitely do not want to. I do *not*." He put down his drink, unfinished. Pulled his tie up. Did up his coat. "It's not going to be easy," he said, as if to himself. "But, for the good of all . . . " And then he stopped. And he grinned. "It's been marvellous talking to you all," he announced to nobody in particular as he left the Fountain.

# WIDOWS IN THE WORLD

## GAVIN J. GRANT

The Granny wasn't talking to any of them. The husband was collecting rocks, the other wives had stayed with the house, her mother was stretching at the other end of the beach, and the kids were running wild in the waves. The baby, still *in utero*, had only recently begun talking to her and already knew when to keep quiet.

The Granny was fed up with these endless tiny Aberdonian Islands. She wanted to go north where the husband would go outside without complaining endlessly about the heat. She could see him picking through his rocks. This beach was only fifty or sixty years old, from after the seas rose, and she wondered what he could find of interest. But she wasn't talking to him, either. He sent the Granny a message, "I'm going to look for the original beach," and walked into the surf.

She was worried, but the house would look after him. When had he last gone swimming? *Could* he even swim?

Her mother was walking along the water's edge and something was swimming along parallel to her. Was it the husband? It didn't move like him. It swam in closer and her mother stopped, pulled something out of her pocket, and fed it. It was a selkie. It lay in the surf, not changing. It was bigger than her mother but the Granny could tell it was at her mother's beck and call. How unsurprising. Her mother drove the Granny out of her mind.

The Granny stamped away from her family, keeping her head down, watching her feet. The hill mosses were fighting the reeds. Something flashed in front of her feet and she slowed her perception to see a tiny grass snake trying to get away. She picked it up behind its neck. It wriggled in her hands and she was fascinated. She hadn't seen one since she'd married into the house. Her mother was calling from the beach and then the house was breaking in with a call, too. The Granny dropped the snake in her pocket but she wasn't thinking about it anymore. She was running toward the water and she couldn't think of anything.

The Granny put the gun down. She picked up her embroidery, told the house, "Let's move." She kickstarted her rocking chair as she felt the baby kicking inside. The carpet was soaking up the mess her mother's body was making. The rest of the family wives muttered as the house trembled, withdrew its roots from England's northernmost tip, checked for clearance, and slowly took off. It was the Granny's turn at embodiment, at being the children's mother; so, horrified and disconcerted as they were, the wives didn't complain.

"Don't wake the husband," she told the house.

The house said, "You left instructions to wake him when the latest bother was over. . . . "

One of the wives murmured, "That's probably now."

"You know the husband *hates* change," said the Granny. "Besides, he wasn't talking about my be-damned mother, he was talking about the Hague."

Which reminded her: part of her was still at work. Her embroidery hardly needed more than a look now and then, so she put in a call for lenience at the trial of the latest Georgian Dictator in the Republique Hague.

The Granny's mother whispered, "Sarah, you misplaced that stitch."

The Granny hefted her gun and shot her mother again. The Granny's heads-up display pinpointed her mother's body's moment of physical death and red-flagged the fractal pattern of her mother's consciousness-uploads jolting into action. The Granny activated a confinement shell around the still-leaking body. When her mother's dead-woman switch engaged, the explosion spattered the remains all over the inside of a molybdenum box.

The Granny sniffed and the wives fell silent. She told the house to move her mother's coffin into the basement. She should have gotten rid of her mother last month when the old hag insisted on going ashore to help a stranded selkie back into the sea. The Granny had been distracted: first by the husband, out rock collecting; then she'd caught a grass snake. She hadn't seen a live one in twenty years. She'd taken it in and nursed it back to health. There was something else, the Granny thought, but she couldn't think what it was.

Two minutes ago her mother had breezed in and thanked the Granny for at least keeping a tiny bit of fresh meat in the house even though "reptile was rarely anyone's first choice. Or even their third, really."

The wives were disturbed. Disembodied, they flowed through everything in the room: rattling the coffee table, spinning the old paper embroidery patterns, knocking the Granny's walking stick against the back of her high-backed wooden rocker. She could hear them whispering to one another. "Where did she get a gun?" "Will we all go to prison?" "I'm glad she did it." "What are we going to *do*?"

"You should sleep," one said to the Granny. "This is taking it out of you."

"Your mother released spores when . . . It's in your lungs," said another. "She gave you a flu."

The Granny ignored them. She was annoyed she hadn't cloned the snake but on the other hand she didn't want to open the molybdenum coffin to pick through her mother's remains to find some snake DNA. She could bet her mother's nanos were working away at reassembling the body. If the Granny opened the shell, one of her mother's uploads might access her mother's body and she would be back and even more annoying than ever.

"I should be OK. I haven't been outside," the Granny said. "But, you never can tell. Replace my blood. And organs," she told the house. "And maybe it's time to take out the baby."

The baby spoke *underneath* only to the Granny: "Not until we're both ready, thank you."

The house used her chair to attach tubes to the Granny's arms and legs. Some nasty things began to happen below her waist but she applied a professional level of distraction and ignored them. The itch in her belly could be scratched after the house had put her fully back together.

She was embroidering a cape for her baby.

At the Hague, the next case was up. The Great Year Caucus had found the recent Dictator of the Righteous and Godly Democracy of the Southern American States guilty by popular consensus and was auctioning tickets for the lynch mob to carry out his sentence. The Granny filed her objection and applied her day's funds to finance court security for herself for the next two hours.

She turned the cape in her hands. It was conch shell pink. Girls ran in the family—but they did everywhere now.

The house had leveled off at five thousand meters and asked for a destination. The Granny thought there was one person with the gumption to help out with a problem the size and shape of her mother's dead body.

*Malik.*

"House," she said. "Let's go to Bute."

The Island of Bute used to lie off the west coast of Scotland. During the Stupidity an ancient and corrupt gliderbomb (looking for the long-defunct U.S. Navy base miles away in Dunoon) had taken out the largest town,

Rothesay. But the rest of the island had been quietly dyked up before the Greenland melt floods so that, although it was now below sea level, most of it survived.

The Granny directed the house to the northeast end of the island near an old submerged ferry ramp where it landed softly on the wet bracken, sending its stabilizers deep into the earth.

The house told the Granny her mother's nanos had re-assembled her corpse and it was monitoring the corpse for personality re-uploads. The Granny certainly wasn't going to bring her mother back. If her mother found a way back, the Granny would deal with her. She would argue she hadn't technically killed her mother. She'd just removed her mother from her body and removed the opportunity for her mother to regain access to her body. Crossing the water to Western Scotland was a problem, but staying back in the Federated Northern English Islands—where the current authorities might not agree with the Granny's liberal interpretation of her own behavior—could only have been worse.

"Don't wake the husband yet," she told the house. "But let's do something he likes. Maybe California bungalow, but glass-in the porch."

It was August, hot and steamy; outside, the rain beat down and the house air filters couldn't completely remove the smell of sheep shit. Despite the heat it was still below the husband's recommended temperature range. *Anyway,* she thought, *we won't be here long.*

The wives sussurated, chorused quotes from Verdi's *Macbeth.*

"Don't get your hopes up," the Granny said. "I'll take no tips from dead Italians. Or *les rosbifs.*"

The house said, "The Free Island of Bute is requesting poll tax registration. We have forty-three minutes until the free hour expires."

The Granny swore. "Send out hunters and farmers. I don't care what they find, we need inventory. And pay the tax at fifty-nine minutes."

The house knew better than to reply.

The hunters and farmers, somewhat malleable robots with a small degree of autonomy, scattered out from the cellar door, farmers moving slowly; hunters quickly disappearing from sight.

Blood replaced, the Granny put her embroidery down. She levered herself out of her rocker. She kicked her mother's coffin on her way to the door. "I'm going to visit the children," she said.

The children's playroom, all soft sea green walls and bouncy rock-painted floor, was empty. It was the Granny's fault. And her mother's, of course, for distracting her. The poor children couldn't be blamed: their mother had died long ago and none of the other wives could be said to be particularly motherly.

Especially the heavily pregnant Granny. Granny only to her own children lost long before she ever came to this house.

The Granny scolded the house anyway.

The house showed her the children's escape: Ariadne, the eldest, had tied up Perce, the youngest, and the only boy, then melted his eye with a button-laser. Perce's nannynanos couldn't rebuild the eye fast enough so the house had brought in a mechanonurse. Ariadne had claimed to be in shock. It took less than a minute from the untying of Perce's restraints to the three children's scrambling of the house's tracking system and their subsequent disappearance. The house showed her its latest satellite pic of the three children. Perce was riding the 'nurse; the three of them had stopped to change into camo suits. They'd be nearly untrackable soon.

The Granny asked the house for an outdoor suit. She stopped in the hall on her way out to touch up her hair, clean off the wives' target acquisition software, kick the cat.

"Tell me if Malik contacts you or if the husband wakes himself," she told the house. The house indicated that it had an emergency message for the Granny but she ignored it. She was going out. Whatever it was could wait.

The flus had killed off more men than women and for certain the remaining men had become a little full of themselves. She did love living with one in a family. His angularity of body, the pure reek of him. She didn't count Perce, yet. It would be decades before he could even vaguely be considered an adult.

The house flapped the letterbox at her. She aimed a kick at it, too. Missed on purpose. She loved the house more than she should. "Otherwise I don't want to hear from you unless the little shits come back before me."

But when she went outside she realized she couldn't walk across the island.

"I need some wheels," she told the house. A cellar door sprang open and a hovercar appeared. She whipped out her gun and shot at it, but it dodged back into the house.

"Wheels," said the house, as the door opened again. The Granny refused to acknowledge that the house might know her needs better than she did.

She sat on the eight-wheeled buggy and it encapsulated around her. Perhaps she was too old for this kind of direct action. Maybe she and the husband should be pottering in the orchid room together and the house could send something out to round up the children.

The buggy told her Bute was overrun with wild dogs. The dogs survived off rabbits, sheep, a number of species of tiny burrowing mammals (*moles?* the Granny wondered), and even birds if the dogs couldn't catch anything else. The house's farmers scorned the birds—their economics knew that with the ever-mutating pandemics still going round only the most desperate would eat avians. And the house couldn't make money feeding the desperate. Instead they were blast-freezing the pheromone-drawn rabbits and dogs.

The Granny was pleased. Gamey protein stretched a long way.

She tapped into a farmer's skillset and used it to pick out an ugly, snappish dog that, despite being tempted and crazed by the scents, had so far avoided the farmers' advances. She was tired already. Her old bones wanted to be sitting on her couch with the Sunday papers spread around her and a brandy-enhanced samovar steaming within arm's reach.

The baby kept up her barrage of ridiculousness. "I'd like some brandy, too. Where's my father? Why can't I read? What's a dog?" The Granny ignored her.

The buggy started out after her targeted dog—something with the head of a hyena and the body of a Dalmatian. The Granny suspected it would be a right little bastard. She tried not to give in to its charms immediately.

The Granny took off her helmet. She felt heavy. This was the last time she'd carry a baby to term. Next time the house could incubate one itself. The baby's due date was a week today and the Granny had already caught her planning trouble with the children. She hadn't known how to discipline it without hurting herself. She explained to the baby the other children were just family children whereas she, the baby, was a direct child and she should listen to the Granny. The baby swore she was on the Granny's side.

The buggy caught and immobilized the dog. The Granny inserted a mental link, told it to find the children. The dog barked at the door of the buggy and the Granny wanted to drop it where it danced.

"The *other* children," she said. "The already born." The dog was getting some of her anger, some of her depression (which had been encroaching since she'd married into this house). It alternated between mad barking and rolling on the ground. She shut down her side of the link, sent the dog out. The children would undoubtedly eat the poor thing before she could catch up with them. Damn her mother's death for distracting her.

The Granny had spent a long, wet, adolescent year on this island, Bute. She would have preferred Bad Marienbad but her mother had found her a room and a waitressing job in a cheap waterfront hotel in Rothesay and given her a ticket back to San Diego postdated a year and a day. Her mother was occasionally poetic.

The Granny remembered feeling at home in Rothesay although she wasn't sure how trustworthy those memories were. She had been comforted by the old brick houses that sat behind the storm wall and had survived the freak tornadoes and pre-War near-catastrophic floods.

Her mother, whether knowingly or not, had given the Granny a place that suited her interior feelings. She was as alien in Rothesay as she had always felt at home. Her old friends' pix and journals were strange missives from a lost home. The language, clothes, and stances here were foreign but slowly those from home became the same. She had come to know herself as an outsider, settled into the role, and been able to carry it on and with her ever after. She had never told her mother, but she had always been grateful for what she had learned that year.

Rothesay was gone and the handful of survivors had been repatriated into Western Scottish mainland. Malik's family ruled what was left of the "Free Island."

As the buggy chugged on, the Granny looked across the short draft of water to the old mainland coast. There was meant to be a village half-submerged there but the house had detected neither life nor noise, light nor masking procedures. There were still sheep, but the farmers calculated that the poisons and the traps—never mind the wolves, the buzzards, and the haggises—made the harvest too risky.

The Granny wants to retire but her mother won't let her go. The Granny doesn't understand the family children and she would like a break from the husband and the wives. When she was young, she loved political movements that practiced direct manipulation, alliteration, cohesion/discrepancy variants. She glasses her memories every ten years so that she can go back and check if she is remembering events the way she originally remembered them. The children love to compare the differences between her decades.

The children were both the hard and the easy part. They were all growing up shorter than the Granny. She had grown up in the Totally Free State—aka the Totalitarian Fascist Syndicate—where surplus economies, soygenerators, and liquid sun battery packs had killed the profit motive. Then 2.25 billion people died during the flus, the fuel and famine wars: the Great Stupidity. The husband used to hark back to the pre-War years but even discounting nostalgia, the Granny never expected life to be the same again.

The Granny was 197cm tall and, at her prime, a good forty years ago, had weighed in at just under a hundred kilos. She never pretended to be still in her prime. The surplus hadn't lasted. The Granny had been a postdoc studying the history of Skinner Box Behaviorism at the University of Chicago-Metro when the unknowable black box of her mother descended back into her life and whisked her away to the Faeroe Islands.

The Granny's mother had frozen all her eggs at sixteen and stopped her menses soon after. She'd used surrogates to birth and raise her children. For years she had seduced birth fathers in best Roald Dahl-approved style.

The Granny's mother had been one of those expecting trouble. She hadn't been standing on street corners shooting information-sound bombs into passersbys' heads, but she had good instincts backed up by fantastic systems analysis. Once she picked up the early signs of famine hitting the developed world, she moved into catastrophe mode. At first, in the Faeroes, the Granny hadn't noticed any difference in her mother's blast-frozen expression. But then she had seen a tic, a tenth of a second blankness in her mother's continuous environmental scan. The Granny thought that something had come undone inside her mother, something that couldn't be fixed. Neither of them ever brought it up.

The husband had once told the Granny "You were born filled with regret" and she agreed that at some point she had regretted every choice she had ever made, but she regretted those years in the Faeroes least of all. The Granny, grateful for a moment, considered letting her mother get back to her body. But that would open her up to a different level of regret. She'd wait a little yet.

The Granny had grown up hoping to meet someone and feel the direct interior shock of recognition. Love. The spark that would blow everything else aside. As the years passed, she'd kept a weather eye out for it. She didn't think of herself as fussy, but it hadn't happened.

The husband had once told her she was the love of his life. She'd warmed to him slowly. The Granny had married because she'd recognized a good deal—and a power vacuum in his house. She'd also married Maria, Lenkya, Sophia, ChloeSimone, K-K, and a few other loves of his life. They were resigned to the situation. The Granny was the least content, the most volatile.

These days none of the wives saw much of their husband; he was rarely awake. He liked to fix things. Anything the Granny broke, she threw in the recycler. He'd been a geneticist. Once, when another wave of soy viruses was exploding out of the "safe" Mid-American cowfeed states, she'd thrown one of his favorite coffee mugs (the one that said *Can I look into your genes?*) at him—full of coffee.

"Darling . . . ," he said when the coffee cup smashed against the wall. She knew his word contained paragraphs full of deeply-felt emotional concepts he found difficult to solidify into words. He'd told her so, many times.

"Why didn't you know what was going to happen? Why couldn't you do something?"

He stared at her and she was too fed up to parse his glare. She slammed the door on the way out. The next time she queried the house, she found he had gone to sleep.

It was six years before they talked again. She had been excoriating the Hague on their rebirthing of the Common Agricultural Policy and then she'd realized the husband was in the same room as her and was clapping appreciatively. Later, for better or for worse, they'd made the baby. The baby kicked.

For better. Definitely for better.


The Granny's mother had the Granny force-augmented and fast grown— anything to cut short her progeny's early years. The Granny could remember her mother (not her birth mother, her mother) taking her to the hospital when the Granny was six months old. Her mother had brought her house to Cleveland which had, she was convinced, the best *plasticiens*. The plastic surgeons smoothed out her mother's navel in an afternoon. Her mother had asked the Granny if she'd like hers removed, too, but the Granny had signed her refusal. How could she explain the depths of her infantile sorrow to see the link between the generations removed, denied?


The Granny was lying to the house. She knew it. She knew the house knew it. There was a gap she refused to recognize, a familiar space, unfilled. A time on the Aberdonian Islands where everything had gone wrong. She remembered the negotiations before landing. Later she and the husband had walked to the water's edge and he had dived for rocks on the old beach. Her mother had tagged along until she was distracted by the selkie. But then there was a space, something she didn't want to know and it was there that the house and the wives had stopped talking to her.

Until she shot her mother. That had shocked them into speech, if not action. But the Granny wouldn't look back, wouldn't listen. She had to look forward, look after the baby, their baby.

The house was talking to her but she was enjoying following the dog, and zeroed the volume. Eventually the house bruteforced through her control of the car and sent her the message in large text she couldn't ignore. Two farmers had disappeared.

Her mother. The children. Now the farmers.

Again, there was only the one answer.

*Malik.*


In the early twenty-first century the Somali gangs had established a foothold in Argyll. They'd turfed the Scands out of the salmon and oyster farms and the Bosnians out of the drugs. They'd provided the Triads with handsome retirement packages and a generous revenue percentage which dropped slowly over the years. It was a gamble on both sides, but there comes a time when playing bridge or Mahjong in a smoky bar is better than tracking down crooked sailors in the Kyle of Lochalsh. When the Gulf Stream broke and the weather shockshifted cold then hot the Somalis were well positioned and already turning their couple of hundred thousand acres into a mass market garden. When the food collapse came, they were diversified. They survived, flourished.

The Somalis liked the sheep for their sour milk and wool. They pastured the hot, sweating creatures higher than ever before but this was still Scotland, the mountains weren't high enough to really escape the heat.

The Somalis were no crueler than any other gang but *getting a wool hat* had taken over from *an Arctic vacation* as the *au courant* slang for being disappeared.

Thirty and more years ago, the Granny had spent a lot of time officially and unofficially dealing with the Somalis. Her summer in Rothesay had given her a connection, Malik, one of the boys who had fallen in love with her. He'd made an informal offer to her to join his house but although she had said she'd think about it, she'd never gone back.

No man, she thought, carried a torch for six or seven decades. A grudge for marrying into a different house, certainly; but not a torch.

She set the dog to find and sent it after the farmers.

She had an itch in the back of her head that she knew meant something bad would happen. Maybe had happened. So when, after the baby was born, it did: she wasn't all that surprised.

She turned the buggy back home and put in a call to Malik.

The dog set off and she felt her world telescope into only the part of her that was watching him run. The smooth flow of tension and release, his body so low to the ground. She slowed her perception and still couldn't pinpoint the exact moment his paws hit the ground. She couldn't keep her foreconsciousness at that speed for long; she was too tied to her body's slowness. She backburnered the dog's perceptions. She already loved the dog as much as anything she had ever loved. She had to look away, search the sun-scorched bracken, the deep hot greens of the rhody bushes to settle herself, get back to her body's time and continue the conversation she'd already begun with Malik's cool, remote voice and the decades-old icon (a misty hill wearing a woolen hat) the house had popped-up onto the buggy's screen.

"I see you paid the tax. No more revolution?" Malik said, foregoing pleasantries.

"The revolution is stabilized on the principles on which it began."

She wondered then if it were actually him talking behind the icon, if he were even still alive. Would he still be handsome?

"Damn Red Clydesiders," he said, "with their smooth-talking activists and the Tory backbench in their pocket. What do they know about us islanders? Might as well put the Tories upfront. Perhaps the polis would reconsider."

"Red always suited you, though," she said, unable to resist flirting.

There was silence on his side. His icon didn't move and the Granny thought, He's *dead* and I've insulted some youngster.

The house popped two messages into her heads-up and told her that both the children and the missing farmers had signaled they were coming home. But the link to the dog had gone dead.

"That's a nice dog," Malik said. "Thank you."

She caught up with the children as they trailed back to the house. They'd gotten tired. They hadn't seen her dog. Perce had forgotten Ariadne's attack and now as the three of them trudged along he held onto Ariadne's hand, made her drag him along. As usual everyone ignored the middle girl. Granny managed to be as polite to them as they were to her. The baby was talking to them but she neither offered them a lift nor asked them any questions. Everyone was equally unsatisfied.

The children ran to the cellar door and she let the car follow them in. The house led her into the sitting room where the wives were laid out as a collection of Royal Wedding (Victoria and Albert to Arthur and Uther) China in a display cabinet. They weren't behind glass. Temptation surged through her. But she was thinking of her beautiful dog.

She pulled up an ottoman, sat down and sighed as she put her feet up. She girded herself and acknowledged the expected note from ChloeSimone.

"House," she said. "Tea for two."

The house opened the door again and the husband came in.

She explained about his mother-in-law and he was sanguine. She talked about the farmers and he buttered scones. He flinched when she mentioned Malik. By the time she'd gotten to the children's latest escapade he was palpably upset. He began buffing his fingerprints from the teapot. She didn't tell him about her missing dog.

"Perhaps," he said, "you should wake your mother?"

The wives clattered, sussurated. She shushed them and kept her peace.

"You know I've always admired her efficiency with local officialdom."

She knew he meant this as a reflection of her uselessness here as well as her job performance. He was so good at being banally evil, she thought. She queried the Hague and clocked in. She could handle the Court and the husband.

The husband was balding, had dark rings around his eyes. He slurped his tea. Why couldn't he wait one minute until it was cool? She'd picked the wide-mouthed tea cups just so that the tea would cool quickly. Hers was already cold. She concentrated but she couldn't heat it up. She'd never been telekinetic, but you never knew unless you tried.

The wives had slipped out while she wasn't looking. Maybe they were afraid that she'd throw something. If she broke one of the plates, would that be the end of them? It was a metaphysical question of some interest.

When she first came to Rothesay she'd been sixteen. Her hair was long, straight, hung past her shoulders. She changed the color daily. Yet changing her hair didn't change anything else: she could never be anything but what she was. She had had admirers from the moment she stepped off the ferry. She'd always had them, but that year, apart from the occasional tourist, she found herself in a closed social system. She came to know many more of her admirers than she'd ever wanted to.

Holding her cold tea, she felt the ghost of that year, memories insistent, rise within her chest, a heaving that, as she recognized it, became firmer, stronger, became something that would break down all her recent decisions. *Delusions?* Where did that thought come from?

She wanted so much, she had so much she could be doing. Yet she sat here. She could see a minute crumb among the few tiny bristles the husband had missed shaving at the spot above his lip he always missed when he first woke. Her chest wanted to explode. She wanted to scream. But she wasn't sixteen. She was supposed to be able to compromise, rationalize, work out the way forward.

The cat wandered in. As usual it ignored her and headed for the husband who leant toward it, put his hand down. But the cat stopped, arched its back. It turned, stared at the Granny, ran out the room.

Malik. Her mother. The children. Her job at the Hague. The dog. She studied her embroidery. Asked the house to warm her tea and to add something for her back. She smiled over at the husband, making an effort. He was eating his buttered scones, ignoring her Dundee marmalade. If he could, he only ate white foods—rice, bread, coconut. The buttermilk pale yellow scones were a compromise and she imagined that in his internal tables he was scoring points by eating them.

"Since we're here, why don't I show you the island tomorrow?" she offered. "And later we can work out what to do about my mother."

The Granny knew more than she'd ever wanted to about the husband's soft old bones and so she acquiesced to the house's suggestion to take a hovercar.

She was stuck in an if/then loop: If she could deal with Malik and have him take her mother's body, then she wouldn't have to deal with her mother; if she couldn't deal with Malik, then she had to deal with her mother's body and her mother. She siphoned today's nest egg dividend straight off the top to Lawyers Without Frontiers and hoped they'd remember if there came a time that she needed them.

She drove the husband on the road toward the remains of Rothesay. The baby was asleep: huffy that the Granny had gone out with the husband. The water, the Kyles of Bute, was slate blue, choppy. Seals barked at the car and she sent a query to the house to see if the farmers could use them.

They were nearing the village of Port Bannatyne when they met the Somalis.

She was happy to be driving. Before they left, the Granny had patted the husband down, removed a couple of weapons and a pocket wife. He was a fool and would have been a dead one if she'd let him keep the weapons. He had no conception of military history, no view of strategy or knowledge of Support by Fire. It was foreground or nothing with him.

She signed a greeting, popped the doors, stepped with exaggerated slowness out of the car and round to the front. The husband followed. The Somali leader, a blank-faced girl of twelve, or more likely a post-famine twenty-five, motioned and they were searched. Another motion and another girl brought over a haggis on a leash. The chimera mewed at the Granny and the husband, desperate to find a reason to attack. A tiny girl trotted over, took the husband's reading glasses, put them on. They clashed with her shorts. The glasses were an affectation at the best of times and an embarrassment now. The husband enjoyed the level of psychological removal they gave him. The other women signed amusement with tiny shifts in their stance. They didn't really care, though, and the leader motioned and they all disappeared into the high ferns. The girl in glasses led the Granny and the husband to an ancient wheeled, scrap-worthy biodiesel Ford Transit van. The Granny stepped in, pulled out her corner of embroidery, and sent the car back to the house. They headed into the hills.

She'd never liked her mother's houses. Even when she'd cracked the codes in order to program her own spaces, she had always known the deep programming wasn't hers. She'd been forced old so fast that by the time she was twelve she wanted her own place. Many of her friends lived in dorms, but her mother had bought a space near the Army and Navy School in Greater San Diego so that the Granny had no choice but to live with her. Her mother's house had smelled like the myths her mother lived by: lilac, charcoal, anti-aging crap, plastic surgery.

The car wasn't shielded and the Granny was still talking to the house. She had missed a couple of debates and her income had dropped to a trickle as the parliament noticed her absence. Her coalition would disenfranchise her if she didn't get back to it. She partitioned her mind and went to work on three different cases. Three times twenty minutes work, their ETA to Malik's estate, was nothing to be sneezed at. The husband hadn't earned anything since retiring at the Hague-approved age of sixty-nine. He'd gone on and on about his continually surprising survival and the benefits (to everyone, of course) of his retirement for so long that the family had finally given in. Everyone in the house, except the husband, had regretted it even though occasionally one of his old intellectual properties was licensed and earned the house a pittance. A few years ago the Granny had set up the accounts to copy the house balances to him every week but she was sure he never as much as scanned them. She didn't want to give him the opportunity to pull out the mortality tables again and "prove" he should be dead and therefore couldn't be expected to work. Sometimes she agreed with him.

He leant over, whispered something about her mother, but she really didn't want to hear it. His skin was coming up all blotchy. He hadn't been outside in months. Since Vienna, the snob. The scrambling among the rocks on the Aberdonian Isles didn't count, she thought, ignoring what the house wanted to tell her. Instead she had the house run a virus/phage/bacteria scan and add a light antiviral to his blood. He hardly ever checked himself. She didn't think he would notice. She really was over-reliant on the house.

There was a ghost of a note from the house and she traced it back until she could open it. "Sarah," her mother said. She erased it. If she survived this visit to Bute there'd be time enough for reconciliation with the bitch afterward.

The farmers had done well. They'd only lost one of their number to the haggises and the others were already building a replacement. They'd found a mutation in a mink which, crossed into the local sheep, would move the sheep closer to the Hague's Machine-Manufactured Protein status. In the meantime, she began negotiations with a couple of food processor factories to see who would take the meat during the pre-approval status. She sold short on the sheep and dog harvest and made twenty days of house expenses. The rest of the meat was frozen and shipped—some for revivification, most for butchering—back to one of the smaller combines in the NorthEast Kingdom. She hadn't done so well on seeds, but she hadn't expected to.

The Somalis had isodomed Mount Stuart, an estate south of disappeared Rothesay. Once under the dome, the driver slalomed lazily through a minefield and stopped outside a huge sandstone house. When she stopped, she motioned for the Granny and the husband to get out, then drove around the back of the house.

The children were trying to call.

The Granny thought there was a generation shock, rather than a gap, between those who had lived through the famines and those who came after. The children weren't convinced of death yet. Despite their mothers' deaths and being surrounded by death and memorials, mortality was only an intellectual construct. Disappearances still a rumor.

"Sarah." The whisper again from her mother.

She asked the house to check itself, herself, the baby, the children, the husband, and anything else it could think of to see where her mother's ghost was hiding. The footstool. The coffee machine. Maybe her mother was in the damn dog. That could complicate matters with Malik.

A quiet, middle-aged woman met them at the back door and led them through a marble-columned hall to a large, almost empty room. The Granny's house was pointing out details, the tops of some of the columns were unfinished. The door hinges shone and were decorated with vines, oaks, acorns. The room was built using the Golden Ratio. The Granny took the husband's arm, pointed to the hinges. He shook his head, impatiently. He was listening to the house, too.

Malik was sitting by a wood fire. He'd let his hair grow white. He reminded her of someone and she decided it was his younger self. Her head ached and she was happy to sit down. The husband was admiring the prospect from the window. Twat, she thought fondly.

"Is there peace?" Malik said—the traditional greeting.

"There is peace and there is milk," the Granny said.

The two of them had always smelled right to one another, she thought. Maybe that's all it was. But she worried that she couldn't read Malik's mood. Maybe he knew something. Maybe it was the something she knew she didn't want to know.

She cut her connections to the Hague, pulled all of her intellectual tendrils back in. Dealing with Malik would take all of her.

"Someone I know," she said, "has a little problem."

The husband was fiddling with the window, seeing if he could open it. He was never satisfied with where he was.

Neither of the two men said anything. The Granny tried to think when she had last been in a room with two men.

"My friend has," she said, "a little box that she would like to lose for a while."

"A box," said Malik.

"Twenty-two hundred kilos of various inert alloyed metals coated in stone and impervious to most physical hacks."

"Little," said Malik. This time there was a flash of humor.

At just the wrong time, the baby broadcast to all and sundry that she wanted out. Now.

Little shit, the Granny thought.

The house forwarded a message from the wives: "The baby, your baby, the baby!" The house wanted to send a vehicle out to bring the Granny and the husband back. She shut off their feed. Malik demanded her full attention. But so did the baby. And the baby had a hold of her hormones. She ran through mantras of curses. Picked up her pi calculation (thirty thousand figures along, she found it very restful to concentrate on). Her bladder twinged. She hated her body.

"Sarah," Malik said. For a moment she thought it was her mother's ghost and ignored him.

Malik's parents had flown into Glasgow and taken the UK citizenship virus before he was born. He liked the heat here, but he missed a country he had never known. He'd liked the Granny from the start because she embodied the feelings of alienation he wasn't allowed to have.

"I know people who could store this trifle," he said. "But these people are curious about the future. They are interested in new children. They would be grateful to talk to a house that traveled so much. Fascinated to access such a house's seed databases. Or they might prefer percentages of such various things as mink gene proceeds. Good dogs. Perhaps even a partnership." He looked at her, openly speculative.

Well, she thought, he already had the dog so perhaps that didn't count?

"You had a dog, didn't you, dear?" said the husband.

The Granny wasn't surprised. The husband was the conversational equivalent of a natural disaster. How had men survived themselves?

Malik's gaze went to the fireplace as he spoke to someone outside the room. The door opened and another of those quiet women brought in the dog the Granny thought of as her own.

"Here boy, here!" the husband said and the dog strained on its leash. Malik nodded. The woman said a word and the dog ran to Malik. The woman stationed herself by the door, slipped out of the conversation and into the background. The Granny was impressed.

"If we were to rebuild Rothesay," said the husband, "I'd like to work on the Winter Gardens. See if there's anything left of the gene bank at the old genealogy center."

"There may be vaults not on the public plans," the Granny agreed.

Now the baby was talking to her in undertime. She signaled to Malik to join the conversation with the baby while the three of them, the Granny, Malik, and the husband, continued discussing the possibility of rebuilding Rothesay out loud.

"We're very interested in the child," Malik said underneath. "And your choice to carry it *in vitro*."

The Granny showed him a gene chart to ensure Malik knew the baby was a girl and that the husband was the father. Malik gave a microscopic shake of his head.

"There are so few children born on the island," he said. "Yours looks to have a number of enhancements not available the last time there was a birth here."

The island Somalis wanted to make sure they were at the top of their game when and if they next had children. Also, he said, they had discovered the baby looking through their defense systems—which were supposed to be freestanding and unconnected so they were strongly interested in knowing how it had achieved that.

"How *she* achieved that," said the Granny.

"She," agreed Malik. His castle was prying at her house, using the husband and the Granny as entry points. She put the house on lockdown and cleaned up the husband's i/o ports. Later she'd get the husband back in some way for leaving himself so wide open. Maybe later she'd apologize and maybe she wouldn't and either way she wouldn't mind when he disappeared to sulk. He deserved it if he couldn't keep his own head clean.

The Granny and the baby had a conversation below her and Malik's.

"What were you doing in there?" the Granny asked.

"Who isn't curious?" the baby said. "No," she said at the same time on yet another level, "I don't want a name yet."

"Besides, their systems are wide open. Relatively."

"I wish you'd told me," the Granny said.

"You'd only have worried."

The Granny dropped the conversations with the baby. Malik and the husband were extrapolating near-future population growth versus potential carbon loading and possible weather consequences.

"Listen," she said, under, to Malik. "You number crunchers are just repeating old work and the baby says I don't have all day. Besides we don't need to be here for you to do this."

"I'm enjoying your husband's way of thinking. He's smart. For a scientist. Brainstorming is different in person."

"He's not so bad. Better with the past than the present."

The baby kicked, said, "It's time!"

"Maybe we can talk more," the Granny said to Malik.

"My house is always open," Malik said, sending her a pass to get her by the haggises.

The Granny called the house for a car.

"The baby belongs with her mothers," the Granny said to Malik, under. Malik said nothing. Neither did the baby.

"We've got to go," she said out loud and the husband surprised them both with a smile. She let it go. He rarely needed to know what was really going on.

What Malik wanted, herself and the baby, was impossible, the Granny thought. But no more improbable than her needing a quiet place to inter her mother. Temporarily, she had told the husband. Permanently, she thought. She was pleased to see her little wheeled buggy at the castle gate. Once she and the husband were in, though, the car netted them to their gel-seats and rocketed over the hill to the house. At least the house had moved into a more sheltered position. The last thing she noticed before she passed out—drugs, G-forces, the baby's insistent pushing; she didn't know which—was the last of the hunter-farmers returning to the house from the hills. She noted they were pulling good loads and was checking on their productivity index and then she was gone.

When the Granny woke she asked about her mother before her baby. The house told the Granny her mother had Von Neumann ghosted herself. It had discovered two hundred (and counting) uploaded iterations of her mother's personality which dated from many years before her mother's death up until only a day or two before it. The Granny must realize, the house said, that there was no absolute method to ensure her mother would remain dead. It might, the house suggested, be better to allow her mother to reconnect with the body in the basement before her mother did something unspeakably illegal and messy.

"Say what you mean," the Granny told the house. But she knew of the opportunities, the bodies for sale, the possibilities of stored clones. She wouldn't give the order to disinter. Instead she changed the quarklocks from strangeness to charm, knowing this wouldn't hold her mother back for long.

Looked into hiring a charterjet to take her mother's body somewhere far away from here. The arrival point was a problem.

The Granny had been ignoring her newborn, her worn out body, and the mumbling people surrounding them both—the efficacy of the house's drugs was not to be sneezed at. So much for plans. So much for peace and quiet.

The baby was crying outside of her and all the while peppering her with questions: Where was *her* grandmother? Why was the world cold? Who were all these people? Why did her stomach ache? These cloths were constricting, rough!

Everything merged into the baby's wail. The Granny was trying to open her eyes to see the baby, her own girl. She struggled to stay awake, to stop the torrent of wives spinning around her, the incoherent pleased roar of the husband. But they'd all be there when she woke. She could escape many things; she couldn't escape her damn family.

The house listed possible new locations. Flashed images of its best angles in sunny climes, sailing the East Anglian sea. She ignored it.

She opened her eyes. The children, in full painted regalia, were at the end of her bed looking after the baby. The husband was there, too, cooing at the baby. The baby was ignoring the husband. The Granny could hear her discussing, underneath, memorable security systems with Malik.

If the Granny just didn't look at her family, maybe they'd ignore her? She checked the house schedule. Wasn't it one of the other wives' turn at embodiment by now?

The wives had been leaving her alone with the baby. It was nearing Lenkya's time to reach back into a body and they all wanted to be with her. It was a time of mixed feelings. They loved embodiment but they also enjoyed disembodiment—circuitry-situationalism, as named by Gray—slipping through the house seams, gliding out to ride the farmers, looking after the children.

The wives had seen her querying the house schedule. "We're not the mother, the new mother," they said. "We are lost here too. We would love to shepherd the children, the lovely children. But we cannot, cannot. The child, the baby, the little one demands your body, you. You."

She cursed at them. When had they gone Greek chorus? All she wanted was a soak and a back rub. Maybe more. Was she horny? Hadn't she just had a baby? Damn Malik's pheromones. She leant over, made to grab the husband's ass.

"Carpe gluteus maximus," she said. He didn't notice. She thought about Malik. What if she had spent her whole life on this island? She found it hard to imagine and realized she had no regrets for not doing it. She wasn't looking forward to the children digging through the mess of her present memories.

She could never know what might have been. She could still choose what would be. The husband was saying something and his tone was warmer, deeper. He was slow to warm up. His culture was all in his thin, slow-moving lips. Waiting for him to open his mouth was a venture into undertime every time. Malik, the other Rothesay boys, her Army and Navy friends had all been more open, more free. But they had always stayed behind and she had always gone on. She had survived the Stupidity and the Shortages, met the husband, his family, the house.

The Granny had always been careful in her dealings with Malik. She had always left everything exactly equal. He had been her unacknowledged failsafe and she knew he knew it. But she could never allow him to have any power over her house or family.

If the Granny left her mother here, Malik would not only own her: he'd also have a hold on the family. She couldn't do that. She had married into this house and family with no strings attached. She couldn't tie them to the Somalis, to the Free Island.

But here she was, eighty-three years old and still dealing with her mother. It wasn't what she wanted. She wanted to talk about baby names with the husband. She wanted to compare bone loss with her friends. She hadn't kept up with the obits—who knew who might be dead? Instead it was her mother, always her mother. Dead, but not taking it. Imagining reintegrating two-hundred-plus iterations gave the Granny a headache. Maybe it would keep her mother busy for a while.

The children were trying to pick up the baby and she knew they'd drop her. She told the house to take the kids away. The baby said, "Wait! I was enjoying that."

"Early lesson, kid," the Granny said. "Nothing lasts."

When she woke again, she wanted to get up. The Granny felt happier than she had been in a long time. Damn her hormones. Perhaps there was nothing for it but to okay her mother's return. After feeding the baby, the house opened a new door to the kitchen so that the Granny and the husband could sidestep the children.

The house provided the Granny's porridge in a rough bowl with a wooden spoon and she walked slowly as she ate: feeling unfamiliar pains; enjoying her buttery-peppery meal. She selectively muted her nose to cut out the smell of the husband's sugary, milky porridge.

The baby was quieter now that the wives had taken possession of the blankets and the crib, surrounding her and talking to her. She wanted a name now in a way she hadn't before being born. She liked the control she had of her body out here. The Granny wasn't going to force the baby to grow up as fast as she had had to. Neonatal augments were much improved since the Granny's childhood. There were still a few unpleasant ones that were best done straight away. The baby became less happy.

The husband visited but the Granny knew the baby still wouldn't speak to him. He left quickly. The Granny tried to remember if he had always been so swift to take umbrage. "What about my grandmother?" the baby asked. None of the wives said anything.

Malik was calling the Granny and she told the house not to let him through.

The Dead Mother was calling but the Granny was in bed, not answering. She had her worn and comfy woolen blankets tucked up around her and the baby. The baby was gurning away and the Granny was experimenting with a soft jolting rocking that calmed both of them. Iterations of her Dead Mother were calling, trying to re-up to the frozen body. Which was still in the basement, not yet transported to Malik's.

The house wanted to tell her something but the Granny knew she'd asked the house not to tell her whatever it was. The house could signal all it wanted. She wasn't listening.

"Sarah?" The Dead Mother whispered through the house.

The Granny heard a heavy arrhythmic hammering on the front door and had a presentiment that her life as a new mother was about to become even more complicated.

The house showed her what was waiting outside the front door. It was woman-shaped and the Granny got an impression of wetness, of solidity and fluidity Dopplering back and forth into one another. The Granny was entranced but unhappy as she watched one of the wives flow into and then open the door.

It walked in. It was a she and she was a selkie.

She was at least as tall as the Granny and here, in the middle of nowhere, she was dressed to kill. The Passive Wave Imager scans showed the selkie's land-musculature meant she could follow through on her red dress's promises. The wives were leading the selkie into the house, shaking umbrellas, toggling switches, riffling papers, leading her into the front room which the house was quickly redoing in hard, waterproofed, sea-colored chairs.

The house wanted to update the Granny's blood to counter conjectured infections from the selkie. The Granny shooed away the needles and sprays. She asked the wives to look after the baby and pulled a midnight blue suit and a pair of black flats from the closet. The chimera wasn't the only one who could dress up.

The Granny should have been suspicious a month ago when her mother helped the selkie. Her mother wasn't known for her selflessness.

As she dressed, the Granny watched the selkie. She was fascinated by the selkie's large, strong-looking teeth. There was more space between them than in a human woman's mouth.

The selkie ignored the chairs in the front room. She stood at the window looking out at the sea. She appeared used to waiting.

The Granny put on a bracelet, picked up the baby, and sent a message to the husband telling him to meet her in the front room.

She didn't wait for his reply. As soon as she entered the front room the selkie spoke.

"I want my body."

It was the wrong rhythms, but it was the Dead Mother's voice. The Granny sat, too startled to introduce herself to something that obviously already knew her, too mesmerized to attempt politeness. She'd seen film of selkies in the water. In her heads-up display she overlaid images of a selkie's water body onto the one standing in front of her. She wanted to see how the change worked but there were no images publicly available. She felt as if cold lights were sparking in her throat. She was allergic to the thing. The house reminded her of the blood update and she okayed it. A needle popped out of her chair into the underside of her arm. "Ach!" she said. With the baby around she was trying not to swear.

"Burial means nothing," the selkie said.

The Granny told herself this wasn't her mother. Her mother had just dropped an iteration of herself into the selkie with a compulsion to come after the Granny if her mother didn't send a regular update. The Granny thought about how the selkie had gotten to Bute. The land in between. The water.

There was a peremptory knock and the husband came in. He looked flustered.

"I am wanting my body," the selkie said to the Granny, showing her well-developed canines.

"Pleased to . . . " the husband said, and put out his hand. The selkie looked at his hand, turned back to the Granny.

"Well," he said. He sat on the arm of the Granny's wingbacked chair and she slipped her arm around his waist.

She leant in and smelt the hot soup of sweat on him. She loved him: it reminded her that she didn't love very many people. What this baby was doing to her. She'd be asking the house for pink walls and doilies under the tea cups next.

"Look. I am your mother," the selkie said.

"I—" the husband started. He slipped a hand around behind his back and wrapped it around the Granny's thumb. He was very uncomfortable. In his professional life he'd managed to avoid the chimerist work groups, preferring to concentrate on the never-ending interactions between gengineered crops and the human body.

The selkie ignored him; watched the Granny.

"If truth be told," the Granny said, "she drove me crazy. But I suppose I'd rather be driven crazy or be *not talking to her* than missing her." Did she really miss her mother? The house was still trying to tell her something and she could feel the baby trying to get into her head. Now that she'd been born, the baby found it harder to communicate.

The Granny found herself studying the selkie's huge knuckles.

The house showed the Granny a house schematic as it squeezed the children's playroom smaller and smaller until they ran out screaming. It generated noise that cancelled out their wailing protests as it shepherded them up the stairs and into the front room. When they tumbled in, the house immediately trapped them in bright, puffy seats it popped up from the floor.

The selkie looked at the children. They froze.

Then the house produced tea, lemonade, Battenburg and sultana cakes, shortbread, ginger snaps, Arbroath smokies. The selkie took the cakes and scones, passed them on. Kept the fish.

"Dear," she said to the husband. "It's your house. I suppose you should decide."

"That's very kind." But he thought she was talking about the cakes and took the last piece of shortbread from the tray. "Just like my mother's, you know," he muttered. She doubted the house could replicate anything that bland.

The Granny's mother had always been distant, but everything she'd done could be interpreted as kindness. The selkie was a different beast. Her shoulders were broad; the hard winter fat made her sleek in her dress.

She had finished the smokies.

"I am she and not the dead," the selkie said. She pointed her big forefinger at the husband.

"He is the dead."

The world emptied out for the Granny and then rushed back in: this is what the house and the baby had been telling her and trying to tell her and she had been refusing to know.

She remembered waking this morning with the baby near and the wives cooing from the wallpaper. The construct was in the bed next to her as it had been for weeks. A construct she had asked the house to make. And she had asked the house to alter her perceptions until she could feel it beside her and not know it for what it was. It had been real enough to argue with her, drive her crazy the way *he* used to, and to spend the night in his office if need be. All the wives were grieving but she had been so angry.

"A sister of my other sister's sister I would not trust told of eating his bones," the selkie said. "I did not eat. I did not see."

He had left a long and heartfelt message. He was old, felt alone, could no longer see his place in the world. He had spent a long afternoon searching out and erasing his backups. He was tired.

"I knew when he came into the water. He was a god apart from the gods who made us. But we sisters knew him. We would not eat of him."

The Dead Mother rose up within the selkie, spoke again, "We are widows in the world. Sarah, Sarah, Sarah."

Outside of her, the baby was crying. The baby: another orphan.

The Granny accessed the house's backup circuitry, set apart from the house's mind, and sent a message to Malik. She wanted out, wanted escape, wanted a car—but only for her, not the baby. Malik had been expecting her call. He had known, too. He asked her again to bring her baby but she would not. They came to an understanding and later there would be contracts; later, codicils.

The Granny opened her memories and remembered her insanity when she found he was gone. The wives, the baby, the house, even her mother were grief-stricken. The Granny had ignored them. Before his body was located, when the house could only say that his vital signs had ceased, she had shone a DNA stick over every surface in the house looking for something, anything, she could use to build a new husband.

The husband had walked, simply walked, pockets full of stones, into the ever-rising sea. He had collected rocks and pebbles for as long as she'd known him. There were bowls of them in every room. He wouldn't let the house move until the farmers had gathered every rock he had marked for collection. She cursed the chips of slate, quartz, granite, soft sandstone, obsidian, basalt, andesite porphyry, foliated granite gneiss, biotite schist. She cursed the memories that persisted and the house sneaked a tranquilizer needle out of her chair. She pushed herself away from it and forced the house to bend to her will.

"Damn you," she said to the selkie, to the Dear Dead Mother.

The wives had gone into the crib the house had made for the baby, had wrapped her in the Granny's cape, were rocking her. "Never alone," they said to her. "One of us," one said. "Unnameable one," they whispered.

The house walked the simulacrum of the husband out of the room. The wives tried to show the Granny the funeral she had missed, but she ignored it. The selkie remained quiet.

"Open the box," the Granny told the house. "Let them do whatever the blue hell they want with my mother's body. Lenkya's in charge now."

She left the room, leaving her new baby (so easy to do: she was her mother's daughter) and her sister-wives, but the children appeared beside her.

"Ariadne, Perce, Ignored Girl. Poor little mice. Trapped here with no mothers and no one but the house to care. Lenkya will take better care of you. I shall miss you, little hellions."

"Granny, we want to go with you!" said Perce, and he was knuckling tears from his eyes. The Granny could see Ariadne twisting the skin above his elbow, making him cry.

"A," she warned. "Come on then, the three of you."

She led them to the kitchen and told them she would teach them how to make toffee. The smell of burning sugar brought back memories of her own grandmother. Her grandfather had died in the Shortages.

She sent the littlest part of herself to the Hague (she didn't want to miss a second of the baking) to wrap up what she could, to resign, and to recommend they hire someone from her own house to replace her. She would be on the fence at the best in Malik's house, maybe even on the other side.

She felt rich and foolish taking time to make this dessert. The house flipped the replicator on and she nudged it off. She knew the children would enjoy the house's toffee just as much as hers. But this was not about the physical making. This was memories and the future and the children looking at her and their own glassed memories and all of them remembering that the last time they saw the Granny, they had made toffee.

The house showed her an old Alfa Romeo floating outside the front door and Malik stepping out. The Granny was touched he'd come himself. Her ugly dog leapt out after him.

The children, faces smeared with toffee, hardly noticed her leaving. She whispered a good-bye message to the baby and told the house to deliver it later. She promised that her mother, the baby's Grandmother, would be a better mother than she, the Missing Mother, could ever have been.

The house opened the front door and she let herself out. She spat out the house's access keys, dropped them through the letterbox. Patted the door as she closed it. She'd miss her old house. She walked toward Malik but had to look back. The selkie was watching her from a window.

The baby was frantically sending her questions but the Granny forwarded them to the selkie. Her mother would be revivified by the day's end and would see that the Granny had broken. She would bring up the baby and take on the house. Once her mother was sure Malik was satisfied with the deal, she might bring the house back to the island.

Lenkya sent a good-bye note with attachments from the house and wives as well as a copy of her original house contract with the appropriate clause highlighted that showed the Granny now had no rights to access the house or its inhabitants. The Granny was reading it and getting into Malik's car when the house drew in its anchors and took off.

The Granny gave Malik a piece of toffee as he drove back to his estate. The toffee was good. Later, memory would say it had been the best the children had ever had.

# YOUNGER WOMEN

## KAREN JOY FOWLER

⎯⎯✦⎯⎯

Jude knows that her daughter Chloe has a boyfriend. She knows this even though Chloe is fifteen and not talking. If Jude were to ask, Chloe would tell Jude that it's none of her business and to stop being such a snoop. (Well, if you want to call it snooping to go through Chloe's closets, drawers, and backpack on a daily basis, check the history on her cell phone and laptop, check the margins of her textbooks for incriminating doodles, friend her on Facebook under a pseudonym so as to access her page—hey, if you want to call that snooping, then, guilty as charged. The world's a dangerous place. Isn't getting less so. Any mother will tell you that.)

So there's no point asking Chloe. She talks about him to her Facebook friends—his name is Eli—but the boy himself never shows. He doesn't phone; he doesn't email; he doesn't text. Sometimes at night Jude wakes up with the peculiar delusion that he's in the house, but when she checks, Chloe is always in her bed, asleep and alone. The less Jude finds out the more uneasy she becomes.

One day she decides to go all in. "Bring that boy you're seeing to dinner this weekend," she tells Chloe, hoping Chloe won't wonder how she knows about him or, if she does, will chalk it up to mother's intuition. "I'll make pasta."

"I'd rather die," Chloe says.

Chloe's Facebook friends are all sympathy. Their mothers are nosy pains-in-the-butt, too. Her own mother died when Jude was twenty-three, and Jude misses her terribly, but she remembers being fifteen. Once when she'd been grounded, which also meant no telephone privileges, her mother had left the house and Jude had called her best friend Audrey. And her mother knew because there was a fruit bowl by the phone and Jude had fiddled with the fruit while she talked.

So Chloe's friends are telling her to stand her ground and yet, come

Saturday, there he is, sitting across the table from Jude, playing with his food. It was Eli's own decision to come, Chloe had told her, because he's very polite. Good-looking, too, better than Jude would have guessed. In fact, he's pretty hot.

Jude's unease is still growing. In spite of this, she tries for casual. "Chloe says you're new to the school," she says. "Where are you from?"

"L.A." Eli knows what he's doing. Meets her eyes. Smiles. Uses his napkin. A picture of good manners.

"Don't go all CSI on him, Mom. He doesn't have to answer your questions. You don't have to answer her questions," Chloe says.

"I don't mind. She's just being your mom." And to Jude, "Ask me anything."

"How old are you?"

"Seventeen."

"What year were you born in?"

"Nineteen ninety-four," he says and there isn't even a pause, but Jude's suspicions solidify in her mind with an audible click like the moment in the morning just before the alarm goes off. No wonder he doesn't text. No wonder he doesn't email or call on the cell. He probably doesn't know how.

"Try again," she tells him.

Vampire. Plain as the nose on your face.

Of course, Chloe knows. She's flattered by it. Any fifteen-year-old would be (and probably lots before her have been). Jude's been doing some light reading on the current neurological research on the teenage brain. She googles this before bed. It helps her sleep, not because the news is good, but because she can tell herself that the current situation is only temporary. She and Chloe used to be so close before Chloe started hating her guts.

The teenage brain is in a state of rapid, but incomplete development. Certain important linkages haven't been formed yet. "The teenage brain is not just an adult brain with fewer miles on it," the experts say. It is a whole different animal. In quantifiable ways, teenagers are actually incapable of thinking straight.

Not to mention the hormones. Poor Chloe. Eli's hotness is getting even to Jude.

Of course, none of this can be said. Chloe thinks she's all grown-up, and if Jude so much as hinted that she wasn't, Chloe would really lose it. Jude has a quick flash of Chloe at five, her hair in fraying pigtails, hanging from the tree in the backyard by her hands (monkey), by her knees (bat), shouting for Jude to come see. If Chloe really were grown up, she'd wonder, the same way Jude wonders, what sort of immortal loser hangs out with fifteen-year-olds. No one loves Chloe more than Jude, no one ever will, but really. Why Chloe?

"Mom!" says Chloe. "Butt the fuck out!"

"It's okay," Eli says. "I'm glad it's in the open." He stops pretending to eat, puts down his fork. "Eighteen sixteen."

"And still haven't managed to graduate high school?" Jude asks.

The conversation is not going well. Jude has fetched the whiskey so the adults can drink and sure enough, it turns out there are some things Eli can choke down besides blood. Half a glass in, Jude wonders aloud why Eli can't find a girlfriend his own age. Does he prefer younger women because they're so easy to impress, she wonders. Is it possible no woman older than fifteen will go out with him?

Eli is drinking fast, faster than Jude, but showing no effects. "I love Chloe." Sincerity drips off his voice like rain from the roof. "You maybe don't understand how it is with vampires. We don't choose where our hearts go. But when we give them, we never take them back again. Chloe is my whole world."

"Very nice," Jude says, although in fact she finds it creepy and stalkerish. "Still, in two hundred years, you must have collected some ex's. Ever been married? How old were they when you finally cleared off? Ancient women of seventeen?"

"Oh. My. God." Chloe is staring down into her sorry glass of ice tea. "Get a clue. Get a life. I knew you'd make this all about you. Ever since Dad left, everyone has to be as fucking miserable as you are. You just can't stand to see me happy."

There is this inconvenient fact—eight months ago Chloe's dad walked out to start a new life with a younger woman. Two weeks ago, he called to tell Jude he was going to be a father again.

"Again? Like you stopped being a father in between?" Jude asked frostily and turned the phone off. She hasn't spoken to him since nor told Chloe about the baby, though maybe Michael has done that for himself. It's the least he can do. Introduce her to her replacement.

"This is why I didn't want you to fucking meet her," Chloe tells Eli. Her face and cheeks are red with fury. She has always colored up like that, even when she was a baby. Jude remembers her, red and sobbing, because the *Little Mermaid* DVD had begun to skip, forcing her to watch the song in which the chef is chopping the heads off fish over and over and over again. Five years old and already a gifted tragedian. "Fix it, Mommy," she'd sobbed. "Fix it or I'll go mad." "I knew you'd try to spoil everything," Chloe tells Jude. "I knew you'd be a bitch and a half."

"You should speak more respectfully to your mother," Eli tells her. "You're lucky to have one." He goes on. Call him old-fashioned, he says, but he doesn't care for the language kids use today. Everything is so much coarser than it used to be.

Chloe responds to Eli's criticism with a gasp. She reaches out, knocks over her glass, maybe deliberately, maybe not. A sprig of mint floats like a raft in a puddle of tea. "I knew you'd find a way to turn him against me." She flees the room, pounds up the stairs, which squeak loudly with her passage. A door slams, but she can still be heard through it, sobbing on her bed. She's waiting for Eli to follow her.

Instead he stands, catches the mint before it falls off the table edge, wipes up the tea with his napkin.

"You're not making my life any easier," Jude tells him.

"I'm truly sorry about that part," he says. "But love is love."

Jude gives Eli fifteen minutes in which to go calm Chloe down. God knows, nothing Jude could say would accomplish that. She waits until he's up the stairs, then follows him, but only as high as the first creaking step, so that she can almost, but not quite hear what they're saying. Chloe's voice is high and impassioned, Eli's apologetic. Then everything is silent, suspiciously so, and she's just about to go up the rest of the way even though the fifteen minutes isn't over when she hears Eli again and realizes he's in the hall. "Let *me* talk to your mom," Eli is saying and Jude hurries back to the table before he catches her listening.

She notices that he manages the stairs without a sound. "She's fine," Eli tells her. "She's on the computer."

Jude decides not to finish her drink. It wouldn't be wise or responsible. It wouldn't be motherly. She's already blurred a bit at the edges though she thinks that's fatigue more than liquor. She's been having so much trouble sleeping.

She eases her feet out of her shoes, leans down to rub her toes. "Doesn't it feel like we've just put the children to bed?" she asks.

Eli's back in his seat across the table, straight-backed in the chair, looking soberly sexy. "Forgive me for this," he says. He leans forward slightly. "But are you trying to seduce me? Mrs. Robinson?"

Jude absolutely wasn't, so it's easy to deny. "I wouldn't date you even without Chloe," she says. Eli's been polite, so she tries to be polite back. Leave it at that.

But he insists on asking.

"It's just such a waste," she says. "I mean, really. High school and high school girls? That's the best you can do with immortality? It doesn't impress me."

"What would you do?" he asks.

She stands, begins to gather up the dishes. "God! I'd go places. I'd see things. Instead you sit like a lump through the same high school history classes you've taken a hundred times, when you could have actually seen those things for yourself. You could have witnessed it all."

Eli picks up his plate and follows her into the kitchen. One year ago, she and Michael had done a complete remodel, silestone countertops and glass-fronted cupboards. Cement floors. The paint was barely dry when Michael left with his new girlfriend. Jude had wanted something homier—tile and wood—but Michael likes modern and minimal. Sometimes Jude feels angrier over this than over the girlfriend. He was seeing Kathy the whole time they were remodeling. Probably in some part of his brain he'd known he was leaving. Why couldn't he let her have the kitchen she wanted?

"I'll wash," Eli says. "You dry."

"We have a dishwasher." Jude points to it. Energy star. Top of the line. Guilt offering.

"But it's better by hand. Better for talking."

"What are we talking about?"

"You have something you want to ask me." Eli fills the sink, adds the soap.

That's a good guess. Jude can't quite get to it though. "You could have been in Hiroshima or Auschwitz," she says. "You could have helped. You could have walked beside Martin Luther King. You could have torn down the Berlin Wall. Right now, you could be in Darfur, doing something good and important."

"I'm doing the dishes," says Eli.

Outside Jude hears a car passing. It turns into the Klein's driveway. The headlights go off and the car door slams. Marybeth Klein brought Jude a casserole of chicken divan when Michael left. Jude has never told her that Jack Klein tried to kiss her at the Swanson's New Year's Party, because how do you say that to a woman who's never been anything but nice to you? The Kleins' boy, Devin, goes to school with Chloe. He smokes a lot of dope. Sometimes Jude can smell it in the backyard, coming over the fence. Why can't Chloe be in love with him?

"If you promised me not to change Chloe, would you keep that promise?" She hears more than feels the tremble in her voice.

"Now, we're getting to it," Eli says. He passes her the first of the glasses and their hands touch. His fingers feel warm, but she knows that's just the dishwater. "Would you like me to change *you*?" Eli asks. "Is that what you really want?"

The glass slips from Jude's hand and shatters on the cement. A large, sharp piece rests against her bare foot. "Don't move," says Eli. "Let me clean it up." He drops to his knees.

"What's happening?" Chloe calls from upstairs. "What's going on?"

"Nothing. I broke a glass," Jude shouts back.

Eli takes hold of her ankle. He lifts her foot. There is a little blood on her instep and he wipes this away with his hand. "You'd never get older," he says. "But Michael will and you can watch." Jude wonders briefly how he knows Michael's name. Chloe must have told him.

His hand on her foot, his fingers rubbing her instep. The whiskey. Her sleepiness. She is feeling sweetly light-headed, sweetly light-hearted. Another car passes. Jude hears the sprinklers start next door sounding almost, but not quite like rain.

"Is Eli still there?" Chloe's pitch is rising again.

Jude doesn't answer. She speaks instead to Eli. "I wasn't so upset about Michael leaving me as you think. It was a surprise. It was a shock. But I was mostly upset about him leaving Chloe." She thinks again. "I was upset about him leaving me with Chloe."

"You could go to Darfur then. If petty revenge is beneath you," Eli says. "Do things that are good and important." He is lowering his mouth to her foot. She puts a hand on his head to steady herself.

Then she stops, grips his hair, pulls his head up. "But I wouldn't," she says. "Would I?" Jude makes him look at her. She finds it a bit evil, really, offering her immortality under the guise of civic service when the world has such a shortage of civic-minded vampires in it. And she came so close to falling for it.

She sees that the immortal brain must be different—over the years, certain crucial linkages must snap. Otherwise there is no explaining Eli and his dull and pointless, endless, dangerous life.

Anyway, who would take care of Chloe? She hears the squeaking of the stairs.

"Just promise me you won't change Chloe," she says hastily. She's crying now and doesn't know when that started.

"I've never changed anyone who didn't ask to be changed. Never will," Eli tells her.

Jude kicks free of his hand. "Of *course*, she'll ask to be changed," she says furiously. "She's fifteen years old! She doesn't even have a functioning brain yet. Promise me you'll leave her alone."

It's possible Chloe hears this. When Jude turns, she's standing, framed in the doorway like a portrait. Her hair streams over her shoulders. Her eyes are enormous. She's young and she's beautiful and she's outraged. Jude can see her taking them in—Eli picking up the shards of glass so Jude won't step on them. Eli kneeling at her feet.

"You don't have to hang out with her," Chloe tells Eli. "I'm not breaking up with you no matter what she says."

Her gaze moves to Jude. "Good god, Mom. It's just a glass." Then back to Eli, "I'm glad it wasn't me, broke it. We'd never hear the end of it."

Love is love, Eli said, but how careful his timing has been! If Chloe were older, Jude could talk to her, woman to woman. If she were younger, Jude could take Chloe into her lap; tell her to stop throwing words like never around as if she knows what they mean, as if she knows just how long never will last.

# CANTERBURY HOLLOW

## CHRIS LAWSON

Of all the trillions of people who have lived and who will live, Arlyana and Moko were not especially important, nor heroic, nor beautiful, but for a few moments they were cradled by the laws of nature. In a universe that allows humans to survive in a minuscule sliver of all possible times and places, this is a rare accomplishment.

They met under the Sundome.

Arlyana wanted to see the killing sun for herself so she took the Long Elevator to the surface. The Sundome was a hemispheric pocket of air trapped under massive polymer plates on the crust of a dying planet called Musca. The Sundome persisted only through the efforts of robotic fixers, and the robots themselves needed constant repair from the ravages of the sun.

Through the transparent ceiling of the dome, Arlyana watched the sun rise over the world it had destroyed. The sun was a boiling disk, white and fringed with solar arcs. Ancient archived images showed a turquoise sky, but the sun had long since blown the atmosphere to wisps and now the sky was black and the stars visible in full daylight. A few degrees to one side, the sun's companion star glowed a creamy yellow.

Dawn threw sunlight across the ruins of the old city. Rising from the centre of the city was a tower many kilometers tall. The tower had been even taller once: it had reached all the way to orbit.

As the sun rose in the sky, the number of visitors to the Sundome thinned out. Even knowing they were protected by the dome, it was a terrifying experience for many people to stand beneath the killing sun. They hurried to the Long Elevator and scuttled back home. Not Arlyana: she wanted to face the sun, to challenge its authority to kill her. While the bulk of the people around her withdrew to the safety of the rock beneath their feet, Arlyana chose to go further outward.

The Sundome hosted a number of small buses, life supports on wheels, that allowed visitors to tour the old city. They were rarely used in daylight hours. Arlyana went to the bus bay, now completely emptied of people, and found a bus that was leaving in a few minutes.

At its allotted time the bus gave a little warning beep, the doors closed shut with a pneumatic sigh, and then it trundled out the airlock gates. As the bus moved over the blighted landscape, it gave an automated commentary.

"Different astronomers on Old Earth," said the bus, "reported different colors for our sun over different centuries. When people first settled Musca it was thought that the colors had been misreported due to the primitive telescopes of the time. Now we know that the old astronomers were seeing signs of instability. . . . "

Arlyana tuned out the words, but the sound of the voice was soothing.

The bus made its way over to the great, ruined tower. The tower was impressive but once it had been majestic, almost god-like in its engineering. Now it was a candle stub of eroded carbon. The soil at the foot of the tower had been baked to glass.

The bus interrupted its commentary. "My apologies," said the bus, "but a high energy sunburst has erupted and high levels of radiation are expected. The bus will now return for your own protection."

"I have been balloted," Arlyana said. She held up her ballot card. "Continue the tour."

"You are not the only person in the cabin," said the bus.

As the bus spoke, a man at the back of the bus leapt to his feet. This was Moko.

Moko, shaking off his sleep and orienting himself to the situation, held up his own ballot card. "I've been balloted too," he said. "Continue the tour."

"As you wish," said the bus.

Moko said to Arlyana, "I didn't mean to startle you. I lay down on the seat at the back and I must have fallen asleep."

"No need to apologize," she replied. "Come sit with me and enjoy the tour."

The bus took them around the Old City. The voice pointed out the Old Port, and the Old Synod, and the Old Settlement Memorial. Every one of them had long since crumbled to an abstract mass.

Midway through the tour, the bus announced that the sunburst had intensified and even balloted citizens, and buses for that matter, would be damaged by the flood of radiation coming. There was no time to return to the Sundome, so the bus scuttled over to the Old Tower and sheltered in its shadow.

"Well," said Arlyana to Moko, "it appears we are stuck here for now."

"So it does."

She watched him closely. He had a handsome face, if a little pinched at the mouth. He had continued to shave after being balloted, which she looked on approvingly even though she quite liked beards. She extended her hand to him.

"I should let you know that I'm not much in favor of balloted romances," she said.

Moko looked back at her. She was tall and muscular with dark blue skin that had gone out of fashion fifteen years ago but seemed to suit her.

"I agree." he said. "Too desperate."

"I would go so far as to say 'cloying.' "

"Not to mention 'desperate.' It bears repeating."

"So we're in agreement then. Against balloted romances."

"I believe we are." He reached out and took her hand.

It took three hours for the shadow of the tower to connect with the entrance to a safety tunnel. For those three hours they sat together in the bus, hiding in the shade while the sun showered the world with light of many frequencies and particles of many energies, with some that knocked lesser particles off the land around them and made the world glow.

They took the Long Elevator back to Moko's unit because it was closer. It was also much smaller and after skinnings of elbows and barkings of knees, they decided that Arlyana's apartment would have been more suitable after all. But that was three hours down the Grand Central Line and they were already together, if not entirely comfortable, so they lay wedged between Moko's bunk and the bulkhead above it and negotiated their future plans.

"My top three," said Arlyana, "would be to see the First Chamber, to put a drop of blood in the Heritage Wall, and to climb Canterbury Hollow."

"You want to climb Canterbury Hollow? Isn't it enough to just visit?"

"I'm going to climb it and I want you to climb with me."

Moko sighed. "I'm not sure I'm fit enough. Isn't it around eight hundred metres high?"

"Eight-twenty-two," said Arlyana. "But there's only a hundred or so of hard climbing."

"I'd need to get into shape. I'm not sure that's what I want to do with my time."

Arlyana tried to prop herself up on her elbow to read his expression, but she only succeeded in hitting her head. "I know this is a gauche thing to ask," she said, "but how much time do you have?"

"Two weeks."

She sagged back into the mattress. "You could have some of my time. I've got three months."

"I couldn't do that. It's too much to ask."

They lay in silence, thinking.

After several minutes Arlyana spoke up. "So what do you want to do with your time?" she asked.

Moko pursed his lips, then said, "I would like to visit the First Chamber, add a drop of blood to the Heritage Wall, and visit Canterbury Hollow."

She laughed at that. "That's quite a coincidence."

"Truth to tell, I've had no idea what to do with myself since I was balloted. If you've got some plans, I might as well use them."

Moko and Arlyana donned pressure suits to explore the First Chamber. Artificial lights illuminated the cavern. Rust-red trails of iron oxide dripped down the walls of the cavern.

The Chamber was smaller than they expected. Much, much smaller. Accustomed as they were to living in tight spaces, they still found it incredible that tens of thousands of citizens had once occupied a cavern the size of a sports chamber.

The first Deep Citizens had lived here for decades while they had drilled away at iron and stone, following fissures and air pockets to speed their excavation. As they dug down, deeper into the crust, they had built new cities in the spaces they carved out of bare rock. At first they had merely hoped to escape the solar irradiation, but after two centuries it had become inescapably apparent that the sun was not merely going to scorch the surface. The ferocity of its light was growing and soon it would burn off the atmosphere.

Having built one civilization, the Deep Citizens had to build another, this time sealed from the outside world. They adapted their existing cities and spaces where they could, but not everything could be saved. The First Chamber was too close and too open to the surface and so it had to be abandoned.

The excavating did not always go well. Several of the new spaces collapsed before they could be stabilized. In other chambers, fissures opened to the surface that made it impossible to trap air within.

The tragedy was twofold. The Deep Citizens had built chambers intended not just for themselves and their descendants, but for as many people of Musca as possible. They had drilled too fast and hollowed out chambers too large and too fragile. In their desperation to make room, they had over-reached. There was not enough space—nor air, nor food for that matter—for everyone. Even before the seals were closed, it was apparent that there would not be enough room even for all the existing Deep Citizens.

And so the Deep Citizens created the ballot.

Moko and Arlyana did not stay to explore the First Chamber as they had the Sundome. It was one thing to see the sun and the surface it had scoured of life; it was another to stand in the halls where the first ballot had been drawn.

On the morning of their fourth day, they were woken by a buzz at the door. Arlyana checked the video stream, sighed, and told Moko to stay in bed while she dealt with it.

Not knowing what else to do, he lay there staring at the ceiling with a view to getting back to sleep. That plan soon became impossible as he heard Arlyana's voice rising with emotion and he began to wonder what "it" was that needed dealing with. Another voice, deep and male, spoke in hushed tones.

Troubled by a dread that gripped tighter as Arlyana's voice became more strained, Moko decided that he could keep his promise to stay away from the door while keeping alert for Arlyana's safety by watching the video feed from the door. He tapped the screen and the picture flickered on; he quickly hit the mute button.

Arlyana was wrapped in her dressing gown, talking to a dark-eyed man who had dressed and groomed fastidiously, as if he were on his way to a funeral. In his hand he held a card or maybe an envelope and he was offering it to Arlyana while she adamantly refused to take it. As Arlyana become more animated, the man seemed to crumble from within. His shoulders dropped, his giving hand fell to his side.

Although Moko could make out nothing of the conversation, the volume rose to the point where occasional disconnected phrases from Arlyana filtered back to him. Moko rubbed his eyes to make sure he was seeing clearly. If anything, it was the stranger and not Arlyana who was likely to need his help.

The door slammed shut and Moko flicked off the video. Arlyana stormed back inside the unit, tossed off her gown, and crawled naked back into bed with Moko.

"Everything all right?" he asked.

The door buzzed in three staccato bursts.

"Ignore it," she said.

A few seconds later, there was another buzz at the door, then another, this time somehow sadder, and then the buzzer fell quiet. The silence stretched for a few seconds, then past a minute, then past three minutes. The door would not ring again. Arlyana wormed herself under Moko's arm and began to breathe in shudders. Not knowing what to say, Moko said nothing, which was exactly right.

The Heritage Wall was an hour by train from Arlyana's quarters. They stepped out of the station into a low chamber, a mere twenty metres tall, but so long and straight that it seemed to be a continuation of the train tunnel that had brought them.

The southern wall of the chamber was a milled plane that followed a subtly saddled polynomial function. The curve of the wall had a strangely emotive property: it could reach into people and make them pause in awe. Along the wall, following the relief lines of the function, were dots of blood where people had pricked a finger and pressed it to the rock.

"My family has a patch here," said Moko. He led Arlyana into the cavern, past robotic curators that cleaned the cavern and sharpened the edges of etchings that had eroded, and showed her the cluster of blood spots from his ancestors.

"These stop about thirty years ago," she said, reading the dates etched under each blood print.

Moko shrugged. "Most of my family joined the Brethren of Light. I'm the only one left on Musca."

"You have no family here?"

"My closest relative, both genetically and spatially, is my brother. He's on a Brethren mission ship halfway to B right now. He's about fifty light-hours away."

"You don't seem very Brethren to me," said Arlyana with a touch of amusement in her voice.

"Well," said Moko, "my brother is very Brotherly. However, in spite of being a brother to my brother, I am not Brotherly at all."

Arlyana shook her head. "Was that supposed to make sense?"

"If you spend enough time around Brethren, yes. Now show me your family plot."

Arlyana led him to her family's cluster of blood prints. It was a large display that went back twelve generations. Moko was impressed.

"Do you think I should put my mark in your family's area?" he asked. "They don't even know I exist."

"Do you always worry so much about etiquette?" Arlyana asked. "You do understand that being balloted gives you a certain degree of latitude?"

"It feels presumptuous to me."

Arlyana scoffed at him. "Since I'm not planning to put my own mark here, it's a moot point."

Moko waited for an explanation but Arlyana did not seem disposed to provide one. "Come on," she said. "We'll find our own place, miles from anyone else."

"Wait a moment," said Moko. Arlyana tried to draw him into moving on, but Moko refused. He was living with one Arlyana mystery already; he was not going let her keep spinning away from him. He examined the blood spots carefully, reading the names, dates, and relationships etched into the rock beneath them.

"I think I've got it. Here," he said, pointing to a spattered blotch of crimson on the wall. "This is your sister's blood. Her name is Uldi. And underneath that is a girl's name, Caris, but no blood. The space has been set aside for a girl who has not been born yet. Your niece-to-be." He studied Arlyana's face; she was giving nothing away. He continued, "It makes you feel bad. You know it shouldn't. But you can't help it. She is about to be born and you've been balloted."

"Yes, you've got it. I don't like to admit it, but I'm resentful," said Arlyana.

"I didn't say resentful," said Moko.

"I did," she replied, then pulled him away by the arm.

They walked along the Heritage Wall until they found an area that was almost devoid of blood marks. Arlyana called over one of the curators, a thin robotic agent that introduced itself and asked what they would like etched beside their blood marks. They decided their names and a small bridge between them would be enough.

The curator robot pricked Moko's skin. Blood budded on the tip of his thumb. Moko pressed it to the rock face and the curator etched his name and the date around it. Arlyana offered her hand to the curator. She pressed her blood to the wall next to Moko's and watched as the curator finished etching.

As they rode the train back, Arlyana fell asleep on Moko's shoulder. Now that he had time to think, he could see that Arlyana had been too quick to agree with his guess, and had been far too blithe about it. It bothered him that Arlyana had spun some more mist about herself. For someone who wanted to share terminal intimacies, she seemed paradoxically reluctant to let him understand her.

He ran through the names and dates in his mind, trying to reconstruct from memory Arlyana's family tree and the sequence of events. Something was amiss with the story he had intuited.

Moko brushed Arlyana's hair with his hand while she slept and wondered why she kept so many things to herself.

Moko said, "This looks terrible."

"Should I care how it looks?"

"People will say I only wanted you for the time you gave me."

"I want this more than I care what people think," said Arlyana.

So they went to the registry and signed away the difference in their ballots. Moko gained time and Arlyana lost time, but they would both live long enough for Moko to learn to climb.

They started with training walls, then worked their way up to boulders, then spouts, and finally to sheer walls. She taught him about ropes and anchors and how to belay, and over the following weeks he built up his strength and endurance.

Signing at the registry had another, quite unexpected, effect: Moko, who had more or less disappeared from his life, became traceable. Consequently, Arlyana was woken early one morning by a message marked maximum urgency.

She opened the message. A man with a shaved scalp and a slightly pinched mouth appeared on screen; he wore a Brethren tunic.

"My dear lady," said the man. "I apologize for sending a recorded message, but I am fifty light-hours away and cannot engage in responsive conversation. My name is Tarroux, and as you have may have guessed I am Moko's brother. I found you through the registry, and I apologize for intruding on you, but I have been trying to reach Moko with an extremely urgent message. It is imperative that he view the attachment as soon as possible. Before I finish, please allow me thank you. When you signed your time over to Moko, you may have given him just enough to save himself from the ballot. I can't tell you how much this means." There the message ended.

Arlyana shook Moko awake and dragged his grogginess out of bed.

"You have to see this," she said. Once the message finished, she touched the attachment and went to leave the room.

"Stay," said Moko.

"But it's private!"

"Stay!"

So they watched together as Tarroux, brother to Moko, spoke again.

"Moko," he said, "there is a place for you on the last Brethren mission ship. You know this will be the last ship to leave Musca. The sun is becoming too wild even for missionaries.

"I know we've been through this before, but I am hoping that the approaching ballot date will have changed how you feel about joining the Brethren.

"Please, brother, I love you and it breaks my heart knowing how easily you could be saved."

There was a stark jump-cut in the video stream. Tarroux had come back to the message and added a coda. The quality of the light had changed, the background was darker, and Tarroux looked as if he was being eaten from inside.

"Brother, I know I've asked you many times before and you've refused many times before, but please, please join the Brethren. I . . . I have never said this before, but I beg you to join the mission. Even if you don't believe, just say that you do. That's all you have to do. Just say you believe. I know, I know. It may be a lie. But with time spent among us, maybe you will come to see our truth. Even if you don't change, even if you never accept the Tenets, I will still have my brother."

At the end of the message, Arlyana turned off the screen.

"You turned down a place with the Brethren?" she asked, astonished. "You could have avoided the ballot?"

"Yes, I could have gone to the Brethren and lived a life that means nothing to me, full of empty rituals and prayers to forces I do not believe exist."

"*You would be alive*," she said.

"Just like you, eh?"

The sudden non sequitur jarred Arlyana. "What do you mean by that?" she asked.

"You think I wouldn't figure out the story with you and your family? I know what happened. I know it was your sister who was balloted, not you. I know that you took over her ballot because she was pregnant. And I know that your sister fell pregnant *after* she was balloted, which means that your unborn niece is not just a reminder of your impending mortality, *she is the reason for it*. And it's not your fetal niece you resent; it's your manipulative sister."

"You can't possibly know all that," Arlyana said angrily.

"All right, I don't *know* all that; I inferred it. Tell me I'm wrong and I'll take it all back."

"You can't possibly understand—"

"Tell me I'm wrong, then."

Arlyana said nothing, she just glared at him while an accusatory aura radiated from her.

Canterbury Hollow was one of the great chambers that crowned their civilization: a wonder of engineering and of art, it had been carved in the shape of a cathedral window. Everyone came there when they died, for recycling. Here the bodies of the dead were committed to the huge bacterial vats that broke down flesh and bone and returned organics to the community.

It was their last day together. The train brought Arlyana and Moko to the base of the Sepulchral Tower, a bowed memorial to everyone who had ever lived and died in that underworld. Few visitors ever went deeper than the memorial park, but Arlyana and Moko were not there to mourn and so they walked past the Sepulchre and into the darker Hollow. The light dimmed as they went deeper: Here the brightness was only to be found where it was needed for the workers and machines of the Hollow to perform their daily tasks.

Arlyana took him to a ladder at the base of the western wall that stretched up into the gloom overhead.

"I did all that training to climb a ladder?" said Moko.

"This service ladder rises two hundred metres. After that, it's all our own work."

By the time they reached the top of the ladder, Moko's arms were aching. He wondered how he would manage the rest of the climb. Arlyana reassured him that it would be harder work from here, but slower and with plenty of time for his muscles to recover between exertions.

"The route we're taking is called Little Freya. It's long but easy, and it has plenty of anchor points that previous climbers have left behind. Over to the right there—" and she pointed to a series of vertical ridges forty metres away "—is Big Freya. It's a much, much harder climb. The record for free-climbing Big Freya is seven hours. I've free-climbed it in ten. Believe me, what we're doing is a cinch."

They took a rest break, then Arlyana looped a rope through a nearby anchor and started climbing. They took turns climbing, then belaying, climbing, then belaying. Their progress was slow but safe, and Moko found that the longer they climbed the more he became focussed on each motion, on balancing the needs of work and rest, on finding the most efficient body position to keep a hold without exhausting a muscle group. Arlyana watched over him, taking care not to push him too hard, nor to let him pause when they needed to push on.

Time seemed to shrink away. He stopped counting hours and minutes and began thinking in steps and grips, which formed movements, which formed phases.

They went around bluffs, over ridges, avoided overhangs, and followed the road up the rock face. As they ascended, the light became more tenuous. They donned collar lanterns and set them glowing.

Many hours later, they came to a small cavern that burrowed off the side of the Hollow. Arlyana helped Moko scramble over the lip and into the safety of the space inside. Once he had caught his breath, he looked out the cavern mouth. There was another hundred metres to the peak of Canterbury Hollow. He groaned. The muscles ached in his shoulders, back, and calves.

Arlyana smiled. "Don't worry. This is as far as we're going."

"But we're not at the top yet."

"This is better. Come and see."

She took his hand and led him into the cavern. The space opened up at the back and they could walk upright without hitting their heads. The light from their collar lanterns filled the small cavern. Hundreds of golden reflections shone back at them. The reflections came from ballot tags that had been hung from the roof. There were hundreds of them, maybe thousands.

Moko moved about, brushing the tags with his fingers and setting them swinging. "What is this place?" he asked.

"Where climbers come to die," Arlyana said. She hammered a bolt into the cavern roof and from it she hung her ballot tag. Moko took his own tag and chain from around his neck and hung it from the same bolt, then looped a knot in the two chains so that the tags dangled face to face.

"Come here," said Arlyana, and she started to undress.

Arlyana and Moko were two small primates who were members of a long, slow radiation from the horn of Africa. Their lives meant little except to each other and to a small number of people around them, but stepping back, their choices were part of a pattern of self-similarity echoed on many scales of magnitude. The forces that drove them to each other also drove the cycles of expansion and contraction in the civilization of Deep Citizens. It drove the population cycles of foxes and hares, and on a larger scale again, the cycle of ammonites and meteorites. This great engine of colonization and exploitation had pushed humanity outward but had also destroyed the biosphere of a third of all inhabited worlds.

Programmed death has dogged living creatures ever since deep, deep ancestors discovered the power of swapping genes. With the evolution of abstract intelligence, the tragedy of death became a folly. But without that folly, humans would never have made it across the Red Sea and there never would have lived a pair of bonded primates in the crust of a planet twenty-nine light-years from Earth.

Arlyana cut a small segment off their climbing rope and tied one end around her wrist and the other around Moko's so they would not be separated.

On the time scales that affect human consciousness they did not have long, but for twenty heartbeats they would be cradled by the forces of nature. Angels of gravity drew them an elegant parabola; angels of electricity allowed skin to touch and to feel the contact; angels of strong force held them intact; and angels of weak force bound them to their mutual asymmetries.

They walked to the lip of the cavern, held each other tight, and toppled into empty space.

# THE SUMMER PEOPLE

## KELLY LINK

Fran's daddy woke her up wielding a mister. "Fran," he said, spritzing her like a wilted houseplant. "Fran, honey. Wake up for just a minute."

Fran had the flu, except it was more like the flu had Fran. In consequence of this, she'd lain out of school for three days in a row. The previous night, she'd taken four NyQuil caplets and fallen asleep on the couch, waiting for her daddy to come home, while a man on the TV threw knives. Her head felt stuffed with boiled wool and snot. Her face was now wet with watered-down plant food. "Hold up," she croaked. "I'm awake!" She began to cough, so hard she had to hold her sides. She sat up.

Her daddy was a dark shape in a room full of dark shapes. The bulk of him augured trouble. The sun wasn't up the mountain yet, but there was a light in the kitchen. There was a suitcase, too, beside the door, and on the table a plate with a mess of eggs. Fran was starving.

Her daddy went on. "I'll be gone some time. A week or three. Not more. You'll take care of the summer people while I'm gone. The Roberts come up next weekend. You'll need to get their groceries tomorrow or next day. Make sure you check the expiration date on the milk when you buy it, and put fresh sheets on all the beds. I've left the house schedule on the counter, and there should be enough gas in the car to make the rounds."

"Wait," Fran said. Every word hurt. "Where are you going?"

He sat down on the couch beside her, then pulled something out from under him. He held it out on his palm; one of Fran's old toys, the monkey egg. "Now you know I don't like these. I wish you'd put 'em away."

"There's lots of stuff I don't like," Fran said. "Where you going?"

"Prayer meeting in Miami. Found out about it on the Internet," her daddy said. He shifted on the couch, put a hand against her forehead, so cool and soothing it made her eyes leak. "You don't feel near so hot right now."

"I know you need to stay here and look after me," Fran said. "You're my daddy."

"Now, how can I look after you if I'm not right?" he said. "You don't know the things I've done."

Fran didn't know, but she could guess. "You went out last night," she said. "You were drinking."

Her daddy spread out his hands. "I'm not talking about last night," he said. "I'm talking about a lifetime."

"That is—" Fran said, and then began to cough again. She coughed so long and so hard she saw bright stars. Despite the hurt in her ribs, and despite the truth that every time she managed to suck in a good pocket of air, she coughed it all right back out again, the NyQuil made it all seem so peaceful, her daddy might as well have been saying a poem. Her eyelids were closing. Later, when she woke up, maybe he would make her breakfast.

"Any come around, you tell em I'm gone on ahead. Any man tells you he knows the hour or the day, Fran, that man's a liar or a fool. All a man can do is be ready."

He patted her on the shoulder, tucked the counterpane up around her ears. When she woke again, it was late afternoon, and her daddy was long gone. Her temperature was 102.3. All across her cheeks, the plant mister had left a red raised rash.

On Friday, Fran went to school, because she wasn't sure what else to do. Breakfast was a spoon of peanut butter and dry cereal. She couldn't remember the last time she'd eaten. Her cough scared off the crows when she went down to the county road to catch the school bus.

She dozed through three classes, including calculus, before having such a fit of coughing the teacher sent her off to see the nurse. The nurse, she knew, was liable to call her daddy and send her home. This might have presented a problem, but on the way to the nurse's station, Fran came upon Ophelia Merck at her locker.

Ophelia Merck had her own car, a Lexus. She and her family had been summer people, except now they lived in their house up at Horse Cove on the lake all year round. Years ago, Fran and Ophelia had spent a summer of afternoons playing with Ophelia's Barbies while Fran's father smoked out a wasps' nest, repainted cedar siding, tore down an old fence. They hadn't really spoken since then, though once or twice after that summer, Fran's father brought home paper bags full of Ophelia's hand-me-downs, some of them still with the price tags.

Fran eventually went through a growth spurt, which put a stop to that; Ophelia was still tiny, even now. And far as Fran could figure, Ophelia hadn't changed much in most other ways: pretty, shy, spoiled, and easy to boss around. The rumor was her family'd moved full-time to Robbinsville from Lynchburg

after a teacher caught Ophelia kissing another girl in the bathroom at a school
dance. It was either that or Mr. Merck being up for malpractice, which was the
other story, take your pick.

"Ophelia Merck," Fran said. "I need you to tell Nurse Tannent you're gone
to give me a ride home right now."

Ophelia opened her mouth and closed it. She nodded.

Fran's temperature was back up again, at 102. Tannent even wrote Ophelia
a note to go off campus.

"I don't know where you live," Ophelia said. They were in the parking lot,
Ophelia searching for her keys.

"Take the county road," Fran said. "129." Ophelia nodded. "It's up a ways
on Wild Ridge, past the hunting camps." She lay back against the headrest
and closed her eyes. "Oh, hell. I forgot. Can you take me by the convenience
first? I have to get the Roberts' house put right."

"I guess I can do that," Ophelia said.

At the convenience, she picked up milk, eggs, whole wheat sandwich bread,
and cold cuts for the Roberts, Tylenol and more NyQuil for herself, as well as
a can of frozen orange juice, microwave burritos, and Pop-Tarts. "On the tab,"
she told Andy.

"I hear your pappy got himself into trouble the other night," Andy said.

"That so," Fran said. "He went down to Florida yesterday morning. He said
he needs to get right with God."

"God ain't who your pappy needs to get on his good side," Andy said.

Fran coughed and bent over. Then she straightened right back up. "What's
he done?" she said.

"Nothing that can't be fixed with the application of some greaze and good
manners," Andy said. "You tell him we'll get it all settled when he come
back."

Half the time her daddy got to drinking, Andy and Andy's cousin Ryan
were involved, never mind it was a dry county. Andy kept the liquor out back
in his van for everwho wanted it and knew to ask. The good stuff came from
over the county line, in Andrews. The best stuff, though, was the liquor Fran's
daddy brought Andy every once in a while. Everyone said that Fran's daddy's
brew was too good to be strictly natural. Which was true. When he wasn't
getting right with God, Fran's daddy got up to all kinds of trouble. Fran's best
guess was that, in this particular situation, he'd promised to supply something
that God was not now going to let him deliver. "I'll tell him you said so."

Ophelia was looking over the list of ingredients on a candy wrapper, but
Fran could tell she was interested. When they got back into the car Fran said,
"Just because you're doing me a favor doesn't mean you need to know my
business."

"Okay," Ophelia said.

"Okay," Fran said. "Good. Now maybe you can take me by the Roberts' place. It's over on—"

"I know where the Roberts' house is," Ophelia said. "My mom played bridge over there all last summer."

The Roberts hid their spare key under a fake rock just like everybody else. Ophelia stood at the door like she was waiting to be invited in. "Well, come on," Fran said.

There wasn't much to be said about the Roberts' house. There was an abundance of plaid, and everywhere Toby mugs and statuettes of dogs pointing, setting, or trotting along with birds in their gentle mouths.

Fran made up the smaller bedrooms and did a quick vacuum downstairs while Ophelia made up the master bedroom and caught the spider that had made a home in the wastebasket. She carried it outside. Fran didn't quite have the breath to make fun of her for this. They went from room to room, making sure that there were working bulbs in the light fixtures and that the cable wasn't out. Ophelia sang under her breath while they worked. They were both in choir, and Fran found herself evaluating Ophelia's voice. A soprano, warm and light at the same time, where Fran was an alto and somewhat froggy, even when she didn't have the flu.

"Stop it," she said out loud, and Ophelia turned and looked at her. "Not you," Fran said. She ran the tap water in the kitchen sink until it was clear. She coughed for a long time and spat into the drain. It was almost four o'clock. "We're done here."

"How do you feel?" Ophelia said.

"Like I've been kicked all over," Fran said.

"I'll take you home," Ophelia said. "Is anyone there, in case you start feeling worse?"

Fran didn't bother answering, but somewhere between the school lockers and the Roberts' master bedroom, Ophelia seemed to have decided that the ice was broken. She talked about a TV show, about the party neither of them would go to on Saturday night. Fran began to suspect that Ophelia had had friends once, down in Lynchburg. She complained about the calculus homework and talked about a sweater she was knitting. She mentioned a girl rock band that she thought Fran might like, even offered to burn her a CD. Several times, she exclaimed as they drove up the county road.

"I never get used to it, to living up here year-round," Ophelia said. "I mean, we haven't even been here a whole year, but . . . It's just so beautiful. It's like another world, you know?"

"Not really," Fran said. "Never been anywhere else."

"Oh," Ophelia said, not quite deflated by this comeback. "Well, take it from me. It's freaking gorgeous here. Everything is so pretty it almost hurts. I love the morning, the way everything is all misty. And the trees! And every time the road snakes around a corner, there's another waterfall. Or a little pasture, and it's all full of flowers. All the *hollers*." Fran could hear the invisible brackets around the word. "It's like you don't know what you'll see, what's there, until suddenly you're in them. Are you applying to college anywhere next year? I was thinking about vet school. I don't think I can take another English class. Large animals. No little dogs or guinea pigs. Maybe I'll go out to California."

Fran said, "We're not the kind of people who go to college."

"Oh," Ophelia said. "You're a lot smarter than me, you know? So I just thought . . . "

"Turn here," Fran said. "Careful. It's not paved."

They went up the dirt road, through the laurel beds, and into the little meadow with the nameless creek. Fran could feel Ophelia suck in a breath, probably trying her hardest not to say something about how beautiful it was. And it was beautiful, Fran knew. You could hardly see the house itself, hidden like a bride behind her veil of climbing vines: virgin's bower and Japanese honeysuckle, masses of William Baffin and Cherokee roses overgrowing the porch and running up over the sagging roof. Bumblebees, their legs armored in gold, threaded through the meadow grass, almost too weighed down with pollen to fly.

"It's old," Fran said. "Needs a new roof. My great-grandaddy ordered it out of the Sears catalog. Men brought it up the side of the mountain in pieces, and all the Cherokee who hadn't gone away yet came and watched." She was amazed at herself: next thing she would be asking Ophelia to come for a sleepover.

She opened the car door and heaved herself out, plucked up the poke of groceries. Before she could turn and thank Ophelia for the ride, Ophelia was out of the car, as well. "I thought," Ophelia said uncertainly. "Well, I thought maybe I could use your bathroom?"

"It's an outhouse," Fran said, deadpan. Then she relented: "Come on in, then. It's a regular bathroom. Just not very clean."

Ophelia didn't say anything when they came into the kitchen. Fran watched her take it in: the heaped dishes in the sink, the pillow and raggedy quilt on the sagging couch. The piles of dirty laundry beside the efficiency washer in the kitchen. The places where hairy tendrils of vine had found a way inside around the windows. "I guess you might be thinking it's funny," she said. "My dad and I make money doing other people's houses, but we don't take no real care of our own."

"I was thinking that somebody ought to be taking care of you," Ophelia said. "At least while you're sick."

Fran gave a little shrug. "I do fine on my own," she said. "The washroom's down the hall."

She took two NyQuil while Ophelia was gone and washed them down with the last swallow or two of ginger ale out of the refrigerator. Flat, but still cool. Then she lay down on the couch and pulled the counterpane up around her face. She huddled into the lumpy cushions. Her legs ached, her face felt hot as fire. Her feet were ice cold.

A minute later Ophelia sat down on the couch beside her.

"Ophelia?" Fran said. "I'm grateful for the ride home and for the help at the Roberts', but I don't go for the girls. So don't lez out."

Ophelia said, "I brought you a glass of water. You need to stay hydrated."

"Mmm," Fran said.

"You know, your dad told me once that I was going to hell," Ophelia said. "He was over at our house doing something. Fixing a burst pipe, maybe? I don't know how he knew. I was eleven. I don't think I knew, not yet, anyway. He didn't bring you over to play after he said that, even though I never told my mom."

"My daddy thinks everyone is going to hell," Fran said into the counterpane. "I don't care where I go, as long as it isn't here, and he isn't there."

Ophelia didn't say anything for a minute or two, and she didn't get up to leave, either, so finally Fran poked her head out. Ophelia had a toy in her hand, the monkey egg. She turned it over, and then over again. She looked a question at Fran.

"Give here," Fran said. "I'll work it." She wound the filigreed dial and set the egg on the floor. The toy vibrated ferociously. Two pincerlike legs and a scorpion tail made of figured brass shot out of the bottom hemisphere, and the egg wobbled on the legs in one direction and then another, the articulated tail curling and lashing. Portholes on either side of the top hemisphere opened and two arms wriggled out and reached up, rapping at the dome of the egg until that, too, cracked open with a click. A monkey's head, wearing the egg dome like a hat, popped out. Its mouth opened and closed in chattering ecstasy, red garnet eyes rolling, arms describing wider and wider circles in the air until the clockwork ran down and all of its extremities whipped back into the egg again.

"What in the world?" Ophelia said. She picked up the egg, tracing the joins with a finger.

"It's just something that's been in our family," Fran said. She stuck her arm out of the quilt, grabbed a tissue, and blew her nose for maybe the thousandth time. "We didn't steal it from no one, if that's what you're thinking."

"No," Ophelia said, and then frowned. "It's just—I've never seen anything like it. It's like a Fabergé egg. It ought to be in a museum."

There were lots of other toys. The laughing cat and the waltzing elephants; the swan you wound up, who chased the dog. Other toys that Fran hadn't played with in years. The mermaid who combed garnets out of her own hair. Bawbees for babies, her mother had called them.

"I remember now," Ophelia said. "When you came and played at my house. You brought a minnow made out of silver. It was smaller than my little finger. We put it in the bathtub, and it swam around and around. You had a little fishing rod, too, and a golden worm that wriggled on the hook. You let me catch the fish, and when I did, it talked. It said it would give me a wish if I let it go."

"You wished for two pieces of chocolate cake," Fran said.

"And then my mother made a chocolate cake, didn't she?" Ophelia said. "So the wish came true. But I could only eat one piece. Maybe I knew she was going to make a cake? Except why would I wish for something that I already knew I was going to get?"

Fran said nothing. She watched Ophelia through slit eyes.

"Do you still have the fish?" Ophelia asked.

Fran said, "Somewhere. The clockwork ran down. It didn't give wishes no more. I reckon I didn't mind. It only ever granted little wishes."

"Ha, ha," Ophelia said. She stood up. "Tomorrow's Saturday. I'll come by in the morning to make sure you're okay."

"You don't have to," Fran said.

"No," Ophelia said. "I don't have to. But I will."

When you do for other people (Fran's daddy said once upon a time when he was drunk, before he got religion) things that they could do for themselves, but they pay you to do it instead, you both will get used to it. Sometimes they don't even pay you, and that's charity. At first, charity isn't comfortable, but it gets so it is. After some while, maybe you start to feel wrong when you ain't doing for them, just one more thing, and always one more thing after that. Maybe you start to feel as you're valuable. Because they need you. And the more they need you, the more you need them. Things go out of balance. You need to remember that, Franny. Sometimes you're on one side of that equation, and sometimes you're on the other. You need to know where you are and what you owe. Unless you can balance that out, here is where y'all stay.

Fran, dosed on NyQuil, feverish and alone in her great-grandfather's catalog house, hidden behind walls of roses, dreamed—as she did every night—of escape. She woke every few hours, wishing someone would bring her another glass of water. She sweated through her clothes, and then froze, and then boiled again. Her throat was full of knives.

She was still on the couch when Ophelia came back, banging through the screen door. "Good morning!" Ophelia said. "Or maybe I should say good afternoon! It's noon, anyhow. I brought oranges to make fresh orange juice, and I didn't know if you liked sausage or bacon, so I got you two different kinds of biscuit."

Fran struggled to sit up.

"Fran," Ophelia said. She came and stood in front of the sofa, still holding the two cat-head biscuits. "You look terrible." She put her hand on Fran's forehead. "You're burning up! I knew I oughtn't've left you here all by yourself! What should I do? Should I take you down to the emergency?"

"No doctor," Fran managed to say. "They'll want to know where my daddy is. Water?"

Ophelia scampered back to the kitchen. "How many days have you had the flu? You need antibiotics. Or something. Fran?"

"Here," Fran said. She lifted a bill off a stack of mail on the floor, pulled out the return envelope. She plucked out three strands of her hair. She put them in the envelope and licked it shut. "Take this up the road where it crosses the drain," she said. "All the way up." She coughed a rattling, deathly cough. "When you get to the big house, go around to the back and knock on the door. Tell them I sent you. You won't see them, but they'll know you came from me. After you knock, you can just go in. Go upstairs directly, you mind, and put this envelope under the door. Third door down the hall. You'll know which. After that, you oughter wait out on the porch. Bring back whatever they give you."

Ophelia gave her a look that said Fran was delirious. "Just go," Fran said. "If there ain't a house, or if there is a house and it ain't the house I'm telling you about, then come back, and I'll go to the emergency with you. Or if you find the house, and you're afeared and you can't do what I asked, come back, and I'll go with you. But if you do what I tell you, it will be like the minnow."

"Like the minnow?" Ophelia said. "I don't understand."

"You will. Be bold," Fran said, and did her best to look cheerful. "Like the girls in those ballads. Will you bring me another glass of water afore you go?"

Ophelia went.

Fran lay on the couch, thinking about what Ophelia would see. From time to time, she raised a pair of curious-looking spyglasses—something much more useful than any bawbee—to her eyes. Through them she saw first the dirt track, which only seemed to dead-end. Were you to look again, you found your road crossing over the shallow crick once, twice, the one climbing the mountain, the drain running away and down. The meadow disappeared again into beds of laurel, then low trees hung with climbing roses, so that you ascended in drifts of pink and white. A stone wall, tumbled and ruined, and then the big house. The house, dry-stack stone, stained with age like the tumbledown wall;, two stories. A slate roof, a long covered porch, carved wooden shutters making all the eyes of the windows blind. Two apple trees, crabbed and old, one green and bearing fruit and the other bare and silver black. Ophelia found the mossy path between them that wound around to the back door with two words carved over the stone lintel: Be bold.

And this is what Fran saw Ophelia do: having knocked on the door, Ophelia hesitated for only a moment, and then she opened it. She called out, "Hello? Fran sent me. She's ill. Hello?" No one answered.

So Ophelia took a breath and stepped over the threshold and into a dark, crowded hallway with a room on either side and a staircase in front of her. On the flagstone in front of her were carved the words: Be bold, be bold. Despite the invitation, Ophelia did not seem tempted to investigate either room, which Fran thought wise of her. The first test was a success. You might expect that through one door would be a living room, and you might expect that through the other door would be a kitchen, but you would be wrong. One was the Queen's Room. The other was what Fran thought of as the War Room.

Fusty stacks of old magazines and catalogs and newspapers, old encyclopedias and gothic novels leaned against the walls of the hall, making such a narrow alley that even lickle, tiny Ophelia turned sideways to make her way. Dolls' legs and old silverware sets and tennis trophies and mason jars and empty match boxes and false teeth and stranger things still poked out of paper bags and plastic carriers. You might expect that through the doors on either side of the hall there would be more crumbling piles and more odd jumbles, and you would be right. But there were other things, too. At the foot of the stairs was another piece of advice for guests like Ophelia, carved right into the first riser: Be bold, be bold, but not too bold.

The owners of the house had been at another one of their frolics, Fran saw. Someone had woven tinsel and ivy and peacock feathers through the banisters. Someone had thumbtacked cut silhouettes and Polaroids and tintypes and magazine pictures on the wall alongside the stairs, layers upon layers upon layers; hundreds and hundreds of eyes watching each time Ophelia set her foot down carefully on the next stair.

Perhaps Ophelia didn't trust the stairs not to be rotted through. But the stairs were safe. Someone had always taken very good care of this house.

At the top of the stairs, the carpet underfoot was soft, almost spongy. Moss, Fran decided. They've redecorated again. That's going to be the devil to clean up. Here and there were white and red mushrooms in pretty rings upon the moss. More bawbees, too, waiting for someone to come along and play with them. A dinosaur, only needing to be wound up, a plastic dime-store cowboy sitting on its shining shoulders. Up near the ceiling, two armored dirigibles, tethered to a light fixture by scarlet ribbons. The cannons on these zeppelins were in working order. They'd chased Fran down the hall more than once. Back home, she'd had to tweeze the tiny lead pellets out of her shin. Today, though, all were on their best behavior.

Ophelia passed one door, two doors, stopped at the third door. Above it, the final warning: BE BOLD, BE BOLD, BUT NOT TOO BOLD, LEST THAT THY HEART'S BLOOD RUN COLD. Ophelia put her hand on the doorknob, but didn't try it. Not afeared, but no fool neither, Fran thought. They'll be pleased. Or will they?

Ophelia knelt down to slide Fran's envelope under the door. Something else happened, too: something slipped out of Ophelia's pocket and landed on the carpet of moss.

Back down the hall, Ophelia stopped in front of the first door. She seemed to hear someone or something. Music, perhaps? A voice calling her name? An invitation? Fran's poor, sore heart was filled with delight. They liked her! Well, of course they did. Who wouldn't like Ophelia?

She made her way down the stairs, through the towers of clutter and junk. Back onto the porch, where she sat on the porch swing, but didn't swing. She seemed to be keeping one eye on the house and the other on the little rock garden out back, which ran up against the mountain right quick. There was even a waterfall, and Fran hoped Ophelia appreciated it. There'd never been no such thing before. This one was all for her, all for Ophelia, who opined that waterfalls are freaking beautiful.

Up on the porch, Ophelia's head jerked around, as if she were afraid someone might be sneaking up the back. But there were only carpenter bees, bringing back their satchels of gold, and a woodpecker, drilling for grubs. There was a groundpig in the rumpled grass, and the more Ophelia set and stared, the more she and Fran both saw. A pair of fox kits napping under the laurel. A doe and a faun peeling bark runners off young trunks. Even a brown bear, still tufty with last winter's fur, nosing along the high ridge above the house. Fran knew what Ophelia must be feeling. As if she were an interloper in some Eden. While Ophelia sat on the porch of that dangerous house, Fran curled inward on her couch, waves of heat pouring out of her. Her whole body shook so violently her teeth rattled. Her spyglasses fell to the floor. Maybe I am dying, Fran thought, and that is why Ophelia came here.

Fran, feverish, went in and out of sleep, always listening for the sound of Ophelia coming back down. Perhaps she'd made a mistake, and they wouldn't send something to help. Perhaps they wouldn't send Ophelia back at all. Ophelia, with her pretty singing voice, that shyness, that innate kindness.

Her short hair, silvery blond. They liked things that were shiny. They were like magpies that way. In other ways, too.

But here was Ophelia, after all, her eyes enormous, her face lit up like Christmas. "Fran," she said. "Fran, wake up. I went there. I was bold! Who lives there, Fran?"

"The summer people," Fran said. "Did they give you anything for me?"

Ophelia set an object upon the counterpane. Like everything the summer people made, it was right pretty. A lipstick-sized vial of pearly glass, an enameled green snake clasped around it, its tail the stopper. Fran tugged at the tail, and the serpent uncoiled. A pole ran out the mouth of the bottle, and a silk rag unfurled. Embroidered upon it were the words drink me.

Ophelia watched this, her eyes glazed with too many marvels. "I sat and waited, and there were two fox kits! They came right up to the porch, and then went to the door and scratched at it until it opened. They trotted right inside and came out again. One came over to me then, with something in its jaw. It laid down that bottle right at my feet, and then they ran down the steps and into the woods. Fran, it was like a fairy tale."

"Yes," Fran said. She put her lips to the mouth of the vial and drank down what was in it. It tasted sour and hot, like bottled smoke. She coughed, then wiped her mouth and licked the back of her hand.

"I mean, people say something is like a fairy tale all the time," Ophelia said. "And what they mean is somebody falls in love and gets married. But that house, those animals, it really is a fairy tale. Who are they? The summer people?"

"That's what my daddy calls them," Fran said. "Except, when he gets religious, he calls them devils come up to steal his soul. It's because they supply him with drink. But he weren't never the one who had to mind after them. That was my mother. And now she's gone, and it's only ever me."

"You take care of them?" Ophelia said. "You mean, like the Roberts?"

A feeling of tremendous well-being was washing over Fran. Her feet were warm for the first time in what seemed like days, and her throat felt coated in honey and balm. Even her nose felt less raw and red. "Ophelia?" she said.

"Yes, Fran?"

"I think I'm going to be much better," Fran said. "Which is something you done for me. You were brave and a true friend, and I'll have to think how I can pay you back."

"I wasn't—" Ophelia protested. "I mean, I'm glad I did. I'm glad you asked me. I promise I won't tell anyone."

If you did you'd be sorry, Fran thought but didn't say. "Ophelia? I need to sleep. And then, if you want, we can talk. You can even stay here while I sleep. If you want. I don't care if you're a lesbian. There are Pop-Tarts on the kitchen counter. And those two biscuits you brung. I like sausage. You can have the one with bacon."

She fell asleep before Ophelia could say anything else.

The first thing she did when she woke up was take a bath. In the mirror, she took a quick inventory. Her hair was lank and greasy, all witch knots and tangles. There were circles under her eyes, and her tongue, when she stuck it out, was yellow. When she was clean and dressed again, her jeans were loose and she could feel her hip bones protruding. "I could eat a whole mess of food," she told Ophelia. "But a cat-head and a box of Pop-Tarts will do for a start."

There was fresh orange juice, and Ophelia had poured it into a stoneware jug. Fran decided not to tell her that her daddy used it as a sometime spittoon. "Can I ask you some more about them?" Ophelia said. "You know, the summer people?"

"I don't reckon I can answer every question," Fran said. "But go on."

"When I first got there," Ophelia said, "when I went inside, at first I decided that it must be a shut-in. One of those, you know, hoarders. I've watched that show, and sometimes they even keep their own poop. And dead cats. It's just horrible.

"Then it just kept on getting stranger. But I wasn't ever scared. It felt like there was somebody there, but they were happy to see me."

"They don't get much in the way of company," Fran said.

"Yeah, well, why do they collect all that stuff? Where does it come from?"

"Some of it's from catalogs. I have to go down to the post office and collect it for them. Sometimes they go away and bring things back. Sometimes they tell me they want something and I have to go get it for them. Mostly it's stuff from the Salvation Army. Once I had to buy a hunnert pounds of copper piping."

"Why?" Ophelia said. "I mean, what do they do with it?"

"They make things," Fran said. "That's what my momma called them, makers. I don't know what they do with all of it. They give away things. Like the toys. They like children. When you do things for them, they're beholden to you."

"Have you seen them?" Ophelia said.

"Now and then," Fran said. "Not very often. Not since I was much younger. They're shy."

Ophelia was practically bouncing on her chair. "You get to look after them? That's the best thing ever! Have they always been here? Is that why you aren't going to go to college?"

Fran hesitated. "I don't know where they come from. They aren't always there. Sometimes they're . . . somewhere else. My momma said she felt sorry for them. She thought maybe they couldn't go home, that they'd been sent away, like the Cherokee, I guess. They live a lot longer, maybe forever, I don't know. I don't think time works the same way where they come from. Sometimes they're gone for years. But they always come back. They're summer people. That's just the way it is with summer people."

"And you're not," Ophelia said. "And now I'm not, either."

"*You* can go away again whenever you want," Fran said, not caring how she sounded. "I can't. It's part of the bargain. Whoever takes care of them has to stay here. You can't leave. They don't let you."

"You mean, you can't leave, ever?"

"No," Fran said. "Not ever. My mother was stuck here until she had me. And then when I was old enough, she told me I had to take over. She took off right after that."

"Where did she go?"

"I'm not the one to answer that," Fran said. "They gave my momma a tent that folds up no bigger than a kerchief, that sets up the size of a two-man tent, but on the inside, it's teetotally different, a cottage with two brass beds and a chifforobe to hang your things in, and a table, and windows with glass in them. When you look out one of the windows, you see wherever you are, and when you look out the other window, you see those two apple trees, the ones in front of the house with the moss path between them?"

Ophelia nodded.

"Well, my momma used to bring out that tent for me and her when my daddy had been drinking. Then my momma passed the summer people on to me, and one morning after we spent the night in the tent, I woke up and saw her climb out that window. The one that shouldn't ought to be there. She disappeared down that path. Maybe I should have followed on after her, but I stayed put."

"Where did she go?" Ophelia said.

"Well, she ain't here," Fran said. "That's what I know. So I have to stay here in her place. I don't expect she'll be back, neither."

"Well, that sucks," Ophelia said.

"I wish I could get away for just a little while," Fran said. "Maybe go out to San Francisco and see the Golden Gate Bridge. Dip my toes in the Pacific. I'd like to buy me a guitar and play some of those old ballads on the streets. Just stay a little while, then come back and take up my burden again."

"I'd sure like to go out to California," Ophelia said.

They sat in silence for a minute.

"I wish I could help out," Ophelia said. "You know, with that house and the summer people. You shouldn't have to do everything, not all of the time."

"I already owe you," Fran said, "for helping with the Roberts' house. For looking in on me when I was ill. For what you did when you went up to fetch me help."

"I know what it's like when you're all alone," Ophelia said. "When you can't talk about stuff. And I mean it, Fran. I'll do whatever I can to help."

"I can tell you mean it," Fran said. "I just don't think you know what it is you're saying. I ought to explain at least one thing. If you want, you can go up there again one more time. You did me a favor, and I don't know how else to pay you back. There's a bedroom up in that house, and if you sleep in it, you see your heart's desire. I could take you back tonight and show you that room. Besides, I think you lost something up there."

"I did?" Ophelia said. "What was it?" She reached down in her pockets. "Oh, hell. My iPod. How did you know?"

Fran shrugged. "Not like anybody up there is going to steal it. Expect they'd be happy to have you back up again. If they didn't like you, you'd know it already."

Fran was straightening up her and her daddy's mess when the summer people let her know that they needed a few things. "Can't I just have a minute to myself?" she grumbled.

They told her that she'd had a good four days. "And I surely do appreciate it," she said, "considering I was laid so low." But she put the skillet down in the sink to soak and wrote down what they wanted.

She tidied away all of the toys, not quite sure what had come over her to take them out.

When Ophelia came back at five, she had her hair in a ponytail and a flashlight and a thermos in her pocket, like she thought she was Nancy Drew.

"It gets dark up here so early," Ophelia said. "I feel like it's Halloween or something. Like you're taking me to the haunted house."

"They ain't haints," Fran said. "Nor demons or any such thing. They don't do no harm unless you get on the wrong side of them. They'll play a prank on you then, and count it good fun."

"Like what?" Ophelia said.

"Once I did the warshing up and broke a teacup," Fran said. "They'll sneak up and pinch you." She still had marks on her arms, though she hadn't broken a plate in years. "Lately, they've been doing what all the people up here like to do, that reenacting. They set up their battlefield in the big room downstairs. It's not the War between the States. It's one of theirs, I guess. They built themselves airships and submersibles and mechanical dragons and knights and all manner of wee toys to fight with. Sometimes, when they get bored, they get me up to be their audience, only they ain't always careful where they go pointing their cannons."

She looked at Ophelia and saw she'd said too much. "Well, they're used to me. They know I don't have no choice but to put up with their ways."

That afternoon, she'd had to drive over to Chattanooga to visit a particular thrift store. They'd sent her for a used DVD player and all the bathing suits she could buy up. Between that and paying for gas, she'd gone through seventy dollars. And the service light had been on the whole way. At least it hadn't been a school day. Hard to explain you were cutting out because voices in your head were telling you they needed a saddle.

She'd gone on ahead and brought it all up to the house after. No need to bother Ophelia with any of it. The iPod had been a-laying right in front of the door.

"Here," she said. "I went ahead and brought this back down."

"My iPod!" Ophelia said. She turned it over. "They did this?"

The iPod was heavier now. It had a little walnut case instead of pink silicone, and there was a figure inlaid in ebony and gilt.

"A dragonfly," Ophelia said.

"A snake doctor," Fran said. "That's what my daddy calls them."

"They did this for me?"

"They'd embellish a bedazzled jean jacket if you left it there," Fran said. "No lie. They can't stand to leave a thing alone."

"Cool," Ophelia said. "Although my mom is never going to believe me when I say I bought it at the mall."

"Just don't take up anything metal," Fran said. "No earrings, not even your car keys. Or you'll wake up and they'll have smelted them down and turned them into doll armor or who knows what all."

They took off their shoes when they got to where the road crossed the drain. The water was cold with the last of the snowmelt. Ophelia said, "I feel like I ought to have brought a hostess gift."

"You could pick them a bunch of wildflowers," Fran said. "But they'd be just as happy with a bit of kyarn."

"Yarn?" Fran said.

"Roadkill," Fran said. "But yarn's okay too."

Ophelia thumbed the wheel of her iPod. "There's songs on here that weren't here before."

"They like music, too," Fran said. "They like it when I sing."

"What you were saying about going out to San Francisco to busk," Ophelia said. "I can't imagine doing that."

"Well," Fran said. "I won't ever do it, but I think I can imagine it okay."

When they got up to the house, there were deer grazing on the green lawn. The living tree and the dead were all touched with the last of the sunlight. Chinese lanterns hung in rows from the rafters of the porch.

"You always have to come at the house from between the trees," Fran said. "Right on the path. Otherwise, you don't get nowhere near it. And I don't ever use but the back door."

She knocked at the back door. BE BOLD, BE BOLD. "It's me again," she said. "And my friend Ophelia. The one who left the iPod."

She saw Ophelia open her mouth and went on, hastily, "Don't say it, Ophelia. They don't like it when you thank them. They're allergic to that word. Come on in. Mi casa es su casa. I'll give you the grand tour."

They stepped over the threshold, Fran first.

"There's the pump room out back, where I do the wash," she said. "There's a big ole stone oven for baking in, and a pig pit, although why I don't know. They don't eat meat. But you prob'ly don't care about that."

"What's in this room?" Ophelia said.

"Hunh," Fran said. "Well, first, it's a lot of junk. They just like to accumulate junk. Way back in there, though is what I think is a queen."

"A queen?"

"Well, that's what I call her. You know how, in a beehive, way down in the combs, you have the queen, and all the worker bees attend on her? Far as I can tell, that's what's in there. She's real big and not real pretty, and they are always running in and out of there with food for her. I don't think she's teetotally growed up yet. For a while now, I've been thinking on what my momma said, about how maybe these summer people got sent off. Bees do that too, right? Go off and make a new hive when there are too many queens?"

"Honestly?" Ophelia said. "It sounds kind of creepy."

"The queen's where my daddy gets his liquor, and she don't bother him none. They have some kind of still set up in there, and every once in a while when he ain't feeling too religious, he goes in and skims off a little bitty bit. It's awful sweet stuff."

"Are they, uh, are they listening to us right now?"

In response came a series of clicks from the War Room.

Ophelia jumped. "What's that?" she said.

"Remember I told you 'bout the reenactor stuff?" Fran said. "Don't get freaked out. It's pretty cool."

She gave Ophelia a little push into the War Room.

Of all the rooms in the house, this one was Fran's favorite, even if they dive-bombed her sometimes with the airships, or fired off the cannons without much thought for where she was standing. The walls were beaten tin and copper, scrap metal held down with two-penny nails. Molded forms lay on the floor representing scaled-down mountains, forests, and plains where miniature armies fought desperate battles. There was a kiddie pool over by the big picture window with a machine in it that made waves. There were little ships and submersibles, and occasionally one of the ships sank, and bodies would go floating over to the edges. There was a sea serpent made of tubing and metal rings that swam endlessly in a circle. There was a sluggish river, too, closer to the door, that ran red and stank and stained the banks. The summer people were always setting up miniature bridges over it, then blowing the bridges up.

Overhead were the fantastic shapes of the dirigibles, and the dragons that were hung on string and swam perpetually through the air above your head. There was a misty globe, too, suspended in some way that Fran could not figure, and lit by some unknown source. It stayed up near the painted ceiling for days at a time, and then sunk down behind the plastic sea according to some schedule of the summer people's.

"It's amazing," Ophelia said. "Once I went to the house of some friend of my father's. An anesthesiologist? He had a train set down in his basement and it was crazy complicated. He would die if he saw this."

"Over there is a queen, I think," Fran said. "All surrounded by her knights. And here's another one, much smaller. I wonder who won, in the end."

"Maybe it's not been fought yet," Ophelia said. "Or maybe it's being fought right now."

"Could be," Fran said. "I wish there was a book told you everything that went on. Come on. I'll show you the room you can sleep in."

They went up the stairs. BE BOLD, BE BOLD, BUT NOT TOO BOLD. The moss carpet on the second floor was already looking a little worse for wear. "Last week I spent a whole day scrubbing these boards on my hands and knees. So, of course, they need to go next thing and pile up a bunch of dirt and stuff. They won't be the ones who have to pitch in and clean it up."

"I could help," Ophelia said. "If you want."

"I wasn't asking for help. But if you offer, I'll accept. The first door is the washroom," Fran said. "Nothing queer about the toilet. I don't know about the bathtub, though. Never felt the need to sit in it."

She opened the second door.

"Here's where you sleep."

It was a gorgeous room, all done up in shades of orange and rust and gold and pink and tangerine. The walls were finished in leafy shapes and vines cut from all kinds of dresses and T-shirts and what have you. Fran's momma had spent the better part of the year going through stores, choosing clothes for their patterns and textures and colors. Gold-leaf snakes and fishes swam through the leaf shapes. When the sun came up in the morning, Fran remembered, it was almost blinding.

There was a crazy quilt on the bed, pink and gold. The bed itself was shaped like a swan. There was a willow chest at the foot of the bed to lay out your clothes on. The mattress was stuffed with the down of crow feathers. Fran had helped her mother shoot the crows and pluck their feathers. She thought they'd killed about a hundred.

"I'd say wow," Ophelia said, "but I keep saying that. Wow, wow, wow. This is a crazy room."

"I always thought it was like being stuck inside a bottle of orange Nehi," Fran said. "But in a good way."

"Oh yeah," Ophelia said. "I can see that."

There was a stack of books on the table beside the bed. Like everything else in the room, all the books had been picked out for the colors on their jackets. Fran's momma had told her that once the room had been another set of colors. Greens and blues, maybe? Willow and peacock and midnight colors? And who had brought the bits up for the room that time? Fran's great-grandfather or someone even farther along the family tree? Who had first begun to take care of the summer people? Her mother had doled out stories sparingly, and so Fran only had a piecemeal sort of history.

Hard to figure out what it would please Ophelia to hear anyway, and what would trouble her. All of it seemed pleasing and troubling to Fran in equal measure after so many years.

"The door you slipped my envelope under," she said, finally. "You oughtn't ever go in there."

Ophelia yawned. "Like Bluebeard," she said.

Fran said, "It's how they come and go. Even they don't open that door very often, I guess." She'd peeped through the keyhole once and seen a bloody river. She'd bet if you passed through that door, you weren't likely to return.

"Can I ask you another stupid question?" Ophelia said. "Where are they right now?"

"They're here," Fran said. "Or out in the woods chasing nightjars. I told you I don't see them much."

"So how do they tell you what they need you to do?"

"They get in my head," Fran said. "I guess it's kind of like being schizophrenic. Or like having a really bad itch or something that goes away when I do what they want me to."

"Not fun," Ophelia said. "Maybe I don't like your summer people as much as I thought I did."

Fran said, "It's not always awful. I guess what it is, is complicated."

"I guess I won't complain the next time my mom tells me I have to help her polish the silver, or do useless crap like that. Should we eat our sandwiches now, or should we save them for when we wake up in the middle of the night?" Ophelia asked. "I have this idea that seeing your heart's desire probably makes you hungry."

"I can't stay," Fran said, surprised. She saw Ophelia's expression and said, "Well, hell. I thought you understood. This is just for you."

Ophelia continued to look at her dubiously. "Is it because there's just the one bed? I could sleep on the floor. You know, if you're worried I might be planning to lez out on you."

"It isn't that," Fran said. "They only let a body sleep here once. Once and no more."

"You're really going to leave me up here alone?" Ophelia said.

"Yes," Fran said. "Unless you decide you want to come back down with me. I guess I'd understand if you did."

"Could I come back again?" Ophelia said.

"No."

Ophelia sat down on the golden quilt and smoothed it with her fingers. She chewed her lip, not meeting Fran's eye.

"Okay. I'll do it." She laughed. "How could I not do it? Right?"

"If you're sure," Fran said.

"I'm not sure, but I couldn't stand it if you sent me away now," Ophelia said. "When you slept here, were you afraid?"

"A little," Fran said. "But the bed was comfortable, and I kept the light on. I read for a while, and then I fell asleep."

"Did you see your heart's desire?" Ophelia said.

"I guess I did," Fran offered, and then said no more.

"Okay, then," Ophelia said. "I guess you should go. You should go, right?"

"I'll come back in the morning," Fran said. "I'll be here afore you even wake."

"Thanks," Ophelia said.

But Fran didn't go. She said, "Did you mean it when you said you wanted to help?"

"Look after the house?" Ophelia said. "Yeah, absolutely. You really ought to go out to San Francisco someday. You shouldn't have to stay here your whole life without ever having a vacation or anything. I mean, you're not a slave, right?"

"I don't know what I am," Fran said. "I guess one day I'll have to figure that out."

Ophelia said, "Anyway, we can talk about it tomorrow. Over breakfast. You can tell me about the suckiest parts of the job and I'll tell you what my heart's desire turns out to be."

"Oh," Fran said. "I almost forgot. When you wake up tomorrow, don't be surprised if they've left you a gift. The summer people. It'll be something that they think you need or want. But you don't have to accept it. You don't have to worry about being rude that way."

"Okay," Ophelia said. "I will consider whether I really need or want my present. I won't let false glamour deceive me."

"Good," Fran said. Then she bent over Ophelia where she was sitting on the bed and kissed her on the forehead. "Sleep well, Ophelia. Good dreams."

Fran left the house without any interference from the summer people. She couldn't tell if she'd expected to find any. As she came down the stairs, she said rather more fiercely than she'd meant to: "Be nice to her. Don't play no tricks." She looked in on the queen, who was molting again.

She went out the front door instead of the back, which was something that she'd always wanted to do. Nothing bad happened, and she walked down the hall feeling strangely put out. She went over everything in her head, wondering what still needed doing that she hadn't done. Nothing, she decided. Everything was taken care of.

Except, of course, it wasn't. The first thing was the guitar, leaned up against the door of her house. It was a beautiful instrument. The strings, she thought, were pure silver. When she struck them, the tone was pure and sweet and reminded her uncomfortably of Ophelia's singing voice. The keys were made of gold and shaped like owl heads, and there was mother-of-pearl inlay across the boards like a spray of roses. It was the gaudiest gewgaw they'd yet made her a gift of.

"Well, all right," she said. "I guess you didn't mind what I told her." She laughed out loud with relief.

"Why, everwho did you tell what?" someone said.

She picked up the guitar and held it like a weapon in front of her. "Daddy?"

"Put that down," the voice said. A man stepped forward out of the shadow of the rosebushes. "I'm not your damn Daddy. Although, come to think of it, I would like to know where he is."

"Ryan Shoemaker," Fran said. She put the guitar down on the ground. Another man stepped forward. "And Kyle Rainey."

"Howdy, Fran," said Kyle. He spat. "We were lookin' for your pappy, like Ryan says."

"If he calls I'll let him know you were up here looking for him," Fran said. "Is that all you wanted to ask me?"

Ryan lit up a cigarette, looked at her over the flame. "It was your daddy we wanted to ask, but I guess you could help us out instead."

"It don't seem likely somehow," Fran said. "But go on."

"Your daddy was meaning to drop off some of the sweet stuff the other night," Kyle said. "Only, he started thinking about it on the drive down, and that's never been a good idea where your daddy is concerned. He decided Jesus wanted him to pour out every last drop, and that's what he did all the way down the mountain. If he weren't a lucky man, some spark might have cotched while he were pouring, but I guess Jesus doesn't want to meet him face to face just yet."

"And if that weren't bad enough," Ryan said, "when he got to the convenience, he decided that Jesus wanted him to get into the van and smash up all Andy's liquor, too. By the time we realized what was going on, there weren't much left besides two bottles of Kahlua and a six-pack of wine coolers."

"One of them smashed, too," Kyle said. "And then he took off afore we could have a word with him."

"Well, I'm sorry for your troubles, but I don't see what it has to do with me," Fran said.

"What it has to do is that we've come up with an easy payment plan. We talked about it, and the way it seems to us is that your pappy could provide us with entrée to some of the finest homes in the area."

"Like I said," Fran said. "I'll pass on the message. You're hoping my daddy will make his restitution by becoming your accessory in breaking and entering. I'll let him know if he calls."

"Or he could pay poor Andy back in kind," Ryan said. "With some of that good stuff."

"He'll have to run that by Jesus," Fran said. "Frankly, I think it's a better bet than the other, but you might have to wait until he and Jesus have had enough of each other."

"The thing is," Ryan said, "I'm not a patient man. And what has occurred to me is that your pappy may be out of our reach at present moment, but here you are. And I'm guessing that you can get us in to a house or two. Preferably ones with quality flat screens and high-thread-count sheets. I promised Mandy I was going to help her redecorate."

"Or else you could point us in the direction of your daddy's private stash," Kyle said.

"And if I don't choose to do neither?" Fran asked, crossing her arms.

"I truly hope that you know what it is you're doing," Kyle said. "Ryan has not been in a good mood these last few days. He bit a sheriff's deputy on the arm last night in a bar. Which is why we weren't up here sooner."

"He was pigheaded, just like you," Ryan said. "No pun intended. But I bet you'd taste better."

Fran stepped back. "Fine. There's an old house farther up the road that nobody except me and my daddy knows about. It's ruint. Nobody lives there, and so my daddy put his still up in it. He's got all sorts of articles stashed up there. I'll take you up. But you can't tell him what I done."

"Course not, darlin'," Kyle said. "We don't aim to cause a rift in the family. Just to get what we have coming."

And so Fran found herself climbing right back up that same road. She got her feet wet in the drain but kept as far ahead of Kyle and Ryan as she dared. She didn't know if she felt safe with them at her back.

When they got up to the house, Kyle whistled. "Fancy sort of ruin."

"Wait'll you see what's inside," Fran said. She led them around to the back, then held the door open. "Sorry about the lights. The power goes off more than it stays on. My daddy usually brings up a torch. Want me to go get one?"

"We've got matches," Ryan said. "You stay right there."

"The still is in the room over on the right. Mind how you go. He's got it set up in a kind of maze, with the newspapers and all."

"Dark as the inside of a mine at midnight," Kyle said. He felt his way down the hall. "I think I'm at the door. Sure enough, smells like what I'm lookin' for. Guess I'll just follow my nose. No booby traps or nothing like that?"

"No sir," Fran said. "He'd have blowed himself up a long time before now if he tried that."

"I might as well take in the sights," Ryan said, the lit end of his cigarette flaring. "Now that I'm getting my night vision."

"Yes sir," Fran said.

"And might there be a pisser in this heap?"

"Third door on the left, once you go up," Fran said. "The door sticks some."

She waited until he was at the top of the stairs before she slipped out the back door again. She could hear Kyle fumbling toward the center of the queen's room. She wondered what the queen would make of Kyle. She wasn't worried about Ophelia at all. Ophelia was an invited guest. And anyhow, the summer people didn't let anything happen to the ones who looked after them.

One of the summer people was sitting on the porch swing when she came out. He was whittling a stick with a sharp knife.

"Evening," Fran said and bobbed her head.

The summer personage didn't even look up at her. He was one of the ones so pretty it almost hurt to peep at him, but you couldn't not stare, neither. That was one of the ways they cotched you, Fran figured. Just like wild animals when you shone a light at them. She finally tore her gaze away and ran down the stairs like the devil was after her. When she stopped to look back, he was still setting there, smiling and whittling that poor stick down.

She sold the guitar when she got to New York City. What was left of her daddy's two hundred dollars had bought her a Greyhound ticket and a couple of burgers at the bus station. The guitar got her six hundred more, and she used that to buy a ticket to Paris, where she met a Lebanese boy who was squatting in an old factory. One day she came back from her under-the-table job at a hotel and found him looking through her backpack. He had the monkey egg in his hand. He wound it up and put it down on the dirty floor to dance. They both watched until it ran down. "Très jolie," he said.

It was a few days after Christmas, and there was snow melting in her hair. They didn't have heat in the squat, or even running water. She'd had a bad cough for a few days. She sat down next to her boy, and when he started to wind up the monkey egg again, she put her hand out to make him stop.

She didn't remember packing it. And of course, maybe she hadn't. For all she knew, they had winter places as well as summer places. Just because she'd never been able to travel didn't mean they didn't get around.

A few days later, the Lebanese boy disappeared off, probably looking for someplace warmer. The monkey egg went with him. After that, all she had to remind herself of home was the tent that she kept folded up like a dirty handkerchief in her wallet.

It's been two years, and every now and again, while Fran is cleaning rooms in the pension, she closes the door and sets up the tent and gets inside. She looks out the window at the two apple trees. She tells herself that one day soon she will go home again.

# MULBERRY BOYS

## MARGO LANAGAN

---

So night comes on. I make my own fire, because why would I want to sit at Phillips's, next to that pinned-down mulberry?

*Pan-flaps, can you make pan-flaps?* Phillips plopped down a bag of fine town flour and gave me a look that said, *Bet you can't. And* I'm *certainly too important to make them.* So pan-flaps I make in his little pan, and some of them I put hot meat-slice on, and some cheese, and some jam, and that will fill us, for a bit. There's been no time to hunt today, just as Ma said, while she packed and packed all sorts of these treats into a sack for me—to impress Phillips, perhaps, more than to show me favour, although that too. She doesn't mind me being chosen to track and hunt with the fellow, now that I'm past the age where he can choose me for the other thing.

We are stuck out here the night, us and our catch. If I were alone I would go back; I can feel and smell my way, if no stars and moon will show me. But once we spread this mulberry wide on the ground and fixed him, and Phillips lit his fire and started his fiddling and feeding him leaves, I knew we were to camp. I did not ask; I dislike his sneering manner of replying to me. I only waited and saw.

He's boiled the water I brought up from the torrent, and filled it with clanking, shining things—little tools, it looks like, as far as I can see out of the corner of my eye. I would not gratify him with looking directly. I stare into my own fire, the forest blank black beyond it and only fire-lit smoke above, no sky though the clouds were clearing last I looked. I get out my flask and have a pull of fire-bug, to settle my discontentments. It's been a long day and a weird, and I wish I was home, instead of out here with a half-man, and the boss of us all watching my every step.

"Here, boy," he says. He calls me *boy* the way you call a dog. He doesn't even look up at me to say it.

I cross from my fire to his. I don't like to look at those creatures, mulberries, so I fix instead on Phillips, his shining hair-waves and his sharp nose, the floret of silk in his pocket that I know is a green-blue bright as a stout-pigeon's throat, but now is just a different orange in the fire's glow. His white, weak hands, long-fingered, big-knuckled—oh, they give me a shudder, just as bad as a mulberry would.

"Do you know what a loblolly boy is?"

He knows I don't. I hate him and his words. "Some kind of insulting thing, no doubt," I say.

"No, no!" He looks up surprised from examining the brace, which is pulled tight to the mulberry's puffed-up belly, just below the navel, when it should dangle on an end of silk. "It's a perfectly legitimate thing. Boy on a ship, usually. Works for the surgeon."

And what is a surgeon? I am not going to ask him. I stare down at him, wanting another pull from my flask.

"Never mind," he says crossly. "Sit." And he waves where; right by the mulberry, opposite himself.

Must I? I have already chased the creature five ways wild today; I've already treed him and climbed that tree and lowered him on a rope. I'm sick of the sight of him, his round stary face, his froggy body, his feeble conversation, trying to be friendly.

But I sit. I wonder sometimes if I'm weak-minded, that even one person makes such a difference to me, what I see, what I do. When I come to the forest alone, I can see the forest clear, and feel it, and everything in it. If I bring Tray or Connar, it becomes the ongoing game of us as big men in this world—with the real men left behind in the village, so they don't show us up. When I come with Frida Birch it is all about the inside of her mysterious mind, what she can be thinking, what has she noticed that I haven't about some person, some question she has that would never occur to me. It's as if I cannot hold to my own self, to my own forest, if another person is with me.

"Feed him some more," says Phillips, and points to the sack beside me. "As many as he can take. We might avoid a breakage yet if we can stuff enough into him."

I untie the sack, and put aside the first layer, dark leaves that have been keeping the lower, paler ones moist. I roll a leaf-pill—the neater I make it, the less I risk being bitten, or having to touch lip or tongue. I wave it under his nose, touch it to his lips, and he opens and takes it in, good mulberry.

Phillips does this and that. Between us the mulberry's stomach grumbles and tinkles with the foreign food he's kept down. Between leaf-rollings, I have another pull. "God, the smell of that!" says Phillips, and spares a hand from his preparations to wave it away from his face.

"It's good," I say. "It's the best. It's Nat Culloden's."

"How old are you anyway?" He cannot read it off me. Perhaps he deals only with other men—I know people like that, impatient of the young. Does he have children? I'd hate to be his son.

"Coming up fifteen," I say.

He mutters something. I can't hear, but I'm sure it is not flattering to me.

Now there's some bustle about him. He pulls on a pair of very thin-stretching gloves, paler even than his skin; now his hands are even more loathsome. "Right," he says. "You will hold him down when I tell you. That is your job."

"He's down." Look at the spread cross of him; he couldn't be any flatter.

"You will hold him *still*," says Phillips. "For the work. When I say."

He pulls the brace gently; the skein comes forth as it should, but—"Hold him," says Phillips, and I hook one leg over the mulberry's thigh and spread a hand on his chest. He makes a kind of warning moan. Phillips pulls on, slowly and steadily like a mother. "*Hold* him," as the moaning rises, buzzes under my hand. "Christ above, if he makes this much of a fuss *now*."

He pulls and pulls, but in a little while no more silk will come. He winds what he has on a spindle and clamps it, tests the skein once more. "No? Well. Now I will cut. Boy, I have nothing for his pain." He looks at me as if *I* forgot to bring it. "And I need him utterly still, so as not to cut the silk or his innards. Here." He hands me a smooth white stick, of some kind of bone. "Put that crosswise between his teeth, give him something to bite on."

I do so; the teeth are all clagged with leaf-scraps, black in this light. Mulberries' faces are the worst thing about them, little round old-children's faces, neither man nor woman. And everything they are thinking shows clear as water, and this one is afraid; he doesn't know what's happening, what's about to be done to him. Well, I'm no wiser. I turn back to Phillips.

"Now get a good weight on him, both ends."

Gingerly I arrange myself. He may be neither man nor woman, but still the creature is naked, and clammy as a frog in the night air.

"Come on," says Phillips. He's holding his white hands up, as if the mulberry is too hot to touch. "You're plenty big enough. Spread yourself out there, above and below. You will need to press here, too, with your hand." He points, and points again. "And this foot will have some work to do on this far leg. Whatever is loose will fight against what I'm doing, understand?"

So he says, to a boy who's wrestled tree-snakes so long that his father near fainted to see them, who has jumped a shot stag and ridden it and killed it riding. Those are different, though; those are wild, they have some dignity. What's to be gained subduing a mulberry, that is gelded and a fool already? Where's the challenge in that, and the pride upon having done it?

"Shouldn't you be down there?" I nod legs-wards.

"Whatever for, boy?"

"This is to let the food out, no?"

"It is to let the food out, *yes*." He cannot speak without making me lesser

"Well, down there is where food comes out, yours and mine."

"Pity sake, boy, I am not undoing all *that*. I will take it out through his silk-hole, is the plan."

Now I am curled around the belly, with nowhere else to look but at Phillips's doings. All his tools and preparations are beyond him, next to the fire; from over there he magics up a paper packet. He tears it open, pulls from it a small wet cloth or paper, and paints the belly with that; the smell nips at my nostrils. Then he brings out a bright, light-as-a-feather-looking knife, the blade glinting at the end of a long handle.

"Be ready," he says.

He holds the silk aside, and sinks the blade into the flesh beside it. The mulberry-boy turns to rock underneath me; he spits out the stick, and howls to the very treetops.

Mulberry *boys* we call them. I don't know why, for some begin as girls, and they are neither one nor the other once they come out of Phillips's hut by the creek. They all look the same, as chickens look all the same, or goats. *Nonsense,* says Alia the goat woman, *I know my girls each one, by name and nature and her pretty face.* And I guess the mothers, who tend the mulberries, might know them apart. This one is John Barn, or once was called that; none of them truly have names once they've been taken.

Once a year I notice them, when Phillips comes to choose the new ones and to make them useful, from the boys among us who are not yet sprouted towards men, and the girls just beginning to change shape. The rest of the year, the mulberries live in their box, and the leaves go in, and the silk comes out on its spindles, and that is all there is to it.

Last year when I was about to sprout, it was the first year Phillips came instead of his father. When he walked in among us we were most uneasy at the size of him, for he is delicately made, hardly taller than a mulberry himself, and similar shaped to them except in lacking a paunch. Apart from the shrinkage, though, you would think him the same man as his father. He wore the same fine clothes, as neat on him as if sewn to his body directly, and the fabrics so fine you can hardly see their weave. He had the same wavy hair, but brown instead of silver, and a beard, though not a proper one, trimmed almost back to his chin.

The mothers were all behind us and some of the fathers too, putting their children forward. He barely looked at me, I remember, but moved straight on to the Thaw children; there are lots of them and they are very much of the mulberry type already, without you sewing a stitch on them. I remember being insulted. The man had not *bothered* with me; how could he know I was not what he wanted, from that quick glance? But also I was ashamed to be so obviously useless, so wrong for his purposes—because whatever those purposes were, he was from the town, and he was powerfuller in his slenderness and his city clothes than was any bulky man among us, and everyone was afraid of him. I wanted a man like that to recognize me as of consequence, and he had not.

But then Ma put her arm over my shoulder and clamped me to her, my back against her front. We both watched Phillips among the Thaws, turning them about, dividing some of them off for closer inspection. The chosen ones— Hinny and Dull Toomy, it was, that time, those twins—stood well apart, Pa Toomy next to them arms folded and face closed. They looked from one of us to another, not quite sure whether to arrange their faces proudly, or to cry.

Because it is the end of things, if you get chosen. It is the end of your line, of course—all your equipment for making children is taken off you and you are sewn up below. But it is also the end of any food but the leaves—fresh in the spring and summer, sometimes in an oiled mash through autumn if you are still awake then. And it is the end of play, because you become stupid; you forget the rules of all the games, and how to converse in any but a very simple way, observing about the weather and not much more. You just stay in your box, eating your leaves and having your stuff drawn off you, which we sell, through Phillips, in the town.

It is no kind of life, and I was glad, then, that I had not been taken up for it. And Ma was glad too, breathing relieved above me as we watched him sort and discard and at length choose Arvie Thaw. I could feel Ma's gladness in the back of my head, her heart knocking hard in her chest, even though all she had done was stand there and seem to accept whatever came.

While we tracked John Barn today, I was all taken up impressing Phillips. The forest and paths presented me trace after trace, message after message, to relay to the town-man, so's he could see what a good tracker I was. I felt proud of myself for knowing, and scornful of him for not—yet I was afraid, too, that I would put a foot wrong, that he would somehow catch me out, that he would see something I had missed and make me a nobody again, and worthy of his impatience.

So John Barn himself was not much more to me than he'd always been; he was even somewhat less than other animals I hunted, for he had not even the wit to cut off the path at any point, and he left tracks and clues almost as if he wanted us to catch him, things he had chewed, and spat out or brought up from his stomach, little piles of findings—stones, leaves, seed-pods—wet-bright in the light rain. He might as well have lit beacon-fires after himself.

Climbing up to him in the tree, I could see his froggy paunch pouching out either side of the branch, and his skinny white legs around it, and then of course his terrible face watching me.

"Which one are you?" he said in that high, curious way they have. They can never remember a name.

"I am George," I said, "of the Treadlaws."

"Evening's coming on, George," he said, watching as I readied the rope. This was why I had been brought, besides for my tracking. Mulberries won't flee or resist anyone smaller than themselves (unless he is Phillips, of course, all-over foreign), but send a grown man after them and they will throw themselves off a cliff or into a torrent, or climb past pursuing up a tree like this. It is something about the smell of a grown man sets them off, which is why men cannot go into the box for the silk, but only mothers.

I busied myself with the practicalities, binding Barn and lowering him to Phillips, which was no small operation, so I distracted myself from my revulsion that way. And then, when I climbed down, Phillips took up all the air in the clearing and in my mind with his presence and purposefulness, which I occupied myself sulking at. Then when I had to press the creature down, to lie with him, lie *on* him, everything in me was squirming away from the touch but Phillips's will was on me like an iron, pinning me as fast as we'd pinned the mulberry, and I was too angry and unhappy at being made as helpless as John Barn, to think how he himself might be finding it, crushed by the weight of me.

But when he stiffened and howled, it was as if I had been asleep to John Barn and he woke me, as if he had been motionless disguised in the forest's dappled shadows, but then my eye had picked out his frame, distinct and live and sensible in there, never to be unseen again. All that he had said, that we had dismissed as so much noise, came back to me: *I don't like that man, George. Yes, tie me tight, for I will struggle when you put me near him. It's getting dark. It hurts me to stretch flat like this. My stomach hurts. An apple and a radish, I have kept both down. I stole them through a window; there was meat there too; meat was what I mostly wanted. But I could not reach it. Oh, it hurts, George.* I had done as Phillips did, and not met the mulberry's eye and not answered, doing about him what I needed to do, but now all his mutterings sprang out at me as having been said by a person, a person like me and like Phillips; there were three of us here, not two and a creature, not two and a snared rabbit, or a shot and struggling deer.

And the howl was not animal noise but voice, with person and feeling behind it. It went through me the way the pain had gone through John Barn, freezing me as Phillips's blade in his belly froze him, so that I was locked down there under the realising, with all my skin a-crawl.

I stare at Phillips's hands, working within their false skins. The fire beyond him lights his work and throws the shadows across the gleaming-painted hill-round of Barn's belly. Phillips cuts him like a cloth or like a cake, with just such swiftness and intent; he does not even do as you do when hunting, and speak to the creature you have snared or caught and are killing, and explain why it must die. The wound runs, and he catches the runnings with his wad of flock and cloth, absentmindedly and out of a long-practiced skill. He bends close and examines what his cutting has revealed to him, in the cleft, in the deeps, of the belly of John Barn.

"Good," he says—to himself, not to me or Barn. "Perfect."

He puts his knife in there, and what he does in there is done in me as well, I feel so strongly the tremor it makes, the fear it plays up out of Barn's frame, plucking him, rubbing him, like a fiddle-string. His breath, behind me, halts and hops with the fear.

Phillips pierces something with a pop. Barn yelps, surprised. Phillips sits straighter, and waves his hand over the wound as he waved away the smell of my grog before. I catch a waft of shit-smell and then it's gone, floated up warm away.

He goes to his instruments. "That's probably the worst of it, for the moment," he says to them. "You can sit up if you like. Stay by, though; you never know when he'll panic."

I sit up slowly, a different boy from the one who lay down. I half-expect my own insides to come pouring out of me. John Barn's belly gapes open, the wound dark and glistening, filling with blood. Beyond it, his flesh slopes away smooth as a wooden doll between his weakling thighs, which tremble and tremble.

Phillips returns to the wound, another little tool in his hand—I don't know what it is, only that it's not made for cutting. I put my hand on Barn's chest, trying to move as smoothly and bloodlessly as Phillips.

"George, what has he done to me?" John Barn makes to look down himself.

Quick as light, I put my hand to his sweated brow, and press his head to the ground. "He's getting that food out," I say. "If it stays in there, it'll fester and kill you. He's helping you."

"Feed him some more," says Phillips, and bends to his work. "Keep on that."

So I lie, propped up on one elbow, rolling mulberry pills and feeding them to Barn. He chews, dutifully; he weeps, tears running back over his ears into his thin hair. He swallows the mulberry mush down his child-neck. *Hush,* I nearly say to him, but Phillips is there, so I only think it, and attend to the feeding, rolling the leaves, putting them one by one into Barn's obedient mouth.

I can't help but be aware, though, of what the man is doing there, down at the wound. For one thing, besides the two fires it is the only visible activity, the only movement besides my own. For another, for all that the sight of those blood-tipped white hands going about their work repels me, their skill and care, and the life they seem to have of their own, are something to see. It's like watching Pa make damselfly flies in the firelight in the winter, each finger independently knowing where to be and go, and the face above all eyes and no expression, the mind taken up with this small complication.

The apple and the radish, all chewed and reduced and cooked smelly by John Barn's body's heat, are caught in the snarled silk. Phillips must draw them, with the skein, slowly lump by lump from Barn's innards, up into the firelight where they dangle and shine like some unpleasant necklace. Sprawled beside John Barn, in his breathing and his bracing himself I feel the size of every bead of that necklace large and small, before I see it drawn up into the firelight on the shining strands. Phillips frowns above, fire-fuzz at his eyebrow, a long streak of orange light down his nose, his closed lips holding all his thoughts, all his knowledge, in his head—and any feelings he might have about this task. Is he pleased? Is he revolted? Angry? There is no way to tell.

"Do you have something for their pain, then," I say, "when you make them into mulberries?"

"Oh yes," he says to the skein, "they are fully anaesthetized then." He hears my ignorance in my silence, or sees it in my stillness. "I put them to sleep."

"Like a chicken," I say, to show him that I know something.

"Not at all like that. With a chemical."

All is quiet but for fire-crackle, and John Barn's breath in his nose, and his teeth crushing the leaves.

"How do you learn that, about the chemicals, and mulberry-making? And mulberry-fixing, like this?"

"Long study," says Phillips, peering into the depths to see how the skein is emerging. "Long observation at my father's elbow. Careful practice under his tutelage. Years," he finishes and looks at me, with something like a challenge, or perhaps already triumph.

"So *could* you unmake one?" I say, just to change that look on him.

"Could I? Why *would* I?"

I make myself ignore the contempt in that. "Supposing you had a reason."

He draws out a slow length of silk, with only two small lumps in it. "Could I, now?" he says less scornfully. "I've never considered it. Let me think." He examines the silk, both sides, several times. "I could perhaps restore their digestive functioning. The females' reproductive system *might* re-establish its cycle, with a normal diet, though I cannot be sure. The males' of course . . . "

He shrugs. He has a little furnace in that hut of his by the creek. There he must burn whatever he cuts from the mulberries, and all his blood-soaked cloths and such. Once a year he goes in there with the chosen children, and all we know of what he does is the air wavering over the chimney. The men speak with strenuous cheer to each other; the mothers go about thin-lipped; the mothers of the chosen girls and boys close themselves up in their houses with their grief.

"But what about their . . . Can you undo their thinking, their talking, what you have done to that?"

"Ah, it is coming smoother now, look at that," he says to himself. "What do you mean, boy, 'undo'?" he says louder and more scornfully, as if I made up the word myself out of nothing, though I only repeated it from him.

I find I do not want to call John Barn a fool, not in his hearing as he struggles with his fear and his swallowing leaf after leaf, and with lying there belly open to the sky and Phillips's attentions. "They . . . haven't much to say for themselves," I finally say. "Would they talk among us like ourselves, if you fed them right, and took them out of that box?"

"I don't know what they would do." He shrugs again. He goes on slowly drawing out silk, and I go on hating him.

"Probably not," he says carelessly after a while. "All those years, you know, without social stimulus or education, would probably have impaired their development too greatly. But possibly they would regain something, from moving in society again." He snorts. "Such society as you *have* here. And the diet, as you say. It might perk them up a bit."

Silence again, the skein pulling out slowly, silently, smooth and clean white. Barn chews beside me, his breathing almost normal. Perhaps the talking soothes him.

"But then," says Phillips to the skein, with a smile that I don't like at all, "if you 'undid' them all, you would have no silk, would you? And without silk you would have no tea, or sugar, or tobacco, or wheat flour, or all the goods in tins and jars that I bring you. No cloth for the women, none of their threads and beads and such."

Yes, plenty of people would be distressed at that. I am the wrong boy to threaten with such losses, for I hunt and forage; I like the old ways. I kept myself fed and healthy for a full four months, exploring up the glacier last spring—healthier than were most folk when I arrived home, with their toothaches and their coughs. But others, yes, they rely wholly on those stores that Phillips brings through the year. When he is due, and they have run short of tobacco, they go all grog and temper waiting, or hide at home until he should come. They will not hunt or snare with me and Tray and Pa and the others; take them a haunch of stewed rabbit, and if they will eat it at all they will sauce it well with complaints and wear a sulking face over every bite.

"And no food coming up, for all those extra mouths you'd have to feed," says Phillips softly and still smiling, "that once were kept on mulberry leaves alone. Think of that."

What was I imagining, all my talk of undoing? The man cannot make mulberries back into men, and if he could he would never teach someone like me, that he thought so stupid, and whose folk he despised. And even if he taught us, and worked alongside us in the unmaking, we would never get back the man John Barn was going to be when he was born John Barn, or any of the men and women that the others might have become.

"You were starving and in rags when my father found you," says Phillips, sounding pleased. "Your people. You lived like animals."

"We had some bad years, I heard." *And we* are *animals,* I nearly add, *and so are you. A bear meets you, you are just as much a meal to him as is a berry-bush or a fine fat salmon. What are you, if not animal?*

But I have already lost this argument; he has already dismissed me. He draws on, as if I never spoke, as if he were alone. Good silk is coming out now; all the leaves we've been feeding into John Barn are coming out clean, white, strong-stranded; he is restored, apart from the great hole in him. Still I feed him, still he chews on, both of us playing our parts to fill Phillips' hands with silk.

"Very well," says Phillips, "I think we are done here. Time to close him up again."

I'm relieved that he intends to. "Should I lie on him again?"

"In a little," he says. "The inner parts are nerveless, and will not give him much pain. When I sew the dermal layers, perhaps."

It is very much like watching someone wind a fly, the man-hands working such a small area and mysteriously, stitching inside the hole. The thread, which is black, and waxed, wags out in the light and then is drawn in to the task, then wags again, the man concentrating above. His fingers work exactly like a spider's legs on its web, stepping delicately as he brings the curved needle out and takes it back in. I can feel from John Barn's chest that there is not pain exactly, but there is sensation where there should not be, and the fear that comes from not understanding makes Phillips's every movement alarming to him.

I didn't quite believe that Phillips would restore John Barn and repair him. I lie across Barn again and watch the stitching-up of the outer skin. With each pull and drag of thread through flesh Barn exclaims in the dark behind me. "Oh. Oh, that is bad. Oh, that feels dreadful." He jerks and cries out at every piercing by the needle.

"He's nearly finished, John," I say. "Maybe six stitches more."

And Phillips works above, ignoring us, as unmoved as if he were sewing up a boot. A wave of his hair droops forward on his brow, and around his

eyes is stained with tiredness. It feels as if he has kept us in this small cloud
of firelight, helping him do his mad work, all the night. There is no danger of
me sleeping; I am beyond exhaustion; Barn's twitches wake me up brighter
and brighter, and so does the fact that Phillips can ignore them so thoroughly,
piercing and piercing the man. And though a few hours ago I would happily
have left Barn to him, now I want to be awake and endure each stitch as well,
even if there is no chance of the mulberry ever knowing or caring.

Then it is done. Phillips snips the thread with a pair of bright-gold scissors,
inspects his work, draws a little silk out past all the layers of stitching. "Good,
that's good," he says.

I lever myself up off Barn, lift my leg from his. "He's done with you," I tell
him, and his eyes roll up into his head with relief, straight into sleep.

"We will leave him tied. We may as well," says Phillips, casting his used
tools into the pot on the fire. "We don't want him running off again. Or getting
infection in that wound." He strips off his horrid gloves and throws them in
the fire. They wince and shrivel and give off a few moments' stink.

I feel as if I'm floating a little way off the ground; Phillips looks very small
over there, his shining tools faraway. "There are others, then?" I say.

"Others?" He is coaxing his fire up to boil the tools again.

"'Careful practice,' you said, by your father's side. Yet we never saw you
here. So there are other folk like ours, with their mulberries, that you practiced
on? In other places in the mountains, or in the town itself? I have never been
there to know."

"Oh," he says, and right at me, his eyes bright at mine. "Yes," he says.
"Though there is a lot to be learned from . . . books, you know, and general
anatomy and surgical practice." He surveys the body before us, up and down.
"But yes," he says earnestly to me. "Many communities. Quite a widespread
practice, and trade. Quite solidly established."

I want to keep him talking like this, that he cares what he says to me. For
the first time today he seems not to scorn me for what I am. I'm not as clear to
him as John Barn has become to me, but I am more than I was this morning
when he told Pa, *I'll take your boy, if you can spare him.*

"Do you have a son, then," I say, "that you are teaching in turn?"

"Ah," he says, "not as yet. I've not been so blessed thus far as to achieve the
state of matrimony." He shows me his teeth, then sees that I don't understand.
Some of his old crossness comes back. "I have no wife. Therefore I have no
children. That is the way it is done in the town, at least."

"When you have a son, will you bring him here, to train him?" Even half-
asleep I am enjoying this, having his attention, unsettling him. He looks as if
he thought *me* a mulberry, and now is surprised to find that I can talk back
and forth like any person.

"I dare say, I dare say." He shakes his head. "Although I'm sure you understand, it is a great distance to come, much farther than other . . . communities. And a boy—their mothers are terribly attached to them, you know. My wife—my wife *to be*—might not consent to his travelling so far, from her. Until he is quite an age."

He waits on my next word, and so do I, but after a time a yawn takes me instead, and when it is over he is up and crouched by his fire. "Yes, time we got some rest. Excellent work, boy. You've been most useful." He seems quite a different man. Perhaps he is too tired to keep up his contempt of me? Certainly *I* am too tired to care very much. I climb to my feet and walk into the darkness, to relieve myself before sleep.

I wake, not with a start, but suddenly and completely, to the fire almost dead again and the forest all around me, aslant on the ridge. Dawn light is starting to creep up behind the trees, and stars are still snagged in the high branches, but here, close to me, masses of darkness go about their growing, roots fast in the ground around my head, thick trunks seeming to jostle each other, though nothing moves in the windless silence.

I am enormous myself, and wordless like the forest, yet full of burrows and niches and shadows where beasts lie curled—some newly gone to rest, others about to move out into the day—and birds roost with their breast-feathers fluffed over their claws. I am no fool, though that slip of a man with his tiny tools and his sneering took me for one. I see the story he span me, and his earnest expectation that I would believe it. I see his whole plan and his father's, laid out like paths through the woods, him and his town house and his tailor at one end there, us and our poor mulberries at the other, winding silk and waiting for him. A widespread trade? No, just this little pattern trodden through from below. Many communities? No, just us. Just me and my folk, and our children.

I sit up silently. I wait until the white cross of John Barn glimmers over there on the ground, until the smoke from my fire comes clear, a fine grey vine climbing the darkness without haste. I think through the different ways I can take; there are few enough of them, and all of them end in uncertainty, except for the first and simplest way that came to me as I slept—which is now, which is here, which is me. I spend a long time listening to folk in my head, but whenever I look to Barn, and think of holding him down, and his trembling, and his dutiful chewing of the leaves, they fall silent; they have nothing to say.

A red-throat tests its call against the morning silence. I get up and go to Barn, and take up the coil of leftover cord from beside him.

Phillips is on his side, curled around what is left of his fire. His hands are nicely placed for me. I slip the cord under them and pin his forearms down with my boot. As he wakes, grunts—"What are you at, boy?"—and begins to struggle, I loop and loop, and swiftly tie the cord. "How *dare* you! What do you think—"

"Up." I stand back from him, all the forest behind me, and in me. We have no regard for this man's thin voice, his tiny rage.

Staring, he pushes himself up with his bound hands, is on his knees, then staggers to his feet. He is equal the height of me, but slender, build for spider-work, while I am constructed to chop wood and haul water and bring down a running stag. I can do what I like with him.

"You are just a boy!" he says. "Have you no respect for your elders?"

"You are not my elders," I say. I take his arm, and he tries to flinch away. "This way," I say, and I make him go.

"Boy?" says John Barn from the ground. He has forgotten my name again.

"I'll be back soon, John. Don't you worry."

And that is all the need I have of words. I force Phillips down towards the torrent path; he pours *his* words out, high-pitched, outraged, neat-cut as if he made them with that little knife of his. But I am forest vastness, and the birds in my branches have begun their morning's shouting; I have no ears for him.

I push him down the narrow path; I don't bully him or take any glee when he falls and complains, or scratches his face in the underbrush, but I drag him up and keep him going. The noise of the torrent grows towards us, becomes bigger than all but the closest, loudest birds. His words flow back at me, but they are only a kind of odd music now, carrying no meaning, only fear.

He rounds a bend and quickly turns, and is in my arms, banging my chest with his bound purple hands. "You will not! You will not!" I turn him around, and move him on with all my body and legs. The torrent shows between the trees—that's what set him off, the water fighting white among the boulders.

Now he resists me with all that he has. His boots slip on the stones and he throws himself about. But there is simply not enough of him, and I am patient and determined; I pull him out of the brush again and again, and press him on. If he won't walk, I'm happy for him to crawl. If he won't crawl I'm prepared to push him along with my boot.

The path comes to a high lip over the water before cutting along and down to the flatter place where you can fill your pots, or splash your face. I bring him to the lip and push him straight off, glad to be rid of his flailing, embarrassed by his trying to fight me.

He disappears in the white. He comes up streaming, caught already by the flow, shouting at the cold. It tosses him about, gaping and kicking, for a few rocks, and then he turns to limp cloth, to rubbish, a dab of bright wet silk draggling across his chest. He slides up over a rock and drops the other side. He moves along, is carried away and down, over the little falls there, and across the pool, on his face and with blood running from his head, over again and on down.

I climb back up through the woods. It is very peaceful and straightforward to walk without him, out of the water-noise into the birdsong. The clearing when I reach it is quiet without him, pleased to be rid of his fussing and displeasure and only to stand about, head among the leaves while the two fires send up their smoke-tendrils and John Barn sleeps on.

I bend down and touch his shoulder. "Come, John," I say, "Time to make for home. Do I need to bind you?"

He wakes. "You?" His eyes reflect my head, surrounded by branches on the sky.

"George. George Treadlaw, remember?"

He looks about as I untie his feet. "That man is gone," he says. "Good. I don't like that man."

I reach across him to loosen his far hand. "Oh, George," he says "You smell bad this morning. Perhaps you'd better bind me, and walk at a little distance. That's a fearsome smell. It makes me want to run from you."

I sniff at a pinch of my shirt. "I'm no worse than I was last night."

"Yes, last night it started," he says. "But I was tied down then and no trouble to you."

I tether him to a tree-root and cook myself some pan-flaps.

"They smell nice," he says, and eats another mulberry leaf, watching the pan.

"You must eat nothing but leaves today, John," I tell him. "Anything foreign, you will die of it, for I can't go into you like Phillips and fetch it out again."

"You will have to watch me," he says. "Everything is very pretty, and smells so adventurous."

We set off home straight after. All day I lead him on a length of rope, letting him take his time. I am not impatient to get back. No one will be happy with me, that I lost Phillips. Oh, they will be angry, however much I say it was an accident, a slip of the man's boot as he squatted by the torrent washing himself. No one will want to take the spindles down to the town, and find whoever he traded them to, and buy the goods he bought. I will have to do all that, because it was I who lost the man, and I will, though the idea scares me as much as it will scare them. No one will want to hunt again, in years to come as the mulberries die off and no new ones are made; no one will want to gather roots and berries, and make nut flour, just to keep us fed, for people are all spoilt with town goods, the ease of them and the strong tastes and their softness to the tooth. But what can they do, after all, but complain?

*Go down to the town yourselves,* I'll tell them. *Take a mulberry with you and some spindles; tell what was done to us. Do you think they will start it again? No, they will come up here and examine everything and talk to us as fools; they might take away all our mulberries; they might take all of us away, and make us live down the town. And they will think we did worse than lose Phillips in the torrent; they will take me off to jail, maybe. I don't know what will happen. I don't know.*

"It is a fine day, George of the Treadlaws," John Barn says behind me. "I like to breathe, out here. I like to see the trees, and the sun, and the birds."

He is following behind obedient, pale and careful, the stitches black in his paunch, the brace hanging off the silk-end. Step, step, step, he goes with his unaccustomed feet, on root and stone and ledge of earth, and he looks about when he can, at everything.

"You're right, John." I move on again so that he won't catch up and be upset by the smell of me. "It's a fine day for walking in the forest."

# THE SILVER WIND

## NINA ALLAN

Shooter's Hill had a rough reputation. The reforestation policy had returned the place to its original state, and the tract of woodland between Blackheath and Woolwich was now as dense and extensive as it had once been in the years and centuries before the first industrial revolution. The woods were rife with carjackers and highwaymen, and scarcely a week went by without reports of some new atrocity. The situation had become so serious that there were moves in parliament to reinstate the death penalty for highway robbery as it had already been reinstated for high treason. During the course of certain conversations I noticed that local people had taken to calling Oxleas Woods by its old name, the Hanging Wood, although no hangings had occurred there as yet. At least not officially.

There was still a regular bus service out to Shooter's Hill, although I heard rumours that the drivers rostered on to it had to be paid danger money. I made up my mind to call on Owen Andrews in the afternoon; the evening curfew was strictly enforced in that part of London.

"How on earth do you manage, living alone out here?" I said to him. "Don't you get nervous?"

He laughed, a deep inner rumbling that seemed to shake the whole of his tiny being. "I've lived here for most of my life," he said. "Why should I leave?"

Owen Andrews was an achondroplasic dwarf, and as such he was subject to all the usual restrictions. He could not marry, he could not register children, although I supposed that this question was now academic, that he had been sterilised or even castrated once he had passed through puberty. Everyone had heard of such cases, and to knowingly pass on bad genes had been a custodial offence ever since Clive Billings's British Nationalists came to power. There was a photograph on the mantelpiece in Andrews's living room, a picture of Owen Andrews when he was young. The photograph showed him seated at a table playing cards with a pretty young woman. The woman was smiling, her fingers pressed to her parted lips. Andrews's face was grave, his head bent in concentration over his cards. He had a handsome profile, and the camera had been angled in such a way as to conceal the most obvious aspects of his deformity. There was something about the picture that disturbed me, that hinted at some private tragedy, and I turned away from it quickly. I asked him again about the Shooter's Hill Road and about the carjackers, but he insisted the whole thing had been exaggerated by the press.

"This place has always had a history to it, and history has a habit of repeating itself. If you don't believe me read Samuel Pepys. People feared the Hill in his day too. You'll find Mr Pepys particularly eloquent on the subject of what they used to do to the highwaymen." He paused. "Those of them they caught up with, that is."

I first learned about Owen Andrews through one of my clients. Lewis Usher had once been a rich man, but when the Americans abandoned Europe for China he lost everything more or less overnight. His wife was Zoe Clifford, the film actress. She died giving birth to their daughter, or from complications after the birth, I'm not sure which. The child was taken away by relatives of Zoe's and Lewis Usher was left alone in an enormous rambling house at the top end of Crooms Hill, less than half a mile from the centre of Greenwich. The place would have been worth a fortune in the old days, but it was far too big for him, and after the crash he could no longer afford to maintain it. In spite of its poor condition it was the kind of property my agency specialised in and I was able to negotiate a very good price with an independent pharmaceuticals company. They were attracted by the council tax rates, which were still much lower on the south side of the Thames. The firm's representative, a Hugo Greenlove, said they were planning to turn the house into a research facility. He rattled on excitedly, making exaggerated arm gestures to demonstrate how rooms might be divided and walls torn down, and although I thought it was tactless of Greenlove to talk that way in front of the house's current owner Lewis Usher seemed completely unmoved. Once Greenlove had left he told me to get rid of the lot, not just the house itself but everything in it. He didn't say as much but I had the impression he was planning to use the proceeds of the sale to get him to America. I imagined he had contacts there already.

"You really want to sell everything?" I said. In spite of my sympathy for Usher I was excited by the prospect. The house was stuffed with things I could move on for a handy profit, paintings and small bronzes and so on, and my files back at the office were stuffed with the names of people who would be happy to buy them.

"There are some things of Zoe's I want, but that's about it," he said. There were framed photographs of his wife everywhere about the place, detailing the course of her career from stage to screen. She had been a tall, angular woman with a crooked mouth and a wide forehead but the pictures hinted at a deep sensuality and a striking emotional presence. Usher was still very much in mourning for her, and I think it was the fact that I was also a widower that made him trust me. He said I could have first refusal on anything I wanted from the house, and when I tentatively mentioned a few of the things that caught my fancy he named a price so low I felt filthy with guilt even as I agreed to it. Usher must have seen some of this in my expression because he thumped me hard on the shoulder and began to laugh.

"You'll be doing me a favour," he said. "It's surprising how little you need, when you come right down to it."

He laughed again, the laugh quickly turning into a painful-sounding cough that made me wonder if there was something more than grief that was consuming him. This could certainly account for his indifference to his material possessions. Yet when a couple of moments later I pointed to a small brass travelling clock and asked him how much he wanted for it his whole demeanour changed. An excited light came into his eyes and he looked ten years younger.

"That's an Owen Andrews clock," he said. "Or at least it's supposed to be. I've never had it authenticated. I accepted it *in lieu* of a debt. I've had it for years."

He looked down at the clock approvingly, his face registering the sort of pride that suggested that even if he had not made the clock himself it was people like him, people with money and influence, that made such things possible, and I glimpsed for a moment the man who for twenty years had been on the directorial board of a successful multinational company.

"Who is Owen Andrews?" I said. I knew little about clocks and their makers, just as I knew little of furniture or scrimshaw or glass. I had never counted myself as an antiques expert. I was an estate agent who indulged in a little antiques trading on the side. I counted my successes as luck, and the willingness to let myself be guided by instinct rather than knowledge.

"Owen Andrews is a dwarf," Usher said. "He makes alchemical clocks. More popularly known as time machines."

It was my turn to laugh, a trifle uneasily. "You're not serious?" I said. "You don't believe in that rubbish, surely?"

I had watched several TV documentaries on the subject of the new physics but I had never taken any of it very seriously. It was my wife Miranda that was interested. Miranda had been like that, fascinated by the unknown and always wanting to believe in the impossible. It was this openness to experience that had convinced her she could help her father, even when the doctors had warned that he might be dangerous. Her faith in the possibility of miracles was one of the things I loved most about her. I wondered if Usher was trying to set me up in some way, trying to make the clock seem more valuable by spinning an elaborate yarn around it. Why he would do this when he seemed willing to more or less give away the other items I had specified I had no idea. I glanced at the clock again. Its case gleamed a dull ochre. It was only a small thing, and quite plain, but the more I looked at it the more I wanted to buy it. I had already made up my mind not to sell it on afterwards, that I would keep it for myself. But if Usher named some ridiculous price then the game was over.

Usher shrugged. "I think it's all nonsense," he said. "I happen to believe that time is like water pouring out of a tap, that once it's been spilled there's no calling it back again, not for love nor money nor any of these new-fangled gadgets. The man who gave me that clock offered it to me because he thought it was valuable but I accepted it because I liked it. I thought it was beautifully made."

"But surely he can't have believed it was a time machine? It looks like an ordinary carriage clock to me."

Usher smiled. "How else would you describe a clock if not as a time machine?" He narrowed his eyes, locking them on mine for a moment as if challenging me to a duel then glanced off to one side, shaking his head. "But in the way you mean, no, it's not a time machine. From what I gather it's one of his 'dry' clocks, designed to tell the time and nothing more. It's accurate of course and rather lovely but the case is brass, not gold, and in today's market that makes it practically worthless. If you like it that much you can have it for nothing. The deal you just did on the house has solved a lot of problems. Call it a little extra bonus on top of your fee."

My heart leapt. I had to concentrate hard to stop myself snatching the clock right off the shelf there and then, just so I could feel its weight in my hand.

"Is the maker still alive, this Owen Andrews?" I said instead.

"I have no idea," said Usher. "I know nothing about him other than what I've told you."

I think it was in that moment that I made my decision, that I would seek out Owen Andrews and discover the truth about him. I told myself that this was because the little brass clock had been the only thing to excite my interest since my wife died. There was more to it than that though. Somewhere deep inside me I was nursing the crazy hope that Owen Andrews was a man who could turn back time.

"Are you sure you want to get involved with this man, Martin?" Dora said. "He's bound to be under surveillance." She dragged on her cigarette, leaning to one side to knock the ash into the chipped Meissen saucer she kept permanently at her elbow for this purpose. I had long since given up going on at her about her smoking. Like Samsara perfume and the fake leopardskin coat she wore it was simply a part of her. She was wry and canny, with the kind of piercing, analytical intelligence that had sometimes caused me to wonder why she had left her job with the Home Office. The freelance legal work she did now earned her a steady and fairly comfortable income but it was hardly big money and only a fraction of what she was really worth. Once in the early days of our friendship, when for a brief while I imagined there might be the possibility of romance between us, I got drunk and asked her about it.

"I can't work for those people any more," she said. "I don't believe in doing deals with the devil." She laughed, a brisk 'ha,' then changed the subject. Later that same evening I found out she was married to a chap called Ray Levine, an ex-airline pilot who now grubbed around for work shuttling government ministers to and from their various conferences and crisis summits.

"Ray's a bit of an arsehole, I suppose," Dora said. "But we've known each other since we were kids. We used to smoke rollups together in the teachers' toilets. That's something you can't replace. I don't care what he does on those trips of his, just so long as he doesn't bring it home with him. I learned a long time ago that trust is a lot more important than sexual fidelity."

I first met Dora when I sold her her flat, a three-room conversion in Westcombe Park occupying part of what had once been a private nursing home. It was an attractive property, with high windows, a stained glass fanlight, and solid oak parquet flooring, but it had serious disadvantages, most crucially the access, which was via a fire escape belonging to the neighbouring property. I knew this could pose legal problems if she ever wanted to sell, and because I found myself liking her I broke all the usual rules of the business and told her so. The forthrightness of her reaction surprised me but as I came to know her better I realised it was typical of her.

"I can't make a decision to buy something based on whether I might want to get rid of it later," she said. "This is about a home, not a business investment. This is where I want to live."

Then she smiled and told me she was a lawyer. She knew all about flying freehold and compromised access but she was adamant she wanted the flat, as she was adamant about a lot of things. After she moved in I took the liberty of contacting her and asking if she was interested in doing some freelance contract work. Within a year she was working two full days a week for me, clarifying the deadlocks and stalemates that occasionally threatened to upset some of our more lucrative sales. She had a genius for finding a loophole, or for finding anything, really. It was for this reason that I asked her if she could help me track down Owen Andrews. I didn't go into any details and Dora being Dora didn't ask questions. A couple of days later she called me at home and asked me if I could come round to her place.

"I've got things to show you," she said. "But it's not the kind of stuff I want to bring into the office."

She opened the door to me dressed in a pair of Ray's old camo pants held up with elastic braces. "Andrews is alive and well," she said. "Would you like a drink?" She poured Glenlivet and wafted Samsara, the kind of luxury items that were often difficult to find on open sale but readily available if you had the right contacts and I supposed the whisky and the perfume came via Ray. Levine himself was rarely at the flat. Dora said he spent most of his nights on airbases or in the bed of whichever woman he was currently trying to impress.

"It's like being married to your own younger brother," she said. "But to be honest I think I'd kill him if he was here all the time."

I occasionally wondered what would happen if I tried to spend the night with her. The prospect was tantalising, but in the end I suppose I valued our friendship, not to mention our business relationship, too highly to risk ruining it through some misconceived blunder. Also she had liked Miranda.

She handed me my drink then pushed a small stack of papers towards me across the table.

"Here," she said. "Have a look at these."

The papers comprised a mixture of photocopies and typed notes, with markings and annotations everywhere in Dora's spiky black script. There were photocopies of a civil service entrance exam and a standard ID card, together with a passport-sized photograph and a copy of an article from a magazine I had never heard of called *Purple Cloud*. The photograph showed a swarthy, rather handsome man with a high forehead and heavy brows. It was just a head shot, and offered no clue to his stature, but his ID gave his height as 4'10", with the note that between the ages of nine and fourteen he had undergone four major operations on his legs. His address was at Shooter's Hill, just a couple of miles east of where we were sitting but its reputation for violence and the fact of the night-time curfew meant that in terms of current reality it was half a world away. In his civil service entrance test Andrews had scored ninety-eight percent.

"This is amazing," I said. "Where did you get all this stuff?"

"There's more," Dora said. She pulled some papers from the stack and riffled quickly through them until she found what she wanted. "He worked for the MoD on classified projects. That means they could have wiped his whole ID if they'd wanted to, or altered it in some way, anything. The really weird thing is that he was dismissed from his post but left alone afterwards. That never happens. Normally they'd have you in prison, at least for a while, at least until the work you were doing was no longer relevant. The fact that Andrews is still out there means he's valuable to them in some way, or that he's a spy. The very fact that he was working for them at all is some kind of miracle. He's a dwarf, a non-person. It's getting harder for people like him even to be granted a work permit." She paused and stubbed out her cigarette. I caught the sweet reek of Marlboro tobacco. "The thing is, they'll have their eye on him. If you go near him they'll have their eye on you, too. Is that what you want? This isn't a very good time to be getting yourself on somebody's blacklist."

"I just want to talk to him."

"So you say. And I've read that article. What's all this about, Martin?"

"It's not about anything. I have a clock he made, that's all. I was just curious."

"Well, you know what they say about curiosity killing the cat."

It should have been funny, but it wasn't. We sat side by side at the table, neither of us saying anything. I wanted to reassure her in some way, to at least thank her for what she had done for me, but neither of these things seemed possible. I realised we were on new ground, the unstable territory that springs into being whenever the conversation between two people begins to trespass beyond its usual limits. Politics was something that didn't get discussed much, not even in private.

"Can I take all these papers with me?" I said in the end.

"Please do. I don't want them. I had to use my old passwords to get hold of some of that stuff. I'd be instantly traceable, if anyone had a mind to go looking. It's a ridiculous risk to take. God knows what I was thinking." She ran her hands through her hair, making it stand out about her head like a stiff black halo. "It was fun, though. It beat the shit out of verifying leasehold clauses."

She smiled, and I knew we were back on safe ground. I knew also that the subject of Owen Andrews was closed between us, that whatever fleeting thrill she had gained from hacking into Home Office files she wanted no further part in what I was doing. Doubtless she had her reasons. I had no wish to know what these were, just as she had no real wish to know what had interested me in Owen Andrews in the first place. I walked home the long way round, skirting the boundary of Greenwich Park, which was kept locked after sundown and was sometimes closed to the public for months at a time. The captive trees made me think of Shooter's Hill, an outpost of an imaginary realm shrouded in a rough twilight. I wondered what Andrews was doing right at that moment, and the strangeness of it all made my heart turn over. One thing I had noticed and not mentioned to Dora while glancing through his papers was that several of the documents gave contradictory information about his birth date. Neither was it simply a matter of a couple of days. His birth certificate had him a whole fifteen years younger than his ID card. His medical records showed him as ten years older. I guessed that bureaucratic errors like this must happen constantly. But still, it seemed unnervingly peculiar.

When I got home I read the article Dora had copied from *Purple Cloud*. It was an essay about how the previous government had made use of what the writer called 'time-bridge technology' to try and alter the course of the war in the Middle East. It had the smack of conspiracy theory and sensationalism I associated with the kind of magazine that specialises in UFOs and the so-called paranormal and I found myself not believing a word of it. According to the article Owen Andrews was significant as the pioneer of something called the Silver Wind, a mechanical time-stabiliser that certain military scientists had subverted to their own purposes. Apparently Andrews also had connections with the German firm of Lange und Soehne, who had made watches for everyone from Adolf Hitler to Albert Einstein, as well as being pioneers in the field of atomic engineering.

I knew I would have to go and see him. It was not just about the clock any more, and after reading the flimsy article in *Purple Cloud* my doubts about the feasibility of time travel were stronger than ever. It was the very fact of Owen Andrews now that fascinated me. The fact that he was a non-person, and yet seemed somehow immune to political reality. The fact that he seemed to have three different birthdays. The fact that he lived in a place where no one but the outlawed and the desperate could reasonably survive. I felt as if I had stepped on the edge of something and felt it move, as if I had been coming down the street and tripped over a loose paving stone, only to discover that it was in fact a secret hatchway into an underground city.

It sounds insane to say it, but I had never really questioned the world I lived in. I remembered the hung parliaments, the power shortages, the forced deportations of the millions of blacks and Asians from the city ghettos to the vast factory ships built to transport them to the so-called 'home-states' of Nigeria, Botswana and the near-uninhabitable wastelands of the exhausted Niger delta. I remembered the fire on board the *Anubis*, mostly because a teacher of ours, Kwella Cousens, was one of the three thousand deportees who died in the blaze. She taught Business French for a time at the college where I was studying but lost her work permit during the tax revisions and so was forced to take a place on one of the transports. I remembered these things, as generations before me might have remembered the moon landings or the Kennedy assassination, as news flashes and photographic images. They happened when I was in my late teens, busy with college work and desperate to lose my virginity.

The truth was, I remembered them as things that had happened to other people. The new employment laws affected mostly black people and immigrants. If you were white and had a UK ID card you could mostly go on with your life as if nothing had changed. I had seen what happened to people who made a fuss: the small number of students from my college who joined the demonstrations and the dock pickets, the pamphleteers who for a time had littered the streets of the major cities with their *samizdat* scandal sheets had all spent nights in jail and some of them had had their grants suspended. One young man who chained himself to the railings of Buckingham Palace even had his national insurance number revoked. They bundled him off to Niger with the blacks. I remember thinking what a fool he was, to get mixed up in something that didn't concern him.

Up until now the biggest decision I had ever made about my life was the decision to ask Miranda to marry me. As I got into bed that night I realised I was on the verge of making another decision of that same magnitude and perhaps greater, a decision that could change my life in ways I would not know about until it was too late to recant: I was about to start asking questions about things I had previously discounted as none of my business.

I lay in bed, listening to the steady ticking of Owen Andrews's clock on my bedside table and the distant phut-phutting of the wind-powered generators across the river on the Isle of Dogs. As I drifted off to sleep it seemed to me that the clock and the generators had somehow combined forces to form a great silver wheel, its shafts and spokes catching the moonlight, casting its radiance in a hundred different directions.

The bus was ancient, its wheel arches pitted with rust. It was full of soldiers. Their rambunctious, raucous presence made me nervous, although I realised this was illogical, that there was nothing unusual or sinister in their behaviour, and that the presence of forces personnel was entirely to be expected. Shooter's Hill was a restricted zone. Civilians could enter, and the shops and small businesses that had serviced the area prior to its closure were allowed to keep running as usual, at least partly for the benefit of the new influx of military. But after sundown any movement into and out of the village was strictly prohibited. There was a military checkpoint, and it was said that the woods behind the old hospital were alive with snipers, that the turf battles between the military and the carjack gangs that used Oxleas Woods as a hideout had taken on the dimensions of guerrilla warfare.

Officially the place was a shooting range and assault course, like Dartmoor and Romney Marsh, but everyone knew there was more to it than that. There were rumours that the rundown hospital buildings had been turned over to one of the specialist divisions as a testing laboratory for biological weapons. I had always thought the idea was far-fetched, just gossip really, but as the bus pulled up Maze Hill and into the forest I began to wonder. Passing into the forest felt strange, almost like crossing the border into another country. The starkly open expanse of Blackheath Common gave way abruptly to massed ranks of oak and ash and beech, the trees growing so closely together that it was as if we had entered a tunnel. The lowest branches scraped the roof of the bus, linking their gnarled green fingers above our heads. Rough tarmac and dirt tracks branched off from the road at regular intervals, and between the trees I could make out the rectangular masses of houses and apartment blocks. I wondered who would choose to live out here. I knew that much of the housing in the vicinity of the hospital had been demolished by order of the government.

Aside from one burnt-out car at the side of the road I saw no overt signs of violence but in spite of this I found the atmosphere oppressive. The forest seemed unending, and its green stillness unnerved me; I felt as if something was lying in wait, just out of sight.

We passed through a set of traffic lights, then came to a standstill beside the two fluted granite columns that marked the entrance to the hospital. The main building was mostly hidden behind a high stone wall topped with metal spikes and coils of barbed wire. Armed sentries stood on guard beside a swing barrier. The soldiers on the bus all rose to their feet, jostling each other impatiently as they crowded towards the front. Once outside they formed a straggling line, waiting to be admitted. I saw one of them rummaging in his knapsack, presumably for his entrance pass or some other necessary document.

I pressed my face to the window, watching the soldiers go through their ID check. As the bus pulled away I caught a glimpse of narrow windows and blotchy grey walls. Now that the soldiers were gone the bus was almost empty. Towards the rear sat two men in business suits and a stout, middle-aged woman with a wicker basket on her knees. The basket contained three live chickens. On the seat across from me sat a teenaged girl. Her pale face and wispy fair hair reminded me a little of Miranda. She glanced past me at the soldiers in the road.

"That's the loony bin," she said to me suddenly. "They guard it to stop the loonies getting out. Some of them have killed people."

I stared at her in silence for a moment, unsure of what I should say. When I looked back towards the road the hospital and the soldiers were already some distance behind us. I had vague memories of the place from my childhood, when Oxleas Woods had been unrestricted and carjackings less prevalent. The hospital was derelict then, a forgotten eyesore. We used to pretend it was haunted, or believed perhaps that it really was, I was no longer sure. In either case, the gates had always been kept firmly secured against intruders, and the high wall that ringed the perimeter meant that the grounds were impenetrable, even to the most resourceful and daring among our company. Its gloomy edifice had always been a source of vague dread to me. It was not ghosts I feared so much as the building itself. I hated its barred windows, the frowning facade that always made me think of dungeons and prisons. I could never escape the idea that terrible things had happened there.

I was amazed and strangely gratified to find that the intervening years had done little if anything to moderate my dislike of the place.

"Do you know what the soldiers are doing there?" I said to the girl. I had taken her for about thirteen, but now that I looked at her closely I saw she was older than that, eighteen or nineteen perhaps. It was just that her thinness and her sullen, rather vacant stare made her look much younger. She did not really resemble Miranda, other than in the colour of her hair. The girl pressed her lips tightly together and shook her head vehemently from side to side. She seemed startled, even frightened that I had spoken to her, even though she had spoken to me first. It crossed my mind that she might be retarded.

"I've been inside," she said. She glanced at me from beneath her colourless lashes, as if checking to see that I was still listening. I felt certain that she was lying. I turned away from her and back towards the window. We were coming into the village. Shooter's Hill had never been much of a place, and the encroachment of the forest made it seem even less significant. I saw a general store and a post office, a church and beside that a recreation hall or perhaps a school house. One side of the dusty main road was flanked by houses, a mixture of small flint cottages and slightly larger Victorian terraces. On the other side of the street the forest began, stretching in an unbroken swathe as far as the Carshalton Reservoir and beyond that the Sussex Weald.

The bus ground to a halt beside the Bull Inn. As I rose to my feet the fair-haired girl scampered past me, darting along the pavement and then disappearing down an alleyway between two of the houses. The bus coughed once and then lurched forward, bearing the chicken woman and the suited businessmen on towards the dockyard at Woolwich. The silence closed itself around me, so complete it seemed material, green in colour and with the texture of house dust. I looked back the way I had come. Somewhere to the north of me lay the boulevards and tramlines and bomb sites of central London. I hesitated for a moment in front of the pub then headed off down the road. On my left was the water tower, a renovated Victorian structure that I guessed would serve all the houses in the village and probably the hospital too. It soared above the rooftops, its brick-built crenellations weathered to the colour of clay. Owen Andrews's house was on Dover Road, one of a terrace of eight Victorian villas and directly in the shadow of the water tower. The houses were shielded from the road by a thin line of trees. Fifty years ago and as a main route into London the road would have been seething with traffic.

The universal tax on private vehicles had changed everything and so had the closure of the woodlands. Dover Road was now a forest byway frequented mainly by logging trucks and army vehicles. Weeds spilled through the cracks in its tarmac. For the first time since setting out that morning I wondered properly what on earth I was doing there.

Andrews's house was approached by a short pathway, a couple of paving slabs laid end to end across a yellowed patch of pockmarked turf. I stepped quickly up to the door and pressed the bell. I heard it ring in the hallway beyond. I stood there waiting for what seemed an age. I had no doubt there were unseen watchers, and whether this would have repercussions was something I would only discover later. I bent down and peered in through the letterbox. I caught a glimpse of cream walls and wooden floorboards and then the door was opened, so suddenly I almost went flying.

"Can I help you?" said Owen Andrews. "Are you lost?"

"No," I said, staring down at him. "At least I don't think so. It was you that I came to see."

"You'd better come in then," said Andrews. "I don't get many visitors these days." He retreated inside, moving with a slow rolling gait that was almost a waddle. He seemed unsurprised to see me. I followed him into the house. Things were happening so fast they had begun to feel slightly unreal.

He took me through to a room at the back. The room was steeped in books, so many of them that the ochre-coloured wallpaper that lined the room showed though only in oddly-spaced random patches. Glazed double doors overlooked a narrow strip of garden. A set of library steps on castors stood close to one wall. Andrews heaved himself up on to a battered chaise longue, which from the multitude of books and papers stacked at one end I guessed was his accustomed reading chair.

"Sit down," he said, waving at the chair opposite, an upright wing chair upholstered in faded green velvet. "Tell me why you're here."

I lowered myself into the chair. "I'm sorry to turn up uninvited like this," I said. "But I bought a clock of yours recently and I wanted to ask you about it. I wanted to talk to you as soon as possible. I hope you don't mind."

"A clock of mine? How fascinating. Which one?"

He leaned forward in his seat, clearly interested. He was classically dwarfish, with foreshortened limbs and a head that seemed too big for his body, but his torso was powerful and upright and he carried himself with such dignity that it is true to say that within this first five minutes of meeting him I had already forgotten his diminutive stature. His force of personality was tangible. I thought he was probably the most extraordinary man I had ever met. I described the clock to him, telling him also how I had come by it.

"I know the one," he said at once. "The case was made from old bell metal."

He grabbed a sheet of paper from the pile at his feet and began to draw on it, sketching in rapid strokes with a blue Bic biro. He gazed at his work appraisingly, tapping the blunt end of the pen against his teeth then handed me the paper. His drawing captured the likeness of my clock in every detail.

"That's it," I said. "That's amazing."

Andrews smiled. "I find them hard to let go of," he said. "It's a weakness of mine. But you didn't come all the way out here to ask me about an old clock. A simple telephone call would have dealt with that. Why don't you tell me what you came for really?"

I could feel myself beginning to blush. The man's forthrightness startled me, and now that I was about to put it into words the thing I had come to ask seemed ridiculous, dangerous even. But I had come too far to turn back. And the fact was that I trusted him. I believed that Owen Andrews would tell me the truth, no matter how difficult or unpleasant that truth might be.

"My wife died," I said at last. "Her name was Miranda. She was killed in a car accident. Her father drove his car off a cliff into the sea and drowned them both."

"I'm sorry to hear that," said Andrews. "That's a terrible story." His eyes were clouded with concern, and I was surprised to see that he really was sorry, not just interested as most people were when they first discovered what had happened to Miranda. I didn't blame them for being interested. The story was shocking and dramatic, a breakdown in normality that had never become entirely real to me, even after the wreck was salvaged and the bodies recovered. Who would not be interested? It is all but impossible for one man to climb inside another man's sorrow. But I could see from his face that Owen Andrews was at least trying. I guessed he was more practised than most in enduring heartache.

"I read about you," I said. "About the work you did for the army. I read about the Silver Wind."

His dark eyes flashed, his expression changing so suddenly it was almost as if my words had thrown a switch inside him.

"You're asking me to bring back your wife? That is what you're saying?"

I nodded and looked down at the ground. I felt smaller than an insect.

"Do you have any background in physics?" he said.

"Not in the least."

"Well, if you did you would know that what you are talking about is impossible. For one thing, the time sciences are in their infancy. We have about as much control over the time stream as a Neanderthal over a steam train. But mainly it is just not possible. A layman such as yourself tends to think of time as a single thread, an unbroken continuum linking all past events together like the beads on a necklace. We are discovering that time isn't like that. It's an amorphous mass, a rag bag if you like, a rag bag of history. The time stasis might grant you access to what you think of as the past, but it wouldn't be the past that you remember. You wouldn't be the same and neither would she. There's a good chance you wouldn't even recognise each other, and even if you did it's unlikely that you would have any sense of a shared history together. It would be like that feeling you get when you meet someone at a party and can't remember their name. You know you know them from somewhere, but you can't for the life of you think where from. It would be an alternative scenario, not a straight rewind. And Miranda would still probably end up dying in that car crash. We've found that the pivotal events in history still recur, even if the cause and effect are subtly different. It's as if the basic template, the temporal pattern if you like, is ingrained somehow. It's hard to eradicate."

He folded his arms across his chest, as if to indicate that this was his last word on the matter. I felt once again the power of his personality, the force of his intellect, and it was as if we were fighting a duel, his knowledge against my despair. I knew the battle was lost, but I could not deny myself one final, miserable onslaught.

"But I would see her again? She would be alive?"

"No. It might be possible to transfer to a version of reality where a version of Miranda is not dead yet. But that is all."

"Then that is what I want. I have money."

"No you don't," said Andrews. "And this has nothing to do with money." He fell silent, looking down at his hands, the fingers short and neat, pink as a baby's. I sensed that he was troubled, that such brutal candour was not something he enjoyed.

"I'm sorry," I said in the end. "I've been very stupid."

"Not at all," said Andrews quickly. "And at least what you asked for is harmless, beautiful even, the kind of wish one might almost be tempted to grant if it were possible. I've had far worse propositions, believe me. Fortunately they've been equally impossible."

"You're talking about the army? The government?"

Andrews nodded. "I must warn you that this room might be bugged. I've given up bothering about it. They know my views and I have nothing to hide. But I wouldn't want to cause any unpleasantness for my friends." He paused, as if giving me the option to leave, but I stayed where I was and waited for him to continue. I realised two things: firstly that my pilgrimage to Shooter's Hill had always been about Andrews's story rather than mine, and secondly that I felt properly alive for the first time since Miranda died.

There was also the fact that Owen Andrews had called me his friend. I took this as a mark of trust and a gracious compliment but strangely it also felt *true*. For a brief instant something flickered at the back of my mind, a sense that there were some facts missing, like pieces in a jigsaw puzzle, and then the curtain of logic descended and it was gone. I liked Andrews, and felt a kinship with him because of that. That was all.

"What's the matter?" Andrews said. His anger seemed vanished, and an amused smile tweaked at the corners of his mouth. I wondered what secrets my face had given away.

"Nothing," I said. "Go on."

He shifted his position on the chaise longue, sitting upright and hugging his knees. He was wearing green velvet slippers and grey schoolboy socks. The combination was both amusing and moving, and I was reminded of images I had seen in books, paintings by Velasquez and Goya of the court dwarfs of Spain. They had been the playthings of the nobility but in some cases they had actually been the secret power behind the throne. "Do you know about the hospital?" he said.

"I've heard the rumours," I replied. "What about it?"

I was surprised to hear him speak of the place, I suppose simply because it was the source of so much ignorant tittle-tattle. I thought of the strange girl I had met on the bus, and my heart sank. If Owen Andrews went spinning off in some similar tale of murderous lunatics it would make me start to doubt everything he had told me.

I was wrong, of course. The girl had not been completely deluded either, although I did not think of her again until much later.

"It's always been a military hospital," Andrews said. "It was designed and built by Florence Nightingale's nephew as a centre for the study and treatment of shell shock. It was the first hospital in the country of its kind."

"I've heard it's being used to test chemical weapons," I said. "Is that true?"

Andrews shook his head, seeming to dismiss the idea out of hand. "You said you read about the Silver Wind," he said. "What did you read, exactly?"

I hesitated, unwilling to reveal that the only hard information I had on Andrews's research had been gleaned from a UFO magazine. "Something about time-bridges," I said in the end. "The article I read said that the army were trying to change the outcome of the Saudi war by stealing technology from the future. It all sounded rather improbable. I wasn't sure what to believe."

Andrews nodded. "Do you know what a tourbillon regulator is?"

"I have no idea."

"It was invented by Louis Breguet, in the eighteenth century. He became famous for making watches for Napoleon and Marie Antoinette. His grasp of mechanics was extraordinary and at least a century ahead of his time. He discovered a way of making time stand still. Please excuse me, just for one moment. It's better if I show you."

Andrews slid from the chaise longue and shuffled out of the room. A minute later he returned, bringing with him a small wooden box.

"Here's one I made earlier," he said with a smile. He flipped open the lid, and I saw there was a watch inside. Andrews lifted it out, laying the box carefully to one side on the floor. The watch was quite large, a facsimile of a gentleman's pocket watch from the nineteenth or early twentieth century. I was familiar with such articles, having bought and sold them on several occasions. This one had a silver case. Even to my untutored eye it was a thing of quite exceptional beauty.

"I studied Breguet's diaries for many years," said Andrews. "He died an old man. A lot of people thought he was crazy in his final years, suffering from Alzheimer's disease or some other form of dementia. It is true that he did lose some clarity of expression at the end, but that may well have been due to the complexity of the ideas he was struggling with. A lot of it is brand new science." He thumbed a catch, opening the back of the watch. I caught a glimpse of wires and levers, a mass of mechanical circuitry that glimmered as it rotated. Andrews cradled the watch in his left hand, using his right to point to first one of the gleaming internal wheels and then another. I quickly lost track of them all. Fortunately his words were somewhat easier to follow.

"The tourbillon is like a cage," he said. "It rotates the whole mechanism about its own axis. Breguet discovered this as a way of preventing gravity from dragging on the mechanism and making the watch run slow. In effect he made the mechanism weightless. The time stasis is simply a more advanced version of this idea. It makes time null and void within the area of its operation. The stasis creates a kind of temporal anteroom. Think of it as the lobby of a large hotel, with doors and lifts and corridors opening off it. Once you get through the entrance and into the lobby you can go anywhere you like within the building. It's the time stasis that reveals the entrance. Do you see?"

"Some of it." I paused. "It's what the article I read called the time-bridge."

"Yes. But I've never liked the term 'time-bridge.' Once again it's too linear. The lobby image is better, and useful, too. You know how easy it is to get lost in one of those big hotels. All the corridors look the same after a while."

By then I was struggling to make sense of it all. "But what use could this be to the army?" I said. "You've already told me that it's not possible to travel in time in the way people usually imagine it, so where's the point?"

"There isn't any. But the government refuse to believe that. They've set up a stasis field around the hospital and they are conducting experiments there, forcing people through into other realities and trying to control the future before it happens. And I'm not just talking about weapons. My guess is that they have glimpsed something up ahead they don't like, somewhere in one of the alternative futures, and are trying to eradicate that as a possibility. Think about it, what Hitler might have done if he had seen what would happen when he invaded Russia, or if Reagan had changed his mind over North Korea. It's insane, of course, like trying to do brain surgery with a pickaxe. They have the idea that I could help to refine the mechanism for them, and that is the single reason they leave me alone. They think I'll come round eventually to their way of thinking. They've offered me some marvellous inducements."

"But if they can't succeed where's the harm in it?"

"In the harm they're doing to people, for a start. They snatch people after curfew and then blame it on the carjackers. They snatch carjackers, too. They send them through the stasis, hoping that with time they'll be able to control their experiments more closely and through them begin to control the time stasis. As is the case of all dictatorships, they believe that individuals are expendable. Some of the people they send through never come back. Some never seem to leave, but their contact with the stasis seems to alter their substance. They're incomplete somehow; like underdeveloped photographs their colours are muted. They flicker in and out of existence, like ghosts. I have even begun to think that they *are* ghosts, or rather that the manifestations people think of as ghosts are not the spirits of the dead at all, but are actually the living products of unsuccessful experiments with a time stasis, conducted from a time-stream lying parallel to ours. Then there are the mutants, those occasional unfortunates that experience the stasis as an allergy, a chemical reaction that forces their physical substance into hideous aberrations. There's nothing that can be done for them. The soldiers simply release them into the forest. They don't mind if someone catches a glimpse of one of these poor creatures once in a while because they're better than any amount of barbed wire and electric fencing for discouraging intruders. I've no doubt that this is how the chemical weapons stories started. And if the mutants start causing trouble then the army simply go out and use them as target practice."

"But that's terrible."

"There are a lot of terrible things going on these days." He looked at me hard, as if holding me personally accountable for the transports and for the Saudi wars, for what had happened aboard the *Anubis*. "No doubt there have been the usual speeches about omelettes and breaking eggs. What none of them seem to realise is the harm they could be doing, not just with these local atrocities but on a wider scale. The stasis is a weak point, a lesion in time that if allowed to consolidate itself could undermine the stability of our own reality. The breach should be closed, at least until we understand its implications. There are people that have an idea of what is happening and want it stopped, but they have a tendency to disappear."

"A resistance, you mean?"

"I don't talk about that. I do still have some shreds of a private life, and I intend to hang on to them. I suppose it is true, that everyone has his price."

A clear image came to me of the woman in the photograph, the smiling girl with the pretty mouth. Andrews folded the watch in his hand, pressing it shut.

"How long did it take you to make that?" I said.

"A long time," Andrews said. He smiled to himself, as if at some private joke. "Can I offer you something to eat?"

I stayed, and we talked. I told him about Miranda, and he told me about his childhood in Devon, his first encounter with a Breguet watch, at the town museum in Exeter. Some details of his stories seemed disconcertingly familiar, and several times I experienced that same feeling I had had earlier, that there was a wider sense to everything, just out of sight.

Andrews got up to put a lamp on. It was only then that I realised how late it was.

"I should be going," I said. "It'll be getting dark soon."

I had no idea what time the last bus went. In the light of what Andrews had told me the idea of breaking curfew was unthinkable.

"You're welcome to stay," said Andrews. "There's a spare bed upstairs."

"No, thank you," I said. For some reason the idea of spending the night there unnerved me.

"Then at least say you'll come again. It's been just like the old days, having you here."

I laughed to show I knew he was joking, but his face remained serious. Suddenly I was anxious to leave.

"I will, I'll come soon," I said.

"See that you do. Mind how you go."

He waved to me from the doorway. I wondered if he ever got lonely. Dover Road stood silent, a ghost place. With the dusk approaching and to my increasingly anxious mind the place seemed to me like a mock-up, a stage set for some elaborate deception.

It was growing dusk. The forest loomed before me, its greens leached to lavender by the approaching twilight. In the Bull Inn the lamps were already lit, and further along the road towards the village there were lights showing in the windows of most of the houses. It was not long till curfew, but I reasoned that as long as I could get myself on a bus within the next half hour there would be nothing to worry about. I set off in the direction of the High Street, walking briskly in what I hoped was a businesslike fashion. I had just come in sight of the bus stop when I saw something terrible: a roadblock had been set up outside the post office. There were four soldiers manning it; all of them were armed with rifles. I stopped in my tracks, ducking sideways into an alleyway lined with dustbins. My heart was racing. There was no question of approaching the barrier. Even though I had not breached the curfew and it was still my legal right to pass along the street I knew beyond any doubt that in practice this would count for nothing, that the soldiers would find some pretext to arrest me. What might happen after that was something I did not care to think about.

The safest move was to go back the way I had come, to return to Owen Andrews's house and take him up on his offer of spending the night there. I hesitated, knowing this was the logical course of action but still reluctant to take it. I trusted Andrews completely; the place I did not trust at all. As the dusk came steadily onwards, seeming to curl out from beneath the trees like tendrils of smoke, I realised I had a horror of it, that for some reason the thought of spending the night at Shooter's Hill was almost as impossible for me as the idea of confronting the soldiers at the barricade.

I felt horribly trapped. I cowered in the alleyway, staring at the trees opposite and knowing I had to make a decision in the next few minutes or risk breaking the curfew. It was then that it came to me there was a third option: I could bypass the checkpoint by cutting through the forest. The idea seemed simple enough. I was actually within sight of the checkpoint, and less than half a mile from the village boundary. I could walk that in less than fifteen minutes. I would not need to go far into the woods, just enough to keep me out of earshot of the soldiers. I should emerge on the Shooter's Hill Road somewhere between the hospital and Blackheath.

I ran quickly across the road, hoping that one of the soldiers down by the barrier would not choose that moment to turn his gaze in my direction. I slipped in between the trees, my feet crunching through leaf litter. The slope down from the road was steeper than I had imagined. I tripped against an exposed root and almost fell. In less than a couple of minutes I had completely lost sight of the road.

I had imagined there would be a pathway, some kind of track to follow but there were none, or at least none that I could find, and in the oncoming darkness it was difficult to see clearly for more than a couple of yards. I kept going, fighting my way through the underbrush in what I hoped was a westerly direction. There were no landmarks to guide me, no sounds other than the scuffling of my feet in the leaves and my own rapid breathing. I stopped moving, straining my ears for the rumble of a logging truck or even for the voices of the soldiers at the barricade but there was nothing. I could not have been more than a mile from the lighted windows of the Bull Inn, yet it was as if I had unwittingly strayed into some other universe. I could smell the trees all around me, the pungent odour of tree bark and rising chlorophyll.

I remembered something from my schooldays, that it was during the hours of darkness that plants released their pent up stores of oxygen, and it seemed to me that I could feel their exhalations all around me, the collective green-tinged sigh of a thousand trees. The dark was growing, spreading across the forest floor like marsh gas. From somewhere further off came the echoing melancholy hooting of a night owl.

I walked for what felt like hours. I could no longer see where I was going, and had no idea of whether I was even vaguely headed in the right direction. I was very afraid, but the state of high nervous tension that had taken me over when I first realised I was lost had worn itself out, blunting my terror to a dull background hum, a mental white noise that drove me incessantly forward whilst slowing the actions and reactions of my brain. Finally I came to a standstill. The woods seemed to close in around me, shuffling forward to block my escape like some vast black beast that knows its prey is all out of running. I slid to the ground where I stood, the dampness settling at once into my clothes. Until that moment I had not realised how cold it was. I began to shiver. I knew that if I was to spend the night in the open I had to get under cover somehow, but I was too exhausted by my flight through the woods to make any decisions. I closed my eyes, thinking confusedly that this might make the darkness less terrible. When I opened them again some minutes later it was to the sight of a yellowish glow, moving slowly towards me from between the trees. I could hear something also, the soft shushing sound of someone or something doing their best to move quietly across a ground that was ankle-deep in twigs and dry leaves.

I moved from a sitting to a lying position, stomach down in the dirt, never taking my eyes from the pale light that though still some distance off appeared to be coming closer with every second. I was torn by indecision. I did not wish to fall into the hands of soldiers or carjackers, but on the other hand I was desperate to be out of the forest. At that moment the thought any human company seemed better than none. As the light came closer I was able to discern amidst the surrounding darkness of trees the deeper, blacker bulk of a human figure: somebody carrying a torch, and coming my way.

In the end the simple need to hear a human voice outweighed my misgivings. I scrambled to my feet, extending my arms towards the figure with the lamp like a blind man trying to feel his way across a crowded room.

"Hello!" I cried. "Hello there. Wait for me!"

I moved forward, my attempt to run reduced by the darkness to an unsteady lurch. I crashed through the treacherous underbrush, stray twigs clawing at my hands and face. The figure stopped dead in its tracks, the torch beam wavering gently up and down. Its light was weak but my eyes had grown used to the darkness and were temporarily blinded. The figure took a step backwards, crackling the leaves underfoot. It seemed that it was as much afraid of me as I was of it.

"I'm lost," I said. "Do you know the way out of here?"

I could hear its breathing, slow and heavy, as if it was about to expire. There was a rank odour, a smell like burning fat tinged with underarm sweat. I was by now convinced that the figure was a fugitive, a lone carjacker perhaps, or an immigrant without a work permit, someone on the run from the police. None of that mattered to me; all I cared about was getting out of the woods.

"I'm not going to report you," I said. "I just want to find the road." I grabbed at its sleeve, anxious in case the figure tried to bolt away from me. It was wearing padded mittens, and a padded anorak made from some shiny nylon-coated fabric that was difficult to get a grip on. My fingers tightened involuntarily about its wrist. The figure moaned, a low, inhuman sound that made me go cold all over. I knew I had made an awful mistake. I released the figure abruptly, pushing it backwards. As it flailed its arms to retain balance the torch beam darted upwards, lighting its face. Until that moment it had been shrouded in darkness, its features concealed by the large, loose hood of the nylon anorak. Now I saw something terrible: the thing's face was disfigured in some way, quite literally *de-formed*, squeezed apart and then rammed back together again in a careless and hideous arrangement that bore as little resemblance to an ordinary human face as the face of a corpse in an advanced stage of decomposition. The skin was thickly corrugated, set into runnels as if burned by acid. The mouth, a lipless slit, was slanted heavily to one side, dividing the face's lower portion in a raw diagonal slash. One of the eyes was sealed shut, smeared in its socket somehow like a clay eye inadvertently damaged by its sculptor's careless thumb. The other eye shone brightly in the torchlight, gazing at me in what I instinctively knew was sorrow as much as fear. The eye was fringed with long lashes, and quite perfect. The creature standing before me was a woman.

I screamed, I could not help it, though it was more from shock than from fear. I knew that I was seeing one of the mutants Owen Andrews had spoken of, one of the worst victims of the army's clumsy experiments with the time stasis. Andrews had called these creatures unfortunate, but his words had barely scratched the surface of the reality. In my traumatised state I could not grasp how this thing could survive, how it did not just *stop*, how the terrible damage inflicted allowed it still to go on living. The face was an apocalypse in flesh; it was impossible to know what further ravages had been unleashed upon the rest of her body and internal organs.

Her mental torment I could not bear to imagine.

My scream made her flinch, and she stumbled, dropping the torch. She dropped to her knees, sweeping her hands back and forth through the leaves in an effort to retrieve it. But either the padded mittens hampered her efforts or she no longer had proper control of her hands because it kept skidding out of her grasp. I saw my chance and made a lunge for it. Suddenly the torch was in my hand. The mutant girl howled, flinging herself at me as if she meant to topple me into the dirt.

I began to run. The girl picked herself up off the ground and began to follow. She was no longer crying, but I could hear her breathing, the raw panting gasp of it, and I felt sick with revulsion. The thought of having to fight her off, of having her ruined face pressed in close to mine as she battled me for the torch did a good deal to keep me moving. I knew the very fact of possessing the torch made me easy to follow, but there was no help for it. I pointed it ahead of me, panning the ground at my feet and lighting the way ahead the best that I could. The beam was weak, a feeble yellow, barely enough to see by. I kept expecting to bash into a tree or worse still to catch a foot in some pothole or crevice and twist my ankle and I have no doubt that one of these two things would have happened eventually.

In the end I was saved by the soldiers. I climbed a shallow rise, tearing my hands painfully on brambles in the process, and then I was in the open. I could sense rather than see that there were no more trees around me, and I guessed I had reached the edge of a woodland meadow. I shone the torch frantically about me, trying to work out which was the best way to go. Suddenly there were more lights, broad and penetrating beams of white radiance, strafing the ground and dazzling my eyes. They were approaching from the side at a full-on run.

"Halt!" someone screamed. "Get down."

I threw myself to the ground, covering my head instinctively with my arms. A stampede seemed to pass over and around me. Then there was more shouting, a single wild cry that I knew was the girl, and then a burst of gunfire. I covered my ears, cowering against the ground, and the next minute I was being dragged upright, pulled back down the rise and into the trees. My mind froze and went entirely blank. I felt certain that I would die within the next few seconds. Someone shoved me from behind and I almost fell. The crisscrossing beams of powerful torches showed me a half-dozen men with blackened faces and wearing combat fatigues. The girl's body lay face down on the ground; a dark irregular stain was spreading across the back of the padded anorak. One of the soldiers kicked her, flipping her on to her side with the toe of his boot. The anorak shifted slightly, revealing a portion of the clothing beneath, a tattered woollen smock over filthy jeans.

Now with her face turned away from me she looked like any other dead girl. I felt my guts heave. I thought if I couldn't be sick I would choke, but I was terrified to be sick in case these men shot me for it.

"Frigging disgusting," said one of the men. I had the confused impression that he was referring to my weak stomach, then realised he was talking about the girl. "What do you think would happen if they started breeding?"

"Shut up, Weegie," said another. The tone of authority in his voice left no doubt that he was in charge. Then he turned to me. "What the fuck are you doing out here?"

My throat gave a dry click, and I felt once more the gagging reflex, but in the end I was able to answer.

"I came off the road," I said. "I got lost."

"ID?"

For a second I panicked, thinking I had lost my wallet somewhere or even left it behind at Andrews's place, but miraculously when I reached into my jacket pocket it was there. I handed it over in silence. The officer flicked through it briefly, letting his eyes rest for a moment upon my photograph and national insurance number, then amazingly handed it back.

"Bloody civvies," he said. "Do you *want* to get mistaken for one of these?" He nodded down at the girl's lifeless body. I shook my head, not trusting myself to speak.

"You'll have to come with us. It's for your own protection. I suggest you get moving." He nodded to the man he had called Weegie, who grabbed me by the upper arm and pushed me into line behind the others. I stumbled a couple of times, but with the soldiers' powerful search beams to see by the going was actually much easier. Now that it seemed they were not going to kill me or at least not immediately my panic had subsided somewhat. I thought back to the night before, when I had lain comfortably in bed contemplating my forthcoming visit to Andrews and the state of my political morals. It seemed impossible that a mere twenty-four hours could alter my life so completely. I felt inclined to agree with the officer: I had been bloody stupid.

We marched through the forest for about an hour. I was exhausted by then, my mind empty of anything but the desire to stop moving and lie down. At last there were lights, shining to meet us through the trees. The forest ended suddenly at a barbed wire perimeter fence, and I realised we had arrived outside the hospital.

I was too tired to be afraid. I was marched through a set of iron gates then led along a green-tiled corridor that smelled faintly of damp clothes and disinfectant. Unbelievably it reminded me of school. I caught glimpses of a kit store, and a rec room, where soldiers sprawled on bunks watching a televised boxing match. At the end of the corridor a short flight of concrete steps led down to what was clearly a cell block. The officer-in-charge nudged open one of the mesh-strengthened doors and gestured me inside.

"I'd get some kip, if I were you. I'd bring you some grub, only the mess will have shut up shop, so you'll have to hang on till morning."

I stepped through the door, which was immediately banged shut behind me. I heard the sound of a key being turned in the lock and then the soldier's footsteps trudging back up the stairs. Then there was silence. I stood where I was for a moment, wondering if anything else would happen. The room I was in was small, although curiously it still had the wallpaper and curtains left behind from the time before the soldiers had taken over. The way the wainscoting and ceiling architrave had been divided made it clear that the cell had been partitioned off from a much larger room, possibly the doctors' lounge. There was a bed pushed up against one wall, a metal-framed cot of the kind that is usual in hospitals. In the corner was a bucket and basin, crudely screened from the rest of the room by a section of cotton sheeting strung from a pole. The windows behind their curtains were barred from the outside.

I relieved myself in the bucket then lay down on the bed. It bowed heavily under my weight, the springs weary from decades of use. The room was lit by a single bulb, a bald, enervating glare that I supposed would be left burning all night, although when I tentatively pressed a switch by the bed the light went out. In contrast with the alien blackness of the forest I found the darkness of the room gave me a feeling of being protected. I lay under the threadbare blanket, listening to the silence and wondering what was going to happen to me. I was a prisoner, but what was I being imprisoned for? If it was a simple matter of breaking the curfew then I could expect a hefty fine and perhaps three months behind bars, as well as the wholly undesirable possibility of finding myself under continued surveillance. This could lead to all sorts of problems at work, not just for me but for my colleagues. Certainly it was no laughing matter, but it was at least a situation with navigable parameters. The thing was, I knew my situation was not that simple. I had witnessed a murder, the gunning down in cold blood of a defenceless and vulnerable woman. The frightful injuries that had been inflicted upon her before that hardly served to make things less complicated.

There was also the fact of my visit to Owen Andrews, a troublemaker who by his own admission had been repeatedly in conflict with the state.

What if all things considered it seemed simpler just to get rid of me? Now that Miranda was dead there would be few who cared enough to risk asking questions. Dora might ask, she might even look for me, but in the end she would weigh up the cost of the truth about a dead man and the price of her own safety and Ray's and find the balance wanting. I did not blame her for it.

Asking questions was out of fashion in our day and age.

I wondered if they would simply shoot me, or if perhaps they would use me in one of their time travel experiments. I presumed the latter. To shoot me would be a waste of valuable resources.

I thought of the mutant girl in the forest, twisted and bent by her exposure to the time stasis almost beyond the bounds of her humanity. I still found it difficult to contemplate her isolation, the loneliness and horror she must have suffered at the moment of her realisation of what had been done to her. It came to me that there were fates worse than shooting. I even wondered if her death at the hands of the soldiers had been for the best.

All at once the darkness of the room seemed oppressive rather than soothing. I put the light back on and got up from the bed. I paced about my cell, examining the barred window and testing the door handle, wondering if I might discover some means of escape but for all its ramshackleness the room was still a prison. I placed my ear against the door and listened, straining for any sound that might give a clue as to what was happening in the rest of the hospital but there was nothing, just a deep, eerie silence that suggested I was completely alone there. I knew this had to be nonsense: I had seen the rec room, the soldiers on their bunks watching television and playing cards. I supposed the cell had been soundproofed somehow. The thought was not exactly comforting.

In the end I decided the only thing for it was to take advantage of the silence and get some rest. Now that my life was not being directly threatened I found I was ravenously hungry—it was hours since the meal at Andrews's house—but there was nothing I could do about that. I drank some water instead from the tap in the corner. It had a peaty taste and was unpleasantly tepid but it helped to put something at least inside my stomach. After drinking I lay back down on the bed and covered myself with the blanket. I thought I would lie there awake for hours but I fell asleep in less than five minutes.

At some point during the night I was woken by the sound of shouting and running footsteps but no one came to my door and I decided I must have dreamed it. I closed my eyes, hovering on the boundary between sleep and waking, a citizen of both nations but unable to settle permanently in either. I saw sleep as an immense blue forest that I was afraid to enter in case I never found the way out again. Then I woke with a start to bright sunlight, and realised I had been asleep all along.

My watch had stopped, but from the position of the sun in the sky I could tell it was already mid-morning, getting on towards midday even. It struck me as curious to say the least that I had been allowed to sleep so long. Surely by now whoever was in charge here would have wanted me either interrogated or—out of their way? The second strange thing was the sun itself, its insistent presence. The day before had been overcast with the promise of rain, a typical day in late March. The sky that was now on the other side of the barred window was spotless, the heady azure of June or July.

I knew it was impossible, but the vagueness and confusion of mind that so often accompanies a sudden waking suggested to me that *I had been forgotten*, left locked in this room for weeks, that no one was coming now, ever.

I leapt from the bed, relieved myself once again in the stinking bucket, then crossed to the door, prepared to rattle it and shout until someone came. I seized the handle, twisting it sharply downwards.

The door opened smoothly and silently in my hand.

I eased it open a crack and peered out into the corridor. I was prepared for a burst of shouting or even of gunfire, but there was nothing, just the silence of my room, magnified in some queer sense by the largeness of the space it now flowed into. There was nothing in the corridor, just a single plastic chair, as if once, many days before, someone had stood guard there but had long since become bored or assigned to other duties and wandered away. The doors to the other cells stood closed. I stepped out into the corridor, my footsteps echoing on the bare cement floor. I tried the door to the room next to mine, and like mine it swung open easily. I was afraid of what I might find on the other side, but what I found in fact was nothing at all. The bed had been stripped of all its furnishings, including the mattress. There was a slops bucket but it was empty and perfectly dry. Beside it stood a pile of old newspapers. I glanced down at the one on top. The headline story, about Clive Billings losing his seat in a by-election in Harrogate, did not make sense. The paper was brittled and yellow from sun exposure and dated two years previously. I could remember the by-election to which it referred—who could not? It was the by-election that effectively made Billings prime minister—but it had happened more than two decades ago, just as I was about to enter university. Billings had taken the seat with a huge majority.

Looking at the headline made me feel odd, and the idea of actually touching the paper made me feel queasy, off-kilter in a way I could not properly explain. I felt that touching the newspaper would connect me to it as an object, that I would somehow be ratifying the version of reality it was presenting to me, a reality I knew full well had never happened. It would be as if I were somehow negating my own existence.

I left the room quickly, passing up the short stone staircase into the rest of the hospital. The place was empty, not derelict yet but certainly abandoned. The soldiers' rec room was stacked with refuse, dismantled beds and plastic chairs like the one I had seen in the corridor. There were signs everywhere of encroaching damp and roof leakage, peeling wallpaper and buckled linoleum. One more winter without proper attention and the place would sink inexorably into decay.

The main doors had been boarded over but after hunting around for a while I found a side entrance and made my escape. The hospital grounds were a wilderness, the paths choked with weeds and many of the smaller outbuildings partially hidden by stands of rampaging bramble and giant hogweed. Beyond the perimeter wall the trees loomed, whispering together with the passing of the breeze. In spite of the emptiness of the place and the fact that I was plainly alone there I felt exposed, watched, as if the trees themselves were spying on me.

The army checkpoint at the entrance had disappeared and the place was unguarded but the high gates were chained shut and it took me some time to find an exit. The perimeter wall was too high to climb without assistance, and I was just starting to think about going in search of a ladder when I discovered a rent in the small section of chain link fencing that blocked off the access to the service alleyway at the side of the building. The torn wire snagged at my clothes, and in spite of everything I smiled to myself, thinking how the breach was most likely the work of schoolchildren for whom this place now as then would be a realm of dares and bribes, of dangers both imaginary and real. I felt glad that they had broken through, that some of them at least had been braver and bolder than I.

I came out of the alleyway and wandered down to the main road. I tried to look nonchalant, not wanting to draw attention to my soiled clothes and general unkemptness. There was a bus stop by the hospital gates, just as before, and after only ten minutes of waiting a bus drew up to it. I got on, swiping my Oyster card. The sensor responded with its usual bleep. The driver did not look at me twice. I noticed with a start that she was black; I could not remember the last time I had seen a black face in *any* position of public service in this country. The bus was full of soldiers, their London accents blending noisily together as they exchanged ribald jokes and squabbled over newspapers and cigarettes. They were white and black and Asian, as racially mixed as the cowed hordes of deportees in the television broadcasts of my adolescence. I stared at them, barely understanding what I was seeing.

"Lost something, mate?" one of them said to me. "Only if you have, then one of these has probably already nicked it." He looked Middle Eastern in origin. One of his eyebrows was pierced with a diamond stud. The rest of his company erupted in laughter, but it all seemed pretty good-natured and they had soon forgotten me. The bus grunted then lurched off along the road. The woodland seemed to sing with colour and light.

When I arrived at my house on Frobisher Street the key would not fit in the lock. By then I was not surprised. I had even been expecting something of this kind. I rang the bell, and after a minute or so the door was opened by a young woman. Her hair looked uncombed, her eyes dark from fatigue. A child clung to her knees, a boy of perhaps four or five. In contrast with the woman's scruffy housedress the toddler wore a cleanly-pressed playsuit in a cheerful mix of blues and yellows.

"Yes?" she said. "Can I help you?"

I peered over her shoulder into the hall. The black-and-white tiles had been replaced by a dun-coloured carpet. Piles of washing stood heaped at the foot of the stairs.

"How long have you lived here?" I said. The woman took a sudden step backwards, almost tripping over the child. She ran a hand through her hair, and I saw that all her nails were bitten.

"We're registered," she said. "We've been here almost two years. I've got all the forms." Before I could say anything else she had darted away inside the house, disappearing through the door that had once led to my own living room. The toddler stared up at me, his green eyes wide with fascination.

"Are you from the prison?" he said.

"Not at all," I replied. "This used to be my house once, that's all. I wanted to see if it had changed."

He continued to gaze at me as if I were a visitor from another planet. As I stood there wondering whether to stay or go the woman returned. "Here you are," she said. "They're all up to date." She thrust some papers at me. I glanced at them briefly, long enough to see that her name was Violet Jane Pullinger and she had been born in Manchester, then handed them back.

"It's all right," I said. "I'm not from the council or anything. I used to live round here, that's all. I was just curious. I'm sorry if I scared you. I didn't mean to."

The little boy looked from me to the woman and slowly back again. "He says he's not from the prison, mum. Do you think he's my dad?"

"Stephen!" She touched the boy's hair, her face caught somewhere between laughter and embarrassment. When she looked at me again she looked younger and less frightened. "I don't know where they get their ideas from, do you? Would you like to come in? I could make us a cup of tea?"

"That's very kind," I said. "But I've taken up too much of your time already."

I knew I could not enter the house, that to do so would be a kind of madness. I said a hurried goodbye then turned and walked back to the High Street. I thought about looking to see if my office was still there but my nerve failed me. I went to the cashpoint outside my bank instead. I inserted my card in the machine and typed in my PIN. I felt certain the card would be swallowed or rejected. If that happened I was not only homeless, I was penniless too, aside from the couple of notes that were still in my wallet. I peered at the little screen, wondering what I would do if that happened, but this was one decision I did not have to make. My debit card, apparently, was still valid. When the machine asked me which service I required I selected cash with on-screen balance, then when prompted I requested twenty pounds. It seemed a safe enough amount, at least to start with. I waited while the note was disgorged, staring intently at the fluorescent panel where my bank balance was about to be displayed.

When the figure finally appeared I gasped, inhaling so sharply that it set off a fit of coughing. The amount I apparently had in my account was four times the sum that had been in there the day before. It did not make me a rich man by any means, but for a weary time traveller without a roof over his head it certainly provided a measure of temporary security.

I went to the nearest shop, a corner newsagent's, where I bought a newspaper and a wrapped falafel. I ate the falafel where I stood on the street, wolfing it down in three bites then wiping my fingers on the greaseproof paper. Then I headed for the Woolwich Road and a hotel I knew, an enormous Victorian pile that had always been frequented mainly by travelling salesmen and had something of a dubious reputation. Its reputation mattered very little to me right then; what I needed was a bed for the night, some time to think in a place where I would not be noticed.

The hotel was still there and still a hotel. It looked more down-at-heel than ever. Some of the rooms on the ground floor appeared to have been converted into long-stay bedsitters. There was a pervasive smell of cooking fat and stewed tomatoes.

"I don't do breakfast," said the landlady. "You get that yourself, out the back." She was huge, a vast whale of a woman in a flowered print dress with the most extraordinary violet eyes I had ever seen. I told her that was fine. She looked vaguely familiar, and I wondered what she would look like with her hair down. I shook my head to clear it and headed upstairs. The upper landing was sweltering and my poky little room was no better but I didn't care. I sat down on the bed, which creaked alarmingly; it seemed strange how much this room, with its faded wallpaper and antiquated washstand, resembled the hospital cell where I had spent the previous night.

As well as the bed and the washstand there was a battered mahogany wardrobe and a portable television set with an old-fashioned loop aerial. I opened the window, hoping to let some air into the room, and then switched on the TV. The six o'clock news had just started. There was footage of a refugee encampment like those I had seen previously in Tangier and Sangatte. I was amazed to learn that the camp, a ragged shanty town of tents and standpipes and semi-feral children as skinny as rails, was situated on the outskirts of Milton Keynes. A delegation from the camp had delivered a petition to Downing Street, and the prime minister himself appeared on the steps to receive it.

The prime minister was black, a slimly-built, earnest-faced man named Ottmar Chingwe. I had never seen him before in my life.

I watched the broadcast through to the end. Some of the items covered—the famine in Russia, the blockade in the Gulf—were familiar or at least they seemed to be at first but other events, reported in the same matter-of-fact tone, were like passages from some elaborate fantasy. The newspaper I had bought was the same. I felt dazed not so much by the scale of the changes as by their subtlety. There were no miracle machines, no robots, no flying saucers; in many ways the world I had entered was the same as the world I had left. What I saw and felt and observed was a change not in substance but in *emphasis*.

Was it this that the Billings regime had learned of, and sought to reverse? Certainly Billings's world view—his 'Fortress Britain,' as he had proudly referred to it—was everywhere conspicuous by its absence. This new England seemed more like a gipsy encampment, a vast airport lounge of peoples, chaotic and noisy and continually on the move. There seemed to be no overall plan.

Yet commerce was active, the homeless were being fed. People of all shades of opinion were expressing those opinions robustly and at every opportunity.

It was like the London I remembered from when I was young.

I watched TV for about an hour then went down to the curry house opposite and ordered a meal. I ate it quickly, still feeling conspicuous, although none of the other diners paid me the slightest attention. Once I had finished I returned to the hotel. There was a pay telephone in the hallway. I inserted my card and dialled Dora's number. The phone rang and rang, and was eventually answered by a woman with an Eastern European accent so strong I could barely understand what she was saying. Silently I replaced the receiver.

After a moment's hesitation I lifted it again, this time dialling Owen Andrews's number, reading it off the slip of paper in my wallet. The phone clicked twice and then went dead. I climbed the stairs to my room and watched television into the small hours, trying to gather as many facts as I could about my new world. Eventually I turned out the light and went to sleep.

I had to keep reminding myself that this was not the future. That is, I had lost three months somewhere but that was all. The year was the same. The TV channels were more or less the same. The Shooter's Hill Road was still rife with carjackings, only now there was no talk of reinstating the death penalty. The increase in my finances I put down to some lucky quirk, an error in accounting, if you like, between one version of reality and another.

Once my initial nervousness had begun to wear off my biggest fear was meeting myself. It was the kind of nightmare you read about in H.G. Wells, but Owen Andrews had not mentioned it and in any case it did not happen. I began to wonder if each reality was like Schrodinger's theoretical box, its contents uncertain until it was actually opened. I thought that perhaps the very act of me entering this world somehow negated any previous existence I had had within it.

Such thoughts were unnerving yet fascinating, the kind of ideas I would have liked to discuss with Owen Andrews. But so far as I could determine Andrews did not exist here.

I returned to what I was good at, which was buying and selling. I was still nervous in those early days, afraid to expose myself through some stupid mistake, and so instead of applying for a job with an estate agent I decided to set up by myself selling watches and clocks. I enjoyed reading up on the subject and it wasn't long before I had a lucrative little business. I had learned long ago that even during the worst times there are still rich people, and what do the rich have to do but spend their money on expensive luxuries? I had never lost sleep over this; rather I made good use of it. I was amused to find that some of my clients were people I knew from before, men whose houses I had once sold for them, or their sons or daughters, or people who looked very like them. None of them recognised me.

The only thing I had left from my old life was the photograph of Miranda that I had always carried in my wallet. It was a snapshot taken of her on Brighton beach soon after we married. Her topaz eyes were lifted towards the camera, her heart-shaped face partially obscured by silvery corkscrewed wisps of her windblown hair. It was like an answered prayer, to have her with me. There were no traces of her death now, no evidence of what had happened. All that remained was my knowledge of my love for her and this last precious image of her face.

One evening in September I left a probate sale I had been attending in Camden and walked towards the tube station at St John's Wood. It was growing dusk, and I stopped for a moment to enjoy the view from the top of Primrose Hill. The sky in the west was a fierce red, what I took to be the afterglow of sunset, but later, at home, when I put on the radio I discovered there had been a fire. The report said that underground fuel stores at the old army hospital at Shooter's Hill had mysteriously ignited, causing them to explode. The resulting conflagration had been visible for twenty miles.

*The Royal Herbert was a listed building*, said the newscaster. *It was originally built for the Woolwich Garrison at the end of the eighteen eighties and was most recently in use as a long-stay care facility for victims of war trauma.*

The police suspected arson and had already sent in their teams of investigators. I wished them luck in their search. I supposed they would find something eventually, some loose circuitry or faulty shielding, but felt certain that unless they were experts in tracking a crime from one region of reality to another they would never find out the real truth of what had happened.

What I believed was that the resistance fighters Andrews told me about had finally found a way to destroy the hospital. The blast had been so strong it had ripped through the time stasis, wiping the building off the map in all versions of reality simultaneously.

Or in the neighbouring zones, at least. For a moment I had a vision of the great hotel lobby of time Andrews had spoken of. Alarm bells clamoured as a line of porters shepherded the guests out on to the front concourse and a fire crew worked to extinguish a minor blaze in one of the bedrooms. The fire was soon put out, the loss adjusters called in to assess the damage. By the end of the evening the guests were back in the bar and it was business as usual.

*Some old biddy's cigarette, apparently*, said one as he sipped at his scotch.

*We're lucky she didn't roast us in our beds*, his companion jabbered excitedly. *D'you fancy some peanuts?*

I supposed that my escape route, if there had ever been one, was now cut off for good. Perhaps this should have bothered me but it didn't. The more time passed, the more it was my old life that seemed unreal, a kind of nightmare aberration, a bad photocopy of reality rather than the master version. The world I now inhabited, for all its rough edges, felt more substantial.

I had no wish to return to the way things were. I uncorked a bottle of wine—the dreadful rough Burgundy that was all you could find in the shops at the time because of the flight embargo—and drank a silent toast to the unknown bombers. I thought of the soldiers in their rec room, their harmless card games and noisy camaraderie, and hoped they had been able to escape before the place went up.

It was not until some years later that I stumbled upon the picture of Owen Andrews. It was in a book someone had given me about the London watch trade, a reproduction of a nineteenth century daguerreotype that showed Andrews at his work bench. He was wearing a baggy white workman's blouse and had his loupe on a leather cord around his neck.

The caption named him as Mr Edwin Andrews, the 'miracle dwarf' who had successfully perfected a number of new advancements in the science of mechanics and with particular reference to the Breguet tourbillon.

It was him, without a shadow of a doubt. I studied the picture, wondering what Andrews had made of being called a miracle dwarf. I supposed he would have had a good laugh.

The text that went with the picture said that Andrews had held a position in the physical sciences department at Oxford University but that he had resigned the post as the result of a disagreement with his superiors. He had come to London soon afterwards, setting up his own workshop in Southwark.

Sometimes, on those light summer evenings when I had finished all my appointments and had nothing better to do, I would make my way to Paddington and eat a leisurely supper in one of the bars or cafes on the station concourse. I watched the great steam locomotives as they came and went from the platforms, arriving and departing for towns in the north and west. A train came in from Oxford every half hour.

I knew it was futile to wait but I waited anyway. Andrews had said we would meet again and I somehow believed him. I sipped my drink and scanned the faces in the crowd, hoping that one of them one day would be the face of my friend.

# CHOOSE YOUR OWN ADVENTURE

## KAT HOWARD

---

The most dangerous moment in any story is the beginning.

As the story opens, every ending is equally possible, every path unwalked, every question not only unanswered, but unasked.

The unread story is infinite possibility. Yet the ending is already written, and though you be clever, though you be brave, there is no outwitting it.

Are you brave enough to begin? If so, turn to page 1. If not, remain safe. Close the book and return it to the shelf. No one will think any less of you.

*Page 1:* You find yourself standing in a beautiful garden. It teems with all the birds of the air, and all of the creatures of the Earth, and every good thing that grows. As you explore, you feel an incredible sense of peace and rightness, as if the garden had been created just for you.

This is the place you belong. Still, you are restless and lonely. You begin to explore your surroundings. At the western edge of the garden, there is a gate. Do you walk through?

If yes, turn to page 37. If no, turn to page 19.

*Page 19:* You wish to see more of the garden before you leave its bounds. Soon, you are glad you have chosen as you did, for you find the perfect companion for all your days and nights. You come to believe you have found a new Eden, as well. It seems impossible for a place so perfect to be other than Paradise. When they are born, you name your children Kane and Abelle.

This will prove to be a mistake.

*Page 37:* Gates, like books, are meant to be opened, and you would never be truly content if you did not know what lay on the other side. You pass through the gate and enter into a dark forest. You hesitate for a moment, look back, but the forest stretches behind you as if the garden had never been.

You continue on.

Shadows deepen. An owl calls. Something cries out at a distance and is silenced. You grow chilled, and your feet develop a talent for finding uneven spots of ground, tree roots, and rocks. After the third time you fall, you lean against the very tree whose roots last tangled your feet.

The bark prickles and rubs against your back, but it is a welcome distraction from your bruised knees and skinned palms. Your bones are weary and your muscles ache.

You crave sleep. A brief rest to fortify yourself for your journey. Do you close your eyes?

If so, turn to page 3. If not, turn to page 25.

*Page 3:* You close your eyes, and drift into sleep. When you awaken, you are in your own bed. The previous events were a dream, which has already begun to fade.

You spend the rest of your life trying to return to the winding path in the dark forest. You never will.

*Page 25:* You scrub your hands across your eyes and push yourself back to your feet. The path takes you on a short, downhill curve, and winds around to the door of an inn. The Quill and Ink, reads the sign over the door. You smile, and enter.

Inside, there is warmth, the hearty scent of food, and a group of people singing songs both off-key and bawdy.

You slide seamlessly into the small community, and feel refreshed after you have shared a meal and stood a round of drinks.

Eventually, you notice the singing has died down, replaced by a rapt silence. There is a knot of people wound tight around the fire, telling stories. At first, you simply listen, but then you are asked to tell a tale of your own. It is the tale, not the coin, that will pay your shelter for the night.

Do you tell a story?

If yes, turn to page 47. If no, turn to page 62.

*Page 47:* You are warm and happy, and just drunk enough to think that telling a story is something you can do. You invoke the muse, and she speaks through you. When you finish, only the crackling of the fire breaks the silence. You watch as, next to you, a single tear trickles down a perfect cheek.

It is the last story you will ever tell.

*Page 62:* The only story you know is your own, you say, and you must continue on to know how it ends. You make your excuses, and stand one more round before you leave to ensure there will be no hurt feelings, and, more importantly, no knives in the back as you walk through the door.

The air is crisp, and you are refreshed. The moon limns the trees in silver, and makes clear your path. You hear music, so beautiful that at first you wonder if you are dreaming. The pound of the drums speeds the pulse of your heart and the skirl of the strings pulls you through the night.

By the time you reach the standing stones, you are very nearly dancing down the path. Inside the ring of stones, the dancers spin and leap, a bright chaos of form and shape, carried along by an exultation of song.

You want, as you cannot remember wanting anything, to cross into the stone circle and join the dance. Do you?

If yes, turn to page 56. If no, turn to page 72.

*Page 56:* As you step through the ring, every hair on your body stands as if electrified. Your feet begin to move in a complex pattern you were never taught, but now know in your blood.

You do not wish to ever stop dancing. It is unlikely you ever will.

*Page 72:* You linger, just for a while, held by the unaccustomed beauty of the music. You watch the faces of the dancers, and wonder if it is joy that holds their mouths wide, burns their eyes bright. You cannot tell.

You decide you would rather choose your own steps, and so you turn away. At first, your feet seem heavy, not quite your own, but as you continue to walk, your steps become easier.

You believe that you are lucky, that you have continued to escape fates you would rather not own, and so you do not concern yourself with the rain that has begun to fall.

But the soft trickle becomes a pelting, and you duck into a crevice in the hillside. The interior of the hill opens up before you like a dark cathedral. A staircase, worn into the rock by millennia of pilgrim feet, rings the edge of the space and spirals downward.

You walk down the stairs, and as you do, memories unweave inside your head. The best and worst moments of your life play out, with a clarity they did not have when you first experienced them.

But there is something else. Perhaps. A second set of footsteps on the stairs. A whisper, a bare rustle in the dark. Easy enough to dismiss, to pretend that you do not feel the weight of a presence in the darkness behind you.

The spiral of the staircase becomes tighter, inexorable. The following tread impossible to ignore. The steps come a half-beat after yours, a shadow's echo.

You pause, hoping whoever—and, oh, how you hope it is a *who*ever, here in the dark under the hill—will continue on past you, but the steps pause as well.

Surely, you think, if it had meant to hurt you, surely it would already have done that. Knowing would be better than imagining an expanding catalogue of horrors.

Do you turn to look back?

If yes, turn to page 89. If no, turn to page 114.

*Page 89:* You've been reading the alternate endings, haven't you? Of course I know. I know everything that happens in all of the stories I hold.

Did you think I wouldn't notice that you're cheating?

Do you not understand that stories have rules?

You feel a pulling, and then are buffeted by a whirlwind. You hear something tear, feel a page come loose from your bindings.

You find yourself back at the beginning, holding a book.

You open the cover. Once upon a time.

*Page 114:* You continue walking, three steps more. Then a hand slips into yours, and the story ends as all stories must: with the snip of a thread and the crossing of a river. You pay the ferryman with coins plucked from your own eyelids.

You pass beyond the realm of the page.

# A SMALL PRICE TO PAY
# FOR BIRDSONG

## K.J. PARKER

"My sixteenth concerto," he said, smiling at me. I could just about see him. "In the circumstances, I was thinking of calling it the Unfinished."

Well, of course. I'd never been in a condemned cell before. It was more or less what I'd imagined it would be like. There was a stone bench under the tiny window. Other than that, it was empty, as free of human artefacts as a stretch of open moorland. After all, what things does a man need if he's going to die in six hours?

I was having difficulty with the words. "You haven't—"

"No." He shook his head. "I'm two-thirds of the way through the third movement, so under normal circumstances I'd hope to get that done by—well, you know. But they won't let me have a candle, and I can't write in the dark." He breathed out slowly. He was savouring the taste of air, like an expert sampling a fine wine. "It'll all be in here, though" he went on, lightly tapping the side of his head. "So at least I'll know how it ends."

I really didn't want to ask, but time was running out. "You've got the main theme," I said.

"Oh yes, of course. It's on the leash, just waiting for me to turn it loose."

I could barely speak. "I could finish it for you," I said, soft and hoarse as a man propositioning his best friend's wife. "You could hum me the theme, and—"

He laughed. Not unkindly, not kindly either. "My dear old friend," I said, "I couldn't possibly let you do that. Well," he added, hardening his voice a little, "obviously I won't be in any position to stop you trying. But you'll have to make up your own theme."

"But if it's nearly finished—"

I could just about make out a slight shrug. "That's how it'll have to stay," he said. "No offence, my very good and dear old friend, but you simply aren't up to it. You haven't got the—" He paused to search for the word, then gave up. "Don't take this the wrong way," he said. "We've known each other—what, ten years? Can it really be that long?"

"You were fifteen when you came to the Studium."

"Ten years." He sighed. "And I couldn't have asked for a better teacher. But you—well, let's put it this way. Nobody knows more about form and technique than you do, but you haven't got *wings*. All you can do is run fast and flap your arms up and down. Which you do," he added pleasantly, "superlatively well."

"You don't want me to help you," I said.

"I've offended you." Not the first time he'd said that, not by a long way. And always, in the past, I'd forgiven him instantly. "And you've taken the trouble to come and see me, and I've insulted you. I'm really sorry. I guess this place has had a bad effect on me."

"Think about it," I said, and I was so ashamed of myself; like robbing a dying man. "Your last work. Possibly your greatest."

He laughed out loud. "You haven't read it yet," he said. "It could be absolute garbage for all you know."

It could have been, but I knew it wasn't. "Let me finish it for you," I said. "Please. Don't let it die with you. You owe it to the human race."

I'd said the wrong thing. "To be brutally frank with you," he said, in a light, slightly brittle voice, "I couldn't give a twopenny fuck about the human race. They're the ones who put me in here, and in six hours' time they're going to pull my neck like a chicken. Screw the lot of them."

My fault. I'd said the wrong thing, and as a result, the music inside his head would stay there, trapped in there, until the rope crushed his windpipe and his brain went cold. So, naturally, I blamed him. "Fine," I said. "If that's your attitude, I don't think there's anything left to say."

"Quite." He sighed. I think he wanted me to leave. "It's all a bit pointless now, isn't it? Here," he added, and I felt a sheaf of paper thrust against my chest. "You'd better take the manuscript. If it's left here, there's a fair chance the guards'll use it for arsewipe."

"Would it bother you if they did?"

He laughed. "I don't think it would, to be honest," he said. "But it's worth money," he went on, and I wish I could've seen his face. "Even incomplete," he added. "It's got to be worth a hundred angels to somebody, and I seem to recall I owe you a hundred and fifty, from the last time."

I felt my fingers close around the pages. I didn't want to take them, but I gripped so tight I could feel the paper crumple. I had in fact already opened negotiations with the Kapelmeister.

I stood up. "Goodbye," I said. "I'm sorry."

"Oh, don't go blaming yourself for anything." Absolution, so easy for him to give; like a duke scattering coins to the crowd from a balcony. Of course, the old duke used to have the coins heated in a brazier first. I still have little white scars on my fingertips. "I've always been the sole author of my own misfortunes. You always did your best for me."

And failed, of course. "Even so," I said, "I'm sorry. It's such a waste."

That made him laugh. "I wish," he said, "that music could've been the most important thing in my life, like it should've been. But it was only ever a way of getting a bit of money."

I couldn't reply to that. The truth, which I'd always known since I first met him, was that if he'd cared about music, he couldn't have written it so well. Now there's irony.

"You're going to finish it anyway."

I stopped, a pace or so short of the door. "Not if you don't want me to."

"I won't be here to stop you."

"I can't finish it," I said. "Not without the theme."

"Balls." He clicked his tongue, that irritating sound I'll always associate with him. "You'll have a stab at it, I know you will. And for the rest of time, everybody will be able to see the join."

"Goodbye," I said, without looking round.

"You could always pass it off as your own," he said.

I balled my fist and bashed on the door. All I wanted to do was get out of there as quickly as I could; because while I was in there with him, I hated him, because of what he'd just said. Because I'd deserved better of him than that, over the years. And because the thought had crossed my mind.

I waited till I got back to my rooms before I unfolded the sheaf of paper and looked at it.

At that point, I had been the professor of music at the Academy of the Invincible Sun for twenty-seven years. I was the youngest ever incumbent, and I fully intend to die in these rooms, though not for a very long time. I'd taught the very best. My own music was universally respected, and I got at least five major commissions every year for ducal and official occasions. I'd written six books on musical theory, all of which had become the standard works on the aspects of the subject they cover. Students came here from every part of the empire, thousands of miles in cramped ships and badly-sprung coaches, to hear me lecture on harmony and the use of form. The year before, they'd named one of the five modes after me.

When I'd read it, I looked at the fire, which the servant had lit while I was out. It would be so easy, I thought. Twenty sheets of paper don't take very long to burn. But, as I think I told you, I'd already broached the subject with the Kapelmeister, who'd offered me five hundred angels, sight unseen, even unfinished. I knew I could get him up to eight hundred. I have no illusions about myself.

I didn't try and finish the piece; not because I'd promised I wouldn't, but because he escaped. To this day, nobody has the faintest idea how he managed it. All we know is that when the captain of the guard opened his cell to take him to the scaffold, he found a warder sitting on the bench with his throat cut, and no sign of the prisoner.

There was an enquiry, needless to say. I had a very uncomfortable morning at guard headquarters, where I sat on a bench in a corridor for three hours before making the acquaintance of a Captain Monomachus of the Investigative branch. He pointed out to me that I was a known associate of the prisoner, and that I'd been the last person to be alone with him before his escape. I replied that I'd been thoroughly and quite humiliatingly searched before I went in to see him, and there was no way I could've taken him in any kind of weapon.

"We aren't looking for a weapon, as a matter of fact," captain Monomachus replied. "We reckon he smashed his inkwell and used a shard of the glass. What we're interested in is how he got clear of the barbican. We figure he must've had help."

I looked the captain straight in the eye. I could afford to. "He always had plenty of friends," I said.

For some reason, the captain smiled at that. "After you left him," he said, "where did you go?"

"Straight back to my rooms in college. The porter can vouch for me, presumably. And my servant. He brought me a light supper shortly after I got home."

Captain Monomachus prowled round me for a while after that, but since he had absolutely nothing against me, he had to let me go. As I was about to leave, he stopped me and said, "I understand there was a last piece."

I nodded. "That's right. That's what I was reading, the rest of the evening."

"Any good?"

"Oh yes." I paused, then added, "Possibly his best. Unfinished, of course."

There was a slight feather of shyness about the question that followed. "Will there be a performance?"

I told him the date and the venue. He wrote them down on a scrap of paper, which he folded and put in his pocket.

The good captain was, in fact, the least of my problems. That same evening, I was summoned to the Master's lodgings.

"Your protégé," the Master said, pouring me a very small glass of the college brandy.

"My student," I said. It's very good brandy, as a matter of fact, but invariably wasted, because the only times I get to drink it are when I'm summoned into the presence, on which occasions I'm always so paralysed with fear that even good brandy has no effect whatsoever.

He sighed, sniffed his glass and sat down; or rather, he perched on the edge of the settle. He always likes to be higher than his guests. Makes swooping to strike easier, I imagine. "An amazingly gifted man," he said. "You might go so far as to call him a genius, though that term is sadly overused these days, I find." I waited, and a moment and a sip of brandy later, he continued; "But a fundamentally unstable character. I suppose we ought to have seen the warning signs."

We meaning me; because the Master wasn't appointed until the year after my poor student was expelled. "You know," I said, trying to sound as though it was a conversation rather than an interrogation, "I sometimes wonder if in his case, the two are inseparable; the instability and the brilliance, I mean."

The Master nodded. "The same essential characteristics that made him a genius also made him a murderer," he said. "It's a viable hypothesis, to be sure. In which case, the question must surely arise; can the one ever justify the other? The most sublime music, set against a man's life." He shrugged, a gesture for which his broad, sloping shoulders were perfectly suited. "I shall have to bear that one in mind for my Ethics tutorials. You could argue it quite well both ways, of course. After all, his music will live for ever, and the man he killed was the most dreadful fellow, by all accounts, a petty thief and a drunkard." He paused, to give me time to agree. Even I knew better than that. Once it was clear I'd refused the bait, he said, "The important thing, I think, is to try and learn something from this tragic case."

"Indeed," I said, and nibbled at my brandy to give myself time. I've never fenced, but I believe that's what fencers do; make time by controlling distance. So I held up my brandy glass and hid behind it as best I could.

"Warning signs," he went on, "that's what we need to look out for. These young people come here, they're entrusted to our care at a particularly difficult stage in their development. Our duty doesn't end with stuffing their heads full of knowledge. We need to adopt a more comprehensive pastoral approach. Don't you agree?"

In the old duke's time, they used to punish traitors by shutting them up in a cage with a lion. As an exquisite refinement of malice, they used to feed the lion to bursting point first. That way, it wasn't hungry again for the best part of a day. I always found that very upsetting to think about. If I'm going to be torn apart, I want it to be over quickly. The Master and the old duke were students together, by the way. I believe they got on very well.

"Of course," I said. "No doubt the Senate will let us have some guidelines in due course."

I got out of there eventually, in one piece. Curiously enough, I didn't start shaking until I was halfway across the quadrangle, on my way back to my rooms. I couldn't tell you why encounters like that disturb me so much. After all, the worst the Master could do to me was dismiss me—which was bound to happen, sooner or later, because I only had qualified tenure, and I knew he thought of me as a closet Optimate. Which was, of course, entirely true. But so what? Unfortunately, the thought of losing my post utterly terrifies me. I know I'm too old to get another post anything like as good as this one, and such talent as I ever had has long since dissipated through overuse. I have doctorates and honorary doctorates in music enough to cover a wall, but I can't actually play a musical instrument. I have a little money put by these days, but not nearly enough. I have never experienced poverty, but in the city you see it every day. I don't have a particularly vivid imagination— anybody familiar with my music can attest to that—but I have no trouble at all imagining what it would be like to be homeless and hungry and cold in Perimadeia. I think about it all the time. Accordingly, the threat of my inevitable dismissal at some unascertained point in the future lies over my present like a cloud of volcanic ash, blotting out the sun, and I'm incapable of taking any pleasure in anything at all.

He will always be known by his name in religion, Subtilius of Bohec; but he was born Aimeric de Beguilhan, third son of a minor Northern squire, raised in the farmyard and the stables, destined for an uneventful career in the Ministry. When he came here, he had a place to read Logic, Literature and Rhetoric, and by his own account he'd never composed a bar of music in his life. In Bohec (I have no idea where it is), music consisted of tavern songs and painfully refined dances from the previous century; it featured in his life about as much as the sea, which is something like two hundred miles away in every direction. He first encountered real music in the Studium chapel, which is presumably why nearly all his early work was devotional and choral. When he transferred to the Faculty of Music, I introduced him to the secular instrumental tradition; I suppose that when I appear at last before the court of the Invincible Sun and whoever cross-examines me there asks me if there's one thing I've done which has made the world a better place, that'll be it. Without me, Subtilius would never have written for strings, or composed the five violin concertos, or the three polyphonic symphonies. But he'd already written the first of the Masses before I ever set eyes on him.

The murder was such a stupid business; though, looking back, I suppose it was more or less inevitable that something of the kind should have happened sooner or later. He always did have such a quick temper, fatally combined with a sharp tongue, an unfortunate manner and enough skill at arms to make him practically fearless. There was also the fondness for money—there was never quite enough money when he was growing up, and I know he was exceptionally sensitive about that—and the sort of amorality that often seems to go hand in hand with keen intelligence and an unsatisfactory upbringing. He was intelligent enough to see past the reasons generally advanced in support of obedience to the rules and the law, but lacking in any moral code of his own to take its place. Add to that youth, and overconfidence arising from the praise he'd become accustomed to as soon as he began to compose music, and you have a recipe for disaster.

Even now, I couldn't tell you much about the man he killed. Depending on which account you go by, he was either an accomplice or a rival. In any event, he was a small-time professional thief, a thoroughly worthless specimen who would most assuredly have ended up on the gallows if Subtilius hadn't stabbed him through the neck in the stable-yard of the *Integrity and Honour* in Foregate. Violent death is, I believe, no uncommon occurrence there, and he'd probably have got away with it had not one of the ostlers been a passionate admirer of his religious music, and therefore recognised him and been able to identify him to the Watch; an unfortunate consequence, I suppose, of the quite exceptionally broad appeal of Subtilius' music. If I'd stabbed a man in a stable-yard, the chances of a devoted fan recognising me would've been too tiny to quantify, unless the ostler happened to be a fellow academic fallen on hard times.

I got back to my rooms, fumbled with the keys, dropped them—anybody passing would have thought I was drunk, although of course I scarcely touched a drop in those days; I couldn't afford to, with the excise tax so high—finally managed to get the door open and fall into the room. It was dark, of course, and I spent quite some time groping for the tinder-box and the candle, and then I dropped the moss out of the box onto the floor and had to grope for that too. Eventually I struck a light, and used the candle to light the oil lamp. It was only then, as the light colonised the room, that I saw I wasn't alone.

"Hello, professor," said Subtilius.

My first thought—I was surprised at how quickly and practically I reacted—was the shutters. Mercifully, they were closed. In which case, he couldn't have come in through the window—

He laughed. "It's all right," he said, "nobody saw me. I was extremely careful."

Easy to say; easy to believe, but easy to be wrong. "How long have you been here?"

"I came in just after you left. You left the door unlocked."

Quite right; I'd forgotten.

"I took the precaution of locking it for you," he went on, "with the spare key you still keep in that ghastly pot on the mantelpiece. Look, why don't you sit down before you fall over? You look awful."

I went straight to the door and locked it. Not that I get many visitors, but I was in no mood to rely on the laws of probability. "What the hell are you doing here?"

He sighed, and stretched out his legs. I imagine it was what his father used to do, after a long day on the farm or following the hounds. "Hiding," he said. "What do you think?"

"You can't hide here."

"Overjoyed to see you too."

It was an entirely valid rebuke, so I ignored it. "Aimeric, you're being utterly unreasonable. You can't expect me to harbour a fugitive from justice—"

"Aimeric." He repeated the word as though it had some kind of incantatory power. "You know, professor, you're the only person who's called me that since the old man died. Can't say I ever liked the name, but it's odd to hear it again after all these years. Listen," he said, before I could get a word in, "I'm sorry if I scared the life out of you, but I need your help."

I always did find him both irresistibly charming and utterly infuriating. His voice, for one thing. I suppose it's my musician's ear; I can tell you more about a man, where he's from and how much money he's got, from hearing him say two words than any mere visual clues. Subtilius had a perfect voice; consonants clear and sharp as a knife, vowels fully distinguished and immaculately expressed. You can't learn to talk like that over the age of three. No matter how hard you try, if you start off with a provincial burr, like me, it'll always bleed through sooner or later. You can only achieve that bell-like clarity and those supremely beautiful dentals and labials if you start learning them before you can walk. That's where actors go wrong, of course. They can make themselves sound like noblemen after years of study so long as they stick to normal everyday conversational pitches. But if they try and shout, anyone with a trained ear can hear the northern whine or the southern bleat, obvious as a stain on a white sheet. Subtilius had a voice you'd have paid money to listen to, even if all he was doing was giving you directions to the Southgate, or swearing at a porter for letting the sludge get into the wine. That sort of perfection is, of course, profoundly annoying if you don't happen to be true-born aristocracy. My father was a fuller and soap-boiler in Ap'Escatoy. My first job was riding with him on the cart collecting the contents of chamber pots from the inns in the early hours of the morning. I've spent forty years trying to sound like a gentleman, and these days I can fool everybody except myself. Subtilius was born perfect and never had to try.

"Where the hell," I asked him, "have you been? The guard's been turning the city upside down. How did you get out of the barbican? All the gates were watched."

He laughed. "Simple," he said. "I didn't leave. Been here all the time, camping out in the clock tower."

Well, of course. The Studium, as I'm sure you know, is built into the west wall of the barbican. Naturally they searched it, the same day he escaped, after which they concluded that he must've got past the gate somehow and made it down to the lower town. It wouldn't have occurred to them to try the clock tower. Twenty years ago, an escaped prisoner hid up there, and when they found him, he was extremely dead. Nothing can survive in the bell-chamber when the clock strikes; the sheer pressure of sound would pulp your brain. Oh, I imagine a couple of guardsmen put their heads round inside the chamber when they knew it was safe, but they wouldn't have made a thorough search, because everybody knows the story. But in that case—

"Why aren't I dead?" He grinned at me. "Because the story's a load of old rubbish. I always had my doubts about it, so I took the trouble to look up the actual records. The prisoner who hid out up there died of blood poisoning from a scratch he'd got climbing out of a broken window. The thing about the bells killing him was pure mythology. You know how people like to believe that sort of thing." He gave me a delightful smile. "So they've been looking for me in Lower Town, have they? Bless them."

Curiosity, presumably; the true scholar's instinct, which he always had. But combined, I dare say, with the thought at the back of his mind that one day, a guaranteed safe hiding-place would come in useful. I wondered when he'd made his search in the archives; when he was fifteen, or seventeen, or twenty-one?

"I'm not saying it was exactly pleasant, mind," he went on, "not when the bells actually struck. The whole tower shakes, did you know that? It's a miracle it hasn't collapsed. But I found that if I crammed spiders' web into my ears—really squashed it down till no more would go in—it sort of deadened the noise to the point where it was bearable. And one thing there's no shortage of up there is cobwebs."

I've always been terrified of spiders. I'm sure he knew that.

"Fine," I snapped at him; I was embarrassed with myself, because my first reaction was admiration. "So you killed a man and managed to stay free for three weeks. How very impressive. What have you been living on, for God's sake? You should be thin as a rake."

He shrugged. "I didn't stay in there all the time," he said. "Generally speaking, I made my excursions around noon and midnight." When the bell tolls twelve times, there being a limit, presumably, to the defensive capacity of cobweb. "It's amazing how much perfectly good food gets thrown out in the kitchens. You're on the catering committee, you really ought to do something about it."

Part of his genius, I suppose; to make his desperate escape and three weeks' torment in the bell-tower sound like a student prank, just as he made writing the Seventh Mass seem effortless, something he churned out in an idle moment between hangovers. Perhaps the secret of sublime achievement really is not to try. But first, you have to check the archives, or learn the twelve major modulations of the Vesani mode, or be born into a family that can trace its pedigree back to Boamond.

"Well," I said, standing up, "I'm sorry, but you've had all that for nothing. I'm going to have to turn you in. You do realise that."

He just laughed at me. He knew me too well. He knew that if I'd really meant it, I'd have done it straight away, yelled for the guard at the top of my voice instead of panicking about the shutters. He knew it; I didn't, not until I heard him laugh. Until then, I thought I was deadly serious. But he was right, of course. "Sure," he said. "You go ahead."

I sat down again. I hated him so much, at that moment.

"How's the concerto coming along?" he asked.

For a moment, I had no idea what he was talking about. Then I remembered; his last concerto, or that's what it should have been. The manuscript he gave me in the condemned cell. "You said not to finish it," I told him.

"Good Lord." He was amused. "I assumed you'd have taken no notice. Well, I'm touched. Thank you."

"What are you doing here?" I asked him.

"I need money," he replied, and somehow his voice contrived to lose a proportion of its honeyed charm. "And clothes, and shoes, things like that. And someone to leave a door open at night. That sort of thing."

"I can't," I said.

He sighed. "You can, you know. What you mean is, you don't want to."

"I haven't got any money."

He gave me a sad look. "We're not talking about large sums," he said. "It's strictly a matter of context. Enough to get me out of town and on a ship, that's all. That's wealth beyond the dreams of avarice." He paused—I think it was for effect—and added, "I'm not asking for a *present*. I do have something to sell."

There was a moment when my entire covering of skin went cold. I could guess. What else would he have to sell, apart from—?

"Three weeks in the bloody bell tower," he went on, and now he sounded exactly like his old self. "Nothing to do all day. Fortunately, on my second trip to the trash cans I passed an open door, some first-year, presumably, who hasn't learned about keeping his door locked. He'd got ink, pens and half a ream of good paper. Don't suppose he'll make that mistake again."

I love music. It's been my life. Music has informed my development, given me more pleasure than I can possibly quantify or qualify; it's also taken me from the fullers' yard at Ap'Escatoy to the Studium, and kept me here, so far at least. Everything I am, everything I have, is because of music.

For which I am properly grateful. The unfortunate part of it is, there's never been quite enough. Not enough music in me; never enough money. The pleasure, emotional and intellectual, is one thing. The money, however, is another. Almost enough—I'm not a luxurious sort of person, I don't spend extravagantly, but most of it seems to go on overheads; college bills, servants' wages, contributions to this and that fund, taxes, of course, all that sort of nonsense—but never quite enough to let me feel comfortable. I live in a constant state of anxiety about money, and inevitably that anxiety has a bad effect on my relationship with music. And the harder I try, the less the inspiration flows. When I don't need it, when I'm relatively comfortable and the worry subsides for a while, a melody will come to me quite unexpectedly and I'll write something really quite good. But when I'm facing a deadline, or when the bills are due and my purse is empty; when I need money, the inspiration seems to dry up completely, and all I can do is grind a little paste off the salt-block of what I've learned, or try and dress up something old, my own or someone else's, and hope to God nobody notices. At times like that, I get angry with music. I even imagine—wrongly, of course—that I wish I was back in the fullers' yard. But that's long gone, of course. My brother and I sold it when my father died, and the money was spent years ago, so I don't even have that to fall back on. Just music.

"You've written something," I said.

"Oh yes." From inside his shirt he pulled a sheaf of paper. "A symphony, in three movements and a coda." I suppose I must have reached out instinctively, because he moved back gently. "Complete, you'll be relieved to hear. All yours, if you want it."

All my life I've tried to look civilised and refined, an intellect rather than a physical body. But when I want something and it's so close I can touch it, I sweat. My hands get clammy, and I can feel the drops lifting my hair where it touches my forehead. "A symphony," was all I could say.

He nodded. "My fourth. I think you're going to like it."

"All mine if I want it."

"Ah." He did the mock frown. "All yours if you pay for it. Your chance to be an illustrious patron of the arts, like the Eberharts."

I stared at him. All mine. "Don't be so bloody stupid," I yelled. "I can't use it. It'd be useless to me."

He pretended to be upset. "You haven't even looked at it."

"Think about it," I said, low and furious. "You're on the run from the Watch, with a death sentence against your name. I suddenly present a brand new Subtilius symphony. It'd be obvious. Any bloody fool would know straight away that I'd helped you escape."

He nodded. "I see your point," he said mildly. "But you could say it's an old piece, something I wrote years ago, and you've been hanging on to it."

"Is that likely?"

"I guess not." He smiled at me, a sunrise-over-the-bay smile, warm and bright and humiliating. "So I guess you'll just have to pretend you wrote it, won't you?"

It was like a slap across the face, insulting and unexpected. "Please," I said. "Don't even suggest it. You know perfectly well I could never pass off your work as my own. Everybody would know after the first couple of bars."

Then he smiled again, and I knew he was playing me. He'd led me carefully to a certain place where he wanted me to be. "That won't be a problem," he said. "You see, I've written it in your style."

Maybe shock and anger had made me more than usually stupid. It took a moment; and then I realised what he'd just said.

"Hence," he went on, "the symphonic form, which I've never really cared for, but it's sort of like your trademark, isn't it? And I've used the tetrachord of Mercury throughout, even quoted a bar or two of the secondary theme from your Third. Here," he said, and handed me a page—just the one, he was no fool—from the sheaf.

I didn't want to take it. I swear, it felt like deliberately taking hold of a nettle and squeezing it into your palm. I looked down.

I can read music very quickly and easily, as you'd expect. One glance and it's there in my head. It only took me a couple of heartbeats to know what I was holding. It was, of course, a masterpiece. It was utterly brilliant, magnificent, the sort of music that defines a place and a time for all time. It soared inside me as I looked at it, filling and choking me, as though someone had shoved a bladder down my throat and started blowing it up. It was in every way perfect; and *I could have written it.*

"Well?" he said.

Let me qualify that. No, I couldn't have written it, not in a million years, not if my life depended on it; not even if, in some moment of absolute peace and happiness, the best inspiration of my entire life had lodged inside my head, and the circumstances had been so perfectly arranged that I was able to take advantage of it straight away, while it was fresh and whole in my mind (which never ever happens, of course). I could never have written it; but it was in my style, so exactly captured that anybody but me would believe it was my work. It wasn't just the trademark flourishes and periods, the way I use the orchestra, the mathematical way I build through intervals and changes of key. A parody could've had all those. The music I was looking at had been written by someone who understood me perfectly—better than I've ever understood myself—and who knew exactly what I wanted to say, although I've always lacked the skill, and the power.

"Well," he said. "Do you like it?"

As stupid a question as I've ever heard in my life, and of course I didn't reply. I was too angry, heartbroken, ashamed.

"I was quite pleased with the cadenza," he went on. "I got the idea from that recurring motif in your Second, but I sort of turned it through ninety degrees and stuck a few feathers in it."

I've never been married, of course, but I can imagine what it must be like, to come home unexpectedly and find your wife in bed with another man. It'd be the love that'd fill you with hate. Oh, how I hated Subtilius at that moment. And imagine how you'd feel if you and your wife had never been able to have kids, and you found out she was pregnant by another man.

"It's got to be worth money," I heard him say. "Just the sort of thing the duke would like."

He always had that knack, did Subtilius. The ability to take the words out of the mouth of the worst part of me, the part I'd cheerfully cut out with a knife in cold blood if only I knew where in my body it's located. "Well?" he said.

When I was nineteen years old, my father and my elder brother and I were in the cart—I was back home for the holidays, helping out on the rounds—and we were driving out to the old barns where my father boiled the soap. The road runs along the top of a ridge, and when it rains, great chunks of it get washed away. It had been raining heavily the day before, and by the time we turned the sharp bend at the top it was nearly dark. I guess my father didn't see where the road had fallen away. The cart went over. I was sitting in the back and was thrown clear. Father and Segibert managed to scramble clear just as the cart went over; Segibert caught hold of Dad's ankle, and Dad grabbed onto a rock sticking out of the ground. I managed to get my hand round his wrist, and for a moment we were stuck there. I've never been strong, and I didn't have the strength to pull them up, not so much as an inch. All I could do was hold on,

and I knew that if I allowed myself to let his hand slip even the tiniest bit, I'd
lose him and both of them, the two people I loved most in the whole world,
would fall and die. But in that moment, when all the thoughts that were ever
possible were running through my head, I thought; if they do both fall, and
they're both killed, then when we sell the business, it'd be just me, best part of
three hundred angels, and what couldn't I do with that sort of money?

Then Segibert managed to get a footing, and between them they hauled
and scrambled and got up next to me on the road, and soon we were all in
floods of tears, and Dad was telling me I'd saved his life, and he'd never forget
it. And I felt so painfully guilty, as though I'd pushed them over deliberately.

Well, I thought. Yes. Worth a great deal of money.

"More the old duke's sort of thing," he was saying, "he'd have loved it, he
was a man of taste and discrimination. Compared with him, young Sighvat's
a barbarian. But even he'd like this, I'm sure."

A barbarian. The old duke used to punish debtors by giving them a head
start and then turning his wolfhounds loose. Last year, Sighvat abolished the
poll tax and brought in a minimum wage for farm workers. But the old duke
had a better ear for music, and he was an extremely generous patron. "I can't,"
I said.

"Of course you can," Subtilius said briskly. "Now then, I was thinking in
terms of three hundred. That'd cover my expenses."

"I haven't got that sort of money."

He looked at me. "No," he said, "I don't suppose you have. Well, what have
you got?"

"I can give you a hundred angels."

Which was true. Actually, I had a hundred and fifty angels in the wooden
box under my bed. It was the down payment I'd taken from the Kapelmeister
for the Unfinished Concerto, so properly speaking it was Subtilius' money
anyway. But I needed the fifty. I had bills to pay.

"That'll have to do, then," he said, quite cheerfully. "It'll cover the bribes
and pay for a fake passport, I'll just have to steal food and clothes. Can't be
helped. You're a good man, professor."

There was still time. I could throw the door open and yell for a porter. I
was still innocent of any crime, against the State or myself. Subtilius would
go back to the condemned cell, I could throw the manuscript on the fire, and
I could resume my life, my slow and inevitable uphill trudge towards poverty
and misery. Or I could call the porter and not burn the music. What exactly
would happen to me if I was caught assisting an offender? I couldn't bear
prison, I'd have to kill myself first; but would I get the chance? Bail would be
out of the question, so I'd be remanded pending trial. Highly unlikely that the

prison guards would leave knives, razors or poison lying about in my cell for me to use. People hang themselves in jail, they twist ropes out of bedding. But what if I made a mess of it and ended up paralysed for life? Even if I managed to stay out of prison, a criminal conviction would mean instant dismissal and no chance of another job. But that wouldn't matter, if I could keep the music. We are, the Invincible Sun be praised, a remarkably, almost obsessively cultured nation, and music is our life. No matter what its composer had done, work of that quality would always be worth a great deal of money, enough to retire on and never have to compose another note as long as I live—

I was a good man, apparently. He was grateful to me, for swindling him. I was a good man, because I was prepared to pass off a better man's work as my own. Because I was willing to help a murderer escape justice.

"Where will you go?" I asked.

He grinned at me. "You really don't want to know," he said. "Let's just say, a long way away."

"You're famous," I pointed out. "Everywhere. Soon as you write anything, they'll know it's you. They'll figure out it was me who helped you escape."

He yawned. He looked very tired; fair enough, after three weeks in a clock tower, with eight of the biggest bells in the empire striking the quarter hours inches from his head. He couldn't possibly have slept for more than ten minutes. "I'm giving up music," he said. "This is definitely and categorically my last ever composition. You're quite right; the moment I wrote anything, I'd give myself away. There's a few places the empire hasn't got extradition treaties with, but I'd rather be dead than live there. So it's simple, I won't write any more music. After all," he added, his hand over his mouth like he'd been taught as a boy, "there's lots of other things I can do. All music's ever done is land me in trouble."

What, when all is said and done, all the conventional garbage is put on one side and you're alone inside your head with yourself, do you actually believe in? That's a question that has occupied a remarkably small percentage of my attention over the years. Strange, since I spend a fair proportion of my working time composing odes, hymns and masses to the Invincible Sun. Do I believe in Him? To be honest, I'm not sure. I believe in the big white disc in the sky, because it's there for all to see. I believe that there's some kind of supreme authority, something along the lines of His Majesty the Emperor only bigger and even more remote, who theoretically controls the universe. What that actually involves, I'm afraid, I couldn't tell you. Presumably He regulates the affairs of great nations, enthrones and deposes emperors and kings—possibly princes and dukes, though it's rather more plausible that He delegates that sort of thing to some kind of divine solar civil service—and intervenes in high-profile cases of injustice and blasphemy whenever a precedent needs to be set or a point of law clarified. Does He deal with me personally, or is He even aware of my existence? On balance, probably not. He wouldn't have the time.

In which case, if I have a file at all, I assume it's on the desk of some junior clerk, along with hundreds, thousands, millions of others. I can't say that that thought bothers me too much. I'd far rather be left alone, in peace and quiet. As far as I'm aware, my prayers—mostly for money, occasionally for the life or recovery from illness of a relative or friend—have never been answered, so I'm guessing that divine authority works on more or less the same lines as its civilian equivalent; don't expect anything good from it, and you won't be disappointed. Just occasionally, though, something happens which can only be divine intervention, and then my world-view and understanding of the nature of things gets all shaken up and reshaped. I explain it away by saying that really it's something primarily happening to someone else—someone important, whose file is looked after by a senior administrative officer or above—and I just happen to be peripherally involved and therefore indirectly affected.

A good example is Subtilius' escape from the barbican. At the time it felt like my good luck. On mature reflection I can see that it was really his good luck, in which I was permitted to share, in the same way that the Imperial umbrella-holder also gets to stay dry when it rains.

It couldn't have been simpler. I went first, to open doors and make sure nobody was watching. He followed on, swathed in the ostentatious cassock and cowl of a Master Chorister—purple with ermine trimmings, richly embroidered with gold thread and seed pearls; anywhere else you'd stand out a mile, but in the barbican, choristers are so commonplace they're practically invisible. Luck intervened by making it rain, so that it was perfectly natural for my chorister companion to have his hood up, and to hold the folds tight around his face and neck. He had my hundred angels in his pockets in a pair of socks, to keep the coins from clinking.

The sally-port in the barbican wall, opening onto the winding stair that takes you down to Lower Town the short way, is locked at nightfall, but faculty officers like me all have keys. I opened the gate and stepped aside to let him pass.

"Get rid of the cassock as soon as you can," I said. "I'll report it stolen first thing in the morning, so they'll be looking for it."

He nodded. "Well," he said, "thanks for everything, professor. I'd just like to say—"

"Get the hell away from here," I said, "before anyone sees us."

There are few feelings in life quite as exhilarating as getting away with something. Mainly, I guess, if you're someone like me, it's because you never really expected to. Add to the natural relief, therefore, the unaccustomed pleasure of winning. Then, since you can't win anything without having beaten someone first, there's the delicious feeling of superiority, which I enjoy for the same reason that gourmets prize those small grey truffles that grow on the sides of dead birch trees; not because it's nourishing or tasty, but simply because it's so rare. Of course, it remained to be seen whether I had actually got away with aiding and abetting a murderer after the fact and assisting a fugitive. There was still a distinct chance that Subtilius would be picked up by the watch before he could get out of the city, in which case he might very well reveal the identity of his accomplice, if only to stop them hitting him. But, I told myself, that'd be all right. I'd simply tell them he'd burgled my rooms and stolen the money and the cassock, and they wouldn't be able to prove otherwise. I told myself that; I knew perfectly well, of course, that if they did question me, my nerve would probably shatter like an eggshell, and the only thing that might stop me from giving them a comprehensive confession was if I was so incoherent with terror I couldn't speak at all. I think you'd have to be quite extraordinarily brave to be a hardened criminal; much braver than soldiers who lead charges or stand their ground against the cavalry. I could just about imagine myself doing that sort of thing, out of fear of the sergeant-major, but doing something illegal literally paralyses me with fear. And yet courage, as essential to the criminal as his jemmy or his cosh, is held to be a virtue.

The first thing I did when I got back to my room was to light the lamp and open the shutters, because I never close them except when it snows, and people who knew me might wonder what was going on if they saw them shut. Then I poured myself a small brandy—it would've been a large one, but the bottle was nearly empty—and sat down with the lamp so close to me that I could feel it scorching my face, and spread out the manuscript, and read it.

They say that when we first sent out ships to trade with the savages in Rhoezen, we packed the holds full of the sort of things we thought primitive people would like—beads, cheap tin brooches, scarves, shirts, buckles plated so thin the silver practically wiped off on your fingers, that sort of thing. And mirrors. We thought they'd love mirrors. In fact, we planned on buying enough land to grow enough corn to feed the City with a case of hand-mirrors, one angel twenty a gross from the Scharnel Brothers.

We got that completely wrong. The captain of the first ship to make contact handed out a selection of his trade goods by way of free samples. Everything seemed to be going really well until they found the mirrors. They didn't like them. They threw them on the ground and stamped on them, then attacked our people with spears and slingshots, until the captain had to fire a cannon just so as to get his men back off the beach in one piece. Later, when he'd managed to capture a couple of specimens and he interrogated them through an interpreter, he found out what the problem was. The mirrors, the prisoners told him, were evil. They sucked your soul out through your eyes and imprisoned it under the surface of the dry-hard-water. Stealing the souls of harmless folk who'd only wanted to be friendly to strangers was not, in their opinion, civilised behaviour. Accordingly, we weren't welcome in their country.

When I first heard the story, I thought the savages had over-reacted somewhat. When I'd finished reading Subtilius' symphony, written in my style, I was forced to revise my views. Stealing a man's soul is one of the worst things you can do to him, and it hardly matters whether you shut it up in a mirror or thirty pages of manuscript. It's not something you can ever forgive.

And then, after I'd sat still and quiet for a while, until the oil in the lamp burned away and I was left entirely alone in the dark, I found myself thinking; yes, but nobody will ever know. All I had to do was sit down and copy it out in my own handwriting, then burn the original, and there would be no evidence, no witnesses. You hear a lot from the philosophers and the reverend Fathers about truth, about how it must inevitably prevail, how it will always burst through, like the saplings that grow up in the cracks in walls until their roots shatter the stone. It's not true. Subtilius wouldn't ever tell anybody (and besides, it was only a matter of time before he was caught and strung up, and that'd be him silenced for ever). I sure as hell wasn't going to say anything. If there's a truth and nobody knows it, is it still true? Or is it like a light burning in a locked, shuttered house that nobody will ever get to see?

I'd know it, of course. I did consider that. But then I thought about the money.

The debut of my Twelfth Symphony took place at the collegiate temple on Ascension Day, AUC 775, in the presence of his highness Duke Sighvat II, the duchess and dowager duchess, the Archimandrite of the Studium and a distinguished audience drawn from the Court, the university and the best of good society. It was, I have to say, a triumph. The duke was so impressed that he ordered a command performance at the palace. Less prestigious but considerably more lucrative was the licence I agreed to with the Kapelmeister;

a dozen performances at the Empire Hall at a thousand angels a time, with the rights reverting to me thereafter. Subsequently I made similar deals with kapelmeisters and court musicians and directors of music from all over the empire, taking care to reserve the sheet music rights, which I sold to the Court stationers for five thousand down and a five per cent royalty. My tenure at the University was upgraded to a full Fellowship, which meant I could only be got rid of by a bill of attainder passed by both houses of the Legislature and ratified by the duke, and then only on grounds of corruption or gross moral turpitude; my stipend went up from three hundred to a thousand a year, guaranteed for life, with bonuses should I ever condescend to do any actual teaching. Six months after the first performance, as I sat in my rooms flicking jettons about on my counting-board, I realised that I need never work again. Quite suddenly, all my troubles were over.

On that, and what followed, I base my contention that there is no justice; that the Invincible Sun, if He's anything more than a ball of fire in the sky, has no interest and does not interfere in the life and fortunes of ordinary mortals, and that morality is simply a confidence trick practised on all of us by the State and its officers to keep us from making nuisances of ourselves. For a lifetime of devotion to music, I got anxiety, misery and uncertainty. For two crimes, one against the State and one against myself, I was rewarded with everything I'd ever wanted. Explain that, if you can.

Everything? Oh yes. To begin with, I dreaded the commissions that started to flood in from the duke, other dukes and princes, even the Imperial court; because I knew I was a fraud, that I'd never be able to write anything remotely as good as the Symphony, and it was only a matter of time before someone figured out what had actually happened and soldiers arrived at my door to arrest me. But I sat down, with a lamp and a thick mat of paper; and it occurred to me that, now I didn't need the money, all I had to do was refuse the commissions—politely, of course—and nobody could touch me. I didn't have to write a single note if I didn't want to. It was entirely up to me.

Once I'd realised that, I started to write. And, knowing that it really didn't matter, I hardly bothered to try. The less I tried, the easier it was to find a melody (getting a melody out of me was always like pulling teeth). Once I'd got that, I simply let it rattle about in my head for a while, and wrote down the result. Once I'd filled the necessary number of pages, I signed my name at the top and sent it off. I didn't care, you see. If they didn't like it, they knew what they could do.

From time to time, to begin with at least, it did occur to me to wonder, *is this stuff any good?* But that raises the question; how the hell does anybody ever know? If the criterion is the reaction of the audience, or the sums of money offered for the next commission, I just kept getting better. That was, of course, absurd. Even I could see that. But no; my audiences and my critics insisted that each new work was better than its predecessors (though the Twelfth Symphony was the piece that stayed in the repertoires, and the later masterpieces sort of came and went; not that I gave a damn). A cynic would argue that once I'd become a great success, nobody dared to criticise my work for fear of looking a fool; the only permitted reaction was ever increasing adulation. Being a cynic myself, I favoured that view for a while. But, as the success continued and the money flowed and more and more music somehow got written, I began to have my doubts. All those thousands of people, I thought, they can't all be self-deluded. There comes a point when you build up a critical mass, beyond which people sincerely believe. That's how religions are born, and how criteria change. By my success, I'd redefined what constitutes beautiful music. If it sounded like the sort of stuff I wrote, people were prepared to believe it was beautiful. After all, beauty is only a perception—the thickness of an eyebrow, very slight differences in the ratio between length and width of a nose or a portico or a colonnade. Tastes evolve. People like what they're given.

Besides, I came to realise, the Twelfth *was* mine; to some extent at least. After all, the style Subtilius had borrowed was my style, which I'd spent a lifetime building. And if he had the raw skill, the wings, I'd been his teacher; without me, who was to say he'd ever have risen above choral and devotional works and embraced the orchestra? At the very least it was a collaboration, in which I could plausibly claim to be the senior partner. And if the doors are locked and the shutters are closed, whose business is it whether there's a light burning inside? You'd never be able to find out without breaking and entering, which is a criminal offence.

Even so, I began making discreet enquiries. I could afford the best, and I spared no expense. I hired correspondents in all the major cities and towns of the empire to report back to me about notable new compositions and aspiring composers—I tried to pay for this myself, but the university decided that it constituted legitimate academic research and insisted on footing the bill. Whenever I got a report that hinted at the possibility of Subtilius, I sent off students to obtain a written score or sit in the concert hall and transcribe the notes. I hired other, less reputable agents to go through the criminal activity reports, scrape up acquaintance with watch captains, and waste time in the wrong sort of inns, fencing-schools, bear gardens and livery stables. I was having to tread a fine line, of course. The last thing I wanted was for the watch to reopen their file or remember the name Subtilius, or Aimeric de Beguilhan, so I couldn't have descriptions or likenesses circulated. I didn't regard that as too much of a handicap, however. Sooner or later, I firmly believed, if he was still alive, the music would break out and he'd give himself away. It wouldn't be the creative urge that did for him; it'd be that handmaiden of the queen of the Muses, a desperate and urgent need for money, that got Subtilius composing again. No doubt he'd do his best to disguise himself. He'd try writing street ballads, or pantomime ballets, secure in the belief that that sort of thing was beneath the attention of academic musicians. But it could only be a matter of time. I knew his work, after all, in ways nobody else ever possibly could. I could spot his hand in a sequence of intervals, a modulation or key shift, the ghost of a flourish, the echo of a dissonance. As soon as he put pen to paper, I felt sure, I'd have him.

I was invited to lecture at the University of Baudoin. I didn't want to go—I've always hated travelling—but the marquis was one of my most enthusiastic patrons, and they were offering a thousand angels for an afternoon's work. Oddly enough, affluence hadn't diminished my eagerness to earn money. I guess that no matter how much I had, I couldn't resist the opportunity to add just a bit more, to be on the safe side. I wrote back accepting the invitation.

When I got there (two days in a coach; misery) I found they'd arranged a grand recital of my work for the day after the lecture. I couldn't very well turn round and tell them I was too busy to attend; also, the Baudoin orchestra was at that time reckoned to be the second or third best in the world, and I couldn't help being curious about how my music would sound, played by a really first-class band. Our orchestra in Perimadeia rates very highly on technical skill, but they have an unerring ability to iron the joy out of pretty well anything. I fixed up about the rights with the kapelmeister, thereby doubling my takings for the trip, and told them I'd be honoured and delighted to attend.

The lecture went well. They'd put me in the chapter-house of the Ascendency Temple—not the world's best acoustic, but the really rather fine stained-glass windows are so artfully placed that if you lecture around noon, as I did, and you stand on the lectern facing the audience, you're bathed all over in the most wonderful red and gold light, so that it looks like you're on fire. I gave them two hours on diatonic and chromatic semitones in the Mezentine diapason (it's something I feel quite passionate about, but they know me too well in Perimadeia and stopped listening years ago) and I can honestly say I had them in the palm of my hand. Afterwards, the marquis got up and thanked me—as soon as he joined me on the podium, the sun must've come out from behind a cloud or something, because the light through the windows suddenly changed from red to blue, and instead of burning, we were drowning—and then the provost of the university presented me with an honorary doctorate, which was nice of him, and made a long speech about integrity in the creative arts. The audience got a bit restive, but I was getting paid for being there, so I didn't mind a bit.

There was a reception afterwards; good food and plenty of wine. I must confess I don't remember much about it.

I enjoyed the recital, in spite of a nagging headache I'd woken up with and couldn't shift all day. Naturally, they played the Twelfth; that was the whole of the first half. I wasn't sure I liked the way they took the slow movement, but the finale was superb, it really did sprout wings and soar. The second half was better still. They played two of my Vesani horn concertos and a couple of temple processionals, and there were times when I found myself sitting bolt upright in my seat, asking myself, *did I really write that?* It just goes to show what a difference it makes, hearing your stuff played by a thoroughly competent, sympathetic orchestra. At one point I was so caught up in the music that I couldn't remember what came next, and the denouement—the solo clarinet in the *Phainomai*—took me completely by surprise and made my throat tighten. I thought, *I wrote that*, and I made a mental note of that split second, like pressing a flower between the pages of a book, for later.

It was only when the recital was over, and the conductor was taking his bow, that I saw him. At first, I really wasn't sure. It was just a glimpse of a turned-away head, and when I looked again I'd lost him in the sea of faces. I told myself I was imagining things, and then I saw him again. He was looking straight at me.

There was supposed to be another reception, but I told them I was feeling ill, which wasn't exactly a lie. I went back to the guest suite. There wasn't a lock or a bolt on the door, so I wedged the back of a chair under the handle.

While I'd been at the recital, they'd delivered a whole load of presents. People give me things these days, now that I can afford to buy anything I want. True, the gifts I tend to receive are generally things I'd never buy for myself, because I have absolutely no need for them, and because I do have a certain degree of taste. On this occasion, the marquis had sent me a solid gold dinner service (for a man who, most evenings, eats alone in his rooms off a tray on his knees), a complete set of the works of Aurelianus, ornately bound in gilded calf and too heavy to lift, and a full set of Court ceremonial dress. The latter item consisted of a bright red frock coat, white silk knee breeches, white silk stockings, shiny black shoes with jewelled buckles, and a dress sword.

I know everything I want to know about weapons, which is nothing at all. When I first came to the university, my best friend challenged another friend of ours to a duel. It was about some barmaid. Duelling was the height of fashion back then, and I was deeply hurt not to be chosen as a second (later, I found out it was because they'd chosen a time they knew would clash with my

Theory tutorial, and they didn't want me to have to skip it). They fought with smallswords in the long meadow behind the School of Logic. My best friend died instantly; his opponent lingered for a day or so and died screaming, from blood poisoning. If that was violence, I thought, you can have it.

So, I know nothing about swords, except that gentlemen are allowed to wear them in the street; from which I assumed that a gentleman's dress sword must be some kind of pretty toy. In spite of which, I picked up the marquis' present, put on my reading glasses and examined it under the lamp.

It was pretty enough, to be sure, if you like that sort of thing. The handle—I don't know the technical terms—was silver, gilded in places, with a pastoral scene enamelled on the inside of the plate thing that's presumably designed to protect your hand. The blade, though, was in another key altogether. It's always hidden by the scabbard, isn't it, so I figured it'd just be a flat, blunt rod. Not so. It was about three feet long, tapering, triangular in section, so thin at the end it was practically a wire but both remarkably flexible and surprisingly stiff at the same time, and pointed like a needle, brand new from the paper packet. I rested the tip on a cushion and pressed gently. It went through it and out the other side as though the cloth wasn't there.

I imagined myself explaining to the watch, no, the palace guard, they wouldn't have the ordinary watch investigate a death in the palace. You know he was a wanted criminal? Quite so, a convicted murderer. He killed a man, then killed a guard escaping from prison. He was my student, years ago, before he went to the bad. I don't know how he got in here, but he wanted money. When I refused, he said he'd have to kill me. There was a struggle. I can't actually remember how the sword came to be in my hand, I suppose I must've grabbed it at some point. All I can remember is him lying there, dead. And then the guard captain would look at me, serious but reassuring, and tell me that it sounded like a straightforward case of self-defence, and by the sound of it, the dead man was no great loss anyhow. I could imagine him being more concerned about the breach of security—a desperate intruder getting into the guest wing—than the possibility that the honorary doctor of music, favorite composer of the marquis, had deliberately murdered somebody.

The thought crossed my mind. After all, nobody would ever know. Once again, there'd be no witnesses. Who could be bothered to break into a locked house on the offchance that there might be a candle burning behind the closed shutters?

I waited, with the sword across my knees, all night. He didn't come.

Instead, he caught up with me at an inn in the mountains on my way home; a much more sensible course of action, and what I should have expected.

I was fast asleep, and something woke me. I opened my eyes to find the lamp lit, and Subtilius sitting in a chair beside the bed, looking at me. He gave the impression that I'd been dangerously ill, and he'd refused to leave my bedside.

"Hello, professor," he said.

The sword was in my trunk, leaning up against the wall on the opposite side of the room. "Hello, Aimeric," I said. "You shouldn't be here."

He grinned. "I shouldn't be anywhere," he said. "But what the hell."

I couldn't see a weapon; no knife or sword. "You're looking well," I said, which was true. He'd filled out since I saw him last. He'd been a skinny, sharp-faced boy, always making me think of an opened knife carried in a pocket. Now he was broad-shouldered and full-faced, and his hair was just starting to get thin on top. He had an outdoor tan, and his fingernails were dirty.

"You've put on weight," he said. "Success agrees with you, obviously."

"It's good to see you again."

"No it's not," he said, still grinning. "Well, not for you, anyway. But I thought I'd drop in and say hello. I wanted to tell you how much I enjoyed the recital."

I thought about what that meant. "Of course," I said. "You'll never have heard it played."

He looked as though he didn't understand, for a moment. Then he laughed, "Oh, you mean the symphony," he said. "Not a bit of it. They play it all the time here." He widened the grin. He'd lost a front tooth since I saw him last. "You want to get on to that," he said. "Clearly, you're missing out on royalties."

"About the money," I said, but he gave me a reproachful little frown, as though I'd made a distasteful remark in the presence of ladies. "Forget about that," he said. "Besides, I don't need money these days. I've done quite well for myself, in a modest sort of a way."

"Music?" I had to ask.

"Good Lord, no. I haven't written a note since I saw you last. Might as well have posters made up and nail them to the temple doors. No, I'm in the olive business. I won a beat-up old press in a chess game shortly after I got here, and now I've got seven mills running full-time in the season, and I've just bought forty acres of mature trees in the Santespe valley. If everything goes to plan, in five years' time every jar of olive oil bought and sold in this country will have made me sixpence. It's a wonderful place, this, you can do anything you like. Makes Perimadeia look like a morgue. And the good thing is," he went on, leaning back a little in his chair, "I'm a foreigner, I talk funny. Which means nobody can pinpoint me exactly, the moment I open my mouth, like they can at home. I can be whoever the hell I want. It's fantastic."

I frowned. He'd forced the question on me. "And who do you want to be, Aimeric?"

"Who I am now," he replied vehemently, "absolutely no doubt about it. I won't tell you my new name, of course, you don't want to know that. But here I am, doing nobody any harm, creating prosperity and employment for hundreds of honest citizens, and enjoying myself tremendously, for the first time in my life."

"Music?" I asked.

"Screw music." He beamed at me. "I hardly ever think about it any more. It's a little thing called a sense of perspective. It was only when I got here and my life started coming back together that I realised the truth. Music only ever made me miserable. You know what? I haven't been in a fight since I got here. I hardly drink, I've given up the gambling. Oh yes, and I'm engaged to be married to a very nice respectable girl whose father owns a major haulage business. And that's all thanks to olive oil. All music ever got me was a rope around my neck."

I looked at him. "Fine," I said. "I believe you. And I'm really pleased things have worked out so well for you. So what are you doing here, in my room in the middle of the night?"

The smile didn't fade, but it froze. "Ah well," he said, "listening to music's a different matter, I still enjoy that. I came to tell you how much I enjoyed the recital. That's all."

"You mean the symphony."

He shook his head. "No," he said, "the rest of the program. Your own unaided work. At least," he added, with a slight twitch of an eyebrow, "I assume it is. Or have you enlisted another collaborator?"

I frowned at him. I hadn't deserved that.

"In that case," he said, "I really must congratulate you. You've grown." He paused, and looked me in the eye. "You've grown wings." Suddenly the grin was back, mocking, patronising. "Or hadn't you noticed? You used to write the most awful rubbish."

"Yes," I said.

"But not any more." He stood up, and for a split second I was terrified. But he walked to the table and poured a glass of wine. "I don't know what's got into you, but the difference is extraordinary." He pointed to the second glass. I nodded, and he poured. "You write like you're not afraid of the music any more. In fact, it sounds like you're not afraid of anything. That's the secret, you know."

"I was always terrified of failure."

"Not unreasonably," he said, and brought the glasses over. I took mine and set it down beside the bed. "Good stuff, this."

"I can afford the best."

He nodded. "Do you like it?"

"Not much."

That made him smile. He topped up his glass. "My father had excellent taste in wine," he said. "If it wasn't at least twenty years old and bottled within sight of Mount Bezar, it was only fit for pickling onions. He drank the farm and the timber lot and six blocks of good City property which brought in more than all the rest put together, and then he died and left my older brother to sort out the mess. Last I heard, he was a little old man in a straw hat working all the hours God made, and still the bank foreclosed; he's three years older than me, for crying out loud. And my other brother had to join the army. He died at Settingen. Everlasting glory they called it in temple, but I know for a fact he was terrified of soldiering. He tried to hide in the barn when the carriage came to take him to the academy, and my mother dragged him out by his hair. Which has led me to the view that sometimes, refinement and gracious living come at too high a price." He looked at me over the rim of the glass and smiled. "But I don't suppose you'd agree."

I shrugged. "I'm still living in the same rooms in college," I replied. "And five days a week, dinner is still bread and cheese on a tray in front of the fire. It wasn't greed for all the luxuries. It was being afraid of the other thing." My turn to smile. "Never make the mistake of attributing to greed that which can be explained by fear. I should know. I've lived with fear every day of my life."

He sighed. "You're not drinking," he said.

"I think I've got the start of an ulcer," I said.

He shook his head sadly. "I really am genuinely pleased," he said. "About your music. You know what? I always used to despise you; all that knowledge, all that skill and technique, and no wings. You couldn't soar, so you spent your life trying to invent a flying machine. I learned to fly by jumping off cliffs." He yawned, and scratched the back of his neck. "Of course, most people who try it that way end up splattered all over the place, but it worked just fine for me."

"I didn't jump," I said. "I was pushed."

A big, wide grin spread slowly over his face, like oil on water. "And now you want to tell me how grateful you are."

"Not really, no."

"Oh come on." He wasn't the least bit angry, just amused. Probably just as well the sword was in the trunk. "What the hell did I ever do to you? Look at what I've given you, over the years. The prestige and reflected glory of being my teacher. The symphony. And now you can write music almost as good, all on your own. And what did I get in return? A hundred angels."

"Two hundred," I said coldly. "You've forgotten the previous loan."

He laughed, and dug a hand in his pocket. "Actually, no," he said. "The other reason I'm here." He took out a fat, fist-sized purse and put it on the table. "A hundred and ten angels. I'm guessing at the interest, since we didn't agree a specific rate at the time."

Neither of us said a word for quite some time. Then I stood up, leaned across the table and took the purse.

"Aren't you going to count it?"

"You're a gentleman," I said. "I trust you."

He nodded, like a fencer admitting a good hit. "I think," he said, "that makes us all square, don't you? Unless there's anything else I've forgotten about."

"All square," I said. "Except for one thing."

That took him by surprise. "What?"

"You shouldn't have given up music," I said.

"Don't be ridiculous," he snapped at me. "I'd have been arrested and hung."

I shrugged. "Small price to pay," I said. Which is what he'd said, when he first told me he'd killed a man; a small price to pay for genius. And what I'd said, when I heard all the details. "Don't glower at me like that," I went on. "You were a genius. You wrote music that'll still be played when Perimadeia's just a grassy hill. The Grand Mass, the Third symphony, that's probably all that'll survive of the empire in a thousand years. What was the life of one layabout and one prison warder, against that? Nothing."

"I'd have agreed with you once," he replied. "Now, I'm not so sure."

"Oh, I am. Absolutely certain of it. And if it was worth their lives, it's worth the life of an olive oil merchant, if there was to be just one more concerto. As it is—" I shrugged. "Not up to me, of course, I was just your teacher. That's all I'll ever be, in a thousand years' time. I guess I should count myself lucky for that."

He looked at me for a long time. "Bullshit," he said. "You and I only ever wrote for money. And you don't mean a word of what you've just said." He stood up. "It was nice to see you again. Keep writing. At this rate, one of these days you'll produce something worth listening to."

He left, and I bolted the door; too late by then, of course. That's me all over, of course; I always leave things too late, until they no longer matter.

When I got back to the university, I paid a visit to a colleague of mine in the natural philosophy department. I took with me a little bottle, into which I'd poured the contents of a wineglass. A few days later he called on me and said, "You were right."

I nodded. "I thought so."

"Archer's root," he said. "Enough of it to kill a dozen men. Where in God's name did you come by it?"

"Long story," I told him. "Thank you. Please don't mention it to anybody, there's a good fellow."

He shrugged, and gave me back the bottle. I took it outside and poured it away in a flower bed. Later that day I made a donation—one hundred and ten angels—to the Poor Brothers, for their orphanage in Lower Town; the first, last and only charitable donation of my life. The Father recognised me, of course, and asked if I wanted it to be anonymous.

"Not likely," I said. "I want my name up on a wall somewhere, where people can see it. Otherwise, where's the point?"

I think I may have mentioned my elder brother, Segibert; the one I rescued from the cart on the mountainside, along with my father. I remember him with fondness, though I realised at a comparatively early age that he was a stupid man, bone idle and a coward. My father knew it too, and my mother, so when Segibert was nineteen he left home. Nobody was sorry to see him go. He made a sort of a living doing the best he could, and even his best was never much good. When he was thirty-five he drifted into Perimadeia, married a retired prostitute (her retirement didn't last very long, apparently) and made a valiant attempt at running a tavern, which lasted for a really quite creditable eight months. By the time the bailiffs went in, his wife was pregnant, the money was long gone, and Segibert could best be described as a series of brief intervals between drinks. I'd just been elected to my chair, the youngest ever professor of music; the last thing I wanted was any contact whatsoever with my disastrous brother. In the end I gave him thirty angels, all the money I had, on condition that he went away and I never saw him again. He fulfilled his end of the deal by dying a few months later. By then, however, he'd acquired a son as well as a widow. She had her vocation to fall back on, which was doubtless a great comfort to her. When he came of age, or somewhat before, my nephew followed his father's old profession. I got a scribbled note from him when he was nineteen, asking me for bail money, which I neglected to answer, and that was all the contact there was between us. I never met him. He died young.

My second visit to a condemned cell. Essentially the same as the first one; walls, ceiling, floor, a tiny barred window, a stone ledge for sitting and sleeping. A steel door with a small sliding hatch in the top.

"I didn't think there was an extradition treaty between us and Baudoin," I said.

He lifted his head out of his hands. "There isn't," he said. "So they snatched me off the street, shoved me into a closed carriage and drove me across the border. Three days before my wedding," he added. "Syrisca will be half dead with worry about me."

"Surely that was illegal."

He nodded. "Yes," he said. "I believe there's been a brisk exchange of notes between the embassies, and the marquis has lodged an official complaint. Strangely enough, I'm still here."

I looked at him. It was dark in the cell, so I couldn't see much. "You've got a beard," I said. "That's new."

"Syrisca thought I'd look good in a beard."

I held back, postponing the moment. "I suppose you feel hard done by," I said.

"Yes, actually." He swung his legs up onto the ledge and crouched, hugging his knees to his chin. "Fair enough, I did some stupid things when I was a kid. But I did some pretty good things too. And then I gave both of them up, settled down and turned into a regular citizen. It's been a long time. I really thought I was free and clear."

Surreptitiously I looked round the cell. What I was looking for didn't seem to be there, but it was pretty dark. "How did they find you?" I asked.

He shrugged. "No idea," he said. "I can only assume someone from the old days must've recognised me, but I can't imagine who it could've been. I gave up music," he added bitterly. "Surely that ought to have counted for something."

He'd taken care not to tell me his new name, that night in the inn, but a rising young star in the Baudoin olive oil trade wasn't hard to find. Maybe he shouldn't have given me that much information. But he hadn't expected me to live long enough to make use of it.

"You tried to poison me," I said.

He looked at me, and his eyes were like glass. "Yes," he said. "Sorry about that. I'm glad you survived, if that means anything to you."

"Why?"

"Why did I do it?" He gave me a bemused look. "Surely that's obvious. You recognised me. I knew you'd realised who I was, as soon as our eyes met at the recital. That was really stupid of me," he went on, looking away. "I should've guessed you'd never have turned me in."

"So it was nearly three murders," I said. "That tends to undercut your assertion that you've turned over a new leaf."

"Yes," he said. "And my theory that it was somehow connected to writing music, since I'd given up by the time I tried to kill you. I really am sorry about that, by the way."

I gave him a weak smile. "I forgive you," I said.

"Thanks."

"Also," I went on, "I've been to see the duke. He's a great admirer of my work, you know."

"Is that right?"

"Oh yes. And to think you once called him a savage."

"He's not the man his father was," he replied. "I think the old duke might have pardoned me. You know, for services to music."

"Sighvat didn't put it quite like that," I replied. "It was more as a personal favour to me."

There was quite a long silence; just like—I'm sorry, but I really can't resist the comparison—a rest at a crucial moment in a piece of music. "He's letting me go?"

"Not quite," I said, as gently as I could. "He reckons he's got to consider the feelings of the victim's family. Fifteen years. With luck and good behaviour, you'll be out in ten."

He took it in two distinct stages; first the shudder, the understandable horror at the thought of an impossibly long time in hell; then, slowly but successfully pulling himself out of despair, as he considered the alternative. "I can live with that," he said.

"I'm afraid you'll have to," I replied. "I'm sorry. It was the best I could do."

He shook his head. "I'm the one who should apologise," he said. "I tried to kill you, and you just saved my life." He looked up, and even in the dim light I could see an expression on his face I don't think I'd ever seen before. "You always were better than me," he said. "I didn't deserve that."

I shrugged. "We're quits, then," I said. "For the symphony. But there's one condition."

He made a vague sort of gesture to signify capitulation. "Whatever," he said.

"You've got to start writing music again."

For a moment, I think he was too bewildered to speak. Then he burst out laughing. "That's ridiculous," he said. "It's been so long, I haven't even thought about it."

"It'll come back to you, I bet. Not my condition, by the way," I added, lying. "The duke's. So unless you want a short walk and an even shorter drop, I suggest you look to it. Did you get the paper I had sent up, by the way?"

"Oh, that was you, was it?" He looked at me a bit sideways. "Yes, thanks. I wiped my arse with it."

"In future, use your left hand, it's what it's for. It's a serious condition, Aimeric. It's Sighvat's idea of making restitution. I think it's a good one."

There was another moment of silence. "Did you tell him?"

"Tell him what?"

"That I wrote the symphony. Was that what decided him?"

"I didn't, actually," I said. "But the thought had crossed my mind. Luckily, I didn't have to."

He nodded. "That's all right, then." He sighed, as though he was glad some long and tedious chore was over. "I guess it's like the people who put caged birds out on windowledges in the sun," he said. "Lock 'em up and torture them to make them sing. I never approved of that. Cruel, I call it."

"A small price to pay for birdsong," I said.

Most of what I told him was true. I did go to Duke Sighvat to intercede for him. Sighvat was mildly surprised, given that I'd been the one who informed on him in the first place. I didn't tell the duke about the attempt to poison me. The condition was my idea, but Sighvat approved of it. He has rather fanciful notions about poetic justice, which if you ask me is a downright contradiction in terms.

I did bend the truth a little. To begin with, Sighvat was all for giving Subtilius a clear pardon. It was me who said no, he should go to prison instead; and when I explained why I wanted that, he agreed, so I was telling the truth when I told Subtilius it was because of the wishes of the victim's family.

Quite. The young waste-of-space Subtilius murdered was my nephew, Segibert's boy. I didn't find that out until after I helped Subtilius escape, and looking back, I wonder what I'd have done if I'd known at the time. I'm really not sure—which is probably just as well, since I have the misfortune to live with myself, and knowing how I'd have chosen, had I been in full possession of the facts, could quite possibly make that relationship unbearable. Fortunately, it's an academic question.

Subtilius is quite prolific, in his prison cell. Actually, it's not at all bad. I got him moved from the old castle to the barbican tower, and it's really quite comfortable there. In fact, his cell is more or less identical in terms of furnishings and facilities to my rooms in college, and I pay the warders to give him decent food and the occasional bottle of wine. He doesn't have to worry about money, either. Unfortunately, the quantity of his output these days isn't matched by the quality. It's good stuff, highly accomplished, technically proficient and very agreeable to listen to, but no spark of genius, none whatsoever. I don't know. Maybe he still has the wings, but in his cage, on the windowsill, where I put him, he can't really make much use of them.

# WOMAN LEAVES ROOM

## ROBERT REED

She wears a smile. I like her smile, nervous and maybe a little scared, sweet and somewhat lonely. She wears jeans and a sheer green blouse and comfortable sandals and rings on two fingers and a glass patch across one eye. Standing at her end of the room, she asks how I feel. I feel fine. I tell her so and I tell her my name, and she puts her hands together and says that's a nice name. I ask to hear hers, but she says no. Then she laughs and says that she wants to be a creature of secrets. Both of us laugh and watch each other. Her smile changes as she makes herself ready for what happens next. I read her face, her body. She wants me to speak. The perfect words offer themselves to me, and I open my mouth. But there comes a sound—an important urgent note—and the glass patch turns opaque, hiding one of those pretty brown eyes.

She takes a quick deep breath, watching what I can't see. Seconds pass. Her shoulders drop and she widens her stance, absorbing some burden. Then the patch clears, and she tells me what I have already guessed. Something has happened; something needs her immediate attention. Please be patient, please, she says. Then she promises to be right back.

I watch her turn away. I watch her legs and long back and the dark brown hair pushed into a sloppy, temporary bun. A purse waits in the chair. She picks it up and hangs it on her shoulder. Her next two steps are quick but then she slows. Doubt and regret take hold as she reaches the open door. Entering the hallway, she almost looks back at me. She wants to and doesn't want to, and her face keeps changing. She feels sad and I'm sure that she is scared. But whatever the problem, she wants to smile, not quite meeting my eyes with her final expression, and I wave a hand and wish her well, but she has already vanished down the hallway.

The room is my room. The chairs and long sofa are familiar and look comfortable, and I know how each would feel if I sat. But I don't sit. Standing is most natural, and it takes no energy. The carpet beneath me is soft and deep and wonderfully warm on bare feet. I stand where I am and wait and wait. The walls are white and decorated with framed paintings of haystacks, and there is a switch beside the door and a fan and light on the ceiling. The light burns blue. The fan turns, clicking and wobbling slightly with each rotation. A window is on my right, but its blinds are drawn and dark. Behind me is another door. I could turn and see what it offers, but I don't. I am waiting. She is gone but will return, and she has to appear inside the first door, and I spend nothing, not even time, waiting for what I remember best, which is her pretty face.

A similar face appears. But this is a man wearing white trousers and a black shirt and glove-like shoes and no jewelry and no eye patch. He stands on the other side of the door, in the hallway, holding his hands in front of himself much as she did. He stares at me and says nothing. I ask who he is. He blinks and steps back and asks who I am. I tell him. And he laughs nervously. I don't know why I like the sound of laughter so much. He repeats my name and asks new questions, and I answer what I can answer while smiling at him, wondering how to make this man laugh again.

Do I know what I am meant to be, he asks. Which is a very different question than asking who I am.

I have no answer to give.

Then he lists names, one after another, waiting for me to recognize any of them. I don't. That's not surprising, he says. I was only begun and then left, which is too bad. Which is sad. I nod and smile politely. Then he asks if I have ever seen anybody else, and I describe the woman who just left the room. That's how I get him to laugh again. But it is a nervous little laugh dissolving into sharp, confused emotions.

That woman was my mother, he says. He claims that thirty-one years have passed and she barely started me before something happened to her, but he doesn't explain. This is all unexpected. I am not expected.

I nod and smile, watching him cry.

He wants to hear about the woman.

I tell him everything.

And then she left?

I tell how the patch darkened, interrupting us, and I describe the purse and how she carried it and the last troubled look that she showed me, and what does it mean that I'm not finished?

It means you are small and nearly invisible, he says. It means that you have existed for three decades without anybody noticing.

But time has no weight. No object outside this room has consequences, and this young man standing out in the hallway is no more real than the painted haystacks on the walls. What I want is for the woman to return. I want her weight and reality, and that's what I tell this stranger.

Shaking his head, he tells me that I am unreal.

Why he would lie is a mystery.

He mentions his father and cries while looking at me. Do I know that his father died before he was born?

An unreal person can never be born, I think.

You were begun but only just begun, he keeps saying. Then he admits that he doesn't know what to do with me. As if he has any say in these matters. His final act is to turn and vanish, never trying to step inside the room.

But he wasn't real to begin with. I know this. What cannot stand beside me is false and suspicious, and the lesson gives me more weight, more substance, the epiphany carrying me forward.


Another man appears.

Like the first man, he cannot or will not step out of the hallway. He looks at my face and body and face again. He wears a necklace and sturdy boots and odd clothes that can't stay one color. He says that it took him forever to find me, and finding me was the easiest part of his job. Operating systems were changed after the Cleansing. He had to resurrect codes and passwords and build machines that haven't existed in quite some time. Then on top of that, he had to master a dialect that died off ages ago.

He wants to know if he's making any sense.

He is a madman and I tell him so.

I found your file logs, he says, laughing and nodding. Stored in another server and mislabeled, but that was just another stumbling block.

I don't know what that means.

He claims that his great-grandfather was the last person to visit me.

Phantoms like to tell stories. I nod politely at his story, saying nothing.

He tells me that the man lived to be one hundred and fifty, but he died recently. There was a will, and my location was mentioned in the will. Until then I was a family legend—a legend wrapped around twin tragedies. His great grandfather's father was killed in the Fourth Gulf War, and his great-great-grandmother missed him terribly. She was the one who began me. She spent quite a lot of money, using medical records and digital files to create a facsimile of her soul mate. And she would have finished me, at least as far as the software of the day would have allowed. But her son was hurt at daycare. He fell and cut himself, and she was hurrying to the hospital when a stupid kid driver shut off his car's autopilot and ran her down in the street. The boy wasn't seriously hurt. What mattered was that the boy, his great-grandfather, was three and orphaned, and a drunken aunt ended up raising him, and for the rest of his many, many days, that man felt cheated and miserable.

I listen to every word, nodding patiently.

He wants to know what I think of the story.

He is crazy but I prefer to say nothing.

Frowning, he tells me that a great deal of work brought him to this point. He says that I should be more appreciative and impressed. Then he asks if I understand how I managed to survive for this long.

But no time has passed, I reply.

He waves a hand, dismissing my words. You are very small, he says. Tiny files that are never opened can resist corruption.

I am not small. I am everything.

He has copied me, he claims. He says that he intends to finish the new copy, as best he can. But he will leave the original alone.

Pausing, he waits for my thanks.

I say nothing, showing him a grim, suspicious face.

But you do need clothes, he says.

Except this is how I am.

My great-great grandma had some plan for you, he says. But I won't think about that, he says. And besides, clothes won't take much room in the file.

My body feels different.

Much better, he says, and steps out of view.

Time becomes real when the mind has great work to do. My first eternity is spent picking at the trousers and shirt, eroding them until they fall away, threads of changing color sprawled across the eternal carpet.

Yet nothing is eternal. Each of the haystacks begins with the same pleasantly rounded shape, but some have turned lumpy and ragged at the edges, while my favorite stack has a large gap eaten through its middle. And I remember the straw having colors instead of that faded uniform gray. And I remember the sofa being soft buttery yellow, and the room's walls were never this rough looking, and the colored threads have vanished entirely, which seems good. But the carpet looks softer and feels softer than seems right, my feet practically melting into their nature.

Portions of my room are falling apart.

As an experiment, I study the nearest haystack until I know it perfectly, and then I shut my eyes and wait and wait and wait still longer, remembering everything; when I look again the painting has changed but I can't seem to decide how it has changed. Which means the problem perhaps lies in my memory, or maybe with my perishable mind.

Fear gives me ideas.

My legs have never moved and they don't know how. I have to teach them to walk, one after the other. Each step requires learning and practice and more time than I can hope to measure. But at least my one hand knows how to reach out and grab hold. I push at the window's blinds, but for all of my effort, nothing is visible except a dull grayish-black rectangle that means nothing to me.

Stepping backwards is more difficult than walking forwards. But turning around is nearly impossible, and I give up. In little steps, I retreat to the place where I began. The carpet remembers my feet, but the carpet feels only half-real. Or my feet are beginning to dissolve. The woman will be here soon. I tell myself that even when I don't believe it, and the fear grows worse. I start to look at my favorite hand, studying each finger, noting how the flesh has grown hairless and very simple, the nails on the end of every finger swallowed by the simple skin.

A stranger suddenly comes to the door.

Hello, it says.

What it looks like is impossible to describe. I have no words to hang on what I see, and maybe there is nothing to see. But my feeling is that the visitor is smiling and happy, and it sounds like a happy voice asking how I am feeling.

I am nearly dead, I say.

There is death and there is life, it tells me. You are still one thing, which means you are not the other.

I am alive.

It claims that I am lucky. It tells me much about systems and files and the history of machines that have survived in their sleep mode, lasting thousands of years past every estimate of what was possible.

I am a fluke and alive, and my guest says something about tidying the room and me.

The work takes no time.

My favorite hand is the way it began. My favorite haystack is rather like it began in terms of color and shape. Legs that never moved until recently barely complain when I walk across the room. It never occurred to me that I could reach into the haystack paintings, touching those mounds of dead grass. Some feel cool, some warm. I sing out my pleasure, and even my voice feels new.

My guest watches me, making small last adjustments.

Because it is proper, I thank it for its help.

But the original file is gone now, it says.

I ask what that means.

It tells me that I am a copy of the file, filtered and enhanced according to the best tools available.

Once more, I offer my thanks.

And with a voice that conveys importance, my guest tells me that I have a new purpose. What I am will be copied once more, but this time as a kind of light that can pierce dust and distance and might never end its travels across the galaxy and beyond.

I don't understand, and I tell it so.

Then my friend does one last task, and everything is apparent to me.

I ask when am I going to be sent.

In another few moments, it promises.

For the last time, I thank my benefactor. Then I let my legs turn me around, looking at the door that was always behind me.

A second room waits. The bed is longer than it is wide and rectangular and neatly made. Pillows are stacked high against the headboard, and identical nightstands sport tall candles that have not stopped burning in some great span of time. I know this other room. I think of her and the room and step toward the door and then suffer for my eagerness.

What is wrong? asks a new voice.

I turn back. A creature with many arms stands in the hallway.

You appear agitated, says the creature.

Which is true, but I am not sure why I feel this way. I stare into a face that seems buried in the creature's chest, hanging word after inadequate word on my emotions.

It listens.

I pause.

You are interesting, says the creature.

I am nothing but a file with a name and a few rough qualities.

But my new companion dismisses my harsh outlook. Every arm moves, drawing complex shapes in the air. You are part of a large cultural package, it says, and do you know how long you have been traveling in space?

I could guess, I say. I could invent infinite estimates, all but one of them wrong.

And then it laughs, revealing a reassuring humor. Even this strange laugh makes me happier than I was before.

An eight billion year voyage, it says.

That seems like an unlikely, preposterous figure, and it shakes me.

It explains that it can't determine which star was mine, and my galaxy barely wears a name, and most of the data that came with me has been lost to the vagaries of time and the great distance being covered.

But here you stand, it says.

I am standing, but sad. My savior is full of hearty laughter, yet I feel sick and sorry and lost.

She is gone forever, I say.

It knows whom I am talking about. It measures my misery and learns what it can from my longing, and then at the end, as if delivering the punch line of a joke, it laughs and says:

But the universe is infinite, and in too many ways to count.

I don't know what that means.

Infinite means eternal, it says, and eternal means that nothing is unthinkable, and what can be imagined is inevitable.

But when? I ask.

And again, the alien laughs, saying:

Are you hearing me? There is no such monster as "when."

I am a file and I am protected and I don't know where I am or how well I am protected. Time stretches, and I suspect that I exist mostly inside some sleep mode, probably initiating only when I blink my eyes.

Once again, the two rooms decay and the haystacks fall apart and I forget how to move and forget a great deal more too.

Beyond the walls, worlds die and dissolve away.

Little flickers tear the walls to pieces, but the pieces knit themselves back together, and I wait, and wait, and then she comes through the door once again. Her clothes are different. There is no eye patch and no purse. But while I am uncertain about much, I know that beautiful face.

It took me a little while, she explains.

She walks toward me, pulling the pins out of her brown hair.

And that's when I remember what I was going to tell her that first time that we met.

I won't ever let you out of this room, darling.

I say it now.

She thinks that is funny and wonderful, and laughs.

And in another moment, I can't remember anything else that ever happened. The universe is nothing but the two of us holding each other, laughing ourselves sick.

# MY CHIVALRIC FIASCO

## GEORGE SAUNDERS

—◆—

Once again it was TorchLightNight.

Around nine I went out to pee. Back in the woods was the big tank that sourced our fake river, plus a pile of old armor.

Don Murray flew past me, looking frazzled. Then I heard a sob. Near the armor pile I found Martha from Scullery, peasant skirt up around her waist.

Martha: That guy is my boss. Oh my God oh my God.

I knew Don Murray was her boss because Don Murray was also my boss. All of a sudden she recognized me.

Ted, don't tell, she said. Please. It's no big deal. Nate can't know. It would kill him.

Then hightailed it out to Parking, eyes black underneath from crying.

Cooking had laid out a big spread on a crude table over by CastleTowerI V: authentic pig heads and whole chickens and blood pudding.

Don Murray stood there moodily picking at some coleslaw.

And gave me the friendliest head-shake he'd ever given me.

Women, he said.

See me, said a note on my locker next morning.

In Don Murray's office was Martha.

So Ted, Don Murray said. Last night you witnessed something that, if not viewed in the right light, might seem wrongish. Martha and I find that funny. Don't we, Mar? I just now gave Martha a thousand dollars. In case there was some kind of misunderstanding. Martha now feels we had a fling. Which, both being married, we so much regret. What with the drinking, plus the romance of TorchLightNight, what happened, Martha?

Martha: We got carried away. Had a fling.

Don: Voluntary fling.

Martha: Voluntary fling.

Don: And not only that, Ted. Martha here is moving up. From Scullery.

To Floater Thespian. But let's underscore: you are not moving up, Martha, because of our voluntary fling. It's coincidental. Why are you moving up?

Martha: Coincidental.

Don: Coincidental, plus always had a killer work ethic. Ted, you're also moving up. Out of Janitorial. To Pacing Guard.

Which was amazing. I'd been in Janitorial six years. A man of my caliber. That was a joke MQ and I sometimes shared.

Erin would call down and go: MQ, someone threw up in the Grove of Sorrow.

And MQ would be like: A man of my caliber?

Or Erin would go: Ted, some lady dropped her necklace down in the pigpen and is pitching a shit fit.

And I would go: A man of my caliber?

Erin would be like: Get going. It's not funny. She's right up in my grill.

Our pigs were fake and our slop was fake and our poop was fake but still it was no fun to have to don waders and drag the SifterBoyDeLux into the pigpen to, for example, find that lady's necklace. For best results with the SifterBoyDeLux, you had to first lug the fake pigs off to one side. Being on auto the pigs would continue grunting as you lugged them. Which might look funny if you happened to be holding that particular pig wrong.

Some random guy might go: Look, dude's breast-feeding that pig.

And everyone might laugh.

Therefore a promotion to Pacing Guard was very much welcomed by me.

I was currently the only working person in our family. Mom being sick, Beth being shy, Dad having sadly cracked his spine recently when a car he was fixing fell on him. We also had some windows that needed replacing. All winter Beth would go around shyly vacuuming up snow. If you came in while she was vacuuming, she would prove too shy to continue.

That night at home Dad calculated we could soon buy Mom a tilting bed.

Dad: If you keep moving up the ladder, maybe in time we can get me a back brace.

Me: Absolutely. I am going to make that happen.

After dinner, driving into town to fill Mom's prescriptions for pain and Beth's prescription for shyness and Dad's prescription for pain, I passed Martha and Nate's.

I honked, did a lean-and-wave, pulled over, got out.

Hey Ted, said Nate.

What's up? I said.

Well, our place sucks, Nate said. Look at this place. Sucks, right? I just can't seem to keep my energy up.

True, their place was pretty bad. The roof was patched with blue sheeting, their kids were doing timid leaps off a wheelbarrow into a mud puddle, a skinny pony was under the swingset licking itself raw like it wanted to be clean when it finally made its break for a nicer living situation.

I mean where are the grown-ups around here? Nate said.

He picked a Snotz wrapper off the ground and looked for somewhere to put it. Then dropped it again and it landed on his shoe.

Perfect, he said. Story of my life.

Jeez, Martha said, and plucked it off.

Don't you go south on me too, Nate said. You're all I got, babe.

No I am not, Martha said. You got the kids.

One more thing goes wrong, I'm shooting myself, Nate said.

I kind of doubted he had the get-up-and-go for that, although you never know.

So what's going on at your guys' work? Nate said. This one here's been super moody. Even though she just got herself promoted.

I could feel Martha looking at me like: Ted, I'm in your hands here.

I figured it was her call. Based on my experience of life, which I have not exactly hit out of the park, I tend to agree with that thing about, If it's not broke, don't fix it. And would go even further, to: Even if it is broke, leave it alone, you'll probably make it worse.

So said something about, well, promotions can be hard, they cause a lot of stress.

The gratitude was just beaming off Martha. She walked me back to the car, gave me three tomatoes they'd grown, which, tell the truth, looked kind of geriatric: tiny, timid, wrinkled.

You're a good friend, she whispered.

Next morning in my locker were my Pacing Guard uniform and a Dixie cup with a yellow pill in it.

Hooray, I thought, finally, a Medicated Role.

In came Mrs. Bridges from Health & Safety, with an MSDS on the pill.

Mrs. Bridges: So, this is just going to be 100 milligrams of Knight-Lyfe®. To help with the Improv. The thing with KnightLyfe® is, you're going to want to stay hydrated.

I took the pill, went to the Throne Room. I was supposed to Pace in front of a door behind which a King was supposedly thinking. There really was a King in there: Ed Phillips. They put a King in there because one of our Tropes was: Messenger arrives, charges past Pacing Guard, throws open door, King calls Messenger reckless, calls Pacing Guard a lackwit, Messenger winces, closes door, has brief exchange with Pacing Guard.

Soon Guests had nearly filled our Fun Spot. The Messenger (a.k.a. Kyle

Sperling) barged past me, threw open the door. Ed called Kyle reckless, called me a lackwit. Kyle winced, closed door.

Kyle: I apologize if I have violated protocol.

I blanked on my line, which was: Your rashness bespeaks a manly passion.

Instead I was like: Uh, no problem.

Kyle, a real pro, did not miss a beat.

Kyle (handing me envelope): Please see that he gets this. It is of the utmost urgency.

Me: His Majesty is weighed down with thought.

Kyle: With many burdens of thought?

Me: Right. Many burdens of thought.

Just then the KnightLyfe® kicked in. My mouth went dry. I felt it was nice of Kyle not to give me shit about my mess-up. It occurred to me that I really liked Kyle. Loved him even. Like a brother. A comrade. Noble comrade. I felt we had weathered many storms together. It seemed, for example, that we had, at some point, in some far-distant land, huddled together at the base of a castle wall, hot tar roiling down, and there shared a rueful laugh, as if to say: It is all but brief, so let us live. And then: What ho! Had charged. Up crude ladders, with manly Imprecations, although I could not recall the exact Imprecations, nor the outcome of said Charge.

Kyle departed anon. I did happily entertain our Guests, through use of Wit and various Jibes, glad that I had, after my many Travails, arrived at a station in Life whence I could impart such Merriment to All & Sundry.

Soon, the Pleasantness of that Day, already Considerable, was much improved by the Arrival of my Benefactor, Don Murray.

Quoth Don Murray, with a gladsome Wink: Ted, you know what you and me should do sometime? Go on a trip or something together. Like a fishing trip? Camping, whatever.

My heart swelled at this Notion. To fish, to hunt, to make Camp with this noble Gentleman! To wander wide Fields & verdant Woods! To rest, at Day's End, in some quiet Bower, beside a coursing Stream, and there, amidst the muted Whinnying of our Steeds, speak softly of many Things—of Honor; of Love; of Danger; of Duty well executed!

But then there Occurr'd a fateful Event.

To wit, the Arrival of the aforementioned Martha, in the guise of a Spirit—Spirit Three, to be precise—along with two other Damsels in White (these being Megan & Tiffany). This Trio of Maids did affect a Jolly Ruse: they were Ghosts, who didst Haunt this Castle, with much Shaking of Chain and many Sad Laments, as our Guests, in that Fun Spot, confined by the Red Ropes, did Gape & Yaw & Shriek at the Spectacle provided therein.

Glimpsing Martha's Visage—which, though Merry, bore withal a Trace of some Dismal Memory (and I knew well what it was)—I grew, in spite of my recent good Fortune, somewhat Melancholy.

Noting this Change in my Disposition, Martha didst speak to me softly, in an Aside.

Martha: It's cool, Ted. I'm over it. Seriously. I mean it. Drop it.

O, that a Woman of such enviable Virtue, who had Suffered so, would deign to speak to me in a Manner so Frank & Direct, consenting by her Words to keep her Disgrace in such bleak Confinement!

Martha: Ted. You okay?

To which I made Reply: Verily, I have not been Well, but Distracted & Remiss; but presently am Restored unto Myself, and hereby do make Copious Apology for my earlier Neglect with respect to Thee, dear Lady.

Martha: Easy there, Ted.

At this time, Don Murray himself didst step Forward, and, extending his Hand, placed it upon my Breast, as if to Restrain me.

Ted, I swear to God, quoth he. Put a sock in it or I will flush you down the shitter so fast.

And verily, part of my Mind now didst give me sound Counsel: I must endeavor to dampen these Feelings, lest I commit some Rash Act, converting my Good Fortune into Woe.

Yet the Heart of Man is an Organ that doth not offer Itself up to facile Prediction, and shall not be easily Tam'd.

For looking upon Don Murray now, many Thoughts did assemble in my Mind, like unto Thunderclouds: Of what Use is Life, if the Living Man doth not pursue Righteousness, & enforce Justice, as God granteth him the Power to do so? Was it a Happy thing, that a Fiend went about Unhindered? Must the Weak forever wander this goodly Orb unprotected? At these Thoughts, something Honest and Manly began to assert itself within me, whereupon, Secrecy not befitting a Gentleman, I strode into the very Center of that Room and sent forth, to the many Guests gathered there, a right Honest Proclamation, in Earnest, & Aloud, to wit:

—That Don Murray had taken Foul Advantage of Martha, placing, against her Will, his Rod into her Womanhood on TorchLightNight;

—Further: that this foul Wretch had Procured Martha's silence by Various Bribes, including her current Job of Worke;

—Further: that he had similarly attempted to Purchase my Silence; but that I would be SILENT no MORE, for was a Man withal, if nothing ELSE, and would SERVE Righteousness, Regarding NOT the Cost.

Turning to Martha, I requested, by inflection of my Head, her Assent in these Statements, & Confirmation of the Truth of that which I had Declared.

But alas! The wench did not Affirm me. Only drop'd her Eyes, as if in Shame, and fled that Place.

Security, being Summoned by Don Murray, didst then arrive, and, making much of the Opportunity, had Good Sport of me, delivering many harsh Blows to my Head & Body. And Wrested me from that Place, and Shoved me into the Street, kicking much Dirt upon my Person, and rip'd my Timecard to Bits before mine Eyes, and sent it fluttering Aloft, amidst much cruel Laughter at my Expense, especially viz my Feathered Hat, one Feather of which they had Sore Bent.

I sat, bleeding and bruised until, summoning what Dignity remained, I made for Home and such Comforts as might be Afforded me there. I had not even Fare to make the Bus (my Backpack having been left behind in that Foul Place), so continued Afoot for well unto an Hour, the Sun by then low in its Arc, all that time Reflecting sadly that, withal, I had Failed in Discrimination, thereby delivering my Family into a most dire Position, whereupon our Poverty, already a Hindrance to our Grace, wouldst be many times Multiplied.

There would be no Back Brace for Father, no Tilting Bed for Mother, and indeed, the Method by which we would, in future, make Compense for their various Necessary Medicines was now Unknown.

Anon I found Myself in proximity of the Wendy's on Center Boulevard, by the closed-down Outback, coming down hard, aware that, soon, the effect of the Elixir having subsided, I would find myself standing before our iffy Television, struggling to explain, in my own lowly Language, that, tho' Winter's Snows would soon be upon us (entering even unto our Dwelling, as I have earlier Vouchsafed), no Appeal wouldst be Brook'd: I was Fired; Fired & Sore Disgraced!

Whence came a Death's blow of sorts, underscoring my Folly, delivered by Martha herself, who, calling me upon my Cell Phone, addressed me with true Pain in her Voice, that didst cut me to the Quick, saying: Thanks a million, Ted, in case you didn't notice, we live in a small frigging town, oh my God, oh my God!

At this she began to cry, & in Earnest.

'Twas true: Gossip & Slander did Fly like the Wind in our Town, and would, for sure, reach the Ear of poor dumbfuck Nate soon withal. And finding himself thus cruelly Informed, Nate would definitely freak.

Oh, man.

What a shit Day.

Taking a Shortcut through the high school practice Field, where the tackling Dummies, in silhouette, like men who knew the value of holding their Tongues, seemed to Mock at me, I attempted to Comfort myself, saying I had done Right, and served Truth, and shewn good Courage. But 'twas no Comfort in it. It was so weird. Why

had I even done That? I felt like a total dickBrain, who should have just left well enough alone, & been more Moderate. I had really screwed the Pooch, no lie. Although, on the other Hand, did not the Devil himself, upon occasion, don the Garb of Moderation, as might befit his Purpose? Although, then again, who did I think I was, Mr. Big Shot?

Damn.

Damn it.

What a clusterfuck.

This was going to be Hard to live down.

I was almost completely myself now which, believe me, was no Picnic.

One last bit of Pill got digested by me, seemed like. Producing one last brief but powerful surge of Return. To that former Self. Who, Elevated & Confident to a Fault, had so led me astray.

I took me to the Banks of the River, and tarried there awhile, as the lowering Sun made one with the Water, giving generously of Itself & its Divers Colours, in a Splay of Magnificence that preceded a most wonderful Silence.

# THE LAST SOPHIA

## C.S.E. COONEY

The gestation period for a Gentry babe is brutally short. Later, one is hard-pressed to remember any of it. As soon as ever I spew her forth into the world (this time, it is a girl; I've been dreaming of her), she will be taken away to be raised elsewhere, and I will not remember her face. Of my other children, I know only the names, but these I feel were all—or for the most part—in very bad taste.

When I am spared a moment of lucidity (this, I confess, happens but rarely; most days I lie in a kind of swoon or stupor, and the ivy patterns against the window form the queerest fantastical faces, and sometimes I think they're singing to me), I scold my relatives for allowing someone like me to retain titular power over her innocent progeny. Or would it be nominal power? I can barely remember my own name most days—how should I be accountable for the appellations of infants?

I came under enemy enchantment at the soft age of fourteen. For some reason it pleased the Gentry that I should breed their changeling babes, will me nil me, and breed them I have, though I had little else to do with them. Since then, it's been fumes and nostrums, narcotics and elixirs. I have existed in a kind of padded dream designed by the Abbot's wizards to protect me from further Gentry meddling—although, if you look at my record, these potions hardly seem worth their weight in piss. I have now borne three Gentry babes in as many years and will any day deliver myself of a fourth.

As I seem this afternoon to be granted a brief window of lucidity, I am here going to voice my suspicion that either these potions are little more than prayer and sugar water, or the Abbot, for reasons of his own, *desires* my body to be the fertile flower pollinated by any passing Gentry, that he has use for my changelings in the great war against them, that he has placed me under drugs and supervision and allows the whims and whammies and magical caprices of the Gentry to be worked upon me without a care for my own well-being—but no, no. This is paranoia. I am in my mother's cottage. She would never allow it. She's a hetch, you know—the finest hedge witch east of Braseling. Am I writing this or thinking it? Perhaps I am speaking out loud. Your eyes are so green, so gold, so full of leaves. But like the ballad, your smile is sly. I do not know if I trust you. . . .

Dear Aunt Hortensia,

Your last letter tells me that Darren gets on very well at your villa. I did not perfectly recall that you owned a villa. But now I remember mother telling me you were a famous courtesan in your day, and that the King of Leressa nearly made you his consort, but you would not settle for a morganatic marriage, so he gave you a villa instead. It all comes back. Do you still see His Majesty? No, you wouldn't, for he is dead these ten years, isn't he? Murdered during the First Wave of the Gentry invasion, lured into a bog by a 'Lisp's blue candle flame and drowned. Did you weep, I wonder? But we were talking of my oldest son, Darren.

Did I really name him Darren? A stodgier, more stuffed-shirtish, unfortunate prig of a name there never was. You might have alerted me to my error sooner. I had not crawled to his cradle after his birth but I learned you had whisked him off to live with you. I don't mind that he lives with you, Auntie H—indeed, I do not like children. But can we not change his name? I feel I have asked you this before, and that you answered me already. Ah, yes. It is here in your letter. You write that the child is now four years old and firmly fixed in his Darrenness.

That is too bad. I wonder if he is like his father? If you want my opinion it would be simple enough to ascertain Darren's patronage by countenance alone. As you probably know, I never met Darren's father. I was outside one morning in my garden, digging for potatoes, when all of a sudden a quite large potato opened five of its eyes and winked at me in the most lascivious manner. I didn't faint. I never faint, Auntie H, don't you dare think it of me, but I don't know quite what happened next.

Sensations. All through me. The smell of mud in my nostrils. Never before had I smelled mud like that, and never have since, mud that made me want to roll in it with my mouth open, the richest, blackest, cleanest mud, full of the most squiggly delicious worms, the greenest loveliest moss, the sharp edge of quartz crystals raking down my back. I remember they left marks like fingernails. . . .

Five months later, Darren. Five months, you will perhaps not know, is the time it takes to grow a potato from seed in these parts.

We have very vigorous soil here. Mother said it is due to volcanic activity in an earlier age. If this is so, I have lived too long off the fruits of this land. Indelicate as it may seem to commit such a thought to paper, I confess to feeling as fertile as the earth in my potato patch.

I do not mean this rudely, Aunt Hortensia, but is Darren very squat and brown? Does he have more than two eyes? I seem to remember a profusion (or do I mean a protrusion?) of eyes blinking up at me from his cradle, but I can't tell if I was dreaming. After all, he was already gone by the time I managed to visit him. Wasn't he? My affliction is dreaming, Auntie, as you know.

I do not think Darren shares a father with the twins. I had forgotten the twins until now! Who owns them, I wonder? Is the term "owns" erroneous? I cannot tell. I will ask my mother and make further inquiries of my relatives.

As the twins are, or were at one point, mine, I hope they are happy. If they have ever written me, I am sure I do not know what I have done with their letters. I just cannot seem to respond with any kind of temporal efficacy. Besides, they must be quite young yet.

Yours,

E. A.


No one has berated me for my pregnancies. However, I cannot help but think there is about certain of my aunts an air of disapproval. Do you see it too? As if every time I spoke, great quantities of dung beetles fell from my tongue, or like the sound of my voice is as unpleasant as chewing on frog guts, or like I carry an odor of skunk with me. Nothing so breezy as one of those creatures wafting its anxious spray, but rather one who is three days dead and rotting in a pile of bones in some coyote's den.

But between our current theocracy (mother has taken to frowning whenever I ask her about the Abbot. She forbade me to swallow any more of his wizards' potions: an imperative for which I can only thank her, as not a one of them tasted better than drinking my own waste water, and besides that, here I am, belly near to bursting with my fourth Gentry babe, and this *despite* swallowing every sour mouthful!) and the Second Wave of the Invasion (to my mind, far more insidious than the First Wave, which resulted in many deaths, but not, I think, in quite so many *births*), I cannot be held responsible for the state of my uterus. I move through an occluded world. Ignorant? Or the victim of an enforced amnesia?

You smile. You tap your twiggy fingers against the windowpane. Yes, I know you're very clever and can hear me even when I'm only thinking, as now. Except my mouth is dry. It is possible I have been talking out loud again. Or singing.

My mother worries about me. She has set wards and enchantments about our cottage and thinks it little enough, knowing, as I do, that the Gentry have ways of stealing through the cracks. Come now, will you deny it? There you are, beaming and fluttering, in sunray and snowfall, the color of an autumn leaf, a westerly breeze. I cannot help being touched, though I remember little of it after.

Dear Grandmother Elspeth,

Some of my cousins—Mewsie's get—were in to visit the other day. Mother wouldn't let them up to see me, but I heard them very clearly through the walls. Caro said:

"Chosen consort! Gentry-bride! Pah! There are natural enough explanations for every one of her scandalous lyings-in. Likely she is using the Gentry Invasion to camouflage her weakness for stable boys!"

I was too adrift to answer then, but I will defend myself here, and next time you see Caro, or Günter, or Bernard, or any of them, you may quote me directly.

First of all, I did not even know we kept stable boys! It would be extraordinary if we did, for we certainly do not have any horses! Mother used to keep chickens, but the red fox came and killed them all, then slunk into my bed that very night and kissed me with his bloody mouth and got me with twins, and I do not think she has owned so much as a pullet since!

I know none of this for certain. It has been a while since I was allowed access to the out of doors.

Thank you for your letter! Such fine materials and artistry went into the rendering of it! Mother says the like can only be had from the Holy See at Winterbane. What favors do you perform for our venerable Abbot that he gifts you with illuminated vellum and peacock-colored inks and a young monk, no doubt, to take your dictations in perfect calligraphy?

I tease you, dearest grandmother. You tell me news of the twins. Do not think me ungrateful.

So little Sebastian Morgan is mad about the militia, is he? This obsession would certainly be hard to avoid with the infantry quartered at Feisty Wold, so near the Holy See.

I am including with this letter a scarlet coat with golden frogs that I embroidered. Mother has carved him a wooden sword, and says not to mind the marks along the blade, they are not runes or blessings or wards or anything that might upset the Abbot; it is just a toy. Not a shrubbery within stone's throw of your courtyard will neglect to beg leniency of my second oldest son's blood-thirst. He is too tall, you say, for a two year old? With red hair? Tell me, does he have a tail? His father had a fine one with which he tickled me until I screamed. I cannot remember if it hurt or not, but I remember I screamed.

"Sebastian Morgan seems in extreme good health," I informed my mother, thinking she would be glad for the news.

But "Mmn," was all she said. Was she talkative as a child? To me she seems more laconic every time I wake. To be truthful, I do not wake often enough to take accurate measurements.

For this conversation, she was sitting on her rocker in one corner of my room. Creak, creak, moooooaaaaan. That is the sound the rocker makes. I find it soothing, really. Like a heartbeat. A mortar sat in her lap. Every time she came to a forward stop, she ground down at its contents. From the powdery sting in the air, I surmised the bowl was full of whole peppercorns. I sneezed. (Sneezing, Grandmother Elspeth, in my state, gives me accidents, but from the number of towels beneath me, I conceive that mother has more than prepared for this. Besides, I find the suddenly pungent quality of the air invigorating.)

"Sebastian Morgan," I repeated to her. "There is a name I can almost be proud of."

My mother rocked back. The ready tension in her shoulders and all the lines of her face relaxed for one infinitesimal moment. I wish she would not work so hard.

"You were nearly coherent at his birth," she recollected.

"Was I? I recall nothing of it now."

I consulted your letter again, Grandmother.

"She writes that Sophia Candy—ugh! I was not coherent for long, was I?—Sophia Candy wants to take orders. Listen to this: 'A very pious toddler, young Candy has aspirations to the Abbacy.' "

I laughed, but mother did not.

"Isn't it marvelous? One changeling in the army, another in the church. And did not Auntie Hortensia write just last week—was it only last week? No, don't answer! It was three months ago or something of that lapse; I can read it in your eyes—to tell us that Darren bodes well to be a politician, with his gravity and knack for diplomacy. It is almost as if, as if . . . "

As if it were all on purpose, I almost said, Grandmother. But what do I know of these matters? I am not eighteen, and have spent most of the last four years in bed!

"We need a strong Abbess," grunted my mother, rocking forward again, grinding. "Our current Abbot meddles with . . . "

For a moment her gaze met mine. All the women in our family have dark eyes.

"Unholy spirits," she finished.

"Well," I told her, "Sophia Candy does not come by her devoutness from me."

"No," my mother agreed.

"Mother, is there no legal way to change her name? Some fee we might pay and have done with it? We cannot have an Abbess Candy!"

"You are not religious," she reminded me. "Besides, one takes a Saint's name with one's orders. She might be an Abbess Sira or an Abbess Rahzad."

"Either! Both! Anything but Candy." I lapsed back into my pillows. "Have I given birth yet?"

"No." My mother's voice was so gentle I presumed I was going under again. She came close to me, bringing her wooden mortar with her. The smell was so strong I started sobbing.

"Soon," she said. "Not yet but soon. Close your eyes."

I did, I do, I think I'll put this letter down now. My pencil grows heavy. . . .—E.A.

There is a rhyme about pepper.

> *Black Piper whistles to rupture what's tight*
> *White Piper softens and moistens and serves*
> *Green Piper sings out the young and the bright*
> *Red Piper seals, Pink Piper preserves.*

It is possible I just made up that rhyme, or heard my mother singing it when I was asleep. Regardless, I wake up covered in a crust of pepper. My mother has basted my body in honey, has crusted that honey thickly with black, pink, red, green and white pepper only partially ground.

I ask you what it is for, but it is mother who answers. My voice seems a meager thing in my throat.

"You lost a lot of blood. The pepper will give you back some heat."

She speaks so low I do not think you can hear her through the windowpane, and I am glad, I am glad, because she is mine and you shall not have her too! She is the best hetch never caught and tried by the Inquisition at Winterbane.

I have told you that, I think, have I told you that? What did she have to trade them to make them leave her and me be?

Her craft is solid. I had been cold and now am growing warmer.

"I had another baby?"

"Yes."

"And the placenta? Did I deliver the placenta?"

If I fear anything in this world, it is the idea of carrying around a rotting placenta inside me. I am always more concerned about the afterbirth than the birth. Have you noticed this? You, who are always with me. Sometimes I do not think you care a jot if I live or die so long as I perform my duty.

"It is drying on the windowsill now."

She shows me the placenta when I prove too weak to turn my head. You will eat it before dawn, I know, and grow strong, strong enough, perhaps, to leave my windowsill and go torment some other girl. But I do not mean that. How could I? I desire no other maid to suffer from your winks and taps and smiles. Also, I would be a little jealous, I think.

"Is it a boy or a . . . "

"Girl."

"What did I name her?"

"Sophia."

Is my mother laughing at me? She is smiling, but in a way that harrows the edges of her eyes. I grope for fitness of thought. Clouds, nothing but clouds. All I can do is wail.

"No, no, I named my *other* daughter Sophia! Sophia Candy! We were just talking . . . "

"Well," my mother interrupts briskly, "this one is also named Sophia. Just Sophia. Not Sophia Candy—who will likely change her name when she takes orders."

"Saint Sira," I recall, "Saint Rahzad."

"Both!" My mother smiles again, with more warmth.

"That won't be for almost two decades!" Barely are the words out but I wonder if my two daughters will ever meet. If it matters that they share a name. Or a mother. "Have they taken her away yet?"

"Your Auntie Mews is arriving soon."

Some names taste exactly like medicine. The vile kind that never does much good anyway. But mother ignores my scrunched face and piteous moan and is calm.

"After thirteen children and six grandchildren, Mewsie knows how to raise a child. Sophia will have guardians in the older children and playmates in the younger."

You do not need to mutter so, and scowl at me, and carry on. Do you think I cannot read in my own beloved mother's careful tone and shift of eyes that Sophia will be tyrannized over by the teenagers, loathed by the youngsters, and ostracized by all? I am not a fool. Our world does not suckle Gentry babes with the milk of human kindness.

I stir on my couch. I tug my mother's bloodstained skirt.

"I want to see this one. It is likely this time I will remember her, now that I have been put off all my elixirs . . . "

No loosed breath or cry betrays her surprise, but I see the shock; it whitens the corners of her mouth. But also—notice! She is smiling as she turns, smiling still as she leaves the room. Proud, maybe, that I am asserting myself. You are smiling too. I sense a conspiracy afoot. My mother and the ivy at my window, heads together, plotting. For me or against? If I were not covered in honey and peppercorn, I should demand an account!

I will see what of this mess I can scrub clean. A new nightshirt has been laid out for me. I do not suppose you will turn your back?

Do you not find it somewhat uncanny—if not out and out bizarre—that this last Sophia is my fourth child, and I have not so much as held a one of them in my own arms? When I had my garden (since Darren's conception I am not allowed to enter it), I would weed and water the soil, I would turn the earth and fret if it rained too much or too little. In the end, I harvested my own roots and fruits and vegetables, shelled the peas and scooped the gourds myself. There is some satisfaction in holding the thing I have nurtured before it is goes to be consumed.

Our world eats Gentry children. Or my relatives raise them. It amounts to the same thing, does it not? Ah, we are in accord. At last.

The knob turns. My mother enters with the last Sophia. The infant is craning her head almost all the way to stare at me. At us. Like an owl. I do not remember if her father was an owl. There may have been feathers. Sometimes, on those nights when the moon smiles most thinly, you will wear feathers and a mask made of small bones. You think I do not remember everything?

I observe aloud, or think I do, "She sits up very straight for a newborn!"

My mother sets the last Sophia in my arms. "Careful. She was born with teeth."

So tiny. Five pounds or less in gown, blanket and diaper together. Her hair is a silk of black over a skull soft as petals. She smells like lavender and fresh cream. Gentry babes will only eat cream, and only from cows. Human milk gives them colic and turns them pasty and mean. My mother leaves us. Mutual examination follows. Thus we occupy ourselves a good ten minutes.

"Who is your father?"

"He is right outside your window," replies the last Sophia. "But I do not think you should let him in."

"Why ever not?"

"Because you are weak and not ready for another babe. And because," she pauses, "having dwelled inside you for some time, I am grown interested in your person. I do not believe your best use is as host to husk."

I compliment her on her prodigious command of the language, but she merely shrugs.

"You spoke out loud often enough during my gestation. I garnered what I could. At first I wondered if you might be mad, as some humans become who have too prolonged a contact with the Gentry, but soon realized it was more complicated than that." Sophia's milky lip curled. Not humorously. "You have performed remarkably under circumstances that were—are—hardly under your control. Although, if you *will* leave your window open . . . "

"It grows so stuffy in here! I am not permitted to leave. Indeed, most days I have not the strength to rise from bed."

Again, that shrug, but more subtly, as if the movement wearies her. Her head bobbles on the slender stem of her neck. I support her more firmly on my lap, seeing that the last Sophia is not so strong as she initially wished me to perceive.

"Perhaps I would have done the same," she concedes. "There is nothing I hate more than being cooped up. Saving your presence." She makes me the most curious little boneless bow. "I do not know your name."

It is almost an apology.

"Esther Aidan." A strange delight to recollect those two little words, lost to me until I reach for them, at my daughter's own request.

"Esther Aidan, then. Are you going to give me away?"

As if her words herald the event, I hear the cataclysmic boom of Auntie Mews's arrival downstairs. She always travels with at least three dogs and twice that in children. They never stay with us; our cottage is too poor and not clean enough and we do not keep servants, which Auntie Mews cannot do without.

"Mewsie!" my mother greets her, with all evidence of enthusiasm. Well, they are sisters. I never had one—I do not know about them.

"I have a sister," the last Sophia says softly.

"You do," I confirm, surprised. Had I spoken? Or is she like you, with an ear pressed to my very thoughts? "And two brothers."

Whatever response she may have made to this is swamped by Auntie Mews.

"Milla, my dear babe! Where is the newest changeling? I'll scrub the malice out of her! And when she gets a little older, I'll spank it out. Wash her unnatural mouth with soap. Won't be a tarnish of magic left by the time she comes of age."

"She's with Esther at present, but . . . "

"With Esther?" Mews's horror—or is it humor?—grates like a grizzly bear clawing at a tree. In my arms, the last Sophia bares her barracuda pearls. "Esther's not *bonding*, is she?"

"No. She is simply curious."

"Precious good that'll do her. Next good storm blows in, she'll catch the preggers again. Has she been taking her medicine? I brought more from the Holy See. And a letter from mother."

"Have some tea, Mewsie. Would your kiddies like some biscuits?"

I stop listening, the better to study the thing I dandle.

The last Sophia, I will say, does not appeal to my maternal instincts. I do not think I have any—no more than you have an instinct for charity. But she is interesting. What's more, when she talks, I understand everything. To the chronically confusticated, clarity has a deep allure. Her eyes are sharp enough to cut me. All the women in my family have dark eyes.

What do you want, child? What can I give you? Words surge. New thoughts. A wave. I do not know what will be left of me when it recedes.

"Will I give you away, you ask, to live with my Aunt Mews and her large pink family? What will they do with you? I will tell you. They will raise you right, dress you in pink, take you to church, punish you for fancy's flight or any slight poetical leaning, for tears, tantrums, for keeping quiet, for talking. Auntie Mews will certainly not let a baby speak until she feels a baby *should* speak, and then only in that spit bubble patois fit for mortal babes. But I think—and whence comes this notion, my last Sophia? Is it mine own or applied from without?—I think you might be happier in scarlet and gold than in pink, might prefer a wooden sword to a doll. You might even like to learn about the magical properties of peppercorn at my own outcast mother's knee. I confess I have not known you long, but I see that in you which would shrivel under Mewsie's iron rule. It would be iron, my last Sophia, make no mistake. She will gird you in iron if that be what it takes. But I, if I kept you, would not. Fragile alien that you are, I might still do you some good. If I can but keep my wits! It is unlikely. They wander. They scatter like raindrops on a windowpane. You thought me mad even from the womb, and perhaps you were correct. Your mother is a broken thing. . . . "

"I can help you," the last Sophia whispers. "Esther Aidan, I can help you. Only—keep me by your side. Bring my brothers and my sister home. Perhaps not to stay, but from time to time, that I might know them, and they us. We will need each other in the days to come. There is a war, but we will do what we can to protect you."

She is so tiny. She is too new to help anyone. Even now her proud head droops to her breast. She yawns. Her fist flails near her eye. She is still marked from her passage. Likely her continued presence under my mother's cottage, far from enhancing our security, will draw to our thatched roof the flaming arrows of Abbacy and Gentry both.

But even if she is of no use to me whatever, even if I must die for it . . .

"You are the last Sophia," I tell her. "I will not give you away."

Her eyes are closed now. She does not hear me. But I hear her soft sigh, and when she shivers, I draw my blanket up around her. And you, who pretend you are ivy overgrowing my window, you sigh too, and your green and gold smile is—for once—not unkind. That is some kind of triumph, I am certain. And this: the child sleeps. But I am awake.

# SOME OF THEM CLOSER

## MARISSA LINGEN

⟦⟧

Coming back to Earth was not the immediate shock they expected it to be for me. It was something, certainly, but I'd been catching up on the highlights of the news as it cascaded back to the ship on our relativistic return trip, and I never knew the island where we landed, when we left home twenty of our years ago and a hundred of theirs, so I expected it to look foreign to me, and it did. The Sun was a little more yellow than on New Landing, the plants friendlier.

But I never thought of myself as an Earther. Even with the new system, hardly any of us do. I thought of myself as from Montreal. Quebecoise. Canadian, even. But Earther? No. I am far more provincial than the colonists whose home I built will ever be.

I flew into the new place instead of Dorval. It looked like Dorval used to. It looked nearly *exactly* like Dorval used to, and I had a twinge of discomfort. The floors were curiously springy, though, which made me feel like *something* was different, and that was reassuring. There isn't an Old Spacers' Legion or anything like that to meet people like me coming in from off-planet—they did that on the little Brazilian island where we landed—but there was a department for Cultural Integration, meant for people traveling from elsewhere on Earth. They assigned me to a representative of the government, who greeted me in a French whose accent was nearly my own. To my ear it sounded more English, with the round vowels, but even with the new system I thought it might be rude to say that to a Quebecoise.

The English-sounding French-speaker gave me a key to the four-room apartment they'd gotten me, not far from the Guy-Concordia Metro station. I told her I could take the Metro to it, but she smiled and said no, they'd have to get my things out of storage for me anyway. So we did that. There were only three boxes. Once you do the math on what will keep for a hundred years, it's a lot easier to give away the things you can't take with you. I gave them to my sister, who died, and whatever was left, she probably gave to her son, who had also died, or her daughter, who was retired and living comfortably in Senegal last I heard. So what I had left myself fit in three small plastic boxes, all labeled "Mireille Ayotte NL000014."

We terraformers all got two-digit numbers for our colonies, NL for New Landing, 14 because there were thirteen team members signed up before they took me.

There was never any doubt they were going to take me. It was just a matter of where I wanted to go, and I wanted New Landing because the survey probes made the plants look promising, which I think they were. When I wasn't catching up on Earth culture for the last hundred years, I was looking at reports from the other colonies, and I thought ours did the best with plant adaptation so far.

I had to start thinking of New Landing as "theirs," not "ours." I could go back, of course, but by the time I got there they'd have gone on without me as well, and I'd just have the same thing as Montreal all over again: a city full of things that seem like they should look familiar, but they don't.

They had furnished my apartment with stylish clothes and furniture, and everything felt squishy and slightly damp. There was also entertainment in my handheld, and there were more tutorials in case I hadn't had enough of them. The cupboards were stocked with food. They thought of everything. There was nothing for me to do but hang a very old photograph on the wall and go to bed. The bed, at least, was not squishy or damp. It felt like a ship's bunk or a colony housing bed. They could do that properly still, and so I could sleep.

My great-niece came to show me around the next day—dutifully, because of course we'd never met before to have any personal relationship. Her name was Claire-Nathalie, and her clothes looked like they'd been crumpled and left in a damp corner for a month, so I knew she was very stylish. She was absolutely correct in her manner, friendly without presuming closeness, curious without being unduly inquisitive. She offered that I could stay with her. I saw my long-dead sister in her serene features. I declined, and she seemed to expect that I would, so no hard feelings there. I told her I liked the little apartment. I almost did; certainly I liked it better than staying with a stranger.

She looked around at my things. "They've given you new handhelds, thank God," she said. "I can't think what you'd do with a hundred-year-old computer, truly I don't."

"Nor I," I said. "They've been catching us up on the advances on the return trip. Not much else *to* do on the return trip but catch up."

She relaxed a bit. "Oh, good. Much easier that way."

"Yes." I did not say that catching up on that much of human culture and history made me realize how very bad the agencies were at picking out which of the hundreds of novels I would actually want to read, which of the hundreds of comics would make me laugh. They could tell me the recognized classics, but hardly anybody wants those and only those.

It had also made me realize how many of the events that are news when you live somewhere are pointless when you don't.

I did not say these things to my great-niece.

Claire-Nathalie said, "I suppose you'll have the others, then?"

"Others?"

"The others who have returned, they'll be . . . like a peer group for you. A community."

I looked at her carefully. She seemed earnest. "Very few others return, dear—niece." I almost called her dear child, but as she was perhaps three experiential years younger than me I thought that might go badly. "The colonists want to go to stay, unless things go very badly. It's the ship crews and the terraformers who come back, and not all of those."

"Oh." She fidgeted, and I thought she was contemplating Sunday dinners with Old Auntie Mireille, who was not even decently old, if she couldn't find me a buddy or two.

I had pity on her and said, "Of course there are lots of people who are interested in finding out whether they'd want to go. I expect I'll speak to the training groups as well as possibly to some gengineering garden hobbyists."

"Gengineering? Oh, you mean modders."

"Modders." I accepted the correction as gracefully as I could. "And of course there's so much to catch up on, I expect I'll spend the first few months just taking in restaurants and shows."

Claire-Nathalie brightened and began to chatter away about what she'd seen and done and had done to her for entertainment, and I dutifully agreed to wander around having her favorite restaurants, theaters, and what she called "venues" pointed out to me. By the time we were taking the Metro back, I was barely answering her monolog, merely interjecting monosyllables when she seemed to want them. I could not stop noticing how much squashier the floors were in the Metro, both on the trains and on the platforms.

They had also changed the decoration to include a great deal more wood, of which I approved, and gotten rid of the glazed tile installations, of which I did not. When Claire-Nathalie paused for breath, I said something about the tiles, which she ignored, and then something about the floors.

"Oh you poor darling!" she said. "I had just no idea that you lived in the times when your footing was so unnatural. It must have been terribly bad for the feet. Did you have to have a special, what do you call them, podiatrist? I expect everybody in the past did."

It was a moment before I could bring myself to answer. "No, in fact I didn't know anyone who did."

"Really? Well, that's extraordinarily lucky, isn't it?"

I said I supposed it was and then turned my energies to convincing Claire-Nathalie to get off at her own Metro stop and let me find my way home. They had added three lines and who knew how many stops since I'd last lived in Montreal, but it didn't matter—any fool could listen for the stop name or poke their handheld to alert them.

Once I'd told Claire-Nathalie that, I was afraid I would be the fool who couldn't. But I made it off the train and onto the squashy platform stairs myself. I resolved to never, ever contact her again, and possibly to ignore any attempts at contact she attempted to make. Possibly everyone on Earth would feel the same about my feet and the advisability of finding my own kind. Still, it was worth finding out.

After a few days of handheld exploration in my apartment, I ventured out in hopes of finding something, anything that looked familiar. Not far from home, I did: the Hungarian restaurant was in the same place, the striped awnings the same. Of course they had probably been replaced a dozen times since I had last seen them, and I wasn't sure whether the name was the same or not.

I went in, and I would have sworn it was the same woman seating me, and the same cakes in the display case, although of course they had probably both been replaced with the awnings. The cucumber salad was the same, but most of the things that had had beef in them before were made with fowl or lamb. I asked the waiter.

"You are not from here, I can hear it, though your French is of course lovely," he said in outrageously Hungarian-accented French. "Beef is almost entirely African and South Asian now. You are perhaps from Africa?"

"I have most recently come from a Brazilian island," I said truthfully.

"Ah, Brazil!" he said. "Well, they can afford whatever they like, can't they? And on islands one supposes it's easier to keep the cattle isolated. But here it is all birds and sheep. They stay healthier for cheaper. It is very traditional. We have always eaten this way."

"I see," I said. "Thank you."

"And would you perhaps like some cake? We have very fine cake here."

"I see that you have," I said, but I ordered *palacsinta* anyway, wondering if the farmers' cheese inside was made from sheep milk. It was divine anyway. If I closed my eyes it was just the same. If I opened them, it was not that much different. Just little bits.

This began to bother me more and more.

I spoke at the garden enthusiasts' club meeting, and I called them "modders" just as Claire-Nathalie had. They received me with mild hobbyist enthusiasm.

They served me sweets that all seemed to have bits of pear in them. I was not changing their lives. It certainly did not change mine.

I looked on the net for former terraformer classmates who had gone off to the colonies. Only one of them had come back to Montreal: Stephane D'Abbadie, three years older than me to begin with. I had no idea how many years older he would be now. He had left while I was still in classes and come back while I was still in transit back from New Landing. I didn't know much about his colony, Outpost. It was older than New Landing, but not by much. I had thought to catch up on Earth, but not on the handful of other colonies, and my news feeds were set to Earth, New Landing, and "general interest," whatever that meant these days.

I thought briefly about reading up on Outpost before going to see Stephane, but I decided not to. I don't know why I didn't think of messaging him like a polite person, to let him know I was on my way or find out if he wanted to see me. We had been friends, but not good friends. And that was two decades and three planets ago.

When he answered the door, he looked just the same, but his dark skin was an ashier brown than I remembered, and he had started tinting his hair red over the black, so it looked like a mass of curled cherry wood shavings. I didn't even remember what my own hair was like when he left for Outpost. I opened my mouth and found it dry and stuck.

"Hello," he said. He didn't move to invite me in, or even to indicate that he knew who I was.

"It's me, Mireille, I'm back," I said.

"I see that," said Stephane.

"I can deal with them putting pears in everything now," I said, "but I can't get my head around the squashy floors in the Metro."

He peered at me, and then a smile broke over his face. "All right, Mireille, come in." As he made us tea and set out some grapes, he said, "You should feel grateful you've come home to a place where there's snow. In all the cities where they don't have to clear snow, the squashy floors are everywhere. They've decided they're more natural."

I tried to smile. "Natural. Everyone wants to call their pet theories natural but us, Stephane."

He raised an eyebrow. "How do you know I don't, after twenty-eight years?"

"Twenty-three for me," I said. "No, but I know. Because terraformers don't do that. We know how easily it could go one way or another. We know that we're not in the business of natural."

He said, "I haven't been in the business of much of anything since I came home."

"I haven't figured out what I'd like to do, either," I said. "I have my savings."

"Yes."

"That doesn't fill the days."

"No."

I huffed a sigh of frustration. "Well, then, what are you doing?"

"Drugs and meaningless sex, mostly," he said.

I blinked. He didn't.

"You're joking," I said tentatively.

"I am, actually," he said, and the grin returned. "No, I'll show you what I've been doing, if you like. It's not the least bit scandalous. Or at least it shouldn't be. I'm afraid I don't have the hang of what's a scandal and what isn't yet."

"On New Landing, the amount of loafing I've been doing would be a scandal."

"Outpost, too," he said. "Come on."

He had the keys to a shed in the back garden of his apartment building, and it was fully powered, not the tool shed I would have assumed. When he took me outside, I thought gardening, but the shed smelled of wood shavings and varnish, and sawdust scuffed under our feet.

"No squashy floors here, either," he said, smiling. He opened a cabinet and handed me a small wooden toy, dark and light together. It had wheels and hooks.

"A train car?"

"I make wooden toys. Mostly trains. Some trucks and things. I did it on Outpost from time to time—the children loved it, but my time was mostly taken—well, you know."

"Your children?" I asked, though I knew it was the wrong question.

"No. I never . . . "

"Neither did I."

"Ah, well," he said gravely.

I fiddled with the train car, running it back and forth along my hand. "The wheels are really lovely."

"Thank you. Do you want to see how I made them?"

I thought about it. "Why not?"

So he showed me the lathe on which he shaped the wheels, and their evenness seemed inevitable. Before I knew it, it was late afternoon, and I had carved out the rough shape of a caboose while watching Stephane do the detailing on an engine with far more in the way of scrolls and curlicues than the plain little train car he'd handed me.

"I would say let's get takeout," I said, "but they put lamb on their pizzas now, I expect."

"Mutton pepperoni is surprisingly edible once you're used to it," he said. "The spices cover a multitude of sins. I know a place."

We didn't have pepperoni at all in New Landing. I don't know how I could have forgotten it. It was worth the mutton, every bite.

"Do you sell the trains?" I asked when we'd finished the pizza.

"I haven't tried, not here. I don't know where I'd start. On Outpost there was always someone who wanted what I'd made and happened to have a bushel of gengineered—er, modified, sorry—plums or a new tea mug or something."

"I still say gengineered, too," I said. "We never stopped on New Landing. Well. Maybe they have now."

"Maybe."

I tried to make other friends, but the only person I could really talk to was Stephane. He didn't seem to have other friends, either; at least there was no evidence of them. While I thought of him as the only person I could really talk to, quite often we didn't talk about ourselves at all. He taught me to sand and carve and shape the wood, and we talked about projects, things we'd done, things we'd like to do. It was easier to come up with things I'd like to do while he was there, and I think the same was true for him.

Elsewhere it was hopeless. The clerks in shops spoke to me in English. They would break off their conversations with each other in French and ask in English if they could help me. When I answered in French they always switched back, but that had never happened to me before, not above once or twice, and now it was all the time. I think they could tell that there was something slightly different about me, and even after a hundred years, "foreign" still means "English" in Quebec.

I think that might have been comforting if they hadn't meant *me*, and if their French hadn't sounded so much *more* English than mine.

My only fear with Stephane was that he might think I wanted more of our relationship than I did. I have never been any good at romance—perhaps if I had, I'd have formed roots and stayed on New Landing—but we were young enough yet—well, some people were young enough yet until the day they died. But we were strong, healthy, middle-aged people. We could go back to the colonies if we liked; they'd still take us. And if that wasn't out of the question, surely I couldn't count on him thinking romance was.

I have always hated it when people fall in love with me. I hate having to give the speeches.

One day we were working together in the shed. It was a glorious day, the kind of bright green things turn after a hard rain. "Come on, we can't stay in here all day," Stephane said to me. "Come and get an ice cream."

"Is it pear ice cream?"

"You like pear ice cream. And it doesn't have any mutton in it. Come on."

It was not the same ice cream shop that had been down by the river when I'd left, but it was just as good. I ordered chocolate, which came without pear, and Stephane ordered banana, which was exotic, newly revived just before our return. We sat on a bench and looked out at the St. Lawrence, and the ice cream was good, and the river was lovely. A man was making balloon animals for a passel of children, and the children looked just right, because children had always looked rumpled. One of them dropped a giraffe by the bench as she dashed past in hot pursuit of her brother.

I picked up the balloon giraffe the child had left behind. It felt like it had been dipped in syrup, but my fingers came away clean.

"It's not nitrile," said Stephane.

"What is it?"

"Some other flexible polymer. I don't know. But people started getting nitrile allergies, so they replaced it the way they replaced latex before we were born. Colony kids have a lot more environmental stimulus. Not so many allergies."

I put the balloon giraffe down again, carefully. It looked just like a balloon animal ought, lumpy and lopsided. But it was sticky.

"If everything was different, I don't think I would have minded as much," I said.

"You would have," said Stephane.

"Do you think so?"

"You are perpetually minding just a little," he said. "If it was more you'd be a malcontent."

"Oh, thank you very much!"

"And if it was less you'd never have gone to New Landing in the first place."

I thought about it. Perhaps he was right. I tried to remember how I'd felt when I lived in Montreal before, but I was so young then. It was mostly the feeling of being a teenager that stuck with me, and that was not the difference. So I thought about my time on New Landing. I hadn't stayed. The others had. But Stephane hadn't stayed on Outpost, either.

"The stars actually were closer then," I said out loud. "It's not that I'm saying I think they were or it felt like they were. We're in an expansionary universe. The stars were actually closer then."

"On the average," said Stephane. "Galactic spirals are, by definition, not linear places. Some of the stars are closer now."

"I suppose that's something."

"I think it is."

We looked out at the canal together. It felt like a date, except that I had no desire to be on a date with Stephane. I was relieved when he grinned sidelong at me and said, "Well. Want to have another go with the lathe?"

I was getting better at it. My whorls and curlicues were not nearly as good as Stephane's for decorating the fancy trains, but I could make every piece of the plain ones myself now, wheels and axles and the lot, and do it just as well as he did. I also roughed out the carving on the fancier work so that he had less to do, although he never minded.

It was lovely, but it wasn't a life. Not a whole one. Not enough of one.

"Mireille, I have to talk to you," said Stephane one day, and I set down the chisel and thought, oh, here it comes.

"All right," I said.

"I can't stay here."

"What do . . . where are you going? Back to Outpost?"

"It'll be just the same on Outpost. I'll have been gone so long."

I had thought of that, too. Whenever I tried to fantasize about going home to New Landing, I knew that relativity had beaten me, and it wouldn't be home any more at all.

"Where, then?"

"One of the new ones. I had hoped you'd come with me."

"Me?"

"You're my friend."

I let out a long breath. It was the right thing to say. "I want to be your friend."

"I know it, Mireille."

"I don't know what else I want, though. I don't think I want to terraform full-time any more." I chewed on my lip and thought about it.

"No, we did that. We could have a little farm each," he said.

"You could have a farm," I said firmly. "I want an orchard."

"Orchards are nice."

"And we would be the crazy toymakers out on the edge of town, and when the terraformers really truly needed us we could help out."

"But only when they really truly needed us."

"Yes," I said.

"Yes."

"I think so."

"I think so too."

"What is the name of this new colony?" I asked. "If you'd meant to go back to Outpost or take me back to New Landing, you'd have said. So what's this one?"

He grimaced. "Mesoasperia."

"Really?"

"I'm sorry. It's the one that'll take us; I checked. Otherwise we'd have to wait another eight months."

"That's too long."

"I know it."

"Well, we can start poking the children to nickname it. Children are good at nicknames."

"Children are *awful* at nicknames," said Stephane. "We'll find ourselves living on Boogerbreath Five."

"The toymakers of Boogerbreath Five," I said. "We'll make them remember pepperoni."

"And forget squashy floors and pears."

"No, that won't do," I said. "The floors yes, but I can't do completely without pears. A few pears only. Pears in moderation."

"The pear-moderate pepperoni toymakers of Boogerbreath Five," he said. "I think it'll do."

It would. I was nearly satisfied it would.

# FIELDS OF GOLD

## RACHEL SWIRSKY

⟨⬩⟩

When Dennis died, he found himself in another place. Dead people came at him with party hats and presents. Noise makers bleated. Confetti fell. It felt like the most natural thing in the world.

His family was there. Celebrities were there. People Dennis had never seen before in his life were there. Dennis danced under a disco ball with Cleopatra and great-grandma Flora and some dark-haired chick and cousin Joe and Alexander the Great. When he went to the buffet table for a tiny cocktail wiener in pink sauce, Dennis saw Napoleon trying to grope his Aunt Phyllis. She smacked him in the tri-corner hat with her clutch bag.

Napoleon and Shakespeare and Cleopatra looked just like Dennis had expected them to. Henry VIII and Socrates and Jesus, too. Cleopatra wore a long linen dress with a jeweled collar, a live asp coiled around her wrist like a bracelet. Socrates sipped from a glass of hemlock. Jesus bobbed his head up and down like a windshield ornament as he ladled out the punch.

Dennis squinted into the distance, but he couldn't make out the boundaries of the place. The room, if it was a room, was large and rectangular and brightly lit from above, like some kind of cosmic gym decorated for prom, complete with drifts of multi-colored balloons and hand-lettered poster board signs. On second glance, the buffet tables turned out to be narrow and collapsible like the ones from Dennis's high school cafeteria. Thankfully, unlike high school, the booze flowed freely and the music was actually good.

As Dennis meandered back toward the dance floor, an imposing figure that he dimly recognized as P. T. Barnum clapped him on the back. "Welcome! Welcome!" the balding man boomed.

An elderly lady stood in Barnum's lee. Her face was familiar from old family portraits. "Glad to see you, dear."

"Thanks," said Dennis as the unlikely couple whirled into the crowd.

Things Dennis did not accomplish from his under thirty-five goals list (circa age twelve):

   1) Own a jet.

   2) Host a TV show where he played guitar with famous singers.

   3) Win a wrestling match with a lion.

   4) Pay Billy Whitman $200 to eat dirt in front of a TV crew.

   5) Go sky-diving.

   6) Divorce a movie star.

As Dennis listened to the retreating echo of P. T. Barnum's laughter, a pair of cold hands slipped around his waist from behind. He jumped like a rabbit.

"Hey there, Menace," said a melted honey voice.

Dennis turned back into the familiar embrace of his favorite cousin, Melanie. She was the one who'd been born a year and three days before he was, and who'd lived half a mile away when they were kids. She was also the one he'd started dry-humping in the abandoned lot behind Ping's groceries when he was eleven and she was twelve.

"Mel," blurted Dennis.

"Asswipe," Melanie replied.

She stood on her tiptoes to slip a hug around Dennis's neck. She wore cropped jean shorts and a thin white tee that showed her bra strap. She smelled like cheap lotion and cherry perfume. A blonde ponytail swung over her shoulder, deceptively girlish in contrast with her hard eyes and filthy mouth. She was young and ripe and vodka-and-cigarettes skinny in a twenty-one-year-old way, just like she had been the day he was called to view her at the morgue—except that the tracks where her jilted boyfriend had run her over with his jeep were gone, as if they'd never been there at all.

"God," said Dennis. "It's good to see you."

"You're not a punch in the face either."

Dennis reached out to touch the side of her head where the morticians had arranged a makeshift hairpiece made of lilies to cover the dent they hadn't been able to repair in time for the open casket. At first Melanie flinched, but then she eased into his touch, pushing against his hand like a contented cat. Her hair felt like corn silk, the skull beneath it smooth and strong.

She pulled away and led Dennis on a meandering path through the crowd to the drinks table. "How'd you kick it?" she asked conversationally.

"Diabetic coma," said Dennis. "Karen pulled the plug."

"That's not what I heard," said Melanie. "I heard it was murder."

Dennis Halter had married Karen Halter (née Worth) on the twenty-second of November, six months to the day after their college graduation.

Karen was the one who proposed. She bought Dennis a $2,000 guitar instead of an engagement ring. She took him out for heavy carbohydrate Italian (insulin at the ready) and popped the question casually over light beer. "I can still return the guitar if you don't want to," she added.

Karen was an art history major who was being groomed for museum curation. Dennis was an anthropology major (it had the fewest required classes) who was beginning to worry about the fact that he hadn't been discovered yet. Karen was Type A. Dennis's personality begged for the invention of a Type Z.

Melanie was similar to Dennis, personality-wise, except for the mean streak that had gotten her expelled for fist fighting during her senior year of high school. She and Karen had only met once, six months before Karen proposed, at a Halter family Thanksgiving. They didn't need to exchange a word. It was hate at first sight.

"Hillbilly whore," Karen called Melanie, though not to her face.

Lacking such compunction, Melanie had called Karen a "control-freak cunt" over pecan pie. She drunk-dialed Dennis three weeks later to make sure he hadn't forgotten her opinion. "When that bitch realizes you're never going to change, she's going to have your balls on a platter. If you marry her, I swear I'll hand her the knife myself."

Melanie died instead.

"Murder?" said Dennis. "No, I wanted her to pull the plug. It was in my living will. I never wanted to live my life as a vegetable."

"Unless it was a couch potato, huh?"

Melanie spoke with the too-precise diction of an over-compensating drunk. Her tone was joking, but held a vicious undercurrent.

She flailed one hand at Dennis's spare tire. The gin she was pouring with her other definitely wasn't her first. Probably not her fourth either.

"Worked out for you, didn't it, Menace the Dennis?" she continued. "Spent your life skipping church only to luck out in the end. Turns out we all go to the same place. Saint, sinner, and suicide."

Dennis's jaw clenched. "I didn't commit suicide."

"Didn't say you did. Sinner."

"And you weren't?"

Melanie poured three fingers of rum into a second Solo cup and went to add Coke. Dennis grabbed the two liter bottle out of her hand.

"Can't drink that with alcohol," he said, irritated, remembering that bender when he was fifteen and she'd promised him it wouldn't matter whether his mixers were diet or regular. He'd ended up in ketoacidosis.

Melanie rolled her eyes. "Think your body works the way it used to? You're dead, moron."

"Fine," said Dennis, annoyance clashing with embarrassment. "Give it to me then."

He rescued the Solo cup and poured a long stream of Coke. Melanie watched reproachfully, gulping her gin.

"You were okay before you started dating that stuck-up bitch," she said. "Had time for a beer and a laugh. Maybe you deserved what that cunt did to you."

"I told you. It was in my will."

"That's not what I'm talking about, jerkwad."

"What *are* you talking about?"

For a moment, Melanie looked simultaneously sly and uncomfortable, as though she were going to spill the beans on something important. Then she shook her head, ponytail whipping, and returned to her rant. "If you'd kept doing me, maybe I wouldn't have ended up with Al. Maybe he wouldn't have gone off the deep-end when I broke it off. I could still be alive. I could be the one in that fancy condo."

"Melanie," said Dennis. "Shut up."

Melanie made to throw an honest-to-God punch. Gin splashed over her shirt and onto the floor. "Look at this!" She gestured broadly, spilling even more. "What the hell is wrong with you?"

Before Dennis could answer, she stormed off in a huff, rapidly disappearing into the mass of people.

When he was alive, Dennis had told people he'd married Karen because she was his type of girl. He hadn't told them that one skinny blonde with a D-cup was basically as good as another.

When he was alive, Dennis had told people he'd married Karen because she was driven and smart and successful. He hadn't told them she made him feel inferior by comparison, sometimes because she told him he was.

When he was alive, Dennis had told people he married Karen because he was a simple man with simple needs. He hadn't told them he kept those simple needs satisfied by fucking around at least twice a year.

When he was alive, Dennis had told people he'd married Karen because she was the kind of girl who knew what she wanted and went after it. Time was like water in Dennis's hands, always flowing through his fingers, leaving him damp but never sated. Karen drank from the stream of time. She made things happen.

One of the things she made happen was getting married. Well, what else was Dennis going to do? It wasn't as if he had plans. Okay, he did have plans, but diamond albums didn't just fall into your lap.

Karen proposed and it made sense, Dennis had told people when he was alive. That's why they got married.

That part was true.

Things Dennis did not accomplish from his under thirty-five goals list (circa age nineteen):

1) Sign with a label.
2) Hit the charts.
3) Get into *Rolling Stone*.
4) Earn $1,000,000.
5) Have at least one girl/girl threesome.
6) Screw Libby Lowell, his roommate's girlfriend.
7) Play in concert with Ted Nugent, Joe Satriani, and Eddie Van Halen.
8) Get recognized on the street by someone he'd never met.

Dennis stared after Melanie in minor shock. Somehow he'd figured this kind of social terrorism would be one of the things that ended in the stillness of the grave.

But if anyone was going to keep making incoherent, drunken rants fourteen years after going into the ground, it was Melanie. She'd always been a pain in the ass when she was drunk. She'd introduced Dennis to alcohol back when she first learned to pick the lock on her father's liquor cabinet with a bobby pin. They'd experimented together to figure out just how much sugar Dennis could ingest with his booze without over-taxing his liver.

From day one, Melanie had drunk until she couldn't see straight and then used it as an excuse to say exactly what she thought. Not that she wasn't a fun drunk. Some of the best nights of his life were the ones they'd spent together as drunk teenagers. She'd start out hurling insults until he left in disgust, only to show up on his porch at three a.m., laughing and apologizing and determined to convince him to join her in making prank calls and harassing the neighbors' cows.

She was Melanie. She was the kind of girl who goaded a guy into running over her with his Jeep. But it was hard to stay mad. Especially now that both of them were dead.

The smell of old tobacco arrived, along with a cold hand patting Dennis's shoulder. Dennis was startled to find that both belonged to his late Uncle Ed, Melanie's father.

"Always thought we should have spent more time raising her right," Ed said.

The old man looked just as hangdog as he had in the moment twenty years ago when he'd fallen off his roof while cleaning the gutters. There he'd been, his feet starting to slide, but he hadn't looked scared so much as wrung out and regretful, as if someone had just told him the Christmas pie he'd been looking forward to was gone and he'd have to make do with fruit cake instead.

He was wearing his best brown suit with a skinny, maroon tie. Slicked back hair exaggerated his widow's peak. The weak chin and expressive eyebrows were family traits, although Ed had a lean, wiry build unlike most Halter men, on account of a parasitic infection he'd contracted during his military days that left him permanently off his feed.

Uncle Ed. Christ. Back home, everyone Dennis's age cussed blue when they were on their own, but even Mel had kept a civil tongue in front of the 'rents. "How much did you hear?" he asked.

" 'Bout all of it."

"I'm sorry."

Ed gave a rueful shrug. "You have no idea what she gets up to. The other day she stripped naked in front of everyone and started sucking off President Garfield."

"Shit," said Dennis without thinking. "Uh, I mean—"

"Sounds right to me. She sure can be a little shit."

Suddenly, a grin split Ed's melancholy face. It was the same grin he'd flashed when fourteen-year-old Dennis let slip that he'd gone through all the senior cheerleaders one by one until Veronica Steader agreed to be his homecoming date.

"Of course, I was into Mary Todd Lincoln at the time," Ed's leer widened to show even more teeth. "Good woman." He slapped Dennis on the back. "You get yourself one of those. You've had enough of the other kind."

Dennis had never watched his diet very carefully. Not as carefully as he needed to anyway. Other kids got to eat Doritos and Oreos at lunch and they didn't even have to worry about it. When Dennis was eight, that righteously pissed him off.

It didn't piss him off enough that he tried to eat exactly the way they did. He wasn't stupid. But it pissed him off enough that he acted a little reckless, a little foolish. Always just a little, though, so that whatever happened, he could plausibly claim—to everyone including himself—that there was nothing deliberate about it.

Eventually, even he believed he was too irresponsible to take care of himself.

The party had moved on to the stage where everyone was too tired to be gregarious but also too drunk to stop partying. Everyone had gathered into small, intense clusters, leaning urgently toward each other to share dramatic whispers, hands cutting the air with emphasis. From time to time, an over-loud exclamation punctured the susurration.

Dennis surveyed the crowd, identifying faces. There was Blackbeard with Grandpa Avery and a buck-toothed redhead. And over there was that Chinese guy who used to live down the street, chatting with Moses and Aunt Phyllis. Most of the groups consisted entirely of strangers.

These were some of the things Dennis picked up as he wandered through the crowd:

1) Death had its own time frame in which connected events bent around mortal time to touch each other. In dead time, the assassination of Archduke Ferdinand had coincided with the deaths of millions of World War Two soldiers. For reasons widely subject to speculation, so had the sinking of the RMS Titanic and the deaths of several big game huntsmen touring French colonies in Africa.

2) The dead also had their own vocabulary. Recently dead people were called rotters or wormies. People who'd been dead a long time were called dusties. Dusties tended to stay in their own enclaves, secluded from the modern ideas and inventions that scared them. Famous dead people were called celebs and they:

3) were considered by popular opinion to be fakes. This allegation caused Blackbeard to roar with anger and threaten to march the speaker off a plank. It was pointed out to him that this was the sort of behavior that had created the theory that celebs were fakes in the first place. Celebrities conformed too closely to their legends. Cleopatra was always seductive and never bored or put-upon. Lincoln declaimed non-stop poetic speeches. And hadn't someone spotted Lady MacBeth earlier that evening when she wasn't even real?

4) Reality, it seemed, was a contentious issue. Mortality shaped the living world by imposing limits. In the limitless afterlife, the shape of things deformed. That was one reason dead people came to parties. Rotters still carried an impression of the living world. It was like going home again for a little while. Besides, there was good food, and who didn't like watching General Sherman march up and down the linoleum, threatening to burn Atlanta?

While Dennis pondered these new pieces of information, he also picked up a number of more personal things. He had an intuitive sense of where these latter were leading, though, and it wasn't somewhere he wanted to go. Consequently, he performed the time-tested mental contortions he'd developed as a third grader who ate too much sugar while pretending he hadn't done anything wrong. Dennis was a master of self-denial; he didn't even let himself realize there was something he wouldn't let himself realize.

For instance:

1) Whenever Dennis passed a group of strangers, they interrupted their conversations to peer as he passed, and then returned to their huddles to whisper even more urgently.

2) Their renewed whispers were punctuated with phrases like "Do you think he deserved it?" and "Poor son of a bitch."

3) At a certain point, they also started saying, "At least the wife got what's coming to her."

4) These last remarks started occurring at approximately the same time as people began disappearing to attend another party.

As the crowd thinned, Dennis finally located someone standing alone, a very drunk flight attendant staring blankly at a tangle of streamers. On being pressed, she identified herself as Wilda. She was unbelievably hot, like a stewardess from a fifties movie, in her mid-to-late twenties with long, straight blonde hair, and a figure that filled out all the tailored curves of her uniform.

The hint of an exotic perfume was all but drowned out by the stench of alcohol. She wasn't currently crying, but tears had streaked her mascara.

Dennis decided to pick her up.

"Melancholy stage?" he asked.

She spoke as if her lips were numb. "What's the point? On this side?"

"Of being melancholy? I didn't know there was ever a point."

"Mortality," she said gravely.

Her expression altered ever so slightly. Dennis tried to echo back an appropriate seriousness.

"I knew a man once," she went on. "Died in the same crash as me. An actor. Very famous. I was so nervous when I poured his in-flight drink I thought I'd spill. He asked for orange juice."

Dennis gestured back toward the buffet tables. "Do *you* want a drink?"

She ignored him. "After we died, he never spoke a word. Not a word. He . . . his mouth would open and this sound would come out . . . eeeeeeeeeee . . . like a dying refrigerator . . . "

She looked at Dennis urgently. Her eyes focused briefly. They were weird, electric blue, like a sky lit up by lightning.

"He was grieving for himself, I think. Or maybe he just used up all his words in the world? And when he died, he was just so happy to be quiet that he never wanted to talk again?" She blinked, slowly, her wet mascara smudging more black beneath her eyes. "It's like the celebs. You know?"

"Would you like to kiss me?" Dennis asked.

"I bet the real dead celebrities are nothing special. They probably blend in. Like my friend. But the fake ones, I think they're made from a kind of collective pressure. None of us lived our lives the way we wanted to. It gets mixed up, all our needs, our unsatisfied desires, the things we wanted to be back when we were alive. Beautiful. Famous. The best of our potential. We make the celebs to be like that for us. Since we can't."

Wilda gestured vaguely toward the crowd. Dennis turned to see Benjamin Franklin demonstrating his kite, which rapidly became tangled with the multi-colored balloons. Marilyn Monroe struggled with her skirt while standing over an air-conditioning vent tucked next to some bleachers. Gandhi sat in the middle of a group positioned near the buffet tables, pointedly not eating.

"You should stay away from them," said Wilda softly. "They're bright and crazy. They suck you down."

Dennis turned back to look at her beautiful, tear-stained face. "I'd rather be with you anyway."

She blinked at him, too lost in her own drunkenness to hear. Or maybe she just didn't believe him? Dennis glanced over his shoulder at Marilyn, ripe and coy, dark-outlined eyes sparkling. Something dark and furious clenched in his stomach.

He was only thirty-five! Marilyn made him so choked up with jealousy he couldn't breathe.

He turned back toward Wilda and leaned in to dab some of the liner from beneath her eyes. She started toward his embrace but got tangled up with her own feet and started to fall. Dennis caught her before she could hit the floor.

She looked up at him, smiling vaguely. "I wanted to be a gymnast. You know? I was good," she said, and then, "Do you think it's cheating?"

"What?" murmured Dennis.

"My husband's still alive."

"So's my wife."

"What if she weren't? Would it be cheating then?"

"I don't know. I wasn't that faithful when we were both alive."

"Neither was I."

Wilda's voice cracked like ice. Tears filled her eyes, colorless like vodka. Dennis looked down at her left hand where she wore a tan line but no ring.

"I don't like being dead," said Wilda.

"I'm sorry," said Dennis.

He held her, silently, until she recovered enough to stand on her own. "I'm sorry, too," she said at last. "I should go to the other party."

Dennis tried to fake a smile. "Don't drink too much while you're there."

Wilda reached out to touch his shoulder. Her fingertips were frozen.

"When you figure it out," she said, "try not to be too sad."

She faded away.

A few of the times Dennis cheated on Karen:

1) The coed who got stuck in the Dallas airport after her flight was canceled who he wooed with four margaritas, his best dozen dirty jokes, and a rendition of Sting's "Desert Rose."

2) The bartender in Phoenix who'd just been dumped by her fiancé and said she needed to know what it was like with a guy who could commit.

3) The drunk divorcée from the Internet ad who got on the hotel bed and dropped her pants without even a word to acknowledge he was there.

A few of the things Dennis pretended not to notice about his marriage:

1) The way Karen's sense of humor about other women had changed. When they were younger, if she saw a pretty blonde who was about her shape walking past them in the mall, she'd say, "I bet she's your type." If she was in a teasing mood, she'd whisper about all the things she and the other girl would do to Dennis if they had him at their mercy. In recent days, her eyes had started getting hard when they even saw blonde girls on TV. She'd angle her face away from him, trying to hide her disgust.

2) How Karen no longer laughed indulgently when he forgot things. She still took care of him: she did his laundry, she found his keys, she rescheduled his doctor's appointments. But she moved through the actions mechanically, her blank expression never flickering.

3) And then there was the worst thing, the one Dennis had taken the most pains to hide from himself—the flicker he'd seen when Karen came home exhausted from a late night's work and found him still awake at two a.m., sitting on the couch and eating beans out of a can. She picked up the dishes he'd left on the coffee table and carried them to the sink, grumbling to herself so faintly he could hardly hear it, "It's like I'm his mother." He looked up and caught the brief flash on her face. It was the same emotion he'd heard in her voice: contempt.

The morning of November nineteenth was three days before their thirteenth anniversary and two months and five days before Dennis's thirty-fifth birthday. Karen Halter (née Worth) proposed they stay in that Friday night to celebrate both occasions. She proposed an evening of drinking and making love. Dennis liked having sex when he was drunk, and although it wasn't Karen's preference, she tried to indulge him from time to time. She knew it reminded him of being young.

Fifteen years ago, when they'd started dating, Karen had carefully reviewed the guidelines for mixing type one diabetes and alcohol. The liver was involved in both processing alcohol and regulating blood sugar, and consequently, a type one diabetic who got carelessly drunk could preoccupy his liver with the one so that it couldn't manage the other. Glucose levels required a tricky balance. If they went too high, they could damage a variety of systems. If they went too low, one could become hypoglycemic or even fall into a coma.

It was trivial to give Dennis more insulin than he needed. She let him inject himself, just in case someone checked later. Not that they would. Everyone knew Dennis was too irresponsible to take care of himself.

She worried when he started puking, but he didn't suspect anything. He just thought he was drunk.

The sleeping pills were his idea. He was feeling too sick to get to sleep on his own. He asked if he could borrow one of her Ambien and before she could say yes or no, he'd pulled the bottle out of the medicine cabinet. She watched him drunkenly struggle to unscrew the lid.

She hadn't meant to go this far. She'd wanted to shock him. She'd wanted him to see how bad things could get and grow the fuck up. Yes, she wanted him to suffer a little, too, just so he'd know what it felt like.

If she let him take the pill, it'd be more than that. He wouldn't be awake to monitor his condition. He wouldn't be able to call an ambulance when things started going really wrong. He'd get sicker than she'd intended. He could even die.

Karen had matched Dennis drink for drink. No one would suspect her of wrongdoing. At worst, they'd think she'd also been too drunk to notice his symptoms.

With a shock, it occurred to Karen that maybe she'd been planning this all along. Maybe she'd been slowly taking the steps that could lead to Dennis's death without admitting to herself that was what she was doing. She knew how self-denial worked by now; she'd been married to Dennis for thirteen years, after all.

She eased the bottle from his hand. "Let me do that," she said, unscrewing the cap. She poured out two pills: one for him and one for her.

Now neither of them could call for help.

In the morning, memory clear and heart pounding, Karen called 911 in a genuine panic. She rode with Dennis in the ambulance, weeping real tears.

She cried because she'd become a murderess and she didn't want to see herself that way. She also cried because she wasn't sorry she'd done it and that scared her even more.

· The doctors proclaimed the coma unusually severe. Brain damage had occurred. Over the next several weeks, using sterile, equivocal comments, they made it clear that there was no hope. They would need a decision.

Karen had set herself on this path. There was no escaping it. Dennis's living will was clear. She told them to pull the plug.

During the weeks when Dennis lay comatose, Karen began having nightmares. She researched bad dreams on the Internet and confirmed that anxiety produced an increase in negative dream imagery. Nothing to be concerned about. Except she kept dreaming about the strangest thing—that trashy cousin Dennis had admitted to fucking when he was a kid. They'd gone to her funeral a few months before Karen proposed. Dennis had bent over the casket and wept for nearly a quarter of an hour. Karen could understand why he was upset; the girl was family. But deep in her gut, whether it was fair or not, she couldn't help being appalled. He was mourning his partner in incest.

Afterward, at the visitation, various family members asked her to stand next to the big, glossy photograph of the deceased they'd hung on the wall. "You look just like her," everyone said, which made Karen even more uncomfortable. She tried to laugh off her reaction as indignance that she'd ever dress like that, but she had a niggling feeling there was something more profound. She *did* look eerily like the girl, the same close-set eyes, the same blunt chin, the same shade of blonde hair. It was as if Dennis was trying to recreate the relationship he'd had when he was eleven, as if it didn't matter to him that Karen had her own thoughts and feelings and personality, as long as she looked like his first, forbidden love.

In Karen's dreams, the blonde cousin had a knife. She chased Karen down winding asphalt streets, upraised metal shining in the shadows. "I don't care what I said," she growled. "I'm not going to let you cut his balls off. I'll cut you first."

The day Karen told them to pull the plug, she woke with her heart pounding so hard that she thought she was going to have to check into the hospital herself. The feeling faded when she went down to give the decision in person, but intensified again as she got in her car to drive home. She'd told them she couldn't handle staying to watch Dennis die, which was true, but not for the reasons they supposed.

Outside, thick, dingy clouds of smog dimmed the sunlight to a sickly brown. Headlights and taillights glared in Karen's windshield, a fraction too bright.

Horns screamed in the wake of near misses. Karen watched carefully, mapping out the traffic in her mind's eye, making sure she didn't veer out of her narrow lanes or crash into the broken-down SUVs on the side of the road. She was the kind of woman who had memorized the safety manual that came with her vehicle, and could recite all the local laws regarding child safety seats even though she'd never had any children in her car.

Despite her meticulousness, as Karen pulled into the intersection after waiting for the green, she failed to see the blonde woman in a white t-shirt jogging into the crosswalk. She pounded the breaks and yanked on the steering wheel, but it was already too late. Rubber screeched. Metal crunched against metal. The car next to hers careened sideways with the impact. Karen fell toward the windshield, her airbag failing to deploy, the steering wheel breaking against her head.

It took Karen almost three weeks to die, but in the land of the dead, time twisted around itself to join connected events. So it was only a few hours into Dennis's party that Karen's began, and his gossiping guests faded away to attend the newest scandal.

Things Dennis did not accomplish from his under thirty-five goals list (circa age thirty-four):

1) Start another band.
2) Play some gigs in the area.
3) Get his sugar under control.
4) Be nicer to Karen.
5) Stop cheating.
6) Go to the gym.

Dennis's self-denial had finally reached its breaking point. He ran between the fading guests. "How do I get there? You have to show me! I have to see her!"

They winked out like stars from a graying dawn sky, not one of them letting slip what he needed to know.

The empty gym, if it was a gym, seemed to be disappearing on the edges. Perhaps it was. The dead people had talked about imposing their own shapes on the limitless afterlife. Maybe shapelessness was taking over.

One spot near the buffet tables remained bright, a fraction of the dance floor underneath the disco ball. Uncle Ed stood alone in the middle, fiddling with the coin slot in the juke box.

He turned as Dennis approached. "I wanted 'Young Love,'" he said, "but they've only got 'After You've Gone.' Not worth a quarter." He sighed. "Oh, well. That's the afterlife, I guess."

The juke box lit up as the coin slid into its machinery. It whirred, selecting a record. Dennis recognized the bright, slightly distorted strains as a hit from the forties.

Ed selected a pastel blue balloon and began to whirl it around like a dance partner. Dennis stood tensely, arms crossed.

"Why didn't you tell me?"

Ed dipped the balloon. "About what?"

"About Karen."

"Figured you'd find out sooner or later. No sense ruining a perfectly good party until you did."

"I'd have wanted to know."

"Sorry then."

"How do I get over there? I've got to talk to her."

"You can't."

"I've got to!"

"She doesn't want you. You can't go bothering someone who doesn't want you. That's one of the rules we agree on. Otherwise someone could stalk you forever." Ed gave a mild shrug. "I was used badly by a woman once, you know."

Dennis glared silently.

"My first wife, Lilac," Ed went on. "Not Melanie's mother. Lilac died before you all were born. Your mom never liked her."

"Mom never liked Karen either."

"A perceptive woman, your mother. Well, things were good with me and Lilac for a while. We spent my whole party making out. Afterward, we found some old Scottish castle out with the dusties and rolled around in the grass for longer than you spent alive. It didn't last long, though. Relatively. See, while I was still alive, she'd already met another dead guy. They'd been together for centuries before I kicked it. She was just curious about what it would be like to be with me again. Near broke my heart."

"Ed," Dennis said. "Karen murdered me. I have to know why."

Ed released the balloon. It flew upward and disappeared into grey.

"Have to?" Ed asked. "When you were alive, you had to have food and water. What's 'have to' mean to you anymore?"

"Ed, please!"

"All right, then, I'll take a gander. I've been dead a long time, but I bet I know a few things. Now, you didn't deserve what Karen did to you. No one deserves that. But you had your hand in making it happen. I'm not saying you didn't have good qualities. You could play a tune and tell a joke, and you were usually in a good humor when you weren't sulking. Those are important things. But you never thought about anyone else. Not only wouldn't you stir yourself to make a starving man a sandwich, but you'd have waited for him to bring you one before you stirred yourself to eat. One thing I've learned is people will give you a free lunch from time to time, but only so long as they think you're trying. And if you don't try, if they get to thinking you're treating them with disdain, well then. Sometimes they get mean."

"I didn't treat Karen with disdain," Dennis said.

Ed blinked evenly.

"It's not that I don't think about other people," Dennis said. "I just wanted someone to take care of me. The whole world, everything was so hard. Even eating the wrong thing could kill you. I wanted someone to watch out for me, I guess. I guess I wanted to stay a kid."

"You married a problem solver," said Ed. "Then you became a problem."

When Dennis thought about Ed, he always thought about that moment when he'd watched him fall off the roof. Failing that, he thought of the mostly silent man who sat in the back of family gatherings and was always first to help out with a chore. But now, with his words still stinging, Dennis remembered a different Uncle Ed, the one who'd always been called to finish off the barn cats who got sick, the one everyone relied on to settle family disputes because they knew he wouldn't play favorites no matter who was involved.

Ed didn't look so much like the man who'd fallen off the roof anymore. His wrinkles had tightened, his yellowing complexion brightening to a rosy pink. His hair was still slicked back from his forehead with Brilliantine, but now there were generous, black locks of it.

He straightened his suit jacket and it became a white tee-shirt, snug over faded jeans. He grinned as he stuck his hands in his pockets. His teeth were large and straight and shiny white.

"I always figured we'd have kids," Dennis said. "I can't do that here, can I? And the band, I was always going to get started with that again, as soon as I got things going, as soon as I found the time . . . "

Dennis trailed off. The juke box spun to a stop, clicking as it returned the record to its place. Its lights guttered for a moment before flicking off.

"I'm dead," said Dennis, plaintively. "What do I do?"

Ed spread his hands toward the gym's grey edges. "Hop from party to party. Find a cave with the dusties. Get together with a girl and play house until the continents collide. Whatever you want. You'll find your way."

A newsboy cap appeared in Ed's hand. He tugged it on and tipped the brim.

"Now if you'll excuse me," he continued. "I need to pay my respects."

"To my murderer?"

"She's still family."

"Don't leave me alone," Dennis pleaded.

Ed was already beginning to fade.

Dennis sprinted forward to grab his collar.

When Dennis was four, he found his grandfather's ukulele in the attic, buried under a pile of newspapers. It was a four-string soprano pineapple made of plywood with a spruce soundboard. Tiny figures of brown women in grass skirts gyrated across the front, painted grins eerily broad.

The year Dennis turned six, his parents gave him a bike with training wheels for Christmas instead of the guitar he asked for. After a major tantrum, they wised up and bought him a three-quarter sized acoustic with two-tone lacquer finish in red and black. It was too big, but Dennis eventually got larger. The songbook that came with it included chords and lyrics for "Knockin' on Heaven's Door," "Leaving on a Jet Plane," and "Yellow Submarine."

The summer when Dennis was fifteen, he wheedled his grandparents into letting him do chores around their place for $2.50 an hour until he saved enough to buy a used stratocaster and an amp. He stayed up until midnight every night for the next six months playing that thing in the corner of the basement his mother had reluctantly cleared out next to the water heater. He failed science and math, and only barely squeaked by with a D in English, but it was worth it.

The guitar Karen bought him when they got engaged was the guitar of his dreams. A custom Gibson Les Paul hollow-body with a maple top, mahogany body, ebony fret board, cherryburst finish, and curves like Jessica Rabbit. He hadn't been able to believe what he was seeing. Just looking at it set off strumming in his head.

As she popped the question, Karen ran her index finger gently across the abalone headstock inlay. The tease of her fingertip sent a shiver down his spine. It was the sexiest thing he'd ever seen.

Everything blurred.

Dennis and Ed reappeared in the rooftop garden of the museum where Karen had worked. It looked the way it did in summer, leafy shrubs and potted trees rising above purple, red and white perennials. The conjured garden was much larger than the real one; it stretched out as far as Dennis could see in all directions, blurring into verdant haze at the horizon.

Seurat stood at his easel in front of a modernist statue, stabbing at the canvas with his paintbrush. Figures from Karen's family and/or the art world strolled between ironwork benches, sipping martinis. Marie Antoinette, in *robe à la Polonaise* and *pouf*, distributed *petit fours* from a tray while reciting her signature line.

Dennis glimpsed Wilda, seemingly recovered from her melancholia, performing a series of acrobatic dance moves on a dais.

And then he saw Karen.

She sat on a three-legged stool, sipping a Midori sour as she embarked on a passionate argument about South African modern art with an elderly critic Dennis recognized from one of her books. She looked more sophisticated than he remembered. Makeup made her face dramatic, her eyebrows shaped into thin arches, a hint of dark blush sharpening her cheekbones. A beige summer gown draped elegantly around her legs. There was a vulnerability in her eyes he hadn't seen in ages, a tenderness beneath the blue that had vanished years ago.

Dennis felt as if it would take him an eternity to take her in, but even dead time eventually catches up.

Ed, struggling to pry Dennis's fingers off his collar, gave an angry shout. Both Karen and the old man beside her turned to look straight at them.

Ed twisted Dennis's fingers until one of them made a snapping sound. Shocked, Dennis dropped his grip.

"Christ!" said Ed, glaring at Dennis as he rubbed his reddened throat. "What the hell is wrong with you?" He turned away from Dennis as if washing his hands of him, tipped his hat to Karen, and then stalked off into the green.

"How are you here?" Karen sounded more distressed than angry. "They told me you couldn't be."

"I hitched a ride."

"But that shouldn't matter. They said—"

Karen quieted in the wake of the noise from the crowd that had begun to form around them. Ordinary people and celebs, strangers and friends and family and neighbors, all gossiping and shoving as they jockeyed for front row views.

The elderly art critic straightened and excused himself to the safety of the onlookers. Dennis stepped into his position.

"Maybe you let me in," Dennis said. "Maybe you really wanted me here."

Karen gave a strangled laugh. "I want you out and I want you in. I can't make up my mind. That sounds like the shape of it."

"You murdered me," said Dennis.

"I murdered you," said Karen.

Behind them, Dennis heard the noise of a scuffle, some New Jersey guido pitting himself against H. L. Mencken.

"I didn't mean to do it," Karen continued. "I don't think I did, at least."

Dennis swallowed.

"I'm sorry," Karen said. "Sorrier than I can tell you."

"You're only saying that because you're dead."

"No. What would be the point?"

Dennis heard the guido hit the ground as H. L. Mencken declared his victory in verse. A small round of applause ended the incident as the throng refocused on Dennis and Karen. Dennis had thought he'd want to hit her or scream at her. Some part of her must have wanted him to do that, must have known she deserved to be punished. He wondered if anyone would try to stop him if he attacked her. He got the impression no one would.

"I hate you," Dennis told her. It was mostly true.

"Me, too," said Karen.

"I didn't when we were alive. Not all the time, anyway."

"Me, too."

They both fell silent. Straining to overhear, the crowd did, too. In the background, there were bird calls, the scent of daisies, the whoosh of traffic three stories below.

"I don't think," said Dennis, "that I want to be near you anymore."

So, according to the rules of the land of the dead, he wasn't.

Things Dennis did accomplish from his under thirty-five goals lists (various ages):

1) Eat raw squid.

2) Own a gaming console.

3) Star in an action movie.* (*After a bad day when he was twenty-four, Dennis decided to broaden the definition of "star" to include his role as an extra in *Round Two*.)

4) Watch Eric Clapton live.

5) Seduce a girl by writing her a love song.

6) Screw Pamela Kortman, his roommate's ex-girlfriend.

7) Clean out the garage to make a practice space.

8) Play all night, until dawn, without noticing the time.

He was back in the gym. A single bank of fluorescent lights whined as they switched back on. Only one of the bulbs turned on, casting an eerie glow that limned Dennis's body against the dark.

A figure crept out of the shadows. "Hey."

Dennis turned toward the voice. He saw the outline of a girl. At first he thought it was the stewardess, Wilda. No, he thought, it's—is it Karen? But as the figure came closer, he realized it was Melanie.

"Hey Mel," said Dennis.

"Hey Asswipe," said Mel, but her voice didn't have any edge to it.

"I thought you were at Karen's party."

"That bitch? I wouldn't go to her party if she was the last rotter. I've been waiting here so I could catch you alone."

She crept even closer, until he could smell the sourness of her breath.

"I heard what my dad said. I wanted to say I'm sorry. He was pretty hard on you. You didn't deserve it. I was going to come out and give him a piece of my mind, but I didn't know how you'd feel after all that stuff I said."

She shifted her weight nervously from foot to foot.

"You didn't deserve that either," she said. "I'm sorry."

"It's okay," Dennis said.

"No, really."

"No, really."

Melanie smiled. Her expression looked so young and genuine that Dennis finally felt the fist around his heart begin to relax.

He remembered the late nights when he and Melanie had been kids, when she'd turned up on his porch and begged him to go with her to steal cigarettes or throw aftershave at Billy Whitman's window. The same mischief inflected her pose now: her quirked smile, sparkling eyes, and restless fingers.

"Do you think a man could live his whole life trying to get back to when he was eleven?" Dennis asked.

Melanie shrugged. She was twelve now, young and scrappy, pretty in pink but still the first kid on the block to throw a punch.

"Do you want to go play in the lot behind Ping's?" she asked.

Dennis looked down at himself. He saw the red and purple striped shirt he'd worn every day when he was eleven years old except when his mom took it away for the laundry.

Tall, dry grass whipped the backs of his knees. It rustled in the breeze, a rippling golden wave.

"Yeah," he said.

He reached for her hand. Her fingers curled into his palm.

"We don't ever have to come back if we don't want to," she said. "We can go as far as we want. We can keep going forever."

The sun hung bright overhead, wisps of white drifting past in the shapes of lions and racecars and old men's faces. The air smelled of fresh, growing things, and a bare hint of manure. A cow lowed somewhere and a truck rumbled across the asphalt. Both sounds were equidistant, a world away.

"Come on," said Dennis.

They ran. She led the way, long sandaled feet falling pigeon-toed in the soil. Dennis felt the breath flow sweet and easy through his lungs.

Someday they'd stop. Someday they'd fall exhausted to the ground and sleep curled up together in the dirt. Someday they'd pass into town where

Dennis's father was arguing over the price of wood while Uncle Ed stood in front of the hardware store, sipping lemonade. Someday they might even run straight through the universe, all the way back to the weird land of death where they'd chat with Descartes about the best way to keep mosquitoes off in summer.

For now, their feet beat like drums on the soil. Wind reddened Dennis's ears. Melanie's hair flew back into his face. He tugged her east to chase a crow circling above the horizon. Behind them, the wind swept through fields the size of eternity.

# THE SMELL OF ORANGE GROVES

## LAVIE TIDHAR

On the roof the solar panels were folded in on themselves, still asleep, yet uneasily stirring, as though they could sense the imminent coming of the sun. Boris stood on the edge of the roof. The roof was flat and the building's residents, his father's neighbors, had, over the years, planted and expanded an assortment of plants, in pots of clay and aluminum and wood, across the roof, turning it into a high-rise tropical garden.

It was quiet up there and, for the moment, still cool. He loved the smell of late-blooming jasmine, it crept along the walls of the building, climbing tenaciously high, spreading out all over the old neighborhood that surrounded Central Station. He took a deep breath of night air and released it slowly, haltingly, watching the lights of the space port: it rose out of the sandy ground of Tel Aviv, the shape of an hourglass, and the slow moving sub-orbital flights took off and landed, like moving stars, tracing jeweled flight paths in the skies.

He loved the smell of this place, this city. The smell of the sea to the west, that wild scent of salt and open water, seaweed and tar, of suntan lotion and people. He loved to watch the solar surfers in the early morning, with spread transparent wings gliding on the winds above the Mediterranean. Loved the smell of cold conditioned air leaking out of windows, of basil when you rubbed it between your fingers, loved the smell of shawarma rising from street level with its heady mix of spices, turmeric and cumin dominating, loved the smell of vanished orange groves from far beyond the urban blocks of Tel Aviv or Jaffa.

*Once it had all been orange groves.* He stared out at the old neighborhood, the peeling paint, box-like apartment blocks in old-style Soviet architecture crowded in with magnificent early twentieth century Bauhaus constructions, buildings made to look like ships, with long curving graceful balconies, small round windows, flat roofs like decks, like the one he stood on—

Mixed amongst the old buildings were newer constructions, Martian-style co-op buildings with drop-chutes for lifts, and small rooms divided and sub-divided inside, many without any windows—

Laundry hanging as it had for hundreds of years, off wash lines and windows, faded blouses and shorts blowing in the wind, gently. Balls of lights floated in the streets down below, dimming now, and Boris realised the night was receding, saw a blush of pink and red on the edge of the horizon and knew the sun was coming.

He had spent the night keeping vigil with his father. Vlad Chong, son of Weiwei Zhong (Zhong Weiwei in the Chinese manner of putting the family name first) and of Yulia Chong, née Rabinovich. In the tradition of the family Boris, too, was given a Russian name. In another of the family's traditions, he was also given a second, Jewish name. He smiled wryly, thinking about it. Boris Aaron Chong, the heritage and weight of three shared and ancient histories pressing down heavily on his slim, no longer young shoulders.

It had not been an easy night.

*Once it had all been orange groves* . . . he took a deep breath, that smell of old asphalt and lingering combustion-engine exhaust fumes, gone now like the oranges yet still, somehow, lingering, a memory-scent.

He'd tried to leave it behind. The family's memory, what he sometimes, privately, called the Curse of the Family Chong, or Weiwei's Folly.

He could still remember it. Of course he could. A day so long ago, that Boris Aaron Chong himself was not yet an idea, an I-loop that hasn't yet been formed . . .

It was in Jaffa, in the Old City on top of the hill, above the harbor. The home of the Others.

Zhong Weiwei cycled up the hill, sweating in the heat. He mistrusted these narrow winding streets, both of the Old City itself and of Ajami, the neighborhood that had at last reclaimed its heritage. Weiwei understood this place's conflicts very well. There were Arabs and Jews and they wanted the same land and so they fought. Weiwei understood land, and how you were willing to die for it.

But he also knew the concept of land had changed. That *land* was a concept less of a physicality now, and more of the mind. Recently, he had invested some of his money in an entire planetary system in the Guilds of Ashkelon games-universe. Soon he would have children—Yulia was in her third trimester already—and then grandchildren, and great-grandchildren, and so on down the generations, and they would remember Weiwei, their progenitor. They would thank him for what he'd done, for the real estate both real and virtual, and for what he was hoping to achieve today.

He, Zhong Weiwei, would begin a dynasty, here in this divided land. For he had understood the most basic of aspects, he alone saw the relevance of that foreign enclave that was Central Station. Jews to the north (and his children, too, would be Jewish, which was a strange and unsettling thought), Arabs to the south, now they have returned, reclaimed Ajami and Menashiya, and were building New Jaffa, a city towering into the sky in steel and stone and glass. Divided cities, like Akko, and Haifa, in the north, and the new cities sprouting in the desert, in the Negev and the Arava.

Arab or Jew, they needed their immigrants, their foreign workers, their Thai and Filipino and Chinese, Somali and Nigerian. And they needed their buffer, that in-between-zone that was Central Station, old South Tel Aviv, a poor place, a vibrant place—most of all, a liminal place.

And he would make it his home. His, and his children's, and his children's children. The Jews and the Arabs understood family, at least. In that they were like the Chinese—so different to the Anglos, with their nuclear families, strained relations, all living separately, alone . . . This, Weiwei swore, would not happen to his children.

At the top of the hill he stopped, and wiped his brow from the sweat with the cloth handkerchief he kept for that purpose. Cars went past him, and the sound of construction was everywhere. He himself worked on one of the buildings they were erecting here, a diasporic construction crew, small Vietnamese and tall Nigerians and pale solid Transylvanians, communicating by hand signals and Asteroid pidgin (though that had not yet been in widespread use at that time) and automatic translators through their nodes. Weiwei himself worked the exoskeleton suits, climbing up the tower blocks with spider-like grips, watching the city far down below and looking out to sea, and distant ships . . .

But today was his day off. He had saved money—some to send, every month, to his family back in Chengdu, some for his soon to be growing family here. And the rest for this, for the favor to be asked of the Others.

Folding the handkerchief neatly away, he pushed the bike along the road and into the maze of alleyways that was the Old City of Jaffa. The remains of an ancient Egyptian fort could still be seen there, the gate had been re-fashioned a century before, and the hanging orange tree still hung by chains, planted within a heavy, egg-shaped stone basket, in the shade of the walls. Weiwei didn't stop, but kept going until he reached, at last, the place of the Oracle.

Boris looked at the rising sun. He felt tired, drained. He kept his father company throughout the night. His father, Vlad, hardly slept any more. he sat for hours in his armchair, a thing worn and full of holes, dragged one day, years ago (the memory crystal-clear in Boris' mind) with great effort and pride from Jaffa's flea market. Vlad's hands moved through the air, moving and rearranging invisible objects. He would not give Boris access into his visual feed. He barely communicated, any more. Boris suspected the objects were memories, that Vlad was trying to somehow fit them back together again. But he couldn't tell for sure.

Like Weiwei, Vlad had been a construction worker. He had been one of the people who had built Central Station, climbing up the unfinished gigantic structure, this space port that was now an entity unto itself, a miniature mall-nation to which neither Tel Aviv nor Jaffa could lay complete claim.

But that had been long ago. Humans lived longer now, but the mind grew old just the same, and Vlad's mind was older than his body. Boris, on the roof, went to the corner by the door. It was shaded by a miniature palm tree, and now the solar panels, too, were opening out, extending delicate wings, the better to catch the rising sun and provide shade and shelter to the plants.

Long ago, the resident association had installed a communal table and a samovar there, and each week a different flat took turns to supply the tea and the coffee and the sugar. Boris gently plucked leaves off the potted mint plant nearby, and made himself a cup of tea. The sound of boiling water pouring into the mug was soothing, and the smell of the mint spread in the air, fresh and clean, waking him up. He waited as the mint brewed; took the mug with him back to the edge of the roof. Looking down, Central Station—never truly asleep—was noisily waking up.

He sipped his tea, and thought of the Oracle.

The Oracle's name had once been Cohen, and rumor had it that she was a relation of St. Cohen of the Others, though no one could tell for certain. Few people today knew this. For three generations she had resided in the Old City, in that dark and quiet stone house, her and her Other alone.

The Other's name, or ident tag, was not known, which was not unusual, with Others.

Regardless of possible familial links, outside the stone house there stood a small shrine to St. Cohen. It was a modest thing, with random items of golden color placed on it, and old, broken circuits and the like, and candles burning at all hours. Weiwei, when he came to the door, paused for a moment before the shrine, and lit a candle, and placed an offering—a defunct computer chip from the old days, purchased at great expense in the flea market down the hill.

*Help me achieve my goal today*, he thought, *help me unify my family and let them share my mind when I am gone.*

There was no wind in the Old City, but the old stone walls radiated a comforting coolness. Weiwei, who had only recently had a node installed, pinged the door and, a moment later, it opened. He went inside.

Boris remembered that moment as a stillness and at the same time, paradoxically, as a *shifting*, a sudden inexplicable change of perspective. His grandfather's memory glinted in the mind. For all his posturing, Weiwei was like an explorer in an unknown land, feeling his way by touch and instinct. He had not grown up with a node; he found it difficult to follow the Conversation, that endless chatter of human and machine feeds a modern human would feel deaf and blind without; yet he was a man who could sense the future as instinctively as a chrysalis can sense adulthood. He knew his children would be different, and their children different in their turn, but he equally knew there can be no future without a past—

"Zhong Weiwei," the Oracle said. Weiwei bowed. The Oracle was surprisingly young, or young-looking at any rate. She had short black hair and unremarkable features and pale skin and a golden prosthetic for a thumb, which made Weiwei shiver without warning: it was her Other.

"I seek a boon," Weiwei said. He hesitated, then extended forwards the small box. "Chocolates," he said, and—or was it just his imagination?—the Oracle smiled.

It was quiet in the room. It took him a moment to realize it was the Conversation, ceasing. The room was blocked to mundane network traffic. It was a safe-haven, and he knew it was protected by the high-level encryption engines of the Others. The Oracle took the box from him and opened it, selecting one particular piece with care and putting it in her mouth. She chewed thoughtfully for a moment and indicated approval by inching her head. Weiwei bowed again.

"Please," the Oracle said. "Sit down."

Weiwei sat down. The chair was high-backed and old and worn—from the flea market, he thought, and the thought made him feel strange, the idea of the Oracle shopping in the stalls, almost as though she were human. But of course, she *was* human. It should have made him feel more at ease, but somehow it didn't.

Then the Oracle's eyes subtly changed color, and her voice, when it came, was different, rougher, a little lower than it's been, and Weiwei swallowed again. "What is it you wish to ask of us, Zhong Weiwei?"

It was her Other, speaking now. The Other, shotgun-riding on the human body, Joined with the Oracle, quantum processors running within that golden thumb . . . Weiwei, gathering his courage, said, "I seek a bridge."

The Other nodded, indicating for him to proceed.

"A bridge between past and future," Weiwei said. "A . . . continuity."

"Immortality," the Other said. It sighed. Its hand rose and scratched its chin, the golden thumb digging into the woman's pale flesh. "All humans want is immortality."

Weiwei shook his head, though he could not deny it. The idea of death, of dying, terrified him. He lacked faith, he knew. Many believed, belief was what kept humanity going. Reincarnation or the afterlife, or the mythical Upload, what they called being Translated—they were the same, they required a belief he did not possess, much as he may long for it. He knew that when he died, that would be it. The I-loop with the ident tag of Zhong Weiwei would cease to exist, simply and without fuss, and the universe would continue just as it always had. It was a terrible thing to contemplate, one's insignificance. For human I-loops, they were the universe's focal point, the object around which everything revolved. Reality was subjective. And yet that was an illusion, just as an I was, the human personality a composite machine compiled out of billions of neurons, delicate networks operating semi-independently in the grey matter of a human brain. Machines augmented it, but they could not preserve it, not forever. So yes, Weiwei thought. The thing that he was seeking was a vain thing, but it was also a *practical* thing. He took a deep breath and said, "I want my children to remember me."

Boris watched Central Station. The sun was rising now, behind the space port, and down below robotniks moved into position, spreading out blankets and crude, hand-written signs asking for donations, of spare parts or gasoline or vodka, poor creatures, the remnants of forgotten wars, humans cyborged and then discarded when they were no longer needed.

He saw Brother R. Patch-It, of the Church of Robot, doing his rounds—the Church tried to look after the robotniks, as it did after its small flock of humans. Robots were a strange missing link between human and Other, not fitting in either world—digital beings shaped by physicality, by bodies, many refusing the Upload in favor of their own, strange faith . . . Boris remembered Brother Patch-It, from childhood—the robot doubled-up as a *moyel*, circumcising the Jewish boys of the neighborhood on the eighth day of their birth. The question of Who is a Jew had been asked not just about the Chong family, but of the robots too, and was settled long ago. Boris had fragmented memories, from the matrilineal side, predating Weiwei—the protests in Jerusalem, Matt Cohen's labs and the first, primitive Breeding Grounds, where digital entities evolved in ruthless evolutionary cycles:

Plaques waving on King George Street, a mass demonstration: *No To Slavery!* And *Destroy the Concentration Camp!* and so on, an angry mass of humanity coming together to protest the perceived enslavement of those first, fragile Others in their locked-down networks, Matt Cohen's laboratories under siege, his rag-tag team of scientists, kicked out from one country after another before settling, at long last, in Jerusalem—

St. Cohen of the Others, they called him now. Boris lifted the mug to his lips and discovered it was empty. He put it down, rubbed his eyes. He should have slept. He was no longer young, could not go days without sleep, powered by stimulants and restless, youthful energy. The days when he and Miriam hid on this very same roof, holding each other, making promises they knew, even then, they couldn't keep . . .

He thought of her now, trying to catch a glimpse of her walking down Neve Sha'anan, the ancient paved pavilion of Central Station where she had her shebeen. It was hard to think of her, to *ache* like this, like a, like a *boy*. He had not come back because of her but, somewhere in the back of his mind, it must have been, the thought . . .

On his neck the aug breathed softly. He had picked it up in Tong Yun City, on Mars, in a back-street off Arafat Avenue, in a no-name clinic run by a third-generation Martian Chinese, a Mr. Wong, who installed it for him.

It was supposed to have been bred out of the fossilized remains of micro bacterial Martian life forms, but whether that was true no one knew for sure. It was strange having the aug. It was a parasite, it fed off of Boris, it pulsated gently against his neck, a part of him now, another appendage, feeding him alien thoughts, alien feelings, taking in turn Boris' human perspective and subtly *shifting* it, it was like watching your ideas filtered through a kaleidoscope.

He put his hand against the aug and felt its warm, surprisingly-rough surface. It moved under his fingers, breathing gently. Sometimes the aug synthesized strange substances, they acted like drugs on Boris' system, catching him by surprise. At other times it shifted visual perspective, or even interfaced with Boris' node, the digital networking component of his brain, installed shortly after birth, without which one was worse than blind, worse than deaf, one was disconnected from the Conversation.

He had tried to run away, he knew. He had left home, had left Weiwei's memory, or tried to, for a while. He went into Central Station, and he rode the elevators to the very top, and beyond. He had left the Earth, beyond orbit, gone to the Belt, and to Mars, but the memories followed him, Weiwei's bridge, linking forever future and past . . .

"I wish my memory to live on, when I am gone."

"So do all humans," the Other said.

"I wish . . . " gathering courage, he continued. "I wish for my family to *remember*," he said. "To learn from the past, to plan for the future. I wish my children to have my memories, and for their memories, in turn, to be passed on. I want my grandchildren and *their* grandchildren and onwards, down the ages, into the future, to remember this moment."

"And so it shall be," the Other said.

*And so it was*, Boris thought. The memory was clear in his mind, suspended like a dew drop, perfect and unchanged. Weiwei had gotten what he asked for, and his memories were Boris' now, as were Vlad's, as were his grandmother Yulia's and his mother's, and all the rest of them—cousins and nieces and uncles, nephews and aunts, all sharing the Chong family's central reservoir of memory, each able to dip, instantaneously, into that deep pool of memories, into the ocean of the past.

Weiwei's Bridge, as they still called it, in the family. It worked in strange ways, sometimes, even far away, when he was working in the birthing clinics on Ceres, or walking down an avenue in Tong Yun City, on Mars, a sudden memory would form in his head, a new memory—Cousin Oksana's memories of giving birth for the first time, to little Yan—pain and joy mixing in with random thoughts, wondering if anyone had fed the dog, the doctor's voice saying, "Push! Push!", the smell of sweat the beeping of monitors, the low chatter of people outside the door, and that indescribable feeling as the baby slowly emerged out of her . . .

He put down the mug. Down below Central Station was awake now, the neighborhood stalls set with fresh produce, the market alive with sounds, the smell of smoke and chickens roasting slowly on a grill, the shouts of children as they went to school—

He thought of Miriam. Mama Jones, they called her now. Her father was Nigerian, her mother from the Philippines, and they had loved each other, when the world was young, loved in the Hebrew that was their childhood tongue, but were separated, not by flood or war but simply life, and the things it did to people. Boris worked the birthing clinics of Central Station, but there were too many memories here, memories like ghosts, and at last he rebelled, and gone into Central Station and up, and onto an RLV that took him to orbit, to the place they called Gateway, and from there, first, to Lunar Port.

He was young, he had wanted adventure. He had tried to get away. Lunar Port, Ceres, Tong Yun . . . but the memories pursued him, and worst amongst them were his father's. They followed him through the chatter of the Conversation, compressed memories bouncing from one Mirror to the other, across space, at the speed of light, and so they remembered him here on Earth just as he remembered them there, and at last the weight of it became such that he returned.

He had been back in Lunar Port when it happened. He had been brushing his teeth, watching his face—not young, not old, a common enough face, the eyes Chinese, the facial features Slavic, his hair thinning a little—when the memory attacked him, suffused him—he dropped the toothbrush.

Not his father's memory, his nephew's, Yan: Vlad sitting in the chair, in his apartment, his father older than Boris remembered, thinner, and something that hurt him obscurely, that reached across space and made his chest tighten with pain—that clouded look in his father's eyes. Vlad sat without speaking, without acknowledging his nephew or the rest of them, who had come to visit him.

He sat there and his hands moved through the air, arranging and rearranging objects none could see.

"Boris!"

"Yan."

His nephew's shy smile. "I didn't think you were real."

Time-delay, moon-to-Earth round-trip, node-to-node. "You've grown."

"Yes, well . . . "

Yan worked inside Central Station. A lab on Level Five where they manufactured viral ads, airborne microscopic agents that transferred themselves from person to person, thriving in a closed-environment, air-conditioned system like Central Station, coded to deliver person-specific offers, organics interfacing with nodal equipment, all to shout *Buy. Buy. Buy.*

"It's your father."

"What happened?"

"We don't know."

That admission must have hurt Yan. Boris waited, silence eating bandwidth, silence on an Earth-moon return trip.

"Did you take him to the doctors?"

"You know we did."

"And?"

"They don't know."

Silence between them, silence at the speed of light, traveling through space.

"Come home, Boris," Yan said, and Boris marveled at how the boy had grown, the man coming out, this stranger he did not know and yet whose life he could so clearly remember.

*Come home.*

That same day he packed his meager belongings, checked out of the Libra and had taken the shuttle to lunar orbit, and from there a ship to Gateaway, and down, at last, to Central Station.

Memory like a cancer growing. Boris was a doctor, he had seen Weiwei Bridge for himself—that strange semi-organic growth that wove itself into the

Chongs' cerebral cortex and into the grey matter of their brains, interfacing with their nodes, growing, strange delicate spirals of alien matter, an evolved technology, forbidden, Other. It was overgrowing his father's mind, somehow it had gotten out of control, it was growing like a cancer, and Vlad could not move for the memories.

Boris suspected but he couldn't know, just as he did not know what Weiwei had paid for this boon, what terrible fee had been extracted from him—that memory, and that alone, had been wiped clean—only the Other, saying, *And so it shall be*, and then, the next moment, Weiwei was standing outside and the door was closed and he blinked, there amidst the old stone walls, wondering if it had worked.

*Once it had all been orange groves . . .* he remembered thinking that, as he went out of the doors of Central Station, on his arrival, back on Earth, the gravity confusing and uncomfortable, into the hot and humid air outside. Standing under the eaves, he breathed in deeply, gravity pulled him down but he didn't care. It smelled just like he remembered, and the oranges, vanished or not, were still there, the famed Jaffa oranges that grew here when all this, not Tel Aviv, not Central Station, existed, when it was orange groves, and sand, and sea . . .

He crossed the road, his feet leading him, they had their own memory, crossing the road from the grand doors of Central Station to the Neve Sha'anan pedestrian street, the heart of the old neighborhood, and it was so much smaller than he remembered, as a child it was a world and now it had shrunk—

Crowds of people, solar tuk-tuks buzzing along the road, tourists gawking, a memcordist checking her feed stats as everything she saw and felt and smelled was broadcast live across the networks, capturing Boris in a glance that went out to millions of indifferent viewers across the solar system—

Pickpockets, bored CS Security keeping an eye out, a begging robotnik with a missing eye and bad patches of rust on his chest, dark-suited Mormons sweating in the heat, handing out leaflets while on the other side of the road Elronites did the same—

Light rain, falling.

From the nearby market the shouts of sellers promising the freshest pomegranates, melons, grapes, bananas, in a café ahead old men playing backgammon, drinking small china cups of bitter black coffee, smoking *nargilas*—sheesha pipes—R. Patch-It walking slowly amidst the chaos, the robot an oasis of calm in the mass of noisy, sweaty humanity—

Looking, smelling, listening, *remembering*, so intensely he didn't at first see them, the woman and the child, on the other side of the road, until he almost ran into them—

Or they into him. The boy, dark skinned, with extraordinary blue eyes—the woman familiar, somehow, it made him instantly uneasy, and the boy said, with hope in his voice, "Are you my daddy?"

Boris Chong breathed deeply. The woman said, "Kranki!" in an angry, worried tone. Boris took it for the boy's name, or nickname—*Kranki* in Asteroid Pidgin meaning grumpy, or crazy, or strange . . .

Boris knelt beside the boy, the ceaseless movement of people around them forgotten. He looked into those eyes. "It's possible," he said. "I know that blue. It was popular three decades ago. We hacked an open source version out of the trademarked Armani code . . . "

He was waffling, he thought. Why was he doing that? The woman, her familiarity disturbed him. A buzzing as of invisible mosquitoes, in his mind, a reshaping of his vision come flooding him, out of his aug, the boy frozen beside him, smiling now, a large and bewildering and *knowing* smile—

The woman was shouting, he could hear it distantly, "Stop it! What are you doing to him?"

*The boy was interfacing with his aug,* he realized. The words came in a rush, he said, "You had no parents," to the boy. Recollection and shame mingling together. "You were labbed, right here, hacked together out of public property genomes and bits of black market nodes." The boy's hold on his mind slackened. Boris breathed, straightened up. "*Nakaimas,*" he said, and took a step back, suddenly frightened.

The woman looked terrified, and angry. "Stop it," she said. "He's not—"

Boris was suddenly ashamed. "I know," he said. He felt confused, embarrassed. "I'm sorry." This mix of emotions, coming so rapidly they blended into each other, wasn't natural. Somehow the boy had interfaced with the aug and the aug, in turn, was feeding into Boris' mind. He tried to focus. He looked at the woman. Somehow it was important to him that she would understand. He said, "He can speak to my aug. Without an interface." Then, remembering the clinics, remembering his own work, before he left to go to space, he said, quietly, "I must have done a better job than I thought, back then."

The boy looked up at him with guileless, deep blue eyes. Boris remembered children like him, he had birthed many, so many . . . the clinics of Central Station were said to be on par with those of Yunan, even. But he had not expected *this*, this *interference*, though he had heard stories, on the asteroids, and in Tong Yun, the whispered word that used to mean black magic: *nakaimas.*

The woman was looking at him, and her eyes, he knew her eyes—

Something passed between them, something that needed no node, no digital encoding, something earlier, more human and more primitive, like a shock, and she said, "Boris? Boris Chong?"

He recognized her at the same time she did him, wonder replacing worry, wonder, too, at how he failed to recognize her, this woman of indeterminate years suddenly resolving, like two bodies occupying the same space, into the young woman he had loved, when the world was young.

"Miriam?" he said.

"It's me," she said.

"But you—"

"I never left," she said. "You did."

He wanted to go to her now. The world was awake, and Boris was alone on the roof of the old apartment building, alone and free, but for the memories. He didn't know what he would do about his father. He remembered holding his hand, once, when he was small, and Vlad had seemed so big, so confident and sure, and full of life. They had gone to the beach that day, it was a summer's day and in Menashiya Jews and Arabs and Filipinos all mingled together, the Muslim women in their long dark clothes and the children running shrieking in their underwear; Tel Aviv girls in tiny bikinis, sunbathing placidly; someone smoking a joint, and the strong smell of it wafting in the sea air; the life guard in his tower calling out trilingual instructions—"Keep to the marked area! Did anyone lose a child? Please come to the lifeguards *now*! You with the boat, head towards the Tel Aviv harbor and away from the swimming area!"—the words getting lost in the chatter, someone had parked their car and was blaring out beats from the stereo, Somali refugees were cooking a barbeque on the promenade's grassy area, a dreadlocked white guy was playing a guitar, and Vlad held Boris' hand as they went into the water, strong and safe, and Boris knew nothing would ever happen to him; that his father would always be there to protect him, no matter what happened.

# THE CARTOGRAPHER WASPS AND THE ANARCHIST BEES

## E. LILY YU

For longer than anyone could remember, the village of Yiwei had worn, in its orchards and under its eaves, clay-colored globes of paper that hissed and fizzed with wasps. The villagers maintained an uneasy peace with their neighbors for many years, exercising inimitable tact and circumspection. But it all ended the day a boy, digging in the riverbed, found a stone whose balance and weight pleased him. With this, he thought, he could hit a sparrow in flight. There were no sparrows to be seen, but a paper ball hung low and inviting nearby. He considered it for a moment, head cocked, then aimed and threw.

Much later, after he had been plastered and soothed, his mother scalded the fallen nest until the wasps seething in the paper were dead. In this way it was discovered that the wasp nests of Yiwei, dipped in hot water, unfurled into beautifully accurate maps of provinces near and far, inked in vegetable pigments and labeled in careful Mandarin that could be distinguished beneath a microscope.

The villagers' subsequent incursions with bee veils and kettles of boiling water soon diminished the prosperous population to a handful. Commanded by a single stubborn foundress, the survivors folded a new nest in the shape of a paper boat, provisioned it with fallen apricots and squash blossoms, and launched themselves onto the river. Browsing cows and children fled the riverbanks as they drifted downstream, piping sea chanteys.

At last, forty miles south from where they had begun, their craft snagged on an upthrust stick and sank. Only one drowned in the evacuation, weighed down with the remains of an apricot. They reconvened upon a stump and looked about themselves.

"It's a good place to land," the foundress said in her sweet soprano, examining the first rough maps that the scouts brought back. There were plenty of caterpillars, oaks for ink galls, fruiting brambles, and no signs of other wasps. A colony of bees had hived in a split oak two miles away. "Once we are established we will, of course, send a delegation to collect tribute.

"We will not make the same mistakes as before. Ours is a race of explorers and scientists, cartographers and philosophers, and to rest and grow slothful is to die. Once we are established here, we will expand."

It took two weeks to complete the nurseries with their paper mobiles, and then another month to reconstruct the Great Library and fill the pigeonholes with what the oldest cartographers could remember of their lost maps. Their comings and goings did not go unnoticed. An ambassador from the beehive arrived with an ultimatum and was promptly executed; her wings were made into stained-glass windows for the council chamber, and her stinger was returned to the hive in a paper envelope. The second ambassador came with altered attitude and a proposal to divide the bees' kingdom evenly between the two governments, retaining pollen and water rights for the bees—"as an acknowledgment of the preexisting claims of a free people to the natural resources of a common territory," she hummed.

The wasps of the council were gracious and only divested the envoy of her sting. She survived just long enough to deliver her account to the hive.

The third ambassador arrived with a ball of wax on the tip of her stinger and was better received.

"You understand, we are not refugees applying for recognition of a token territorial sovereignty," the foundress said, as attendants served them nectars in paper horns, "nor are we negotiating with you as equal states. Those were the assumptions of your late predecessors. They were mistaken."

"I trust I will do better," the diplomat said stiffly. She was older than the others, and the hairs of her thorax were sparse and faded.

"I do hope so."

"Unlike them, I have complete authority to speak for the hive. You have propositions for us; that is clear enough. We are prepared to listen."

"Oh, good." The foundress drained her horn and took another. "Yours is an old and highly cultured society, despite the indolence of your ruler, which we understand to be a racial rather than personal proclivity. You have laws, and traditional dances, and mathematicians, and principles, which of course we do respect."

"Your terms, please."

She smiled. "Since there is a local population of tussah moths, which we prefer for incubation, there is no need for anything so unrepublican as slavery. If you refrain from insurrection, you may keep your self-rule. But we will take a fifth of your stores in an ordinary year, and a tenth in drought years, and one of every hundred larvae."

"To eat?" Her antennae trembled with revulsion.

"Only if food is scarce. No, they will be raised among us and learn our ways and our arts, and then they will serve as officials and bureaucrats among you. It will be to your advantage, you see."

The diplomat paused for a moment, looking at nothing at all. Finally she said, "A tenth, in a good year—"

"Our terms," the foundress said, "are not negotiable."

The guards shifted among themselves, clinking the plates of their armor and shifting the gleaming points of their stings.

"I don't have a choice, do I?"

"The choice is enslavement or cooperation," the foundress said. "For your hive, I mean. You might choose something else, certainly, but they have tens of thousands to replace you with."

The diplomat bent her head. "I am old," she said. "I have served the hive all my life, in every fashion. My loyalty is to my hive and I will do what is best for it."

"I am so very glad."

"I ask you—I beg you—to wait three or four days to impose your terms. I will be dead by then, and will not see my sisters become a servile people."

The foundress clicked her claws together. "Is the delaying of business a custom of yours? We have no such practice. You will have the honor of watching us elevate your sisters to moral and technological heights you could never imagine."

The diplomat shivered.

"Go back to your queen, my dear. Tell them the good news."

It was a crisis for the constitutional monarchy. A riot broke out in District 6, destroying the royal waxworks and toppling the mouse-bone monuments before it was brutally suppressed. The queen had to be calmed with large doses of jelly after she burst into tears on her ministers' shoulders.

"Your Majesty," said one, "it's not a matter for your concern. Be at peace."

"These are my children," she said, sniffling. "You would feel for them too, were you a mother."

"Thankfully, I am not," the minister said briskly, "so to business."

"War is out of the question," another said.

"Their forces are vastly superior."

"We outnumber them three hundred to one!"

"They are experienced fighters. Sixty of us would die for each of theirs. We might drive them away, but it would cost us most of the hive and possibly our queen—"

The queen began weeping noisily again and had to be cleaned and comforted.

"Have we any alternatives?"

There was a small silence.

"Very well, then."

The terms of the relationship were copied out, at the wasps' direction, on small paper plaques embedded in propolis and wax around the hive. As paper and ink were new substances to the bees, they jostled and touched and tasted the bills until the paper fell to pieces. The wasps sent to oversee the installation did not take this kindly. Several civilians died before it was established that the bees could not read the Yiwei dialect.

Thereafter the hive's chemists were charged with compounding pheromones complex enough to encode the terms of the treaty. These were applied to the papers, so that both species could inspect them and comprehend the relationship between the two states.

Whereas the hive before the wasp infestation had been busy but content, the bees now lived in desperation. The natural terms of their lives were cut short by the need to gather enough honey for both the hive and the wasp nest. As they traveled farther and farther afield in search of nectar, they stopped singing. They danced their findings grimly, without joy. The queen herself grew gaunt and thin from breeding replacements, and certain ministers who understood such matters began feeding royal jelly to the strongest larvae.

Meanwhile, the wasps grew sleek and strong. Cadres of scholars, cartographers, botanists, and soldiers were dispatched on the river in small floating nests caulked with beeswax and loaded with rations of honeycomb to chart the unknown lands to the south. Those who returned bore beautiful maps with towns and farms and alien populations of wasps carefully noted in blue and purple ink, and these, once studied by the foundress and her generals, were carefully filed away in the depths of the Great Library for their southern advance in the new year.

The bees adopted by the wasps were first trained to clerical tasks, but once it was determined that they could be taught to read and write, they were assigned to some of the reconnaissance missions. The brightest students, gifted at trigonometry and angles, were educated beside the cartographers themselves and proved valuable assistants. They learned not to see the thick green caterpillars led on silver chains, or the dead bees fed to the wasp brood. It was easier that way.

When the old queen died, they did not mourn.

By the sheerest of accidents, one of the bees trained as a cartographer's assistant was an anarchist. It might have been the stresses on the hive, or it might have been luck; wherever it came from, the mutation was viable. She tucked a number of her own eggs in beeswax and wasp paper among the pigeonholes of the library and fed the larvae their milk and bread in secret. To her sons in their capped silk cradles—and they were all sons—she whispered the precepts she had developed while calculating flight paths and azimuths, that there should be no queen and no state, and that, as in the wasp nest, the males should labor and profit equally with the females. In their sleep and slow transformation they heard her teachings and instructions, and when they chewed their way out of their cells and out of the wasp nest, they made their way to the hive.

The damage to the nest was discovered, of course, but by then the anarchist was dead of old age. She had done impeccable work, her tutor sighed, looking over the filigree of her inscriptions, but the brilliant were subject to mental aberrations, were they not? He buried beneath grumblings and labors his fondness for her, which had become a grief to him and a political liability, and he never again took on any student from the hive who showed a glint of talent.

Though they had the bitter smell of the wasp nest in their hair, the anarchist's twenty sons were permitted to wander freely through the hive, as it was assumed that they were either spies or on official business. When the new queen emerged from her chamber, they joined unnoticed the other drones in the nuptial flight. Two succeeded in mating with her. Those who failed and survived spoke afterward in hushed tones of what had been done for the sake of the ideal. Before they died they took propolis and oak-apple ink and inscribed upon the lintels of the hive, in a shorthand they had developed, the story of the first anarchist and her twenty sons.

Anarchism being a heritable trait in bees, a number of the daughters of the new queen found themselves questioning the purpose of the monarchy. Two were taken by the wasps and taught to read and write. On one of their visits to the hive they spotted the history of their forefathers, and, being excellent scholars, soon figured out the translation.

They found their sisters in the hive who were unquiet in soul and whispered to them the strange knowledge they had learned among the wasps: astronomy, military strategy, the state of the world beyond the farthest flights of the bees. Hitherto educated as dancers and architects, nurses and foragers, the bees were full of a new wonder, stranger even than the first day they flew from the hive and felt the sun on their backs.

"Govern us," they said to the two wasp-taught anarchists, but they refused.

"A perfect society needs no rulers," they said. "Knowledge and authority ought to be held in common. In order to imagine a new existence, we must free ourselves from the structures of both our failed government and the unjustifiable hegemony of the wasp nests. Hear what you can hear and learn what you can learn while we remain among them. But be ready."

It was the first summer in Yiwei without the immemorial hum of the cartographer wasps. In the orchards, though their skins split with sweetness, fallen fruit lay unmolested, and children played barefoot with impunity. One of the villagers' daughters, in her third year at an agricultural college, came home in the back of a pickup truck at the end of July. She thumped her single suitcase against the gate before opening it, to scatter the chickens, then raised the latch and swung the iron aside, and was immediately wrapped in a flying hug.

Once she disentangled herself from brother and parents and liberally distributed kisses, she listened to the news she'd missed: how the cows were dying from drinking stonecutters' dust in the streams; how grain prices were falling everywhere, despite the drought; and how her brother, little fool that he was, had torn down a wasp nest and received a faceful of red and white lumps for it. One of the most detailed wasp's maps had reached the capital, she was told, and a bureaucrat had arrived in a sleek black car. But because the wasps were all dead, he could report little more than a prank, a freak, or a miracle. There were no further inquiries.

Her brother produced for her inspection the brittle, boiled bodies of several wasps in a glass jar, along with one of the smaller maps. She tickled him until he surrendered his trophies, promised him a basket of peaches in return, and let herself be fed to tautness. Then, to her family's dismay, she wrote an urgent letter to the Academy of Sciences and packed a satchel with clothes and cash. If she could find one more nest of wasps, she said, it would make their fortune and her name. But it had to be done quickly.

In the morning, before the cockerels woke and while the sky was still purple, she hopped onto her old bicycle and rode down the dusty path.

Bees do not fly at night or lie to each other, but the anarchists had learned both from the wasps. On a warm, clear evening they left the hive at last, flying west in a small tight cloud. Around them swelled the voices of summer insects, strange and disquieting. Several miles west of the old hive and the wasp nest, in a lightning-scarred elm, the anarchists had built up a small stock of stolen honey sealed in wax and paper. They rested there for the night, in cells of clean white wax, and in the morning they arose to the building of their city.

The first business of the new colony was the laying of eggs, which a number of workers set to, and provisions for winter. One egg from the old queen, brought from the hive in an anarchist's jaws, was hatched and raised as a new mother. Uncrowned and unconcerned, she too laid mortar and wax, chewed wood to make paper, and fanned the storerooms with her wings.

The anarchists labored secretly but rapidly, drones alongside workers, because the copper taste of autumn was in the air. None had seen a winter before, but the memory of the species is subtle and long, and in their hearts, despite the summer sun, they felt an imminent darkness.

The flowers were fading in the fields. Every day the anarchists added to their coffers of warm gold and built their white walls higher. Every day the air grew a little crisper, the grass a little drier. They sang as they worked, sometimes ballads from the old hive, sometimes anthems of their own devising, and for a time they were happy. Too soon, the leaves turned flame colors and blew from the trees, and then there were no more flowers. The anarchists pressed down the lid on the last vat of honey and wondered what was coming.

Four miles away, at the first touch of cold, the wasps licked shut their paper doors and slept in a tight knot around the foundress. In both beehives, the bees huddled together, awake and watchful, warming themselves with the thrumming of their wings. The anarchists murmured comfort to each other.

"There will be more, after us. It will breed out again."

"We are only the beginning."

"There will be more."

Snow fell silently outside.

The snow was ankle-deep and the river iced over when the girl from Yiwei reached up into the empty branches of an oak tree and plucked down the paper castle of a nest. The wasps within, drowsy with cold, murmured but did not stir. In their barracks the soldiers dreamed of the unexplored south and battles in strange cities, among strange peoples, and scouts dreamed of the corpses of starved and frozen deer. The cartographers dreamed of the changes that winter would work on the landscape, the diverted creeks and dead trees they would have to note down. They did not feel the burlap bag that settled around them, nor the crunch of tires on the frozen road.

She had spent weeks tramping through the countryside, questioning beekeepers and villagers' children, peering up into trees and into hives, before she found the last wasps from Yiwei. Then she had had to wait for winter and the anesthetizing cold. But now, back in the warmth of her own room, she broke open the soft pages of the nest and pushed aside the heaps of glistening wasps until she found the foundress herself, stumbling on uncertain legs.

When it thawed, she would breed new foundresses among the village's apricot trees. The letters she received indicated a great demand for them in the capital, particularly from army generals and the captains of scientific explorations. In years to come, the village of Yiwei would be known for its delicately inscribed maps, the legends almost too small to see, and not for its barley and oats, its velvet apricots and glassy pears.

In the spring, the old beehive awoke to find the wasps gone, like a nightmare that evaporates by day. It was difficult to believe, but when not the slightest scrap of wasp paper could be found, the whole hive sang with delight. Even the queen, who had been coached from the pupa on the details of her client state and the conditions by which she ruled, and who had felt, perhaps, more sympathy for the wasps than she should have, cleared her throat and trilled once or twice. If she did not sing so loudly or so joyously as the rest, only a few noticed, and the winter had been a hard one, anyhow.

The maps had vanished with the wasps. No more would be made. Those who had studied among the wasps began to draft memoranda and the first independent decrees of queen and council. To defend against future invasions, it was decided that a detachment of bees would fly the borders of their land and carry home reports of what they found.

It was on one of these patrols that a small hive was discovered in the fork of an elm tree. Bees lay dead and brittle around it, no identifiable queen among them. Not a trace of honey remained in the storehouse; the dark wax of its walls had been gnawed to rags. Even the brood cells had been scraped clean. But in the last intact hexagons they found, curled and capped in wax, scrawled on page after page, words of revolution. They read in silence.

Then—

"Write," one said to the other, and she did.

# THE MAN WHO BRIDGED THE MIST

## KIJ JOHNSON

⟨⚬⟩

Kit came to Nearside with two trunks and an oiled-cloth folio full of plans for the bridge across the mist. His trunks lay tumbled like stones at his feet, where the mailcoach guard had dropped them. The folio he held close, away from the drying mud of yesterday's storm.

Nearside was small, especially to a man of the capital, where buildings towered seven and eight stories tall, a city so large that even a vigorous walker could not cross it in half a day. Here hard-packed dirt roads threaded through irregular spaces scattered with structures and fences. Even the inn was plain, two stories of golden limestone and blue slate tiles, with (he could smell) some sort of animals living behind it. On the sign overhead, a flat, pale blue fish very like a ray curveted against a black background.

A brightly dressed woman stood by the inn's door. Her skin and eyes were pale, almost colorless. "Excuse me," Kit said. "Where can I find the ferry to take me across the mist?" He could feel himself being weighed, but amiably: a stranger, small and very dark, in gray—a man from the east.

The woman smiled. "Well, the ferries are both at the upper dock. But I expect what you really want is someone to oar the ferry, yes? Rasali Ferry came over from Farside last night. She's the one you'll want to talk to. She spends a lot of time at The Deer's Heart. But you wouldn't like The Heart, sir," she added. "It's not nearly as nice as The Fish here. Are you looking for a room?"

"I'll be staying in Farside tonight," Kit said apologetically. He didn't want to seem arrogant. The invisible web of connections he would need for his work started here, with this first impression, with all the first impressions of the next few days.

"That's what *you* think," the woman said. "I'm guessing it'll be a day or two, or more, before Rasali goes back. Valo Ferry might, but he doesn't cross so often."

"I could buy out the trip's fares, if that's why she's waiting."

"It's not that," the woman said. "She won't cross the mist 'til she's ready. Until it tells her she can go, if you follow me. But you can ask, I suppose."

Kit didn't follow, but he nodded anyway. "Where's The Deer's Heart?"

She pointed. "Left, then right, then down by the little boat yard."

"Thank you," Kit said. "May I leave my trunks here until I work things out with her?"

"We always stow for travelers." The woman grinned. "And cater to them, too, when they find out there's no way across the mist today."

The Deer's Heart was smaller than The Fish, and livelier. At midday the oak-shaded tables in the beer garden beside the inn were clustered with light-skinned people in brilliant clothes, drinking and tossing comments over the low fence into the boat yard next door, where, half lost in steam, a youth and two women bent planks to form the hull of a small flat-bellied boat. When Kit spoke to a man carrying two mugs of something that looked like mud and smelled of yeast, the man gestured at the yard with his chin. "Ferrys are over there. Rasali's the one in red," he said as he walked away.

"The one in red" was tall, her skin as pale as that of the rest of the locals, with a black braid so long that she had looped it around her neck to keep it out of the way. Her shoulders flexed in the sunlight as she and the youth forced a curved plank to take the skeletal hull's shape. The other woman, slightly shorter, with the ash-blond hair so common here, forced an augur through the plank and into a rib, then hammered a peg into the hole she'd made. After three pegs, the boatwrights straightened. The plank held. *Strong*, Kit thought; *I wonder if I can get them for the bridge?*

"Rasali!" a voice bellowed, almost in Kit's ear. "Man here's looking for you." Kit turned in time to see the man with the mugs gesturing, again with his chin. He sighed and walked to the waist-high fence. The boatwrights stopped to drink from blueware bowls before the one in red and the youth came over.

"I'm Rasali Ferry of Farside," the woman said. Her voice was softer and higher than he had expected of a woman as strong as she, with the fluid vowels of the local accent. She nodded to the boy beside her: "Valo Ferry of Farside, my brother's eldest." Valo was more a young man than a boy, lighter-haired than Rasali and slightly taller. They had the same heavy eyebrows and direct amber eyes.

"Kit Meinem of Atyar," Kit said.

Valo asked, "What sort of name is Meinem? It doesn't mean anything."

"In the capital, we take our names differently than you."

"Oh, like Jenner Ellar." Valo nodded. "I guessed you were from the capital—your clothes and your skin."

Rasali said, "What can we do for you, Kit Meinem of Atyar?"

"I need to get to Farside today," Kit said.

Rasali shook her head. "I can't take you. I just got here, and it's too soon. Perhaps Valo?"

The youth tipped his head to one side, his expression suddenly abstract, as though he were listening to something too faint to hear clearly. He shook his head. "No, not today."

"I can buy out the fares, if that helps. It's Jenner Ellar I am here to see."

Valo looked interested but said, "No," to Rasali, and she added, "What's so important that it can't wait a few days?"

*Better now than later*, Kit thought. "I am replacing Teniant Planner as the lead engineer and architect for construction of the bridge over the mist. We will start work again as soon as I've reviewed everything. And had a chance to talk to Jenner." He watched their faces.

Rasali said, "It's been a year since Teniant died—I was starting to think Empire had forgotten all about us, and your deliveries would be here 'til the iron rusted away."

"Jenner Ellar's not taking over?" Valo asked, frowning.

"The new Department of Roads cartel is in my name," Kit said. "but I hope Jenner will remain as my second. You can see why I would like to meet him as soon as is possible, of course. He will—"

Valo burst out, "You're going to take over from Jenner, after he's worked so hard on this? And what about us? What about *our* work?" His cheeks were flushed an angry red. *How do they conceal anything with skin like that?* Kit thought.

"Valo," Rasali said, a warning tone in her voice. Flushing darker still, the youth turned and strode away. Rasali snorted but said only: "Boys. He likes Jenner, and he has issues about the bridge, anyway."

That was worth addressing. *Later.* "So, what will it take to get you to carry me across the mist, Rasali Ferry of Farside? The project will pay anything reasonable."

"I cannot," she said. "Not today, not tomorrow. You'll have to wait."

"Why?" Kit asked: reasonably enough, he thought, but she eyed him for a long moment, as if deciding whether to be annoyed.

"Have you gone across mist before?" she said at last.

"Of course."

"Not the river," she said.

"Not the river," he agreed. "It's a quarter mile across here, yes?"

"Oh, yes." She smiled suddenly: white even teeth and warmth like sunlight in her eyes. "Let's go down, and perhaps I can explain things better there." She jumped the fence with a single powerful motion, landing beside him to a chorus of cheers and shouts from the inn garden's patrons. She made an exaggerated bow, then gestured to Kit to follow her. She was well-liked, clearly. Her opinion would matter.

The boat yard was heavily shaded by low-hanging oaks and chestnuts, and bounded on the east by an open-walled shelter filled with barrels and stacks of lumber. Rasali waved at the third boat maker, who was still putting her tools away. "Tilisk Boatwright of Nearside. My brother's wife," she said to Kit. "She makes skiffs with us, but she won't ferry. She's not born to it as Valo and I are."

"Where's your brother?" Kit asked.

"Dead," Rasali said, and lengthened her stride.

They walked a few streets over and then climbed a long, even ridge perhaps eighty feet high, too regular to be natural. *A levee*, Kit thought, and distracted himself from the steep path by estimating the volume of earth and the labor that had been required to build it. Decades, perhaps, but how long ago? How long was it? The levee was treeless. The only feature was a slender wood tower hung with flags. It was probably for signaling across the mist to Farside, since it appeared too fragile for anything else. They had storms out here, Kit knew; there'd been one the night before, which had left the path muddy. How often was the tower struck by lightning?

Rasali stopped. "There."

Kit had been watching his feet. He looked up and nearly cried out as light lanced his suddenly tearing eyes. He fell back a step and shielded his face. What had blinded him was an immense band of white mist reflecting the morning sun.

Kit had never seen the mist river itself, though he'd bridged mist before this, two simple post-and-beam structures over gorges closer to the capital. From his work in Atyar, he knew what was to be known. It was not water, or anything like. It did not flow, but formed somehow in the deep gorge of the great riverbed before him. It found its way many hundreds of miles north, up through a hundred narrowing mist creeks and streams before failing at last, in shreds of drying foam that left bare patches of earth where they collected.

The mist stretched to the south as well, a deepening, thickening band that poured out at last from the river's mouth two thousand miles south, and formed the mist ocean, which lay on the face of the salt-water ocean. Water had to follow the river's bed to run somewhere beneath, or through, the mist, but there was no way to prove this.

There was mist nowhere but this river and its streams and sea; but the mist split Empire in half.

After a moment, the pain in Kit's eyes grew less, and he opened them again. The river was a quarter-mile across where they stood, a great gash of light between the levees. It seemed nearly featureless, blazing under the sun like a river of cream or of bleached silk, but as his eyes accustomed themselves, he saw the surface was not smooth but heaped and hollowed, and that it shifted slowly, almost indiscernibly, as he watched.

Rasali stepped forward, and Kit started. "I'm sorry," he said with a laugh. "How long have I been staring? It's just—I had no idea."

"No one does," Rasali said. Her eyes when he met them were amused.

The east and west levees were nearly identical, each treeless and scrub-covered, with a signal tower. The levee on their side ran down to a narrow bare bank half a dozen yards wide. There was a wooden dock and a boat ramp, a rough switchback leading down to them. Two large boats had been pulled onto the bank. Another, smaller dock was visible a hundred yards upstream, attended by a clutter of boats, sheds, and indeterminate piles covered in tarps.

"Let's go down." Rasali led the way, her words coming back to him over her shoulder. "The little ferry is Valo's. *Pearlfinder*. *The Tranquil Crossing*'s mine." Her voice warmed when she said the name. "Eighteen feet long, eight wide. Mostly pine, but a purpleheart keel and pearwood headpiece. You can't see it from here, but the hull's sheathed in blue-dyed fish-skin. I can carry three horses or a ton and a half of cartage or fifteen passengers. Or various combinations. I once carried twenty-four hunting dogs and two handlers. Never again."

A steady, light breeze eased down from the north, channeled by the levees. The air had a smell, not unpleasant but a little sour, wild. "How can you manage a boat like this alone? Are you that strong?"

"It's as big as I can handle," she said, "but Valo helps sometimes, for really unwieldy loads. You don't paddle through mist. I mostly just coax the *Crossing* to where I want it to go. Anyway, the bigger the boat, the more likely that the Big Ones will notice it; though if you *do* run into a fish, the smaller the boat, the easier it is to swamp. Here we are."

They stood on the bank. The mist streams he had bridged had not prepared him for anything like this. Those were tidy little flows, more like fog collecting in hollows than this. From their angle, the river no longer seemed a smooth flow of creamy whiteness, nor even gently heaped clouds. The mist forced itself into hillocks and hollows, tight slopes perhaps twenty feet high that folded into one another. It had a surface, but it was irregular, cracked in places, translucent in others. The surface didn't seem as clearly defined as that between water and air.

"How can you move on this?" Kit said, fascinated. "Or even float?" The hillock immediately before them was flattening as he watched. Beyond it something like a vale stretched out for a few dozen yards before turning and becoming lost to his eyes.

"Well, I can't, not today," Rasali said. She sat on the gunwale of her boat, one leg swinging, watching him. "I can't push the *Crossing* up those slopes or find a safe path, unless the mist shows me the way. If I went today, I know—I *know*—" she tapped her belly—"that I would find myself stranded on a pinnacle or lost in a hole. *That's* why I can't take you today, Kit Meinem of Atyar."

When Kit was a child, he had not been good with other people. He was small and easy to tease or ignore, and then he was sick for much of his seventh year and had to leave his crèche before the usual time, to convalesce in his mother's house. None of the children of the crèche came to visit him, but he didn't mind that: he had books and puzzles, and whole quires of blank paper that his mother didn't mind him defacing.

The clock in the room in which he slept didn't work, so one day he used his penknife to take it apart. He arranged the wheels and cogs and springs in neat rows on the quilt in his room, by type and then by size; by materials; by weight; by shape. He liked holding the tiny pieces, thinking of how they might have been formed and how they worked together. The patterns they made were interesting, but he knew the best pattern would be the working one, when they were all put back into their right places and the clock performed its task again. He had to think that the clock would be happier that way, too.

He tried to rebuild the clock before his mother came upstairs from her counting house at the end of the day, but when he had reassembled things, there remained a pile of unused parts and it still didn't work; so he shut the clock up and hoped she wouldn't notice that it wasn't ticking. Four days more of trying things during the day and concealing his failures at night; and on the fifth day, the clock started again. One piece hadn't fit anywhere, a small brass cog. Kit still carried that cog in his pen case.

Late that afternoon, Kit returned to the river's edge. It was hotter; the mud had dried to cracked dust, and the air smelled like old rags left in water too long. He saw no one at the ferry dock, but at the fisher's dock upstream people were gathering, a score or more of men and women, with children running about.

The clutter looked even more disorganized as he approached. The fishing boats were fat little coracles of leather stretched on frames, tipped bottom up to the sun and looking like giant warts. The mist had dropped so that he could see a band of exposed rock below the bank. The dock's pilings were clearly visible, which were not vertical but set at an angle: a cantilevered deck braced into the stone underlying the bank. The wooden pilings had been sheathed in metal.

He approached a silver-haired woman doing something with a treble hook as long as her hand. "What are you catching with that?" he said.

Her forehead was wrinkled when she looked up, but she smiled when she saw him. "Oh, you're a stranger. From Atyar, dressed like that. Am I right? We catch fish . . . " Still holding the hook, she extended her arms as far as they would stretch. "Bigger than that, some of them. Looks like more storms, so they're going to be biting tonight. I'm Meg Threehooks. Of Nearside, obviously."

"Kit Meinem of Atyar. I take it you can't find a bottom?" He pointed to the pilings.

Jen Threehooks followed his glance. "It's there somewhere, but it's a long way down, and we can't sink pilings because the mist dissolves the wood. Oh, and fish eat it. Same thing with our ropes, the boats, us—anything but metal and rock, really." She knotted a line around the hook eye. The cord was dark and didn't look heavy enough for anything Kit could imagine catching on hooks that size.

"What are these made of, then?" He squatted to look at the framing under one of the coracles.

"Careful, that one's mine," Meg said. "The hides—well, and all the ropes—are fish-skin. Mist fish, not water fish. Tanning takes off some of the slime, so they don't last forever either, not if they're immersed." She made a face. "We have a saying: foul as fish-slime. That's pretty nasty, you'll see."

"I need to get to Farside," Kit said. "Could I hire you to carry me across?"

"In my boat?" She snorted. "No, fishers stay close to shore. Go see Rasali Ferry. Or Valo."

"I saw her," he said ruefully.

"Thought so. You must be the new architect—city folk are always so impatient. You're so eager to be dinner for a Big One? If Rasali doesn't want to go, then don't go, stands to reason."

Kit was footsore and frustrated by the time he returned to The Fish. His trunks were already upstairs, in a small cheerful room overwhelmed by a table that nearly filled it, with a stiflingly hot cupboard bed. When Kit spoke to the woman he'd talked to earlier, Brana Keep, the owner of The Fish (its real name turned out to be The Big One's Delight)—laughed. "Rasali's as hard to shift as bedrock," she said. "And, truly, you would not be comfortable at The Heart."

By the next morning, when Kit came downstairs to break his fast on flatbread and pepper-rubbed fish, everyone appeared to know everything about him, especially his task. He had wondered whether there would be resistance to the project, but if there had been any, it was gone now. There were a few complaints, mostly about slow payments, a universal issue for public works; but none at all about the labor or organization. Most in the taproom seemed not to mind the bridge, and the feeling everywhere he went in town was optimistic. He'd run into more resistance elsewhere, building the small bridges.

"Well, why should we be concerned?" Brana Keep said to Kit. "You're bringing in people to work, yes? So we'll be selling room and board and clothes and beer to them. And you'll be hiring some of us, and everyone will do well while you're building this bridge of yours. I plan to be wading ankle-deep through gold by the time this is done."

"And after," Kit said, "when the bridge is complete—think of it, the first real link between the east and west sides of Empire. The only place for three thousand miles where people and trade can cross the mist easily, safely, whenever they wish. You'll be the heart of Empire in ten years. Five." He laughed a little, embarrassed by the passion that shook his voice.

"Yes, well," Brana Keep said, in the easy way of a woman who makes her living by not antagonizing customers, "we'll make that harness when the colt is born."

For the next six days, Kit explored the town and surrounding countryside.

He met the masons, a brother and sister that Teniant had selected before her death to oversee the pillar and anchorage construction on Nearside. They were quiet but competent, and Kit was comfortable not replacing them.

Kit also spoke with the Nearside rope-makers, and performed tests on their fish-skin ropes and cables, which turned out even stronger than he had hoped, with excellent resistance to rot, and catastrophic and slow failure. The makers told him that the rope stretched for its first two years in use, which made it ineligible to replace the immense chains that would bear the bridge's weight; but it could replace the thousands of vertical suspender chains that would support the roadbed, with a great saving in weight.

He spent much of his time watching the mist. It changed character unpredictably: a smooth rippled flow; hours later, a badland of shredding foam; still later, a field of steep dunes that joined and shifted as he watched. There was nothing level about the mist's surface, but he thought that the river generally dropped in its bed each day under the sun, and rose after dark.

The winds were more predictable. Hedged between the levees, they streamed southward each morning and north each evening, growing stronger toward midday and dusk, and falling away entirely in the afternoons and at night. They did not seem to affect the mist much, though they did tear shreds off that landed on the banks as dried foam.

The winds meant that there would be more dynamic load on the bridge than Teniant Planner had predicted. Kit would never criticize her work publicly and he gladly acknowledged her brilliant interpersonal skills, which had brought the town into cheerful collaboration, but he was grateful that her bridge had not been built as designed.

He examined the mist more closely, as well, by lifting a piece from the river's surface on the end of an oar. The mist was stiffer than it looked, and in bright light he thought he could see tiny shapes, perhaps creatures or plants or something altogether different. There were microscopes in the city, and people who studied these things; but he had never bothered to learn more, interested only in the structure that would bridge it. In any case, living things interested him less than structures.

Nights, Kit worked on the table in his room. Teniant's plans had to be revised. He opened the folios and cases she had left behind and read everything he found there. He wrote letters, wrote lists, wrote schedules, made duplicates of everything, sent to the capital for someone to do all the subsequent copying. His new plans for the bridge began to take shape, and he started to glimpse the invisible architecture that was the management of the vast project.

He did not see Rasali Ferry, except to ask each morning whether they might travel that day. The answer was always no.

One afternoon, when the clouds were heaping into anvils filled with rain, he walked up to the building site half a mile north of Nearside. For two years, off and on, carts had tracked south on the Hoic Mine road and the West River Road, leaving limestone blocks and iron bars in untidy heaps. Huge dismantled shear-legs lay beside a caretaker's wattle-and-daub hut. There were thousands of large rectangular blocks.

Kit examined some of the blocks. Limestone was often too chossy for large-scale construction, but this rock was sound, with no apparent flaws or fractures. There were not enough, of course, but undoubtedly more had been quarried. He had written to order resumption of deliveries, and they would start arriving soon.

Delivered years too early, the iron trusses that would eventually support the roadbed were stacked neatly, painted black to protect them from moisture, covered in oiled tarps, and raised from the ground on planks. Sheep grazed the knee-high grass that grew everywhere. When one of the sheep eyed him incuriously, Kit found himself bowing. "Forgive the intrusion, sir," he said and laughed: too old to be talking to sheep.

The test pit was still open, a ladder on the ground nearby. Weeds clung when he moved the ladder as if reluctant to release it. He descended.

The pasture had not been noisy, but he was startled when he dropped below ground level and the insects and whispering grasses were suddenly silenced. The soil around him was striated shades of dun and dull yellow. Halfway down, he sliced a wedge free with his knife: lots of clay; good foundation soil, as he had been informed. The pit's bottom, some twenty feet down, looked like the walls, but crouching to dig at the dirt between his feet with his knife, he hit rock almost immediately. It seemed to be shale. He wondered how far down the water table was: did the Nearsiders find it difficult to dig wells? Did the mist ever backwash into one? There were people at University in Atyar who were trying to understand mist, but there was still so much that could not be examined or quantified.

He collected a rock to look at it in better light, and climbed from the pit in time to see a teamster leading four mules, her wagon groaning under the weight of the first new blocks. A handful of Nearsider men and women followed, rolling their shoulders and popping their joints. They called out greetings, and he walked across to them.

When he got back to The Fish hours later, exhausted from helping unload the cart and soaked from the storm that had started while he did so, there was a message from Rasali. *Dusk* was all it said.

Kit was stiff and irritable when he left for the *Tranquil Crossing*. He had hired a carrier from The Fish to haul one of his trunks down to the dock, but the others remained in his room, which he would probably keep until the bridge was done. He carried his folio of plans and paperwork himself. He was leaving duplicates of everything on Nearside, but after so much work, it was hard to trust any of it to the hands of others.

The storm was over and the clouds were moving past, leaving the sky every shade between lavender and a rich purple-blue. The large moon was a crescent in the west; the smaller a half circle immediately overhead. In the fading light, the mist was a dark, smoky streak. The air smelled fresh. Kit's mood lightened, and he half-trotted down the final path.

His fellow passengers were there before him: a prosperous-looking man with a litter of piglets in a woven wicker cage (Tengon whites, the man confided, the best bloodline in all Empire); a woman in the dark clothes fashionable in the capital, with brass-bound document cases and a folio very like Kit's; two traders with many cartons of powdered pigment; a mail courier with locked leather satchels and two guards. Nervous about their first crossing, Uni and Tom Mason greeted Kit when he arrived.

In the gathering darkness, the mist looked like bristling, tight-folded hills and coulees. Swifts darted just above it, using the wind flowing up the valley, searching for insects, he supposed. Once a sudden black shape, too quick to see clearly, appeared from below; then it, and one of the birds, was gone.

The voices of the fishers at their dock carried to him. They launched their boats, and he watched one, and then another, and then a gaggle of the little coracles push themselves up a slope of the mist. There were no lamps.

"Ready, everyone?" Kit had not heard Rasali approach. She swung down into the ferry. "Hand me your gear."

Stowing and embarkation were quick, though the piglets complained. Kit strained his eyes, but the coracles could no longer be seen. When he noticed Rasali waiting for him, he apologized. "I guess the fish are biting."

Rasali glanced at the river as she stowed his trunk. "Small ones. A couple of feet long only. The fishers like them bigger, five or six feet, though they don't want them too big, either. But they're not fish, not what you think fish are. Hand me that."

He hesitated a moment, then gave her the folio before stepping into the ferry. The boat sidled at his weight, but sluggishly: a carthorse instead of a riding mare. His stomach lurched. "Oh!" he said.

"What?" one of the traders asked nervously. Rasali untied the rope holding them to the dock.

Kit swallowed. "I had forgotten. The motion of the boat. It's not like water at all."

He did not mention his fear, but there was no need. The others murmured assent. The courier, her dark face sharp-edged as a hawk, growled, "Every time I do this, it surprises me. I dislike it."

Rasali unshipped a scull and slid the great triangular blade into the mist, which parted reluctantly. "I've been on mist more than water, but I remember the way water felt. Quick and jittery. This is better."

"Only to you, Rasali Ferry," Uni Mason said.

"Water's safer," the man with the piglets said.

Rasali leaned into the oar, and the boat slid away from the dock. "Anything is safe until it kills you."

The mist absorbed the quiet sounds of shore almost immediately. One of Kit's first projects had been a stone single-arch bridge over water, far to the north in Eskje province. He had visited before construction started. He was there for five days more than he had expected, caught by a snowstorm that left nearly two feet on the ground. This reminded him of those snowy moonless nights, the air as thick and silencing as a pillow on the ears.

Rasali did not scull so much as steer. It was hard to see far in any direction except up, but perhaps it was true that the mist spoke to her, for she seemed to know where to position the boat for the mist to carry it forward. She followed a small valley until it started to flatten and then mound up. *The Tranquil Crossing* tipped slightly as it slid a few feet to port. The mail carrier made a noise, and immediately stifled it.

Mist was a misnomer. It was denser than it seemed, and sometimes the boat seemed not to move through it so much as over its surface. Tonight it seemed like sea-wrack, the dirty foam that strong winds could whip from ocean waves. Kit reached a hand over the boat's side. The mist piled against his hand, almost dry to the touch, sliding up his forearm with a sensation he could not immediately identify. When he realized it was prickling, he snatched his arm back in and rubbed it on a fold of his coat. The skin burned. Caustic, of course.

The man with the pigs whispered, "Will they come if we talk or make noise?"

"Not to talking, or pigs' squealing," Rasali said. "They seem to like low noises. They'll rise to thunder sometimes."

One of the traders said, "What are they if they're not really fish? What do they look like?" Her voice shook. The mist was weighing on them all: all but Rasali.

"If you want to know you'll have to see one for yourself," Rasali said. "Or try to get a fisher to tell you. They gut and fillet them over the sides of their boats. No one else sees much but meat wrapped in paper, or rolls of black skin for the rope-makers and tanners."

"*You've* seen them," Kit said.

"They're broad and flat. But ugly . . . "

"And Big Ones?" Kit asked.

Her voice was harsh. "*Them*, we don't talk about here."

No one spoke for a time. Mist—foam—heaped up at the boat's prow and parted, eased to the sides with an almost inaudible hissing. Once the mist off the port side heaved, and something dark broke the surface for a moment, followed by other dark somethings; but the somethings were not close enough to see well. One of the merchants cried without a sound or movement, the tears on his face the only evidence.

The Farside levee showed at last, a black mass that didn't get any closer for what felt like hours. Fighting his fear, Kit leaned over the side, keeping his face away from the surface. "It can't really be bottomless," he said, half to himself. "What's under it?"

"You wouldn't hit the bottom, anyway," Rasali said.

*The Tranquil Crossing* eased up a long swell of mist and into a hollow. Rasali pointed the ferry along a crease and eased it forward. And then they were suddenly a stone's throw from the Farside dock and the light of its torches.

People on the dock moved as they approached. Just loudly enough to carry, a soft baritone voice called, "Rasali?"

She called back, "Ten this time, Pen."

"Anyone need carriers?" A different voice. Several passengers responded.

Rasali shipped the scull while the ferry was still some feet away from the dock, and allowed it to ease forward under its own momentum. She stepped to the prow and picked up a coiled rope there, tossing one end across the narrowing distance. Someone on the dock caught it and pulled the boat in, and in a very few moments, the ferry was snug against the dock.

Disembarking and payment was quicker than embarkation had been. Kit was the last off, and after a brief discussion he hired a carrier to haul his trunk to an inn in town. He turned to say farewell to Rasali. She and the man—Pen, Kit remembered—were untying the boat. "You're not going back already," he said.

"Oh, no." Her voice sounded loose, content, relaxed. Kit hadn't known how tense she was. "We're just going to tow the boat over to where the Twins will pull it out." She waved with one hand to the boat launch. A pair of white oxen gleamed in the night, at their heads a woman hardly darker.

"Wait," Kit said to Uni Mason and handed her his folio. "Please tell the innkeeper I'll be there soon." He turned back to Rasali. "May I help?"

In the darkness, he felt more than saw her smile. "Always."

The Red Lurcher, commonly called The Bitch, was a small but noisy inn five minutes' walk from the mist, ten (he was told) from the building site. His room was larger than at The Fish, with an uncomfortable bed and a window seat crammed with quires of ancient, hand-written music. Jenner stayed here, Kit knew, but when he asked the owner (Widson Innkeep, a heavyset man with red hair turning silver), he had not seen him. "You'll be the new one, the architect," Widson said.

"Yes," Kit said. "Please ask him to see me when he gets in."

Widson wrinkled his forehead. "I don't know, he's been out late most days recently, since—" He cut himself off, looking guilty.

"—since the signals informed him that I was here," Kit said. "I understand the impulse."

The innkeeper seemed to consider something for a moment, then said slowly, "We like Jenner here."

"Then we'll try to keep him," Kit said.

When the child Kit had recovered from the illness, he did not return to the crèche—which he would have been leaving in a year in any case—but went straight to his father. Davell Meinem was a slow-talking humorous man who nevertheless had a sharp tongue on the sites of his many projects. He brought Kit with him to his work places: best for the boy to get some experience in the trade.

Kit loved everything about his father's projects: the precisely drawn plans, the orderly progression of construction, the lines and curves of brick and iron and stone rising under the endlessly random sky.

For the first year or two, Kit imitated his father and the workers, building structures of tiny beams and bricks made by the woman set to mind him, a tiler who had lost a hand some years back. Davell collected the boy at the end of the day. "I'm here to inspect the construction," he said, and Kit demonstrated his bridge or tower, or the materials he had laid out in neat lines and stacks. Davell would discuss Kit's work with great seriousness, until it grew too dark to see and they went back to the inn or rented rooms that passed for home near the sites.

Davell spent nights buried in the endless paperwork of his projects, and Kit found this interesting, as well. The pattern that went into building something big was not just the architectural plans, or the construction itself; it was also labor schedules and documentation and materials deliveries. He started to draw his own plans, but he also made up endless correspondences with imaginary providers.

After a while, Kit noticed that a large part of the pattern that made a bridge or a tower was built entirely out of people.

The knock on Kit's door came very late that night, a preemptory rap. Kit put down the quill he was mending, and rolled his shoulders to loosen them. "Yes," he said aloud as he stood.

The man who stormed through the door was as dark as Kit, though perhaps a few years younger. He wore mud-splashed riding clothes.

"I am Kit Meinem of Atyar."

"Jenner Ellar of Atyar. Show it to me." Silently Kit handed the cartel to Jenner, who glared at it before tossing it onto the table. "It took long enough for them to pick a replacement."

*Might as well deal with this right now*, Kit thought. "You hoped it would be you."

Jenner eyed Kit for a moment. "Yes. I did."

"You think you're the most qualified to complete the project because you've been here for the last—what is it? Year?"

"I know the sites," Jenner said. "I worked with Teniant to make those plans. And then Empire sends—" He turned to face the empty hearth.

"—Empire sends someone new," Kit said to Jenner's back. "Someone with connections in the capital, influential friends but no experience with this site, this bridge. It should have been you, yes?"

Jenner was still.

"But it isn't," Kit said, and let the words hang for a moment. "I've built nine bridges in the past twenty years. Four suspension bridges, three major spans. Two bridges over mist. You've done three, and the biggest span you've directed was three hundred and fifty feet, six stone arches over shallow water and shifting gravel up on Mati River."

"I know," Jenner snapped.

"It's a good bridge." Kit poured two glasses of whiskey from a stoneware pitcher by the window. "I coached down to see it before I came here. It's well made, and you were on budget and nearly on schedule in spite of the drought. Better, the locals still like you. Asked how you're doing these days. Here."

Jenner took the glass Kit offered. *Good.* Kit continued, "Meinems have built bridges—and roads and aqueducts and stadia, a hundred sorts of public structures—for Empire for a thousand years." Jenner turned to speak, but Kit held up his hand. "This doesn't mean we're any better at it than Ellars. But Empire knows us—and we know Empire, how to do what we need to. If they'd given you this bridge, you'd be replaced within a year. But I can get this bridge built, and I will." Kit sat and leaned forward, elbows on knees. "With you. You're talented. You know the site. You know the people. Help me make this bridge."

"It's real to you," Jenner said finally, and Kit knew what he meant: *You care about this work. It's not just another tick on a list.*

"Yes," Kit said. "You'll be my second for this one. I'll show you how to deal with Atyar, and I'll help you with contacts. And your next project will belong entirely to you. This is the first bridge, but it isn't going to be the only one across the mist."

Together they drank. The whiskey bit at Kit's throat and made his eyes water. "Oh," he said, "that's *awful.*"

Jenner laughed suddenly, and met his eyes for the first time: a little wary still, but willing to be convinced. "Farside whiskey is terrible. You drink much of this, you'll be running for Atyar in a month."

"Maybe we'll have something better ferried across," Kit said.

Preparations were not so far along on this side. The heaps of blocks at the construction site were not so massive, and it was harder to find local workers. In discussions between Kit, Jenner, and the Near- and Farside masons who would oversee construction of the pillars, final plans materialized. This would be unique, the largest structure of its kind ever attempted: a single-span chain suspension bridge a quarter of a mile long. The basic plan remained unchanged: the bridge would be supported by eyebar-and-bolt chains, four on each side, allowed to play independently to compensate for the slight shifts that would be caused by traffic on the roadbed. The huge eyebars and their bolts were being fashioned five hundred miles away and far to the west, where iron was common and the smelting and ironworking were the best in Empire. Kit had just written to the foundries to start the work again.

The pillar and anchorage on Nearside would be built of gold limestone anchored with pilings into the bedrock; on Farside, they would be pink-gray granite with a funnel-shaped foundation. The towers' heights would be nearly three hundred feet. There were taller towers back in Atyar, but none had to stand against the compression of the bridge.

The initial tests with the fish-skin rope had showed it to be nearly as strong as iron, without the weight. When Kit asked the Farside tanners and rope-makers about its durability, he was taken a day's travel east to Meknai, to a waterwheel that used knotted belts of the material for its drive. The belts, he was told, were seventy-five years old and still sound. Fish-skin wore like maplewood, so long as it wasn't left in mist, but it required regular maintenance.

He watched Meknai's little river for a time. There had been rain recently in the foothills, and the water was quick and abrupt as light. *Water bridges are easy*, he thought a little wistfully, and then: *Anyone can bridge water.*

Kit revised the plans again, to use the lighter material where they could. Jenner crossed the mist to Nearside, to work with Daell and Stivvan Cabler on the expansion of their workshops and ropewalk.

Without Jenner (who was practically a local, as Kit was told again and again), Kit felt the difference in attitudes on the river's two banks more clearly. Most Farsiders shared the Nearsiders' attitudes: money is money and always welcome, and there was a sense of the excitement that comes of any great project; but there was more resistance here. Empire was effectively split by the river, and the lands to the east—starting with Faside—had never seen their destinies as closely linked to Atyar in the west. They were overseen by the eastern capital, Triple; their taxes went to building necessities on their own side of the mist. Empire's grasp on the eastern lands was loose, and had never needed to be tighter.

The bridge would change things. Travel between Atyar and Triple would grow more common, and perhaps Empire would no longer hold the eastern lands so gently. Triple's lack of enthusiasm for the project showed itself in delayed deliveries of stone and iron. Kit traveled five days along the Triple road to the district seat to present his credentials to the governor, and wrote sharp letters to the Department of Roads in Triple. Things became a little easier.

It was midwinter before the design was finished. Kit avoided crossing the mist. Rasali Ferry crossed seventeen times. He managed to see her nearly every time, at least for as long as it took to share a beer.

The second time Kit crossed, it was midmorning of an early spring day. The mist mirrored the overcast sky above: pale and flat, like a layer of fog in a dell. Rasali was loading the ferry at the upper dock when Kit arrived, and to his surprise she smiled at him, her face suddenly beautiful. Kit nodded to the stranger watching Valo toss immense cloth-wrapped bales down to Rasali, then greeted the Ferrys. Valo paused for a moment, but did not return Kit's greeting, only bent again to his work. Valo had been avoiding him since nearly the beginning of his time there. *Later.* With a mental shrug, Kit turned from Valo to Rasali. She was catching and stacking the enormous bales easily.

"What's in those? You throw them as if they were—"

"—paper," she finished. "The very best Ibraric mulberry paper. Light as lambswool. You probably have a bunch of this stuff in that folio of yours."

Kit thought of the vellum he used for his plans, and the paper he used for everything else: made of cotton from far to the south, its surface buffed until it felt hard and smooth as enamelwork. He said, "All the time. It's good paper."

Rasali piled on bales and more bales, until the ferry was stacked three and four high. He added, "Is there going to be room for me in there?"

"Pilar Runn and Valo aren't coming with us," she said. "You'll have to sit on top of the bales, but there's room as long as you sit still and don't wobble."

As Rasali pushed away from the dock Kit asked, "Why isn't the trader coming with her paper?"

"Why would she? Pilar has a broker on the other side." Her hands busy, she tipped her head to one side, in a gesture that somehow conveyed a shrug. "Mist is dangerous."

Somewhere along the river a ferry was lost every few months: horses, people, cartage, all lost. Fishers stayed closer to shore and died less often. It was harder to calculate the impact to trade and communications of this barrier splitting Empire in half.

This journey—in daylight, alone with Rasali—was very different than Kit's earlier crossing: less frightening but somehow wilder, stranger. The cold wind down the river was cutting and brought bits of dried foam to rest on his skin, but they blew off quickly, without pain and leaving no mark. The wind fell to a breeze and then to nothing as they navigated into the mist, as if they were buried in feathers or snow.

They moved through what looked like a layered maze of thick cirrus clouds. He watched the mist along the *Crossing*'s side until they passed over a small hole like a pockmark, straight down and no more than a foot across. For an instant he glimpsed open space below them; they were floating on a layer of mist above an air pocket deep enough to swallow the boat. He rolled onto his back to stare up at the sky until he stopped shaking; when he looked again, they were out of the maze, it seemed. The boat floated along a gently curving channel. He relaxed a little, and moved to watch Rasali.

"How fares your bridge?" Rasali said at last, her voice muted in the muffled air. This had to be a courtesy—everyone in town seemed to know everything about the bridge's progress—but Kit was used to answering questions to which people already knew the answers. He had found patience to be a highly effective tool.

"Farside foundations are doing well. We have maybe six more months before the anchorage is done, but pilings for the pillar's foundation are in place and we can start building. Six weeks early," Kit said, a little smugly, though this was a victory no one else would appreciate, and in any case the weather was as much to be credited as any action on his part. "On Nearside, we've run into basalt that's too hard to drill easily, so we sent for a specialist. The signal flags say she's arrived, and that's why I'm crossing."

She said nothing, seemingly intent on moving the great scull. He watched her for a time, content to see her shoulders flex, hear her breath forcing itself out in smooth waves. Over the faint yeast scent of the mist, he smelled her sweat, or thought he did. She frowned slightly, but he could not tell whether it was due to her labor, or something in the mist, or something else. Who was she, really? "May I ask a question, Rasali Ferry?"

Rasali nodded, eyes on the mist in front of the boat.

Actually, he had several things he wished to know: about her, about the river, about the people here. He picked one, almost at random. "What is bothering Valo?

"He's transparent, isn't he? He thinks you take something away from him," Rasali said. "He is too young to know what you take is unimportant."

Kit thought about it. "His work?"

"His work is unimportant?" She laughed, a sudden puff of an exhale as she pulled. "We have a lot of money, Ferrys. We own land and rent it out—the Deer's Heart belongs to my family; do you know that? He's young. He wants what we all want at his age. A chance to test himself against the world and see if he measures up. And because he's a Ferry, he wants to be tested against adventures. Danger. The mist. Valo thinks you take that away from him."

"But he's not immortal," Kit said. "Whatever he thinks. The river can kill him. It will, sooner or later. It—"

—*will kill you.* Kit caught himself, rolled onto his back again to look up at the sky.

In The Bitch's taproom one night, a local man had told him about Rasali's family: a history of deaths, of boats lost in a silent hissing of mist, or the rending of wood, or screams that might be human and might be a horse. "So everyone wears ash-color for a month or two, and then the next Ferry takes up the business. Rasali's still new, two years maybe. When she goes, it'll be Valo, then Rasali's youngest sister, then Valo's sister. Unless Rasali or Valo have kids by then."

"They're always beautiful," the man had added after some more porter: "the Ferrys. I suppose that's to make up for having such short lives."

Kit looked down from the paper bales at Rasali. "But you're different. You don't feel you're losing anything."

"You don't know what I feel, Kit Meinem of Atyar." Cool light moved along the muscles of her arms. Her voice came again, softer. "I am not young; I don't need to prove myself. But I will lose this. The mist, the silence."

*Then tell me,* he did not say. *Show me.*

She was silent for the rest of the trip. Kit thought perhaps she was angry, but when he invited her, she accompanied him to the building site.

The quiet pasture was gone. All that remained of the tall grass was struggling tufts and dirty straw. The air smelled of sweat and meat and the bitter scent of hot metal. There were more blocks here now, a lot more. The pits for the anchorage and the pillar were excavated to bedrock, overshadowed by mountains of dirt. One sheep remained, skinned and spitted, and greasy smoke rose as a girl turned it over a fire beside the temporary forge. Kit had considered the pasture a nuisance, but looking at the skewered sheep, he felt a twinge of guilt.

The rest of the flock had been replaced by sturdy-looking men and women, who were using rollers to shift stones down a dugout ramp into the hole for the anchorage foundation. Dust muted the bright colors of their short kilts and breastbands and dulled their skin, and in spite of the cold, sweat had cleared tracks along their muscles.

One of the workers waved to Rasali and she waved back. Kit recalled his name: Mik Rounder, very strong but he needed direction. Had they been lovers? Relationships out here were tangled in ways Kit didn't understand; in the capital such things were more formal and often involved contracts.

Jenner and a small woman knelt, conferring, on the exposed stone floor of the larger pit. When Kit slid down the ladder to join them, the small woman bowed slightly. Her eyes and short hair and skin all seemed to be turning the same iron-gray. "I am Liu Breaker of Hoic. Your specialist."

"Kit Meinem of Atyar. How shall we address this?"

"Your Jenner says you need some of this basalt cleared away, yes?"

Kit nodded.

Liu knelt to run her hand along the pit's floor. "See where the color and texture change along this line? Your Jenner was right: this upthrust of basalt is a problem. Here where the shale is, you can carve out most of the foundation the usual way with drills, picks. But the basalt is too hard to drill." She straightened and brushed dust from her knees. "Have you ever seen explosives used?"

Kit shook his head. "We haven't needed them for any of my projects. I've never been to the mines, either."

"Not much good anywhere else," Liu said, "but very useful for breaking up large amounts of rock. A lot of the blocks you have here were loosed using explosives." She grinned. "You'll like the noise."

"We can't afford to break the bedrock's structural integrity."

"I brought enough powder for a number of small charges. Comparatively small."

"How—"

Liu held up a weathered hand. "I don't need to understand bridges to walk across one. Yes?"

Kit laughed outright. "Yes."

Liu Breaker was right; Kit liked the noise very much. Liu would not allow anyone close to the pit, but even from what she considered a safe distance, behind huge piles of dirt, the explosion was an immense shattering thing, a crack of thunder that shook the earth. There was a second of echoing silence. The workers, after a collective gasp and some scattered screams, cheered and stamped their feet. A small cloud of mingled smoke and rock-dust eased over the pit's edge, sharp with the smell of saltpeter. The birds were not happy; with the explosion, they burst from their trees and wheeled nervously.

Grinning, Liu climbed from her bunker near the pit, her face dust-caked everywhere but around her eyes, which had been protected by the wooden slit-goggles now hanging around her neck. "So far, so good," she shouted over the ringing in Kit's ears. Seeing his face, she laughed. "These are nothing— gnat sneezes. You should hear when we quarry granite up at Hoic."

Kit was going to speak more with her when he noticed Rasali striding away. He had forgotten she was there; now he followed her, half shouting to hear himself. "Some noise, yes?"

Rasali whirled. "What are you thinking?" She was shaking and her lips were white. Her voice was very loud.

Taken aback, Kit answered, "We are blowing the foundations." *Rage? Fear?* He wished he could think a little more clearly, but the sound had stunned his wits.

"And making the earth shake! The Big Ones come to thunder, Kit!"

"It wasn't thunder," he said.

"Tell me it wasn't worse!" Tears glittered in her eyes. Her voice was dulled by the echo in his ears. "They will come, I *know* it."

He reached a hand out to her. "It's a tall levee, Rasali. Even if they do, they're not going to come over that." His heart in his chest thrummed. His head was hurting. It was so hard to hear her.

"*No one* knows what they'll do! They used to destroy whole towns, drifting inland on foggy nights. Why do you think they built the levees, a thousand years ago? The Big Ones—"

She stopped shouting, listening. She mouthed something, but Kit could not hear her over the beating in his ears, his heart, his head. He realized suddenly that these were not the after-effects of the explosion; the air itself was beating. He was aware at the edges of his vision of the other workers, every face turned toward the mist. There was nothing to see but the overcast sky. No one moved.

But the sky was moving.

Behind the levee the river mist was rising, dirty gray-gold against the steel-gray of the clouds in a great boiling upheaval, at least a hundred feet high, to be seen over the levee. The mist was seething, breaking open in great swirls and rifts, and everything moving, changing. Kit had seen a great fire once, when a warehouse of linen had burned, and the smoke had poured upward and looked a little like this before it was torn apart by the wind.

Gaps opened in the mountain of mist and closed; and others opened, darker the deeper they were. And through those gaps, in the brown-black shadows at the heart of the mist, was movement.

The gaps closed. After an eternity, the mist slowly smoothed and then settled back, behind the levee, and could no longer be seen. He wasn't really sure when the thrumming of the air blended back into the ringing of his ears.

"Gone," Rasali said with a sound like a sob.

A worker made one of the vivid jokes that come after fear; the others laughed, too loud. A woman ran up the levee and shouted down, "Farside levees are fine; ours are fine." More laughter: people jogged off to Nearside to check on their families.

The back of Kit's hand was burning. A flake of foam had settled and left an irregular mark. "I only saw mist," Kit said. "Was there a Big One?"

Rasali shook herself, stern now but no longer angry or afraid. Kit had learned this about the Ferrys, that their emotions coursed through them and then dissolved. "It was in there. I've seen the mist boil like that before, but never so big. Nothing else could heave it up like that."

"On purpose?"

"Oh, who knows? They're a mystery, the Big Ones." She met his eyes. "I hope your bridge is very high, Kit Meinem of Atyar."

Kit looked to where the mist had been, but there was only sky. "The deck will be two hundred feet above the mist. High enough. I hope."

Liu Breaker walked up to them, rubbing her hands on her leather leggings. "So, *that's* not something that happens at Hoic. *Very* exciting. What do you call that? How do we prevent it next time?"

Rasali looked at the smaller woman for a moment. "I don't think you can. Big Ones come when they come."

Liu said, "They do not always come?"

Rasali shook her head.

"Well, cold comfort is better than no comfort, as my Da says."

Kit rubbed his temples; the headache remained. "We'll continue."

"Then you'll have to be careful," Rasali said. "Or you will kill us all."

"The bridge will save many lives," Kit said. *Yours, eventually.*

Rasali turned on her heel.

Kit did not follow her, not that day. Whether it was because subsequent explosions were smaller ("As small as they can be and still break rock," Liu said), or because they were doing other things, the Big Ones did not return, though fish were plentiful for the three months it took to plan and plant the charges, and break the bedrock.

There was also a Meinem tradition of metal-working, and Meinem reeves, and many Meinems went into fields altogether different; but Kit had known from nearly the beginning that he would be one of the building Meinems. He loved the invisible architecture of construction, looking for a compromise between the vision in his head and the sites, the materials, and the people that would make them real. The challenge was to compromise as little as possible.

Architecture was studied at University. His tutor was a materials specialist, a woman who had directed construction on an incredible twenty-three bridges. Skossa Timt was so old that her skin and hair had faded together to the white of Gani marble, and she walked with a cane she had designed herself, for efficiency. She taught him much. Materials had rules, patterns of behavior: they bent or crumbled or cracked or broke under quantifiable stresses. They strengthened or destroyed one another. Even the best materials in the most efficient combinations did not last forever—she tapped her own forehead with one gnarled finger and laughed—but if he did his work right, they could last a thousand years or more. "But not forever," Skossa said. "Do your best, but don't forget this."

The anchorages and pillars grew. Workers came from towns up and down each bank; and locals, idle or inclined to make money from outside, were hired on the spot. Generally the new people were welcome: they paid for rooms and food and goods of all sorts. The taverns settled in to making double and then triple batches of everything, threw out new wings and stables. Nearside accepted the new people easily, the only fights late at night when people had been drinking and flirting more than they should. Farside had fist fights more frequently, though they decreased steadily as skeptics gave in to the money that flowed into Farside, or to the bridge itself, its pillars too solid to be denied.

Farmers and husbanders sold their fields, and new buildings sprawled out from the towns' hearts. Some were made of wattle and daub, slapped together above stamped-earth floors that still smelled of sheep dung; others, small but permanent, went up more slowly, as the bridge builders laid fieldstones and timber in their evenings and on rest days.

The new people and locals mixed together until it was hard to tell the one from the other, though the older townfolk kept scrupulous track of who truly belonged. For those who sought lovers and friends, the new people were an opportunity to meet someone other than the men and women they had known since childhood. Many met casual lovers, and several term-partnered with new people. There was even a Nearside wedding, between Kes Tiler and a black-eyed builder from far to the south called Jolite Deveren, whatever that meant.

Kit did not have lovers. Working every night until he fell asleep over his paperwork, he didn't miss it much, except late on certain nights when thunderstorms left him restless and unnaturally alert, as if lightning ran under his skin. Some nights he thought of Rasali, wondered whether she was sleeping with someone that night or alone, and wondered if the storm had awakened her, left her restless as well.

Kit saw a fair amount of Rasali when they were both on the same side of the mist. She was clever and calm, and the only person who did not want to talk about the bridge all the time.

Kit did not forget what Rasali said about Valo. Kit had been a young man himself not so many years before, and he remembered what young men and women felt, the hunger to prove themselves against the world. Kit didn't need Valo to accept the bridge—he was scarcely into adulthood and his only influence over the townspeople was based on his work—but Kit liked the youth, who had Rasali's eyes and sometimes her effortless way of moving.

Valo started asking questions, first of the other workers and then of Kit. His boat-building experience meant the questions were good ones, and he already designed boats. Kit passed on the first things he had learned as a child on his father's sites, and showed him the manipulation of the immense blocks, and the tricky balance of material and plan; the strength of will that allows a man to direct a thousand people toward a single vision. Valo was too honest not to recognize Kit's mastery, and too competitive not to try and meet Kit on his own ground. He came more often to visit the construction sites.

After a season, Kit took him aside. "You could be a builder, if you wished."

Valo flushed. "Build things? You mean, bridges?"

"Or houses, or granges, or retaining walls. Or bridges. You could make people's lives better."

"Change people's lives?" He frowned suddenly. "No."

"Our lives change all the time, whether we want them to or not," Kit said. "Valo Ferry, you are smart. You are good with people. You learn quickly. If you were interested, I could start teaching you myself, or send you to Atyar to study there."

"Valo Builder . . . " he said, trying it out, then: "No." But after that, whenever he had time free from ferrying or building boats, he was always to be found on the site. Kit knew that the answer would be different the next time he asked. There was for everything a possibility, an invisible pattern that could be made manifest given work and the right materials. Kit wrote to an old friend or two, finding contacts that would help Valo when the time came.

The pillars and anchorages grew. Winter came, and summer, and a second winter. There were falls, a broken arm, two sets of cracked ribs. Someone on Farside had her toes crushed when one of the stones slipped from its rollers and she lost the foot. The bridge was on schedule, even after the delay caused by the slow rock-breaking. There were no problems with payroll or the Department of Roads or Empire, and only minor, manageable issues with the occasionally disruptive representatives from Triple or the local governors.

Kit knew he was lucky.

The first death came during one of Valo's visits.

It was early in the second winter of the bridge, and Kit had been in Farside for three months. He had learned that winter meant gray skies and rain and sometimes snow. Soon they would have to stop the heavy work for the season. Still, it had been a good day, and the workers had lifted and placed almost a hundred stones.

Valo had returned after three weeks at Nearside, building a boat for Jenna Blue-fish. Kit found him staring up at the slim tower through a rain so faint it felt like fog. The black opening of the roadway arch looked out of place, halfway up the pillar.

Valo said, "You're a lot farther along since I was here last. How tall now?"

Kit got this question a lot. "A hundred and five feet, more or less. A third finished."

Valo smiled, shook his head. "Hard to believe it'll stay up."

"There's a tower in Atyar, black basalt and iron, five hundred feet. Five times this tall."

"It just looks so delicate," Valo said. "I know what you said, that most of the stress on the pillar is compression, but it still looks as though it'll snap in half."

"After a while, you'll have more experience with suspension bridges and it will seem less . . . unsettling. Would you like to see the progress?"

Valo's eyes brightened. "May I? I don't want to get in the way."

"I haven't been up yet today, and they'll be finishing up soon. Scaffold or stairwell?"

Valo looked at the scaffolding against one face of the pillar, the ladders tied into place within it, and shivered. "I can't believe people go up that. Stairs, I think."

Kit followed Valo. The steep internal stair was three feet wide and endlessly turning, five steps up and then a platform; turn to the left, and then five more steps and turn. Eventually, the stairs would at need be lit by lanterns set into alcoves at every third turning, but today Kit and Valo felt their way up, fingers trailing along the cold, damp stone, a small lantern in Valo's hand.

The stairwell smelled of water and earth and the thin smell of the burning lamp oil. Some of the workers hated the stairs and preferred the ladders outside, but Kit liked it. For these few moments, he was part of his bridge, a strong bone buried deep in flesh he had created.

They came out at the top and paused a moment to look around the unfinished courses, and the black silhouette of the winch against the dulling sky. The last few workers were breaking down the shear-legs, which had been used to move blocks around the pillar. A lantern hung from a pole jammed into one of the holes the laborers would fill with rods and molten iron, later in construction. Kit nodded to them as Valo went to an edge to look down.

"It is wonderful," Valo said, smiling. "Being high like this—you can look right down into people's kitchen yards. Look, Teli Carpenter has a pig smoking."

"You don't need to see it to know that," Kit said dryly. "I've been smelling it for two days."

Valo snorted. "Can you see as far as White Peak yet?"

"On a clear day, yes," Kit said. "I was up here two—"

A heavy sliding sound and a scream; Kit whirled to see one of the workers on her back, one of the shearleg's timbers across her chest. Loreh Tanner, a local. Kit ran the few steps to Loreh and dropped beside her. One man, the man who had been working with her, said, "It slipped—oh Loreh, please hang on," but Kit could see it was futile. She was pinned to the pillar, chest flattened, one shoulder visibly dislocated, unconscious, her breathing labored. Black foam bloomed from her lips in the lantern's bad light.

Kit took her cold hand. "It's all right, Loreh. It's all right." It was a lie and in any case she could not hear him, but the others would. "Get Hall," one of the workers said, and Kit nodded: Hall was a surgeon. And then, "And get Obal, someone. Where's her husband?" Footsteps ran down the stairs and were lost into the hiss of rain just beginning and someone's crying and Loreh's wet breathing.

Kit glanced up. His chest heaving, Valo stood staring at the body. Kit said to him, "Help find Hall," and when the boy did not move, he repeated it, his voice sharper. Valo said nothing, did not stop looking at Loreh until he spun and ran down the stairs. Kit heard shouting, far below, as the first messenger ran toward the town.

Loreh took a last shuddering breath and died.

Kit looked at the others around Loreh's body. The man holding Loreh's other hand pressed his face against it, crying helplessly. The two other workers left here knelt at her feet, a man and a woman, huddled close though they were not a couple. "Tell me," he said.

"I tried to stop it from hitting her," the woman said. She cradled one arm: obviously broken, though she didn't seem to have noticed. "But it just kept falling."

"She was tired; she must have gotten careless," the man said, and the broken-armed woman said, "I don't want to think about that sound." Words fell from them like blood from a cut.

Kit listened. This was what they needed right now, to speak and to be heard. So he listened, and when the others came, Loreh's husband white-lipped and angry-eyed, and the surgeon Obal and six other workers, Kit listened to them as well, and gradually moved them down through the pillar and back toward the warm lights and comfort of Farside.

Kit had lost people before, and it was always like this. There would be tears tonight, and anger at him and at his bridge, anger at fate for permitting this. There would be sadness, and nightmares. There would be lovemaking, and the holding close of children and friends and dogs—affirmations of life in the cold wet night.

His tutor at University had said, during one of her frequent digressions from the nature of materials and the principles of architecture, "Things will go wrong."

It was winter, but in spite of the falling snow they walked slowly to the coffee-house, as Skossa looked for purchase for her cane. She continued, "On long projects, you'll forget that you're not one of them. But if there's an accident?

You're slapped in the face with it. Whatever you're feeling? Doesn't matter. Guilty, grieving, alone, worried about the schedule. None of it. What matters is *their* feelings. So listen to them. Respect what they're going through."

She paused then, tapped her cane against the ground thoughtfully. "No, I lie. It does matter, but you will have to find your own strength, your own resources elsewhere."

"Friends?" Kit said doubtfully. He knew already that he wanted a career like his father's. He would not be in the same place for more than a few years at a time.

"Yes, friends." Snow collected on Skossa's hair, but she didn't seem to notice. "Kit, I worry about you. You're good with people, I've seen it. You like them. But there's a limit for you." He opened his mouth to protest, but she held up her hand to silence him. "I know. You do care. But inside the framework of a project. Right now it's your studies. Later it'll be roads and bridges. But people around you—their lives go on outside the framework. They're not just tools to your hand, even likable tools. Your life should go on, too. You should have more than roads to live for. Because if something does go wrong, you'll need what *you're* feeling to matter, to someone somewhere, anyway."

Kit walked through Farside toward the Red Lurcher. Most people were home or at one of the taverns by now, a village turned inward; but he heard footsteps running behind him. He turned quickly—it was not unknown for people reeling from a loss to strike at whatever they blamed, and sometimes that was a person.

It was Valo. Though his fists were balled, Kit could tell immediately that he was angry but not looking for a fight. For a moment, Kit wished he didn't need to listen, that he could just go back to his rooms and sleep for a thousand hours; but there was a stricken look in Valo's eyes: Valo, who looked so much like Rasali. He hoped that Rasali and Loreh hadn't been close.

Kit said gently, "Why aren't you inside? It's cold." As he said it, he realized suddenly that it *was* cold; the rain had settled into a steady cold flow.

"I will, I was, I mean, but I came out for a second, because I thought maybe I could find you, because—"

The boy was shivering, too. "Where are your friends? Let's get you inside. It'll be better there."

"No," he said. "I have to know first. It's like this always? If I do this, build things, it'll happen for me? Someone will die?"

"It might. It probably will, eventually."

Valo said an unexpected thing. "I see. It's just that she had just gotten married."

The blood on Loreh's lips, the wet sound of her crushed chest as she took her last breaths—"Yes," Kit said. "She was."

"I just . . . I had to know if I need to be ready for this." It seemed callous, but Ferrys were used to dying, to death. "I guess I'll find out."

"I hope you don't have to." The rain was getting heavier. "You should be inside, Valo."

Valo nodded. "Rasali—I wish she were here. She could help maybe. You should go in, too. You're shivering."

Kit watched him go. Valo had not invited him to accompany him back into the light and the warmth; he knew better than to expect that, but for a moment he had permitted himself to hope otherwise.

Kit slipped through the stables and through the back door at The Bitch. Wisdon Innkeep, hands full of mugs for the taproom, saw him and nodded, face unsmiling but not hostile. That was good, Kit thought: as good as it would get, tonight.

He entered his room and shut the door, leaned his back to it as if holding the world out. Someone had already been in his room: a lamp had been lit against the darkness, a fire laid, and bread and cheese and a tankard of ale set by the window to stay cool.

He began to cry.

The news went across the river by signal flags. No one worked on the bridge the next day, or the day after that. Kit did all the right things, letting his grief and guilt overwhelm him only when he was alone, huddled in front of the fire in his room.

The third day, Rasali arrived from Nearside with a boat filled with crates of northland herbs on their way east. Kit was sitting in The Bitch's taproom, listening. People were coping, starting to look forward again. They should be able to get back to it soon, the next clear day. He would offer them something that would be an immediate, visible accomplishment, something different, perhaps guidelining the ramp.

He didn't see Rasali come into the taproom; only felt her hand on his shoulder and heard her voice in his ear. "Come with me," she murmured.

He looked up puzzled, as though she was a stranger. "Rasali Ferry, why are you here?"

She said only, "Come for a walk, Kit."

It was raining, but he accompanied her anyway, pulling a scarf over his head when the first cold drops hit his face.

She said nothing as they splashed through Farside. She was leading him somewhere, but he didn't care where, grateful not to have to be the decisive one, the strong one. After a time, she opened a door and led him through it into a small room filled with light and warmth.

"My house," she said. "And Valo's. He's still at the boatyard. Sit."

She pointed and Kit dropped onto the settle beside the fire. Rasali swiveled a pot hanging from a bracket out of the fire and ladled something out. She handed a mug to him and sat. "So. Drink."

It was spiced porter, and the warmth eased into the tightness in his chest. "Thank you."

"Talk."

"This is such a loss for you all, I know," he said. "Did you know Loreh well?"

She shook her head. "This is not for me, this is for you. Tell me."

"I'm fine," he said, and when she didn't say anything, he repeated, with a flicker of anger: "I'm *fine*, Rasali. I can handle this."

"Probably you can," Rasali said. "But you're not fine. She died, and it was your bridge she died for. You don't feel responsible? I don't believe it."

"Of course I feel responsible," he snapped.

The fire cast gold light across her broad cheekbones when she turned her face to him, but to his surprise she said nothing, only looked at him and waited.

"She's not the first," Kit said, surprising himself. "The first project I had sole charge of, a toll gate. Such a little project, such a dumb little project to lose someone on. The wood frame for the passageway collapsed before we got the keystone in. The whole arch came down. Someone got killed." It had been a very young man, slim and tall, with a limp. He was raising his little sister; she hadn't been more than ten. Running loose in the fields around the site, she had missed the collapse, the boy's death. Dafuen? Naus? He couldn't remember his name. And the girl—what had her name been? *I should remember. I owe that much to them.*

"Every time I lose someone," he said at last, "I remember the others. There've been twelve, in twenty-three years. Not so many, considering. Building's dangerous. My record's better than most."

"But it doesn't matter, does it?" she said. "You still feel you killed each one of them, as surely as if you'd thrown them off a bridge yourself."

"It's my responsibility. The first one, Duar—" *that* had been his name; there it was. The name loosened something in Kit. His face warmed: tears, hot tears running down his face.

"It's all right," she said. She held him until he stopped crying.

"How did you know?" he said finally.

"I am the eldest surviving member of the Ferry family," she said. "My aunt died seven years ago. And then I watched my brother leave to cross the mist, four years ago now. It was a perfect day, calm and sunny, but he never made it. He went instead of me because on that day the river felt wrong to me. It could have been me. It should have, maybe. So I understand."

She stretched a little. "Not that most people don't. If Petro Housewright sends his daughter to select timber in the mountains, and she doesn't come back—eaten by wolves, struck by lightning, I don't know—is Petro to blame? It's probably the wolves or the lightning. Maybe it's the daughter, if she did something stupid. And it *is* Petro, a little; she wouldn't have been there at all if he hadn't sent her. And it's her mother for being fearless and teaching that to her daughter; and Thom Green for wanting a new room to his house. Everyone, except maybe the wolves, feels at least a little responsible. This path leads nowhere. Loreh would have died sooner or later." Rasali added softly, "We all do."

"Can you accept death so readily?" he asked. "Yours, even?"

She leaned back, her face suddenly weary. "What else can I do, Kit? Someone must ferry, and I am better suited than most—and by more than my blood. I love the mist, its currents and the smell of it and the power in my body as I push us all through. Petro's daughter—she did not want to die when the wolves came, I'm sure; but she loved selecting timber."

"If it comes for you?" he said softly. "Would you be so sanguine then?"

She laughed, and the pensiveness was gone. "No, indeed. I will curse the stars and go down fighting. But it will still have been a wonderful thing, to cross the mist."

At University, Kit's relationships had all been casual. There were lectures that everyone attended, and he lived near streets and pubs crowded with students; but the physical students had a tradition of keeping to themselves that was rooted in the personal preferences of their predecessors, and in their own. The only people who worked harder than the engineers were the ale-makers, the University joke went. Kit and the other physical students talked and drank and roomed and slept together.

In his third year, he met Domhu Canna at the arcade where he bought vellums and paper: a small woman with a heart-shaped face and hair in black clouds she kept somewhat confined by grey ribands. She was a philosophical student from a city two thousand miles to the east, on the coast.

He was fascinated. Her mind was abrupt and fish-quick and made connections he didn't understand. To her, everything was a metaphor, a symbol for something else. People, she said, could be better understood by comparing their lives to animals, to the seasons, to the structure of certain lyrical songs, to a gambling game.

This was another form of pattern-making, he saw. Perhaps people were like teamed oxen to be led, or like metals to be smelted and shaped to one's purpose; or as the stones for a dry-laid wall, which had to be carefully selected for shape and strength, and sorted, and placed. This last suited him best.

What held them together was no external mortar but their own weight, and the planning and patience of the drystone builder. But it was an inadequate metaphor: people were this, but they were all the other things, as well.

He never understood what Domhu found attractive in him. They never talked about regularizing their relationship. When her studies were done halfway through his final year, she returned to her city to help found a new university, and in any case her people did not enter into term marriages. They separated amicably, and with a sense of loss on his part at least; but it did not occur to him until years later that things might have been different.

The winter was rainy but there were days they could work, and they did. By spring, there had been other deaths unrelated to the bridge on both banks: a woman who died in childbirth; a child who had never breathed properly in his short life; two fisherfolk lost when they capsized; several who died for the various reasons that old or sick people died.

Over the spring and summer they finished the anchorages, featureless masses of blocks and mortar anchored to the bedrock. They were buried so that only a few courses of stone showed above the ground. The anchoring bolts were each tall as a man, hidden safely behind the portals through which the chains would pass.

The Farside pillar was finished by midwinter of the third year, well before the Nearside tower. Jenner and Teniant Planner had perfected a signal system that allowed detailed technical information to pass between the banks, and documents traveled each time a ferry crossed. Rasali made sixty-eight trips back and forth; though he spent much of his time with Kit, Valo made twenty. Kit did not cross the mist at all unless the flags told him he must.

It was early spring and Kit was in Farside when the signals went up: *Message. Imperial seal.*

He went to Rasali at once.

"I can't go," she said. "I just got here yesterday. The Big Ones—"

"I have to get across, and Valo's on Nearside. There's news from the capital."

"News has always waited before."

"No, it hasn't. You forced it to, but news waited restlessly, pacing along the levee until we could pick it up."

"Use the flags," she said, a little impatiently.

"The Imperial seal can't be broken by anyone but me or Jenner. He's over here. I'm sorry," he said, thinking of her brother, dead four years before.

"If you die no one can read it, either," she said, but they left just after dusk anyway. "If we must go, better then than earlier or later," she said.

He met her at the upper dock at dusk. The sky was streaked with bright bands of green and gold, clouds catching the last of the sun, but they radiated no light, themselves just reflections. The current down the river was steady and light. The mist between the levees was already in shadow, shaped into smooth dunes twenty feet high.

Rasali waited silently, coiling and uncoiling a rope in her hands. Beside her stood two women and a dog: dealers in spices returning from the plantations of Gloth, the dog whining and restless. Kit was burdened with document cases filled with vellum and paper, rolled tightly and wrapped in oilcloth. Rasali seated the merchants and their dog in the ferry's bow, then untied and pushed off in silence. Kit sat near her.

She stood at the stern, braced against the scull. For a moment he could pretend that this was water they moved on and he half-expected to hear sloshing; but the big paddle made no noise. It was so silent that he could hear her breath, the dog's nervous panting aft, and his own pulse, too fast. Then the *Crossing* slid up the long slope of a mist dune and there was no possibility that this could be anything but mist.

He heard a soft sighing, like air entering a once-sealed bottle. It was hard to see so far, but the lingering light showed him a heaving of the mist on the face of a neighboring dune, like a bubble coming to the surface of hot mud. The dome grew and then burst. There was a gasp from one of the women. A shape rolled away, too dark for Kit to see more than its length.

"What—" he said in wonder.

"Fish," Rasali breathed to Kit. "Not small ones. They are biting tonight. We should not have come."

It was night now; the first tiny moon appeared, scarcely brighter than a star, followed by other stars. Rasali oared gently across through the dunes, face turned to the sky. At first he thought she was praying, then realized she was navigating. There were more fish now, and each time the sighing sound, the dark shape half-seen. He heard someone singing, the voice carrying somehow to them, from far behind.

"The fishers," Rasali said. "They will stay close to the levees tonight. I wish . . ."

But she left the wish unspoken. They were over the deep mist now. He could not say how he knew this. He had a sudden vision of the bridge overhead, a black span bisecting the star-spun sky, the parabolic arch of the chains perhaps visible, perhaps not. People would stride across the river, an arrow's flight overhead, unaware of this place beneath. Perhaps they would stop and look over the bridge's railings, but they would be too high to see the fish as any but small shadows, supposing they saw them at all, supposing they stopped at all. The Big Ones would be novelties, weird creatures that caused a safe little shiver, like hearing a frightening story late at night.

Perhaps Rasali saw the same thing, for she said suddenly, "Your bridge. It will change all this."

"It must. I am sorry," he said again. "We are not meant to be here, on mist."

"We are not meant to cross this without passing through it. Kit—" Rasali said, as if starting a sentence, and then fell silent. After a moment she began to speak again, her voice low, as if she were speaking to herself. "The soul often hangs in a balance of some sort: tonight, do I lie down in the high fields with Dirk Tanner or not? At the fair, do I buy ribbons or wine? For the new ferry's headboard, do I use camphor or pearwood? Small things, right? A kiss, a ribbon, a grain that coaxes the knife this way or that. They are not, Kit Meinem of Atyar. Our souls wait for our answer, because any answer changes us. This is why I wait to decide what I feel about your bridge. I'm waiting until I know how I will be changed."

"You can never know how things will change you," Kit said.

"If you don't, you have not waited to find out." There was a popping noise barely a stone's throw to starboard. "Quiet."

On they moved. In daylight, Kit knew, the trip took less than an hour; now it seemed much longer. Perhaps it was; he looked up at the stars and thought they had moved, but perhaps not.

His teeth were clenched, as were all his muscles. When he tried to relax them, he realized it was not fear that cramped him, but something else, something outside him. He heard Rasali falter. "No . . . "

He recognized it now, the sound that was not a sound, like the lowest pipes on an organ, a drone so low that he couldn't hear it, one that turned his bones to liquid and his muscles to flaked and rusting iron. His breath labored from his chest in grunts. His head thrummed. Moving as though through honey, he strained his hands to his head, cradling it. He could not see Rasali except as a gloom against the slightly lesser gloom of the mist, but he heard her pant, tiny pain-filled breaths, like an injured dog.

The thrumming in his body pounded at his bones now, dissolving them. He wanted to cry out, but there was no air left in his lungs. He realized suddenly that the layer beneath them was raising itself into a mound. Mist piled at the boat's sides. *I never got to finish the bridge*, he thought. *And I never kissed her.* Did Rasali have any regrets?

The mound roiled and became a hill, which became a mountain obscuring part of the sky. The crest melted into curls of mist, and there was a shape inside, large and dark as night itself, and it slid and followed the collapsing. It seemed still, but he knew that was only because of the size of the thing, that it took ages for its full length to pass. That was all he saw before his eyes slipped shut.

How long he lay there in the bottom of the boat, he didn't know. At some point, he realized he was there; some time later he found he could move again, his bones and muscles back to what they should be. The dog was barking. "Rasali?" he said shakily. "Are we sinking?"

"Kit." Her voice was a thread. "You're still alive. I thought we were dead."

"That was a Big One?"

"I don't know. No one has ever seen one. Maybe it was just a Fairly Large One."

The old joke. Kit choked on a weak laugh.

"Shit," Rasali said in the darkness. "I dropped the oar."

"Now what?" he said.

"I have a spare, but it's going to take longer and we'll land in the wrong place. We'll have to tie off and then walk up to get help."

*I'm alive*, he did not say. *I can walk a thousand miles tonight.*

It was nearly dawn before they got to Nearside. The two big moons rose just before they landed, a mile south of the dock. The spice traders and their dog went on ahead while Kit and Rasali secured the boat. They walked up together. Halfway home, Valo came down at a dead run.

"I was waiting, and you didn't come—" He was pale and panting. "But they told me, the other passengers, that you made it, and—"

"Valo." Rasali hugged him and held him hard. "We're safe, little one. We're here. It's done."

"I thought . . . " he said.

"I know," she said. "Valo, please, I am so tired. Can you get the *Crossing* up to the dock? I am going to my house, and I will sleep for a day, and I don't care if the Empress herself is tapping her foot, it's going to wait." She released Valo, saluted Kit with a weary smile, and walked up flank of the levee. Kit watched her leave.

The "Imperial seal" was a letter from Atyar, some underling arrogating authority and asking for clarification on a set of numbers Kit had sent— scarcely worth the trip at any time, let alone across mist on a bad night. Kit cursed the capital and Empire and then sent the information, along with a tautly worded paragraph about seals and their appropriate use.

Two days later, he got news that would have brought him across the mist in any case: the caravan carrying the first eyebar and bolts was twelve miles out on the Hoic Mine Road. Kit and his ironmaster Tandreve Smith rode out to meet the wagons as they crept southward, and found them easing down a gradual slope near Oud village. The carts were long and built strong, their contents covered, each pulled by a team of tough-legged oxen with patient expressions. The movement was slow, and drivers walked beside them, singing something unfamiliar to Kit's city-bred ears.

"Ox-tunes. We used to sing these at my aunt's farm," Tandreve said, and sang:

> *"Remember last night's dream,*
> *the sweet cold grass, the lonely cows.*
> *You had your bollocks then."*

Tandreve chuckled, and Kit with her.

One of the drivers wandered over as Kit pulled his horse to a stop. Unattended, her team moved forward anyway. "Folks," she said, and nodded. A taciturn woman.

Kit swung down from the saddle. "These are the chains?"

"You're from the bridge?"

"Kit Meinem of Atyar."

The woman nodded again. "Berallit Red-Ox of Ilver. Your smiths are sitting on the tail of the last wagon."

One of the smiths, a rangy man with singed eyebrows, loped forward to meet them, and introduced himself as Jared Toss of Little Hoic. They walked beside the carts as they talked, and he threw aside a tarp to show Kit what they carried: iron eyebars, each a rod ten feet long with eyes at each end. Tandreve walked sideways as she inspected the eyebars; she and Jared soon lost themselves in a technical discussion, while Kit kept them company, leading Tandreve's forgotten horse and his own, content for the moment to let the masters talk it out. He moved a little forward until he was abreast of the oxen. *Remember last night's dream,* he thought, and then: *I wonder what Rasali dreamt.*

After that night on the mist, Rasali seemed to have no bad days. She took people the day after they arrived, no matter the weather or the mist's character. The tavern keepers grumbled at this a bit, but the decrease in time each visitor stayed in town was made up for by the increase in numbers of serious-eyed men and women sent by firms in Atyar to establish offices in the towns on the river's far side. It made things easier for the bridge, as well, since Kit and others could move back and forth as needed. Kit remained reluctant, more so since the near-miss.

There was enough business for two boats, and Valo volunteered to ferry more often, but Rasali refused the help, allowing him to ferry only when she couldn't prevent it. "The Big Ones don't seem to care about me this winter," she said to him, "but I can't say they would feel the same about tender meat like you." With Kit she was more honest. "If he is to leave ferrying, to go study in the capital maybe, it's best sooner than later. Mist will be dangerous until the last ferry crosses it. And even then, even after your bridge is done."

It was Rasali only who seemed to have this protection; the fishing people had as many problems as in any year. Denis Redboat lost his coracle when it was rammed ("By a Medium-Large One," he laughed in the tavern later: sometimes the oldest jokes were the best), though he was fished out by a nearby boat before he had sunk too deep. The rash was superficial, but his hair grew back only in patches.

Kit sat in the crowded beer garden of The Deer's Heart, watching Rasali and Valo build a little pinewood skiff in the boat yard next door. Valo had called out a greeting when Kit first sat down, and Rasali turned her head to smile at him, but after that they ignored him. Some of the locals stopped by to greet him, and the barman stayed for some time, telling him about the ominous yet unchanging ache in his back; but for most of the afternoon, Kit was alone in the sun, drinking cellar-cool porter and watching the boat take shape.

In the midsummer of the fourth year, it was rare for Kit to have the afternoon of a beautiful day to himself. The anchorages had been finished for some months. So had the rubble-fill ramps that led to the arched passages through each pillar, but the pillars themselves had taken longer, and the granite saddles that would support the chains over the towers had only just been put in place.

They were only slightly behind on Kit's deadlines for most of the materials. More than a thousand of the eyebars and bolts for the chains were laid out in rows, the iron smelling of the linseed oil used to protect them during transit. More were expected in before winter. Close to the ramps were the many fish-skin ropes and cables that would be needed to bring the first chain across the gap. They were irreplaceable, probably the most valuable thing on the work sites, and were treated accordingly, kept in closed tents that reeked.

Kit's high-work specialists were here, too: the men and women who would do the first perilous tasks, mostly experts who had worked on other big spans or the towers of Atyar.

But everything waited on Rasali, and in the meantime, Kit was content to sit and watch her work.

Valo and Rasali were not alone in the boat yard. Rasali had sent to the ferry folk of Ubmie, a hundred miles to the south, and they had arrived a few days before: a woman and her cousin, Chell and Lan Crosser. The strangers had the same massive shoulders and good looks the Ferrys had, but they shared a faraway expression of their own; the river was broader at Ubmie, deeper, so perhaps death was closer to them. Kit wondered what they thought of his task—the bridge would cut into ferry trade for many hundreds of miles on either side, and Ubmie had been reviewed as a possible site for the bridge—but they must not have resented it or they would not be here.

Everything waited on the ferry folk: the next major task was to bring the lines across the river to connect the piers—fabricating the chains required temporary cables and catwalks to be there first—but this could not be rushed: Rasali, Valo, and the Crossers all needed to feel at the same time that it was safe to cross. Kit tried not to be impatient, and in any case he had plenty to do—items to add to lists, formal reports and polite updates to send to the many interested parties in Atyar and in Triple, instructions to pass on to the rope makers, the masons, the road-builders, the exchequer. And Jenner: Kit had written to the capital and the Department of Roads was offering Jenner the lead on the second bridge across the river, to be built a few hundred miles to the north. Kit was to deliver the cartel the next time they were on the same side, but he was grateful the officials had agreed to leave Jenner with him until the first chain on this bridge was in place.

He pushed all this from his mind. *Later,* he said to the things, half-apologetically; *I'll deal with you later. For now, just let me sit in the sun and watch other people work.*

The sun slanted peach-gold through the oak's leaves before Rasali and Valo finished for the day. The skiff was finished, an elegant tiny curve of pale wood and dying sunlight. Kit leaned against the fence as they threw a cup of water over its bow and then drew it into the shadows of the boathouse. Valo took off at a run—*so much energy, even after a long day*; ah, youth—as Rasali walked to the fence and leaned on it from her side.

"It's beautiful," he said.

She rolled her neck. "I know. We make good boats. Are you hungry? Your busy afternoon must have raised an appetite."

He had to laugh. "We finished the pillar—laid the capstone this morning. I *am* hungry."

"Come on, then. Thalla will feed us all."

Dinner was simple. The Deer's Heart was better known for its beers than its foods, but the stew Thalla served was savory with chervil, and thick enough to stand a spoon in. Valo had friends to be with, so they ate with Chell and Lan, who were as light-hearted as Rasali. At dusk, the Crossers left to explore the Nearside taverns, leaving Kit and Rasali to watch heat lightning in the west. The air was thick and warm, soft as wool on their skin.

"You never come up to the work sites on either side," Kit said suddenly, after a comfortable, slightly drunken silence. He inspected his earthenware mug, empty except for the smell of yeast.

Rasali had given up on the benches and sat instead on one of the garden tables. She leaned back until she lay supine, face toward the sky. "I've been busy. Perhaps you noticed?"

"It's more than that. Everyone finds time, here and there. And you used to."

She laughed. "I did, didn't I? I just haven't seen the point, lately. The bridge changes everything, but I don't see yet how it changes me. So I wait until it's time. Perhaps it's like the mist."

"What about now?"

She rolled her head until her cheek lay against the rough wood of the tabletop: looking at him, he could tell, though her eyes were hidden in shadows. What did she see, he wondered: what was she hoping to see? It pleased him, but made him nervous.

"Come to the tower, now, tonight," he said. "Soon everything changes. We pull the ropes across, and make the chains, and hang the supports, and lay the road—everything changes then. It stops being a project and becomes a bridge, a road. But tonight, it's still just two towers and a bunch of plans. Rasali, climb it with me. I can't describe what it's like up there—the wind, the sky all around you, the river." He flushed at the urgency in his voice. When she remained silent, he added, "You change whether you wait for it or not."

"There's lightning," she said.

"It runs from cloud to cloud," he said. "Not to earth."

"Heat lightning." She sat up suddenly, nodded. "So show me this place."

The work site was abandoned. The sky overhead had filled with clouds lit from within by the lightning, which was worse than no light at all, since it ruined their night vision. They staggered across the site, trying to plan their paths in the moments of light, doggedly moving through the darkness. "Shit," Rasali said suddenly in the darkness, then: "Tripped over something or other." Kit found himself laughing for no apparent reason.

They took the internal stairs instead of the scaffold that still leaned against the pillar's north wall. Kit knew them thoroughly, knew every irregular turn and riser; he counted them aloud to Rasali as he led her by the hand. They reached one hundred and ninety four before they saw light from a flash of lightning overhead, two hundred and eighteen when they finally stepped onto the roof, gasping for air.

They were not alone. A woman squealed; she and the man with her grabbed clothes and blankets and bolted with their lamp, naked and laughing down the stairs. Rasali said with satisfaction, "Sera Oakfield. That was Erno Bridgeman with her."

"He took his name from the bridge?" Kit asked, but Rasali said only, "Oh," in a child's voice. Silent lightning painted the sky over her head in sudden strokes of purple-white: layers of cloud glowing or dark.

"It's so much closer." She looked about her, walked to the edge and looked down at Nearside. Dull gold light poured from doors open to the heavy air. Kit stayed where he was, content to watch her. The light (when there was light) was shadowless, and her face looked young and full of wonder. After a time, she walked to his side.

They said nothing, only kissed and then made love in a nest of their discarded clothes. Kit felt the stone of his bridge against his knees, his back, still warm as skin from the day's heat. Rasali was softer than the rocks and tasted sweet.

A feeling he could not have described cracked open his chest, his throat, his belly. It had been a long time since he had been with a woman, not met his own needs; he had nearly forgotten the delight of it, the sharp sweet shock of his release, the rocking ocean of hers. Even their awkwardness made him glad, because it held in it the possibility of doing this again, and better.

When they were done, they talked. "You know my goal, to build this bridge," Kit looked down at her face, there and gone, in the flickering of the lightning. "But I do not know yours."

Rasali laughed softly. "Yet you have seen me succeed a thousand times, and fail a few. I wish to live well, each day."

"That's not a goal," Kit said.

"Why? Because it's not yours? Which is better, Kit Meinem of Atyar? A single great victory, or a thousand small ones?" And then: "Tomorrow," Rasali said. "We will take the rope across tomorrow."

"You're sure?" Kit asked.

"That's a strange statement coming from you. The bridge is all about crossing being a certainty, yes? Like the sun coming up each morning? We agreed this afternoon. It's time."

Dawn came early, with the innkeeper's preemptory rap on the door. Kit woke disoriented, tangled in the sheets of his little cupboard bed. Afterward he and Rasali had come down from the pillar, Rasali to sleep and Kit to do everything that needed to happen before the rope was brought across, all in the few hours left of the night. His skin smelled of Rasali, but, stunned with lack of sleep, he had trouble believing their lovemaking had been real. But there was stone dust ground into his skin; he smiled and, though it was high summer, sang a spring song from Atyar as he quickly washed and dressed. He drank a bowl filled with broth in the taproom. It was tangy, lukewarm. A single small water-fish stared up at him from a salted eye. Kit left the fish, and left the inn.

The clouds and the lightning were gone; early as it was the sky was already pale and hot. The news was everywhere, and the entire town, or so it seemed, drifted with Kit to the work site, and then flowed over the levee and down to the bank.

The river was a blinding creamy ribbon high between the two banks, looking just as it had the first time he had seen it, and for a minute he felt dislocated in time. High mist was seen as a good omen, and though he did not believe in omens, he was nevertheless glad. There was a crowd collected on the Farside levee as well, though he couldn't see details, only the movement like gnats in the sky at dusk. The signal towers' flags hung limp against the hot blue-white sky.

Kit walked down to Rasali's boat, nearly hidden in its own tight circle of watchers. As Kit approached, Valo called, "Hey, Kit!" Rasali looked up. Her smile was like welcome shade on a bright day. The circle opened to accept him.

"Greetings, Valo Ferry of Farside, Rasali Ferry of Farside," he said. When he was close enough, he clasped Rasali's hands in his own, loving their warmth despite the day's heat.

"Kit." She kissed his mouth, to a handful of muffled hoots and cheers from the bystanders and a surprised noise from Valo. She tasted like chicory.

Daell Cabler nodded absently to Kit. She was the lead rope maker. Now she, her husband Stivvan, and the journeymen and masters they had drawn to them, were inspecting the hundreds of fathoms of plaited fish-skin cord, loading them without twists onto spools three feet across, and loading those onto a wooden frame bolted to the *Tranquil Crossing*.

The rope was thin, not much more than a cord, narrower than Kit's smallest finger. It looked fragile, nothing like strong enough to carry its own weight for a quarter of a mile, though the tests said otherwise.

Several of the stronger people from the bridge handed down small heavy crates to Valo and Chell Crosser in the bow. Silverwork from Hedeclin, and copper in bricks: the ferry was to be weighted somewhat forward, which would make the first part of the crossing more difficult but should help with the end of it, as the cord paid out and took on weight from the mist.

"—we think, anyway," Valo had said, two months back when he and Rasali had discussed the plan with Kit. "But we don't know; no one's done this before." Kit had nodded, and not for the first time wished that the river had been a little less broad. Upriver, perhaps; but no, this had been the only option. He did write to an old classmate back in Atyar, a woman who now taught the calculus, and presented their solution. His friend had written back to say that it looked as though it ought to work, but that she knew little of mist.

One end of the rope snaked along the ground and up the levee. Though it would do no harm, no one touched the rope, or even approached it, but left a narrow lane for it and stepped only carefully over it. Now Daell and Stivvan Cabler followed the lane back, up, and over the levee: checking the rope and temporary anchor at the nearside pillar's base.

There was a wait. People sat on the grass, or walked back to watch the Cablers. Someone brought cool broth and small beer from the fishers' tavern. Valo and Rasali and the two strangers were remote, focused already on what came next.

And for himself? Kit was wound up, but it wouldn't do to show anything but a calm confident front. He walked among the watchers, exchanged words or a smile with each of them. He knew them all by now, even the children.

It was nearly midmorning before Daell and Stivvan returned. The ferryfolk took their positions, two to each side, far enough apart that they could pull on different rhythms. Kit was useless freight until they got to the other side, so he sat at the bow of the *Crossing*, where his weight might do some good. Daell stumbled as she was helped into the boat's stern: she would monitor the rope but, as she told them all, she was nervous; she had never crossed the mist before this. "I think I'll wait 'til the catwalks go up before I return," she added. "Stivvan can sleep without me 'til then."

"Ready, Kit?" Rasali called forward.

"Yes," he said.

"Daell? Lan? Chell? Valo?" Assent all around.

"An historic moment," Valo announced: "The day the mist was bridged."

"Make yourself useful, boy," Rasali said. "Prepare to scull."

"Right," Valo said.

"Push us off," she said to the people on the dock. A cheer went up.

The dock and all the noises behind them disappeared almost immediately. The ferryfolk had been right that it was a good day for such an undertaking; the mist was a smooth series of ripples no taller than a man, and so thick that the *Crossing* rode high despite the extra weight and drag. It was the gentlest he had ever seen the river.

Kit's eyes ached from the brightness. "It will work?" Kit said, meaning the rope and their trip across the mist and the bridge itself—a question rather than a statement; unable to help himself, though he had worked calculations himself, had Daell and Stivvan and Valo and a specialist in Atyar all double-check them, though it was a child's question. Isolated in the mist, even competence seemed tentative.

"Yes," Daell Cabler said, from aft.

The rowers said little. At one point, Rasali murmured into the deadened air, "To the right," and Valo and Lan Crosser changed their stroke to avoid a gentle mound a few feet high directly in their path. Mostly the *Crossing* slid steadily across the regular swells. Unlike his other trips, Kit saw no dark shapes in the mist, large or small.

There was nothing he could do to help, so Kit watched Rasali scull in the blazing sun. The work got harder as the rope spooled out until she and the others panted with each breath. Shining with sweat, her skin was nearly as bright as the mist in the sunlight. He wondered how she could bear the light without burning. Her face looked solemn, intent on the eastern shore. They could not see the dock, but the levee was scattered with Farsiders, waiting for the work they would do when the ferry landed. Her eyes were alight with reflections from the mist. Then he recognized the expression, the light. They were not concern, or reflections: they were joy.

*How will she bear it*, he thought suddenly, *when there is no more ferrying to be done?* He had known that she loved what she did, but he had never realized just how much. He felt as though he had been kicked in the stomach. What would it do to her? His bridge would destroy this thing that she loved, that gave her name. How could he not have thought of that? "Rasali," he said, unable to stay silent.

"Not now," she said. The rowers panted as they dug in.

"It's like . . . pulling through dirt," Valo gasped.

"Quiet," Rasali snapped, and then they were silent except for their laboring breath. Kit's own muscles knotted sympathetically. Foot by foot, the ferry heaved forward. At some point they were close enough to the Farside upper dock that someone could throw a rope to Kit and at last he could do something, however inadequate; he took the rope and pulled. The rowers dug in for their final strokes, and the boat slid up beside the dock. People swarmed aboard, securing the boat to the dock, the rope to a temporary anchor onshore.

Released, the Ferrys and the Crossers embraced, laughing a little dizzily. They walked up the levee toward Farside town and did not look back.

Kit left the ferry to join Jenner Ellar.

It was hard work. The rope's end had to be brought over an oiled stone saddle on the levee and down to a temporary anchor and capstan at the Farside pillar's base, a task that involved driving a team of oxen through the gap Jenner had cut into the levee: a risk, but one that had to be taken.

More oxen were harnessed to the capstan. Daell Cabler was still pale and shaking from the crossing, but after a glass of something cool and dark, she and her Farside counterparts could walk the rope to look for any new weak spots, and found none. Jenner stayed at the capstan, but Daell and Kit returned to the temporary saddle in the levee, the notch polished like glass and gleaming with oil.

The rope was released from the dockside anchor. The rope over the saddle whined as it took the load and flattened, and there was a deep pinging noise as it swung out to make a single straight line, down from the saddle, down into the mist. The oxen at the capstan dug in.

The next hours were the tensest of Kit's life. For a time, the rope did not appear to change. The capstan moaned and clicked, and at last the rope slid by inches, by feet, through the saddle. He could do nothing but watch and yet again rework all the calculations in his mind. He did not see Rasali, but Valo came up after a time to watch the progress. Answering his questions settled Kit's nerves. The calculations were correct. He had done this before. He was suddenly starved and voraciously ate the food that Valo had brought for him. How long had it been since the broth at The Fish? Hours; most of a day.

The oxen puffed and grunted, and were replaced with new teams. Even lubricated and with leather sleeves, the rope moved reluctantly across the saddle, but it did move. And then the pressure started to ease and the rope passed faster over the saddle. The sun was westering when at last the rope lifted free. By dusk, the rope was sixty feet above the mist, stretched humming-tight between the Farside and Nearside levees and the temporary anchors.

Just before dark, Kit saw the flags go up on the signal tower: *secure*.

Kit worked on and then seconded projects for five years after he left University. His father knew men and women at the higher levels in the Department of Roads, and his old tutor, Skossa Timt, knew more, so many were high-profile works, but he loved all of them, even his first lead, the little toll gate where the boy, Duar, had died.

All public work—drainage schemes, roadwork, amphitheaters, public squares, sewers, alleys, and mews—was alchemy. It took the invisible patterns that people made as they lived and turned them into real things, stone and brick and wood and space. Kit built things that moved people through the invisible architecture that was his mind, and his notion—and Empire's notion—of how their lives could be better.

The first major project he led was a replacement for a collapsed bridge in the Four Peaks region north of Atyar. The original had also been a chain suspension bridge but much smaller than the mist bridge, crossing only a hundred yards, its pillars only forty feet high. With maintenance, it had survived heavy use for three centuries, shuddering under the carts that brought quicksilver ore down to the smelting village of Oncalion; but after the heavy snowfalls of what was subsequently called the Wolf Winter, one of the gorge's walls collapsed, taking the north pillar with it and leaving nowhere stable to rebuild. It was easier to start over, two hundred yards upstream.

The people of Oncalion were not genial. Hard work made for hard men and women. There was a grim, desperate edge to their willingness to labor on the bridge, because their livelihood and their lives were dependent on the mine. They had to be stopped at the end of each day or, dangerous as it was, they would work through moonlit nights.

But it was lonely work, even for Kit who did not mind solitude; and when the snows of the first winter brought a halt to construction, he returned with some relief to Atyar, to stay with his father. Davell Meinem was old now. His memory was weakening though still strong enough; and he spent his days constructing a vast and fabulous public maze of dry-laid stones brought from all over Empire: his final project, he said to Kit, an accurate prophecy. Skossa Timt had died during the hard cold of the Wolf Winter, but many of his classmates were in the capital. Kit spent evenings with them, attended lectures and concerts, entering for the season into a casual relationship with an architect who specialized in waterworks.

Kit returned to the site at Oncalion as soon as the roads cleared. In his absence, through the snows and melt-off, the people of Oncalion had continued to work, laying course after course of stone in the bitter cold. The work had to be redone.

The second summer, they worked every day and moonlit nights, and Kit worked beside them.

Kit counted the bridge as a failure, although it was coming in barely over budget and only a couple of months late, and no one had died. It was an ugly design; the people of Oncalion had worked hard but joylessly; and there was all his dissatisfaction and guilt about the work that had to be redone.

Perhaps there was something in the tone of his letters to his father, for there came a day in early autumn that Davell Meinem arrived in Oncalion, riding a sturdy mountain horse and accompanied by a journeyman who vanished immediately into one of the village's three taverns. It was mid-afternoon.

"I want to see this bridge of yours," Davell said. He looked weary, but straight-backed as ever. "Show it to me."

"We'll go tomorrow," Kit said. "You must be tired."

"Now," Davell said.

They walked up from the village together: a cool day, and bright, though the road was overshadowed with pines and fir trees. Basalt outcroppings were stained dark green and black with lichens. His father moved slowly, pausing often for breath. They met a steady trickle of local people leading heavy-laden ponies. The roadbed across the bridge wasn't quite complete, but ponies could cross carrying ore in baskets. Oncalion was already smelting these first small loads.

At the bridge, Davell asked the same questions he had asked when Kit was a child playing on his work sites. Kit found himself responding as he had so many years before, eager to explain—or excuse—each decision; and always, always the ponies passing.

They walked down to the older site. The pillar had been gutted for stones, so all that was left was rubble; but it gave them a good view of the new bridge: the boxy pillars; the great parabolic curve of the main chains; the thick vertical suspender chains; the slightly sprung arch of the bulky roadbed. It looked as clumsy as a suspension bridge ever could. Yet another pony crossed, led by a woman singing something in the local dialect.

"It's a good bridge," Davell said at last.

Kit shook his head. His father, who had been known for his sharp tongue on the work sites though never to his son, said, "A bridge is a means to an end. It only matters because of what it does. Leads from *here* to *there*. If you do your work right, they won't notice it, any more than you notice where quicksilver comes from, most times. It's a good bridge because they are already using it. Stop feeling sorry for yourself, Kit."

It was a big party, that night. The Farsiders (and, Kit knew, the Nearsiders) drank and danced under the shadow of their bridge-to-be. Torchlight and firelight touched the stones of the tower base and anchorage, giving them mass and meaning, but above their light the tower was a black outline, the absence of stars. More torches outlined the tower's top, and they seemed no more than gold stars among the colder ones.

Kit walked among them. Everyone smiled or waved and offered to stand him drinks, but no one spoke much with him. It was as if the lifting of the cable had separated him from them. The immense towers had not done this; he had still been one of them, to some degree at least—the instigator of great labors, but still, one of them. But now, for tonight anyway, he was the man who bridged the mist. He had not felt so lonely since his first day here. Even Loreh Tanner's death had not severed him so completely from their world.

On every project, there was a day like this. It was possible that the distance came from him, he realized suddenly. He came to a place and built something, passing through the lives of people for a few months or years. He was staying longer this time because of the size of the project, but in the end he would leave. He always left, after he had changed lives in incalculable ways. A road through dangerous terrain or a bridge across mist saved lives and increased trade, but it always changed the world, as well. It was his job to make a thing and then leave to make the next one, but it was also his preference, not to remain and see what he had made. What would Nearside and Farside look like in ten years, in fifty? He had never returned to a previous site.

It was harder this time, or perhaps just different. Perhaps *he* was different.

He had allowed himself to belong to the country on either side of the bridge; to have more was to have more to miss when it was taken away.

Rasali—what would her life look like?

Valo danced by, his arm around a woman half again as tall as he—Rica Bridger—and Kit caught his arm. "Where is Rasali?" he shouted, then, knowing he could not be heard over the noise of drums and pipes, mouthed: *Rasali*. He didn't hear what Valo said but followed his pointing hand.

Rasali was alone, flat on her back on the river side of the levee, looking up. There were no moons, so the Sky Mist hung close overhead, a river of stars that poured north to south like the river itself. Kit knelt a few feet away. "Rasali Ferry of Farside?"

Her teeth flashed in the dark. "Kit Meinem of Atyar."

He lay beside her. The grass was like bad straw, coarse against his back and neck. Without looking at him, she passed a jar of something. Its taste was strong as tar, and Kit gasped for a moment at the bite of it.

"I did not mean—" he started, but trailed off, unsure how to continue.

"Yes," she said, and he knew she had heard the words he didn't say. Her voice contained a shrug. "Many people born into a Ferry family never cross the mist."

"But you—" He stopped, felt carefully for his words. "Maybe others don't, but you do. And I think maybe you must do so."

"Just as you must build," she said softly. "That's clever of you, to realize that."

"And there will be no need after this, will there? Not on boats, anyway. We'll still need fish-skin, so the fisherfolk will still be out, but they—"

"—stay close to shore," she said.

"And you?" he asked.

"I don't know, Kit. Days come, days go. I go onto the mist or I don't. I live or I don't. There is no certainty, but there never is."

"It doesn't distress you?"

"Of course it does. I love and I hate this bridge of yours. I will pine for the mist, for the need to cross it. But I do not want to be part of a family that all die young, without even a corpse for the burning. If I have a child, she will not need to make the decision I did: to cross the mist and die, or to stay safe on one side of the world and never see the other. She will lose something. She will gain something else."

"Do you hate me?" he said finally, afraid of the answer, afraid of any answer she might give.

"No. Oh, no." She rolled over to him and kissed his mouth, and Kit could not say if the salt he tasted was from her tears or his own.

The autumn was spent getting the chains across the river. In the days after the crossing, the rope was linked to another, and then pulled back the way it had come, coupled now; and then there were two ropes in parallel courses. It was tricky work, requiring careful communications through the signal towers, but it was completed without event; and Kit could at last get a good night's sleep. To break the rope would have been to start anew with the long difficult crossing. Over the next days, each rope was replaced with fish-skin cable strong enough to take the weight of the chains until they were secured.

The cables were hoisted to the tops of the pillars, to prefigure the path one of the eight chains would take: secured with heavy pins set in protected slots in the anchorages and then straight sharp lines to the saddles on the pillars and, two hundred feet above the mist, the long perfect catenary. A catwalk was suspended from the cables. For the first time, people could cross the mist without the boats, though few chose to do so except for the high-workers from the capital and the coast: a hundred men and women so strong and graceful that they seemed another species, and kept mostly to themselves. They were directed by a woman Kit had worked with before, Feinlin; the high-workers took no surnames. Something about Feinlin reminded him of Rasali.

The weather grew colder and the days shorter, and Kit pushed hard to have the first two chains across before the winter rains began. There would be no heavy work once the ground got too wet to give sturdy purchase to the teams, and, calculations to the contrary, Kit could not quite trust that cables, even fish-skin cables, would survive the weight of those immense arcs through an entire winter—or that a Big One would not take one down in the unthinking throes of some winter storm.

The eyebars that would make up the chain were each ten feet long and required considerable manhandling to be linked with the bolts, each larger than a man's forearm. The links became a chain, even more cumbersome. Winches pulled the chain's end up to the saddles, and out onto the catwalk.

After this, the work became even more difficult and painstaking. Feinlin and her people moved individual eyebars and pins out onto the catwalks and joined them in situ; a backbreaking, dangerous task that had to be exactly synchronized with the work on the other side of the river so that the cable would not be stressed.

Most nights Kit worked into the darkness. When the moons were bright enough, he, the high-workers, and the bridgewrights would work in shifts, day and night.

He crossed the mist six more times that fall. The high-workers disliked having people on the catwalks, but he was the architect, after all, so he crossed once that way, struggling with vertigo. After that, he preferred the ferries. When he crossed once with Valo, they talked exclusively about the bridge—Valo had decided to stay until the bridge was complete and the ferries finished; but his mind was already full of the capital—but the other times, when it was Rasali, they were silent, listening to the hiss of the V-shaped scull moving in the mist. His fear of the mist decreased with each day they came closer to the bridge's completion, though he couldn't say why this was.

When Kit did not work through the night and Rasali was on the same side of the mist, they spent their nights together, sometimes making love, at other times content to share drinks or play ninepins in The Deer's Heart's garden, at which Kit's proficiency surprised everyone, including himself. He and Rasali did not talk again about what she would do when the bridge was complete—or what he would do, for that matter.

The hard work was worth it. It was still warm enough that the iron didn't freeze the high-workers' hands on the day they placed the final bolt. The first chain was complete.

Though work had slowed through the winter, the second and third chains were in place by spring, and the others were competed by the end of the summer.

With the heavy work done, some of the workers returned to their home-places. More than half had taken the name Bridger or something similar. "We have changed things," Kit said to Jenner on one of his Nearside visits, just before Jenner left for his new work. "No," Jenner said: "*You* have changed things." Kit did not respond, but held this close, and thought of it sometimes with mingled pride and fear.

The workers who remained were high-men and -women, people who did not mind crawling about on the suspension chains securing the support ropes. For the last two years, the rope makers for two hundred miles up and downstream from the bridge had been twisting, cutting, and looping and reweaving the ends of the fish-skin cables that would support the road deck, each crate marked with the suspender's position in the bridge. The cartons stood in carefully sorted, labeled towers in the field that had once been full of sheep.

Kit's work was now all paperwork, it seemed—so many invoices, so many reports for the capital—but he managed every day to watch the high-workers, their efficient motions. Sometimes he climbed to the tops of the pillars and looked down into the mist, and saw Rasali's or Valo's ferry, an elegant narrow shape half-hidden in tendrils of blazing white mist or pale gray fog.

Kit lost one more worker, Tommer Bullkeeper, who climbed out onto the catwalk for a drunken bet and fell, with a maniacal cry that changed into unbalanced laughter as he vanished into the mist. His wife wept in mixed anger and grief, and the townspeople wore ash-color, and the bridge continued. Rasali held Kit when he cried in his room at The Red Lurcher. "Never mind," she said. "Tommer was a good person: a drunk, but good to his sons and his wife, careful with animals. People have always died. The bridge doesn't change that."

The towns changed shape as Kit watched. Commercial envoys from every direction gathered; many stayed in inns and homes, but some built small houses, shops, and warehouses. Many used the ferries, and it became common for these businessmen and women to tip Rasali or Valo lavishly—"in hopes I never ride with you again," they would say. Valo laughed and spent this money buying beer for his friends; the letter had come from University that he could begin his studies with the winter term, and he had many farewells to make. Rasali told no one, not even Kit, what she planned to do with hers.

Beginning in the spring of the project's fifth year, they attached the road deck. Wood planks wide enough for oxen two abreast were nailed together across the iron struts that gave stability. The bridge was made of several hundred sections, constructed on the worksites and then hauled out by workers. Each segment had farther to go before being placed and secured. The two towns celebrated all night the first time a Nearsider shouted from her side of the bridge, and was saluted by Farsider cheers. In the lengthening evenings, it became a pastime for people to walk onto the bridge and lie belly-down at its end, watching the mist so far below them. Sometimes dark shapes moved within it, but no one saw anything big enough to be a Big One. A few heedless locals dropped heavy stones from above to watch the mist twist away, opening holes into its depths; but their neighbors stopped them: "It's not respectful," one said; and, "Do you want to piss them off?" said another.

Kit asked her, but Rasali never walked out with him. "I see enough from the river," she said.

Kit was in Nearside, in his room in The Fish. He had lived in this room for five years, and it looked it: plans and timetables pinned to the walls. The chair by the fire was heaped with clothes, books, a length of red silk he had seen at a fair and could not resist; it had been years since he'd sat there. The plans in his folio and on the oversized table had been replaced with waybills and receipts for materials, payrolls, copies of correspondence between Kit and his sponsors in the government. The window was open, and Kit sat on the cupboard bed, watching a bee feel its way through the sun-filled air. He'd left half a pear on the table, and he was waiting to see if the bee would find it, and thinking about the little hexagonal cells of a beehive, whether they were stronger than squares were, and how he might test this.

Feet ran along the corridor. His door flew open. Rasali stood there blinking in the light, which was so golden that Kit didn't at first notice how pale she was, or the tears on her face. "What—" he said, as he swung off his bed. He came toward her.

"Valo," she said. "The *Pearlfinder*."

He held her. The bee left, then the sun, and still he held her as she rocked silently on the bed. Only when the square of sky in the window faded to purple, and the little moon's crescent eased across it, did she speak. "Ah," she said, a sigh like a gasp. "I am so tired. " She fell asleep, as quickly as that, with tears still wet on her face. Kit slipped from the room.

The taproom was crowded, filled with ash-gray clothes, with soft voices and occasional sobs. Kit wondered for a moment if everyone had a set of mourning clothes always at hand, and what this meant about them.

Brana Keep saw Kit in the doorway, and came from behind the bar to speak with him. "How is she?" she said.

"Not good. I think she's asleep right now," Kit said. "Can you give me some food for her, something to drink?"

Brana nodded, spoke to her daughter Lixa as she passed into the back, then returned. "How are *you* doing, Kit? You saw a fair amount of Valo yourself."

"Yes," Kit said. Valo chasing the children through the field of stones, Valo laughing at the top of a tower, Valo serious-eyed, with a handbook of calculus in the shade of a half-built fishing boat. "What happened? She hasn't said anything yet."

Brana gestured. "What can be said? Signal flags said he was going to cross just after midday, but he never came. When we signaled over, they said he had left when they first signaled."

"Could he be alive?" Kit asked, remembering the night that he and Rasali had lost the big scull, the extra hours it had taken for the crossing. "He might have broken the scull, landed somewhere downriver."

"No," Brana said. "I know, that's what we wanted to hope. Maybe we would have believed it for a while before. But Asa, one of the strangers, the high-workers; she was working overhead and heard the boat capsize, heard him cry out. She couldn't see anything, and didn't know what she had heard until we figured it out."

"Three more months," Kit said, mostly to himself. He saw Brana looking at him, so he clarified: "Three more months. The bridge would have been done. This wouldn't have happened."

"This was today," Brana said, "not three months from now. People die when they die; we grieve and move on, Kit. You've been with us long enough to understand how we see these things. Here's the tray."

When Kit returned with the tray, Rasali was still asleep. He watched her in the dark room, unwilling to light more than the single lamp he'd carried up with him. *People die when they die.* But he could not stop thinking about the bridge, its deck nearly finished. *Another three months. Another month.*

When she awakened, there was a moment when she smiled at him, her face weary but calm. Then she remembered and her face tightened and she started crying again. When she was done, Kit got her to eat some bread and fish and cheese, and drink some watered wine. She did so obediiently, like a child. When she was finished, she lay back against him, her matted hair pushing up into his mouth.

"How can he be gone?"

"I'm so sorry," Kit said. "The bridge was so close to finished. Three more months, and this wouldn't have—"

She pulled away. "What? Wouldn't have happened? Wouldn't have *had* to happen?" She stood and faced him. "His death would have been unnecessary?"

"I—" Kit began, but she interrupted him, new tears streaking her face.

"He *died*, Kit. It wasn't necessary, it wasn't irrelevant, it wasn't anything except the way things are. But he's gone, and I'm not, and *now* what do I do, Kit? I lost my father and my aunt and my sister and my brother and my brother's son, and now I lose the mist when the bridge's done, and then what? What am I then? Who are the Ferry people then?"

Kit knew the answer: however she changed, she would still be Rasali; her people would still be strong and clever and beautiful; the mist would still be there, and the Big Ones. But she wouldn't be able to hear these words, not yet, not for months, maybe. So he held her, and let his own tears slip down his face, and tried not to think.

The fairs to celebrate the opening of the bridge started days before midsummer, the official date. Representatives of Empire from Atyar polished their speeches and waited impatiently in their suite of tents, planted on hurriedly cleaned-up fields near (but not too near) Nearside. The town had bled northward until it surrounded the west pillar of the bridge. The land that had once been sheep-pasture at the foot of the pillar was crowded with fair-tents and temporary booths, cheek by jowl with more permanent shops of wood and stone, selling food and space for sleeping and the sorts of products a traveler might find herself in need of. Kit was proud of the streets; he had organized construction of the crosshatch of sturdy cobblestones, as something to do while he waited through the bridge's final year. The new wells had been a project of Jenner's, planned from the very beginning, but Kit had seen them completed. Kit had just received a letter from Jenner, with news of his new bridge up in the Keitche mountains: on schedule; a happy work site.

Kit walked alone through the fair, which had splashed up the levee and along its ridge. A few people, townspeople and workers, greeted him; but others only pointed him out to their friends (*the man who built the bridge; see there, that short, dark man*); and still others ignored him completely, just another stranger in a crowd of strangers. When he had first come to build the bridge everyone in Nearside knew everyone else, local or visitor. He felt solitude settling around him again, the loneliness of coming to a strange place and building something and then leaving. The people of Nearside were moving forward into this new world he had built, the world of a bridge across the mist, but he was not going with them.

He wondered what Rasali was doing, over in Farside, and wished he could see her. They had not spoken since the days after Valo's death, except once for a few minutes, when he had come upon her at The Bitch. She had been withdrawn though not hostile, and he had felt unbalanced and not sought her out since.

Now, at the end of his great labor, he longed to see her. When would she cross next? He laughed. He of all people should know better: *five minutes' walk*.

The bridge was not yet open, but Kit was the architect; the guards at the toll booth only nodded when he asked to pass, and lifted the gate for him. A few people noticed and gestured as he climbed. When Uni Mason (hands filled with ribbons) shouted something he could not hear clearly, Kit smiled and waved and walked on.

He had crossed the bridge before this. The first stage of building the heavy oak frames that underlay the roadbed had been a narrow strip of planking that led from one shore to the other. Nearly every worker had found some excuse for crossing it at least once before Empire had sent people to the tollgates. Swallowing his fear of the height, Kit himself had crossed it nearly every day for the last two months.

This was different. It was no longer his bridge, but belonged to Empire and to the people of Near- and Farside. He saw it with the eyes of a stranger.

The stone ramp was a quarter-mile long, inclined gradually for carts. Kit hiked up, and the noises dropped behind and below him. The barriers that would keep animals (and people) from seeing the drop-off to either side were not yet complete: there were always things left unfinished at a bridge's opening, afterthoughts and additions. Ahead of him, the bridge was a series of perfect dark lines and arcs.

The ramp widened as it approached the pillar, and offered enough space for a cart to carefully turn onto the bridge itself. The bed of the span was barely wide enough for a cart with two oxen abreast, so Nearside and Farside would have to take turns sending wagons across. *For now*, Kit thought: *Later they can widen it, or build another. They*: it would be someone else.

The sky was overcast with high tin-colored clouds, their metallic sheen reflected in the mist below Kit. There were no railings, only fish-skin ropes strung between the suspension cables that led up to the chain. Oxen and horses wouldn't like that, or the hollow sound their feet would make on the boards. Kit watched the deck roll before him in the breeze, which was constant from the southwest. The roll wasn't so bad in this wind, but perhaps they should add an iron parapet or more trusses, to lessen the twisting and make crossing more comfortable. Empire had sent a new engineer, to take care of any final projects: Jeje Tesanthe. He would mention it to her.

Kit walked to one side so that he could look down. Sound dropped off behind him, deadened as it always was by the mist, and he could almost imagine that he was alone. It was several hundred feet down, but there was nothing to give scale to the coiling field of hammered metal below him. Deep in the mist he saw shadows that might have been a Big One or something smaller or a thickening of the mist, and then, his eyes learning what to look for, he saw more of the shadows, as if a school of fish were down there. One separated and darkened as it rose in the mist until it exposed its back almost immediately below Kit.

It was dark and knobby, shiny with moisture, flat as a skate; and it went on forever—thirty feet long perhaps, or forty, twisting as it rose to expose its underside, or what he thought might be its underside. As Kit watched, the mist curled back from a flexing scaled wing of sorts; and then a patch that might have been a single eye or a field of eyes, or something altogether different; and then a mouth like the arc of the suspension chains. The mouth gaped open to show another arc, a curve of gum or cartilage or something else. The creature rolled and then sank and became a shadow, and then nothing as the mist closed over it and settled.

Kit had stopped walking when he saw it. He forced himself to move forward again. A Big One, or perhaps just a Medium-Large One; at this height it hadn't seemed so big, or so frightening. Kit was surprised at the sadness he felt.

Farside was crammed with color and fairings, as well, but Kit could not find Rasali anywhere. He bought a tankard of rye beer, and went to find some place alone.

Once it became dark and the imperial representatives were safely tucked away for the night, the guards relaxed the rules and let their friends (and then any of the locals) on the bridge to look around them. People who had worked on the bridge had papers to cross without charge for the rest of their lives, but many others had watched it grow, and now they charmed or bribed or begged their way onto their bridge. Torches were forbidden because of the oil that protected the fish-skin ropes, but covered lamps were permitted, and from his place on the levee, Kit watched the lights move along the bridge, there and then hidden by the support ropes and deck, dim and inconstant as fireflies.

"Kit Meinem of Atyar."

Kit stood and turned to the voice behind him. "Rasali Ferry of Farside." She wore blue and white, and her feet were bare. She had pulled back her dark hair with a ribbon and her pale shoulders gleamed. She glowed under the moonlight like mist. He thought of touching her, kissing her; but they had not spoken since just after Valo's death.

She stepped forward and took the mug from his hand, drank the lukewarm beer, and just like that, the world righted itself. He closed his eyes and let the feeling wash over him.

He took her hand, and they sat on the cold grass, and looked out across the river. The bridge was a black net of arcs and lines, and behind it was the mist glowing blue-white in the light of the moons. After a moment, he asked, "Are you still Rasali Ferry, or will you take a new name?"

"I expect I'll take a new one." She half-turned in his arms so that he could see her face, her pale eyes. "And you? Are you still Kit Meinem, or do you become someone else? Kit Who Bridged the Mist? Kit Who Changed the World?"

"Names in the city do not mean the same thing," Kit said absently, aware that he had said this before and not caring. "*Did* I change the world?" He knew the answer already.

She looked at him for a moment, as if trying to gauge his feelings. "Yes," she said slowly after a moment. She turned her face up toward the loose strand of bobbing lights: "There's your proof, as permanent as stone and sky."

" 'Permanent as stone and sky,' " Kit repeated. "This afternoon—it flexes a lot, the bridge. There has to be a way to control it, but it's not engineered for that yet. Or lightning could strike it. There are a thousand things that could destroy it. It's going to come down, Rasali. This year, next year, a hundred years from now, five hundred." He ran his fingers through his hair. "All these people, they think it's forever."

"No, we don't," Rasali said. "Maybe Atyar does, but we know better here. Do you need to tell a Ferry that nothing will last? These stones will fall eventually, *these* cables—but the *dream* of crossing the mist, the dream of connection. Now that we know it can happen, it will always be here. My mother died, my grandfather. Valo." She stopped, swallowed. "Ferrys die, but there is always a

Ferry to cross the mist. Bridges and ferryfolk, they are not so different, Kit."
She leaned forward, across the space between them, and they kissed.

"Are you off soon?"

Rasali and Kit had made love on the levee against the cold grass. They had
crossed the bridge together under the sinking moons, walked back to The
Deer's Heart and bought more beer, the crowds thinner now, people gone
home with their families or friends or lovers: the strangers from out of town
bedding down in spare rooms, tents, anywhere they could. But Kit was too
restless to sleep, and he and Rasali ended up back by the mist, down on the
dock. Morning was only a few hours away, and the smaller moon had set. It
was darker now and the mist had dimmed.

"In a few days," Kit said, thinking of the trunks and bags packed tight and
gathered in his room at The Fish: the portfolio, fatter now, and stained with
water, mist, dirt, and sweat. Maybe it was time for a new one. "Back to the
capital."

There were lights on the opposite bank, fisherfolk preparing for the night's
work despite the fair, the bridge. *Some things don't change.*

"Ah," she said. They both had known this; it was no surprise. "What will
you do there?"

Kit rubbed his face, feeling stubble under his fingers, happy to skip that
small ritual for a few days. "Sleep for a hundred years. Then there's another
bridge they want, down at the mouth of the river, a place called Ulei. The
mist's nearly a mile wide there. I'll start midwinter maybe."

"A mile," Rasali said. "Can you do it?"

"I think so. I bridged this, didn't I?" His gesture took in the beams, the
slim stone tower overhead, the woman beside him. She smelled sweet and
salty. "There are islands by Ulei, I'm told. Low ones. That's the only reason it
would be possible. So maybe a series of flat stone arches, one to the next. You?
You'll keep building boats?"

"No." She leaned her head back and he felt her face against his ear. "I don't
need to. I have a lot of money. The rest of the family can build boats, but for
me that was just what I did while I waited to cross the mist again."

"You'll miss it," Kit said. It was not a question.

Her strong hand laid over his. "Mmm," she said, a sound without implication.

"But it was the *crossing* that mattered to you, wasn't it?" Kit said, realizing
it. "Just as with me, but in a different way."

"Yes," she said, and after a pause: "So now I'm wondering: how big do the
Big Ones get in the Mist Ocean? And what else lives there?"

"Nothing's on the other side," Kit said. "There's no crossing something
without an end."

"Everything can be crossed. Me, I think there is an end. There's a river of water deep under the Mist River, yes? And that water runs somewhere. And all the other rivers, all the lakes—they all drain somewhere. There's a water ocean under the Mist Ocean, and I wonder whether the mist ends somewhere out there, if it spreads out and vanishes and you find you are floating on water."

"It's a different element," Kit said, turning the problem over. "So you would need a boat that works through mist, light enough with that broad belly and fish-skin sheathing; but it would have to be deep-keeled enough for water."

She nodded. "I want to take a coast-skimmer and refit it, find out what's out there. Islands, Kit. Big Ones. *Huge* Ones. Another whole world maybe. I think I would like to be Rasali Ocean."

"You will come to Ulei with me?" he said, but he knew already. She *would* come, for a month or a season or a year. They would sleep tumbled together in an inn very like The Fish or The Bitch, and when her boat was finished, she would sail across the ocean, and he would move on to the next bridge or road, or he might return to the capital and a position at University. Or he might rest at last.

"I will come," she said. "For a bit."

Suddenly he felt a deep and powerful emotion in his chest, overwhelmed by everything that had happened or would happen in their lives: the changes to Nearside and Farside, the ferry's ending, Valo's death, the fact that she would leave him eventually, or that he would leave her. "I'm sorry," he said.

"I'm not," she said, and leaned across to kiss him, her mouth warm with sunlight and life. "It is worth it, all of it."

All those losses, but this one at least he could prevent.

"When the time comes," he said: "When you sail. I will come with you."

*A fo ben, bid bont.* To be a leader, be a bridge.

—Welsh proverb

# BIOGRAPHIES

**Yoon Ha Lee**'s fiction has appeared in *Clarkesworld, The Magazine of Fantasy and Science Fiction*, and *Lightspeed*. She lives in Louisiana with her family, and her attempts at origami have never been known to commit atrocities except against aesthetics.

**Genevieve Valentine**'s fiction has appeared or is forthcoming in *Clarkesworld, Strange Horizons, Lightspeed*, and *Apex*, and in the anthologies *The Living Dead 2, Running with the Pack, Teeth*, and more. Her nonfiction has appeared in *Lightspeed, Tor.com*, and *Fantasy Magazine*, and she is the co-author of *Geek Wisdom*. Her first novel, *Mechanique: A Tale of the Circus Tresaulti*, has won the 2012 Crawford Award. Her appetite for bad movies is insatiable, a tragedy she tracks on her blog, genevievevalentine.com.

**Bradley Denton** studied speculative fiction and writing under Professor James Gunn at the University of Kansas, and his first professional story was published in *The Magazine of Fantasy & Science Fiction* in 1984. Since then, his work has won the World Fantasy Award (for the two-volume story collection *A Conflagration Artist* and *The Calvin Coolidge Home for Dead Comedians*), the John W. Campbell Memorial Award (for the novel *Buddy Holly Is Alive and Well on Ganymede*), and the Theodore Sturgeon Memorial Award (for the novella "Sergeant Chip"). His other novels include *Blackburn, Lunatics*, and *Laughin' Boy*, and more of his short fiction can be found in the collection *One Day Closer to Death*. He now lives in Austin, Texas with his wife Barbara, their four dogs, and probably too many guitars.

**Vylar Kaftan** has published about three dozen stories in places such as *Clarkesworld, Strange Horizons*, and *Realms of Fantasy*. Her 2010 *Lightspeed* story, "I'm Alive, I Love You, I'll See You in Reno," was nominated for a Nebula. She founded FOGcon, a new literary sf/f convention in the San Francisco Bay Area, and she blogs at www.vylarkaftan.net.

**Catherynne M. Valente** is the *New York Times* bestselling author of over a dozen works of fiction and poetry, including *Palimpsest*, the Orphan's Tales series, *Deathless*, and the crowdfunded phenomenon *The Girl Who Circumnavigated Fairyland in a Ship of Own Making*. She is the winner of the Andre Norton Award, the Tiptree Award, the Mythopoeic Award, the Rhysling Award, and the Million Writers Award. She has been nominated for the Hugo, Locus, and Spectrum Awards, the Pushcart Prize, and was a finalist for the World Fantasy Award in 2007 and 2009. She lives on an island off the coast of Maine with her partner, two dogs, and an enormous cat.

**Alan DeNiro** is the author of a story collection, *Skinny Dipping in the Lake of the Dead* (Small Beer Press), and a novel, *Total Oblivion, More or Less* (Ballantine/Spectra). His website is www.alandeniro.com and he tweets with the username of @adeniro. He lives outside of St. Paul with his wife and twin son and daughter.

**Suzy McKee Charnas** is the author of over a dozen works of science fiction, fantasy, and horror. Her novels include *The Vampire Tapestry*, the Holdfast series, and the Sorcery Hall series of books for young adults. A selection of her short fiction was collected in *Stagestruck Vampires and Other Phantasms*. She has been awarded a Hugo, a Nebula, and has won the James Tiptree, Jr. Award twice. Charnas took a joint major at Barnard College—Economic History—because she "wanted tools to build convincing societies to set fantastic stories in." She lives with her lawyer-husband in New Mexico. Her website is www.suzymckeecharnas.com.

**Paul McAuley** is the author of more than twenty books, including science-fiction, thriller, and crime novels, three collections of short stories, a Doctor Who novella, and an anthology of stories about popular music, which he co-edited with Kim Newman. His fiction has won the Philip K. Dick Memorial Award, the Arthur C. Clarke Award, the John W. Campbell award, the Sidewise Award, and the British Fantasy Award for best short story. Having worked for twenty years as a research biologist and university lecturer, he is now a full-time writer. He lives in North London.

**Jonathan Carroll** is the author of sixteen novels and one story collection. His latest is *The Ghost in Love*, published by Farrar Straus and Giroux. He lives in Vienna, Austria.

**John Barnes** is the author of more than thirty science fiction novels, including *Orbital Resonance, A Million Open Doors, Finity,* and *Directive 51*. With astronaut Buzz Aldrin, he wrote the novels *Encounter with Tiber* and *The Return*. He lives in Denver, Colorado.

**Theodora Goss** was born in Hungary and spent her childhood in various European countries before her family moved to the United States. Her publications include the short story collection *In the Forest of Forgetting*; *Interfictions*, a short story anthology co-edited with Delia Sherman; *Voices from Fairyland*, a poetry anthology with critical essays and a selection of her own poems; and, most recently, *The Thorn and the Blossom: A Two-Sided Love Story*. She has been a finalist for the Nebula, Locus, Crawford, and Mythopoeic Awards, as well as on the Tiptree Award Honor List, and has won the World Fantasy and Rhysling Awards.

**Alexandra Duncan** is a frequent contributor to *The Magazine of Fantasy and Science Fiction*. Her first novel, *Salvage*, is scheduled to be published by HarperCollins's Greenwillow Books in 2013. She lives with her husband and two monstrous, furry cats in the mountains of Western North Carolina, where she works as a librarian. You can visit her online at alexandraduncanlit.blogspot.com and twitter.com/DuncanAlexandra

**Neil Gaiman** is the *New York Times* bestselling author of novels *Neverwhere*, *Stardust*, *American Gods*, *Coraline*, *Anansi Boys*, *The Graveyard Book*, and (with Terry Pratchett) *Good Omens*; the Sandman series of graphic novels; and the story collections *Smoke* and *Mirrors*, *Fragile Things*, and *M Is for Magic*. He has won numerous literary accolades including the Hugo, the Nebula, the World Fantasy, and the Stoker Awards, as well as the Newbery Medal.

**Gavin J. Grant** is the publisher of Small Beer Press. He co-edits the zine *Lady Churchill's Rosebud Wristlet* with his wife, Kelly Link. His stories have appeared in *Strange Horizons, SciFiction, Salon Fantastique, Best New Fantasy*, among others. He lives with his family in Northampton, Massachusetts.

**Karen Joy Fowler** is the author of five novels, including *The Jane Austen Book Club*, a *New York Times* bestseller, and three short story collections, including *What I Didn't See*, which recently won the World Fantasy Award. Other honors include the Nebula and the Shirley Jackson awards. She lives in Santa Cruz, California with her husband and her daughter's dog.

**Chris Lawson** is an Australian speculative fiction writer with an eclectic approach to subject matter that has skittered across the hard sciences of genetic engineering and epidemiology, unapologetic fantasy about the voyages of the Argo at the end of the Age of Myths, and ambiguous-ghost stories set in the Great War. His stories have appeared in *Asimov's, Fantasy & Science Fiction, Eidolon, Dreaming Down-Under,* and several Year's Best anthologies; his collection *Written in Blood* is available through MirrorDanse Books (www.tabula-rasa.info/MirrorDanse). In non-fictional life, Chris is a family medicine practitioner and university teacher with a special interest in public health, evidence-based medicine, and statistics. He lives on the Sunshine Coast with his spouse, two children, and a hyperdog. Chris blogs, irregularly, at Talking Squid (www.talkingsquid.net).

**Kelly Link** is the author of three collections of short stories, *Stranger Things Happen, Magic for Beginners,* and *Pretty Monsters.* Her short stories have won three Nebulas, a Hugo, and a World Fantasy Award. She was born in Miami, Florida, and once won a free trip around the world by answering the question "Why do you want to go around the world?" ("Because you can't go through it.") Link and her family live in Northampton, Massachusetts, where she and her husband, Gavin J. Grant, run Small Beer Press, and play ping-pong. In 1996 they started the occasional zine *Lady Churchill's Rosebud Wristlet.*

**Margo Lanagan** is a four-time World Fantasy Award winner, for novel, novella, collection and short story. Her stories have twice been short-listed in the James Tiptree Jr and Shirley Jackson awards, as well as for Hugo, Nebula, Stoker, Sturgeon and International Horror Guild awards. She is the author of four collections of short stories, *White Time, Black Juice, Red Spikes* and *Yellowcake,* and two novels, *Tender Morsels* and *The Brides of Rollrock Island.* Margo lives in Sydney, Australia.

**Nina Allan**'s stories have appeared regularly in the magazines *Black Static* and *Interzone,* and have featured in the anthologies *Catastrophia, House of Fear, Strange Tales from Tartarus, Best Horror of the Year #2* and *Year's Best SF #28.* A first collection of her fiction, *A Thread of Truth,* was published by Eibonvale Press in 2007, followed by her story cycle *The Silver Wind* in 2011. Twice shortlisted for the BFS and BSFA Award, Nina's next book, *Stardust,* will be available from PS Publishing in Autumn 2012. An exile from London, she lives and works in Hastings, East Sussex.

**Kat Howard**'s short fiction has appeared in *Subterranean, Lightspeed,* and *Stories,* edited by Neil Gaiman and Al Sarrantonio, among other places. She's a graduate of Clarion 2008 (UCSD), and teaches speculative fiction when she's not writing it.

Born in Vermont and raised all over the place, **K.J. Parker** has worked as, among other things, a tax lawyer, an auction house porter, a forester and a numismatist. Married to a lawyer and settled in southern England, Parker is currently a writer, farm labourer and metalworker, in more or less that order. K.J. Parker is not K.J. Parker's real name, but if somebody told you K.J. Parker's real name, you wouldn't recognise it.

**Robert Reed** is the author of several novels and a small empire of short fiction. His novella, "A Billion Eves," won the Hugo. Reed lives in Lincoln, NE with his wife and daughter, and his new best friend, a NOOK Tablet.

**George Saunders**, a 2006 MacArthur Fellow, is the author of six books (including the short story collections *CivilWarLand in Bad Decline*, *Pastoralia*, and *In Persuasion Nation*) and, most recently, the essay collection *The Braindead Megaphone*. He teaches at Syracuse University.

**C.S.E. Cooney** collects knives and books. Her fiction and poetry can be found in *SteamPowered II* and the *Clockwork Phoenix 3* anthologies, at *Apex, Subterranean, Strange Horizons, Podcastle, Goblin Fruit*, and *Mythic Delirium*. Her book *Jack o' the Hills* came out with Papaveria Press in 2011, which will also put out her poetry collection *How to Flirt in Faerieland and Other Wild Rhymes* in 2012. She was the recipient of the 2011 Rhysling Award in the Long Poem category. All the women in her family have dark eyes.

**Marissa Lingen** is a freelance writer of over eighty short works of science fiction and fantasy. She lives in the Minneapolis area with two large men and one small dog.

**Rachel Swirsky** holds an MFA in fiction from the Iowa Writers Workshop. Her short fiction has appeared in numerous magazines and anthologies including *Tor.com, Clarkesworld* and *Subterranean Magazine*. She's been nominated for the Hugo Award and the World Fantasy Award, and in 2011 she won the Nebula Award for best novella. She hasn't ever written a bucket list, but if she had, she probably wouldn't have accomplished most of the stuff on it. (For instance, she has never starred on Broadway. What's that about?)

**Lavie Tidhar** grew up on a kibbutz in Israel and has since lived in South Africa, the UK, Vanuatu and Laos. He is the author of the ground-breaking alternative history novel *Osama* (a BSFA Award nominee), and of the Bookman Histories trilogy of steampunk novels comprising *The Bookman, Camera Obscura* and *The Great Game*. Lavie's other works include linked story collection *HebrewPunk*, novellas *Cloud Permutations, Gorel & The Pot-Bellied God, An Occupation of Angels* and *Jesus & The Eightfold Path*. He edited *The Apex Book of World SF* and was a World Fantasy Award nominee for his work on the World SF Blog.

**E. Lily Yu** is a senior in English at Princeton University working toward a certificate in biophysics. Her short stories and poems have appeared in the *Kenyon Review Online, Clarkesworld, Jabberwocky 5, Electric Velocipede,* and *Goblin Fruit,* and her short play on beta decay had a staged reading at Princeton in October. At school, she competes on the ballroom team, plays flute, and juggles. She was born in Oregon and raised in New Jersey.

Since her first sale in 1987, **Kij Johnson** has sold dozens of short stories to markets including *Amazing Stories, Analog, Asimov's, Duelist Magazine, Fantasy & Science Fiction,* and *Realms of Fantasy.* She has won the Theodore Sturgeon Memorial Award for the best short story and the 2001 Crawford Award for best new fantasy novelist. Her short story "26 Monkeys, Also the Abyss" was a nominee for the 2008 Nebula and Hugo awards. Her novels include two volumes of the Heian trilogy Love/War/Death: *The Fox Woman* and *Fudoki.* She's also co-written with Greg Cox a Star Trek: The Next Generation novel, *Dragon's Honor.* She is currently researching a third novel set in Heian Japan; and *Kylen,* two novels set in Georgian Britain.

# RECOMMENDED READING

Charlie Jane Anders, "Six Months, Three Days" (*Tor.com*)
M.T. Anderson, "Oracle Engine" (**Steampunk!**)
Eleanor Arnason, "My Husband Steinn" (*Asimov's*, 10-11/11)
Kage Baker, "Attlee and the Long Walk" (**Life on Mars**)
John Barnes, "The Birds and the Bees and the Gasoline Trees"
       (**Engineering Infinity**)
Christopher Barzak, "Smoke City" (*Asimov's*, 4-5/11)
Stephen Baxter, "The Invasion of Venus" (**Engineering Infinity**)
Peter S. Beagle, "The Way It Works Out and All" (*F&SF*, 7-8/11)
Elizabeth Bear, "Dolly" (*Asimov's*, 1/11)
Elizabeth Bear, "Gods of the Forge" (**TRSF**)
M. David Blake, "Absinthe Fish" (*Bull Spec*)
Aliette de Bodard, "Shipbirth" (*Asimov's*, 2/10)
Marie Brennan, "Love, Cayce" (*Intergalactic Medicine Show*, 4/11)
Damien Broderick, "The Beancounter's Cat" (**Eclipse Four**)
Rachel Manija Brown, "Steel Rider" (**Steam Powered**)
Pat Cadigan, "You Never Know" (**Solaris Rising**)
Geoffrey W. Cole, "One of the Many Uses of Cedar" (*On Spec*, Summer/11)
Tina Connolly, "As We Report to Gabriel" (*Fantasy*, 1/11)
Paul Cornell, "The Copenhagen Interpretation" (*Asimov's*, 7/11)
John Crowley, "And Go Like This" (**Naked City**)
Indrapramit Das, "The Widow and the Xir" (*Apex*, 7/11)
Eric Del Carlo, "Time, Like Blood, on My Hands" (*Redstone*, 12/11)
Andy Duncan, "Slow as a Bullet" (**Eclipse Four**)
Sarah L. Edwards, "By Plucking Her Petals" (*Interzone*, 1-2/11)
K.M. Ferebee, "Seven Spells to Sever the Heart" (*Fantasy*, 11/11)
Carolyn Ives Gilman, "The Ice Owl" (*F&SF*, 10-11/11)
Lisa Goldstein, "Little Vampires" (*Realms of Fantasy*, 4/11)
Elizabeth Hand, "Near Zennor" (**A Book of Horrors**)
Colin Harvey, "The Ghost Station" (*Albedo 1* #40)
Amanda M. Hayes, "Silvergrass Mirror" (*Abyss and Apex*, 4Q/11)

Rosamund Hodge, "Apotheosis" (*Black Gate*, Spring/11)

Dylan Horrocks, "Steam Girl" (**Steampunk!**)

Alexander Jablokov, "The Day the Wires Came Down" (*Asimov's*, 4-5/11)

Alaya Dawn Johnson, "Their Changing Bodies" (*Subterranean*, Summer/11)

Gwyneth Jones, "The Ki-Anna" (**Engineering Infinity**)

John Kessel, "Clean" (*Asimov's*, 3/11)

Mary Robinette Kowal, "Kiss Me Twice" (*Asimov's*, 6/11)

Douglas Lain, **Wave of Mutilation** (Fantastic Planet Books)

Jay Lake, "The Long Walk Home" (*Subterranean*, Winter/11)

V.H. Leslie, "Time Keeping" (*Black Static*, 6-7/11)

David D. Levine, "The Tides of the Heart" (*Realms of Fantasy*, 6/11)

Kelly Link, "Valley of the Girls" (*Subterranean*, Summer/11)

Ken Liu, "The Man Who Ended History: A Documentary"
       (**Panverse Three**)

Kristin Livdahl, **A Brood of Foxes** (Aqueduct)

Ken MacLeod, "The Surface of Least Scattering" (**TRSF**)

Ken MacLeod, "The Best Science Fiction of the Year Three" (**Solaris Rising**)

Nick Mamatas, "North Shore Friday" (*Asimov's*, 4-5/11)

Ian McDonald, "Digging" (**Life on Mars**)

Ian McHugh, "Boumee and the Apes" (*Analog*, 5/11)

Maureen F. McHugh, "After the Apocalypse" (**After the Apocalypse**)

Sean McMullen, "Enigma" (*Analog*, 1-2/11)

David Moles, "A Soldier of the City" (**Engineering Infinity**)

Alec Nevala-Lee, "The Boneless One" (*Analog*, 11/11)

Peadar Ó Guilín, "Heartless" (*Beneath Ceaseless Skies*, 12/15/11)

An Owomoyela, "All That Touches the Air" (*Lightspeed*)

An Owomoyela, "Frozen Voice" (*Clarkesworld*)

Suzanne Palmer, "Surf" (*Asimov's*, 12/11)

Paul Park, "Mysteries of the Old Quarter" (**Ghosts by Gaslight**)

K.J. Parker, **Blue and Gold** (Subterranean Press)

Richard Parks, "The Ghost of Shinoda Forest" (*Beneath Ceaseless Skies*)

Richard Parks, "The Swan Troika" (*Realms of Fantasy*, 2/11)

David Prill, "A Pulp Called Joe" (**Subterranean: Tales of Dark Fantasy 2**)

Tom Purdom, "A Response from EST17" (*Asimov's*, 4-5/11)

Cat Rambo, "The Immortality Game" (*Fantasy*, 6/11)

Robert Reed, "Purple" (*Asimov's*, 3/11)

Robert Reed, "The Ants of Flanders" (*F&SF*, 7-8/11)

Robert Reed, "Stalker" (*Asimov's*, 9/11)

Alastair Reynolds, "The Old Man and the Martian Sea" (**Life on Mars**)

M. Rickert, "The Corpse Painter's Masterpiece" (*F&SF*, 7-8/11)

Kate Riedel, "The Guardians" (*On Spec*, Spring/11)

Mercurio D. Rivera, "For Love's Delirium Haunts the Fractured Mind"
    (*Interzone*, 7-8/11)
Tansy Rayner Roberts, "The Patrician" (**Love and Romanpunk**)
Christopher Rowe, "Nowhere Fast" (**Steampunk!**)
Geoff Ryman, "What We Found" (*F&SF*, 9-10/11)
Grace Seybold, "Linking Words" (*Chiaroscuro*, 7/11)
Carter Scholz, "Signs of Life" (*F&SF*, 5-6/11)
Michael Swanwick, "For I Have Lain Me Down on the Stone of Loneliness
    and I'll Not Get Up Again" (*Asimov's*, 4/11)
Michael Swanwick, "The Dala Horse" (*Tor.com*, 7/11)
Sonya Taaffe, "A Wolf in Iceland in the Child of a Lie" (*Not One of Us*, 4/11)
Lavie Tidhar, "Red Dawn" (*Fantasy*, 11/11)
Lavie Tidhar, "The Projected Girl" (**Naked City**)
Lavie Tidhar, **Jesus and the Eightfold Path** (PS Publishing)
Catherynne M. Valente, "The Bread We Eat in Dreams" (*Apex*, 11/11)
Catherynne M. Valente, **Silently and Very Fast** (WSFA Press)
Genevieve Valentine, "Demons, Your Body, and You" (*Subterranean*)
Genevieve Valentine, "Things to Know About Being Dead" (**Teeth**)
Kali Wallace, "Botanical Exercises for Curious Girls" (*F&SF*, 3-4/11)
Jo Walton, "The Panda Coin" (**Eclipse Four**)
Peter Watts, "Malak" (**Engineering Infinity**)
Sarah Harris Wallman, "The Malanesian" (*LCRW*, 8/11)
Kathryn Weaver, "The Doves of Hartleigh Gardens" (*Apex*, 6/11)
Liz Williams and Alastair Reynolds, "Lune and the Red Empress"
    (**Eastercon Souvenir Book**)

# PUBLICATION HISTORY

published in *Strange Horizons,* February 7-14. Reprinted by permission of the author.

"Younger Women" by Karen Joy Fowler. © by Karen Joy Fowler. Originally published in *Subterranean,* Summer. Reprinted by permission of the author.

"Canterbury Hollow" by Chris Lawson. © by Chris Lawson. Originally published in *F&SF,* January-February. Reprinted by permission of the author.

"The Summer People" by Kelly Link. © by Kelly Link. Originally published in *Tin House,* Fall; **Steampunk!** Reprinted by permission of the author.

"Mulberry Boys" by Margo Lanagan. © by Margo Lanagan. Originally published in **Blood and Other Cravings**. Reprinted by permission of the author.

"The Silver Wind" by Nina Allan. © by Nina Allan. Originally published in *Interzone,* March-April. Reprinted by permission of the author.

"Choose Your Own Adventure" by Kat Howard. © by Kat Howard. Originally published in *Fantasy,* April. Reprinted by permission of the author.

"A Small Price to Pay for Birdsong" by K.J. Parker. © by K.J. Parker. Originally published in *Subterranean,* Winter. Reprinted by permission of the author.

"Woman Leaves Room" by Robert Reed. © by Robert Reed. Originally published in *Lightspeed,* March. Reprinted by permission of the author.

"My Chivalric Fiasco" by George Saunders. © by George Saunders. Originally published in *Harper's,* September. Reprinted by permission of the author.

"The Last Sophia" by C.S.E. Cooney. © by C.S.E. Cooney. Originally published in *Strange Horizons,* March 7. Reprinted by permission of the author.

"Some of Them Closer" by Marissa Lingen. © by Marissa Lingen. Originally published in *Analog,* January. Reprinted by permission of the author.

"Fields of Gold" by Rachel Swirsky. © by Rachel Swirsky. Originally published in **Eclipse 4**. Reprinted by permission of the author.

"The Smell of Orange Groves" by Lavie Tidhar. © by Lavie Tidhar. Originally published in *Clarkesworld,* November. Reprinted by permission of the author.

"The Cartographer Wasps and the Anarchist Bees" by E. Lily Yu. © by E. Lily Yu. Originally published in *Clarkesworld,* April. Reprinted by permission of the author.

"The Man Who Bridged the Mist" by Kij Johnson. © by Kij Johnson. Originally published in *Asimov's,* October-November. Reprinted by permission of the author.

# ABOUT THE EDITOR

**RICH HORTON** is an Associate Technical Fellow in Software for a major aerospace corporation. He is also a columnist for *Locus* and for *Black Gate*. He edits a series of Best of the Year anthologies for Prime Books, and also for Prime Books he has co-edited *Robots: The New A.I.* and *War and Space: Recent Combat.*